漢英對照成語詞典

Chinese Idioms And Their English Equivalents

編著：陳永楨　陳善慈

商務印書館

漢英對照成語詞典

Chinese Idioms And Their English Equivalents

編　　著：陳永楨　陳善慈

封面設計：張　毅

出　　版：商務印書館（香港）有限公司
香港筲箕灣耀興道 3 號東滙廣場 8 樓
http://www.commercialpress.com.hk

發　　行：香港聯合書刊物流有限公司
香港新界荃灣德士古道 220－248 號荃灣工業中心 16 樓

印　　刷：美雅印刷製本有限公司
九龍觀塘榮業街 6 號海濱工業大廈 4 樓 A

版　　次：2021 年 6 月新一版第 6 次印刷
1983 年 4 月第一版

ISBN 978 962 07 0278 5
Printed in Hong Kong

ACKNOWLEDGMENT

The authors wish to express their deepest gratitude to Dr. Lee Siu-Kong (李少剛)， Dip. Ed. (H.K.), D.I.C., Ph.D. (London), the second author's husband, for his untiring assistance in the editing of the book and in reading the manuscript, and for his writing of "A Guide to the Use of this Dictionary" and 本詞典使用法 which appear on the pages hereafter.

目　錄
Contents

序　言

學習一種語言，能學會它的語音、詞匯和語法，只能説是掌握了它的基礎，若要精通這種語言，還得掌握大量成語（包括習語、諺語等），因為成語是每一種民族語言的精髓部分。

漢語和英語都有很豐富和精煉的成語。出版的成語典籍委實不少，可惜都屬於註釋性質，難得找到一本漢英成語對照的書，讓兩種成語本身並列對照，相映成趣，藉此可以表現出兩種不同文化的語言的優點。編者正要在這書裏作這種新嘗試。

學習單詞有所謂同義詞、反義詞；編者認為學習漢英成語也可以利用同義成語和反義成語來加深對每個成語的認識，鞏固記憶，和作為逐漸擴大成語範圍的學習手段。

本書收集了可作對照的漢成語 4,079 條，英成語約 7,000 條。為了方便外籍學者學習漢成語，本書把每條成語標上漢語拼音，附上直譯（literal translation），並對有典故和特別艱深的成語提供出處，以增加讀者對中國文學的興趣和鑒賞力。

新嘗試本身就意味着不成熟，加之編者水平有限，謬誤之處在所難免，敬希國內外讀者不吝指正。

此書蒙李博士少剛不辭辛勞，審查成語出處，校閱全稿，並親筆撰“本詞典使用法”一文，謹此致謝。

陳永楨

1981 年 6 月於廣州

FOREWORD

The Chinese people has been considered by the westerners to be a peace-loving people who are philosophical in their attitude toward life. The westerners are often impressed by the wise or ingenious sayings in their everyday expressions in conversation and writing. Indeed Chinese people are fond of wisdom and knowledge which have been handed down by the sages and great philosophers through the ages. Whether they can live up to the ideals and wisdom is another matter, but at least the wise sayings containing advice and warning can serve as a kind of guidance of wisdom and moral codes in their everyday life.

However, idioms and proverbs are not unique to the Chinese language; they exist probably in every language and the English language is reputed for its richness in expressive, idiomatic and proverbial phrases. One English writer said "take fifty of their current proverbial sayings – they embody the concentrated wisdom of the race, and the man who orders his life according to their teaching cannot go far wrong."

What is an idiom? An idiom is a form of expression peculiar to a language. It is formed of a group of words which, in most cases, taken together convey a meaning of its own different from the individual words of the group when they are taken alone. For maintaining the characteristics of brevity, balance in form, or rhyme, the arrangement of words in an idiom is often strange, seemingly illogical, or even grammatically incorrect. It is therefore usually unwise and impossible to translate word by word an idiom from one language into another and yet to maintain the original meaning of the idiom.

When an idiom carries a message of moral or philosophical teaching it becomes a proverb. A proverb is defined as a popular, short, pithy saying with words of advice or warning, or a wise general comment on a situation. These sayings being short, to the point, condensed in form and with positive qualities, are easy to remember. For examples:

(1) Simple and short:
   0051 百煉成鋼 ⟷ Practice makes perfect.
   0298 財可通神 ⟷ Money talks.

(2) Balance in form:
   3719 欲速則不達 ⟷ More haste, less speed.
   3076 先到先得 ⟷ First come, first served.
   3258 旋得旋失 ⟷ Easy come, easy go.

(3) Written in rhyme:
   1095 互忍互讓 ⟷ Live and let live.

3879 只要功夫深，鐵杵磨成針 ⟷ Little strokes fell great oaks.

Idioms and proverbs of both languages, Chinese and English, naturally come from different origins, and in both languages some sayings have been assimilated by the common people and have become so popular that the users are no longer aware of their origins. These sayings express a truth which summarizes everyday experience. For examples:

2907 未雨綢繆 ⟷ Make hay while the sun shines.
3028 勿誤農時 ⟷ Don't miss farming time.
0348 趁熱打鐵 ⟷ Strike while the iron is hot.
0659 鼎力支持 ⟷ Put one's hand to the plough.
1919 牛不喝水，難按得牛頭低 ⟷ You may lead a horse to water, but you cannot make him drink.

All these might have their origins in farm work and would have developed out of common-sense experience of farming.

Many English proverbs come from the English Bible; for examples:

The spirit is willing, but the flesh is weak. ⟷ 力不從心(1602)；心有餘而力不足(3195)
A soft answer turneth away wrath. ⟷ 忍一句，息一怒(2246)
Spare the rod and spoil the child. ⟷ 棒頭出孝子(0076)

Shakespeare, next to the Bible in English language, is definitely the greatest source of English proverbs. Other English sources of proverbs are quotations from the famous writers such as Pope, Herrick and Benjamin Franklin, to quote a few. The following are some of the examples:

A rose by any other name would smell as sweet (Shakespeare). ⟷ 有麝自然香(3665)
Sweet are the uses of adversity. (Shakespeare). ⟷ 塞翁失馬，焉知非福(2301)
A little learning is a dangerous thing (Pope). ⟷ 一知半解(3495)
Gather ye rosebuds while ye may (Herrick). ⟷ 花開堪折直須折，莫待無花空折枝(1104)
Early to bed and early to rise, makes a man healthy, wealthy, and wise (Benjamin Franklin). ⟷ 早眠早起(3764)

Although China has had no national religion, she has quite a number of great scholar-philosophers whose teachings have influenced directly or indirectly the moral and social principles of the people. Among these famous philosophers were Confucius (孔子), Mencius (孟子), and Lao Zi (老子). Confucius is the most well-known and his teaching was recorded in the famous writing, Confucian Analects (論語). For examples:

0235 不念舊惡(論語) ⟷ Forgive and forget.
3013 五十而知天命(論語) ⟷ Life is half spent before we know what it is.
0315 惻隱之心，仁之端也(孟子) ⟷ Milk of human kindness.
3257 玄之又玄(老子) ⟷ Explaining what is unknown by what is still unknown.

The Chinese literary classics which are full of idioms and proverbs, and quotations from different famous scholars and poets, are also sources of many Chinese idiomatic and proverbial sayings. Thus:

2494 士為知己者用(史記) ⟷ Respect a man, he will do the more.
1179 禍兮福所倚(史記) ⟷ Every cloud has a silver lining.
1368 進退維谷(詩經) ⟷ In the horns of a dilemma.
1826 明哲保身(詩經) ⟷ Be worldly wise and play safe.
2228 人微言輕(韓愈) ⟷ Poor man's reasons are not heard.
2398 深思熟慮(蘇軾) ⟷ Put it through the meat grinder.

One important and interesting finding from working on this book is that languages of different cultures, customs, and traditions in countries so far apart geographically and with hardly any communication in ancient times could have developed similar metaphorical idioms and proverbs as can be seen in many examples in this volume. This should not be a surprise if the proverbial sayings represent the accumulated wisdom of the people acquired through experiences in life, as human nature is the same every-where and has undergone very little change in the human history.

Many who come to either of the two languages as a foreigner, e.g. a Chinese to the English language, may be able to see in the idioms and proverbs of a foreign language the old truths in a different light and also may develop a deeper understanding of the foreign culture and mentality.

Idioms are not a separate part of a language but rather they form quite an essential part of the general vocabulary of the language. The general tendencies of present-day language usage are towards more idiomatic expressions in speaking and writing. This collection of over 4,000 Chinese idioms and proverbs and 7,000 English ones is aimed at guiding the learners of either language to the correct use of these idioms and proverbs. Of course mastery of them comes only through constant practice and experience, and especially communication with the people of the language.

In closing, a word about the story of how this work has come to realization of a wish of the authors may not be out of place. In late 1979 the first author of this book, my elder brother, sent me from Canton, China, the preliminary manuscript, a collection of thousands of Chinese idioms and their English equivalents for my comments. This interested me tremendously, and I earnestly thought, and naturally still think, that the collection should be made into a book-form for publication so as to let the scholars and students of the same interest all over the world share the fruit of many years' work and our joint effort.

Spring Chen

University of Hong Kong
28 August, 1981

本詞典使用法

本書共收漢成語 4,079 條，及與其意義相同、可作相互對照之英成語約 7,000 條。此處成語一詞包括習語、諺語、俚語、常用語等。中國人日常生活中所講的，報紙雜誌上所閱讀到的，及普通書籍所引用的漢成語都包括在內。

排列次序是按每條成語句首該漢字之漢語拼音字母、聲調、及其筆畫數而定。從書首之音序表內可以看出，先是按漢語拼音字母順序排列；若字母相同則要看其聲調，依照陰平ー，陽平ˊ，上聲ˇ，去聲ˋ之次序而排列；若字母聲調兩者均同，則再按筆畫數之多少而排列。本書每條漢成語自有一個條目號碼（Code Number），冠在成語之前；全書條目號碼由 0001 起至 4079 止。

在每條漢成語後，先標出其漢語拼音及聲調符號（陰平ー，陽平ˊ，上聲ˇ，去聲ˋ，輕聲則不用符號）。其次把成語直譯成英語，盡可能逐字譯出，後面用（1it.）縮語表示。漢語拼音及漢英直譯主要是供外國讀者之用，但中國讀者亦可藉此確知該漢成語之標準讀音，並通過直譯複習英語詞匯與擴大詞匯量。

其後便開列出與該漢成語相對照之英成語，由一條至四、五條不等。各條英成語間在意義上可有若干差別；外國讀者可藉此以增加對漢成語之了解，而中國讀者可由此學習表達同一漢成語之不同英文句子。英成語句中遇有某詞可用其他詞代替的，本書把可代用之詞用括號附入。此外，所列英成語有些是以介詞如 of，to，with 等結尾的，為的是可隨時靈活套用，因此末端概不加句點（full stop）。

再後便是同義成語及反義成語，先漢後英，每條附有條目號碼以便翻閱參考；由一同義或反義成語可引至另一同義或反義成語，起着連鎖作用，由是增大成語量並加深對該成語含義的認識。但並非每一漢成語必有同義成語和反義成語。

漢成語不少源出於古詩文，或有典故。了解成語來源可增加對漢語古籍的認識，培養對中國古典文學的鑒賞能力，故結尾一項是該漢成語的出處與典故。

下面是本書幾條項目較齊全的漢英成語對照例子：

同甘共苦 tóng gān gòng kǔ 2767

Sharing joy and sorrow together. (lit.)

Friendships multiply joys and divide griefs.

A sorrow shared is but half a trouble, but a joy that is shared is a joy made double.

In weal or woe.

同 有福同享，有禍同當（3647）For better or for worse.

反 有酒有肉多兄弟，急難何曾見一人（3651）In time of prosperity friends will be plenty; in time of adversity not one among twenty.

源 晉書．應詹傳：“詹與分甘共苦，情若兄弟。”

求人不如求己 qiú rén bù rú qiú jǐ 2145

Asking others for help is not as good as asking oneself. (lit.)

Better do it than wish it done.

Better spare to have thine own than ask of other men.

同 事必躬親（2506）If you want a thing done well, do it yourself.

反 因人成事（3574）Come in through the cabin window.

源 貴耳集：“宋孝宗見觀音像，手持數珠，問何用，僧淨輝對曰，念觀世音菩薩。問自念則甚，對曰，求人不如求己。”

如魚得水 rú yú dé shuǐ 2145

Like fish getting water. (lit.)

Feel oneself at home.

Like a duck to water.

To be in one's element.

同 優哉悠哉（3631）Free and easy.

反 涸轍之鮒（1054）A fish out of water.

源 三國志．蜀志．諸葛亮傳：“孤（劉備自稱）之有孔明，猶魚之有水也。”

若要找尋某漢成語是否在本書內，可查音序表或漢成語條目筆畫索引。此索引按成語首字筆畫數目多少而排列，由一畫至二十九畫。同畫數之字很多，則又須看該字如何起筆而定。起筆分七種，按、（點）、一（橫）、乛（橫折）、丨（直）、𠃊（直折）、丿（撇）、𠃋（撇折）先後次序排列。若起筆亦相同，如同為〔、〕起的，又將偏旁與頂蓋分為冫，氵，宀，亠，广，疒 各組排列，以便易於找尋。首漢字完全相同之各成語則按第二漢字筆畫多少而定先後。若為首兩漢字均相同，則按第三漢字之筆畫多少排列，餘類推。

若要找尋某一英成語是否在本書內，可查書末之英成語索引。此索引按英文字母順序（alphabetical order）編排。但成語以冠詞 a，an，the 開始，或以不定動詞（infinitive）的標記 to 與 to be 開始的，則不在計算之內。中國讀者從這索引可找到與之相當的漢成語以了解該英成語之意義，外國讀者找到了相當的漢成語後還可在其下看見其他與之相對照的若干英成語，加深對該漢成語之認識。

本詞典可供下列四種讀者使用：（一）學習英國語文的中國人；（二）母語為英語而欲學習漢語文者；（三）漢英與英漢翻譯工作者；（四）學習漢英兩種語文的外國學者。無論對於哪一類讀者，這詞典都是一本有用的工具書。

A Guide to the Use of This Dictionary

This book contains just over 4,000 entries of the most well-known Chinese phrases, idioms and proverbs and nearly 7,000 entries of their English equivalents. These are the Chinese idioms one would use or come across in ordinary spoken language, in newspapers, and in other reading materials – in short, in everyday life of the Chinese people in the past and present.

Each entry of the Chinese idiom is followed by the phonetical transcription of each character based on the latest standardized romanization, i.e. the Hanyu Pinyin (漢語拼音), and then the literal translation, (lit.), of the idiom. The literal translation given here is to translate as nearly as possible the Chinese idiom word by word into English so that the readers could learn not only the meaning of the individual characters but also the gist of the idiom without consulting a Chinese dictionary.

Now comes the English equivalent of the Chinese idiom; to each Chinese entry there may be one, two, three or more English idioms. Non-Chinese readers may find these equivalents helpful to further understand the meaning of the Chinese idiom whereas the Chinese readers can learn the different ways of expressing an idiom in good and proper English. Even synonyms in both languages often have subtle differences in meaning between them.

Then follows a Synonym or an Antonym or both; in the latter case the Synonym comes first. Each Chinese Synonym and Antonym is also followed by English equivalent. These synonym and antonym idioms, Chinese or English, may be in some rare cases new additions, or may have been cited more than once. However, the readers will become more familiar with them, the more frequently the idioms appear.

Lastly, whenever available, there appears the origin of the Chinese idiom, being a quotation from some Chinese classics or literature.

Here are a few examples of the entries:

1224 集思廣益 jí sī guǎng yì
Collecting ideas to broaden benefits.
Lay our heads together.
Two heads are better than one.
In the multitude of counsellors there is safety.

同 一人計短，二人計長（3447）Four eyes see more than two.
反 獨斷獨行（0677）Take the law into one's own hand.
源 諸葛丞相集：“夫參署者，集眾思廣忠益也。”

既往不咎 jì wǎng bú jiù 1234

What is past is not condemned. (lit.)

Let bygones be bygones.

Let the dead bury the dead.

Forgive and forget.

同 不念舊惡（0235）Bury the hatchet.

反 翻老賬（0739）Rake out old grievances.

源 論語．八佾："成事不說，遂事不諫，既往不咎。"

如願以償 rú yuàn yǐ cháng 2280

To have fulfilled one's wish. (lit.)

The prayer is answered.

Long looked for comes at last.

A dream comes true.

To have one's will.

Bring home the bacon.

同 正中下懷（3845）After one's own heart.

反 大失所望（0550）Fish for herring and catch a sprat.

源 黃庭堅："政當為公乞如願。"

Quoting the origins is meant to arouse literary interest and appreciation of the Chinese Classics in which the beauty of the language is abundantly revealed.

The Chinese idioms of this book are arranged according to the alphabetical order of their first character and where the first character of more than one idiom is the same, they are arranged according to the alphabetical order of the second character, or of the third, and so on. Where the alphabetical order of the first character of the idioms is the same, they are arranged according to the tonic order of the first character (cf. Yinxubiao,音序表). Each entry is given a code number, in increasing order (0001–4079).

For looking up a Chinese idiom, a Chinese Index according to the number of strokes of the first character is provided and each idiom is followed by the entry's code number. In this Index, the Chinese entries are arranged according to the increasing number of strokes of the first character. Where the number of strokes of the first character in more than one entry is the same, they are then arranged according to the increasing number of strokes of the second character, or of the third, and so on.

In the English Index, also provided, the English idioms are arranged in alphabetical order of the first word (except the articles, 'a', 'an', and 'the'; 'to' and 'to be') in each expression. At the end of each English idiom, one or more code numbers of one or more Chinese entries are quoted where the English idiom may be found.

This book may be used by 4 categories of readers:

(1) Chinese scholars learning English;

(2) Non-Chinese scholars of English-speaking countries learning Chinese;

(3) Scholars who are doing translation work of these two languages;

(4) Scholars other than the above categories who are using these two languages.

It is hoped that they may all find this book interesting and useful.

Lee Siu Kong
D.I.C. Ph. D (London)

August, 1981
Hong Kong

音序表

YINXUBIAO —— Tonic Order Table

按成語句首漢字之漢語拼音字母、聲調及筆畫數之次序排列。表中左邊為聲調符號，中為句首漢字，數字為條目號碼。

An Explanatory Note on Yīn Xù Biǎo

The page is vertically divided into three columns in succession of increasing code numbers. In the Table, the extreme left column gives the tonic symbols in the order of the four variations of tone indicated by the symbols ━, ╱, ∨, ╲. The next small column gives the first Chinese characters of the Chinese idioms of which the code numbers are listed against these Chinese characters. The 4,079 entries of Chinese idioms of the book are arranged in accordance with the alphabetical order of romanization, tonic order, and the number of strokes of the first Chinese characters of the Chinese idioms.

A

a

━阿 0001

ai

━哀 0002
╱挨 0003
╲愛 0004－0007

an

━安 0008－0017
╲按 0018－0021
╲暗 0022－0030
╲黯 0031

ang

╱昂 0032

ao

╲傲 0033

B

ba

━八 0034－0035
╱拔 0036

bai

╱白 0037－0045
∨百 0046－0063
∨擺 0064－0065
╲拜 0066

ban

━班 0067
━搬 0068
∨板 0069
╲半 0070－0075

bang

╲棒 0076

bao

━包 0077－0078
∨保 0079－0081
∨飽 0082－0086
∨寶 0087
╲抱 0088－0090
╲暴 0091－0092

bei

━杯 0093－0094
━卑 0095
━悲 0096－0098

C

D

N

O

P

條目筆劃索引

Chinese Characters Strokes Index

、（點） 一（橫） ㄱ（橫折） ｜（直） ㄴ（直折） ㇒（撇） ㄥ（撇折）

一 畫

〔一 起〕

二畫

〔一起〕

〔㇕起〕

〔丿起〕

三 畫

〔、起〕

〔一起〕

四　畫

〔一 起〕

五　畫

七　畫

〔、起〕

〔一 起〕

〔㇕起〕

九　畫

〔一 起〕

十　畫

〔ㄥ 起〕

十一　畫

〔、 起〕

〔ㄥ起〕

十二　畫

〔、起〕

〔一起〕

〔乛起〕

〔丨起〕

〔丿起〕

〔ㄥ起〕

十三　畫

〔、起〕

〔一起〕

十五　畫

〔、起〕

十七　畫

〔、起〕

〔一起〕

〔㇕起〕

〔丨起〕

〔丿起〕

〔㇜起〕

A

阿聾送殯 ā lóng sòng bìn

The deaf attends the funeral (implying that he can't hear the music). (lit.)

Turn a deaf ear to

As deaf as a post.

同 充耳不聞（0384）None so deaf as those who won's hear.

反 洗耳恭聽（3053）To be all ears. 0001

哀莫大於心死 āi mò dà yú xīn sǐ

Sadness is not as great as heart's death. (lit.)

He begins to die that quits his desires.

The wound that bleedeth inwardly is most dangerous.

源 莊子："哀莫大於心死，而身死次之。" 0002

挨鬥 ái dòu

To be beaten. (lit.)

Stand the gaff.

Run the gauntlet.

反 批鬥（1965）Haul over the coals. 0003

愛莫能助 ài mò néng zhù

Love but can't help. (lit.)

The spirit is willing, but the flesh is weak.

Beyond one's tether.

源 詩經："維仲山甫舉之，愛莫助之。" 0004

愛屋及烏 ài wū jí wū

Love one's house and extend love to the crows on the roof. (lit.)

Love me, love my dog.

He that loves the tree loves the branch.

同 幼吾幼以及人之幼（3684）Charity begins at home.

源 說苑："臣聞愛其人者，兼愛及屋上之烏。" 0005

愛憎分明 ài zēng fēn míng

Love and hatred separate clearly. (lit.)

Separate the sheep from the goats.

反 認賊作父（2248）Set a fox to keep one's geese. 0006

0007 **愛之欲其生，惡之欲其死**
ài zhī yù qí shēng, wù zhī yù qí sǐ
Loving him wish him alive, hating him wish him dead. (lit.)
The greatest hate springs from the greatest love.

源 論語．顏淵："愛之欲其生，惡之欲其死，既欲其生，又欲其死，是惑也。"

0008 **安步當車** ān bù dàng chē
Walking step by step is as good as riding in a carriage. (lit.)
Ride the shoe leather express.
On shanks' mare.
To leg it.
Ride in the marrow-bone coach.

同 乘十一路車（0363）Ride on the horse with ten toes.
源 戰國策："晚食以當肉，安步以當車。"

0009 **安分守己** ān fèn shǒu jǐ
Keep one's duty and have self control. (lit.)
Know one's distance.
Know where to draw a line.
Mind one's own business.

同 循規蹈矩（3280）Walk the chalk.
反 橫行無忌（1069）Throw one's weight about.
源 蘇軾詩："胡不安其份，但聽物所誘。"

0010 **安家落戶** ān jiā luò hù
To settle down with the family. (lit.)
To settle down.
To domicile oneself in

反 萍蹤無定（1997）Here today and gone tomorrow

0011 **安貧樂道** ān pín lè dào
Willing to accept poverty and be happy with the right track. (lit.)
Poverty is not a shame but the being ashamed of it.

同 不戚戚於貧賤，不汲汲於富貴（0241）Better go to heaven in rags than to hell in embroidery.

0012 **安然無恙** ān rán wú yàng
Safe and no illness. (lit.)
In (With) a whole skin.
To escape with life and limb.
To be safe and sound.
Save one's bacon.
Land on both feet.

反 遍體鱗傷（0134）Beaten black and blue.

安如磐石 ān rú pán shí 0013
Firm as a great rock. (lit.)
As firm as a rock.

反 搖搖欲墜（3348）Hang by a thread.
源 史記："此所謂磐石之安也。"

安如泰山 ān rú tài shān 0014
As stable as Tai Shan (Mt. Tai in the west of Shantung Province, China). (lit.)
Safe upon the solid rock.

同 固若金湯（0946）As firm as a rock.
反 危在旦夕（2876）Hang on by the eyelids.
源 文選·枚乘諫吳王書："乘所欲為，易於反掌，安於泰山。"

安下金鈎 ān xià jīn gōu 0015
Lay down a golden hook. (lit.)
Lay an ambush.

同 打埋伏（0493）A put-up job.

安於現狀 ān yú xiàn zhuàng 0016
Content with the present situation. (lit.)
Let well alone.
Stick in the mud.

同 既來之，則安之（1233）Take the world as it is.
反 野心勃勃（3364）To level at the moon.

安之若素 ān zhī ruò sù 0017
At ease as usual. (lit.)
To be well at ease.
To be well adapted to

同 既來之，則安之（1233）Take things as they come.
反 突兀不安（2806）Get hot under the collar.

按兵不動 àn bīng bú dòng 0018
Keep the troops unmoved. (lit.)
Stay one's hand.
Bide one's time.
To mark time.

源 史記："王按兵毋出。"

按部就班 àn bù jiù bān 0019
To follow according to the prescribed way. (lit.)
In apple-pie order.
A place for everything, and everything in its place.

同 井井有條（1402）Keep everything ship-shape.
反 亂作一團（1708）All in a huddle.
源 文選·陸機文賦："然後選義按部，老辭就班。"

0020 按老皇曆辦事
àn lǎo huáng lì bàn shì
According to the old Imperial way to do things. (lit.)
Ride a method to death.
To keep a custom you hammer the anvil still, though you have no iron.

同 陳陳相因（0344）Follow the beaten track.
反 另起爐灶（1671）Break fresh ground.

0021 按下不提 àn xià bù tí
Put it down unmentioned. (lit.)
To leave it at that.

0022 暗藏敵人 àn cáng dí rén
A secretly hidden enemy. (lit.)
A snake in the grass.

反 過街老鼠（0998）Everybody points an accusing finger at

0023 暗渡陳倉 àn dù chén cāng
Secretly pass through the old barn. (lit.)
To steal a march upon

0024 暗箭傷人 àn jiàn shāng rén
A secret arrow injures a man. (lit.)
A stab in the back.
Hit below the belt.

同 明槍易躲，暗箭難防（1822）Better be stung by a nettle than pricked by a rose.
反 公開挑戰（0918）Throw down the gauntlet.
源 宋 · 劉炎邇言："暗箭中人，其深次骨，人之怨之，亦必次骨。"

0025 暗結珠胎 àn jié zhū tāi
Secretly forming a pearl embryo. (lit.)
To be in the family way.
In an interesting condition.
To be in trouble.

0026 暗送秋波 àn sòng qiū bō
Secretly send autumn waves (beauty's eyes are as bright as autumn lake water or waves). (lit.)
Make eyes at
Cast sheep's eyes at

同 眉目傳情（1776）Leer one's eyes at

暗中埋伏 àn zhōng mái fú
Ambush in the dark. (lit.)
Lie in wait.

同 佈下伏兵（0294）Lay an ambush.

0027

暗中摸索 àn zhōng mō suǒ
To reach by feeling in the dark. (lit.)
Grope in the dark.
Feel one's way.

0028

暗中示意 àn zhōng shì yì
Hint an idea. (lit.)
Drop a hint.
Put a bug in one's ear.

反 開誠佈公（1466）Put one's cards on the table.

0029

暗中行事 àn zhōng xíng shì
Secretly take action. (lit.)
On the sly.
With closed doors.
Under the rose.
Hole and corner.

同 偷偷摸摸（2784）Up to some hangky-pangky.
反 光明磊落（0981）To be open and aboveboard.

0030

黯然失色 àn rán shī sè
Sadly losing colour. (lit.)
The moon is not seen where the sun shines.
Pale beside another.
To be cast into the shade.

同 相形見絀（3113）Make one shrink small.
反 毫無遜色（1030）Sustain comparison with another.

0031

昂首雲外 áng shǒu yún wài
To lift up the head beyond the cloud. (lit.)
Hold one's head high.
Have one's nose in the air.
As proud (vain) as a peacock.
Hold one's head up.

同 自命不凡（3986）Pique oneself on.
反 得縮頭時且縮頭（0616）When you bow, bow low.

0032

傲骨嶙峋 ào gǔ lín xún
Haughty bone uneven with notches. (lit.)
As hard as a bone.

同 威武不屈（2879）Die in the last ditch.
反 卑躬屈節（0095）Bow and scrape.

0033

B

0034 **八面玲瓏** bā miàn líng lóng

Eight faces transparent. (lit.)

All things to all men.

Dance and sing all weathers.

His mill will go with all winds.

同 圓滑周旋（3733）Smooth and suave.

反 到處碰壁（0599）Driven from pillar to post.

源 元 · 馬熙詩句："八面玲瓏得月多。"

0035 **八月十五是中秋，有人快活有人愁** bā yuè shí wǔ shì zhōng qiū, yǒu rén kuài huó yǒu rén chóu

August the 15th is the midautumn, there are people happy and people sad. (lit.)

It is no play where one weeps and another laughs.

0036 **拔苗助長** bá miáo zhù zhǎng

Pull up the seedling to help its growth. (lit.)

Too much zeal spoils all.

A watched pot never boils

同 欲速則不達（3719）Haste makes waste.

源 孟子 · 公孫丑上："揠苗助長。"

0037 **白費唇舌** bái fèi chún shé

Sheer waste of lips and tongue. (lit.)

Waste one's breath.

0038 **白費氣力** bái fèi qì lì

Sheer waste of air and strength. (lit.)

Beat the air.

Find a mare's nest.

Wash a blackamoor white.

同 徒勞無功（2807）Plow the sands and sow the waves.

0039 **白刃戰** bái rèn zhàn

White dagger war. (lit.)

Fight hilt to hilt.

同 短兵相接（0687）Fight at close quarters.

白日作夢 bái rì zuò mèng
Making dreams in broad daylight. (lit.)
To be day-dreaming.
In a brown study.

同 想入非非（3116）Build castles in the air.
反 頭腦清醒（2798）To be all there.

0040

白手起家 bái shǒu qǐ jiā
Start a family with empty hand. (lit.)
Start from scratch.
A self-made man.

反 家道中落（1252）To be worse off.

0041

白頭宮女在，閒話説玄宗
bái tóu gōng nǚ zài, xián huà shuō xuán zōng
The white-haired court girls in the palace gossip about Xuan Zong (an emperor in the Tang Dynasty). (lit.)
Strike up the old tune.

0042

白頭偕老 bái tóu xié lǎo
To grow old together with white hair. (lit.)
At their silver wedding.
A Darby and Joan.

0043

白雲蒼狗 bái yún cāng gǒu
The white cloud changes into a grey dog. (lit.)
It is the unforeseen that always happens.

同 變幻無常（0136）As changeable as the weather.
源 杜甫詩："天上浮雲如白衣，斯須變幻如蒼狗。"

0044

白紙黑字 bái zhǐ hēi zì
White paper and black writing. (lit.)
It's all in black and white.

0045

百般愚弄 bǎi bān yú nòng
To fool by hundred ways. (lit.)
Pull someone's leg.

0046

0047 **百步穿楊** bǎi bù chuān yáng
Hit the willow from a hundred steps. (lit.)
Hit the bull's-eye.

0048 **百尺竿頭，更進一步**
bǎi chǐ gān tóu, gèng jìn yī bù
To the top of a hundred-foot pole, one step further up. (lit.)
Make further efforts.
Break one's own record.

同 精益求精（1397）Though good is good, yet better is better.
反 吃老本（0371）Rest on one's laurels.
源 傳燈錄：“百尺竿頭須進步，十方世界是全身。”

0049 **百川歸海** bǎi chuān guī hǎi
Hundred rivers return to the sea. (lit.)
Follow the river and you'll get to the sea.
The sea refuses no river.
All rivers do what they can for the sea.
All roads lead to Rome.

同 異途同歸（3558）There are more ways to the wood than one.
源 淮南子・氾論訓：“百川異源，而皆歸於海。”

0050 **百發百中** bǎi fā bǎi zhòng
Hundred shoots and hundred hits. (lit.)
Every shot told.
Every time a bull's eye.

反 無的放矢（2954）Draw a bow at a venture.
源 史記：“楚有養由基者，善射者也。去柳葉百步而射之，百發而百中。”

0051 **百煉成鋼** bǎi liàn chéng gāng
Tempering for hundred times makes steel. (lit.)
Steeled and tempered.
Practice makes perfect.

源 漢・應劭漢官儀：“今取堅鋼，百煉而不耗。

0052 **百鳥歸巢** bǎi niǎo guī cháo
Hundred birds returning to nests. (lit.)
To sing off beat.
Sing out of tune.

同 亂作一團（1708）It was hell broken loose.
反 步調一致（0292）To be in step.

0053 **百忍成金** bǎi rěn chéng jīn
Hundred patience makes gold. (lit.)
All good things come to those who wait.

反 小不忍則亂大謀（3134）Anger and haste hinder good counsel.

百舍重繭 bǎi shè chóng jiǎn

Hundred housing and double cocoon. (lit.)

To be dead beat.

More dead than alive.

同 筋疲力竭（1348）To be worn out. 0054

反 生龍活虎（2415）Alive and kicking.

源 莊子天道："百舍重繭而不敢息。"

百事通 bǎi shì tōng

Hundred things through. (lit.)

A know-all.

反 一竅不通（3440）A babe in the wood. 0055

百萬雄師 bǎi wàn xióng shī

Million brave soldiers. (lit.)

Their name is legion.

反 烏合之眾（2944）Rag, tag and bobtail. 0056

百聞不如一見 bǎi wén bù rú yí jiàn

Hearing of hundred times is not like seeing once. (lit.)

Seeing is believing.

One eye-witness is better than ten ear-witnesses.

同 耳聞不如目睹（0726）The eyes believe themselves, the ears believe other people. 0057

百無禁忌 bǎi wú jìn jì

No taboo for hundred things. (lit.)

To ride whip and spur.

同 不管三七二十一（0196）Let the world wag as it will. 0058

反 投鼠忌器（2792）Burn not your house to rid the mouse.

百無聊賴 bǎi wú liáo lài

Out of hundred things nothing one wants to do. (lit.)

It's more pain to do nothing than something.

Have time hanging on one's hands.

Bored stiff.

同 閒極無聊（3092）Twiddle one's thumbs. 0059

反 忙不過來（1758）Have too many irons in the fire.

百務羈身 bǎi wù jī shēn

Body is tied down by hundred things. (lit.)

To be up to one's ears in work.

To have one's hands full.

同 忙得不可開交（1759）Not to have a moment one can call one's own. 0060

反 閒極無聊（3092）Bored to death.

0061 **百依百順** bǎi yī bǎi shùn
Follow and obey hundred times. (lit.)
At one's beck and call.
Dance after someone's pipe.
Have a nose of wax.
Feed (eat) out of someone's hands.

同 言聽計從（3306）Go all out on a person.
反 拂逆人意（0824）Go against the grain with one.

0062 **百折不撓** bǎi zhé bù náo
Undeterred by hundred setbacks. (lit.)
Fight for it tooth and nail.
Get at it hammer and tongs.
Never say die.
Stick it out.

同 不屈不撓（0243）Firm and unyielding.
反 俯首就範（0832）Give one's head for the washing.
源 漢 · 蔡邕："有百折不撓，臨大節而不可奪之風。"

0063 **百足之蟲，死而不殭**
bǎi zú zhī chóng, sǐ ér bù jiāng
An insect of hundred feet (a centipede) even dies yet not get stiff. (lit.)
Even a worm will turn.

源 淮南子："百足之蟲，至死不僵。"

0064 **擺臭架子** bǎi chòu jià zi
To put up smelly shelf. (lit.)
Cock one's chest like a half-pay admiral.
Throw one's weight about.

同 盛氣凌人（2433）To be overbearing.
反 畢恭畢敬（0121）Cap in hand.

0065 **擺架子** bǎi jià zi
To put up a shelf. (lit.)
Put on side (airs, frills).
Wear a high hat.
On the high horse.

同 神氣十足（2407）Puffed up with pride.
反 平易近人（1994）Have a taking way with one.

0066 **拜把兄弟** bài bǎ xiōng dì
To be brothers by oath and handshaking. (lit.)
Sworn brothers.

班門弄斧 bān mén nòng fǔ

To wield an axe at the door of Lu Ban. (lit.)

Teach one's grandmother how to suck eggs.

Bend the bow of Ulysses.

It is hard to halt before a cripple.

***Ban was a famous mechanic of Lu State and is now worshipped as the god of carpenter.**

源 梅之渙題李白墓詩："采石江邊一堆土，李白之名高千古，來來往往一首詩，魯班門前弄大斧。" 0067

搬起石頭打自己的腳

bān qǐ shí tóu dǎ zì jǐ de jiǎo

Carrying up the stone hits oneself's feet. (lit.)

To be hoisted with one's own petard.

同 自作自受（4017）Fry in one's own grease. 0068

板起面孔 bǎn qǐ miàn kǒng

To harden one's countenance like a board. (lit.)

Pull a long face.

Keep a straight face.

同 冷若冰霜（1595）As cold as ice. 0069

反 笑逐顏開（3155）Beam with joy.

半斤八兩 bàn jīn bā liǎng

Half a catty and eight ounces. (lit.)

Six of one and half a dozen of the other.

To be as broad as it is long.

Tweedledum and tweedledee.

同 不相上下（0258）Break even. 0070

反 天淵之別（2737）A far cry from

半絲半縷，恆念物力維艱

bàn sī bàn lǚ, héng niàn wù lì wéi jiān

Half a thread of silk, half a piece of string, always remember things and efforts are difficult (to produce). (lit.)

Waste not, want not.

He that will not stoop for a pin shall never be worth a pound.

See a pin and let it lie, you're sure to want before you die.

同 來之不易（1543）Hard to come by 0071

0072 **半途而廢** bàn tú ér fèi
Abandon half way. (lit.)
Do things by halves.
Drop (fall) by the wayside.
Not go the whole hog.

反 堅持到底（1265）Stick it out.
源 禮記："君子遵道而行，半途而廢，吾弗能已矣。"

0073 **半吞半吐** bàn tūn bàn tǔ
Half-swallowing, half-spitting. (lit.)
To mince matters.
To hum and haw.

同 欲説還休（3718）To shut up shop.
反 暢所欲言（0333）Speak one's mind.

0074 **半心半意** bàn xīn bàn yì
Half heart and half mean. (lit.)
Half heart is no heart.

同 心猿意馬（3197）Run with the hound and hold with the hare.
反 全心全意（2164）Heart and soul.

0075 **半信半疑** bàn xìn bàn yí
Half belief, half doubt. (lit.)
Half in doubt.
Take with a grain of salt.

同 姑妄聽之（0931）Take the story for what it is worth.
反 深信不疑（2400）Feel it in one's bones.

0076 **棒頭出孝子** bàng tóu chū xiào zǐ
The head of a rod brings out filial son. (lit.)
Spare the rod and spoil the child.

0077 **包藏禍心** bāo cáng huò xīn
Conceal an evil heart. (lit.)
The bait hides the hook.

同 笑裏藏刀（3151）Velvet paws hide sharp claws.
源 左傳："無乃包藏禍心以圖之。"

0078 **包打聽** bāo dǎ tīng
Guarantee to pry. (lit.)
Have an itching ear.
A rubber neck.
A nosey parker.
Paul Pry is on the spy.

反 充耳不聞（0384）None so deaf as those who won't hear.

0079 **保持鎮靜** bǎo chí zhèn jìng
Maintain calm. (lit.)
Keep one's hair on.
Keep one's head.
Keep cool.
As cool as a cucumber.
Keep one's shirt on.

同 頭腦冷靜（2797）Have one's brains on ice.
反 驚惶失措（1399）Like ducks in a thunder storm.

保留一手 bǎo liú yì shǒu
Reserve the master hand. (lit.)
Reserve the master-blow.

反 竭盡所能（1329）To the best of one's abilities. 0080

保留意見 bǎo liú yì jiàn
Reserve one's opinion. (lit.)
Keep one's own counsel. 0081

飽餐一頓 bǎo cān yí dùn
Eat a full hearty meal. (lit.)
Gorge oneself.
Eat like a horse.
Grease the gills.
To tuck in.

反 飢腸轆轆（1197）As hunger as a hunter. 0082

飽經風霜 bǎo jīng fēng shuāng
Fully experienced in wind and frost. (lit.)
Gone through thick and thin.
Gone through deep waters.

同 曾經滄海（0317）To have sailed the seven seas.
反 初見世面（0424）Babes in the woods. 0083

飽慳私囊 bǎo qiān sī náng
Fill private pocket to the full. (lit.)
Line one's pocket.
Feather one's nest.

同 貪污腐化（2675）Have an itching palm. 0084

飽食終日，無所用心
bǎo shí zhōng rì, wú suǒ yòng xīn
Eating to the full all day and never use the heart. (lit.)
A belly full of gluttony will never study willingly.
A full belly neither fights nor flies well.
Highly fed and lowly taught.
Fat paunches make lean pates.
He is better fed than nurtured

同 行屍走肉（3216）Idle men are dead all their life long.
反 孜孜不倦（3961）Keep one's nose to the grind-stone.
源 論語："飽食終日，無所用心，難矣哉。" 0085

飽以老拳 bǎo yǐ lǎo quán
To satisfy (him) with old fist. (lit.)
Give one a good licking.
Land a person one.
Comb a person's head.
Dust someone's jacket.

同 狠揍一頓（1061）Knock the daylight out of one.
源 晉書．石勒載記："孤昔日厭卿老拳，卿亦飽孤毒手。" 0086

0087 **寶刀未老** bǎo dāo wèi lǎo

Precious sword is not yet old. (lit.)

There's many a good tune played on an old fiddle.

同 老當益壯（1562）There is fight in the old dog yet.

反 吾老矣，無能為也矣（2945）Old bees yield no honey.

0088 **抱殘守缺** bào cán shǒu quē

Cherish broken and worn out articles. (lit.)

Stick-in-the-mud.

反 改弦更張（0855）Start with a clean slate.

源 漢書 · 劉歆傳："猶欲抱殘守缺。"

0089 **抱頭鼠竄** bào tóu shǔ cuàn

Hold the head and skulk away like a rat. (lit.)

Show a clean pair of shoes.

源 漢書："常山王奉頭鼠竄以歸漢王。"

0090 **抱恙在身** bào yàng zài shēn

Carry sickness of the body. (lit.)

To be taken ill.

To be laid up.

To be out of sorts.

同 身體違和（2388）To be under the weather.

反 久病新瘥（1416）To pull through.

0091 **暴虎馮河** bào hǔ píng hé

To attack a tiger without weapons, cross a river without a boat. (lit.)

Zeal without knowledge is fire without light.

To go it blind.

Fool-hardiness.

同 有勇無謀（3679）Have more guts than brains.

源 論語："暴虎馮河，死而無悔者，吾不與也。"

0092 **暴跳如雷** bào tiào rú léi

Jump up like a thunderbolt. (lit.)

Fly into a passion.

To go berserk.

Hit the ceiling.

Get one's monkey up.

In a towering rage.

Stamp with fury.

Have a tantrum.

Blow one's top (stack).

同 怒不可遏（1928）To hit the roof.

反 平心靜氣（1993）Collect oneself.

杯弓蛇影 bēi gōng shé yǐng 0093

Mistake the shadow of a bow in a glass for a snake. (lit.)

Take every bush for a bugbear.

同 疑神疑鬼（3520）Harbour suspicions.

源 晉書・樂廣傳："廣賜客酒，杯中有蛇，既而疾，廣意廳壁角弓影，復置酒，客頓愈。"

杯水車薪 bēi shuǐ chē xīn 0094

A cup of water (to put out burning) a cartload of firewood. (lit.)

A drop in the bucket.

同 僧多粥少（2321）Not enough to go round.

源 孟子："猶以一杯水，救一車薪之火也。"

卑躬屈節 bēi gōng qū jié 0095

Bow low and humiliate oneself. (lit.)

Bow and scrape.

Lick the ground.

Lick someone's shoes.

同 奴顏婢膝（1926）Grovel at the feet of

反 昂首雲外（0032）Have one's nose in the air.

悲不自勝 bēi bú zì shèng 0096

To grieve beyond one's control. (lit.)

Be overcome with grief.

Abandon one's self to grief.

A lump in the throat.

反 喜氣洋洋（3059）Beam with joy.

悲歡離合 bēi huān lí hé 0097

Grief and joy; partings and reunions. (lit.)

Sadness and gladness succeed each other.

源 蘇軾詞："人有悲歡離合，月有陰晴圓缺。"

悲痛欲絕 bēi tòng yù jué 0098

Grief to pain that one wants to die. (lit.)

Eat one's heart out.

Torn with grief.

Feel all mops and brooms.

Go to pieces.

同 心如刀割（3188）Cut one to the heart.

反 欣喜若狂（3202）Frantic with joy.

背城借一 bèi chéng jiè yī 0099

Borrow one with one's back on the wall (to fight). (lit.)

Fight with one's back to the wall.

Make a spoon or spoil a horn.

Fight to the last ditch.

同 破釜沉舟（2003）Burn one's boats.

源 左傳・成二年："請收合餘燼，背城借一。"

0100 **背道而馳** bèi dào ér chí
To run, turning the back on. (lit.)
Run counter to
Look one way and row another.
To be diametrically opposed to

同 南轅北轍（1877）Poles apart.
反 方向對頭（0753）On the right tack.
源 蘇軾詩："仙山佛國本同歸，世跡玄關兩背馳。"

0101 **背誦如流** bèi sòng rú liú
Repeat from memory as fluently as a stream. (lit.)
To rattle off.
Know a lesson off pat.
To reel off.
Get something down cold.
Know by heart.

0102 **背信棄義** bèi xìn qì yì
Unfaithful to and a breach of faith. (lit.)
Go back on a person.
To back out.
Play one false.
A breach of promise.
Go back on.

反 忠心耿耿（3910）As true as the dial to the sun.

0103 **悖入悖出** bèi rù bèi chū
Wrongly in and wrongly out. (lit.)
Ill got, ill spent.
What is gotten over the devil's back is spent under his belly.

源 大學："言悖而出者，亦悖而入，貨悖而入者，亦悖而出。"

0104 **備受奚落** bèi shòu xī luò
Suffer much from jeers and sneers. (lit.)
Get the cold shoulder.
To get the goose.
To be sneezed at
To be looked down upon.

0105 **本地薑不辣** běn dì jiāng bú là
Local ginger is not hot. (lit.)
A prophet is not without honour, save in his own country and his own home.
Grass is always greener on the other side of the fence (hill).

反 月是故鄉明（3744）Dry bread at home is better than roast meat abroad.

本來無一物，何處惹塵埃 0106

běn lái wú yí wù, hé chù rě chén āi

Originally there wasn't a thing, where came the dust? (lit.)

Out of nothing comes nothing.

源 六祖佛偈詩："菩提本無樹，明鏡亦非台，本來無一物，何處惹塵埃。"

本末倒置 běn mò dào zhì 0107

The first and last turn around. (lit.)

Put the cart before the horse.

Turn topsy-turvy.

同 冠履倒置Turn things upside down.

反 撥亂反正（0167）Put things back to order.

源 大學："物有本末，事有終始。"

笨頭笨腦 bèn tóu bèn nǎo 0108

Stupid head, stupid brain. (lit.)

Dead from the neck up.

Mickle head, little wit.

A block-head.

同 獃頭獃腦（呆頭呆腦）（0570）To be muddle-headed.

反 聰明伶俐（0459）Have a good head on one's shoulders.

蹦蹦跳跳 bèng bèng tiào tiào 0109

Hopping and Jumping. (lit.)

Jump like parched peas.

As playful as a kitten.

同 生龍活虎（2415）Alive and kicking.

反 呆若木雞（0569）To be rooted to the spot.

逼供信 bī gòng xìn 0110

Compel one to give the truth. (lit.)

Give one the third degree.

Grill a person.

Extort confession.

逼近眉睫 bī jìn méi jié 0111

Forcing near eyebrow and lashes. (lit.)

Hang over one's head.

同 危在旦夕（2876）Sword of Damocles.

鼻子朝天 bí zi cháo tiān 0112

Nose up towards sky. (lit.)

Cock up the nose.

Have one's nose in the air.

同 目空一切（1871）Turn a blind eye to

反 五體投地（3014）Fall on one's knees.

0113 **比比皆是** bǐ bǐ jiē shì
Here and there all is the same. (lit.)
Right and left.
Here and there and everywhere.

同 滿坑滿谷（1746）As thick as blackberries.
反 寥若晨星（1641）Few and far between.
源 明．陶宗儀．輟耕錄：“朝為師生而暮若途人者，比比皆是。”

0114 **彼此對立** bǐ cǐ duì lì
Facing each other. (lit.)
To be at odds.

同 冰炭不相容（0155）At loggerheads with one another.
反 水乳交融（2593）To be hand and glove with another.

0115 **彼此交惡** bǐ cǐ jiāo è
Exchange ill-feeling toward each other. (lit.)
There is no love lost between them.

反 互忍互讓（1095）Live and let live.

0116 **筆走龍蛇** bǐ zǒu lóng shé
Pen runs like snake and dragon. (lit.)
Write a fair hand.
To write with a flourish.

同 龍飛鳳舞（1691）Write a good fist.
源 溫庭筠詩：“落筆龍蛇滿壞牆。”

0117 **必恭必敬** bì gōng bì jìng
Certainly one will stoop and respect. (lit.)
Cap in hand.

同 維恭維謹（2898）Bow and scrape.
源 論語：“有子曰恭近於禮，遠恥辱也。”

0118 **敝帚自珍** bì zhǒu zì zhēn
Value even one's worn-out broom. (lit.)
All his geese are swans.
There's nothing like leather.
The crow thinks her bird fairest.
The smoke of a man's own house is better than the fire of another's.

源 魏文帝典論：“里語曰，家有敝帚，享之千金。”

0119 **閉口不言** bì kǒu bù yán
Shut the mouth saying nothing. (lit.)
Zip one's lip.
Hold one's peace.
Not to breathe a syllable.
Keep mum.
Button up one's lip.

同 默不作聲（1857）As mute as a fish.
反 信口開河（3207）Shoot off one's mouth.

閉門謝客 bì mén xiè kè
Close the door and refuse receiving guests. (lit.)
Not at home.
Sport one's oak.

同 餉以閉門羹（3117）Leave one on the mat.
反 夾道歡迎（1246）Roll out the red carpet for

0120

畢恭畢敬 bì gōng bì jìng
Salute and bow deeply. (lit.)
Cap in hand.

同 維恭維謹（2898）Bow and scrape.
反 毫不客氣（1022）With gloves off

0121

裨益不淺 bì yì bù qiǎn
Get benefit not thin. (lit.)
Stand one in good stead.
Be of great benefit.

反 後患無窮（1079）The devil and all to pay.

0122

弊多利少 bì duō lì shǎo
More trouble, less benefit. (lit.)
More kicks than halfpence.

0123

避而不答 bì ér bù dá
Keep away and not answer. (lit.)
To take the fifth.
Turn the pigs into the clover.

同 王顧左右而言他（2862）To fob off

0124

避繁就簡 bì fán jiù jiǎn
Avoid the complicated and take the simple. (lit.)
For shortness'sake.
To simplify matters.

同 執簡馭繁（3868）Take care of the pence and the pounds will take care of themselves.

0125

避難就易 bì nán jiù yì
Evade the difficult and take the easy. (lit.)
Cross the stream where it is shallowest.
Where the hedge is lowest men leap over.
Follow the line of least resistance.

反 知難而進（3855）Never shirk the hardest work

0126

0127 避之則吉 bì zhī zé jí

It's auspicious to avoid it. (lit.)

The best remedy against an ill man is much ground between.

To be out of harm's way.

Steer clear of

Fight shy of

Give a wide berth to

同 敬而遠之（1403）Keep one at a respectful distance.

反 惹禍上身（2179）Wake a sleeping dog.

0128 避重就輕 bì zhòng jiù qīng

Avoid the heavy and take the light. (lit.)

To ride off side issues.

It is better to fall from the window than from the roof.

Of two evils choose the least.

反 首當其衝（2552）Bear the brunt of

0129 篳路藍縷 bì lù lán lǚ

Beating through a path in rags. (lit.)

Blaze the trail.

反 步人後塵（0293）Follow the beaten track.

源 左傳．宣十二年："篳路藍縷，以啟山林。"

0130 邊幹邊學 biān gàn biān xué

In doing, it is learnt. (lit.)

In doing we learn.

0131 邊說邊幹 biān shuō biān gàn

While saying, do it. (lit.)

No sooner said than done.

Suit the action to the word.

同 身體力行（2387）Practise what one preaches.

反 誇誇其談（1522）The greatest talkers are always the least doers.

0132 鞭長莫及 biān cháng mò jí

Even a long lash will not reach him. (lit.)

Beyond one's grasp.

Out of reach.

同 遠水不救近火（3738）Water afar off quencheth not fire.

反 信手拈來（3208）Come in handy.

源 左傳："雖鞭之長，不及馬腹。"

0133 鞭闢入裏 biān pì rù lǐ

Whip through the inside. (lit.)

Cut to the quick.

同 入木三分（2286）Leave an indelible impression on

反 蜻蜓點水（2120）Skim over.

遍體鱗傷 biàn tǐ lín shāng 0134
Covered with scaly wounds all over the body. (lit.)
Beaten black and blue.

同 體無完膚（2709）With cuts and bruises.
反 安然無恙（0012）To be safe and sound.

變幻莫測 biàn huàn mò cè 0135
Illusory an unfathomable changes. (lit.)
The unexpected always happens.

同 天有不測之風雲（2735）Though the sun shines, leave not your cloak at home.
反 一成不變（3380）Hard and fast.

變幻無常 biàn huàn wú cháng 0136
Illusory and inconstant changes. (lit.)
As changeable as the weather.
A woman's mind and winter change oft.

同 天有不測之風雲，人有霎時之禍福（2736）It is the unforeseen that always happens.

表裏如一 biǎo lǐ rú yī 0137
Surface and interior as one. (lit.)
What the heart thinks the tongue speaks.

同 心口如一（3174）Mean what one says.
反 當面是人，背後是鬼（0588）Who flatters me to my face will speak ill of me behind my back.

別高興得過早 0138
bié gāo xìng dé guò zǎo
Don't be pleased too early. (lit.)
He laughs best that laughs last.
Don't hallo till you are out of the wood.

別管閒事 bié guǎn xián shì 0139
Never mind other's business. (lit.)
Pull in your ears.
Mind your own business.

同 安分守己（0009）Know where to draw a line.

別和他一般見識 0140
bié hé tā yì bān jiàn shí
Don't share the same opinion with him. (lit.)
If a donkey brays at you, don't bray at him.

0141 **别假手於人** bié jiǎ shǒu yú rén
Don't borrow others' hand. (lit.)
Send not a cat for lard.

同 親力親為（2106）If you want a thing done well, do it yourself.

0142 **別具一格** bié jù yī gé
Possesses a style of one's own. (lit.)
To be a class by itself.

同 不同凡響（0252）Out of the common run.

0143 **別開生面** bié kāi shēng miàn
Especially open a new face. (lit.)
Break fresh ground.
Strike out in another direction.

反 襲人故智（3052）Take a leaf out of another's book.
源 杜甫詩："將軍下筆開生面。"

0144 **別杞人憂天** bié qǐ rén yōu tiān
Don't be like the man of Qi State worrying about the fall of the sky. (lit.)
Don't cross a bridge before you come to it.
Don't meet the trouble half way.

源 列子："杞國有人，憂天崩墜，身無所寄，廢寢食者。"

0145 **別輕舉妄動** bié qīng jǔ wàng dòng
Don't behave lightly and move rashly. (lit.)
Look before you leap.

0146 **別挑肥揀瘦** bié tiāo féi jiǎn shòu
Don't pick out the fat and choose the lean. (lit.)
You must take the fat with the lean.

0147 **別無他法** bié wú tā fǎ
Simply no other way. (lit.)
To have nothing for it but

同 事不得已（2507）If the mountain will not come to Mahomet, Mahomet must go to the mountain.
反 滿腹妙計（1742）To be full of wrinkles.

0148 **別瞎指揮** bié xiā zhǐ huī
Don't blindly direct. (lit.)
Let the cobbler stick to his last.

別洩氣 bié xiè qì
Don't let air leak. (lit.)
Never say die.
Never say die! Up man, and try!

同 一鼓作氣（3396）Come to the scratch. 0149

別有用心 bié yǒu yòng xīn
To have an ulterior motive in heart. (lit.)
Have an axe to grind.
With an ulterior purpose.
Have an end in view.
Have something up one's sleeve.

反 心地光明（3162）Have one's heart in the right place. 0150

彬彬有禮 bīn bīn yǒu lǐ
Ceremoniously polite. (lit.)
To stand on ceremony.

同 文質彬彬（2924）Manners make the man. 0151
反 粗口爛舌（0471）Swear like a trooper.
源 論語："文質彬彬，然後君子。"

賓至如歸 bīn zhì rú guī
The guests feel at home. (lit.)
Keep open house.
A home from home.
Feel at home.

源 左傳·襄三十一年："賓至如歸，無寧災患。" 0152

鬢髮斑白 bìn fà bān bái
The hair with white patches. (lit.)
Silver threads among the gold.

反 乳臭未乾（2283）One's mouth is full of pap. 0153

冰凍三尺，非一日之寒 0154
bīng dòng sān chǐ, fēi yí rì zhī hán
To be frozen in three feet ice is not due to the cold for one day. (lit.)
Ill habits gather by unseen degrees.
The tree falls not at the first stroke.
An oak is not felled at one stroke.

冰炭不相容 bīng tàn bù xiāng róng
Ice and charcoal do not mix. (lit.)
At loggerheads with one another.
Like oil and water.

同 格格不入（0895）Out of keeping with 0155
源 鹽鐵論："冰炭不同器，日月不並明。"

0156 **冰消瓦解** bīng xiāo wǎ jiě
Ice melting and tiles disintegrating. (lit.)
Sink differences.
To melt away.

源 五燈會元詩："兒孫不是無料理，要見冰消瓦解時。"

0157 **兵不血刃** bīng bú xuè rèn
The soldiers did not stain their swords with blood. (lit.)
To win hands down.
Without striking a blow.

反 短兵相接（0687）Fight hilt to hilt.
源 荀子："兵不血刃，遠爾來服。"

0158 **兵諫** bīng jiàn
Negotiation by arm force. (lit.)
The persuasion of cold steel.

源 左傳："楚鬻拳諫文王，王不聽，臨之以兵，懼而從之。

0159 **兵來將擋，水來土掩**
bīng lái jiàng dǎng, shuǐ lái tǔ yǎn
Soldiers coming shall be stopped by soldiers, water coming shall be stopped by the soil (land). (lit.)
Measure for measure.
Give tit for tat.

0160 **兵戎相見** bīng róng xiāng jiàn
Military confrontation. (lit.)
At sword's points with each other.
At daggers drawn.

同 短兵相接（0687）Fight hilt to hilt.
反 化干戈為玉帛（1113）Beat swords into ploughshares, and spears into pruning hooks.

0161 **並駕齊驅** bìng jià qí qū
Riding in horse carriages abreast. (lit.)
Keep abreast (pace) with
Shoulder to shoulder.

同 齊頭並進（2035）Neck and Neck
反 遙遙領先（3349）Streets ahead of
源 劉勰・文心雕龍："並駕齊驅，而一轂統輻。"

0162 **並肩作戰** bìng jiān zuò zhàn
Fight shoulder by shoulder. (lit.)
Fight side by side.
Fight shoulder to shoulder.

病從口入 bìng cóng kǒu rù ◀0163
Sickness enters from the mouth. (lit.)
Gluttony kills more than the sword.

源 晉傅玄 · 口銘："病從口入，禍從口出。"

病入膏肓 bìng rù gāo huāng ◀0164
The disease has entered the vital regions. (lit.)
Too far gone.
Beyond remedy.

同 無可救藥（2974）There is no medicine against death.
反 久病新痊（1416）Take a fresh lease of life.
源 左傳 · 成十年："病入膏肓，不可為也。"

病休 bìng xiū ◀0165
Sick rest. (lit.)
To lie up.
To be laid up.

剝去偽裝 bō qù wěi zhuāng ◀0166
Strip off false decoration. (lit.)
Take the gilt off the gingerbread.
Cut someone down to size.

同 原形畢露（3732）Come out in one's true colours.
反 喬裝打扮（2096）Sail under false colours.

撥亂反正 bō luàn fǎn zhèng ◀0167
To restore the disorder to order. (lit.)
Square accounts.
Put things back to order.
Set things right side up.
Right the wrong.
Put something to rights.

反 顛倒是非（0644）Stand truth on its head.
源 公羊傳："撥亂世反諸正。"

勃然大怒 bó rán dà nù ◀0168
Abruptly burst into a great rage. (lit.)
Go black in the face.
Fly into a rage.
Fly off the handle.
Hit the ceiling.
Flare up.
Go off the top.

同 大發雷霆（0516）Explode with rage.
反 啞然失笑（3291）Burst out laughing.

博學多才 bó xué duō cái ◀0169
To be of great learning and talent. (lit.)
Know a thing or two.
Know what's what.
Well-read

同 多才多藝（0694）To be all-round.
反 胸無點墨（3232）Not to know A from a windmill.

0170 **駁得體無完膚** bó dé tǐ wú wán fū
Dress one down till his body has no full skin. (lit.)
Leave a person flat.
Take someone to pieces.
Have a person on toast.
Cut the ground from under someone's feet.
Argue someone down.
Knock the bottom out of
Wipe the floor with one.
Make mincemeat of

反 無言可對（3001）Come to a nonplus.

0171 **薄利多銷** bó lì duō xiāo
Thin profit, more sales. (lit.)
Small profits and quick returns.

同 貨如輪轉（1172）Sell like hot cakes.
反 血本無歸（3273）Sell one's hens on a rainy day.

0172 **捕風捉影** bǔ fēng zhuō yǐng
To seize wind and grasp the shadow. (lit.)
Take every bush for a bugbear.
All bulrushes are bugbears to him.

源 朱子全書．學一：“若悠悠地，似做不做，捕風捉影，有甚長進。”

0173 **不必拘禮** bù bì jū lǐ
No need to mind courtesy. (lit.)
Make yourself at home.
Don't stand on ceremony.

0174 **不辨菽麥** bù biàn shū mài
Cannot distinguish wheat from the beans. (lit.)
Not know chalk from cheese.

源 左傳：“周子有兄而無慧，不能辨菽麥。”

0175 **不表態** bù biǎo tài
No expression of attitude. (lit.)
Keep a straight face.
Not to commit oneself.

反 開誠佈公（1466）Wear one's heart on one's sleeve.

不恥下問 bù chǐ xià wèn 0176

Not ashamed to ask of one's inferiors. (lit.)

Bow down thy ear.

Though old and wise, yet still advise.

It is lawful to learn even from an enemy

反 剛愎自用（0875）Reckon without one's host.

源 論語："敏而好學，不恥下問。"

不揣冒昧 bù chuǎi mào mèi 0177

Without considering being presumptuous. (lit.)

Take the liberty to

不辭而別 bù cí ér bié 0178

Left without bidding farewell. (lit.)

Take French leave.

同 揚長而去（3334）Make oneself scarce.

不辭勞苦 bù cí láo kǔ 0179

Spare neither toil nor painstaking. (lit.)

Take great pains.

Up hill and down dale.

Take the trouble (to)

不到黃河心不死 0180

bù dào huáng hé xīn bù sǐ

Having not reached Yellow River, the heart won't die. (lit.)

See Naples and then die.

Hang on like grim death.

不得其所 bù dé qí suǒ 0181

Unable to obtain the way. (lit.)

Feel out of one's depth. (element).

A fish out of water.

To be out of one's latitude.

Out of place.

同 方鑿圓枘（0752）A square peg in a round hole.

反 得其所哉（0614）In one's own element.

0182 不得要領 bù dé yào lǐng

Cannot get the important point. (lit.)

Miss the point.

Beside the mark.

Not get the gist.

同 莫名其妙（1851）Can make neither head nor tail of

反 找着竅門（3817）Get the hang of it.

源 史記・大宛列傳："騫（張騫）不得其要領。"

0183 不懂裝懂 bù dǒng zhuāng dǒng

Not understand but pretend to know. (lit.)

Assume a knowing air.

Tyro and smatterer.

反 大智若愚（0568）No man can play the fool so well as the wise man.

0184 不動聲色 bù dòng shēng sè

Not raising voice and colour. (lit.)

Set one's face like a flint.

Keep a straight face./ Keep one's countenance.

Bit one's lips.

Keep quiet.

As quiet as a mouse.

同 面不改容（1794）Without turning a hair.

反 虛張聲勢（3249）Barking dogs seldom bite.

0185 不費吹灰之力 bù fèi chuī huī zhī lì

Require not the effort of blowing the ash off. (lit.)

A lift of the finger.

There's nothing to it.

Can do it on one's head.

As easy as pie.

同 易如反掌（3556）As easy as winking.

反 九牛二虎之力（1411）Move heaven and earth to

0186 不分勝負 bù fēn shèng fù

Undecided win or loss. (lit.)

A dead heat.

A drawn battle (game).

同 勢均力敵（2534）Nip and tuck.

0187 不孚眾望 bù fú zhòng wàng

Not satisfying people's expectation. (lit.)

Fall short of public expectation.

0188 不甘罷休 bù gān bà xiū

Not willing to give up. (lit.)

Go to great lengths.

同 不到黃河心不死（0180）See Naples and then die.

反 洗手不幹（3054）Wash one's hands of the business.

不甘後人 bù gān hòu rén ◀0189
Not willing to be behind others. (lit.)
Not to be outdone.
Keep one's end up.
Hold one's own.

反 甘拜下風（0860）Take a back seat.

不甘就範 bù gān jiù fàn ◀0190
Not willing to be disciplined. (lit.)
Kick over the traces.

反 俯首就範（0832）Give one's head for the washing.

不敢望其項背 bù gǎn wàng qí xiàng bèi ◀0191
Not dare to look at his back. (lit.)
Not in the same street as
Not fit to hold a candle to

同 瞠乎其後（0351）Lag far behind.
反 迎頭趕上（3601）To overtake one.

不共戴天之仇 bù gòng dài tiān zhī chóu ◀0192
Not to live together (with hatred) under the same sky. (lit.)
Sworn enemy.
Deadly feud.
Inveterate enemy.

反 莫逆之交（1852）A bosom friend.
源 禮記："父之讎勿以共戴天。"

不苟言笑 bù gǒu yán xiào ◀0193
Gareful not to talk and laugh. (lit.)
First think and then speak.
A man of few words.

同 非禮勿言，非禮勿動（0766）Speak fitly, or be silent wisely.
反 輕舉妄動（2125）To rush headlong.
源 禮記："不苟笑。"

不顧一切 bù gù yí qiè ◀0194
Disregard everything. (lit.)
Neck or nothing.
Stick at nothing.

同 置生死於度外（3901）Heedless of consequences.
反 瞻前顧後（3778）Take a look around.

不管好歹 bù guǎn hǎo dǎi ◀0195
Don't mind good or bad. (lit.)
Sink or swim.
Rain or shine.
For better or for worse.

0196 不管三七二十一
bù guǎn sān qī èr shí yī
Not bothering three times seven equals twenty one. (lit.)
Rain or shine.
Let the world wag as it will.
Come what may.
For good or ill.

反 瞻前顧後（3778）Take a look around.

0197 不過如此 bù guò rú cǐ
Nothing more than that. (lit.)
That is all there is to it.

0198 不害臊 bù hài sào
Not feel blushing. (lit.)
To blush like a dog.

同 恬不知恥（2741）Have no sense of shame.

0199 不寒而慄 bù hán ér lì
Trembling without being cold. (lit.)
Make one's teeth chatter.
Make one's flesh creep.

源 史記．酷吏列傳："是日皆報殺四百餘人，其後郡中不寒而慄。"

0200 不合時宜 bù hé shí yí
Not agree with the time. (lit.)
Out of season (date, fashion).
Behind the times.
As seasonable as snow in summer.
Ill-timed.

反 當時得令（0590）Everything is good in its season.
源 志林："朝雲曰，公一肚皮不合時宜，東坡大笑。"

0201 不慌不忙 bù huāng bù máng
Neither fearful nor busy. (lit.)
Take one's time.
Take it easy.
Keep one's head.
At one's ease.

同 慢條斯理（1755）Make two bites of a cherry.
反 驚惶失措（1399）Stand aghast.

0202 不急之務 bù jí zhī wù
An un-urgent affair. (lit.)
That can wait.

反 事不宜遲（2510）It brooks no delay.

不加按語 bù jiā àn yǔ 0203
Without adding comments. (lit.)
Refrain from comment.
Pass over in silence.

同 不表態（0175）Not to commit oneself.

不假思索 bù jiǎ sī suǒ 0204
No time to think. (lit.)
Speak impromptu.
Do (Say) something off-hand.

同 脱口而出（2829）Escape one's lips.
反 挖空心思（2833）Rack（Cudgel）one's brains.

不解之仇 bù jiě zhī chóu 0205
Unresolved hatred. (lit.)
Irreconciliable enmity.

反 刎頸之交（2929）Damon and Pythias.

不進則退 bù jìn zé tuì 0206
Not to advance is to retreat. (lit.)
Not to advance is to go back.

不經之談 bù jīng zhī tán 0207
An unfounded talk. (lit.)
Talk rubbish.
A tale of tub.

反 引經據典（3584）Give chapter and verse.
源 史記："其語閎大不經。"

不脛而走 bù jìng ér zǒu 0208
Run without legs. (lit.)
Spread like wildfire.
Catch on fast.
Make (Go) the round.

源 列子："珠無脛而行，玉無翼而飛。"

不堪一擊 bù kān yì jī 0209
Cannot stand a blow. (lit.)
The earthen pot must keep clear of the brass vessel.

反 固若金湯（0946）As firm as a rock.

不堪造就 bù kān zào jiù 0210
Could not be educated. (lit.)
Ill beef never made good broth.
Of a pig's tail you can never make a good shaft.
You cannot make a silk purse out of a sow's ear.

同 朽木不可雕（3241）No man can make a good coat with bad cloth.
反 孺子可教（2282）There's a good boy!

0211 不可等閒視之
bù kě děng xián shì zhī
Cannot wait for leisure to see it. (Cannot belittle it.) (lit.)
Not to be sneezed (sniffed) at.

反 不屑一顧（0260）Shut one's eyes to

0212 不可或缺 bù kě huò quē
Cannot be lacking or without. (lit.)
Part and parcel (of)

0213 不可救藥 bù kě jiù yào
Cannot be saved by medicine. (lit.)
Beyond remedy.
If physic do not work, prepare for the kirk.

同 病入膏肓（0164）Too far gone.
反 微感不適（2883）To feel off colour.
源 詩經．大雅：“多將熇熇，不可救藥。”

0214 不可企及 bù kě qǐ jí
Cannot see ahead. (lit.)
Beyond one's reach.
Not fit to hold a candle to

同 望塵莫及（2870）To be nowhere.
反 後來居上（1082）He finished first though he began last.

0215 不可輕敵 bù kě qīng dí
Do not take enemy lightly.
Despise not your enemy.

0216 不可輕視 bù kě qīng shì
Do not slight (any one or thing). (lit.)
Not to be taken lightly.
Not to be sneezed at.

0217 不可勝數 bù kě shèng shǔ
Cannot be counted. (lit.)
More than one could shake a stick at.
Beyond calculation.

同 恒河沙數（1063）As numberless as the sands.
源 墨子．非攻中：“百姓之道疾病而死者，不可勝數。”

0218 不可收拾 bù kě shōu shí
Cannot be gathered together. (lit.)
All the fat is in the fire.
Go to pot.

源 韓愈：“泊與淡相遭，頹墮委靡，潰敗不可收拾。”

不可同日而語 bù kě tóng rì ér yǔ
Can't be mentioned on the same day. (lit.)
Not to be mentioned in the same breath.
Not to be lumped together.

反 相提並論（3112）Place on par.
源 漢書．息夫躬傳：“臣與祿（公孫祿）異議，未可同日語也。” 0219

不可外傳 bù kě wài chuán
Cannot be spread outside. (lit.)
Off the record.
Between ourselves.

同 不足為外人道（0289）Between you and me.
反 一人傳十，十人傳百（3445）Pass from mouth to mouth. 0220

不可挽回 bù kě wǎn huí
Cannot be recovered. (lit.)
To be too far gone.

反 力挽狂瀾（1606）Save the situation. 0221

不可為外人道 bù kě wèi wài rén dào
Cannot tell others. (lit.)
Between you, me and the gatepose.

同 不可外傳（0220）Off the record.
反 一人傳十，十人傳百（3445）Flow from lip to lip. 0222

不可言狀 bù kě yán zhuàng
Cannot describe with words. (lit.)
Beggar description.

同 難以形容（1882）Beyond description. 0223

不可一概而論 bù kě yí gài ér lùn
Cannot be generalised in mentioning it. (lit.)
Every shoe fits not every foot.
All are not thieves that dogs bark at.

反 等量齊觀（0627）Six of one and half a dozen of the other.
源 劉知幾．史通．敘事：“而作者安可以今為古，一概而論得失。” 0224

不可一世 bù kě yí shì
Can't be in a life time.
As proud (vain) as a peacock.
Puffed up with pride.
As proud as Lucifer.

同 昂首雲外（0032）Have one's nose in the air.
反 無面目見江東父老（2981）To fly from the face of men. 0225

不吭一聲 bù kēng yì shēng
Not breathe a sound. (lit.)
Not to breathe a syllable.

同 默不作聲（1857）As mute as a fish.
反 大叫大嚷（0532）Cry at the top of one's voice. 0226

0227 不勞動，不得食 bù láo dòng, bù dé shí
No work, get no food. (lit.)
No pains, no gains.
No bees, no honey; no work, no money.
They must hunger in frost that will not work in heat.
A close mouth catches no flies.

反 自己動手，豐衣足食（3982）He that will eat the kernel must crack the nut.

0228 不露才華 bù lù cái huá
Not to show off talents. (lit.)
Hide one's talents under a bushel.

同 深藏若虛（2396）Still waters run deep.
反 大顯身手（0557）Show one's metal.

0229 不露鋒芒 bù lù fēng máng
Not to show the sharp edge and shining (of knife). (lit.)
Draw in one's horns.
Hide one's light (candle) under a bushel.

反 張牙舞爪（3794）Show one's claw（teeth）.

0230 不倫不類 bù lún bú lèi
Neither this group nor that class. (lit.)
Neither fish, flesh, nor fowl, nor good red herring.
Neither rhyme nor season.

同 非驢非馬（0767）Neither hawk nor buzzard.
源 禮記："儗人不於其倫。"
晉書："抗明威以懾不類。"

0231 不明所以 bù míng suǒ yǐ
Not understand why it is so. (lit.)
All at sea.

0232 不名一文 bù míng yì wén
Having not a single penny. (lit.)
Have not a penny to bless oneself with.
Have no face but one's own.
Not a feather to fly with.
To be on the hocks.

同 阮囊羞澀（2291）Not to have a bean.
反 腰纏萬貫（3344）Roll in wealth.
源 漢書 · 鄧通傳："竟不得名一錢，寄死人家。"

不謀而合 bù móu ér hé 0233

Agree without plan. (lit.)

To see eye to eye.

同 英雄所見略同（3596）Great minds think like.

反 意見分歧（3561）Opinions are divided.

源 蘇軾．朱壽昌梁武讖贊偈："如磁石鐵，不謀而合。"

不能容物 bù néng róng wù 0234

Cannot tolerate things. (lit.)

A little pot is soon hot.

同 心胸狹隘（3191）To be narrow-minded.

反 將相頭上堪走馬，公侯肚裏好撐船（1300）To take in good part.

不念舊惡 bù niàn jiù è 0235

Not harbouring old hatred. (lit.)

Forgive and forget.

Bury the hatchet.

Let bygones be bygones.

同 既往不咎（1234）Let the dead bury the dead.

反 永記血淚仇（3613）To nurse vengeance.

源 論語．公冶長："伯夷叔齊，不念舊惡，怨是用希。"

不怕官，最怕管 bù pà guān, zuì pà guǎn 0236

Not afraid of officials, but most afraid of being bossed. (lit.)

Better trust in God than in his saints.

不偏不倚 bù piān bù yǐ 0237

Neither inclining nor leaning. (lit.)

Hold the scale even.

Sit on the rail.

Betwixt and between.

同 一視同仁（3457）Not to make chalk of one and cheese of another.

反 厚此薄彼（1076）Make chalk of one and cheese of the other.

不破不立 bù pò bù lì 0238

Without destruction, no construction. (lit.)

You can't make an omelet without breaking eggs.

A house pulled down is half rebuilt.

0239 **不期而遇** bù qī ér yù
To meet unexpectedly. (lit.)
To happen upon
To meet up with
To chance upon
To come across
Bump into someone.
Fall in with

同 邂逅相遇（3157）Run into someone.
源 穀梁傳．隱八年："不期而會曰遇。"

0240 **不戚戚於貧賤** bù qī qī yú pín jiàn
Not worry to be poor and low. (lit.)
Poverty is not a shame, but the being ashamed of it.

0241 **不戚戚於貧賤，不汲汲於富貴**
bù qī qī yú pín jiàn, bù jí jí yú fù guì
Not worry to be poor and low, nor anxious to be rich. (lit.)
Better go to heaven in rags than to hell in embroidery.

源 漢書："少嗜欲，不汲汲於富貴，不戚戚於貧賤。"

0242 **不求上進** bù qiú shàng jìn
Not seeking progress. (lit.)
Rest on one's laurels.

同 自暴自棄（3968）Stand in one's own light.
反 奮發有為（0795）Shake oneself together.

0243 **不屈不撓** bù qū bù náo
Neither bending nor flinching. (lit.)
Stick to one's colours.
Firm and unyielding.
Fight for it tooth and nail.
Hang on by the eyelashes.
Keep one's chin up.
As steady as a rock.

同 百折不撓（0062）Stick it out.
反 俯首就範（0832）Give one's head for the washing.
源 漢書．敍傳下："樂昌篤實，不撓不屈。"

0244 **不容置疑** bù róng zhì yí
Allow no place to doubt. (lit.)
Beyond all question.
It leaves no room for doubt.

同 毫無疑義（1031）A moral certainty.
反 難以置信（1883）To stagger belief.

不入虎穴，焉得虎子 0245
bù rù hǔ xué, yān dé hǔ zǐ
How to get the cubs without entering the tiger den? (lit.)
Nothing venture, nothing have (gain.)
No pains, no gain.

源 後漢書 · 班超傳："班超使西域，謂其官屬曰，不入虎穴，不得虎子。"

不三不四 bù sān bù sì 0246
Neither three nor four. (lit.)
Neither one thing nor the other.
Neither hawk nor buzzard.
Neither fish nor foul.

不聲不響 bù shēng bù xiǎng 0247
No noise, no sound. (lit.)
As quiet (silent, still) as a mouse.

反 大吵大鬧（0507）To make the fur fly.

不食嗟來之食 bù shí jiē lái zhī shí 0248
Do not eat the food from pity. (lit.)
Better die a beggar than live a beggar.
A forced kindness deserves no thanks.
A civil denial is better than a rude grant.

源 禮記 · 檀弓下："予唯不食嗟來之食，以至於斯也。"

不識抬舉 bù shí tái jǔ 0249
Don't know being appreciated and lifted. (lit.)
Bring a cow to the hall and she will run to the byre.
Give him enough rope and he will hang himself.

同 不堪造就（0210）Of a pig's tail you can never make a good shaft.

不速之客 bù sù zhī kè 0250
Unexpected visitor. (lit.)
An unbidden guest.
A gate-crasher.
Turn up like a bad shilling.
He that comes uncalled sits unserved.
He that comes unbidden goes unthanked.

源 周易 · 需："有不速之客三人來。"

0251 **不通情理** bù tōng qíng lǐ
Not understand common sense. (lit.)
Have no bowels.

反 通情達理（2762）Know what's what.

0252 **不同凡響** bù tóng fán xiǎng
Different from the ordinary tune. (lit.)
Out of the common run.
Out of the ordinary.

同 技藝超倫（1228）Able to kick the eye out of a mosquito.

0253 **不為已甚** bù wéi yǐ shèn
Without doing more, already too much. (lit.)
Pour not water on a drowned mouse.

同 適可而止（2540）Know where to stop.

0254 **不問自取** bù wèn zì qǔ
Without asking, take it for oneself. (lit.)
To make free with something.

同 順手牽羊（2603）Walk away with

0255 **不惜工本** bù xī gōng běn
Spare neither labor nor capital. (lit.)
At all cost.
Spare no expense.

同 該花就花，該省就省（0852）Spend not when you may save; save not when you must spend.

0256 **不先不後** bù xiān bù hòu
Neither before nor after. (lit.)
In the nick of time.
Just on time.

0257 **不相伯仲** bù xiāng bó zhòng
Cannot distinguish who's the first or second. (lit.)
On a par with
Six of one and half a dozen of the other.

同 半斤八兩（0070）Tweedledum and Tweedledee.

反 霄壤之別（3131）A world of difference.

不相上下 bù xiāng shàng xià 0258
It is not altogether up or down. (lit.)
Much of a muchness.
Break even.
On a par with
As well be hanged for a sheep as for a lamb.
A dead heat.
On a dead level with

同 半斤八兩（0070）Six of one and half a dozen of the other.
反 相去十萬八千里（3111）Poles apart.

不向上級伸手 bù xiàng shàng jí shēn shǒu 0259
Not stretching hand to the superior. (lit.)
We must not lie down and cry "God help us".

不屑一顧 bù xiè yí gù 0260
Not worth taking a look at (lit.)
Shut one's eyes to
Snap one's fingers at
Turn up one's nose at
To set at naught.
Fly in the face (teeth) of

同 漠然置之（1855）Look on with unconcern.
反 不可輕視（0216）Not to be taken lightly.

不亞於人 bù yà yú rén 0261
Not inferior to others. (lit.)
Second to none.

同 出人頭地（0410）To be head and shoulders taller.

不言而喻 bù yán ér yù 0262
Comprehend without being told. (lit.)
It goes without saying.
Needless to say.

同 不在話下（0273）To be taken for granted.

不厭其煩 bù yàn qí fán 0263
Not tired of the trouble. (lit.)
Take the trouble.

不以我為德，反以我為仇 0264
bù yǐ wǒ wéi dé, fǎn yǐ wǒ wéi chóu
Not considering my good deed but treat me as an enemy. (lit.)
Lend one's money and lose one's friend.

0265 **不遺餘力** bù yí yú lì

Spare no effort. (lit.)

For all one is worth.

Leave no avenue unexplored.

Leave no stone unturned.

Go to all lengths.

Tooth and nail.

Move heaven and earth.

同 開足馬力（1477）At full steam.

反 袖手旁觀（3242）Stand by with folded arms.

源 戰國策：“王曰，秦之攻我也，不遺餘力矣，必以倦而歸也。”

0266 **不以人廢言** bù yǐ rén fèi yán

Not regarding others' words useless because of the persons. (lit.)

Give the devil his due. /If the counsel be good, no matter who gave it.

Give credit where credit is due.

同 不恥下問（0176）Bow down thy ear.

源 論語 · 衛靈公：“君子不以言舉人，不以人廢言。”

0267 **不以為忤** bù yǐ wéi wǔ

Not to be considered as offensive. (lit.)

Take no offence.

Take something in good part.

0268 **不翼而飛** bù yì ér fēi

Fly away without wings. (lit.)

Vanish from sight.

Nowhere to be found.

源 列子：“珠無脛而行，玉無翼而飛。”

0269 **不義之財** bù yì zhī cái

Money obtained unscrupulously. (lit.)

Ill-gotten wealth (gains.)

Hot money.

Filthy lucre.

0270 **不用提點** bù yòng tí diǎn

No use to mention the points. (lit.)

Send a wise man on an errand, and say nothing to him.

同 舉一反三（1442）A word is enough to the wise.

反 反覆叮嚀（0745）Knock into one's head.

0271 **不由自主** bù yóu zì zhǔ

Have no control over oneself. (lit.)

In spite of oneself.

Can't help.

同 身不由主（2382）The wagon must go whither the horses draw it.

反 獨立自主（0678）Stand on one's feet.

不約而同 bù yuē ér tóng 0272
In agreement without previous arrangement. (lit.)
With one accord.

反 聚訟紛紜（1447）So many men, so many minds.

不在話下 bù zài huà xià 0273
Not in the speaking. (lit.)
It goes without saying.
To be taken for granted.

不在人世 bù zài rén shì 0274
Not in the human world. (lit.)
To be no more.

同 九泉之下（1413）Under the clods.

不擇手段 bù zé shǒu duàn 0275
Without choosing any means. (lit.)
By hook or by crook.
By fair means or foul.
Stop at nothing.
Go to all lengths.

反 有分有寸（3646）Draw the line somewhere.

不折不扣 bù zhé bú kòu 0276
No discount. (lit.)
Out and out.
Every inch.
In every way.
In every sense of the word.

不知好歹 bù zhī hǎo dǎi 0277
Not knowing the good from the bad. (lit.)
Not know chalk from cheese.

反 分清是非（0786）Separate the wheat from the chaff.

不知老之將至 bù zhī lǎo zhī jiāng zhì 0278
Not realising old age soon coming. (lit.)
The insidious approach of age (death).
It's late ere a man comes to know he is old.

不知死活 bù zhī sǐ huó 0279
Not knowing life and death. (lit.)
Heedless of consequences.

0280 **不知所措** bù zhī suǒ cuò

Not knowing what to do. (lit.)

At a loss what to do.

Stand at gaze.

To be at loose ends.

To be up a tree.

同 六神無主（1687）To be all at sea.

反 胸有成竹（3233）Have an ace up one's sleeve.

源 三國志・吳志・諸葛恪傳："哀喜交並，不知所措。"

0281 **不知所云** bù zhī suǒ yún

Not knowing what one has said. (lit.)

Talk thirteen to the dozen.

源 諸葛亮・前出師表："臨表涕泣，不知所云。"

0282 **不知天高地厚** bù zhī tiān gāo dì hòu

Not knowing how high the sky and how thick the earth. (lit.)

To strut like a crow in the gutter.

0283 **不值一提** bù zhí yì tí

Not worth a mention. (lit.)

Nothing to make a song about.

同 何足掛齒（1047）Don't mention it.

反 姑妄言之（0932）From the teeth outwards.

0284 **不置可否** bù zhì kě fǒu

Not to put it yes or no. (lit.)

Not to commit oneself.

同 不表態（0175）Keep a straight face.

反 當機立斷（0584）Take the bull by the horns.

0285 **不着邊際** bù zhuó biān jì

Not reaching the edge. (lit.)

It's neither here nor there.

同 離題萬丈（1598）Wide of the mark.

反 正中要害（3846）Hit the nail on the head.

0286 **不自量力** bù zì liàng lì

Not measure one's own strength. (lit.)

Go beyond one's depth.

Overreach oneself.

Bite off more than one can chew.

Throw straws against the wind.

同 螳臂擋車（2689）Kick against the pricks.

反 人貴有自知之明（2203）Know myself.

源 戰國策・齊策三："荊甚固，而薛亦不量其力。"

0287 **不走彎路** bù zǒu wān lù

Not to walk crooked roads. (lit.)

By the string rather than by the bow.

同 直截了當（3871）Give it to one straight.

反 拐彎抹角（0961）In a round-about way.

不足介意 bù zú jiè yì ◀0288

No need to mind. (lit.)

It doesn't matter.

Of no consequence.

不足為外人道 bù zú wéi wài rén dào ◀0289

Not worth to tell other people. (lit.)

To be off the record.

Between you and me.

步步高升 bù bù gāo shēng ◀0290

Step by step, getting higher and higher. (lit.)

Step by step the ladder is ascended.

同 向上爬（3119）Climb the social ladder.

反 每況愈下（1778）Go down the drain.

步步為營 bù bù wéi yíng ◀0291

Step by step walk with care. (lit.)

Inch forward.

Pick one's steps.

On the alert.

同 穩紮穩打（2931）Slow but sure wins the race.

步調一致 bù diào yí zhì ◀0292

Marching steps in unison. (lit.)

To be in tune.

To be in step.

Keep step with

反 亂作一團（1710）Go haywire.

步人後塵 bù rén hòu chén ◀0293

Follow the dust left by another. (lit.)

Tread in one's footsteps.

Follow upon one's heels.

Take a leaf out of another's book.

Follow the beaten track.

同 蕭規曹隨（3132）Go on in the same old rut.

反 別開生面（0143）Break fresh ground.

佈下伏兵 bù xià fú bīng ◀0294

Lay the hidden soldiers. (lit.)

Lay an ambush.

C

0295 **才藝出眾** cái yì chū zhòng

Artistic talent surpasses the average. (lit.)

To be head and shoulders taller.

0296 **才子佳人** cái zǐ jiā rén

A talented man and a pretty woman. (lit.)

In the husband wisdom, in the wife gentleness.

源 西廂記："這叫做才子佳人信有之。"

0297 **財不可露眼** cái bù kě lù yǎn

Money should not be exposed to eyes. (lit.)

Opportunity makes the thief.

He that shows his purse longs to be rid of it.

0298 **財可通神** cái kě tōng shén

Money can get through to gods. (lit.)

Money talks.

No lock can hold against the power of gold.

Money makes the mare go.

同 有錢能使鬼推磨（3659）Wage will get a page.

0299 **財運亨通** cái yùn hēng tōng

The luck for wealth is prosperous. (lit.)

All he touches turns to gold.

反 手頭拮据（2547）To be hard up.

采聲雷動 cǎi shēng léi dòng 0300
Applause like thunders. (lit.)
Thunders of applause.

採薪之憂 cǎi xīn zhī yōu 0301
Have worry in gathering firewood. (lit.)
To be taken ill.
To be indisposed.

同 抱恙在身（0090）To be out of sorts.
源 孟子：“有采薪之憂。”

參與其事 cān yǔ qí shì 0302
Take part in the business. (lit.)
Have a finger in the pie.
Take part in

同 插上一手（0321）Put in one's oar.
反 置身事外（3900）Stand aloof.

殘羹冷炙 cán gēng lěng zhì 0303
Left-over soup and cold food. (lit.)
The left-over.
Crumbs from a rich man's table.

反 酒池肉林（1421）Beef and ale galore.
源 杜甫詩：“殘杯與冷炙，到處潛悲辛。”

倉猝之間 cāng cù zhī jiān 0304
In a sudden moment. (lit.)
On the spur of the moment.

同 猝然間（0473）All of a sudden.
源 李陵書：“前書倉卒，未盡所懷。”

倉皇失措 cāng huáng shī cuò 0305
Disturbed, not knowing what to do. (lit.)
Lose one's head.
Stand at gaze.
At a loss what to do.

同 不知所措（0280）To be up a tree.
反 泰然自若（2669）With perfect composure.

滄海一粟 cāng hǎi yī sù 0306
A grain in the blue sea. (lit.)
A drop in the ocean.
A drop in the bucket

反 滿坑滿谷（1746）As thick as blackberries.
源 蘇軾．赤壁賦：“寄蜉蝣於天地，渺滄海之一粟。”

操生殺之權 cāo shēng shā zhī quán 0307
Execute the authority of life and death. (lit.)
Tread on the neck of

0308 **操之過急** cāo zhī guò jí
To execute too hastily. (lit.)
Jump the gun.
Draw one's bow before the arrow is fixed.
Leap over the hedge before one comes to the stile.

同 欲速則不達（3719）Haste trips over its own heels.
反 慢條斯理（1755）Make two bites of a cherry.

0309 **操縱自如** cāo zòng zì rú
To control as one likes. (lit.)
Like wax in one's hands.
As clay in the hands of the potter.

反 老鼠拉龜，無處下手（1574）To catch a Tartar.

0310 **草草了事** cǎo cǎo liǎo shì
Finish a thing roughly. (lit.)
To huddle through
Get it over with
Slap (throw) together.

同 敷衍塞責（0821）To muddle through
反 認認真真（2247）In sober earnest.

0311 **草菅人命** cǎo jiān rén mìng
Treat human life as grass. (lit.)
Mow down like grass.
Kill like flies.

源 漢書："其視殺人，若艾草菅然。

0312 **草木皆兵** cǎo mù jiē bīng
Take the grass and the trees as troops. (lit.)
Take every bush for a bugbear.
Fields have eyes, and woods have ears.
Afraid of one's own shadow.

源 東晉書："堅登城望八公山上，草木皆類人形。"

0313 **側耳諦聽** cè ěr dì tīng
Incline the ear and listen attentively. (lit.)
Strain one's ears.
Lend an ear to

同 豎起耳朵（2575）Prick up one's ears.
反 充耳不聞（0384）Turn a deaf ear to

0314 **側目而視** cè mù ér shì
Look with a sidelong glance. (lit.)
Look askance at

源 戰國策："則目而視，則耳而聽。"

惻隱之心 cè yǐn zhī xīn 0315

A heart of sympathy. (lit.)

Milk of human kindness.

Bowels of compassion (mercy).

Sense of pity.

反 嗜殺成性（2537）To be blood thirsty.

源 孟子：“惻隱之心，人皆有之。”

參差不偶 cēn cī bù ǒu 0316

Irregular and uneven. (lit.)

To be in a pretty pickle.

In a sorry plight.

同 處境困難（0429）Like a toad under a barrow.

反 飛黃騰達（0771）Rise in the world.

曾經滄海 céng jīng cāng hǎi 0317

Having travelled over the deep blue sea. (lit.)

To have gone through deep waters.

To have sailed the seven seas.

Go through fire and water.

Go through thick and thin

同 過來人（0999）Have had one's day.

反 初見世面（0424）Babes in the woods.

源 元稹詩：“曾經滄海難為水，除卻巫山不是雲。”

曾經滄海難為水 0318

céng jīng cāng hǎi nán wéi shuǐ

Having travelled over the deep blue sea, it is difficult to show (interest) in water. (lit.)

He that is down needs fear no fall.

I wasn't born in a wood to be scared by an owl.

There is nothing new under the sun.

差強人意 chā qiáng rén yì 0319

Only just satisfy one's wish. (lit.)

Suit one's fancy

反 討厭萬分（2699）Bored to death.

源 後漢書：“吳公差強人意。”

差之毫釐，謬以千里 0320

chā zhī háo lí, miù yǐ qiān lǐ

To miss the mark by an inch is to miss it by thousand li (mile). (lit.)

A miss is as good as a mile.

There is but one step from the sublime to the ridiculous.

Take a farthing from a thousand pounds, it will be a thousand pounds no longer.

A little too late is much too late.

反 恰到好處（2052）To a turn.

源 漢書：“失之毫釐，差以千里。”

0321 **插上一手** chā shàng yì shǒu

Insert one's hand in. (lit.)

Have a finger in the pie.
Poke one's nose into
Have a hand in
Put in one's oar.

同 參與其事（0302）Take part in
反 置身事外（3900）To hold off.

0322 **拆穿西洋鏡** chāi chuān xī yáng jìng

Breaking through the western mirror. (lit.)

Take the mickey out of it.

同 撕開畫皮（2622）Take the gilt off the gingerbread.
反 掩人耳目（3322）Draw the wool over one's eyes.

0323 **豺狼當道** chái láng dāng dào

A wolf bars the road. (lit.)

A lion in the path.
Iron rule.
Rod of iron.

源 後漢書：“豺狼當道，安問狐狸。

0324 **柴米夫妻** chái mǐ fū qī

Firewood and rice, husband and wife (married to get the necessities). (lit.)

Cupboard love.

0325 **饞涎欲滴** chán yán yù dī

Desire of food makes saliva drip. (lit.)

The mouth waters.
Smack the lips.

同 垂涎三尺（0446）To drool over
反 食慾不振（2470）Loss of appetite.

0326 **剷草除根** chǎn cǎo chú gēn

To spade the weeds and remove the roots. (lit.)

Pluck up by the roots.
Nip in the bud.

同 寸草不留（0477）To lay waste.
反 培育成才（1957）Lick into shape.
源 魏收・為侯景叛移梁朝文：“抽薪止沸，翦草除根。”

0327 **長年累月** cháng nián lěi yuè

Long years and accumulated months. (lit.)

Year in and year out.
Year after year.

長驅直入 cháng qū zhí rù ◀0328

Long drive and penetrate directly (into enemy territory). (lit.)

It was just a walk over.

同 勢如破竹（2536）Like a hot knife cutting through butter.

反 到處碰壁（0599）Driven from pillar to post.

源 曹操·勞徐晃令："所聞古之善用兵者，未有長驅直入敵圍者也。"

長袖善舞 cháng xiù shàn wǔ ◀0329

Long sleeves help one to dance well. (lit.)

Wheel and deal.

同 圓滑周旋（3733）Smooth and suave.

源 韓非子·五蠹："鄙諺曰，長袖善舞，多錢善賈。此言多資之易為工也。"

常捨常有 cháng shě cháng yǒu ◀0330

Often give, often have. (lit.)

The hand that gives gathers.

The charitable gives out at the door and God puts in at the window.

Give much to the poor doth increase a man's store.

唱低調 chàng dī diào ◀0331

Sing low tune. (lit.)

Play something down.

同 大題小做（0554）The mountain has brought forth a mouse.

唱反調 chàng fǎn diào ◀0332

Sing the opposite tune. (lit.)

Whistle a different tune.

反 唯唯諾諾（2904）Say ditto.

暢所欲言 chàng suǒ yù yán ◀0333

Freely say what one wishes. (lit.)

Open one's budget.

Speak one's mind.

同 傾吐衷情（2123）Get it off one's chest.

反 半吞半吐（0073）To mince matters.

超塵拔俗 chāo chén bá sú ◀0334

Surpassing the dust and rising above the common lot. (lit.)

Out of the common run.

同 瀟灑出塵（3133）Neat but not gaudy.

反 平平庸庸（1989）Pass in a crowd in a push.

朝上有人好做官 cháo shàng yǒu rén hǎo zuò guān ◀0335

Having a friend in court, it is easy to be an official. (lit.)

With a friend at court.

A friend in court is better than a penny in purse.

0336 徹底打垮 chè dǐ dǎ kuǎ
Knock it down thoroughly. (lit.)
Knock the bottom out of
Knock saucepan out of

反 刀下留情（0595）Pull one's punches.

0337 徹底粉碎 chè dǐ fěn suì
Break it to pieces thoroughly. (lit.)
Smash to smithereens.

0338 徹底交代 chè dǐ jiāo dài
Change over thoroughly. (lit.)
Make a chean breast of

同 低頭認罪（0634）Plead guilty

0339 徹頭徹尾 chè tóu chè wěi
From head to tail. (lit.)
Through and through.
Out and out.
From tip to toe.
To the end of one's little finger.
To the core.
From beginning to end.

源 朱子全書：“聖賢之學，徹頭徹尾，只是一個通字。”

0340 撤職查辦 chè zhí chá bàn
To get the sack, be investigated and punished. (lit.)
To be cast out of the saddle.

反 加官晉爵（1241）A feather in one's cap.

0341 沉得住氣 chén dé zhù qì
Keeping down the air (temper). (lit.)
Keep one's temper.

反 大發脾氣（0517）To lose one's shirt.

0342 沉默寡言 chén mò guǎ yán
Deep silence and rarely talk. (lit.)
Hold one's peace (tongue).
To be a regular oyster.
A person of few words.

同 默不作聲（1857）Refrain from comment.

反 滔滔不絕（2692）Talk oneself out of breath.

0343 沉思默想 chén sī mò xiǎng
Deep thought and silent thinking. (lit.)
To be in a brown study.

陳陳相因 chén chén xiāng yīn 0344
In accordance with old ways. (lit.)
Follow the beaten track.
Ride a method to death.
In the rut

同 食古不化（2467）Stick-in-the-mud.
反 改弦更張（0855）Start with a clean slate.
源 漢書："太倉之粟，陳陳相因。"

陳詞濫調 chén cí làn diào 0345
Hackneyed and abusive phrases. (lit.)
Hackneyed phrases.
Flog the dead horse.
Harp on the same string.

趁火打劫 chèn huǒ dǎ jié 0346
Take the advantage of a fire, rob. (lit.)
Fish in troubled waters.
Avail oneself of another's dilemma.

趁機行事 chèn jī xíng shì 0347
Make use of the opportunity to do things. (lit.)
Catch the tide.
Set sail when the wind is fair.
Make hay while the sun shines.

同 勿失時機（3026）Take fortune at the tide.
反 坐失良機（4055）Miss the boat.

趁熱打鐵 chèn rè dǎ tiě 0348
Strike the iron while it is hot. (lit.)
Strike while the iron is hot.

同 趁機行事（0347）Make hay while the sun shines.
反 賊去關門（3771）Lock the stable door after the horse is stolen.

稱王稱霸 chēng wáng chēng bà 0349
Call oneself king and tyrant. (lit.)
To rule the roost.
To lord it over.
Ordering people about.

同 作威作福（4073）Throw one's weight abou

稱兄道弟 chēng xiōng dào dì 0350
Call each other brothers. (lit.)
Call cousins with
Chum in with
Thick as thieves.

反 倒戈相向（0597）Turn one's coat.

0351 瞠乎其後 chēng hū qí hòu
Fall behind with open eyes. (lit.)
Lag far behind.
To be nowhere.
Not fit to hold a candle to (one).
To be not a patch on a person.

同 倒數第一（0600）To bring up the rear.
反 迎頭趕上（3601）Make up for leeway.
源 莊子．田子方："夫子奔逸絕塵，而回瞠若夫後矣。"

0352 瞠目結舌 chēng mù jié shé
Wide eyes and tongue-tied. (lit.)
Struck dumb.
Stare tongue-tied.
Stunned and speechless.
To be dumb-founded.

同 目瞪口呆（1866）Lose one's tongue.
反 鼓如簧之舌（0944）Wag one's tongue.

0353 成敗利鈍 chéng bài lì dùn
Success or failure, sharp or blunt. (lit.)
Hit or miss.
Make or mar.
Hail, rain or shine.
The ups and downs of life.
Every flow must have its ebb.

同 盛衰榮辱（2435）The vicissitudes of life.
源 諸葛亮．後出師表："成敗利鈍，非臣之明所能逆睹也。"

0354 成千上萬 chéng qiān shàng wàn
The whole thousand, up to tens of thousands. (lit.)
Thousands upon thousands.

0355 成羣結隊 chéng qún jié duì
Forming groups and uniting the ranks. (lit.)
To muster in force.
Flock together.

同 魚貫而出（3690）In Indian file.
反 孤雲野鶴（0938）Keep oneself to oneself.

0356 成則為王，敗則為寇
chéng zé wéi wáng, bài zé wéi kòu
He who conquers is crowned king, he who fails is called vagabond chief. (lit.)
Losers are always in the wrong.
A thief passes for a gentleman when thieving has made him rich.

成竹在胸 chéng zhú zài xiōng 0357

There is a bamboo (image) in the chest (mind of a painter). (lit.)

Have a card (an ace) up one's sleeve.

同 心中有數（3201）Know what's what.

反 一籌莫展（3381）To be at one's wit's end.

源 蘇軾："畫竹必先得成竹在胸中。"

承先啟後 chéng xiān qǐ hòu 0358

Inherit from the ancestors and initiate the descendants. (lit.)

To carry forward.

城門失火，殃及池魚 0359

chéng mén shī huǒ, yāng jí chí yú

The city gate on fire brings calamity to the fish pond. (lit.)

When thy neighbour's house doth burn be careful of thine own.

源 北史："城門失火，殃及池魚。"

城下之盟 chéng xià zhī méng 0360

Sue for peace under the wall of the city. (lit.)

A city that parleys is half gotten.

Treaty signed under duress.

源 左傳："為城下之盟而還。"

乘風破浪 chéng fēng pò làng 0361

Ride the wind and break the waves. (lit.)

Sail before the wind.

Brave the winds and waves.

Carry a bone in the teeth.

Plough the waves.

源 宋書．宗愨傳："願乘長風，破萬里浪。"

乘人不備 chéng rén bú bèi 0362

Catch one unprepared. (lit.)

Catch one off guard.

Catch a person napping.

Catch a weasel asleep.

Take one unaware (at advantage.)

同 出其不意（0408）Take one by surprise

0363 乘十一路車 chéng shí yī lù chē

Ride on bus route 11 (11 looks like two legs). (lit.)

Ride on the horse with ten toes.

Ride the shoe leather express.

同 安步當車（0008）On shanks' mare.

0364 誠實可靠 chéng shí kě kào

Honest and reliable. (lit.)

As true as steel.

To be on the square (level).

To be all wool and a yard wide.

Fair and square.

To be on the up and up.

反 詭計多端（0991）As crooked as a corkscrew.

0365 懲羹吹膾 chéng gēng chuī kuài

Scalded by (hot) broth one blows on (cold) vegetable. (lit.)

Blow first and sip afterwards.

A burnt child dreads the fire.

同 吳牛喘月（2947）The scalded dog fears cold water.

反 玩火自焚（2841）Play with fire.

源 楚辭・九章・惜誦：“懲於羹而吹齏兮。”

0366 懲前毖後 chéng qián bì hòu

Punish the precedent to guard against the future offense. (lit.)

Make an example of one.

源 詩經：“予其懲而毖後患。”

0367 懲一儆百 chéng yī jǐng bǎi

Punish one as a warning to a hundred. (lit.)

He that chastiseth one amendeth many.

Make an example of

Let it be a lesson to

同 懲前毖後（0366）Make an example of one.

源 漢書：“以一警百，使民皆服。”

0368 稱薪而爨 chèng xīn ér cuàn

Weigh the firewood before lighting it to cook. (lit.)

Spare well and spend well.

Pinch and scrape.

同 數米而炊（2571）Skin the flea for its hide and tallow.

反 酒池肉林（1421）Beef and ale galore.

源 淮南子：“秤薪而爨，數米而炊。”

吃得苦中苦，方為人上人 0369
chī de kǔ zhōng kǔ, fāng wéi rén shàng rén
He who can bear the bitterness of hardship can then be man above man. (lit.)
No sweet without sweat.

同 天將降大任於是人也，必先苦其心志，勞其筋骨（2713）Storms make oaks take deeper roots.

吃喝玩樂 chī hē wán lè 0370
Eat, drink and pleasure-seeking. (lit.)
All beer and skittles.
Make merry.

同 尋歡作樂（3279）Go on a spree.
反 艱苦樸素（1272）To hog it.

吃老本 chī lǎo běn 0371
Eat the old capital. (lit.)
Rest on one's laurels (oars).

吃力不討好 chī lì bù tǎo hǎo 0372
The effort is not appreciated. (lit.)
Bite on granite.
Be a fool for one's pains.
A thankless job.
Shoe the goose.
Make bricks without straw.
Get all the kicks and none of the ha'pence.

同 心勞日拙（3176）To find a mare's nest.
反 輕而易舉（2124）Mere child's play.

吃屎吃着豆 chī shǐ chī zhe dòu 0373
Eating faeces, find eating beans. (lit.)
The luck of the devil.

吃西北風 chī xī běi fēng 0374
Eat north west wind. (lit.)
To live like a plover.

反 食前方丈（2468）One's bread is buttered on both side

吃小虧佔大便宜 chī xiǎo kuī zhàn dà pián yí 0375
At a little loss take up a great gain (favour). (lit.)
Sometimes the best gain is to lose.
Venture a small fish to catch a great one.
Take the bit and the buffet with it.

0376 **吃一塹，長一智**
chī yí qiàn, zhǎng yí zhì
Once fallen into a pit, there is a gain in wisdom. (lit.)
A fall into a pit, a gain in your wit.
A stumble may prevent a fall.
Once bitten, twice shy.
Experience must be bought.
Experience is the mother of wisdom.

同 人老精，鬼老靈（2207）Old birds are not caught with chaff.

0377 **癡心妄想** chī xīn wàng xiǎng
Silly heart and vain hopes. (lit.)
Have a bee in one's bonnet.
Hitch one's wagon to a star.
Indulge in wishful thinking.

同 異想天開（3559）Have one's head full of bees.
反 實事求是（2480）Look fact on the face.

0378 **嗤之以鼻** chī zhī yǐ bí
To scorn one with the nose. (lit.)
Turn up one's nose at
Treat with contempt.
Look down one's nose at

反 阿諛諂媚（0712）Tickle someone's ears.

0379 **持之以恒** chí zhī yǐ héng
To maintain it with perseverance. (lit.)
Stick to it.
Keep it up.
Without a break.
Perseverance will prevail.

同 滴水穿石（0637）Constant dripping wears away the stone.
反 三天打魚，兩天曬網（2313）By fits and starts.

0380 **恥食嗟來之食** chǐ shí jiē lái zhī shí
Shame to eat food from pity. (lit.)
Better die a beggar that live a beggar.
A forced kindness deserves no thanks.

同 寧死不辱（1916）Loss of honour is loss of life.
反 飢者易為食（1198）Hungry dogs would eat dirty puddings.

0381 **彳亍街頭** chī chù jiē tóu
Staggering in the street. (lit.)
Have got the key of the street.
Pound the pavement.

同 流離失所（1680）Here today and gone tomorrow.

赤舌燒城 chì shé shāo chéng **0382**
Red tongue burns city. (lit.)
Opinion rules the world.
We are all slaves of opinion.
Fling dirt enough, and some will stick.

同 眾口爍金（3918）If all men say that thou art an ass, then bray.
源 太玄經："赤舌燒城，吐水於瓶。"

赤繩繫足 chì shéng xì zú **0383**
The red cord binds the feet. (lit.)
Marriages are made in heaven.
Marriage comes by destiny.

源 幽怪錄："赤繩繫夫婦之足，雖仇家異域，一繫終不可易。"

充耳不聞 chōng ěr bù wén **0384**
Plugging the ears, one can't hear. (lit.)
None so deaf as those who won't hear.
Turn a deaf ear to

同 耳邊風（0722）In at one ear and out at the other.
反 洗耳恭聽（3053）To be all ears.
源 詩經："叔兮伯兮，褎如充耳。"

沖昏頭腦 chōng hūn tóu nǎo **0385**
Knock the head dizzy. (lit.)
Go to one's head.
To be carried away (by)
Get dizzy with

同 蒙頭轉向（1784）Make one's head swim.
反 頭腦清醒（2798）Keep a level head.

沖天幹勁 chōng tiān gàn jìng **0386**
Zest for work soars to the sky. (lit.)
Be a live wire.

反 老油條（1578）A milk-sop.

衝破藩籬 chōng pò fān lí **0387**
Burst through and break down hedges and fences. (lit.)
Kick over the traces.
To break bounds.

反 固步自封（0945）Stay put.

重為馮婦 chóng wéi féng fù **0388**
Again to be woman Feng (a difficult job that no one likes). (lit.)
Pick up the threads.
Back to the salt mines.

0389 重溫舊夢 chóng wēn jiù mèng
Review old dreams. (lit.)
To chew the cud.
Relive the good old days.
Do it again.

同 白頭宮女在，閒話說玄宗（0042）Strike up the old tune.

0390 重新做人 chóng xīn zuò rén
To be a man anew. (lit.)
Turn over a new leaf.
Start with a clean slate.

同 悔過自新（1153）Make a fresh start.
反 故態復萌（0951）At one's little games again.

0391 重修舊好 chóng xiū jiù hǎo
To restore the good old (friendship). (lit.)
Heal the breach.
Bury the hatchet.

同 握手言歡（2941）To make it up.
反 管寧割蓆（0974）Cut loose from old ties.

0392 重整旗鼓 chóng zhěng qí gǔ
Re-arrange banners and drums. (lit.)
Dig up the hatchet.
Rally one's forces.
Re-shuffle.

0393 抽捐募稅 chōu juān mù shuì
Draw the contribution and collect the tax. (lit.)
To raise the wind.

同 橫徵暴斂（1071）Grind the faces of the people.

0394 抽薪止沸 chōu xīn zhǐ fèi
Pull out the firewood and stop the boiling. (lit.)
Take away fuel, take away flame.
To root up.

反 火上加油（1168）Pour oil on the flame.
源 諺語："揚湯止沸，不若釜底抽薪。"

0395 愁眉不展 chóu méi bù zhǎn
Gloomy eyebrows knitting unhappily. (lit.)
Look blue.
Mope about.
Down in the mouth.
To be in the dumps.

同 鬱鬱不樂（3725）In the blues.
反 笑逐顏開（3155）Beam with joy.

愁眉苦臉 chóu méi kǔ liǎn
Gloomy eyebrows and bitter face. (lit.)
Wear a glum countenance.
Laugh on the other side of one's face.
Pull a long face.

同 哭喪着臉（1513）To sour one's cheeks.
反 笑容可掬（3154）A face wreathed in smiles.

0396

躊躇不決 chóu chú bù jué
Hesitating and uneasy. (lit.)
Between hawk and buzzard.
Like one o'clock half struck.
To be neither fish nor flesh.

同 舉棋不定（1439）Let "I dare not" wait upon "I would"
反 快刀斬亂麻（1523）Cut the Gordian knot.

0397

躊躇滿志 chóu chú mǎn zhì
Irresolute then gratified. (lit.)
To one's heart's content.
To be self-satisfied.
Puffed up with pride.
Look like the cat that ate (swallowed) the canary.

同 心滿意足（3180）After one's own heart.
反 大喊倒霉（0526）Get it in the neck.
源 莊子："為之躊躇滿志。"

0398

臭老九 chòu lǎo jiǔ
Smelly old No. 9. (lit.) (This is a very derogatory term in Chinese.)
Egg-head.
High-brow.

0399

臭罵一頓 chòu mà yí dùn
Scold with dirty words at one length. (lit.)
To call for everything under the sun.
Give one a dressing down.
To roast someone.

反 吹捧上天（0444）Praise to the skies.

0400

出處不如聚處 chū chù bù rú jù chù
Goods in their origin are not so good as those in the place of gathering. (lit.)
Game is cheaper in the market than in the fields and woods.

0401

0402 **出爾反爾** chū ěr fǎn ěr

What comes from you will contradict you. (lit.)

Blow hot and cold.

Play fast and loose.

Go back on one's word.

同 朝令夕改（3811）The law is not the same at morning and night.

反 一言為定（3486）A bargain is a bargain.

源 孟子："戒之戒之，出乎爾者，反乎爾者也。"

0403 **出風頭** chū fēng tóu

Rise to the wind head. (lit.)

Cut a dash.

In the spotlight (limelight).

同 招搖過市（3806）Seek the limelight.

反 獻醜不如藏拙（3102）Hide one's diminished head（ignorance）.

0404 **出乎意外** chū hū yì wài

Out of expectation. (lit.)

Out of one's reckoning.

More than one bargained for.

0405 **出口成章** chū kǒu chéng zhāng

What comes out from his mouth is like a composition. (lit.)

One's tongue is the pen of a ready writer.

反 張口結舌（3793）At a loss for words.

源 蘇軾文："脱口成章，粲莫可耘。"

0406 **出類拔萃** chū lèi bá cuì

Stand out from the class and raise oneself from the rest. (lit.)

Tower above the rest.

Out of the common run.

In a class by itself.

Distinguish oneself.

同 卓爾不羣（3957）Come to the fore.

反 平平庸庸（1989）Pass in a crowd in a push.

源 孟子："出於其類，拔乎其萃。"

0407 **出門不換** chū mén bù huàn

Out of the door, cannot change. (lit.)

Let the buyer beware.

同 姜太公釣魚，願者上鈎（1295）If fools went not to the market, bad wares would not be sold.

0408 **出其不意** chū qí bù yì

Out from his unexpected happening. (lit.)

Take one by surprise.

Take someone unawares.

同 乘人不備（0362）Catch one off his guard.

源 孫子·計篇："攻其不備，出其不意。"

出奇制勝 chū qí zhì shèng

By surprise, to win the battle. (lit.)

To outwit.

Take by surprise.

To cope with

同 智取為上（3897）Contrivance is better than force.

源 史記：“兵以正合，出奇制勝，善之者出其無窮。”

0409

出人頭地 chū rén tóu dì

Tower above one's fellows. (lit.)

To be head and shoulders taller.

Come to the fore.

同 不亞於人（0261）Second to none.

反 無地自容（2955）To be put out of countenance.

源 宋史：“吾當避此人出一頭地。”

0410

出身寒微 chū shēn hán wēi

Emerge from obscurity. (lit.)

Born in low water.

Born with a wooden spoon in one's mouth.

Rise from the gutter.

反 來頭大（1541）He is the bishop's sister's son.

0411

出身好 chū shēn hǎo

Born of good (family). (lit.)

Come of a good stock.

0412

出身望族 chū shēn wàng zú

Born of good ancestry. (lit.)

Born in the purple.

From the top drawer.

同 生於富貴之家（2422）Born with a silver spoon in one's mouth.

0413

出身要看，重在表現

chū shēn yào kàn, zhòng zài biǎo xiàn

Where one comes from should be considered, but what is shown is important. (lit.)

Birth is much, but breeding is more.

0414

出生入死 chū shēng rù sǐ

In and out of life and death. (lit.)

Put one's head in the lion's mouth.

Go through hell and high water.

Go through fire and water.

Carry one's life in one's hands.

源 潘岳：“彼知安而忘危兮，故出生而入死。”

0415

0416 **出師不利** chū shī bú lì
To despatch army in an disadvantageous situation. (lit.)
Step off on the wrong foot.
Begin at the wrong side.

反 旗開得勝（2034）To start with a bang.

0417 **出師未捷身先死**
chū shī wèi jié shēn xiān sǐ
The despatched army hasn't won, the warrior is already dead. (lit.)
Many go out for wool and come back shorn.

源 杜甫詩："出師未捷身先死。"

0418 **出污泥而不染** chū wū ní ér bù rǎn
Rising from dirty soil one does not get stained. (lit.)
Lilies are whitest in a blackamoor's hand.

反 染於蒼則蒼，染於黃則黃（2177）Touch pitch, and you will be defiled.

源 宋．周敦頤．愛蓮說："余獨愛蓮之出污泥而不染，濯清漣而不妖，中通外直，不蔓不枝。"

0419 **出言不遜** chū yán bù xùn
Speak immodestly. (lit.)
Put one's foot in one's mouth.
Drop a clanger.

同 大放厥詞（0519）To let oneself loose.

源 三國志．魏志．張郃傳："郃快軍敗，出言不遜。"

0420 **出洋相** chū yáng xiàng
Showing a "westerner's" face. (lit.)
Make an ass (a fool) of oneslef.
Cut a sorry figure.
Put one's foot into it.

同 當眾出醜（0594）Cut a ridiculous figure.

0421 **初出茅廬** chū chū máo lú
Fresh out of a thatched hut. (lit.)
A raw recruit.
A green horn.
A freshwater sailor.
As green as grass.
Wet behind the ears.

同 少不更事（2366）Not dry behind the ears.

反 老於世故（1579）Know which way the wind blows.

初歸媳婦，落地孩兒 0422
chū guī xí fù, luò dì hái ér
The newly wedded daughter-in-law; a child learning to walk. (lit.)
Best to bend while 'tis a twig.
Train a tree when it is young.
Youth is the time when the seeds of character are sown.

初見成效 chū jiàn chéng xiào 0423
First looks to produce effect. (lit.)
Carry into effect at once.
To ring the bell.

同 開紅門（1472）The first blow is half the battle.

初見世面 chū jiàn shì miàn 0424
First look at the face of the world. (lit.)
Babes in the woods

同 初出茅廬（0421）A green horn.
反 過來人（0999）One of the has-beens.

初露鋒芒 chū lù fēng máng 0425
First expose of knife edge. (lit.)
Fresh from the iron.

初露頭角 chū lù tóu jiǎo 0426
First expose the head and horns. (lit.)
Make one's debut.
Make one's mark in the world.
To find one's feet.

反 重為馮婦（0388）Back to the salt mines.

初生之犢不畏虎 chū shēng zhī dú bú wèi hǔ 0427
A new born calf fears not the tiger. (lit.)
They that know nothing fear nothing.

反 驚弓之鳥（1398）A burned child dreads the fire.
源 三國演義："俗云，初生之犢不畏虎。"

處境尷尬 chǔ jìng gān gà 0428
To be in an awkward situation. (lit.)
In a spot (hole).
To be in a pretty pickle.
To be caught with one's pants down

同 狼狽不堪（1548）One shoe off and one shoe on.
反 得其所哉（0614）In one's own element.

0429 **處境困難** chǔ jìng kùn nán
To be in a difficult position. (lit.)
To be up the spout (pole).
In a scrape.
Hard put to it.
To be in the soup.
Like a toad under a harrow.

同 參差不偶（0316）In a sorry plight.
反 一帆風順（3391）It's all plain sailing.

0430 **處心積慮** chǔ xīn jī lǜ
Store the accumulated worries in the heart. (lit.)
After long deliberation.
By design.

同 深思熟慮（2398）Turn is over in one's mind.
反 心血來潮（3193）On the impulse of the moment.
源 穀梁傳："何甚乎鄭伯，甚鄭伯之處心積慮成於殺也。"

0431 **處之泰然** chǔ zhī tài rán
Attend to it calmly. (lit.)
Take it coolly.

同 漠然置之（1855）Look on with unconcern.
反 耿耿於懷（0915）To take it to heart.

0432 **觸到痛處** chù dào tòng chù
Irritate the painful part. (lit.)
Touch one on the raw.
Sting (Cut) to the quick.
Touch one on a soft (weak) spot.
Touch one on a sore point.

同 擊中要害（1195）Hit one where it hurts.

0433 **川流不息** chuān liú bù xī
Flowing in an endless stream. (lit.)
In rapid succession.
A constant flow.

同 繼續不斷（1239）On and on.
反 停滯不前（2758）Get bogged down.
源 後漢書："處土山積，學者川流。"

0434 **穿針引線** chuān zhēn yǐn xiàn
To thread a needle. (lit.)
Act as a go-between (match-maker).
Pull strings (wires).

0435 **傳之後世** chuán zhī hòu shì
Pass down to later generations. (lit.)
Hand down to
Hand down to posterity.
Hand on the torch.

喘不過氣 chuǎn bù guò qì ◀0436

Panting for not enough breath. (lit.)

Out of breath.

喘息機會 chuǎn xī jī huì ◀0437

Chance to regain one's breath. (lit.)

Abreathing spell(space).

Before one is oneself again.

串門 chuàn mén ◀0438

String the doors together. (lit.)

Go jagging.

反 息交絕遊（3044）Retire into oneself.

闖下彌天大禍 ◀0439

chuǎng xià mí tiān dà huò

Cause a full-sky big calamity. (lit.)

All the fat is in the fire.

吹吹捧捧 chuī chuī pěng pěng ◀0440

Blow and praises. (lit.)

Lay it on with a trowel.

Flatter grossly

同 拍馬屁（1940）Butter someone up.

反 冷嘲熱諷（1592）Laugh to scorn.

吹毛求疵 chuī máo qiú cī ◀0441

Blow the hair to find fault with it. (lit.)

Split hairs.

Pick a hole in one's coat.

Pick to pieces.

Find fault with.

Number the streaks of the tulip.

源 韓非子 · 大體："不吹毛而求小疵，不洗垢而察難知。"

吹牛大王 chuī niú dà wáng ◀0442

King of bluff. (lit.)

Hot air artist.

0443 吹牛皮 chuī niú pí
Blow cow's hide. (lit.)
Talk horse.
Swing and lead.
Brag and bluff.
Talk in high language.
Many talk of Robin Hood that never shot in his bow; and many talk of Little John that never did him know.
To shoot a line.

同 大吹大擂（0510）Bluff and bluster.

0444 吹捧上天 chuī pěng shàng tiān
Blow and praise to the sky. (lit.)
Praise to the skies.
Flatter up to the nines.
Lay it on thick.

反 臭罵一頓（0400）Call one for everything under the sun.

0445 垂頭喪氣 chuí tóu sàng qì
Drooping one's head and desponding. (lit.)
Hang one's head.
Down in the mouth (dumps).
With one's tail between one's legs.
Look crestfallen.

同 沒精打采（1848）With the wind taken out of one's sails.
反 趾高氣揚（3888）Ride the high horse.
源 唐書："失勢者垂頭喪氣。"

0446 垂涎三尺 chuí xián sān chǐ
Saliva dripping three feet. (lit.)
It makes the mouth water.
Show greed for

0447 垂涎欲滴 chuí xián yù dī
Hanging saliva tends to drip. (lit.)
To drool over
The mouth waters.

反 食慾不振（2470）Loss of appetite.

0448 春風滿面 chūn fēng mǎn miàn
One's face is full of spring breeze. (lit.)
Beam with joy.
Spring in the air.

同 笑容可掬（3154）A face wreathed in smiles.

春天不是讀書天，夏日炎炎正好眠，過得秋來冬又至，收拾書卷待明年 chūn tiān bù shì dú shū tiān, xià rì yán yán zhèng hǎo mián, guò dé qiū lái dōng yòu zhì, shōu shí shū juàn dài míng nián 0449

Spring is not the time for study, long summer days are just good for napping, by the time autumn passing through winter comes again, pack up the books and papers for next year. (lit.)

The sluggard's convenient season never comes.

脣槍舌劍 chún qiāng shé jiàn 0450

Lips like spears and tongues like swords. (lit.)

Speak daggers.

Have a sharp tongue.

Exchange heated words.

Break a lance with one.

Cross swords.

源 元曲選 · 武漢臣 · 玉壺春："使心猿意馬，逞舌劍脣槍。"

鶉衣百結 chún yī bǎi jié 0451

like the feathers of a quail, one' s clothes covered with hundred patches. (lit.)

Out at elbows.

Down at heels.

To be threadbare.

Darned and patched.

反 衣冠楚楚（3504）Dressed up to the ninety nines.

源 荀子："子夏貧，衣若鶉鶉。"

蠢如鹿豕 chǔn rú lù shǐ 0452

As stupid as deer and hog. (lit.)

As silly as a goose.

As stupid as a donkey.

Brute beasts that have no understanding.

As dumb as a fish.

同 笨頭笨腦（0108）Dead from the neck up.

反 足智多謀（4033）Fruitful of expedients.

0453 綽綽有餘 chuò chuò yǒu yú
Ample with surplus. (lit.)
Enough and to spare.
One's cup runs over.
Lashings and lavings.

反 借債度日（1336）Live on ticket.
源 詩經・小雅・角弓："綽綽有裕。"

0454 慈母出敗兒 cí mǔ chū bài ér
A kind mother produces spoiled son. (lit.)
Mothers' darlings make but milksop heroes.
Spare the rod and spoil the child.
The road to hell is paved with good intentions.

0455 此起彼伏 cǐ qǐ bǐ fú
This rises and that falls. (lit.)
Wave after wave.

同 一波未平，一波又起（3376）It never rains but it pours.

0456 刺刺不休 cì cì bù xiū
Irritating (ears) incessantly. (lit.)
Talk the bark off a tree.
Talk nineteen to the dozen.

同 絮絮不休（3253）To hold forth.
反 默不作聲（1857）As mute as a fish.
源 管子："孰能弁刺刺而為愕愕乎。"

0457 從容不迫 cóng róng bú pò
Take it leisurely without pressure. (lit.)
Take things easy.
Take one's time.
Cool as a cucumber.

同 慢條斯理（1755）Make two bites of a cherry.
反 急不可待（1208）Eat the calf in the cow's belly.
源 史記："良嘗閒從容步遊下邳圯上。"

0458 從容就義 cóng róng jiù yì
Tread the path of virtue calmly. (lit.)
Die a martyr's death.
Die a martyr to one's principle.

同 視死如歸（2531）Look death in the face.

0459 聰明伶俐 cōng míng líng lì
Intelligent and smart. (lit.)
Have a good head on one's shoulders.

反 笨頭笨腦（0108）Dead from the neck up.

0460 從大處着眼 cóng dà chù zhuó yǎn
Fix one's eye on big place. (lit.)
Have an eye to the main chance.

反 鑽牛角尖（4035）Look at the needle point of things.

從輕發落 cóng qīng fā luò 0461
Send down lightly. (lit.)
Let one off lightly.
Let down gently.

同 刀下留情（0595）Pull one's punches.
反 嚴加懲處（3316）Put it across one.

從善如流 cóng shàn rú liú 0462
Follow goodness like flowing (of water). (lit.)
If the counsel be good, no matter who gave it.

同 三人行必有我師，擇其善者而從之（2309）Keep good men company and you shall be of the number.
源 左傳："從善如流，宜哉。"/國語："從善如登，從惡如崩。"

從勝利走向勝利 cóng shèng lì zǒu xiàng shèng lì 0463
From victory run to victory. (lit.)
Nothing succeeds like success.
A winning streak.

同 無往不利（2997）To get it every way.
反 一蹶不振（3409）Meet one's Waterloo.

從頭到尾 cóng tóu dào wěi 0464
From head to tail. (lit.)
From first to last.
From beginning to end.

同 自始至終（3995）From the egg to the apples.
反 有始無終（3670）Do things by halves.

從頭做起 cóng tóu zuò qǐ 0465
From the beginning, start to work. (lit.)
Start from a clean slate.

從未謀面 cóng wèi móu miàn 0466
Never have (planned to) meet. (lit.)
Not to know one from Adam.

同 緣慳一面（3735）Haven't had the pleasure of meeting one.
反 過從甚密（0994）On intimate terms with

從小到大 cóng xiǎo dào dà 0467
From small to big. (lit.)
Small beginning make great endings.
Every oak must be an acorn.
Great oaks from little acorns grow.

同 天下大事，必作於細（2726）The thin end of the wedge is to be feared.
反 來如風雨，去似微塵（1539）He who swells in prosperity will shrink in adversity.

從中搗亂 cóng zhōng dǎo luàn 0468
Causing disturbance in the midst of (lit.)
Throw a spanner in the works.
Throw a monkey wrench into

反 鼎力支持（0659）Put one's hand to the plough.

0469 **從中作梗** cóng zhōng zuò gěng
Making obstacle in the midst of (lit.)
Put a spoke in one's wheel.

反 為人説項（2916）Put in a good word for

0470 **粗茶淡飯** cū chá dàn fàn
Coarse tea and plain rice. (lit.)
Simple fare.
Pot-luck.

同 家常便飯（1248）Homely fare.
反 酒池肉林（1421）Beef and ale galore.
源 宋・楊萬里詩：“粗茶淡飯終殘年。”

0471 **粗口爛舌** cū kǒu làn shé
Rough mouth and nasty tongue. (lit.)
Swear like a trooper.

反 甜言蜜語（2742）Give one a mouthful of moonshine.

0472 **促膝談心** cù xī tán xīn
Cross the knees and talk from the heart. (lit.)
Get knee to knee with one.
Have a heart-to-heart talk.
Take into confidence

同 推心置腹（2821）From the bottom of one's heart.
反 話不投機半句多（1119）It's ill talking between a full man and a fasting.

0473 **猝然間** cù rán jiān
On a sudden. (lit.)
All of a sudden.
All at once.

同 迅雷不及掩耳（3283）As swift as lightning.

0474 **摧枯拉朽** cuī kū lā xiǔ
Break off a decayed stump and pull a rotten one. (lit.)
Sweep everything before one.

同 勢如破竹（2536）Like a hot knife cutting through butter.
反 羝羊觸藩（0635）To be in a cleft stick.
源 晉書・甘卓傳：“將軍之舉武昌，若摧枯拉朽，何所顧慮乎。

0475 **存乎人者莫良於眸子**
cún hū rén zhě mò liáng yú móu zǐ
That contained in a man is nothing better than his eyes. (lit.)
The eye is the best index of a man's character.
The eye is the mirror of the soul.
The heart's letter is read in the eyes.

源 孟子：“存乎人者，莫良於眸子。”

寸步不離 cùn bù bù lí 0476

Inch step won't leave. (lit.)

At one's elbow (heels).

Hover over

同 緊跟（1351）Follow hard after.

反 避之則吉（0127）Steer clear of

寸草不留 cùn cǎo bù liú 0477

Not an inch of grass left. (lit.)

To lay waste.

Stripped bare.

同 剷草除根（0326）Pluck up by the roots.

寸土不讓 cùn tǔ bú ràng 0478

Not to yield an inch of land. (lit.)

To dispute every inch of ground.

Not budge an inch.

反 退避三舍（2822）Beat a retreat.

寸陰尺璧 cùn yīn chǐ bì 0479

An inch of shade (time, equals to) a foot of jade. (lit.)

Time is money.

Precious time.

源 淮南子："聖人不貴尺之璧，而重寸之陰，時難得而易失也。"

寸陰若歲 cùn yīn ruò suì 0480

Time hangs heavy on one's hand.

It seems ages.

An inch of (light) shadow is as long as a year.

源 北史："相思之甚，寸陰若歲。"

厝火積薪 cuò huǒ jī xīn 0481

Carry a fire under a heap of firewood. (lit.)

He lives unsafely that looks too near on things.

A concealed calamity.

反 曲突徙薪（2146）A stitch in time saves nine.

源 賈誼・新書・數寧："夫抱火厝之積薪之下，而寢其上，火未及燃，因謂之安，偷安者也。"

挫其鋭氣 cuò qí ruì qì 0482

Damp one's sharp air. (lit.)

Take the wind out of one's sails.

Clip the wings of

Take down a notch (peg).

反 養精蓄鋭（3340）Recharge one's mental batteries.

0483 **措手不及** cuò shǒu bù jí
Not in time with one's hand. (lit.)
Caught unawares (off-guard).
Taken by surprise.

0484 **錯怪了人** cuò guài le rén
To blame the wrong person. (lit.)
The boot is on the other leg.

0485 **錯綜複雜** cuò zōng fù zá
Complex and mixed. (lit.)
There are wheels within wheels.
The plot thickens

反 簡單明瞭（1275）As plain as a pikestaff.
源 易經：“參伍以變，錯綜其數。”

D

打抱不平 dǎ bào bù píng
Fight against injustice. (lit.)
Take up the cudgel for another.

同 見義勇為（1283）Do a good turn. 0486

打草驚蛇 dǎ cǎo jīng shé
Beat the grass and frighten the snakes. (lit.)
Wake a sleeping wolf (dog, lion).

反 不動聲色（0184）Keep quiet. 0487

打得火熱 dǎ dé huǒ rè
Beat it hot in flame. (lit.)
Being intimate with
Get on like a house on fire

同 一見如故（3403）Be hail-fellow-well-met with
反 冰炭不相容（0155）At loggerheads with one another. 0488

打定主意 dǎ dìng zhǔ yì
To make up one's mind. (lit.)
Set one's heart upon
Take into one's head.

同 下定決心（3071）Put one's foot down.
反 猶疑不決（3642）Like one o'clock half-struck. 0489

打開天窗說亮話
dǎ kāi tiān chuāng shuō liàng huà
Open the skylight to speak loudly. (lit.)
Place one's cards on the table.
Come out into the open.

同 開誠佈公（1466）Wear one's heart on one's sleeve. 0490

打量一番 dǎ liàng yì fān
To measure one up quite a while. (lit.)
Look a person up and down.
Size one up

同 評頭品足（1995）Pick one to pieces.
反 不屑一顧（0260）Shut one's eyes to 0491

0492 **打亂計劃** dǎ luàn jì huà
Disturb one's plans. (lit.)
Upset one's apple-cart.

0493 **打埋伏** dǎ mái fú
Make an ambush. (lit.)
A put-up job.

同 安下金鈎（0015）Lay an ambush.

0494 **打破砂鍋問到底** dǎ pò shā guō wèn dào dǐ
Breaking an earthenware pot through its bottom (to get answer) of one's question. (lit.)
Get to the bottom of the matter.
Go to the root of

同 追根究底（3952）Get down to rock bottom.
反 隻眼開，隻眼閉（3865）Wink at small faults.

0495 **打起精神** dǎ qǐ jīng shén
To raise one's spirit. (lit.)
Keep up one's spirits.

反 昏昏欲睡（1159）Have a wink in one's eye.

0496 **打他個落花流水** dǎ tā ge luò huā liú shuǐ
To beat one down like flowers dropping and water flowing. (lit.)
Beat someone hollow.
Beat the daylight out of one.
Smite hip and thigh.
Smash into smithereens.
Mop (Wipe) up the floor with one.

源 趙長卿 · 送春詞："落花流水一春休。"

0497 **打他個皮開肉爛** dǎ tā ge pí kāi ròu làn
Beat one till his skin open and flesh torn. (lit.)
Beat one black and blue.

反 救死扶傷（1429）Rescue the perishing.

0498 **打鐵趁熱** dǎ tiě chèn rè
Beat the iron while it is still hot. (lit.)
Strike while the iron is hot.

同 勿失時機（3026）Hoist sail when the wind is fair.
反 坐失良機（4055）Miss the boat.

打退堂鼓 dǎ tuì táng gǔ 0499

Beat the retreat drum. (lit.)

Beat a retreat

同 知難而退（3856）To back out.

反 一馬當先（3421）To be in the van.

打下基礎 dǎ xià jī chǔ 0500

To lay the foundation. (lit.)

Lay the corner stone.

打下他的威風 dǎ xià tā de wēi fēng 0501

Knock down his majestic air. (lit.)

Give one a dressing down.

Take one down a peg or two.

Crop a person's feather.

I'll pluck his goose for him.

同 滅他人志氣（1807）Cut someone's comb.

打，砸，搶 dǎ, zá, qiǎng 0502

Beat, hit, and snatch. (lit.)

Set the heather on fire.

打腫臉充胖子 dǎ zhǒng liǎn chōng pàng zi 0503

Beat one's face swollen to pretend a fat man. (lit.)

Face it out.

Keep up appearances.

Keep up with the Joneses.

Shabby gentility.

打中要害 dǎ zhòng yào hài 0504

To have hit the important and hurting place. (lit.)

To strike home.

同 觸到痛處（0432）Sting to the quick.

反 不着邊際（0285）It's neither here nor there.

大擺架子 dà bǎi jià zi 0505

To put up a big shelf. (lit.)

To have too much side.

Give oneself air.

同 裝腔作勢（3950）Strike a pose.

反 平易近人（1994）Have the common touch.

大飽眼福 dà bǎo yǎn fú 0506

Big feast of the eyes. (lit.)

Glut one's eyes with

0507 **大吵大鬧** dà chǎo dà nào

A big wrangle and quarrel. (lit.)

Fight like cat and dog.

To make the fur (feathers) fly.

Raise cain.

Make a scene.

同 大鬧一場（0543）To raise hell.

反 不聲不響（0247）As quiet as a mouse.

0508 **大吃大喝** dà chī dà hē

Big eat, big drink. (lit.)

To peg and quaff.

Gorge oneself.

Make a beast (pig) of oneself.

同 狼吞虎嚥（1550）Have a wolf in one's stomach.

反 節衣縮食（1327）Pinch and scrape.

0509 **大出風頭** dà chū fēng tóu

Big rise to the wind head. (lit.)

Cut a dash.

Cut a smart figure.

A limelight figure

同 招搖過市（3806）Seek the limelight.

反 收斂起來（2544）Hide one's light under a bushel.

0510 **大吹大擂** dà chuī dà léi

To blow (trumpet) and to beat (drum). (lit.)

Brag about.

Bluff and bluster.

A flourish of trumpets.

Make much of

同 大張旗鼓（0566）With great fanfare.

反 偃旗息鼓（3329）Draw in one's horns.

源 元曲選 · 賈仲名 · 蕭淑蘭：“小的每與我大吹大擂者。”

0511 **大打出手** dà dǎ chū shǒu

Big blows with hands. (lit.)

Come to blows.

Fall together by the ears.

Come to grips with

同 拳腳交加（2165）Cuffs and kicks.

反 相安無事（3103）Get along fairly well.

0512 **大膽創新** dà dǎn chuàng xīn

Big gall, new creation. (lit.)

Take the initiative.

同 另闢蹊徑（1670）Take one's own line.

反 墨守成規（1856）Follow the beaten track.

0513 **大刀闊斧** dà dāo kuò fǔ

A large knife and a broad axe. (lit.)

Go the whole hog.

大動肝火 dà dòng gān huǒ 0514
Big stir of liver fire. (lit.)
To have one's gorge rise.
Fly off the handle.

同 大發脾氣（0517）To lose one's shirt.
反 平心靜氣（1993）Keep one's temper.

大發牢騷 dà fā láo sāo 0515
Speak out grievances furiously. (lit.)
Let off steam.
Chew the fat.

同 怨天尤人（3740）Everyone puts his faults at the times.
反 逆來順受（1898）Grin and bear it.

大發雷霆 dà fā léi tíng 0516
To raise a burst of thunder. (lit.)
Come down like a ton of bricks.
Explode with rage.
Fly into one's tantrums.

同 暴跳如雷（0092）Stamp with fury.
反 忍氣吞聲（2243）Swallow the leek.
源 三國志．吳志．陸遜傳：“今不忍小忿而發雷霆之怒。”

大發脾氣 dà fā pí qì 0517
To raise big temper. (lit.)
Bite a person's head off.
Go off the top.
To lose one's shirt.
As cross as two sticks.
Get one's dander (Irish) up.

同 七竅生煙（2016）Fuming with anger.
反 捺着性子（1876）Bottle up one's feelings.

大發議論 dà fā yì lùn 0518
To raise lot of argument. (lit.)
To enlarge one's self.

同 侃侃而談（1478）Talk the back off a tree.
反 噤若寒蟬（1377）Mute as a fish.

大放厥詞 dà fàng jué cí 0519
To let off loose talk. (lit.)
Speak through the back of one's neck.
To let oneself loose.

源 韓愈．祭柳子厚文：“玉佩瓊琚，大放厥詞。”

大腹便便 dà fù pián pián 0520
Carrying a big paunch. (lit.)
As round as a barrel.
Beef to the heels.
As plump as a partridge.

反 飄飄欲仙（1975）As light as a butterfly.
源 後漢書．邊韶傳：“邊孝先，腹便便。”

0521 **大幹快上** dà gàn kuài shàng
Big job quickly done. (lit.)
To make things hum.

反 廢時失事（0781）Tarry-long brings little home.

0522 **大幹一場** dà gàn yì cháng
One big do. (lit.)
To set the Thames on fire.

同 大顯身手（0557）Show one's mettle.
反 退隱林下（2826）Go to grass.

0523 **大功告成** dà gōng gào chéng
The big job completed. (lit.)
Come off with honours.
Bring home the bacon.
Come through with flying colours.

反 功虧一簣（0924）Another course would have done it.

0524 **大公無私** dà gōng wú sī
For big public justice without selfishness. (lit.)
Fair field and no favour.
The balance distinguishes not between gold and lead.

同 捨己為人（2372）To bell the cat.
反 假公濟私（1256）To practise jobbery.
源 龔自珍．龔定庵集．論私：“且今之大公無私者，有楊墨之賢耶。”

0525 **大海撈針** dà hǎi lāo zhēn
To dredge a needle in a vast sea. (lit.)
Look for a needle in a haystack (a bundle of hay).

0526 **大喊倒霉** dà hǎn dǎo méi
Great cry of bad luck. (lit.)
Get it in the neck.
Get it where the chicken got the axe.

反 躊躇滿志（0398）To one's heart's content.

0527 **大好時機** dà hǎo shí jī
Very good opportunity. (lit.)
High time.
Now is your time

同 千載一時（2068）Now or never.
反 時運不濟（2477）In an evil hour.

0528 **大惑不解** dà huò bù jiě
Perplex and not understandable. (lit.)
Beyond comprehension.
Beyond one.
Can make neither head nor tail of

同 莫名其妙（1851）To be at sea.
反 心中有數（3201）Know what's what.
源 莊子．天地：“大惑者終身不解，大愚者終身不靈。”

大禍臨頭 dà huò lín tóu 0529
Great calamity comes to head. (lit.)
The black ox has trod on one's foot.

同 火燒眉毛（1169）Imminent danger.

大獲全勝 dà huò quán shèng 0530
To gain complete victory. (lit.)
Sweep the board.

反 一敗塗地（3368）To land with a thud.

大雞不吃細米 dà jī bù chī xì mǐ 0531
Large chickens don't eat small rice. (lit.)
The eagle does not catch flies.

大叫大嚷 dà jiào dà rǎng 0532
Big shout, big scream. (lit.)
Cry at the top of one's voice (lungs).
Hue and cry.

反 不吭一聲（0226）Not to breathe a syllable.

大驚失色 dà jīng shī sè 0533
Great terror, losing colour (from one's face). (lit.)
Jump out of one's skin.
Get out of countenance.

反 面不改容（1798）Keep a straight face.

大驚小怪 dà jīng xiǎo guài 0534
Great terror and little astonishment. (lit.)
Much matter of a wooden platter.
Like a hen with one chicken.
A storm in a teacup.
Go off the deep end.
Much ado about nothing.
Look like a dying duck in a thunderstorm.
Make a song and dance about something.

反 若無其事（2295）As if nothing has happened.

大開眼界 dà kāi yǎn jiè 0535
Big eye-opening. (lit.)
Open a person's eyes.
Broaden one's horizon.
See the elephant.
An eye-opener.

反 目光如豆（1869）See no further than one's nose.

0536 **大快朵頤** dà kuài duǒ yí
Big satisfaction of appetite. (lit.)
Eat one's fill.
Tuck in.
Gorge oneself.

同 大吃大喝（0508）Peg and quaff.
反 淺斟低酌（2086）Eat at pleasure, drink by measure.

0537 **大老粗** dà lǎo cū
Big old rough. (lit.)
A rough diamond
A country cousin.

反 文質彬彬（2924）Manners make the man.

0538 **大鳴大放** dà míng dà fàng
Big ringing and big liberating. (lit.)
Say one's piece.
Stand up and be counted.

同 知無不言，言無不盡（3861）Lay one's heart bare.
反 滿懷心腹事，盡在不言中（1744）I say little but I think the more.

0539 **大名鼎鼎** dà míng dǐng dǐng
A very big name. (lit.)
Of great renown.

反 湮沒無聞（3293）Sink into oblivion.

0540 **大謬不然** dà miù bù rán
Great mistake, it is not so. (lit.)
Get hold of the wrong end of the stick.

0541 **大難不死** dà nàn bù sǐ
Big trouble (but) won't die. (lit.)
Have a close brush with death.
Have a charmed life.

同 死裏逃生（2627）Out of the jaws of death.

0542 **大難臨頭** dà nàn lín tóu
Big troubles loom up. (lit.)
To be in hot (deep) waters.

同 危在旦夕（2876）Hang on by the eyelids.
反 平安無事（1983）All is well.

0543 **大鬧一場** dà nào yì cháng
One big quarrel. (lit.)
Raise the devil.
To raise hell.
Kick up a fuss.

大器晚成 dà qì wǎn chéng 0544
Great vessels completed late. (lit.)
Rome was not built in a day.
The best fruits are slowest in ripening

同 十年樹木，百年樹人（2460）A skill is not acquired in a matter of days.
源 老子：“大方無隅，大器晚成。”

大千世界 dà qiān shì jiè 0545
Great thousand of worlds. (lit.)
It takes all sorts to make a world.

大權在握 dà quán zài wò 0546
The great power is within grasp. (lit.)
To be at the helm.
Take the rein into one's hand.
To have in the palm of one's hand.
High and mighty.
Hold the reins.
To be top do

同 炙手可熱（3893）At the Zenith of one's power.
反 人微言輕（2228）Poor men's reasons are not heard.
源 唐書：“京邑如身，王畿如臂，而四海如指，此天子大權也。”

大煞風景 dà shā fēng jǐng 0547
Great kill the scenery. (lit.)
A wet blanket.
A fly in the ointment.
Take all the fun out of

源 李義山．雜纂：“其一曰殺風景。謂清泉濯足，花上曬裩，背山起樓，燒琴煮鶴，對花啜茶，松下喝道也。”

大上其當 dà shàng qí dàng 0548
Get into the big trap. (lit.)
To be done brown.
Swallow the bait.
Rise to the fly.
To be badly taken.

同 入人圈套（2287）Put one's neck into a noose.

大聲疾呼 dà shēng jí hū 0549
Shout at the top of (one's) voice with desperation. (lit.)
A clarion call.
To proclaim from the house-tops.

反 不吭一聲（0226）Not to breathe a syllable.
源 韓愈：“則將大其聲疾呼，而望其人之救也。”

大失所望 dà shī suǒ wàng 0550
Great loss of expectation. (lit.)
Fish for herring and catch a sprat.

反 如願以償（2280）Long looked for comes at last.

0551 **大事渲染** dà shì xuàn rǎn
Greatly exaggerated and coloured. (lit.)
To make much of
Lay on the colours.
Lay it on with a trowel.
Lend colour to

同 加鹽加醋（1244）Tell with unction.
反 輕描淡寫（2126）To skate over

0552 **大勢已去** dà shì yǐ qù
The big situation declines completely. (lit.)
The day (field) is lost.
Come out of the little end of the horn.
Thursday come, and the week is gone.

反 形勢大好（3220）The goose hang high.

0553 **大肆揮霍** dà sì huī huò
Spendthrift in a big way. (lit.)
Dip into one's purse.
Buy a white horse.

同 揮金如土（1148）Play ducks and drakes with one's money.
反 錙銖計較（3964）Skin a flint.

0554 **大題小做** dà tí xiǎo zuò
Big problem little doing. (lit.)
The mountain has brought forth a mouse.

同 輕描淡寫（2126）Touch on lightly.
反 小題大做（3144）A storm in a teacup.

0555 **大體而論** dà tǐ ér lùn
Generally speaking. (lit.)
By and large.
On the whole.

0556 **大同小異** dà tóng xiǎo yì
Great similarity and little difference. (lit.)
Much of a muchness.
There's not a pin to choose between them.

同 不相上下（0258）As well be hanged for a sheep as for a lamb.
反 判若雲泥（1950）A world of difference.
源 唐・盧同・玉川子詩集・與馬異結交："同不同，異自異，是謂大同而小異。"

0557 **大顯身手** dà xiǎn shēn shǒu
Big show off body and hand. (lit.)
Have the field to oneself.
To try one's hand.
Show one's metal (mettle).
Have the field before one.

反 冷眼旁觀（1596）To be outside the ropes.

大獻殷勤 dà xiàn yīn qín 0558

Great offer of attention. (lit.)

Dance attendance on

Serve one hand and foot

同 阿諛逢迎（0713）Butter up a person.

反 給以冷遇（0912）Give one the cold shoulder.

大相徑庭 dà xiāng jìng tíng 0559

A great difference between (a court apart). (lit.)

Poles apart.

The opposite.

At odds with

At loggerheads.

反 同心協力（2772）Unite as one.

源 莊子．逍遙遊：“大有徑庭，不近人情。”

大興問罪之師 dà xīng wèn zuì zhī shī 0560

To send an army to punish (the enemy). (lit.)

Bring someone to book.

Have a bone to pick with one.

Have a crow to pluck with one

反 負荊請罪（0842）Eat humble-pie.

源 左傳：“齊桓公伐楚曰，師出有名，曰問罪之師。”

大雪紛飛 dà xuě fēn fēi 0561

Snowing in great flakes. (lit.)

The old woman is plucking her goose.

大言不慚 dà yán bù cán 0562

Boast without shame. (lit.)

Blow one's own trumpet.

To talk big.

To overshoot oneself.

同 信口雌黃（3206）Talk through one's hat.

源 史記：“劉季固多大言，少成事。”

大魚吃小魚 dà yú chī xiǎo yú 0563

Big fish eats small fish. (lit.)

Great thieves hang little ones.

The little cannot be great unless he devours many.

大雨滂沱 dà yǔ pāng tuó 0564

Heavy rain in cataracts. (lit.)

It's raining cats and dogs.

Fine day for the young ducks.

Rain pitchforks.

同 傾盆大雨（2122）To rain trams and omnibuses.

反 青空一碧（2116）The blue expanse of heaven.

0565 大雨如注 dà yǔ rú zhù
The rain coming down in cataracts.
Rain buckets.

同 傾盆大雨（2122）To rain cats and dogs.

0566 大張旗鼓 dà zhāng qí gǔ
Big display of banners and drums. (lit.)
With great fanfare.
On a grand scale.

反 收斂起來（2544）Draw in one's horns.

0567 大丈夫能屈能伸
dà zhàng fū néng qū néng shēn
A big man can bend and stretch. (lit.)
The boughs that bear most hang lowest.

反 高不成，低不就（0877）He that will not stoop for a pin shall never be worth a pound.

0568 大智若愚 dà zhì ruò yú
The wise man appears like a fool. (lit.)
Still waters run deep.
No man can play the fool so well as the wise man.
He is not a wise man who cannot play the fool on occasion.

同 深藏若虛（2396）To humble oneself.
反 不懂裝懂（0183）Assume a knowing air.
源 老子："大智若愚。"

0569 呆若木雞 dāi ruò mù jī
Dumb like a wooden chicken. (lit.)
To be rooted to the spot.
Stop dead in one's tracks.

反 矯若游龍（1312）As nimble as a squirrel.
源 莊子："望之若木雞矣。"

0570 獃頭獃腦 dāi tóu dāi nǎo
Silly head and simple brain. (lit.)
To be muddle-headed.
Mickle head, little wit.
A dumb-bell.

同 蠢如鹿豕（0452）As stupid as a donkey.

0571 代人受過 dài rén shòu guò
To suffer for the fault of another. (lit.)
To carry the can.

同 當替罪羊（0591）Be made the scapegoat for
反 委過於人（2902）Lay a fault at a person's door.

待機而動 dài jī ér dòng 0572
Waiting for opportunity to make the move. (lit.)
Bide one's time.
Have an eye to the main chance.

反 急不可待（1208）To be bursting to do something.

待價而沽 dài jià ér gū 0573
Waiting for (high) price to sell. (lit.)
On the block.
For sale.
On the long side of the market.

源 論語 · 子罕："求善價而沽諸。"

膽大心細 dǎn dà xīn xì 0574
Having a big gall-bladder but a tiny heart. (lit.)
Discretion is the better part of valour.
Combine courage with wisdom.

源 唐書 · 孫思邈傳："膽欲大而心欲小，智欲圓而行欲方。"

膽小如鼠 dǎn xiǎo rú shǔ 0575
One's gall-bladder is as small as that of a rat. (lit.)
As timid as a mouse.
Cannot say Boo to a goose.
Afraid of one's own shadow.
Have one's heart in a nutshell.
To be chicken-hearted.
As timid as a rabbit

同 前怕狼，後怕虎（2077）Too much taking heed is loss.

反 一身是膽（3453）With plenty of guts.

但看三五日，相見不如初 0576
dàn kàn sān wǔ rì, xiāng jiàn bù rú chū
Only having seen three or five days, the meeting is not like the first. (lit.)
Fish and company stink in three days.
Fish and guests smell at three days old.
A constant guest is never welcome.

同 久住令人賤（1420）To outstay one's welcome.

但聞雷聲，不見雨點 0577
dàn wén léi shēng, bú jiàn yǔ diǎn
Only hearing the sound of thunder, do not see rain drops. (lit.)
You cackle often, but never lay an egg.

同 口惠而實不至（1505）Good words without deeds are rushes and reeds.

0578 **淡泊明志** dàn bó míng zhì

Simple, plain, and clear ambition. (lit.)

Live on simple fare.

Lead a stoical life

同 艱苦樸素（1272）To hog it

反 窮奢極欲（2139）Live on the fat of the land.

源 諸葛亮・戒子書："非淡泊無以明志，非寧靜無以致遠。"

0579 **淡而無味** dàn ér wú wèi

Insipid and tasteless. (lit.)

Milk and wate

同 索然無味（2667）As dull as ditch water.

反 甘之如飴（0861）With relish.

0580 **彈丸之地** dàn wán zhī dì

A pellet of land. (lit.)

Hole-in-the-wall.

Not enough room to swing a cat.

源 戰國策："此彈丸之地，猶不予也。"

0581 **殫精竭慮** dàn jīng jié lǜ

Empty energy and exhaust thinking. (lit.)

Rack one's brains.

同 深思熟慮（2398）Turn it over in one's mind.

反 冒失從事（1774）Buy a pig in a poke.

0582 **當場被捕** dāng cháng bèi bǔ

Caught at once on the spot. (lit.)

To be caught redhanded.

To be caught in the act.

0583 **當二把手** dāng èr bǎ shǒu

To be regarded as second hand. (lit.)

Play second fiddle.

0584 **當機立斷** dāng jī lì duàn

Decide at the opportune moment. (lit.)

Fish or cut bait.

Take the bull by the horns.

To think on one's feet.

Quick to act.

同 快刀斬亂麻（1523）Cut the Gordian knot.

反 猶疑不決（3642）To shilly-shally.

源 文選・陳琳・答東阿王箋："拂鐘無聲，應機立斷。"

0585 **當局者迷** dāng jú zhě mí

The man involved in the business would often be confused. (lit.)

The darkest place is under the candle-stick.

You must go into the country to hear what news at London.

同 只見樹木，不見森林（3877）One can't see the wood for the trees.

反 旁觀者清（1951）Lookers-on see more than the players.

源 唐書・元行沖傳："當局者迷，旁觀必審。"

當面撒謊 dāng miàn sā huǎng
To lie to one's face. (lit.)
To lie in one's throat.

同 大言不慚（0562）To talk big. 0586
源 蔡邕：“筆疏可以當面。”

當面申斥 dāng miàn shēn chì
Comb a person's hair for him.
To blame to one's face. (lit)

同 面斥不雅（1799）Give a person a piece of one's mind. 0587

當面是人，背後是鬼
dāng miàn shì rén, bèi hòu shì guǐ
To other's face, one is a man, behind them he is a ghost. (lit.)
Who flatters me to my face will speak ill of me behind my back.

同 說一套，做一套（3616）Say one thing and do another. 0588
反 有人見，沒人見，一個樣（3663）Do on the hill as you would do in the hall.

當權派 dāng quán pài
The party that exercises authority. (lit.)
The powers that be.
Those at the stern of public affairs.

反 小人物（3140）A small potato. 0589

當時得令 dāng shí dé lìng
At the right time in season. (lit.)
Everything is good in its season.

反 明日黃花（1824）The day after the fair. 0590

當替罪羊dāng tì zuì yáng
Take the place of a scape goat. (lit.)
Carry the can.
Be made the scapegoat for

反 委過於人（2902）Put the blame on someone. 0591

當頭一棒 dāng tóu yí bàng
Strike one blow on the head. (lit.)
Deal a head-on blow.
Strike a telling blow.

同 迎頭痛擊（3602）Deal a telling blow. 0592
源 佛經：“以後接人棒喝交馳。”

當一天和尚，撞一天鐘 dāng yì tiān hé shàng, zhuàng yì tiān zhōng
While one day as a monk, strike one day bell. (lit.)
Come day, go day, God send Sunday.

同 吊兒郎當（0649）Gad about. 0593
反 野心勃勃（3364）To level at the moon.

0594 **當眾出醜** dāng zhòng chū chǒu
To expose one's defect publicly. (lit.)
Cut a ridiculous figure.
Pull a boner.
Drop a brick.

同 出洋相（0420）Make an ass of oneself.
反 全場喝彩（2159）Bring down the house.

0595 **刀下留情** dāo xià liú qíng
Leniency under the guillotine. (lit.)
Pull one's punches.

同 從輕發落（0461）Let one off lightly.
反 毫不留情（1023）Ride rough-shod over one.

0596 **叨叨嘮嘮** dāo dāo láo láo
Muttering and grumbling. (lit.)
To chew the rag

同 喋喋不休（0654）Talk the hind leg off a donkey.
反 言簡意賅（3304）Brevity is the soul of wit.

0597 **倒戈相向** dǎo gē xiāng xiàng
Turn the spear to one's own men. (lit.)
Turn one's coat.

同 反戈一擊（0747）A Parthian shot.
反 稱兄道弟（0350）Chum in with
源 書經：“前徒倒戈，功於後以北。”

0598 **蹈常襲故** dǎo cháng xí gù
Practice the normal rules and follow the tradition. (lit.)
Follow the beaten track.
Stick-in-the-mud.
Attached to old customs.
Conservative-minded

同 陳陳相因（0344）Ride a method to death.
反 另闢蹊徑（1670）Take one's own line.

0599 **到處碰壁** dào chù pèng bì
Everywhere hitting against the wall. (lit.)
Driven from pillar to post.

反 左右逢源（4050）It is good to have friends both in heaven and in hell.

0600 **倒數第一** dào shǔ dì yī
Count backward number one. (lit.)
To bring up the rear.

反 名列前茅（1814）Head the list.

0601 **倒屣相迎** dào xǐ xiāng yíng
To greet (a visitor) with the shoes back to front (in haste). (lit.)
Give one three times three.

反 下逐客令（3072）Show someone the door.
源 三國志：“蔡邕聞粲（王粲）在門，倒屣以迎之。”

倒行逆施 dào xíng nì shī 0602

Act inversely and practice oppositely. (lit.)

Turn things upside down.

After meat, mustard.

After death, the doctor.

Put the cart before the horse.

Put the clock back.

同 本末倒置（0107）Turn topsy-turvy.

反 順應潮流（2605）Go with the tide.

源 史記・伍子胥列傳："吾日暮途遠，吾故倒行而逆施之。"

盜亦有道 dào yì yǒu dào 0603

Robbers also have their virtues. (lit.)

There's honour among thieves.

Dog does not eat dog.

Give the devil his due.

源 莊子："跖之徒問於跖曰，盜亦有道乎。"

道德淪喪 dào dé lún sàng 0604

Perdition of morality. (lit.)

Fall from grace.

Go to the dogs.

同 世風日下，人心不古（2496）The more I see of men, the more I love dogs.

源 禮記："道德仁義，非禮不成。"

道高一尺，魔高一丈 0605

dào gāo yī chǐ, mó gāo yī zhàng

When the truth grows to one foot high, the evil grows to ten feet. (lit.)

Where God has his church, the devil will have his chapel.

同 一法立，一弊生（3389）The more laws, the more offenders.

源 西遊記："道高一尺魔高丈，性亂情昏錯認家。"

道貌岸然 dào mào àn rán 0606

Scholarly appearance, dignified and serious. (lit.)

Look as if butter would not melt in one's mouth.

同 一本正經（3371）Have a serious look.

反 賊眉賊眼（3770）Have the brand of a villian in one's looks.

源 續仙傳："李珏情景恬澹，道貌秀異。"

道聽途説 dào tīng tú shuō 0607

Heard in the street and talked by the road side. (lit.)

Hear something over (through) the grape-vine.

A traveller's tale.

同 街談巷議（1316）Way-side inn gossips.

反 權威人士透露（2167）Straight from the horse's mouth.

源 論語・陽貨："道聽而途説，德之棄也。"

0608 **道吾好者是吾賊，道吾惡者是吾師** dào wú hào zhě shì wú zéi, dào wú wù zhě shì wú shī

Who says good of me is my thief, who says bad of me is my teacher. (lit.)

A friend's frown is better than a fool's smile.

All are not friends that speak us fair.

0609 **得不償失** dé bù cháng shī

The gain does not recompense the loss. (lit.)

The game is not worth the candle.

Give a lark to catch a kite.

Pay dear for the whistle.

More kicks than halfpence.

同 以珠彈雀（3549）Not worth powder and shot.

反 一本萬利（3370）Light gains make heavy purses.

源 蘇軾詩："感時嗟事變，所得不償失。"

0610 **得寸進尺** dé cùn jìn chǐ

Get an inch and go for a foot. (lit.)

Give him an inch and he will take an ell (a mile.)

同 得隴望蜀（0613）Give me a footing and I will find elbow room.

反 退而思其次（2825）If you cannot have the best, make the best of what you have.

源 戰國策："得寸則王之寸，得尺亦王之尺。"

0611 **得過且過** dé guò qiě guò

Can pass, pass it. (lit.)

Let well enough alone.

To muddle along.

同 馬馬虎虎（1729）Fair to middling.

反 一絲不苟（3460）Dot one's i's and cross one's t's.

源 陶宗儀．輟耕錄："寒號蟲至深冬嚴寒之際，自鳴曰，得過且過。"

0612 **得力助手** dé lì zhù shǒu

A capable assistant. (lit.)

A right-hand man.

0613 **得隴望蜀** dé lǒng wàng shǔ

Having captured Long (Shensi province) and hankering after Shu (Szechuan Province). (lit.)

Give me a footing and I will find elbow room.

The more you have, the more you want.

Fly at higher game.

To want jam on it.

同 得寸進尺（0610）Give him an inch and he will take an ell （a mile）.

反 知足常樂（3863）Enough is as good as a feast.

源 晉書："人苦無足，既得隴右，復欲得蜀。"

得其所哉 dé qí suǒ zāi
Got what he wanted. (lit.)
Fall into place.
In one's own element.

同 如魚得水（2279）Like a duck to water.
反 不得其所（0181）A fish out of water.
源 孟子：“得其所哉。”

0614

得勝凱旋 dé shèng kǎi xuán
Getting triumph with victory. (lit.)
Come off with flying colours.
Bring home the bacon.
To carry (win) the day.

反 潰不成軍（1533）To be put to rout.

0615

得縮頭時且縮頭 dé suō tóu shí qiě suō tóu
When it is time to withdraw the head, then withdraw it. (lit.)
When you bow, bow low.

同 能屈能伸（1891）Stretch your legs according to your coverlet.
反 昂首雲外（0032）Have one's nose in the air.

0616

得天獨厚 dé tiān dú hòu
Well endowed by Heaven. (lit.)
Richly endowed by nature.
Flowing with milk and honey.
A land of plenty.

同 天賦之才（2711）To be gifted with

0617

得心應手 dé xīn yìng shǒu
Wish at heart comes to hand. (lit.)
As clay in the hands of the potter.
Get into one's stride.
Take to something like duck to water.

反 心勞日拙（3176）To be a fool for one's pains.
源 莊子・天道：“不徐不疾，得之於手而應於心。”

0618

得意濃時便好休 dé yì nóng shí biàn hǎo xiū
When one's wishes are fully satisfied one may well take leave. (lit.)
Leave off while the play is good. When the play is best, it is best to leave.

0619

0620 得意忘形 dé yì wàng xíng

When one's wishes are satisfied, one tends to forget himself. (lit.)

Leap out of one's skin.

Beside oneself with joy.

Leap with joy.

To tread on air.

Turn one's head.

同 手舞足蹈（2549）Dance for joy.

源 晉書・阮籍傳："當其得意，忽忘形骸。"

0621 得意洋洋 dé yì yáng yáng

The wishes are fulfilled exaltingly. (lit.)

Have one's nose (tail) in the air.

In high feather.

Feel one's oats

同 洋洋自得（3333）To tread on air.

反 心灰意冷（3171）To lose heart.

0622 得魚忘筌 dé yú wàng quán

Having caught the fish, one forgets the trap. (lit.)

Kick down the ladder.

源 莊子・外物："筌者所以在魚，得魚而忘筌。"

0623 登峰造極 dēng fēng zào jí

Climb to the summit and achieve the utmost. (lit.)

At the top of the tree.

Reach the limit.

Reach the top of the ladder.

同 歎為觀止（2687）Nothing can be better.

源 世說新語："簡文云，不知便可登峰造極。"

0624 登門造訪 dēng mén zào fǎng

Ascend (the steps) to the door and pay a visit. (lit.)

Look someone up.

Drop in on a person.

Pay a visit.

Look in on one.

0625 燈芯扛成鐵 dēng xīn káng chéng tiě

A lamp wick being carried (for long time or distance) becomes (as heavy as) iron. (lit.)

Light burdens, long borne, grow heavy.

On a long journey even a straw is heavy.

等待時機 děng dài shí jī 0626
Wait for the opportunity. (lit.)
Bide one's time.

同 伺機而動（2640）Have an eye to the main chance.
反 急不可待（1208）Leap over the hedge before one comes to the stile.

等量齊觀 děng liàng qí guān 0627
Quantitatively equal in the same view. (lit.)
Six of one and half a dozen of the other.
Put on a par.
Draw a parallel between
Place on the same footing.

同 一視同仁（3457）The sun shines upon all alike.
反 另眼相看（1672）Regard with favour.

等閒視之 děng xián shì zhī 0628
Look at it too lightly. (lit.)
Take things lightly.
Make little of
Think nothing of

同 掉以輕心（0651）Make light of
反 鄭重其事（3847）To mean business.

等因奉此 děng yīn fèng cǐ 0629
In view of the reasons mentioned above, therefore...... (lit.)
Red tape.

等着瞧 děng zhe qiáo 0630
Waiting to see. (lit.)
Wait and see.
It remains to be seen.

同 風物長宜放眼量（0810）See which way the cat jumps.

鄧通銅山 dèng tōng tóng shān 0631
Deng-tong (a well known person in history) owned a hill of copper. (lit.)
To be made of money.
As rich as Croesus.
Have money to burn.
Flourish like the green bay-tree.

同 腰纏萬貫（3344）Roll in wealth.
反 阮囊羞澀（2291）Not to have a bean.

低能差勁 dī néng chā jìn 0632
Incapable and lacking of energy. (lit.)
Not worth one's salt.

同 酒囊飯袋（1424）A good-for-nothing.
反 精明強幹（1386）To be up to snuff.

0633 **低聲下氣** dī shēng xià qì
Low voice and modest volume. (lit.)
Pocket one's pride.
When you bow, bow low.

反 盛氣凌人（2433）Throw one's weight about.

0634 **低頭認罪** dī tóu rèn zuì
Lowering down the head to confess one's crime. (lit.)
Cop a plea.
Plead guilty.
Stand in a white sheet.

反 鳴冤叫屈（1832）Plead not guilty.

0635 **羝羊觸藩** dī yáng chù fān
The ram butting the fence gets stuck. (lit.)
To be in a cleft stick.
Get into a nice hobble.

反 摧枯拉朽（0474）Sweep everything before one.
源 周易："羝羊觸藩，不能退，不能遂。"

0636 **滴酒不沾** dī jiǔ bù zhān
Touching not one drop of wine. (lit.)
Drink only with the duck.
Adam's ale is the best brew.

反 酩酊大醉（1833）As drunk as a fiddler.

0637 **滴水穿石** dī shuǐ chuān shí
Drips of water wear through a stone. (lit.)
Constant dripping wears away the stone.
Feather by feather the goose is plucked.
Slow but sure wins the race.
A sheer strength of will.

同 持之以恆（0379）Perseverance will prevail.
反 三天打魚，兩天曬網（2313）By fits and starts.

0638 **抵抗到底** dǐ kàng dào dǐ
To resist to the end. (lit.)
To be dead set against
Die in the last ditch.
Fight tooth and nail.

同 寸土不讓（0478）Not budge an inch.
反 臨陣退縮（1659）Back down at the sight of the enemy.

地球依舊會轉 dì qiú yī jiù huì zhuàn 0639

The earth (sphere) will rotate as ever. (lit.)

It will be all the same a hundred years hence.

地頭蛇 dì tóu shé 0640

Local snake. (lit.)

Cock on his own dunghill.

反 流浪漢（1679）A bird of passage.

第一把手 dì yī bǎ shǒu 0641

The first steering hand. (lit.)

Cock of the walk.

To be at the helm.

第一手材料 dì yī shǒu cái liào 0642

The first hand material. (lit.)

At first hand.

Straight from the horse's mouth.

顛倒黑白 diān dǎo hēi bái 0643

To confound the black and white. (lit.)

Talk (Turn) black into white.

Call black white.

同 指鹿為馬（3881）Swear black is white.

反 黑白分明（1058）The fairer the paper, the fouler the blot.

顛倒是非 diān dǎo shì fēi 0644

To confuse right and wrong. (lit.)

Stand truth on its head.

Confound right with wrong.

Turn things upside down.

反 撥亂反正（0167）Set things right side up.

源 韓愈．施先生墓銘："箋註紛羅，顛倒是非。"

顛沛流離 diān pèi liú lí 0645

Fell and frustrated, wandering with no home. (lit.)

Here today and gone tomorrow.

Have got the key of the street.

Live a vagabond life.

同 流浪漢（1679）A bird of passage.

反 安家落戶（0010）To settle down.

源 論語："造次必如是，顛沛必如是。"

典當度日 diǎn dàng dù rì 0646

Pass the day by pawning. (lit.)

Climb the mountain of piety.

0647 **點石成金** diǎn shí chéng jīn

The stone touched turned gold. (lit.)

All he touches turns to gold.

A golden touch.

反 佛頭着糞（0817）A fly in the ointment.

源 列仙傳：“許遜，南昌人。晉初為旌陽令，點石化金，以足逋賦。”

0648 **點頭朋友** diǎn tóu péng yǒu

A nodding friend. (lit.)

A bowing (nodding) acquaintance.

同 泛泛之交（0750）Just on speaking terms with one another.

反 刎頸之交（2929）Damon and Pythias.

0649 **吊兒郎當** diào ér láng dāng

A Chinese slang somewhat equivalent to 'dilly dally' in English. (lit.)

Gad about.

Dilly dally.

Happy-go-lucky.

Follow the primrose path.

反 鄭重其事（3847）In sober earnest.

0650 **掉頭不顧** diào tóu bù gù

Turn the head away and not care for. (lit.)

Never to look back.

同 不屑一顧（0260）Shut one's eyes to

反 多方照顧（0700）Heap favours upon.

0651 **掉以輕心** diào yǐ qīng xīn

To treat something light-heartedly. (lit.)

Take it lightly.

Make light of

Lower one's guard.

同 毫不在意（1024）To make nothing of

反 嚴陣以待（3319）Poised for action.

源 柳宗元．論師道書：“故吾每為文章，未嘗敢以輕心掉之。”

0652 **調查研究** diào chá yán jiū

To enquire and to investigate. (lit.)

See how the land lies.

See how the cat will jump.

反 想當然（3115）To take for granted.

0653 **調虎離山** diào hǔ lí shān

Lure a tiger out of a mountain. (lit.)

Draw a red herring across the path.

同 引入歧途（3587）Lead one up the garden path.

喋喋不休 dié dié bù xiū 0654

A ceaseless chattering. (lit.)

Hold someone by the button.

Talk a horse's hind leg off.

Talk the hind leg off a donkey.

Chew the rag.

Chatter away.

同 話匣子（1121）A gas bag.

反 欲説還休（3718）To shut up shop.

源 漢書："喋喋利口。"

丁是丁，卯是卯 dīng shì dīng, mǎo shì mǎo 0655

Ding is ding, mao is mao (ding and mao are terms in Chinese chronology). (lit.)

Business is business.

Call a spade a spade.

同 實事求是（2480）Look fact in the face.

反 指鹿為馬（3881）Talk black into white.

源 元曲選："要説個丁一卯二，不許你差三錯四。"

頂呱呱 dǐng guā guā 0656

A Chinese slang somewhat similar to 'thumb's up' in English. (lit.)

All wool and a yard wide.

To be a hot number.

Bang-up.

同 第一流 Of the first water.

頂禮膜拜 dǐng lǐ mó bài 0657

Bow deeply and kneel down. (lit.)

Fall at one's feet.

When you bow, bow low.

同 五體投地（3014）Fall on one's knees.

反 嗤之以鼻（0378）Turn up one's nose at

源 圓覺經疏："以己最勝之頂，禮佛最卑之足，敬之至也。"

頂事 dǐng shì 0658

Do a good job. (lit.)

Serve the prupose (turn).

反 無濟於事（2969）To be of little avail.

鼎力支持 dǐng lì zhī chí 0659

To support with great effort. (lit.)

Stand up for

Stand by a person.

Give one a leg up.

Put one's hand to the plough.

同 熱烈贊助（2185）Carry a torch for

反 從中作梗（0469）Put a spoke in one's wheel.

0660 **東邊日出西邊雨**
dōng biān rì chū xī biān yǔ
The sun rising from the east side while raining at the west side. (lit.)
The devil is beating his wife with a shoulder of mutton.

源 劉禹錫·竹枝詞："東邊日出西邊雨，道是無晴還有晴。"

0661 **東窗事發** dōng chuāng shì fā
A plot of the eastern window was exposed. (lit.)
The murder is out.

源 西湖遊覽志餘："可煩傳語夫人，東窗事發矣。"

0662 **東方發白** dōng fāng fā bái
The eastern side turns white. (lit.)
The day is breaking.

0663 **東方欲曉** dōng fāng yù xiǎo
The eastern side just begin to dawn. (lit.)
The crack of day (dawn).

同 旭日東升（3252）The morning sun rises in the east.
反 夜幕低垂（3367）Under the screen of night.

0664 **東風吹馬耳** dōng fēng chuī mǎ ěr
The east wind blowing (past) the horse's ears. (lit.)
Like water off a duck's back.

反 牢記心頭（1552）Take it to heart.
源 李白詩："世人聞此皆掉頭，有如東風吹馬耳。"

0665 **東郭先生救狼** dōng guō xiān shēng jiù láng
Mr. Dongguo saved the wolf. (lit.)
He that spares the bad injures the good.
Save the thief from the gallows and he will cut your throat.

0666 **東山再起** dōng shān zài qǐ
The eastern mountain rises again. (lit.)
Stage a comeback.
Bob up like a cork.
He that falls today may rise tomorrow.

同 重整旗鼓（0392）Dig up the hatchet.
反 一敗塗地（3368）Down and out.
源 晉書："謝安初隱東山，後入朝，位登台輔。"

東施效顰 dōng shī xiào pín 0667

Dong-Shi imitating the knitting of her brows (in copying Xi-Shi, a beauty in Chinese history) made herself uglier than ever. (lit.)

Ugly women, finely dressed, are uglier.

源 莊子．天運："西子病心而顰，其里之醜人，見而美之，歸亦捧心而效其顰。"

東遊西逛 dōng yóu xī guàng 0668

Playing at east and loitering at west. (lit.)

To moon (mooch) about.

反 埋頭苦幹（1735）Keep one's nose to the grind-stone.

東撞西突 dōng zhuàng xī tū 0669

Bumping to the east and butting to the west. (lit.)

Like a bear with a sore head.

A bull in a china shop.

同 莽莽撞撞（1769）To be harum-scarum.

洞若觀火 dòng ruò guān huǒ 0670

To know as clearly as looking at a fire. (lit.)

See through a thing.

Clear as noonday.

As clear as day.

同 一目了然（3429）Everybody can see that at a glance.

源 書經："予若觀火。"

洞悉內情 dòng xī nèi qíng 0671

Understanding thoroughly the inside situation. (lit.)

To be in the swim.

同 深知底細（2402）Know something like a boot.

反 全不知情（2158）To be in the dark.

動人肺腑 dòng rén fèi fǔ 0672

Move (emotionally) one's lung and viscera. (lit.)

Come home to one's heart.

Sweep one off one's feet.

同 扣人心弦（1512）Tug at one's heartstrings.

動如脫兔 dòng rú tuō tù 0673

Move like an escaped hare. (lit.)

Run like a hare.

As fleet as (a) deer.

同 兔起鶻落（2812）Like a shot.

反 靜如處女（1407）As quiet as a lamb.

源 孫子："是故始如處女，敵人開戶，後如脫兔，敵不及拒。"

0674 動員報告 dòng yuán bào gào
Mobilization report. (lit.)
Pep talk.

0675 斗酒三千恣歡謔 dǒu jiǔ sān qiān zì huān nüè
Enjoy fully the three thousand ladles of wine and laughter. (lit.)
Beer and skittles.

0676 獨步一時 dú bù yī shí
Tread alone at one time. (lit.)
A man of the hour.

同 名噪一時（1817）To rise to fame.
源 宣和畫譜："論者謂熙（郭熙）獨步一時，雖年老落筆益壯，如隨年貌焉。"

0677 獨斷獨行 dú duàn dú xíng
Decide and act alone. (lit.)
Take the law into one's own hand.
Act arbitrarily.
Get one's own way.

同 一意孤行（3488）Go one's own way.
反 集思廣益（1224）In the multitude of counsellors there is safely.
源 管子："獨斷者，微密之營壘也。"

0678 獨立自主 dú lì zì zhǔ
Independence and sovereignty. (lit.)
Stand on one's feet.
Stand on one's own bottom.
To be on one's hook.

反 寄人籬下（1236）To eat out of one's hand.

0679 獨木不成林 dú mù bù chéng lín
A lone tree can't make a forest. (lit.)
One flower makes no garland.
The voice of one man is the voice of no man.

反 眾志成城（3926）Union is strength.
源 漢·崔駰·達旨："高樹靡陰，獨木不林。"

0680 獨善其身 dú shàn qí shēn
Keep one's own virtue to oneself. (lit.)
Better be alone than in ill company.
Solitude is better than ill company.
Keep one's distance.
Keep oneself to oneself.

反 與世浮沉（3708）To drift with the stream.
源 孟子·盡心上："窮則獨善其身，達則兼善天下。"

獨佔鰲頭 dú zhàn áo tóu

Perched alone on the Levia-than's head (big sea turtle). (lit.)

Come out first.

Sweep the board.

Carry off the palm.

Bear away the bell.

同 名列前茅（1814）Head the list. 0681

反 名落孫山（1815）Get plucked.

源 洪北江詩話："俗語謂狀元獨佔鰲頭，非盡無稽。"

獨自謀生 dú zì móu shēng

To earn one's own living. (lit.)

Paddle one's own canoe.

Cut one's own grass.

反 因人成事（3574）Come in through the cabin window. 0682

睹物思人 dǔ wù sī rén 0683

Looking at the thing, think of the person. (lit.)

A token of remembrance.

杜漸防微 dù jiàn fáng wēi

Stop the gradual (change) and prevent minute development. (lit.)

Nip in the bud.

Crush in the egg.

A little fire is quickly trodden out.

The thin end of the wedge is to be feared.

同 防患未然（0755）To take precaution. 0684

源 元史・張楨傳："防微杜漸而禁於未然。"

杜門謝客 dù mén xiè kè

Shut the door and refuse visitors. (lit.)

Sport one's oak.

同 餉以閉門羹（3117）Leave one on the mat. 0685

反 倒屣相迎（0601）Give one three times three.

源 國語："遂趨而退歸，杜門不出。"

渡過難關 dù guò nán guān

To cross the difficult barrier. (lit.)

Over the hump.

Weather a storm.

Tide over difficulties.

Turn the corner.

Pull through.

同 化險為夷（1116）To be out of the woods. 0686

0687 **短兵相接** duǎn bīng xiāng jiē

Soldiers fighting at short distance in confrontation. (lit.)

Fight hilt to hilt.

Fight at close quarters.

Hand-to-hand fight.

同 劍拔弩張（1289）At sword's points with each other.

反 和平共處（1049）Peaceful co-existence.

源 史記．季布傳："丁公逐窘高帝彭城西，短兵相接。"

0688 **斷斷續續** duàn duàn xù xù

Breaking and continuing. (lit.)

Off and on.

同 或作或輟（1171）By fits and starts.

反 一氣呵成（3438）At a breath.

0689 **斷章取義** duàn zhāng qǔ yì

Make interpretation by quoting parts of the essay. (lit.)

Quote out of context.

A garbled quotation (statement).

反 引經據典（3584）Give chapter and verse.

源 孝經．孔傳："斷章取義，上下相成。"

0690 **對牛彈琴** duì niú tán qín

Play the harp to the cow. (lit.)

It is lost labour to play a jig to an old cat.

Cast pearls before swine.

Preach to deaf ears.

源 莊子注："猶是對牛鼓簧耳。"

0691 **對症下藥** duì zhèng xià yào

Prescribe medicine according to the disease. (lit.)

There is a salve for every sore.

Find a right antidote.

Counter with proper measures.

反 飲鴆止渴（3591）The remedy is worse than the disease.

0692 **頓起疑心** dùn qǐ yí xīn

Suddenly doubt rises in the heart. (lit.)

To smell a rat.

反 深信不疑（2400）Feel it in one's bones.

0693 **遁跡空門** dùn jì kōng mén

To conceal oneself in a monastery. (lit.)

Retire into a cloister.

反 與世浮沉（3708）To drift with the stream.

多才多藝 duō cái duō yì 0694

Possessing numerous gifts and considerable arts. (lit.)

To be all-round.

A man of many gifts.

A man of parts.

Many accomplishments.

Gifted in many fields.

同 百事通（0055）A know-all.

反 一無所長（3473）A rolling stone gathers no moss.

源 尚書．金滕："予仁若考，能多才多藝。"

多財善賈 duō cái shàn gǔ 0695

Very rich and know how to do business. (lit.)

Drive a roaring trade.

同 一本萬利（3370）Light gains make heavy purses.

反 虧空破產（1532）Gone through the sieve.

源 韓非子．五蠹："鄙諺曰，長袖善舞，多錢善賈。"

多吃多佔 duō chī duō zhàn 0696

The more one eats the more he takes. (lit.)

Take the lion's share.

同 貪得無厭（2672）As greedy as a wolf.

反 自奉甚薄（3977）Practise self-denial.

多吃飯，少開口 duō chī fàn, shǎo kāi kǒu 0697

Eat more rice, less open mouth (less talk). (lit.)

Save one's breath to cool one's porridge.

多此一舉 duō cǐ yī jǔ 0698

One move too many. (lit.)

Carry coals to Newcastle.

Carry water to the river.

Gild refined gold.

To no purpose.

多多益善 duō duō yì shàn 0699

Plentiful the better. (lit.)

The more the better.

All is fish that comes to his net.

All's grist that comes to the mill.

源 史記．淮陰侯傳："上問曰，如我能將幾何，信曰，不過十萬，上曰，於君何如，曰，臣多多益善耳。"

0700 **多方照顧** duō fāng zhào gù
Taking care from many directions. (lit.)
Heap favours upon
Put one on a pedestal.

同 無微不至（2998）Wait on one hand and foot.
反 要理不理（3357）Give one the cold shoulder.

0701 **多管閒事** duō guǎn xián shì
Minding too much unimportant matters. (lit.)
Poke one's nose into other people's business.
Put one's finger into another's pie.

反 事不關己，高高掛起（2508）I will neither meddle nor make.

0702 **多面手** duō miàn shǒu
Many-sided hand. (lit.)
Jack of all trades.
An all-rounder.

0703 **多謀善斷** duō móu shàn duàn
Plenty of wisdom and good at making right decisions. (lit.)
To be full of wrinkles.
Have the presence of mind.
Equal to the occasion.
Fruitful of expedients.

同 精明強幹（1386）To be up to snuff.
反 束手無策（2573）Throw up one's hands in despair.
源 文選．陸機．辨亡論上：“疇咨俊茂，好謀善斷。”

0704 **多事之秋** duō shì zhī qiū
An eventful autumn (time of troubles). (lit.)
In these eventful days.

同 戰火瀰漫（3786）Fire and sword.
反 太平盛世（2668）The piping times of peace.

0705 **多行不義必自斃**
duō xíng bù yì bì zì bì
The one who does all evil things will himself perish. (lit.)
Every sin brings its punishment with it.
Ill-gotten gains seldom prosper.

反 積善多福（1191）Give much to the poor doth increase a man's store.
源 左傳．隱元年：“多行不義必自斃，子姑待之。”

0706 **多言多敗** duō yán duō bài
More talks more errors. (lit.)
Talk much and err much.

反 少說為佳（2364）Few words are best.

多一事不如少一事
duō yī shì bù rú shǎo yī shì
One more matter is not as good as one matter less. (lit.)
Leave well alone.

反 不厭其煩（0263）Take the trouble.

0707

咄咄逼人 duō duō bī rén
Press and scold others fiercely. (lit.)
Lord it over.
Play the bully.
To be overbearing.

同 盛氣淩人（2433）Throw one's weight about.
反 溫柔敦厚（2920）As harmless as a dove.
源 法書要錄：“王濛子修，善隸行，子敬每者修書云，咄咄逼人。”

0708

踱來踱去 duó lái duó qù
Strolling here and there. (lit.)
Walk the floor.
Pace back and forth.

同 來回往復（1536）To and fro.

0709

躲躲閃閃 duǒ duǒ shǎn shǎn
Hiding and dodging. (lit.)
Wriggle like a cut snake.
Sneaking in and out.
Hole-and-corner.

同 鬼鬼祟祟（0989）Up to some hangky pangky.
反 堂堂正正（2688）On the square.

0710

墮入情網 duò rù qíng wǎng
Fall into a love net. (lit.)
To fall in love.
Lose one's heart to

同 神魂顛倒（2046）To fall for

0711

E

0712 **阿諛諂媚** ē yú chǎn mèi

Flatter and fawn upon. (lit.)

Lick another's boots.

Tickle someone's ears.

反 嗤之以鼻（0378）Turn up one's nose at

0713 **阿諛逢迎** ē yú féng yíng

Flattering and ingratiating manner. (lit.)

Curry favour.

Butter up a person.

Do a person proud.

Dance attendance on a person.

同 奴顏婢膝（1926）Grovel at the feet of

0714 **惡恐人知，便是大惡**

è kǒng rén zhī, biàn shì dà è

The wickedness afraid of others to know, must be a great sin. (lit.)

Dissembled sin is double wickedness.

0715 **惡事傳千里** è shì chuán qiān lǐ

The bad things pass on thousand li (Chinese mile). (lit.)

Ill news runs space.

源 事文類聚："好事不出門，惡事傳千里。"

0716 **惡有惡報** è yǒu è bào

Evil doings get evil returns. (lit.)

Every sin brings its punishment with it.

Sow the wind and reap the whirlwind.

Curses, like chickens, come home to roost.

同 多行不義必自斃（0705）Ill-gotten gains seldom prosper.

反 善有善報（2346）Kindnesses, like grain, increase by sowing.

惡語傷人恨不消 è yǔ shāng rén hèn bù xiāo ◀0717
The wicked words hurting others cause unperishable hatred. (lit.)
Slander leaves a scar behind it.

惡語中傷 è yǔ zhòng shāng ◀0718
Say wicked words to hurt. (lit.)
The tongue is not steel, yet it cuts.
Snap a person's nose (head) off.
Put a nail in a person's coffin.
As sharp as a razor (needle).

反 甜言蜜語（2742）Give one a mouthful of moonshine.

恩將仇報 ēn jiāng chóu bào ◀0719
Requite good with evil. (lit.)
Return evil for good.
Bite the hand that feeds one.
I taught you to swim, and now you'd drown me.
A kick in the pants (teeth).

同 以怨報德（3545）Save a thief from the gallows and he will cut your throat.
反 認賊作父（2248）Set a fox to keep one's geese.

恩威並施 ēn wēi bìng shī ◀0720
Kind deeds and authouity are applied together. (lit.)
To temper justice with mercy.

同 軟硬兼施（2293）Strong in action, gentle in method.

兒孫自有兒孫福，莫為兒孫作馬牛 ér sūn zì yǒu ér sūn fú, mò wèi ér sūn zuò mǎ niú ◀0721
Children and grandchildren will have their own blessings, don't be a horse or an ox for the children and grandchildren. (lit.)
Children are certain cares, but uncertain comforts.

耳邊風 ěr biān fēng ◀0722
The wind that passes one's ears. (lit.)
In at one ear and out at the other.
Turn a deaf ear to

同 聽而不聞（2753）None so deaf as those who won't hear.
反 側耳諦聽（0313）Strain one's ears.
源 南齊書："吾日冀汝美，勿得粉如風過耳，使吾失氣。"

0723 **耳濡目染** ěr rú mù rǎn

What one's ears have soaked (heard) and eyes coloured (seen). (lit.)

He that keeps company with the wolf will learn to howl.

Under the influence of

反 出污泥而不染（0418）Lilies are whitest in a blackamoor's hand.

源 昌黎先生集．清河郡公房公墓碣銘："目濡耳染，不學以能。"

0724 **耳提面命** ěr tí miàn mìng

To ring advice in his ears and to give order to his face. (lit.)

Lead by the nose.

Knock into one's head.

Din into one's ears.

同 反覆叮嚀（0745）To rub in.

源 詩經．大雅．抑："匪面命之，言提其耳。"

0725 **耳聽八方** ěr tīng bā fāng

The ears hearing from eight directions. (lit.)

To bell all ears.

同 豎起耳朵（2575）Prick up one's ears.

反 充耳不聞（0384）None so deaf as those who won't hear.

0726 **耳聞不如目睹** ěr wén bù rú mù dǔ

Hearing is not as good as seeing. (lit.)

One eye-witness is better than ten ear-witnesses.

Seeing is believing.

The eyes believe themselves, the ears believe other people.

源 劉向．說苑．政理："耳聞之不如目見之，目見之不如足踐之。"

0727 **爾虞我詐** ěr yú wǒ zhà

You cunning and I dishonest. (lit.)

Play each other false.

Double-crossing each other.

反 互相信任（1099）Confidence begets confidence.

源 左傳．宣十五年："爾無我詐，我無爾虞。"

0728 **二流子** èr liú zǐ

Second rate son (person). (lit.)

A lay-about.

0729 **二豎所侵** èr shù suǒ qīn

To be attacked by two waiting-lads (who often appear in the dreams of a sick person in Chinese legends). (lit.)

Be taken ill.

Be out of sorts.

同 抱恙在身（0090）To be laid up.

反 久病新痊（1416）To pull through.

源 左傳："晉景公求醫於秦，秦伯使醫緩視之，未至，公夢疾為二豎子。"

二一添作五 èr yī tiān zuò wǔ

Ten divided by two is five. (lit.)

Go fifty-fifty.

Go halves.

同 平分秋色（1988）Share and share alike. 0730

二者不可得兼 èr zhě bù kě dé jiān

Can't have both together. (lit.)

You can't have it both ways.

You cannot burn the candle at both ends.

反 一舉兩得（3408）Kill two flies with one slap. 0731

源 孟子："魚我所欲也，熊掌亦我所欲也，二者不可得兼，舍魚而取熊掌者也。"

F

0732 **發憤圖強** fā fèn tú qiáng

Strive for getting strong. (lit.)

Shake oneself together

同 自力更生（3983）Pull oneself up by the footstraps.

反 自暴自棄（3968）Abandon oneself to despair.

0733 **發號施令** fā hào shī lìng

Give order and execute mandates. (lit.)

Lay down the law.

Call the tune.

同 指手劃腳（3884）To lord it over.

反 唯命是從（2891）Do one's bidding.

源 尚書 · 冏命：“發號施令，罔有不臧。”

0734 **發家致富** fā jiā zhì fù

Expand the family and get rich. (lit.)

Make one's pile.

Keep one's self afloat.

Keep the tail in water.

反 虧空破產（1532）Gone through the sieve.

0735 **發牢騷** fā láo sāo

To make complaints. (lit.)

Let off steam.

Say devil's paternoster.

同 怨天尤人（3740）Everyone puts his faults on the times.

反 捺着性子（1876）Bottle up one's feelings.

0736 **發人深省** fā rén shēn xǐng

Induce one to deep reflection. (lit.)

Set one to thinking.

Provide food for thought.

Give one something to think about.

源 杜甫詩：“欲覺聞晨鐘，令人發深省。”

0737 **幡然悔悟** fān rán huǐ wù

Suddendly turn to realise and remorse. (lit.)

Make a clean break with one's past.

Turn over a new leaf.

同 痛改前非（2779）Mend one's way.

反 故態復萌（0951）Back in the old rut.

翻江倒海 fān jiāng dǎo hǎi 0738

Overturn the river and pour out the sea. (lit.)

Move heaven and earth.

Leave no stone unturned.

To take great trouble.

翻老賬 fān lǎo zhàng 0739

Turn back the old debts. (lit.)

Rip up old sores.

Rake out old grievances.

同 舊事重提（1433）Rake up the past.

反 既往不咎（1234）Let bygones be bygones.

翻臉不認人 fān liǎn bú rèn rén 0740

Turn the face from one without recognizing him. (lit.)

Cut one dead.

Give one the go-by.

Turn one's back to someone.

Cut a person in the street.

同 六親不認（1686）Cut loose from old ties.

反 一見如故（3404）Be hail-fellow-well-met with

翻山越嶺 fān shān yuè lǐng 0741

Scale the mountain and climb over the hill. (lit.)

Over hill and dale.

翻雲覆雨 fān yún fù yǔ 0742

Overturn the clouds and stop the rains. (lit.)

Blow hot and cold.

同 出爾反爾（0402）Play fast and loose.

源 杜甫．貧交行："翻手為雲覆手雨。"

繁文縟節 fán wén rù jié 0743

Complicated rules of etiquette and numerous formalities. (lit.)

Forms and for malities.

Red tape.

同 精兵簡政（1380）I will keep no more cats than will catch mice.

反唇相稽 fǎn chún xiāng jī 0744

Turn the lips and retort each other. (lit.)

Answer back.

Give one a rolling for his all-over.

A Roland for an Oliver.

源 漢書．賈誼傳："婦姑不相悅，則反唇而相稽。"

0745 **反覆叮嚀** fǎn fù dīng níng
Reminding repentedly. (lit.)
Beat into one's head.
To rub in.
Jog a person's memory.
Knock into one's head.

反 不用提點（0270）Send a wise man on errand, and say nothing to him.

0746 **反覆無常** fǎn fù wú cháng
Changeable and inconsistent. (lit.)
Blow hot and cold.
Play fast and loose.

同 風派（0804）The wind keeps not always at one quarter.
反 始終不渝（2483）Stick to it.
源 漢書：“齊夸詐多變，反覆之國。”

0747 **反戈一擊** fǎn gě yì jī
Turn the Ge (ancient Chinese weapon)to make a strike. (lit.)
A parthian shot.

0748 **反正一樣** fǎn zhèn yí yàng
The right and opposite sides the same. (lit.)
It is all one.
As broad as it is long.
As well be hanged for a sheep as a lamb.

同 橫豎一樣（1067）To be much of a muchness.
反 千差萬別（2056）As different as chalk is from cheese.

0749 **返老還童** fǎn lǎo huán tóng
Turn old age back to youth.(rejuvenation). (lit.)
In one's second childhook.
An old man is twice a child.

反 年少老成（1909）An old head on young shoulders.
源 神仙傳：“八公曰，王薄我老，今則少矣，八公皆變為童子。”

0750 **泛泛之交** fàn fàn zhī jiāo
A mere acquaintance. (lit.)
Have only a bowing acquaintance.
Just on speaking terms with one another.

反 管鮑之誼（0972）Damon and Pythias.

0751 **方寸已亂** fāng cùn yǐ luàn
One's square inch (heart) is already confused. (lit.)
Fall into a flutter.
To be greatly upset.
With one's heart going pitpat.

同 心亂如麻（3179）To be in a stew.
反 頭腦冷靜（2797）Have one's brains on ice.
源 三國志：“徐庶曰，今失老母，方寸亂矣。”

方枘圓鑿 fāng ruì yuán zuò

Square handle and round socket. (lit.)

A square peg in a round hole.

同 格格不入（0895）Out of keeping with.

反 貼貼切切（2746）Fit like a glove.

源 史記："持方枘欲納圓鑿，其能入乎。" 0752

方向對頭 fāng xiàng duì tóu

The direction which faces the head. (lit.)

On the right tack.

反 背道而馳（0100）Run counter to 0753

方興未艾 fāng xīng wèi ài

Just starting to flourish but not reaching climax yet. (lit.)

In the bud.

In the ascendant.

On the upgrade.

In infancy.

同 欣欣向榮（3203）Flourish like the green bay-tree.

反 日薄西山（2253）Sinking fast. 0754

防患未然 fáng huàn wèi rán

Precaution in advance. (lit.)

Prevention is better than cure.

Nip in the bud.

Crush in the egg.

To take precaution.

同 杜漸防微（0684）A little fire is quickly trodden out.

反 賊去關門（3771）Lock the stable door after the horse is stolen.

源 漢書．外戚傳："事不當固爭，防禍於未然。" 0755

放長線，釣大魚

fàng cháng xiàn, diào dà yú

Releasing a long line, hook a big fish. (lit.)

Give one line enough.

同 欲擒先縱（3717）Give a thief enough rope and he'll hang himself. 0756

放蕩不羈 fàng dàng bù jī

Profligate and unrestrained. (lit.)

Sow one's wild oats.

Have one's fling.

To forget oneself.

同 放浪形骸（0759）To live fast.

反 循規蹈矩（3280）Toe the line.

源 晉書．王長文傳："少以才學知名，而放蕩不羈。" 0757

放飯流歠 fàng fàn liú chuò

Throw the rice away but keep the crust. (lit.)

Penny wise and pound foolish.

同 揀了芝麻，丟了西瓜（1274）Spare at the spigot and spioll at the bung.

反 從大處着眼（0460）Have an eye to the main chance.

源 孟子："放飯流歠，而問無齒决。" 0758

0759 **放浪形骸** fàng làng xíng hái

Let loose freely one's manner and body. (lit.)

To have one's fling.

To live fast.

反 謹言慎行（1359）Mind one's P's and Q's.

源 王羲之．蘭亭集序："或因寄所托，放浪形骸之外。"

0760 **放冷箭** fàng lěng jiàn

Let off the cold arrow. (lit.)

Stab in the back.

同 暗箭傷人（0024）Hit below the belt.

反 公開挑戰（0918）Throw down the gauntlet.

0761 **放任自流** fàng rèn zì liú

Let it flow its own course. (lit.)

Let it run its course.

Let things drift.

Leave the matter to take its own course.

Laissez-faire.

同 聽其自然（2755）Let thing slide.

反 加緊督促（1242）Put the screws on one.

0762 **放下架子** fàng xià jià zǐ

Let down the frame. (lit.)

Lay off one's lid.

Come off the high horse.

反 擺臭架子（0064）Cock one's chest like a half-pay admiral.

0763 **放之四海而皆準**

fàng zhī sì hǎi ér jiē zhǔn

Let it go to four seas and find universal acceptance. (lit.)

A universal rule.

What is sauce for the goose is sauce for the gander.

What's good for the bee is good for the hive.

0764 **非此即彼** fēi cǐ jí bǐ

Either this or that. (lit.)

The door must be either shut or open.

反 模棱兩可（1842）Betwixt and between.

0765 **非復吳下阿蒙** fēi fù wú xià ā méng

It is no more A Meng (a man in the street) in Wu State. (lit.)

The ugly duckling.

To be past the spoon.

Naughty boys sometimes make good men.

同 士別三日，刮目相看（2493）Wanton kittens may make sober cats.

反 江山易改，本性難移（1294）A leopard can't change its spots.

源 三國志．呂蒙傳注："今者學識英博，非復吳下阿蒙。"

非禮勿言，非禮勿動 0766

fēi lǐ wù yán, fēi lǐ wù dòng

Don't speak impolite things, don't act impolitely. (lit.)

Speak fitly, or be silent wisely.

Say well, or be still.

Quietness is best.

同 謹言慎行（1359）Mind one's P's and Q's.

源 論語．顏淵："非禮勿視，非禮勿聽，非禮勿言，非禮勿動。"

非驢非馬 fēi lǘ fēi mǎ 0767

Neither an ass nor a horse. (lit.)

Neither fish nor fowl.

Neither hawk nor buzzard.

同 不倫不類（0230）Neither rhyme nor reason.

源 漢書．西域傳："驢非驢，馬非馬，若龜茲王所謂騾也。"

非錢莫辦 fēi qián mò bàn 0768

Without money can't do. (lit.)

Nothing for nothing.

源 朝野僉載："當今之選，非錢不行。"

非同小可 fēi tóng xiǎo kě 0769

Is not like a small matter. (lit.)

Something out of the ordinary.

No small matter.

Not to be dismissed lightly.

同 不可輕視（0216）Not to be sneezed at.

反 平淡無奇（1986）Nothing to write home about.

源 元曲選．魔合羅："人命事關天關地，非同小可。"

非我族類，其心必異 0770

fēi wǒ zú lèi, qí xīn bì yì

Not of our clan and race, their hearts must be different. (lit.)

The mice do not play with the cat's son.

反 疏不間親（2565）Blood is thicker than water.

源 左傳．成四年："非我族類，其心必異，楚雖大，非吾族也。"

飛黃騰達 fēi huáng téng dá 0771

Ride a prancing horse (Fei-Huang) to rapid success. (lit.)

Rise in the world.

Flourish like the green bay-tree.

His star was in the ascendant.

Get on in the world.

同 平步青雲（1985）Skyrocket to fame.

反 參差不偶（0316）In a sorry plight.

源 韓愈詩："飛黃騰踏去，不能顧蟾蜍。"

飛毛腿 fēi máo tuǐ 0772

Flying hairy legs. (lit.)

To be fleet of foot.

0773 **飛鳥盡，良弓藏**
fēi niǎo jìn, liáng gōng cáng
No more flying birds, store the good bows. (lit.)
Once on shore, we pray no more.
The nurse is valued till the child has done sucking.

同 狡兔死，走狗烹（1309）Kick down the ladder.
源 史記．越世家："蜚鳥盡，良弓藏，狡兔死，走狗烹。"

0774 **蜚短流長** fēi duǎn liú cháng
Flying gossips spread far. (lit.)
Shoot a paper-bolt.
Start a whispering campaign.

同 謠言滿天飛（3351）Rumour is a great traveller.

0775 **肥缺** féi quē
Fat job. (lit.)
A gravy train.
An armchair job.

0776 **肺腑之言** fèi fǔ zhī yán
The talk from the lungs and bowels (the heart). (lit.)
Speak one's conscience.

同 披肝瀝膽（1967）Lay bare one's heart.
源 史記："田蚡以肺腑為京師相。"

0777 **費力不討好** fèi lì bù tǎo hǎo
Waste the effort and get no appreciation. (lit.)
A thankless job.
Shoe the goose.
Be a fool for one's pains.

同 徒勞無功（2807）A wild goose chase.
反 輕而易舉（2124）Mere child's play.

0778 **費時失事** fèi shí shī shì
Wasting time and losing business. (lit.)
Tarry-long brings little home.

同 吾生待明日，萬事成蹉跎（2946）By the street of By and By one arrives at the house of Never.
反 分秒必爭（0785）Improve each shining hour.

0779 **廢話** fèi huà
Useless words. (lit.)
Stuff and nonsense.
It's all my eye.

反 金玉良言（1343）Good advice is beyond price.

廢話連篇 fèi huà lián piān
Useless words in pages. (lit.)
It's all moonshine.
Talk inutilities.

同 言之無物（3314）A deluge of words and a drop of sense.
反 引經據典（3584）Give chapter and verse.

0780

廢時失事 fèi shí shī shì
Waste time and ruin business. (lit.)
Tarry-long brings little home.

同 吾生待明日，萬事成蹉跎（2946）By the street of By and By one arrives at the house of Never.
反 大幹快上（0521）To make things hum.

0781

分別善惡 fēn bié shàn è
To distinguish good from bad. (lit.)
Separate the sheep from the goats.

反 良莠不分（1622）Not know good from evil.

0782

分道揚鑣 fēn dào yáng biāo
Waving the reins, ride on separate routes. (lit.)
To part company.
Go separate ways.

同 各行其是（0908）Have one's own way.
反 異途同歸（3558）All roads lead to Rome.

0783

分而治之 fēn ér zhì zhī
Divide and then govern. (lit.)
Divide and rule.

0784

分秒必爭 fēn miǎo bì zhēng
Fighting for minutes and seconds. (lit.)
Every minute counts.
Improve each shining hour.
Improve every moment.

同 一萬年太久，只爭朝夕（3467）Never put off till tomorrow what may be done today.
反 虛度時光（3244）Kick one's heels.

0785

分清是非 fēn qīng shì fēi
Distinguish clearly right from wrong. (lit.)
Separate the wheat from the chaff.
Know the right from the wrong.

反 不知好歹（0277）Not know chalk from cheese.

0786

分清主次 fēn qīng zhǔ cì
Distinguish the principal and the secondary. (lit.)
First things first.

反 樣樣都抓，等於不抓（3343）Grasp all, lose all.

0787

0788 **分身乏術** fēn shēn fá shù
Lacking the art of diving oneself. (lit.)
One can't be in two places at once.

同 忙不過來（1758）Have too many irons in the fire.

0789 **分庭抗禮** fēn tíng kàng lǐ
Opposite to each other in separate courts. (lit.)
As one's rival.
Keep at arm's length.
At loggerheads with

同 大相徑庭（0559）At odds with
源 莊子．漁父：“萬乘之主，千乘之君，未嘗不分庭亢禮。”

0790 **分文不值** fēn wén bù zhí
Not worth a penny. (lit.)
Not worth a rap (dump, stitch).

同 賤如糞土（1288）As cheap as dirt.
反 無價之寶（2971）Not to be had for love or money.

0791 **紛至沓來** fēn zhì tà lái
People are coming in great number. (lit.)
Thick and fast.
As thick as hail.

同 接二連三（1314）In rapid succession.
反 作鳥獸散（4071）To flee pell-mell.

0792 **焚膏繼晷** fén gāo jì guǐ
Burning oil till the shadow of the sun (daytime). (lit.)
Burn the candle at both ends.
Burn the midnight oil.

同 晝夜不息（3930）By night and day.
反 虛度時光（3244）Twiddle one's thumbs.
源 韓愈．進學解：“焚膏油以繼晷，恆兀兀以窮年。”

0793 **粉墨登場** fěn mò dēng chǎng
To powder with ink and ascend the stage. (lit.) (Used literally and as a phrase of satire for those who are not fit for their posts.)
Appear before the footlights.

反 退出舞台（2824）Make one's exit.
源 漢書：“今乃傳粉墨，衣綺羅。”

0794 **奮不顧身** fèn bù gù shēn
So brave as to care not one's body (life). (lit.)
Neck or nothing.
At all hazards.
To go all lengths.
Take one's life in one's hands.
Move heaven and earth.

同 捨得一身剮（2372）To tempt providence.
反 畏縮不前（2912）Back out of
源 司馬遷．報任少卿書：“常思奮不顧身，以殉國家之急。”

奮發有為 fèn fā yǒu wéi 0795

Put forth effort for achievement. (lit.)

Shake oneself together.

Rouse oneself to action.

Go all out.

反 遁跡空門（0693）Retire into a cloister.

奮力圖存 fèn lì tú cún 0796

Put forth effort to maintain existence. (lit.)

Keep one's head above water.

同 爭生競存（3834）Self-preservation is the first law of nature.

反 自尋短見（4005）Make away with oneself.

風塵僕僕 fēng chén pú pú 0797

Blown by the wind and covered by dust. (lit.)

Shake off the dust from one's feet.

Travel from place to place.

反 深居簡出（2397）Live in seclusion.

風馳電掣 fēng chí diàn chè 0798

As swift as the blowing wind and the lightning. (lit.)

With lightning speed.

Burn up the road.

Go like a shot.

同 開足馬力（1477）At full speed.

反 慢條斯理（1755）At a snail's pace.

源 六韜 · 龍韜："風馳電掣，不知所由。"

風吹草動 fēng chuī cǎo dòng 0799

The wind blows and grass bends. (lit.)

There's something in the wind.

To smell the rat.

源 敦煌變文集 · 伍子胥變文："風吹草動，即便藏形。"

風捲殘雲 fēng juǎn cán yún 0800

The wind rolls and scatters clouds away. (lit.) (Used for fast eating.)

Polish off a meal.

Gorge oneself.

Everything is cleared up.

同 狼吞虎嚥（1550）Gobble up.

反 食慾不振（2470）Loss of appetite.

風流韻事 fēng liú yùn shì 0801

Romantic and poetic affairs. (lit.)

Love (Romantic) affairs.

0802 **風馬牛不相及**
fēng mǎ niú bù xiāng jí
Wind, horse and cow cannot be compared. (lit.)
As different as chalk is from cheese.
Poles apart.

反 一而二，二而一（3387）One and the same thing.
源 左傳 · 僖四年："君處北海，寡人處南海，唯是風馬牛不相及也。"

0803 **風靡一時** fēng mǐ yī shí
Wind passes for a time. (lit.)
All the rage (vogue).

同 盛極一時（2432）Prevail for a time.

0804 **風派** fēng pài
Windy party. (lit.)
Those sitting on the fence (rail).
A fence-sitter.
The wind keeps not always at one quarter.

反 死硬派（2631）A die-hard.

0805 **風平浪靜** fēng píng làng jìng
Winds calm and waves quiet. (lit.)
After a storm comes a calm.

反 洶湧澎湃（3229）Rolling and billowing.

0806 **風聲鶴唳** fēng shēng hè lì
At the sound of the wind the cranes (scared) cry. (lit.)
In a panic.
Apprehend danger in every sound.

源 晉書 · 謝玄傳："堅眾奔潰，棄甲宵遁，聞風聲鶴唳，皆以為王師。"

0807 **風水先生騙你十年八年，騙不了一世**
fēng shuǐ xiān shēng piàn nǐ shí nián bā nián, piàn bù liǎo yí shì
Professor of geomancy may fool you eight or ten years, but not the whole life. (lit.)
Time trieth truth

源 郭璞："葬者乘生氣也，氣乘則散，界水則止，古人聚之使不散，行之使有止，故謂之風水。"

0808 **風頭火勢** fēng tóu huǒ shì
At the wind head fire is fierce. (lit.)
Like a house afire.

同 如火如荼（2270）In full blast.
反 煙消雲散（3292）Vanish like smoke.

風聞其事 fēng wén qí shì 0809
To hear of the matter from the wind. (lit.)
Get wind of

風物長宜放眼量 0810
fēng wù cháng yí fàng yǎn liáng
Wind and things should always be judged farsightedly. (lit.)
See which way (how) the cat jumps.
Wait and see.

同 等着瞧（0630）It remains to be seen.

風雨故人來 fēng yǔ gù rén lái 0811
Wind and rain, old friends come. (lit.)
A foul weather friend.
A friend in need is a friend indeed.

反 貧來親也疏（1979）Poverty parteth fellowship.

風雨同舟 fēng yǔ tóng zhōu 0812
With wind and rain in the same boat. (lit.)
In the same boat.

同 患難之交（1133）Foul weather friends.
源 孫子．九地："當其同舟而濟，遇風，其相救也如左右手。"

風燭殘年 fēng zhú cán nián 0813
One's failing years (resemble) the candle (before) the wind. (lit.)
The lees of life.

同 日薄西山（2253）The sands are running out.
反 血氣方剛（3275）In one's salad days.

蜂擁而至 fēng yōng ér zhì 0814
Like a swarm of bees coming. (lit.)
Swarm like bees.

同 紛至沓來（0791）Thick and fast.
反 作鳥獸散（4071）To flee helter-skelter.

瘋瘋癲癲 fēng fēng diān diān 0815
Mad and lunatic. (lit.)
As mad as a hatter.
Have bats in the belfry.

豐富多彩 fēng fù duō cǎi 0816
Abundant varieties. (lit.)
Variety is pleasing .
Variety is the spice of life.

同 五花八門（3010）Of every description.

0817 **佛頭着糞** fó tóu zhuó fèn
To put night soil on Buddha's head. (lit.)
A fly in the ointment.

源 范泓．典籍便覽："歐陽修作五代史，或作序冠其前。王安石曰，佛頭上豈可着糞。"

0818 **佛也冒火** fó yě mào huǒ
Even Buddha could shoot fire. (lit.)
Enough to make a saint swear.

0819 **否極泰來** pǐ (fǒu) jí tài lái
（否之讀音為pǐ）
When the worst goes to extreme, peace will come. (lit.)
When things are at the worst, they will mend.
They that sow in tears shall reap in joy.
The darkest hour is that before the dawn.

同 苦盡甘來（1519）Pain past is pleasure.
反 興盡悲來（3225）He who laughs on Friday will weep on Sunday.
源 白居易．遣懷詩："樂往必悲生，泰來猶否極。"

0820 **夫唱婦隨** fū chàng fù suí
Husband sings and wife follows. (lit.)
A good Jack makes a good Jill.

源 關尹子："夫者倡，婦者隨。"

0821 **敷衍塞責** fū yǎn sè zé
Make a display and evade responsibility. (lit.)
Huddle over one's duty.
To muddle throug

反 勉奮從事（1794）Keep one's nose down to the grindstone.

0822 **扶危濟困** fú wēi jì kùn
Support one in danger and give aid to the destitute. (lit.)
Help a lame dog over a stile.
Be a good Samaritan.

同 見義勇為（1283）Do a good turn.
反 落井下石（1719）When a dog is drowing, everyone offers him a drink.
源 水滸記傳奇："宋公明他扶危濟困隱功曹。"

0823 **扶搖直上** fú yáo zhí shàng
Holding (on something) and swaggering he goes straight up. (lit.)
On the upgrade.
Step by step the ladder is ascended.
On the up and up.

同 蒸蒸日上（3837）Grow with each passing day.
反 每況愈下（1778）Out of the flying pan into the fire.
源 莊子．逍遙遊："摶扶搖羊角而上者九萬里。"

拂逆人意 fú nì rén yì 0824

Ruffle against others' feeling (opinion). (lit.)

Rub one up the wrong way.

Go against the grain with one.

Stroke one up.

反 百依百順（0061）Dance after someone's pipe.

服務周到 fú wù zhōu dào 0825

Serve perfectly. (lit.)

Serve (Wait) hand and foot.

同 多方照顧（0700）Put one on a pedestal.

反 給以冷遇（0912）Leave one in the cold.

浮生若夢 fú shēng ruò mèng 0826

Life fleeting like a dream. (lit.)

Life is but a dream.

Man is a bubble.

源 李白・春夜宴桃李園序："浮生若夢，為懽幾何。"

福無雙至 fú wú shuāng zhì 0827

Felicity will not come in pairs. (lit.)

Opportunity seldom knocks twice.

Lightning never strikes twice in the same place.

同 盛筵難再（2436）Opportunity seldom knocks twice.

反 禍不單行（1174）Misfortunes seldom come singly.

源 劉向・說苑・權謀："此所謂福不重至，禍必重來者也。"

福之所在，禍必從之 0828

fú zhī suǒ zài, huò bì cóng zhī

Where fortune is, calamity must follow. (lit.)

He that talks much of his happiness summons grief.

Sadness and gladness succeed each other.

同 有一利必有一弊（3678）No rose without a thorn.

釜底抽薪 fǔ dǐ chōu xīn 0829

Draw away the firewood from below the cauldron. (lit.)

Take away fuel, take away flame (fire).

反 火上加油（1168）Pour oil on the flame.

源 魏收・為侯景叛移梁朝文："抽薪止沸，剪草除根。"

釜底游魚 fǔ dǐ yóu yú 0830

In the bottom of a cauldron, fish swimming. (lit.)

He that is born to be hanged shall never be drowned.

One's fate is sealed.

同 劫數難逃（1320）No flying from fate.

反 人定勝天（2194）Everyone is the maker of his own fate.

源 後漢書・張綱傳："若魚游釜中，喘息須臾間耳。"

0831 **俯拾即是** fǔ shí jí shì

Stooping down to pick it up everywhere. (lit.)

High and low.

Here and there and everywhere.

同 比比皆是（0113）Right and left.

反 千載難逢（2067）It only happens once in a blue moon.

0832 **俯首就範** fǔ shǒu jiù fàn

Bowing the head deeply and subject to command. (lit.)

Give one's head for the washing.

Knuckle under.

反 至死不屈（3890）Die game.

0833 **俯首帖耳** fǔ shǒu tiē ěr

Bow the head and drop the ears. (lit.)

Speak when you're spoken to; come when you're called.

At one's beck and call.

同 百依百順（0061）Have a nose of wax.

反 威武不屈（2879）Die in the last ditch.

源 韓愈 · 應科目時與人書：“若俯首帖耳，搖尾而乞憐者，非我之志也。”

0834 **俯仰之間** fǔ yǎng zhī jiān

Between looking up and down. (lit.)

In a short span.

同 轉瞬之間（3941）In half a jiffy.

反 億萬斯年（3571）Forever and ever.

源 漢書 · 晁錯傳：“以大為小，以強為弱，在俯仰之間耳。”

0835 **腐敗透頂** fǔ bài tòu dǐng

Corrupt through the top. (lit.)

Rotten to the core.

反 盡善盡美（1374）Tip-top.

0836 **付之東流** fù zhī dōng liú

Send it in the eastern flowing streams. (lit.)

Go down the drain.

源 高啟 · 詩：“世情付之東流水。”

0837 **付之一炬** fù zhī yí jù

Send it to the flames. (lit.)

Commit to the flames.

Set fire to

0838 **付之一笑** fù zhī yí xiào

Pass it for a laugh. (lit.)

Laugh it off.

同 一笑置之（3478）Dismiss with a laugh.

源 陸游 · 老學庵筆記：“乃知朝士妄望，自古已然，可付一笑。”

附庸風雅 fù yōng fēng yǎ 0839

Adhere to graceful and cultured (people). (lit.)

Shabby gentility.

Keep up with the Joneses.

赴湯蹈火 fù tāng dǎo huǒ 0840

Go through hot water and tread on fire. (lit.)

Go through fire and water.

同 出生入死（0415）Go through hell and high water.

源 漢書："攻城屠邑，則得其財鹵以富家室，故能使其眾蒙矢石，赴湯火。"

負擔過重 fù dān guò zhòng 0841

The burden is too heavy. (lit.)

The last straw breaks the camel's back.

反 輕而易舉（2124）Can do it on one's head.

負荊請罪 fù jīng qǐng zuì 0842

Bearing a thorn-rod, plead guilty. (lit.)

To kiss the rod.

Eat crow (humble-pie).

反 大興問罪之師（0560）Bring someone to book.

源 史記："廉頗聞之，肉袒負荊，因賓客至藺相如門謝罪。"

負隅頑抗 fù yú wán kàng 0843

Put up a stiff resistance. (lit.)

With one's back to the wall.

Fight to the last.

同 作困獸鬥（4069）To be at bay.

源 孟子·盡心下："有眾逐虎，虎負隅，莫之敢攖。"

負債纍纍 fù zhài lěi lěi 0844

Carry debts like beads strung together. (lit.)

Over head and ears in debt.

One step ahead of the sheriff.

同 債台高築（3776）Up to the ears in debt.

反 腰纏萬貫（3344）Roll in wealth.

源 漢書："通家尚負責（債）數鉅萬。"

富從升合起 fù cóng shēng hé qǐ 0845

The rich starts from savings combined. (lit.)

Little and often fills the purse.

Many a little makes a mickle.

同 勤儉起家（2112）Industry is fortune's right hand, and frugality her left.

反 坐食山空（4056）Always taking out of a meal-tub, and never putting in, soon comes to the bottom.

0846 **富而不驕易，貧而無怨難**
fù ér bù jiāo yì, pín ér wú yuàn nán
Rich yet not arrogant, easy; poor yet not complaining, difficult. (lit.)
Shame of poverty is almost as bad as pride of wealth.
Fat sorrow is better than lean sorrow.

源 論語：“富而無驕。”

0847 **富在深山有遠親**
fù zài shēn shān yǒu yuǎn qīn
The rich even deep in the hills still have distant relatives. (lit.)
Everyone is kin to the rich man.
The rich never want for kindred.
Rich folk have many friends.

同 有酒有肉多兄弟（3650）He that hath a full purse never wanted a friend.
反 貧來親也疏（1980）Poverty parteth fellowship.

0848 **富者愈富** fù zhě yù fù
The rich becomes richer. (lit.)
Money begets (breeds) money.

0849 **腹背受敵** fù bèi shòu dí
Being attacked on both the stomach and back. (lit.)
To be between two fires.
To be in a cleft stick.

源 王明清 · 揮塵三錄：“今則脊尾俱搖，腹背受敵。”

0850 **腹如雷鳴** fù rú léi míng
Belly makes a sound like thunder. (lit.)
As hungry as a hunter.
Have a wolf in the stomach.
Empty as an old drum.

同 飢腸轆轆（1197）As hungry as a wolf.
反 腦滿腸肥（1888）He is better fed than nurtured.

0851 **覆水難收** fù shuǐ nán shōu
Split water is difficult to recollect. (lit.)
It is no use crying over spilt milk.
What is done can't be undone.

源 類林：“太公曰，若能離更合，覆水定難收。”

G

該花就花，該省就省 gāi huā jiù huā, gāi shěng jiù shěng 0852

Ought to spend, spend; ought to save, save. (lit.)

Spend not when you may save; spare not when you must spend.

Spare well and spend well.

同 精打細算（1383）Keep no more cats than will catch mice.

反 不惜工本（0255）At all cost.

改過自新 gǎi guò zì xīn 0853

Repent and start a new life. (lit.)

Wipe the slate chean.

Turn over a new leaf.

同 重新做人（0390）Start with a clean slate.

反 故態復萌（0951）Back in the old rut.

源 史記．吳王濞列傳：“文帝弗忍，因賜几杖，德至厚，當改過自新。”

改頭換面 gǎi tóu huàn miàn 0854

Alter the head and change the face. (lit.)

A new deal.

A changed version.

同 裝點門面（3945）Put up a front.

反 原封不動（3730）To be left intact.

源 古今風謠：“漢似胡兒胡似漢，改頭換面總一般。”

改弦更張 gǎi xián gēng zhāng 0855

Change the chord (of a bow) and adjust the tension. (lit.)

Start with a clean slate.

Make a fresh start.

同 另起爐灶（1671）Break fresh ground.

反 抱殘守缺（0088）Stick-in-the-mud.

源 漢書．禮樂志：“辟之琴瑟不調，甚者必解而更張之，迺可鼓也。”

改邪歸正 gǎi xié guī zhèng 0856

Change the crooked way and return to the righteous. (lit.)

To mend one's way.

同 去惡從善（2156）Eschew evil, and do good.

反 誤入歧途（3042）To have gone astray.

0857 改轉念頭 gǎi zhuǎn niàn tóu

Change round the idea. (lit.)

Think better of it.

To come round.

0858 蓋棺論定 gài guān lùn dìng

Make judgement of one after his coffin is closed. (lit.)

Call no man great before he is dead.

Call no man happy till he dies.

He that would right understand a man must read his whole story.

源 趙翼・詩："蓋棺論自定。"

0859 蓋世無雙 gài shì wú shuāng

No double of the age. (lit.)

Without parallel(peer).

The only one of its kind.

Second to none.

同 無與倫比（3004）Defy all comparison.

反 平平庸庸（1989）Pass in a crowd in a push.

0860 甘拜下風 gān bài xià fēng

Willing to bow low to the wind. (lit.)

Eat humble pie.

Lower one's flag.

Play second fiddle.

Take a back seat.

To sit at a person's feet.

反 不甘後人（0189）Not to be outdone.

源 左傳・僖十五年："皇天后土，實聞君之言，羣臣敢在下風。"

0861 甘之如飴 gān zhī rú yí

Take it as sweet as sugar-plums. (lit.)

Smack one's lips.

With relish.

Lick one's chops.

同 津津有味（1347）With gusto.

反 苦不堪言（1517）As bitter as gall.

源 文天祥・正氣歌："鼎鑊甘如飴，求之不可得。"

0862 肝膽相照 gān dǎn xiāng zhào

Liver and gallbladder facing each other. (lit.)

Heart to heart talk.

The best mirror is an old friend.

源 侯鯖錄："同心相親，照心照膽壽千春。"

乾脆利落 gān cuì lì luò 0863

Dry, crisp, and clear-cut. (lit.)

Cut and dried.

As neat as a new pin.

To be clear-cut.

乾枯無味 gān kū wú wèi 0864

Dried up and tasteless. (lit.)

As dry as dust(a bone).

同 索然無味（2667）As dull as ditch water.

反 津津有味（1347）Smack one's lips.

敢想敢幹 gǎn xiǎng gǎn gàn 0865

Dare to think and dare to do. (lit.)

He was a bold man that first ate an oyster.

Shoot one's wad.

反 畏首畏尾（2911）Full of misgivings.

敢於正視 gǎn yú zhèng shì 0866

Venture to look straight. (lit.)

Look in the eye (face).

反 逃避現實（2694）Bury one's head in the sand.

敢做敢為 gǎn zuò gǎn wéi 0867

Venture to do and dare to act. (lit.)

Take one's courage in both hands.

同 勇挑重擔（3618）Bite off a big chunk.

反 前怕狼，後怕虎（2077）Too much taking heed is loss.

感人肺腑 gǎn rén fèi fǔ 0868

Move (emotionally) one's lung and viscera (heart). (lit.)

Come home to one's heart.

Tug at one's heart strings.

同 扣人心弦（1512）Pluck at one's heartstrings.

趕進度 gǎn jìn dù 0869

Rush to (make) progress. (lit.)

Make up for leeway.

Make up for lost time.

同 迎頭趕上（3601）To catch up with.

反 慢條斯理（1755）Make two bites of a cherry.

趕任務 gǎn rèn wù 0870

Rush to (complete) mission. (lit.)

Working against time.

Make up for lost time.

反 磨洋工（1846）Lie on one's oars.

0871 **趕上時代** gǎn shàng shí dài
Catch up with the times. (lit.)
Keep abreast of the times.

0872 **幹出水平** gàn chū shuǐ píng
Manage to rise above water level. (lit.)
Hit one's stride.
To do oneself justice.
Hit on all cylinders.

0873 **幹得出色** gàn de chū sè
Can do it with flying colour. (lit.)
Do something to advantage.

同 幹出水平（0872）Hit on all cylinders.
反 當眾出醜（0594）Cut a ridiculous figure.

0874 **幹勁沖天** gàn jìn chōng tiān
The zeal for action shoots sky high. (lit.)
To be a live wire.
To be a ball of fire.
Like a whirlwind.

同 大幹快上（0521）To make things hum.
反 老油條（1578）A milk-sop.

0875 **剛愎自用** gāng bì zì yòng
Stubborn and self-willed. (lit.)
Stubborn as a mule.
As tough as nails.
Reckon without one's host.
To be a law unto oneself.

反 不恥下問（0176）Bow down thy ear.
源 蘇東坡後集 · 謝宣召入學士院狀："知臣剛愎自用，雖有寬饒（蓋寬饒）之狂，察臣招摩不移，庶幾長孺之守。"

0876 **高傲自大** gāo ào zì dà
Highly proud of oneself. (lit.)
To be stuck up.
Have a swelled head.
As proud as a dog in a doublet.
Too big for one's breeches.

同 夜郎自大（3366）To be too big for one's boots.
反 虛懷若谷（3245）To humble oneself.

0877 **高不成，低不就**
gāo bù chéng, dī bú jiù
Can't reach high, won't stoop low. (lit.)
He that will not stoop for a pin shall never be worth a pound.

反 能屈能伸（1891）Strech your legs according to your coverlet.

高不可攀 gāo bù kě pān 0878
Too high to climb. (lit.)
At the top of the ladder.
High up in the stirrups.
Could not be had.

源 文選 · 陳琳 · 為曹洪與魏文帝書：“縈帶為垣，高不可登。”

高高興興 gāo gāo xìng xìng 0879
Highly elated and delighted. (lit.)
With a good grace.
Glad of heart.

同 喜氣洋洋（3059）Light up with pleasure.
反 愁眉苦臉（0396）Wear a glum countenance.

高高在上 gāo gāo zài shàng 0880
High up in the air. (lit.)
High and mighty.
High up in the stirrups.

同 位高勢危（2908）He sits not sure who sits too high.
反 敬陪末座（1404）Take a back seat.
源 詩經 · 周頌 · 敬之：“無曰高高在上。”

高人一等 gāo rén yī děng 0881
One class above others. (lit.)
Stand head and shoulders above others.
A cut above others.

同 出人頭地（0410）Come to the fore.

高深莫測 gāo shēn mò cè 0882
Unfathomably high and deep. (lit.)
Out of one's depth.
Beyond understanding.

反 瞭如指掌（1646）As plain as a pikestaff.

高視闊步 gāo shì kuò bù 0883
Look high and walk with wide steps. (lit.)
Prance (swagger) about.
Give oneself airs.
Independent as a hog on ice.
Walk with one's nose in the air.

同 趾高氣揚（3888）Ride the high horse.
反 作揖打拱（4074）Bow and scrape.
源 魏文帝 · 漢文論：“得闊步高談，無危懼之心。”

高談闊論 gāo tán kuò lùn 0884
High-fly talk and lofty comments. (lit.)
To enlarge oneself.
To prate about.

同 談天説地（2680）Talk of everything under the sun.
反 欲説還休（3718）To shut up shop.
源 元曲選 · 賈仲明 · 玉梳記：“倚仗着高談闊論，全用些野狐涎撲子弟，打郎君。”

0885 高壓手段 gāo yā shǒu duàn
High pressure way in handling things. (lit.)
High-handed policy(method).

0886 高瞻遠矚 gāo zhān yuǎn zhǔ
Behold high and look far. (lit.)
Show great foresight.
Have a second sight.

反 目光如豆（1869）See no further than one's nose.

0887 高枕而臥 gāo zhěn ér wò
Sleep on a high pillow. (lit.)
Sleep upon both ears.
To be able to sleep on a clothesline.
Free from cares.

反 輾轉反側（3779）Toss about all night.
源 漢書 · 英布傳："使布出於下計，則陛下可安枕而臥矣。"

0888 高枕無憂 gāo zhěn wú yōu
(Sleep on) high pillow without worry. (lit.)
A good conscience is a soft pillow.
A quiet conscience sleeps in thunder.

同 生平不作虧心事，半夜敲門也不驚（1991）A clear conscience is a coat of mail.
反 坐立不安（4053）Sit on a bag of fleas.

0889 高奏凱旋 gāo zòu kǎi xuán
High tune of victory. (lit.)
Come off with flying colours.

同 從勝利走向勝利（0463）Nothing succeeds like success.
反 潰不成軍（1533）To be put to rout.

0890 膏粱子弟 gāo liáng zǐ dì
Sons of fats and grains. (lit.)
Gilded youth.

同 紈袴子弟（2843）Lounge lizard.
反 莊稼漢（3944）Son of the soil.
源 虞兆漋 · 天香樓偶得："今人謂富貴家曰膏粱子弟，言但知飽食，不諳他務也。"

0891 搞小動作 gǎo xiǎo dòng zuò
Make little actions. (lit.)
Adopt the policy of pin pricks.

0892 告吹 gào chuī
To blow off. (lit.)
To fall through.
Fall flat.

反 大功告成（0523）Come off with honours.

割斷關係 gē duàn guān xì 0893
Cut off relation. (lit.)
Cut loose from old ties.
Sever relations.

同 一刀兩斷（3386）To have done with a person.
反 拉關係（1534）Scrape acquaintance with

歌功頌德 gē gōng sòng dé 0894
Sing merits and praise virtue. (lit.)
Chant the praises of

同 讚不絕口（3762）Lavish praises on
反 喝倒彩（1055）Give a Bronx cheer.

格格不入 gé gé bú rù 0895
It cannot fit in. (lit.)
Not talk the same language.
Go against the grain with one.
Out of keeping with
A square peg in a round hole.

同 話不投機半句多（1119）It's ill talking between a full man and a fasting.
反 氣味相投（2047）Birds of a feather flock together.
源 禮記 · 學記："發然後禁，則扞格而不勝，時過然後學，則勤苦而難成。"

格外賣力 gé wài mài lì 0896
To sell extra effort. (lit.)
To go out of one's way.

同 拼命幹（1976）Work one's fingers to the bone.
反 敷衍塞責（0821）To muddle through.

格物致知 gé wù zhì zhī 0897
Study of matter to gain knowledge. (lit.)
The proof of the pudding is in the eating.
Sermons in stones.

同 實踐出真知（2479）In doing we learn.
源 大學："致知在格物。"

各安本分 gè ān běn fèn 0898
Each stays in his own place. (lit.)
Every sow to its own trough.

同 安分守己（0009）Mind one's own business.

各安天命 gè ān tiān mìng 0899
Each rests in fate. (lit.)
No flying from fate.
Every bullet has its billet.

反 人定勝天（2194）Everyone is the maker of his own fate.

各得其所 gè dé qí suǒ 0900
Each gets what he wants. (lit.)
A place for everything, and everything in its place.

同 得其所哉（0614）Fall into place.
反 不得其所（0181）Out of place.
源 周易 · 繫辭下："交易而退，各得其所。"

0901 各行各業 gè háng gè yè

All trades and all professions. (lit.)

All walks of life.

The butcher, the baker, the candlestick maker.

0902 各盡其能 gè jìn suǒ néng

Each exerts himself according to his ability. (lit.)

When you are an anvil, hold you still; when you are a hammer, strike your fill.

同 有一分熱，發一分光（3677）Do one's utmost.

0903 各取所值 gè qǔ suǒ zhí

Each takes his worth. (lit.)

The labour is worthy of his hire.

0904 各人自掃門前雪 gè rén zì sǎo mén qián xuě

Each sweeps the snow in front of his own door. (lit.)

Sweep before your own door .

Let each tailor mend his own coat.

Let every man skin his own skunk.

Let everyone mind his own business.

同 事不關己，高高掛起（2508）Dogs never go into mourning when a horse dies.

反 通力合作（2761）To pull together.

0905 各式各樣 gè shì gè yàng

Every form, every kind. (lit.)

Of every description.

This, that, and the other .

同 豐富多彩（0816）Variety is the spice of life.

0906 各適其適 gè shì qí shì

Each does as he pleases. (lit.)

One man's meat is another man's poison.

A barley corn is better than a diamond to a cock.

Jack Sprat could eat no fat; and his wife could eat no lean; and so betwixt them both, you see, they lick the platter clean.

各顯神通 gè xiǎn shén tōng 0907

Each tries to show his genius. (lit.)

Each plays his long suit.

Each has his own way.

各行其是 gè xíng qí shì 0908

Each goes his own way. (lit.)

Do as one pleases.

Have one's own way.

同 同心協力（2772）Pull together.

各有打算 gè yǒu dǎ suàn 0909

Everyone has his plans. (lit.)

The horse thinks one thing, and he that saddles him another.

The donkey means one thing, and the driver another.

同 羣策羣力（2173）To pool issues.

各有所好 gè yǒu suǒ hào 0910

Each has his likes. (lit.)

Tastes differ.

Every man to his own taste.

同 仁者見仁，智者見智（2241）Everything is as you take it.

各自打算 gè zì dǎ suàn 0911

Each plans for himself. (lit.)

Strike out for oneself.

同 各人自掃門前雪（0904）Let everyone mind his own business.

反 羣策羣力（2173）Join forces.

給以冷遇 gěi yǐ lěng yù 0912

Give one a cold reception. (lit.)

Leave one in the cold.

Give one the cold shoulder.

同 要理不理（3357）To be standoffish.

反 熱烈歡迎（2184）Give one three times three.

根深蒂固 gēn shēn dì gù 0913

The root deep and the stem strong. (lit.)

Strike (Take) root.

To be deep-rooted.

Run deep.

源 晉書：“深根固蒂，則延祚無窮。”

0914 **更深人靜** gēng shēn rén jìng

In the depth of night while people are quiet. (lit.)

In the dead of night.

In the small hours of the morning.

In the stillness of the night.

源 蔡絛．西清詩話．引楊鸞詩："白日蒼蠅滿飯盤，夜間蚊子又成團，每到更深人靜後，定來頭上咬楊鸞。"

0915 **耿耿於懷** gěng gěng yú huái

Disquieting in the chest (heart). (lit.)

To take to heart.

Rankle in one's heart.

反 寬大為懷（1529）To be large-minded.

0916 **工力悉敵** gōng lì xī dí

Work and strength can resist (enemy). (lit.)

Documents travel. (lit.)

Break even.

Nip and tuck.

Evenly matched.

On a par with

同 旗鼓相當（2033）Six of one and half a dozen of the other.

反 小巫見大巫（3146）To be cast into the shade.

源 全唐詩話："昭容評曰，二詩工力悉敵。"

0917 **工欲善其事，必先利其器**

gōng yù shàn qí shì, bì xiān lì qí qì

A workman wishing to make good his work must first sharpen his tools. (lit.)

A bad workman quarrels with his tools.

0918 **公開挑戰** gōng kāi tiǎo zhàn

Open challenge. (lit.)

Throw down the gauntlet.

反 暗箭傷人（0024）A stab in the back.

0919 **公事公辦** gōng shì gōng bàn

Public matters should be done publicly. (lit.)

Business is business.

反 走後門（4025）Through backstairs influence.

公說公有理，婆說婆有理 0920
gōng shuō gōng yǒu lǐ, pó shuō pó yǒu lǐ
Husband says he has reasons, wife says she has reasons. (lit.)
Wranglers never want words.
There are two sides to a story.

公文旅行 gōng wén lǚ xíng 0921
Documents travel. (lit.)
Play the game of dockets.

功敗垂成 gōng bài chuí chéng 0922
Fail in time of near success. (lit.)
A slip betwixt the cup and the lip.
A flash in the pan.

同 功虧一簣（0924）Look back from the plough.
反 一蹴而就（3383）At one stroke.
源 漢書："垂成之功，敗於一日。"

功多藝熟 gōng duō yì shú 0923
Practice more the art becomes mature. (lit.)
Practice makes perfect.
He that shoots oft shall at last hit the mark.

同 練出功夫（1619）The more you do, the more you may do.

功虧一簣 gōng kuī yí kuì 0924
The success lacks one basket(of earth). (lit.)
Give up when near success.
Look back from the plough.
Another course would have done it.

反 大功告成（0523）Come off with honours.
源 尚書・旅獒："為山九仞，功虧一簣。"

攻其不備 gōng qí bú bèi 0925
Attack one while unprepared. (lit.)
Take one napping.
Take one off his guard.
To catch a weasel asleep.

同 突然襲擊（2804）Swoop down upon
反 鳴鼓而攻之（1831）Beat a charge.
源 孫子・計篇："攻其不備，出其不意。"

攻心為上 gōng xīn wéi shàng 0926
Attack the heart is the best way. (lit.)
Scare a bird is not the way to catch it .

同 智取為上（3897）Contrivance is better than force.
源 蜀志："夫用兵之道，攻心為上，攻城為下，心戰為上，兵戰為下。"

0927 供不應求 gōng bù yìng qiú

The supply does not meet the demand. (lit.)

Supply short of demand.

Demand over supply.

同 僧多粥少（2321）Not enough to go round.

反 取之無禁，用之不竭（2155）The more the well is used, the more water it gives.

0928 苟延殘喘 gǒu yán cán chuǎn

To prolong the fading pant. (lit.)

Keep body and soul together.

Linger on.

同 得過且過（0611）To muddle through.

源 馬中錫 · 中山狼傳："今日之事，何不使我得早處囊中，以苟延殘喘乎。"

0929 狗嘴裏吐不出象牙

gǒu zuǐ lǐ tǔ bù chū xiàng yá

Dog's mouth cannot protrude ivory. (lit.)

What can you expect from a hog but a grunt.

Look not for musk in a dog's kennel.

There came nothing out of the sack but what was there.

0930 沽名釣譽 gū míng diào yù

To buy name and fish for fame. (lit.)

Fish for compliments.

Angle for praise.

Court publicity.

Seek the limelight.

同 嘩眾取寵（1112）Impress people by claptrap.

源 荊釵記傳奇："妾今移心改嫁，前日投江，乃沽名釣譽也。"

0931 姑妄聽之 gū wàng tīng zhī

Anyway, listen to it. (lit.)

Take with a grain of salt.

Take the story for what it is worth.

同 將信將疑（1298）To be half in doubt.

0932 姑妄言之 gū wàng yán zhī

Anyhow, say it. (lit.)

From the teeth outwards.

0933 姑妄言之，姑妄聽之

gū wàng yán zhī, gū wàng tīng zhī

Anyhow, say it; anyway, listen to it. (lit.)

To beg the question.

姑息養奸 gū xī yǎng jiān
Over-indulgence nourishes evil. (lit.)
Spare the rod and spoil the child.

同 慈母出敗兒（0454）Mothers' darlings make but milk-sop heroes.
源 禮記："君子之愛人也以德，細人之愛人也以姑息。" 0934

孤芳自賞 gū fāng zì shǎng
To appreciate one's own solitude fragrance (like a flower). (lit.)
Each bird loves to hear himself sing.

同 自我陶醉（4003）As the fool thinks, so the bell chinks.
反 自慚形穢（3971）He that has a great nose thinks everybody is speaking of it.
源 沈約："貞操與日月也俱懸，孤芳隨山壑共遠。" 0935

孤立無援 gū lì wú yuán
Isolated and helpless. (lit.)
To be left out in the cold.
To be left high and dry.

同 伶仃孤苦（1661）His hat covers his family.
反 人多勢眾（2196）There is safety in numbers. 0936

孤陋寡聞 gū lòu guǎ wén
Isolated, incomplete, less informed. (lit.)
Who does not mix with the crowd knows nothing.

同 一無所知（3475）To be in the dark.
反 消息靈通（3127）Have an ear to the ground.
源 禮記．學記："獨學而無友，則孤陋而寡聞。" 0937

孤雲野鶴 gū yún yě hè
A wild crane in a solitary cloud. (lit.)
Keep oneself to oneself.
live in seclusion.

同 形單影隻（3217）All alone.
源 劉長卿．送方外上人詩："孤雲將野鶴，豈向人間住。" 0938

孤注一擲 gū zhù yí zhì
Bet all on a single throw. (lit.)
Bet one's bottom dollar on.
Put all one's eggs in one basket.
Win the horse or lose the saddle.

同 盡此一舉（1370）Shoot one's bolt.
反 留有一手（1684）Have a second string to one's bow.
源 元史．伯顏傳："今日我宋天下，猶賭博孤注，輸贏在此一擲耳。" 0939

古往今來 gǔ wǎng jīn lái
The ancient past and the present coming-time. (lit.)
From time out of mind.

源 潘岳．西征賦："古往今來，邈矣悠哉。" 0940

骨肉之情 gǔ ròu zhī qíng
The flesh and bones sentiments. (lit.)
Flesh and blood.
Bone of the bone and flesh of the flesh.

源 呂氏春秋："父母之於子，子之於父母，此之謂骨肉之親。" 0941

0942 **骨瘦如柴** gǔ shòu rú chái

Bones as emaciated as firewood. (lit.)

A mere bag of bones.
All skin and bone.
As thin as a lath.

同 瘦骨嶙峋（2561）As lean as a rake.
反 身體發福（2386）Put on flesh.
源 宋・陸佃《埤雅・釋獸》：“骨瘦如豺。豺，柴也。豺體細瘦，故謂之豺。”

0943 **鼓起勇氣** gǔ qǐ yǒng qì

Stir up the courage. (lit.)

Square one's shoulders.
Pluck up one's heart (courage).
Keep a stiff upper lip.
To be on one's mettle.
Take heart .
Bolster up the morale.
Get up the nerve to

同 振作起來（3830）Gird up one's loins.
反 意氣消沉（3563）To be in the doldrum.

0944 **鼓如簧之舌** gǔ rú huáng zhī shé

Rouse the tongue like playing a reed-organ. (lit.)

Wag one's tongue.
Talk one's head off.

同 侃侃而談（1478）Talk the bark off a tree .
反 張口結舌（3793）To be tongue-tied.
源 後漢書：“賢哲鉗口，小人鼓舌。”

0945 **固步自封** gù bù zì fēng

Block one's fixed steps. (lit.)

Stay put.
Get into a groove.
He that stays in the valley shall never get over the hill.
Stand pat.

同 裹足不前（0993）At a standstill.
反 衝破藩籬（0387）Kick over the traces.

0946 **固若金湯** gù ruò jīn tāng

As firm as gold and hot-water (meaning a firmly-held city in war). (lit.)

As firm as a rock.

同 安如泰山（0014）Safe upon the solid rock.
反 不堪一擊（0209）The earthen pot must keep clear of the brass vessel.
源 漢書：“皆為金城湯池，不可攻也。”

0947 **固守陣地** gù shǒu zhèn dì

Holding firmly the defence line. (lit.)

Hold one's own ground.

同 寸土不讓（0478）Not budge an inch.
反 退避三舍（2822）Beat a retreat.

固執己見 gù zhí jǐ jiàn 0948
Holding fast to one's own view. (lit.)
Abide by one's opinion.
Stick to one's gun.
Take the bit in one's teech.
Have a will of one's own.
Nail one's colours to the mast.

同 剛愎自用（0875）Reckon without one's host.
反 收回成命（2543）Eat one's words.
源 宋史．陳宓傳："固執己見，動失人心。"

固執如牛 gù zhí rú niú 0949
Obstinate as a cow. (lit.)
As obstinate as a mule.
A wilful man will have his way.

反 改轉念頭（0857）To come round.

故弄玄虛 gù nòng xuán xū 0950
Purposely make a mystery of it. (lit.)
Keep one guessing.
The magician mutters, and knows not what he mutters.

固態復萌 gù tài fù méng 0951
To resume one's old manner. (lit.)
Return to one's old habit.
Back in the old rut.
At one's little games again.
Return to one's vomit.
He that has done ill once will do it again.
Fall from grace.

同 賊性難改（3773）Once a knave and ever a knave.
反 改過自新（0853）Turn over a new leaf.
源 後漢書："帝曰，狂奴故態也。"

故作鎮靜 gù zuò zhèn jìng 0952
(Purposely) Pretend to be calm. (lit.)
To affect composure.

同 若無其事（2295）As if nothing has happened.

顧此失彼 gù cǐ shī bǐ 0953
Care for one thing and neglect the other. (lit.)
Lose on the swings what one makes on the roundabouts.

反 一箭雙鵰（3404）Kill two birds with one stone.

0954 **顧得東來西又倒**
gù dé dōng lái xī yòu dǎo
When the east is looked after the west collapses. (lit.)
He who hunts two hares leaves one and loses the other.
If you run after two hares, you will catch neither.

同 兩頭落空（1634）Fall between two stools.
源 朱子語錄：“教學者如扶醉人，扶得東來西又倒。”

0955 **顧慮重重** gù lǜ chóng chóng
Full of worries. (lit.)
Full of misgivings.
Too much taking heed is loss.

同 憂心忡忡（3625）To be on the rack .
反 無憂無慮（3003）To be care-free.

0956 **顧盼自雄** gù pàn zì xióng
To gaze around and be proud of oneself. (lit.)
To be full of oneself. /
Preen oneself. /
To be corned with oneself.

同 目空一切（1871）Have one's nose in the air.
反 自慚形穢（3971）Have a sense of inferiority.

0957 **顧全顏面** gù quán yán miàn
Take care of face. (lit.)
To save face.
Keep up appearances.

反 打下他的威風（0501）Give one a dressing down.

0958 **寡廉鮮恥** guǎ lián xiǎn chǐ
Lacking righteousness and little sense of shame. (lit.)
Have no sense of shame .
Brazen faced.

同 恬不知恥（2741）Have the effrontery to
反 內心慚疚（1890）The prick of conscience.
源 史記·司馬相如：寡廉鮮恥，而俗不長厚也。

0959 **掛冠歸里** guà guān guī lǐ
Hang one's cap and return to his village. (lit.)
Go to grass.
Hang up one's axe.
To bow out.

源 催信明詩：“西上君飛蓋，東歸我掛冠。”

掛羊頭，賣狗肉 0960
guà yáng tóu, mài gǒu ròu
Hang the sheep's head but sell dog's meat. (lit.)
Cry up wine and sell vinegar.

同 以假亂真（3530）Foist a thing off on one.

拐彎抹角 guǎi wān mò jiǎo 0961
Go around and turn a corner. (lit.)
In a round-about way.
Beat about the bush.

同 迂迴曲折（3685）Tortuous and devious.
反 直截了當（3871）Give it to one straight.

怪相百出 guài xiàng bǎi chū 0962
Queer appearances come out hundred. (lit.)
To mop and mow.

同 百醜圖A rogue's gallery.

官官相護 guān guān xiāng hù 0963
Officials protect officials. (lit.)
The devil is kind to his own.
Dog does not eat dog.
Crows do not pick crow's eyes.
Caw me, caw thee.
Rou scratch my back and I'll scratch yours.

源 劉鶚 · 老殘遊記："縱然派個委員前來會審，官官相護……你說，這官司打得贏打不贏呢。"

官氣十足 guān qì shí zú 0964
Official air is ten full (ten in Chinese means complete). (lit.)
Jack in office.

同 擺臭架子（0064）Cock one's chest like a half-pay admiral.
反 放下架子（0762）Come off the high horse.

官樣文章 guān yàng wén zhāng 0965
Official forms of writing. (lit.)
Red tape.

源 歸田錄："王安國語予曰，文章須是官樣，豈亦謂有館閣氣耶。"

關鍵時刻 guān jiàn shí kè 0966
The key time. (lit.)
At the critical moment.
In the nick of time.
When the chips are down.

0967 **關鍵所在** guān jiàn suǒ zài
The key point is there. (lit.)
There's the rub (snag).
Where the shoe pinches.
The crux of the matter (question).

同 癥結所在（3838）The crux of the matter.
反 無關宏旨（2962）To be neither here nor there.

0968 **關門大吉** guān mén dà jí
Close the door (of shop) for big luck. (lit.)
To shut up shop.

反 開張大吉（1464）Hang out one's shingle.

0969 **觀今宜鑒古** guān jīn yí jiàn gǔ
To see the present, one must learn from the past. (lit.)
Things present are judged by things past.

同 鑒往知來（1291）He that would know what shall be must consider what has been.

0970 **觀微知著** guān wēi zhī zhù
Observing the small things, one knows the outstanding character. (lit.)
A straw will show which way the wind blows.

同 管中窺豹（0976）You may know by a handful the whole sack.
反 只見樹木，不見森林（3877）One can't see the wood for the trees.

0971 **觀音也落淚** guān yīn yě luò lèi
Even Goddess of Mercy could shred tears. (lit.)
Enough to make the angel weep.

0972 **管鮑之誼** guǎn bào zhī yí
The friendship of Guan (Chung)and Bao (Shu-ya)(an example of true friendship in Chinese history). (lit.)
Damon and Pythias.

同 莫逆之交（1852）A sworn friend.
反 泛泛之交（0750）Have only a bowing acquaintance.
源 史記："管仲之交曰鮑叔牙，仲有生我者父母，知我者鮑叔之言。"

0973 **管窺蠡測** guǎn kuī lí cè
To look (at the sky) through a tube and measure (the sea) with calabash. (lit.)
Have a narrow outlook on things.

同 鼠目寸光（2568）See no further than one's nose.
反 高瞻遠矚（0886）Show great foresight.
源 漢書·東方朔傳："以管窺天，以蠡測海。"

0974

管寧割蓆 guǎn níng gē xí

Guan (Chung) rather cut the mat (than to make friend with a bad person sitting next to him). (lit.)

Cut loose from old ties.

同 分道揚鑣（0783）Part company.

反 重修舊好（0391）Heal the breach.

源 世說新語："管寧分坐，曰子非吾友也。"

0975

管它黑貓白貓，捉住老鼠是好貓 guǎn tā hēi māo bái māo, zhuō zhù lǎo shǔ shì hǎo māo

Never mind whether she is a black cat or white cat, if she catches rats, she is a good cat. (lit.)

The end justifies the means.

A black plum is as sweet as a white.

0976

管中窺豹 guǎn zhōng kuī bào

To look at a leopard through a tube. (lit.)

You may know by a handful the whole sack.

See only one spot.

同 可見一斑（1492）One may see day at a little hole.

源 晉書 · 王獻之傳："此郎亦管中窺豹，時見一斑。"

0977

貫徹始終 guàn chè shǐ zhōng

Go through from beginning to end. (lit.)

Carry through to the end.

Such beginning, such end.

同 一竿到底（3393）To see a thing through.

反 見異思遷（1282）A rolling stone.

0978

光彩奪目 guāng cǎi duó mù

Brilliant and dazzling to the eye. (lit.)

Dazzling to the eye.

同 光可鑒人（0980）Shine like a shittim barn door.

反 黑漆一團（1059）As black as midnight.

0979

光輝燦爛 guāng huī càn làn

Brilliant and very bright. (lit.)

Dazzling to the eye.

同 閃閃發光（2340）As bright as silver.

反 黑漆一團（1059）As black as pitch.

0980

光可鑒人 guāng kě jiàn rén

The shine can serve one like a mirror. (lit.)

Shine like a shittim barn door.

源 左傳："光可以鑒。"

0981 光明磊落 guāng míng lěi luò
As clear as heap of stones falling down. (lit.)
To be open and aboveboard.
As clear as crystal.

同 胸懷坦蕩（3231）As open as the day.
反 鬼鬼祟祟（0989）Up to some hangky-pangky.
源 晉書："大丈夫行為，當磊磊落落，如日月皎然。"

0982 光明正大 guāng míng zhèng dà
Bright and righteous. (lit.)
To be on the square.
Fair and square.

反 偷偷摸摸（2784）On the sly.

0983 光天化日 guāng tiān huà rì
Bright sky and broad daylight. (lit.)
In broad daylight.

反 夜幕低垂（3367）Under screen of night.
源 陸隴其・答仇滄柱太史書："不才庸吏得於光天化日之下，效其馳驅。"

0984 光陰似箭 guāng yīn sì jiàn
Light and shade (day and night) flies like an arrow. (lit.)
Time flies like an arrow.
How time flies.

源 韋莊・關河道中詩："但見時光流似箭，豈知天道曲如弓。"

0985 光陰一去不復返
guāng yīn yí qù bú fù fǎn
Time once gone will not return. (lit.)
Time past cannot be recalled.
Lost time is never found.
One can't put the clock back.
The mill cannot grind with water that is past.

0986 龜兔競走 guī tù jìng zǒu
A running race between a tortoise and a hare. (lit.)
The snail slides up the tower at last, though the swallow mounteth it not.

歸根結蒂 guī gēn jié dì 0987
Revert to the origin (root) and tie together. (lit.)
In the long run.
In the final analysis.
When all is said and done.
As a result.

歸心似箭 guī xīn sì jiàn 0988
Longing at heart to return home like the fleeting of an arrow. (lit.)
Longing for home.

同 鳥倦飛而知還（1913）Home is the sailor, home from sea.
反 流連忘返（1681）Can't tear oneself away.

鬼鬼祟祟 guǐ guǐ suì suì 0989
Ghostly and sneaking. (lit.)
Up to some hangky-pangky.
Hole-and-corner.

同 偷偷摸摸（2784）On the sly.
反 光明磊落（0981）To be open and aboveboard.

鬼斧神工 guǐ fǔ shén gōng 0990
A devil's axe and god's skill. (lit.)
Finished to the finger-nail.

源 吳萊·大食瓶詩："晶熒龍宮獻，錯落鬼斧鐫。"

詭計多端 guǐ jì duō duān 0991
All sorts of treacherous tricks. (lit.)
As crooked as a corkscrew.
Full of guile (tricks).
As crooked as a dog's hind leg.
As tricky as a monkey.

同 老奸巨滑（1568）As cunning as a fox.
反 誠實可靠（0364）Fair and square.

滾瓜爛熟 gǔn guā làn shú 0992
Fallen gourd ripens to rot. (lit.)
Know a lesson off pat.

同 背誦如流（0101）To reel off.

裹足不前 guǒ zú bù qián 0993
Bind the feet and make no advance. (lit.)
Hang back.
Fight shy of
At a standstill.
Drag one's heels.

同 停滯不前（2758）Get bogged down.
反 爭先恐後（3835）The devil take the hindmost.
源 李斯·諫逐客書："使天下之士，退而不敢西向，裹足不入秦。"

0994 過從甚密 guò cóng shèn mì
To be with very intimately. (lit.)
On intimate terms with

同 親密無間（2107）As thick as thieves.
反 雞犬之聲相聞，而老死不相往來（1202）Half the world knows not how the other half lives.

0995 過訪不遇 guò fǎng bú yù
Have visited but not met. (lit.)
Kiss the post.

同 萍水相逢（1996）Merry meet, merry part.

0996 過分樂觀 guò fèn lè guān
Over optimistic. (lit.)
Count one's chickens before they are hatched.
See things through coloured spectacles.

0997 過河拆橋 guò hé chāi qiáo
Dismantle the bridge after crossing the river. (lit.)
Burn the bridge behind.
Kick down the ladder.
Cast aside like an old shoe.

源 元史："參政可謂過河拆橋者矣。"

0998 過街老鼠 guò jiē lǎo shǔ
A rat across the street. (lit.)
A target of attack.
Everybody points an accusing finger at

0999 過來人 guò lái rén
A man with the past. (lit.)
One of the has-beens.
Have had one's day.

同 曾經滄海（0317）To have gone through deep waters.
反 初見世面（0424）Babes in the woods.

1000 過目不忘 guò mù bú wàng
Passing the eyes and not forgetting. (lit.)
Have a memory like an elephant.
A photographic memory.

反 特別健忘（2701）Have a head like a sieve.
源 晉書·苻融傳："苻融下筆成章，耳聞則誦，過目不忘。"

過甚其詞 guò shèn qí cí 1001

Exaggeration of one's words. (lit.)

The devil is not so black as he is painted.

同 言過其實（3303）Stretch the truth.

反 輕描淡寫（2126）To skate over.

過眼煙雲 guò yǎn yān yún 1002

Passing one's eye like smoke and cloud. (lit.)

A flash in the pan

Ephemeral grandeur.

同 曇花一現（2681）Sudden glory soon goes out.

源 蘇軾 · 寶繪堂記："譬之煙雲之過眼，百鳥之感耳。"

過猶不及 guò yóu bù jí 1003

Excess is as bad as deficiency. (lit.)

Overdone is worse than underdone.

The archer who overshoots misses as well as he that falls short.

In excess nectar poisons.

He that makes a thing too fine breaks it.

Double charging will break a cannon.

Too much water drowned the miller.

Too much humility is pride.

同 失之過甚（2448）Carry too far.

反 聊勝於無（1640）A little is better than none.

源 論語 · 先進："過猶不及。"

過則勿憚改 guò zé wù dàn gǎi 1004

Should not be afraid to correct mistakes. (lit.)

It is never too late to mend.

源 論語："過則勿憚改。"

1005 還未落實 hái wèi luò shí

Not yet down sure. (lit.)

In the air.

1006 海底撈針 hǎi dǐ lāo zhēn

Dredge a needle from the bottom of the sea. (lit.)

A waste of effort.

Look for a needle in a haystack.

1007 海上無魚蝦自大

hǎi shàng wú yú xiā zì dà

If there were no fish in the sea, shrimps would become big (important). (lit.)

In the country of the blind the one-eyed man is king.

1008 海市蜃樓 hǎi shì shèn lóu

A mirage on the sea. (lit.)

A fool's paradise.

Castles in the air.

A mirage.

A hallucination.

源 三齊紀略："海上蜃氣，時結樓台，名海市。"

1009 害羣之馬 hài qún zhī mǎ

A horse which is harmful to the herd. (lit.)

A black sheep.

One scabbed (sickly) sheep infects a whole flock.

The rotten apple injures its neighbour.

Bad egg of the community.

源 莊子："夫為天下，亦奚以異乎牧馬哉，亦去其害馬者而已矣。"

害人反害己 hài rén fǎn hài jǐ 1010
Harming others may turn to harm oneself. (lit.)
Curses come home to roost.
Hoist with one's own petard.
Bite off one's own head.

同 惡有惡報（0716）Sow the wind and reap the whirlwind.

害人終害己 hài rén zhōng hài jǐ 1011
Hurting others will hurt oneself in the end. (lit.)
Harm set, harm get.
He that mischief hatcheth mischief catcheth.

同 多行不義必自斃（0705）Ill-gotten gains seldom prosper.
反 厚德載福（1077）Kindnesses, like grain, increase by sowing.

鼾聲如雷 hān shēng rú léi 1012
The snoring sounds like thunder. (lit.)
Drive one's pig to the market.
Snore like a pig in the sun.
Saw wood.

含垢茹辱 hán gòu rú rǔ 1013
Bear slander and tolerate insult. (lit.)
Eat dirt.
Pocket an insult.
Swallow the leek.

同 忍辱負重（2244）Eat boiled crow.
反 昭雪平反（3809）Redress a wrong.
源 後漢書．曹世叔妻傳：“忍辱含垢，常若畏懼。”

含糊其詞 hán hú qí cí 1014
The words used are vague. (lit.)
To be soft-spoken.
Hum and ha.
Beat about the bush.

同 支吾其詞（3849）Speak with one's tongue in one's cheek.
反 毫不含糊（1021）Make no bones of

寒不擇衣 hán bù zé yī 1015
A man feeling cold does not choose about his clothes. (lit.)
Any port in a storm.

同 飢不擇食（1196）Hunger finds no fault with the cookery.
反 挑三揀四（2744）Pick and choose.

1016 汗流浹背 hàn liú jiá bèi

Sweat streams down to trench one's back. (lit.)

All of a muck of sweat.

Drenched with sweat.

In a sweat.

Perspire profusely.

源 後漢書・伏皇后紀："操去，顧左右，汗流浹背。"

1017 行行出狀元 háng háng chū zhuàng yuán

Every trade has its crop of Standouts (Zhuang Yuen = champion of the Imperial Examination). (lit.)

Every one can reach the top of the ladder.

There are many ways to fame.

In every art it is good to have a master.

1018 行伍出身 háng wǔ chū shēn

Risen as a soldier in military service. (lit.)

Risen from the ranks.

1019 沆瀣一氣 hàng xiè yī qì

The dew water-vapour and the night air are the same kind of gas. (lit.) (meaning "united with the same heart". According to the Chinese classics, Hang and Xie were the names of a teacher and his pupil.)

Like draws to like.

同 氣味相投（2047）Like will to like.

反 格格不入（0895）Go against the grain with one.

源 錢易・南部新書："座主門生，沆瀣（主考崔沆，考生崔瀣）一氣。"

1020 毫不動容 háo bù dòng róng

Not the least disturbed in one's face. (lit.)

Keep one's hair on.

Not to bat an eyelid.

Not turn a hair.

反 驚惶失措（1399）Shake in one's shoes.

1021 毫不含糊 háo bù hán hú

Not in the least vague. (lit.)

Make no bones of

同 一清二楚（3442）As clear as day.

反 含糊其詞（1014）Hum and ha.

毫不客氣 háo bù kè qì 1022
Showing no slightest guest manner. (lit.)
With gloves off.
Handle without mittens.

反 畢恭畢敬（0121）Cap in hand.

毫不留情 háo bù liú qíng 1023
Leave no slightest mercy. (lit.)
Ride rough-shod over one.
Pull no punches.

同 嚴加懲處（3316）Put it across one.
反 顧全顏面（0957）To save face.

毫不在意 háo bù zài yì 1024
Not in the least mind. (lit.)
Not to give a damn.
To make nothing of
To set at naught.

反 耿耿於懷（0915）To take to heart.

毫無差異 háo wú chā yì 1025
Not a slightest difference. (lit.)
It makes no odds.
Without a shade of difference.

同 一模一樣（3428）As like as two peas in a pod.
反 相去十萬八千里（3111）A far cry from.

毫無道理 háo wú dào lǐ 1026
Without any reason at all. (lit.)
Without rhyme or reason.

同 無理取鬧（2979）Find fault with a fat goose.
反 言之成理（3313）It stands to reason.

毫無顧慮 háo wú gù lǜ 1027
Have not the slightest worry. (lit.)
Make no scruple of
Without misgivings.

同 無憂無慮（3003）Happy-go-lucky.
反 心有餘悸（3196）Once bitten, twice shy.

毫無價值 háo wú jià zhí 1028
No slightest value. (lit.)
Not worth a hoot (rap, dump, stitch).

同 賤如糞土（1288）As cheap as dirt.
反 無價之寶（2971）Not to be had for love or money.

毫無條件 háo wú tiáo jiàn 1029
Have no conditions at all. (lit.)
With no strings attached.

1030 **毫無遜色** háo wú xùn sè
By no means inferior to (lit.)
Sustain comparison with another.

同 不亞於人（0261）Second to none.
反 黯然失色（0031）The moon is not seen where the sun shines.

1031 **毫無疑義** háo wú yí yì
Have no doubt at all. (lit.)
A moral certainty.
Beyond all doubt.

同 千真萬確（2069）As sure as eggs is eggs.

1032 **毫無用處** háo wú yòng chù
Have no use at all. (lit.)
As much use as a headache.

同 一無是處（3472）Good for nothing.
反 天生我才必有用（2718）Everything is good for something.

1033 **豪言壯語** háo yán zhuàng yǔ
Boasting words and strong phrases. (lit.)
Boom out big words.

反 唱低調（0331）Play something (it) down.

1034 **好歹試試** hǎo dǎi shì shì
Good or bad have a try. (lit.)
To take one's chance.

1035 **好漢不吃眼前虧**
hǎo hàn bù chī yǎn qián kuī
Good fellow does not eat immediate (before eye) loss. (lit.)
Better good afar off than evil at hand.
One pair of heels is often worth two pairs of hands.

反 吃小虧佔大便宜（0375）Sometimes the best gain is to lose.

1036 **好好先生** hǎo hǎo xiān shēng
Mr. Good man. (lit.)
A good scout.
Goody-goody.
A regular brick.
An easy-going fellow.
A yes man.
A regular guy.
A push-over.
Duck soup.

源 譚概："後漢司馬徽不談人短，與人語美惡皆言好。"

好話説盡，壞事做盡 1037

hǎo huà shuō jìn, huài shì zuò jìn

Good words are completely said, bad deeds completely done. (lit.)

The devil can cite Scripture for his purpose.

好景不常 hǎo jǐng bù cháng 1038

Good circumstances never last long. (lit.)

The morning sun never lasts a day.

The longest day must have an end.

Every day is not Sunday.

A wonder lasts but nine days.

反 天下無不散之筵席（2729）Merry meet, merry part.

源 王勃："好景不常，盛筵難再。"

好事不出門，惡事傳千里 1039

hǎo shì bù chū mén, è shì chuán qiān lǐ

Good things do not get out of door, bad things pass to thousand li (Chinese mile). (lit.)

When I did well, I heard it never; when I did ill, I heard it ever.

源 孫光憲．北夢瑣言："好事不出門，惡事傳千里，士君子得不戒之哉。"

好物沉歸底 hǎo wù chén guī dǐ 1040

Good things sink to the bottom. (lit.)

The best fish swim near the bottom.

The best is at the bottom.

同 後來居上（1082）The best is behind.

好吃懶做 hào chī lǎn zuò 1041

Keen to eat but lazy. (lit.)

Eat one's head off.

同 尸位素餐（2444）Feast at the public crib.

反 枵腹從公（3121）Get all the kicks and none of the ha'pence.

好高騖遠 hào gāo wù yuǎn 1042

After something high and far (above). (lit.)

Hitch one's wagon to a star.

Gaze at the moon and fall into the gutter.

Vaulting ambition that overleaps itself.

同 想入非非（3116）To be in the clouds.

反 腳踏實地（1310）Come down to bedrock.

1043 **好管閒事** hào guǎn xián shì

Fond of meddling in others' business. (lit.)

A busybody.
Have an oar in every man's boat.
Poke one's nose into
Grease the fat pig.
A nosey parker.

同 包打聽（0078）Paul Pry is on the spy.

反 事不關己，高高掛起（2508）I will neither meddle nor make.

1044 **合抱之木，生於毫末**

hé bào zhī mù, shēng yú háo mò

A trunk that can be embraced by (two persons) grows up from a tiny thing. (lit.)

Great oaks from little acorns grow.
The thin end of the wedge is to be feared.

同 從小到大（0467）Small beginnings make great endings.

源 老子：“合抱之木，生於毫末。”

1045 **何陋之有** hé lòu zhī yǒu

How can it be shabby? (lit.)

Home is home, be it ever so homely.

同 龍牀不如狗竇（1690）Every bird thinks its own nest charming.

源 論語．子罕：“君子居之，何陋之有。”

1046 **何去何從** hé qù hé cóng

Which way to go and to follow. (lit.)

At a loss what to do.
Torn between.
To be or not to be.

源 楚辭．卜居：“此孰吉孰凶，何去何從。”

1047 **何足掛齒** hé zú guà chǐ

How can it be worth to hang on the teeth. (lit.)

Don't mention it.
Nothing to speak of.

同 不值一提（0283）Nothing to make a song about.

反 膾炙人口（1528）To be in everyone's mouth.

源 史記：“何足掛牙齒間。”

1048 **和藹可親** hé ǎi kě qīn

Affable and accessible. (lit.)

As harmless as a dove.
With a good grace.
Easy to get along with.

同 平易近人（1994）Have a taking way with someone.

反 盛氣凌人（2433）Throw one's weight about.

和平共處 hé píng gòng chǔ 1049

Get on together peacefully. (lit.)

Peaceful co-existence.

同 相安無事（3103）Get along fairly well.

反 訴諸武力（2651）Appeal to arms.

和氣致祥 hé qì zhì xiáng 1050

Peaceful disposition brings blessing. (lit.)

A soft fire makes sweet malt.

源 劉向·上封事："和氣致祥，祥多者其國安。"

和衣而睡 hé yī ér shuì 1051

To sleep with the clothes on. (lit.)

Turn in all standing.

源 楊萬里詩："連拳贏僕和衣睡。"

和衷共濟 hé zhōng gòng jì 1052

Peace and harmony in helping each other. (lit.)

To pull together.

同 互忍互讓（1095）Live and let live.

反 自相殘殺（4004）Gut one another's throats.

源 書經；"同寅協恭，和衷哉。"

河東獅吼 hé dōng shī hǒu 1053

From the east of the river (comes) the roar of the lioness. (lit.)

Wear the breeches.

The grey mare is the better horse.

同 牝雞司晨（1982）Wear the trousers.

反 有季常癖（3649）To be henpecked.

源 蘇軾詩："忽聞河東獅子吼，拄杖落手心茫然。"

涸轍之鮒 hé zhé zhī fù 1054

A fresh-water fish in the dried up track. (lit.)

A fish out of water.

To be dead broke.

To be low in one's pocket.

同 不得其所（0181）To be out of one's latitude.

反 如魚得水（2279）To be in one's element.

源 李商隱："活枯鱗於涸轍。"

喝倒彩 hè dào cǎi 1055

A shot of hoot. (lit.)

Give a Bronx cheer.

Make cat calls.

Boo and hoot.

To hoot at

Give the bird.

反 歌功頌德（0894）Chant the praises of

1056 **鶴立雞羣** hè lì jī qún

A crane standing among a group of chickens. (lit.)

A Triton among the minnows.

Stand head and shoulders above others.

同 出類拔萃（0406）Tower above the rest.

源 世説新語：“嵇延祖卓卓如野鶴之在雞羣。”

1057 **黑暗面** hēi àn miàn

The dark face. (lit.)

The seamy side of life.

1058 **黑白分明** hēi bái fēn míng

A clear distinction between black and white. (lit.)

As plain as the nose on one's face.

The fairer the paper, the fouler the blot.

In sharp contrast.

源 春秋繁露：“黑白分明，然後民知所去就。”

1059 **黑漆一團** hēi qī yī tuán

A patch of black paint. (lit.)

As black as pitch (ink, midnight).

反 光輝燦爛（0979）Dazzling to the eye.

1060 **黑甜鄉** hēi tián xiāng

A dark and sweet village. (lit.)

The Land of Nod.

源 蘇軾詩：“一枕黑甜餘。”

1061 **狠揍一頓** hěn zòu yī dùn

Being beaten up violently. (lit.)

Knock the daylight out of one.

Give a person socks.

同 飽以老拳（0086）Give one a good licking.

1062 **恨之入骨** hèn zhī rù gǔ

Hate one to the bone. (lit.)

Hate one's guts.

Can eat one without salt.

同 咬牙切齒（3354）Gnash one's teeth in anger.

1063 **恆河沙數** héng hé shā shù

As numerous as the sands of Ganges. (lit.)

As numberless as the sands.

反 寥若晨星（1641）Few and far between.

源 金剛經：“諸恆河所有沙數，寧為多不。”

横衝直撞 héng chōng zhí zhuàng 1064
Rush across and dash straight ahead. (lit.)
Run amuck.
Run one's head against a post.
Jostle along.

反 躲躲閃閃（0710）Sneaking in and out.

横加阻撓 héng jiā zǔ náo 1065
To add on the cross to hinder (progress) (lit.)
Cut the grass from under a person's feet.
Throw a spanner in the works.

反 熱烈贊助（2185）Carry a torch for

横眉冷對千夫指 1066
héng méi lěng duì qiān fū zhǐ
Raising his eyebrow, one looked coldly at thousand men's pointing fingers. (lit.)
A valiant man's look is more than a coward's sword.

源 魯迅・自嘲詩："横眉冷對千夫指，俯首甘為孺子牛。"

横豎一樣 héng shù yí yàng 1067
Length and breadth are the same. (lit.)
It's as broad as it's long.
To be much of a muchness.

同 反正一樣（0748）It is all one.
反 相去十萬八千里（3111）As wide as the poles asunder.

横行霸道 héng xíng bà dào 1068
Walk sideways (like a crab) and act in tyrannous manner. (lit.)
Push people around.
Play the bully.
On the high ropes.

同 作威作福（4073）Throw one's weight about.
反 安分守己（0009）Mind one's own business.
源 紅樓夢："一任薛蟠横行霸道。"

横行無忌 héng xíng wú jì 1069
Walk sideways without scruple. (lit.)
Throw one's weight about.
Ride roughshod over

反 投鼠忌器（2792）Take not a musket to kill a butterfly.
源 史記："聚黨數千人，横行天下。"

1070 **橫遭冷遇** héng zāo lěng yù

Unexpected encounter and cold reception. (lit.)

Get the frozen mitt (cold shoulder).

To be left out in the cold.

同 備受奚落（0104）To get the goose.

反 獲人青睞（1180）To get around someone.

1071 **橫徵暴斂** héng zhēng bào liǎn

Irrational levy and extorted taxation. (lit.)

Grind the faces of the people.

Bleed the people white.

1072 **哄動一時** hōng dòng yī shí

To prevail upon for a time. (lit.)

Hell broke loose.

The fat is in the fire.

Make the fur fly.

Make a stir.

1073 **哄堂大笑** hōng táng dà xiào

All present in the hall roared with laughter. (lit.)

Set the room in a roar.

Bring down the house.

1074 **紅到發紫** hóng dào fā zǐ

So red it turns purple. (lit.)

At the zenith of one's power.

同 走運（4032）Hit the jackpot.

反 潦倒一生（1645）Lead a dog's life.

1075 **紅顏易老** hóng yán yì lǎo

Pretty face easily turns old. (lit.)

The fairest silk is soonest stained.

The fairest rose at last is withered.

1076 **厚此薄彼** hòu cǐ bó bǐ

Thick to this and thin to that. (lit.)

Make chalk of one and cheese of the other.

Treat with partiality.

同 區別對待（2150）Make fish of one and flesh of another.

反 一視同仁（3457）The sun shines upon all alike.

厚德載福 hòu dé zài fú 1077

Great virtue bears blessing. (lit.)

Virtue and happiness are mother and daughter.

Kindnesses, like grain, increase by sowing.

同 積善多福（1191）A good deed is never lost.

反 多行不義必自斃（0705）Ill-gotten gains seldom prosper.

源 易經：“地勢坤，君子以厚德載福。”

厚顏無恥 hòu yán wú chǐ 1078

Brazen-faced with no sense of shame. (lit.)

Have plenty of cheek.

As bold as brass.

To brazen out.

Have the effrontery to

同 恬不知恥（2741）Have no sense of shame.

反 羞人答答（3239）Feel like thirty cents.

源 孔稚圭．北山移文：“豈可使芳杜厚顏，薜荔蒙恥。”

後患無窮 hòu huàn wú qióng 1079

Disastrous after-effects are endless. (lit.)

With no end of trouble.

The deuce to pay.

The devil and all to pay.

同 不可收拾（0218）All the fat is in the fire.

後悔莫及 hòu huǐ mò jí 1080

The repentance is not in time (too late). (lit.)

Lock the stable door after the horse is stolen.

Repentance comes too late.

同 悔之晚矣（1154-5）It is too late to grieve when the chance is past.

反 亡羊補牢，未為晚也（2861）It is never too late to mend.

後會有期 hòu huì yǒu qī 1081

There is a date to meet again. (lit.)

Till we meet again.

同 人生何處不相逢（2215）Friends may meet, but mountains never greet.

反 一去不復返（3444）To be going for good and all.

後來居上 hòu lái jū shàng 1082

Those that came last get to higher positions. (lit.)

The best is behind.

He finished first though he began last.

同 迎頭趕上（3601）To overtake one.

反 遙遙領先（3349）Streets ahead of

源 史記．汲鄭列傳：“陛下用羣臣，如積薪耳，後來者居上。”

1083 呼之即來，揮之即去
hū zhī jí lái, huī zhī jí qù
Call, one comes at once; wave hand, one goes away at once. (lit.)
At one's beck and call.

同 頤指氣使（3522）Get someone by the short hairs.
源 蘇軾．王仲儀真贊序："至於緩急之際，決大策，安大眾，呼之即來，揮之即散者，唯世臣巨室為能。"

1084 囫圇吞棗 hú lún tūn zǎo
Swallowed a date whole without thinking. (lit.)
To bone up.
To learn by rote.

同 生吞活剝（2420）Copy blindly.
反 細味品嘗（3063）Enjoy the full gusto of
源 朱子語錄："道是個有條理的，不是囫圇底物。"

1085 狐假虎威 hú jiǎ hǔ wēi
The fox assumes the awe of a tiger. (lit.)
The fly sat upon the axletree of the chariot wheel and said: What a dust do I raise!

同 馬屎憑官勢（1730）Great men's servants think themselves great.
源 庾子山集．哀江南賦："或以隼翼鷃批，虎威狐假。"

1086 胡說八道 hú shuō bā dào
To speak imprudently and talk nonsense. (lit.)
Stuff and nonsense.
Talk through one's hat (the back of one's neck).
Talk twaddle.
Talk rubbish.

反 引經據典（3584）Give chapter and verse.

1087 胡思亂想 hú sī luàn xiǎng
Reckless thoughts and stupid wish. (lit.)
Go off into wild flights of fancy.
Build castles in the air (Spain).
Have a bee in one's bonnet.
To be in the clouds.

同 想入非非（3116）Show him an egg, and instantly the whole air is full of feathers.
源 朱熹："不要如此胡思亂量，過卻日子也。"

糊裏糊塗 hú lǐ hú tú 1088

This is a Chinese slang somewhat equivalent to "in a muddle" in English. (lit.)

To be in a muddle.
To be all at sea.
As clear as mud.
To be muddleheaded.
In a haze (fog).

反 一清二楚（3442）As clear as day.

虎口餘生 hǔ kǒu yú shēng 1089

Life spared from the mouth of a tiger. (lit.)

To be snatched from the jaws of death.
Have a narrow escape (close shave).

同 大難不死（0541）Have a close brush with death.

虎落平陽被犬欺 1090

hǔ luò píng yáng bèi quǎn qī

When a tiger comes down to the plain it is bullied by the dogs. (lit.)

Hares may pull dead lions by the beard.

同 龍游淺水遭蝦戲（1693）He came safe from the East Indies, and was drowned in the Thames.

虎生猶可近，人熟不堪親 1091

hǔ shēng yóu kě jìn, rén shóu bù kān qīn

Live tiger is still approachable but familiar man is not worth to get near. (lit.)

Familiarity breeds contempt.
Too too will in two.
No man is a hero to his valet.

同 但看三五日，相見不如初（0576）A constant guest is never welcome.

虎視眈眈 hǔ shì dān dān 1092

To look fiercely at as a tiger does. (lit.)

As watchful as a hawk.

同 覬覦已久（1238）Cast greedy eyes on

源 周易 · 頤："虎視眈眈，其欲逐逐。"

虎頭蛇尾 hǔ tóu shé wěi 1093

A tiger's head but a snake's tail. (lit.)

Going up like a rocket and coming down like a stick.
Come out at the little end of the horn.
The mountain has brought forth a mouse.
In like a lion, out like a lamb.
A flash in the pan.

同 來如風雨，去似微塵（1539）He who swells in prosperity will shrink in adversity.

反 始終不渝（2483）Keep it up.

源 元曲選 · 李逵負荊："這廝敢狗行狼心，虎頭蛇尾。"

1094 **虎頭捉虱** hǔ tóu zhuō shī

Like catching lice on a tiger's head. (lit.)

Beard the lion in his den.

1095 **互忍互讓** hù rěn hù ràng

Mutual tolerance and allowance. (lit.)

Live and let live.

反 自相殘殺（4004）Cut one another's throats.

1096 **互相衝突** hù xiāng chōng tū

Fight against each other. (lit.)

To be at odds.

At loggerheads with

反 相安無事（3103）Get along fairly well.

1097 **互相吹捧** hù xiāng chuī pěng

Mutual boasting and lifting. (lit.)

Scratch my back, and I will scratch yours.

Claw me, and I'll claw thee.

1098 **互相勾結** hù xiāng gōu jié

Hook and link one another. (lit.)

Play into one another's hands.

同 朋比為奸（1960）Gang up with

1099 **互相信任** hù xiāng xìn rèn

Trust each other. (lit.)

Confidence begets confidence.

反 爾虞我詐（0727）Play each other false.

1100 **怙惡不悛** hù è bù quān

Stick to one's wickedness and refuse to reform. (lit.)

To abide in sin.

To be hard-boiled.

同 堅決不改（1268）To sit tight.

反 從善如流（0462）If the counsel be good no matter who gave it.

源 後漢書・朱暉傳："諱惡不悛，卒至亡滅。

1101 **花多眼亂** huā duō yǎn luàn

Too many flowers the eyes get confused. (lit.)

One can't see the wood for the trees.

1102 **花花公子** huā huā gōng zǐ

A profligate youth. (lit.)

Jack-a-dandy.

同 膏粱子弟（0890）Gilded youth.

花街柳巷 huā jiē liǔ xiàng 1103

Flower street and willow lanes. (lit.)

Red-light district.

源 黃庭堅詞："初綰雲鬟，才勝羅綺，便嫌柳巷花街。"

花開堪折直須折，莫待無花空折枝 1104

huā kāi kān zhé zhí xū zhé, mò dài wú huā kōng zhé zhī

When flowers bloom and worthy of picking, must pick them; do not wait until the branches are empty of flowers. (lit.)

Gather ye rose buds while ye may.

He that will not when he may, when he will he shall have nay.

同 今朝有酒今朝醉（1339）Let us eat and drink, for tomorrow we shall die.

源 杜秋娘・金縷衣："勸君莫惜金縷衣，勸君惜取少年時，花開堪折直須折，莫待無花空折枝。"

花天酒地 huā tiān jiǔ dì 1105

Flowers in heaven and wine on earth. (lit.)

Lead a fast life.

To live fast.

Give nature a fillip.

Indulge in debauchery.

同 窮奢極欲（2139）Live at rack and manger.

花無百日紅 huā wú bǎi rì hóng 1106

Flowers cannot remain red for hundred days. (lit.)

The fairest rose at last is withered.

花枝招展 huā zhī zhāo zhǎn 1107

The flowering branches wave and show off. (lit.)

As gaudy as a peacock.

As fair as a rose.

同 飄飄欲仙（1975）As light as a butterfly.

華而不實 huá ér bù shí 1108

Flowery but bears no fruit. (lit.)

Window dressing.

More sauce than pig.

同 金玉其外，敗絮其中（1345）All is not gold that glitters.

源 左傳："且華而不實，怨之所聚也。"

1109 **華胥國** huá xū guó

In Chinese mythology Hua Xu Guo was a kingdom of peace and prosperity. (lit.)

Utopia.

Land of Nod.

1110 **滑稽可笑** huá jī kě xiào

Comical and laughable. (lit.)

Enough to make a cat laugh.

同 滑天下之大稽（1111）Make a laughing-stock of oneself.

反 可歌可泣（1491）Melt into tears.

1111 **滑天下之大稽** huá tiān xià zhī dà jī

Make oneself the laughing-stock of the world. (lit.)

Make a laughing-stock of oneself.

How ridiculous!

1112 **嘩眾取寵** huá zhòng qǔ chǒng

Make noise to the people to get popularity. (lit.)

To play to the gallery.

Impress people by claptrap.

源 漢書・藝文志："然惑者既失精微，而僻者又隨時抑揚，違離道本，苟以嘩眾取寵。"

1113 **化干戈為玉帛** huà gān gē wéi yù bó

Transform the armour into jade and silk. (lit.)

Beat swords into ploughshares, and spears into pruning hooks.

Peace makes plenty.

Bury the hatchet.

反 訴諸武力（2651）Appeal to arms.

1114 **化為灰燼** huà wéi huī jìn

Changed to ashes. (lit.)

Reduced to ashes.

反 死灰復燃（2626）To rise like the Phoenix.

1115 **化為烏有** huà wéi wū yǒu

Reduced to nothingness. (lit.)

To come to nought (nothing).

Vanish into thin air.

同 煙消雲散（3292）End in smoke.

反 無中生有（3006）Sheer fabrication.

源 蘇軾詩："豈意青州六從事，化為烏有一先生。"

化險為夷 huà xiǎn wéi yí 1116

Turn danger to safety. (lit.)

Weather the storm.

Keep one's head above water.

Escape scotfree.

Fall on one's feet.

Bear a charmed life.

To be out of the woods.

同 絕處逢生（1455）Escape by the skin of one's teeth.

反 晴天霹靂（2134）A bolt from the blue.

畫餅充飢 huà bǐng chōng jī 1117

Sketch cakes to pacify hunger. (lit.)

Hope is the poor man's bread.

A barmecide feast.

Castle in the air.

源 三國志："選舉莫取有名，名如畫地作餅，不可啖也。"

畫蛇添足 huà shé tiān zú 1118

Draw a snake with feet added. (lit.)

Gild refined gold.

Paint the lily.

同 多此一舉（0698）Carry water to the river.

源 戰國策："畫地為蛇，先成者飲，一人蛇先成，引酒，且言吾能為之足，未成，一人蛇成，奪其巵。"

話不投機半句多 1119

huà bù tóu jī bàn jù duō

When the conversation is not agreeable even half a sentence is too much. (lit.)

It's ill talking between a full man and a fasting.

反 與君一夕話，勝讀十年書（3702）Sweet discourse makes short days and nights.

話到嘴邊 huà dào zuǐ biān 1120

Words come to the edge of the mouth. (lit.)

On the tip of one's tongue.

反 脱口而出（2829）Escape one's lips.

話匣子 huà xiá zi 1121

Talking box. (lit.)

A gas bag.

A gasometer.

A chatter-box.

反 沉默寡言（0342）A regular oyster.

1122 **話中有話** huà zhōng yǒu huà
Hidden words in a speech. (lit.)
There's a catch in one's words.

同 字裏行間（3967）Read between the lines.
反 言之無物（3314）A deluge of words and a drop of sense.

1123 **懷才不遇** huái cái bù yù
Having talent but not meeting the (opportune) time. (lit.)
What's the good of a sundial in the shade?
A round peg in a square hole.
Have soul above buttons.

同 英雄無用武之地（3597）A square peg in a round hole.

1124 **懷恨在心** huái hèn zài xīn
Harbour hatred in one's heart. (lit.)
To bear a grudge.

反 不念舊惡（0235）Forgive and forget.

1125 **壞事變好事** huài shì biàn hǎo shì
Bad thing can change to good thing. (lit.)
Even ill-luck is good for something in a wise man's hand.
Sweet are the uses of adversity.

同 塞翁失馬，焉知非福（2301）A blessing in disguise.

1126 **壞事傳千里** huài shì chuán qiān lǐ
Bad doings spread thousand li (Chinese mile). (lit.)
Ill news runs apace.
Ill news travels fast.

1127 **歡天喜地** huān tiān xǐ dì
Heaven and earth full of joy. (lit.)
Seem to tread on air.

同 喜氣洋洋（3059）Light up with pleasure.
反 愁眉苦臉（0396）Wear a glum countenance.
源 西廂記："則見他歡天喜地，謹依來命。"

1128 **歡欣鼓舞** huān xīn gǔ wǔ
Happy and delighted, excited and encouraged. (lit.)
Fly into raptures.
Dance for joy.

同 手舞足蹈（2549）Leap with joy.
源 蘇軾・上王龍圖書："是故莫不歡欣鼓舞之至。"

歡欣若狂 huān xīn ruò kuáng 1129

To be rapt with joy. (lit.)

Walk on air.

Frantic (mad) with joy.

To be on cloud nine.

反 悲痛欲絕（0098）Torn with grief.

宦海浮沉 huàn hǎi fú chén 1130

Floating and sinking in the official seas. (lit.)

Ups and downs of life.

The world is a ladder for some to go up and some down.

同 有人掛冠歸故里，有人臨夜趕科場（3662）The world is a staircase, some are going up and some are going down.

源 仙傳拾遺："不宜自沉於名宦之海。"

患得患失 huàn dé huàn shī 1131

Afraid of (not) gaining and afraid of losing. (lit.)

Not know where one stands.

Too much consulting confounds.

Too much taking heed is loss.

源 論語．陽貨："鄙夫可與事君也歟哉。其未得之也，患得之。既得之，患失之。"

患難相濟 huàn nàn xiāng jì 1132

Share together afflictions. (lit.)

Through foul and fair.

Friends tie their purses with a cobweb thread.

Share weal and woe.

同 同舟共濟（2773）Two in distress make sorrow less.

反 見死不救（1280）Leave one in the lurch.

患難之交 huàn nàn zhī jiāo 1133

Friendship made during adversity. (lit.)

Foul weather friends.

A friend in need is a friend indeed.

同 風雨同舟（0812）In the same boat.

反 酒肉朋友（1425）Fair-weather friends.

煥然一新 huàn rán yī xīn 1134

Shiningly a new one. (lit.)

Look spick and span.

Take on a new look.

反 原封不動（3730）To be left intact.

源 丘崇．重修羅池廟記："煥然一新，觀者嗟異。"

荒謬絕倫 huāng miù jué lún 1135

Absurd and ridiculous of no compare. (lit.)

Absolutely preposterous.

1136 荒唐可笑 huāng táng kě xiào
Absurd and laughable. (lit.)
Enough to make a cat laugh.
Utterly ridiculous.

1137 慌慌張張 huāng huāng zhāng zhāng
Flurried and hurried. (lit.)
Have a bee in one's head.
In a flurry.
Helter-skelter.

同 心慌意亂（3170）With one's heart going pitpat.
反 頭腦冷靜（2797）Have one's brains on ice.

1138 慌作一團 huāng zuò yì tuán
Frightened into a cluster. (lit.)
Struck all of a heap.
Thrown into utter confusion.

反 保持鎮靜（0079）As cool as a cucumber.

1139 惶惶不可終日
huáng huáng bù kě zhōng rì
Nervously can't get the day over. (lit.)
To be kept in suspense.
To be on the rack.

同 坐立不安（4053）Sit on a bag of fleas.
反 無憂無慮（3003）Free from care.

1140 惶恐不安 huáng kǒng bù ān
Fearful, perplexed and uneasy. (lit.)
With one's heart going pit-pat.

反 心安理得（3158）Have an easy conscience.
源 漢書．王莽傳："人民正營，顏師古注，正營，惶恐不安也。"

1141 黃道吉日 huáng dào jí rì
Auspicious and lucky day. (lit.)
A red-letter day.

1142 黃河尚有澄清日，豈可人無得運時 huáng hé shàng yǒu chéng qīng rì, qǐ kě rén wú dé yùn shí
Yellow River still would one day get clear, how could a man not have one day to fulfil his ambition. (lit.)
Fortune knocks once at least at every man's gate.
Every dog has his day, and every man his hour.
There is an hour wherein a man might be happy all his life, could he find it.

黃鼠狼給雞拜年 1143
huáng shǔ láng gěi jī bài nián
Yellow weasel pays New Year greetings to the hen. (lit.)
When the fox preaches, beware the geese.

同 禮多必詐（1600）Full of courtesy, full of craft.

恍然大悟 huǎng rán dà wù 1144
Suddenly there is great understanding. (lit.)
It dawned upon one.
See daylight.

同 如夢初醒（2274）To wake up to
反 如入五里霧中（2276）To be lost in the cloud.

灰心喪志 huī xīn sàng zhì 1145
Disheartened with the loss of ambition. (lit.)
In the dumps.
In black despair.
To lose heart.

同 意氣消沉（3563）Have one's heart in one's boots.
反 發奮有為（0795）Shake oneself together.

恢復神志 huī fù shén zhì 1146
Restore one's spirit and will. (lit.)
To come to.
To recollect oneself.

恢復元氣 huī fù yuán qì 1147
Restore to its former air. (lit.)
To be up and about.
To be on the mend.

反 一蹶不振（3409）Fall flat.

揮金如土 huī jīn rú tǔ 1148
Squander gold like earth. (lit.)
Play ducks and drakes with one's money.
Spend money like water.
Throw money about.

同 恣意揮霍（4018）Money burns a hole in his pocket.
反 守財奴（2550）As tight as a drum.

回頭是岸 huí tóu shì àn 1149
Turn the head around and there lies the shore. (lit.)
It is never too late to mend. (or repent)

源 佛家語："苦海無邊，回頭是岸。"

1150 **回心轉意** huí xīn zhuǎn yì
Change one's mind and views. (lit.)
Think better of it.
A change of heart.

反 堅決不改（1268）To sit tight.

1151 **回（迴）旋之地** huí xuán zhī dì
Ground (room) for turning around. (lit.)
Elbow room.

1152 **悔不當初** huǐ bù dāng chū
Regret for not having done it at first. (lit.)
Come home by weeping cross.
Kick oneself.

同 覆水難收（0851）It is no use crying over spilt milk.
源 唐．薛昭緯．謝銀工詩："早知文字多辛苦，悔不當初學冶銀。"

1153 **悔過自新** huǐ guò zì xīn
Repent and reform oneself. (lit.)
To be on the cot.
Make a fresh start.
Turn over a new leaf.

同 改邪歸正（0856）To mend one's way.
反 堅決不改（1268）To sit tight.
源 唐書．馮元常傳："劍南有光火盜，元常喻以恩信，約悔過自新。"

1154 **悔之莫及** huǐ zhī mò jí
Regretting it (comes) not in times. (lit.)
Lock the stable door after the horse is stolen.

1155 **悔之晚矣** huǐ zhī wǎn yǐ
It is indeed too late to remorse. (lit.)
Repentance comes too late.
It is too late to grieve when the chance is past.

反 亡羊補牢，未為晚也（2861）It is never too late to mend.

1156 **惠而不費** huì ér bú fèi
A favour needs not be expensive. (lit.)
You may light another's candle at your own without loss.
The cost is a mere fleabite.

反 所費不貲（2663）It has dipped into one's pocket.
源 論語："君子惠而不費。"

喙長三尺 huì cháng sān chǐ 1157

Mouth long, three feet. (lit.)

Good at repartee.

A flannel mouth person.

Have the gift of the gab.

同 三寸不爛之舌（2303）Silver tongued.

反 張口結舌（3793）To be tongue-tied.

源 莊子 · 徐無鬼：“丘願有喙長三尺。”

諱莫如深 huì mò rú shēn 1158

Never as deep as he hides (his secret). (lit.)

Breathe not a syllable.

Keep one's own counsel.

Keep mum.

同 隻字不提（3866）Keep it dark.

反 傾吐衷情（2123）Lay one's heart bare.

源 穀梁傳 · 莊三十二年：“諱莫如深，深則隱。”

昏昏欲睡 hūn hūn yù shuì 1159

Drowsy and sleepy. (lit.)

Have a wink in one's eye.

Gather (draw) straws.

Make drowsy.

魂飛魄散 hún fēi pò sàn 1160

Soul flies and spirit scatters. (lit.)

Like a hog in a squall (storm).

Scared out of one's wits.

Stand aghast.

同 神不守舍（2404）Lose one's presence of mind.

源 元曲選 · 百花亭：“可正是船到江心補漏遲，只着我魄散魂飛。”

魂歸天國 hún guī tiān guó 1161

Spirit returns to Heaven. (lit.)

Go to heaven.

Give up the ghost.

Pay the debt of nature.

Go to meet one's Maker.

同 西方極樂世界（3043）The sweet by-and-by.

反 入土為安（2288）Dust unto dust, and under dust to lie.

混水摸魚 hùn shuǐ mō yú 1162

Grope for fish in turbid water. (lit.)

Take advantage of

To fish in troubled waters.

同 鷸蚌相持，漁人得利（3724）Two dogs fight for a bone, and a third runs away with it.

1163 **豁出去** huō chū qù

Suddenly go out. (lit.)

Go for a thing bald-head.
Ride for a fall.
Go all out.
Take one's life in one's hands.

同 置生死於度外（3901）Heedless of consequences.
反 明哲保身（1826）Be worldly wise and play safe.

1164 **活到老，學到老**

huó dào lǎo, xué dào lǎo

Live to old age and learn to old ages. (lit.)

Never too old to learn.
Live and learn.
Art is long, life is short.

同 學無止境（3268）Live and learn.
反 飽食終日，無所用心（0085）A belly full of gluttony will never study willingly.

1165 **活得不耐煩** huó dé bù nài fán

Live impatiently. (lit.)

To tempt providence.
To tempt the fates.

1166 **活該** huó gāi

As it ought to be. (lit.)

Serve one right.
Have only oneself to blame.

1167 **活龍活現** huó lóng huó xiàn

Live dragon appears lively. (lit.)

Vivid with life.

同 栩栩如生（3251）True to life.

1168 **火上加油** huǒ shàng jiā yóu

To add oil on the fire. (lit.)

Pour oil on the flame (fire).
Add fuel to the flames.
Like a red rag to a bull.

同 推波助瀾（2815）Fan the fire.
反 釜底抽薪（0829）Take away fuel, take away flame（fire）.
源 元曲選．陳州糶米：“我從來不劣方頭，恰便是火上澆油。”

1169 **火燒眉毛** huǒ shāo méi máo

Fire burning the eye-brow. (lit.)

A crisis.
Imminent danger.
There's not a moment to lose.

同 燃眉之急（2176）Pressing need.
源 五燈會元：“僧問蔣山佛慧，如何是急切一句。慧曰，火燒眉毛。”

火中取栗 huǒ zhōng qǔ lì 1170
Pull chestnuts out of the fire. (lit.)
Played for a sucker.
Take the chestnut out of the fire with the cat's paw.

或作或輟 huò zuò huò chuò 1171
Either do or stop. (lit.)
Off and on.
By fits and starts (snatches).

反 一氣呵成（3438）At a stretch.

貨如輪轉 huò rú lún zhuǎn 1172
Goods like the turning wheel. (lit.)
Small profits and quick returns.
Sell like hot cakes.

同 生意興隆（2421）Drive a roaring trade.

貨真價實 huò zhēn jià shí 1173
Goods genuine and prices fixed. (lit.)
Worth its weight in gold.

反 掛羊頭，賣狗肉（0960）Cry up wine and sell vinegar.

禍不單行 huò bù dān xíng 1174
Misfortunes never come alone. (lit.)
Misfortunes seldom come singly.
It never rains but it pours.
One misfortune comes on the neck of another.
Troubles never come singly.

同 一波未平，一波又起（3376）Hit one snag after another.
反 福無雙至（0827）Opportunity seldom knocks twice.
源 傳燈錄・紫桐和尚："禍不單行，福無雙至。"

禍從口出 huò cóng kǒu chū 1175
Troubles come forth from the mouth. (lit.)
The tongue talks at the head's cost.

反 病從口入（0163）Gluttony kills more than the sword.
源 傅玄・口銘："病從口入，禍從口出。"

禍福無常 huò fú wú cháng 1176
Misfortune and happiness do not last. (lit.)
Be it weal or be it woe, it shall not be always so.
He who laughs on Friday will weep on Sunday.

同 人有霎時之禍福（2236）Today a man, tomorrow a mouse.

1177 禍福相倚伏 huò fú xiāng yǐ fú
Calamity and blessing are sometimes depending on each other and hidden. (lit.)
Fortune turns like a mill wheel; now you are at the top, and then at the bottom.

源 史記："禍兮福所倚，福兮禍所伏。"

1178 禍福與共 huò fú yǔ gòng
To share both misfortune and happiness. (lit.)
For weal and woe.
Cast in one's lot with

同 同生死，共命運（2770）Cast in one's lot with
反 各人自掃門前雪（0904）Sweep before your own door.

1179 禍為福所倚 huò wèi fú suǒ yǐ
Calamity is what blessing sometimes leans on. (lit.)
Every cloud has a silver lining.

同 塞翁失馬，焉知非福（2301）A blessing in disguise.
源 史記："禍兮福所倚，福兮禍所伏。"

1180 獲人青睞 huò rén qīng lài
Obtain from people a special look. (lit.)
To get around someone.

反 橫遭冷遇（1070）Get the cold shoulder.

J

基本解決 jī běn jiě jué 1181
Basic solution. (lit.)
Break the back of

激起無名火 jī qǐ wú míng huǒ
Provoke a nameless anger. (lit.)
Let a person's hair down.
Put a person's monkey up.
Like a red rag to a bull.
Make one see red.

同 佛也冒火（0818）Enough to make a saint swear. 1182

激起義憤 jī qǐ yì fèn
To stimulate the public indignation. (lit.)
Make one's blood boil.

同 令人髮指（1674）Make one's hair stand on end. 1183

機不可失 jī bù kě shī
Opportunity must not be lost. (lit.)
Take fortune at the tide.
One hour today is worth two tomorrow.

同 勿失時機（3026）Now or never. 1184
反 失之交臂（2449）Miss the bus.
源 舊唐書．李靖傳：“兵貴神速，機不可失。”

機關算盡太聰明
jī guān suàn jìn tài cōng míng
Calculating all the machanisms, one is still too clever. (lit.)
To lose one's reckoning.
He that reckons without one's host must reckon twice.

同 弄巧成拙（1925）Ride one's horse to death. 1185

機會均等 jī huì jūn děng 1186
Equal opportunity. (lit.)
Fair field and no favour.

1187 **機靈果斷** jī líng guǒ duàn

A smart, swift, and determined decision. (lit.)

Have the presence of mind.

同 精明強幹（1386）To be up to snuff.

反 優柔寡斷（3628）To be shilly-shally.

1188 **積不相能** jī bù xiāng néng

Accumulated disagreements cause difficulty (to get on). (lit.)

Not to touch one with a barge pole.

To be at loggerheads.

同 彼此對立（0114）To be at odds.

反 水乳交融（2593）To be hand and glove with another.

源 後漢書 · 吳漢傳：“子與劉公積不相能，而信其虛談，不為之備，終受制矣。”

1189 **積穀防饑** jī gǔ fáng jī

Store up grains to prevent famine. (lit.)

Lay up against a rainy day.

Keep something for a sore foot.

同 未雨綢繆（2907）In fair weather prepare for foul.

1190 **積勞而死** jī láo ér sǐ

Accumulated fatigue causes death. (lit.)

Burn oneself out.

Crack up through overwork.

1191 **積善多福** jī shàn duō fú

Accumulated good deeds (lead to) more blessings. (lit.)

A good deed is never lost.

Give much to the poor doth increase a man's store.

反 多行不義必自斃（0705）Ill-gotten gains seldom prosper.

1192 **積善之家，必有餘慶**

jī shàn zhī jiā, bì yǒu yú qìng

A family with accumulated good deeds must have plenty of blessings. (lit.)

Kindnesses, like grain, increase by sowing.

Virtue and happiness are mother and daughter.

同 善有善報（2346）Sow good work and thou shalt reap gladness.

反 多行不義必自斃（0705）Ill-gotten gains seldom prosper.

源 周易：“積善之家，必有餘慶，積不善之家，必有餘殃。”

積少成多 jī shǎo chéng duō 1193

Accumulating little by little becomes plenty. (lit.)

Every little helps.

Many a little makes a mickle.

Many a mickle makes a muckle.

Penny and penny laid up will be many.

Little and often fills the purse.

同 集腋成裘（1225）Little by little the bird builds its nest.

反 坐食山空（4056）Always taking out of a meal tub, and never putting in, soon comes to the bottom.

源 漢書．董仲舒傳：“聚少成多，積小致巨。”

積重難返 jī zhòng nán fǎn 1194

Accumulated weight is difficult to return (to its original shape.) (lit.)

To be too far gone.

Deeply rooted.

同 難以收拾（1881）All the fat is in the fire.

源 顧炎武．日知錄：“是則民間之田一入於官，而一畝之糧化而為十四畝矣。此固其積重難返之勢。”

擊中要害 jī zhòng yào hài 1195

Hit and cause fatal injury. (lit.)

Hit one where it hurts.

飢不擇食 jī bù zé shí 1196

Too hungry to pick and choose food. (lit.)

Hunger finds no fault with the cookery.

Nothing comes amiss to a hungry man.

Nothing comes wrong to the hungry.

All's good in a famine.

Beggars should not be choosers.

Hunger is the best sauce.

同 寒不擇衣（1015）Any port in a storm.

反 挑三揀四（2744）Pick and choose.

源 水滸傳：“自古有幾般，飢不擇食，寒不擇衣，慌不擇路，貧不擇妻。”

飢腸轆轆 jī cháng lù lù 1197

Starved intestines rumbling.

Have a wolf in the stomach.

As hungry as a hunter (wolf, hawk).

Empty as an old drum.

My belly thinks my throat cut.

同 腹如雷鳴（0850）Empty as an old drum.

飢者易為食 jī zhě yì wéi shí 1198

Hungry man reacts easily to any food. (lit.)

Hungry dogs would eat dirty puddings.

Hunger is the best sauce.

Carry off meat from the graves.

The first dish pleases all.

反 挑三揀四（2744）Pick and choose.

源 孟子：“飢者易為食，渴者易為飲。”

1199 **雞蛋碰石頭** jī dàn pèng shí tóu

Chicken eggs strike the stones. (lit.)

Whether the pitcher strikes the stone, or the stone the pitcher, it is bad for the pitcher.

同 螳臂擋車（2689）Kick against the pricks.

1200 **雞鳴即起** jī míng jí qǐ

To rise immediately with the crow of cocks. (lit.)

To be up with the lark.

反 日上三竿猶未起（2257）A sluggard makes his night till noon.

1201 **雞犬之聲相聞**

jī quǎn zhī shēng xiāng wén

The noise of the chickens and dogs can be heard. (lit.)

Within earshot (hearing).

Within call (calling distance).

同 近在咫尺（1364）Just round the corner.

反 相去十萬八千里（3111）As wide as the poles asunder.

源 老子："鄰國相望，雞犬之聲相聞，民至老死不相往來。"

1202 **雞犬之聲相聞，而老死不相往來**

jī quǎn zhī shēng xiāng wén, ér lǎo sǐ bù xiāng wǎng lái

The noise of fowls and dogs is both heard but the ages till death do not come and go to each other. (lit.)

Half the world knows not how the other half lives.

同 各人自掃門前雪（0904）Sweep before your own door.

反 串門（0438）Go jagging.

1203 **雞腿打來牙鉸軟** jī tuǐ dǎ lái yá jiǎo ruǎn

Beating one with a chicken leg will make his jaw soft. (lit.)

A dog will not howl if you beat him with a bone.

Spread the table and contention will cease.

1204 **及時行樂** jí shí xíng lè

At right time, to have pleasure. (lit.)

In frolics dispose your pounds, shillings and pence, for we shall be nothing a hundred years hence.

There will be sleeping enough in the grave.

同 今朝有酒今朝醉（1339）Let us eat and drink, for tomorrow we shall die.

源 漢樂府 · 西門行："夫為樂，為樂當及時。"

及時雨 jí shí yǔ 1205

Rain at right time. (lit.)

A friend in need.

He gives twice who gives quickly (in a trice).

汲深綆短 jí shēn gěng duǎn 1206

The well is deep and the rope is short. (lit.)

Beyond one's tether.

同 心有餘而力不足（3195）The spirit is willing, but the flesh is weak.

源 淮南子："短綆不可以汲深，器小不可以盛大，非其任也。"

吉人天相 jí rén tiān xiàng 1207

Heaven protects the good man. (lit.)

One's star is in the ascendant.

Bear (Have) a charmed life.

同 走運（4032）Hit the jackpot.

源 方回·詩："釋怒思須報，天終相吉人。"

急不可待 jí bù kě dài 1208

Too urgent to wait. (lit.)

Eat the calf in the cow's belly.

Leap over the hedge before one comes to the stile.

To be bursting to do something.

To be on edge.

同 急如星火（1213）In hot haste.

反 從容不迫（0457）Take things easy.

急不暇擇 jí bù xiá zé 1209

In emergency there is no time to choose. (lit.)

Any port in a storm.

Necessity has no law.

A drowning man will catch a straw.

同 飢不擇食（1196）Hunger finds no fault with the cookery.

反 挑三揀四（2744）Pick and choose.

急功近利 jí gōng jìn lì 1210

Quick success and near profit. (lit.)

Better an egg today than a hen tomorrow.

Better keep now than seek anon.

A bird in hand is worth two in the bush.

One today is worth two tomorrow.

1211 **急流勇退** jí liú yǒng tuì

To retreat bravely from the rapid current. (lit.)

Leave off while the play is good.

A brave retreat is a brave exploit.

反 硬着頭皮幹到底（3603）Face it out.

源 蘇軾詩：“勇退當年正急流。”

1212 **急起直追** jí qǐ zhí zhuī

Rise quickly and chase straightly. (lit.)

To catch up with

Make up for leeway.

Jump on the bandwagon.

同 緊跟（1351）Keep up with

反 裹足不前（0993）At a standstill.

1213 **急如星火** jí rú xīng huǒ

As urgent as (falling) star and fire. (lit.)

In hot haste.

Of great urgency.

同 十萬火急（2462）S O S

反 慢條斯理（1755）As slow as molasses in winter.

源 李密．陳情表：“州司臨門，急於星火。”

1214 **急如雨下** jí rú yǔ xià

As fast as falling rain. (lit.)

Thick and fast.

同 紛至沓來（0791）As thick as hail.

反 細水長流（3062）A bit at a time.

1215 **急時抱佛腳** jí shí bào fó jiǎo

Holding Buddha's feet in urgency. (lit.)

The danger past and God forgotten.

源 劉攽．劉貢父詩話：“王丞相好嘲謔，嘗曰，老欲依僧。客對曰，急則抱佛腳耳。”

1216 **急行軍** jí xíng jūn

Quick movement of army. (lit.)

A forced march.

反 原地踏步 Mark time.

1217 **急中生智** jí zhōng shēng zhì

Emergency produces wits. (lit.)

Necessity is the mother of invention.

In a flash of inspiration.

同 心生一計（3190）Hit upon an idea.

反 無計可施（2968）Up the creek without a paddle.

1218 **即席發言** jí xí fā yán

Speaking from his seat (in a meeting). (lit.)

Speak off the cuff.

Speak impromptu (extempore).

疾風知勁草 jí fēng zhī jìng cǎo 1219
The swift wind reveals sturdy grass. (lit.)
Oaks may fall when reeds stand the storm.
The good seaman is known in bad weather.

同 路遙知馬力（1702）A good seaman is known in bad weather.
源 宋書："故疾風知勁草，嚴霜知貞木。"

疾風知勁草，患難見交情 1220
jí fēng zhī jìng cǎo, huàn nàn jiàn jiāo qíng
The swift wind reveals sturdy grass, and in calamity one sees true feelings. (lit.)
Calamity is man's true touchstone.

源 唐太宗詩："疾風知勁草，板盪識誠臣。"

疾如飛矢 jí rú fēi shǐ 1221
As fast as a flying arrow. (lit.)
As swift as an arrow.
As fleet as (a) deer.
To be off like a shot.

同 兔起鶻落（2812）Like a shot.
反 蝸牛上樹（2935）At a snail's pace.
源 淮南子："疾如錐矢。"

極力討好 jí lì tǎo hǎo 1222
With greatest effort to please. (lit.)
Throw oneself at someone's head.
Lick one's boots.

同 拍馬屁（1940）Eat one's toads.
反 拂逆人意（0824）Stroke one up.

極一時之盛 jí yī shí zhī shèng 1223
Flourish extremely at a time. (lit.)
To be in full flourish.

同 盛極一時（2432）To be all the rage.

集思廣益 jí sī guǎng yì 1224
Collecting ideas to broaden benefits.
Lay our heads together.
Two heads are better than one.
In the multitude of counsellors there is safety.

同 一人計短，二人計長（3447）Four eyes see more than two.
反 獨斷獨行（0677）Take the law into one's own hand.
源 諸葛丞相集："夫參署者，集眾思廣忠益也。"

集腋成裘 jí yè chéng qiú 1225
Gathering little bits of fur (from under forelegs of foxes) to make a fur coat. (lit.)
Many a mickle makes a muckle.
Little by little the bird builds its nest.
Little and often fills the purse.

同 涓滴成河（1450）Every little helps.
源 慎子·知忠："狐白之裘，非一腋之皮也。"

1226 **己所不欲，勿施於人**
jǐ suǒ bú yù, wù shī yú rén
What one does not want for himself must not give to others. (lit.)
Do as you would be done by.
Do not do unto others as you do not like them to do to you.

源 論語．顏淵："其恕乎，己所不欲，勿施於人。"

1227 **擠作一團** jǐ zuò yì tuán
Press into a crowd. (lit.)
Packed like sardines.
Like sardines in a tin.
Like herrings in a barrel.
Jammed together.

反 稀稀落落（3046）Few and far between.

1228 **技藝超倫** jì yì chāo lún
Technique and arts beyond comparison. (lit.)
Able to kick the eye out of a mosquito.

1229 **技止此耳** jì zhǐ cǐ ěr
The skills stop here. (lit.)
At the end of one's tether.
All his goods in the window.

同 黔驢技窮（2085）At the end of one's rope.
反 多才多藝（0694）A man of many gifts
源 柳宗元．黔之驢："驢不勝怒，蹄之，虎因喜，計曰，技止此耳。"

1230 **記了一功** jì le yì gōng
Record a credit. (lit.)
A feather in one's cap.

1231 **記憶猶新** jì yì yóu xīn
Memory still fresh. (lit.)
Fresh in the memory.

同 言猶在耳（3311）Still ring in one's ears.

1232 **既得利益** jì dé lì yì
Since benefit is obtained. (lit.) (meaning the interest already got.)
Vested interest.

既來之，則安之 jì lái zhī, zé ān zhī 1233

Since it comes, let it settle. (lit.)

Take things as they come.

Take things as you find them.

Take the world as it is.

同 隨遇而安（2659）Take what comes and be contented.

反 忐忑不安（2684）Like a hen on a hot griddle.

既往不咎 jì wǎng bú jiù 1234

What is past is not condemned. (lit.)

Let bygones be bygones.

Let the dead bury the dead.

Forgive and forget.

同 不念舊惡（0235）Bury the hatchet.

反 翻老賬（0739）Rake out old grievances.

源 論語．八佾："成事不說，遂事不諫，既往不咎。"

既在矮檐下，怎敢不低頭 1235

jì zài ǎi yán xià, zěn gǎn bù dī tóu

Since staying under the low eaves, how dare not to lower the head. (lit.)

He must stoop that hath a low door.

Everyone bows to the bush that shelters him.

When you bow, bow low.

同 俯首就範（0832）Give one's head for the washing.

反 至死不屈（3890）Die game.

寄人籬下 jì rén lí xià 1236

To stay dependently by someone's fence. (meaning living in someone's house). (lit.)

To eat out of one's hand.

反 自食其力（3994）Shift for oneself.

源 南史．張融傳："大丈夫當刪詩書，制禮樂，何至因循寄人籬下。"

濟弱扶傾 jì ruò fú qīng 1237

To aid the weak and uphold the fallen. (lit.)

Help a lame dog over a stile.

同 扶危濟困（0822）Be a good Samaritan.

覬覦已久 jì yú yǐ jiǔ 1238

Greedily hoping already for a long time. (lit.)

To have a mind for it.

Cast greedy eyes on

同 虎視眈眈（1092）As watchful as a hawk.

1239 **繼續不斷** jì xù bú duàn
Continue without a break. (lit.)
Without a break.
On and on.
Keep it up.
For ever more.
Keep the ball rolling.

同 晝夜不息（3930）Round the clock.
反 半途而廢（0072）Do things by halves.

1240 **加把勁** jiā bǎ jìn
Add extra-effort. (lit.)
Put one's shoulder to the wheel.
Pull one's socks up.
Put one's best foot forward.

反 磨洋工（1846）Lie on one's oars.

1241 **加官晉爵** jiā guān jìn jué
Promoted in rank and advanced in peerage. (lit.)
Win laurels.
A feather in one's cap.

反 掛冠歸里（0959）To go to grass.

1242 **加緊督促** jiā jǐn dū cù
Add extra-speed to push. (lit.)
Put the screws on one.

反 放任自流（0761）Let things slide.

1243 **加快速度** jiā kuài sù dù
To accelerate the speed. (lit.)
Step on the gas.

反 不慌不忙（0201）Take one's time.

1244 **加鹽加醋** jiā yán jiā cù
Add salt, add vinegar. (lit.)
Give colour to the matter.
Tell with unction.
The tale runs as it pleases the teller.
A tale never loses in the telling.

同 大事渲染（0551）To make much of

1245 **加油幹** jiā yóu gàn
Add fuel to work. (lit.)
Buck up!
They are far behind that may not follow.
Go it.

同 加把勁（1240）Pull one's socks up.

夾道歡迎 jiā dào huān yíng 1246
Lining the street to welcome. (lit.)
Roll out the red carpet for

同 隆重接待（1689）Give royal reception.
反 餉以閉門羹（3117）Sport one's oak.

家財萬貫 jiā cái wàn guàn 1247
Family's wealth amounts to tens of thousand. (lit.)
Have money to burn.

同 鄧通銅山（0631）As rich as Croesus.
反 囊空如洗（1885）Dead broke.

家常便飯 jiā cháng biàn fàn 1248
An ordinary family meal (of rice). (lit.)
A common practice.
Potluck.
Order of the day.
Homely fare.

同 粗茶淡飯（0470）Simple fare.
反 食前方丈（2468）Eat high on the hog.
源 獨醒雜志："常調官好做，家常便飯好喫。"

家醜不可外揚 jiā chǒu bù kě wài yáng 1249
The family disgrace cannot be waved about outside. (lit.)
Wash your dirty linen at home.
It's an ill bird that fouls its own nest.

家醜外揚 jiā chǒu wài yáng 1250
The family disgrace is waved outside. (lit.)
Drag the family skeleton out of the cupboard.
Wash one's dirty linen in public.
Cry stinking fish.

家道小康 jiā dào xiǎo kāng 1251
Family's means is a little well off. (lit.)
To be well-off.
Well-to-do.
To be comfortably off.
On easy street.

家道中落 jiā dào zhōng luò 1252
Family's means is declining. (lit.)
Have seen better days.
To be worse off.

反 發家致富（0734）Make one's pile.

1253 **家室之累** jiā shì zhī lèi

Family burden. (lit.)

Wedlock is padlock.

同 一身兒女債，半世老婆奴（3451）Wife and children are bills of charges.

1254 **家徒四壁** jiā tú sì bì

The family possesses mere four walls. (lit.)

There is not a stick of furniture around.

As poor as a church mouse.

同 一無所有（3474）Not a shirt to one's name.

反 家財萬貫（1247）Have money to burn.

源 漢書 · 司馬相如傳："文君夜亡奔相如，相如與馳歸成都，家徒四壁立。"

1255 **家喻戶曉** jiā yù hù xiǎo

Known to every family and house. (lit.)

Pass from mouth to mouth.

On everyone's lips.

Common knowledge.

To be a household word.

To be in everyone's mouth.

Every barber knows that.

The talk of the town.

同 膾炙人口（1528）Enjoy great popularity.

源 宣和畫譜："不出九重深邃之地，使四方萬里朝令夕行，豈家至而戶曉也哉。"

1256 **假公濟私** jiǎ gōng jì sī

In the name of the public to serve one's private purpose. (lit.)

Practise jobbery.

Abuse one's power.

同 飽慳私囊（0084）Line one's pocket.

源 元曲選 · 陳州糶米："他假公濟私，我怎肯和他干罷了也呵。"

1257 **假仁假義** jiǎ rén jiǎ yì

Pretend to be kind and righteous. (lit.)

An idle compliment.

Crocodile tears.

A wolf in sheep's clothing.

Shed crocodile tears.

Carrion crows bewail the dead sheep and then eat them.

同 口蜜腹劍（1506）A honey tongue, a heart of gall.

1258 **假手於人** jiǎ shǒu yú rén

To put a job into the hand of another. (lit.)

Make a cat's paw of someone.

Take the chestnuts out of the fire with the cat's paw.

反 親力親為（2106）If you want a thing done well, do it yourself.

源 左傳："假手於我寡人。"

架子十足 jià zǐ shí zú 1259

The frame in full ten (100%). (lit.)

Wear a high hat.

Have too much side (air).

Throw one's weight about.

Fly at higher game.

同 擺臭架子（0064）Cock one's chest like a half-pay admiral.

反 平易近人（1994）Easy to get along with.

嫁禍於人 jià huò yú rén 1260

To shift one's evil to another. (lit.)

Put the blame on someone.

Lay a fault at a person's door.

反 代人受過（0571）To carry the can.

源 史記·趙世家："韓氏所以不入於秦者，欲嫁禍於趙也。"

駕輕就熟 jià qīng jiù shú 1261

Take a light carriage on a familiar road. (lit.)

An old hand at the game.

Know the ropes.

An old ox makes a straight furrow.

同 老馬識途（1570）An old dog for a hard road.

源 韓愈文："若駟馬，駕輕車，就熟路。"

兼聽則明 jiān tīng zé míng 1262

Hear two sides and then understand. (lit.)

Hear all parties.

源 王符·潛夫論·明暗："君之所以明者兼聽也，其所以暗者，偏信也。"

兼職過多 jiān zhí guò duō 1263

Take too many jobs. (lit.)

Have too many irons in the fire.

同 忙不過來（1758）Have too much on one's plate.

反 無官一身輕（2963）Out of office, out of danger.

堅持不懈 jiān chí bú xiè 1264

Persevere in one's effort untiringly. (lit.)

Peg away at it.

同 始終不渝（2483）Keep it up.

堅持到底 jiān chí dào dǐ 1265

Firmly persevere to the end. (lit.)

Hold out.

Stick it out.

Go through with it.

To the bitter end.

同 貫徹始終（0977）Such beginning, such end.

反 半途而廢（0072）Do things by halves.

1266 **堅持原則** jiān chí yuán zé
Firmly hold the principles. (lit.)
Stick to one's guns.

1267 **堅持原則，講究方法**
jiān chí yuán zé, jiǎng jiū fāng fǎ
Firmly holding the principles, and being critical in the method. (lit.)
Strong in action, gentle in method.
An iron hand in a velvet glove.

1268 **堅決不改** jiān jué bù gǎi
Decided not to change. (lit.)
To sit tight.

反 改過自新（0853）Turn over a new leaf.

1269 **堅韌不拔** jiān rèn bù bá
Firm, tough and not be uprooted. (lit.)
Get at it hammer and tongs.
With might and main.
Brave it out.

同 不屈不撓（0243）Firm and unyielding.
反 知難而退（3856）To back out.

1270 **堅守陣地** jiān shǒu zhèn dì
Firmly hold the field and ground. (lit.)
Hold the field.
Hold one's ground.
Hold the fort.

反 棄甲曳兵而走（2049）Beat a hasty retreat.

1271 **監守自盜** jiān shǒu zì dào
Prison warders themselves steal. (lit.)
The friar preached against stealing and had a goose in his sleeve.

反 以身作則（3538）Practise what you preach.

1272 **艱苦樸素** jiān kǔ pǔ sù
Hardship and plain life. (lit.)
To hog it.

同 自奉甚薄（3977）Live on simple fare.
反 窮奢極欲（2139）Live on the fat of the land.

1273 **剪除羽翼** jiǎn chú yǔ yì
Cut and eliminate the feathers and wings. (lit.)
Clip someone's wings.

揀了芝麻，丟了西瓜 1274

jiǎn le zhī má, diū le xī guā

Pick up the sesame but throw away the water melon. (lit.)

Spare at the spigot and spill at the bung.

Penny wise and pound foolish.

同 捨本逐末（2371）Kill the goose that lay the golden eggs.

反 從大處着眼（0460）Have an eye to the main chance.

簡單明瞭 jiǎn dān míng liáo 1275

Simple and understandable. (lit.)

In words of one syllable.

反 錯綜複雜（0485）There are wheels within wheels.

簡而言之 jiǎn ér yán zhī 1276

Briefly speaking. (lit.)

To make a long story short.

In a nutshell.

It boils down to this.

In short.

同 質而言之（3906）The long and the short of it.

反 詳情細節（3114）The ins and outs.

見機行事 jiàn jī xíng shì 1277

Seeing the chance one acts. (lit.)

Make hay while the sun shines.

Play it by ear.

Opportunity seldom knocks twice.

同 隨機應變（2655）Cut your coat according to your cloth.

反 坐失良機（4055）Miss the boat.

源 周易：“幾者動之微，吉之先見者也，君子見幾而作，不俟終日。”

見利忘義 jiàn lì wàng yì 1278

Seeing profit, forget the moral principles. (lit.)

Double cross one for money.

Honour and profit lie not in one sack.

Two dogs over one bone seldom agree.

源 漢書：“夫賣友者，謂見利而忘義也。”

見事莫說，問事不知 1279

jiàn shì mò shuō, wèn shì bù zhī

Not say about seeing things happening, when asked about them, not know. (lit.)

Keep your mouth shut and your eyes open.

Hear and see and be still.

No wisdom like silence.

1280 見死不救 jiàn sǐ bú jiù

Seeing someone dying, not rescue (save) him. (lit.)

Leave one in the lurch.

反 起死回生（2041）To bring one to.

1281 見微知著 jiàn wēi zhī zhù

Seeing the small things, one knows the important features. (lit.)

A straw will show which way the wind blows.

同 管中窺豹（0976）You may know by a handful of the whole sack.

反 只見樹木，不見森林（3877）One can't see the wood for the trees.

源 白虎通義 · 性情節：“不惑於事，見微而知著也。”

1282 見異思遷 jiàn yì sī qiān

Seeing the difference, wish to change. (lit.)

Grass is always greener on the other side of the fence (hill).

A rolling stone.

反 固步自封（0945）He that stays in the valley shall never get over the hill.

源 國語 · 齊語：“少而習焉，其心安焉，不見異物而思遷焉。”

1283 見義勇為 jiàn yì yǒng wéi

Seeing the righteousness one acts bravely. (lit.)

Help a lame dog over a stile.

Do a good turn.

Be a good Samaritan.

Take heart of grace to

反 見死不救（1280）Leave one in the lurch.

源 論語 · 為政：“見義不為，是無勇也。”

1284 間不容髮 jiàn bù róng fà

The gap cannot hold a hair. (lit.)

By a hair's breadth.

Within an ace.

源 説苑：“其出不出，間不容髮。”

1285 僭隊 jiàn duì

Usurp the queue. (lit.)

Jump the queue.

1286 賤價而沽 jiàn jià ér gū

To sell at cheap price. (lit.)

Go for a song.

反 漫天要價（1757）Quote sky-rocket prices.

賤肉橫生 jiàn ròu héng shēng 1287
Cheap flesh grows broadly. (lit.)
Fall away from a horse-load to a cart-load.

賤如糞土 jiàn rú fèn tǔ 1288
As cheap as manure and earth. (lit.)
As cheap as dirt.

同 分文不值（0790）Not worth a rap.
反 掌上明珠（3798）The apple of one's eye.

劍拔弩張 jiàn bá nǔ zhāng 1289
With swords drawn and bows stretched. (lit.)
At daggers drawn.
To be at sword's points with each other.

同 摩拳擦掌（1845）Roll up one's sleeves.
反 和平共處（1049）Peaceful co-existence.
源 豐道生・賦："弩張劍拔，虎跳龍蟠。"

劍及屨及 jiàn jí jù jí 1290
Where the sword reaches, the boot reaches it. (lit.)
If you want a thing done well, do it yourself.

同 事必躬親（2506）Better do it than wish it done.
反 假手於人（1258）Make a cat's paw of someone.
源 左傳・宣十四年："楚子聞之，投袂而起，屨及於窒息，劍及於寢門之外，車及於蒲胥之市。"

鑒往知來 jiàn wǎng zhī lái 1291
Reviewing the past, one knows the future. (lit.)
Coming events cast their shadows before.
He that would know what shall be must consider what has been.

同 前事不忘，後事之師（2080）Today is yesterday's pupil.

江河日下 jiāng hé rì xià 1292
The river daily decrease their flow. (lit.)
Go from bad to worse.
Go down drain.
Get worse and worse.

同 每況愈下（1778）Out of the frying pan into the fire.
反 蒸蒸日上（3837）Grow with each passing day.
源 王士禎："至於漢魏樂府古選之遺音，蕩然無復存者，江河日下，滔滔不及。"

江郎才盡 jiāng láng cái jìn 1293
Jiang's talent is exhausted. (lit.)
At the end of one's tether.
At one's wit's end.

同 智窮才盡（3896）At the end of one's rope.
反 滿腹妙計（1742）To be full of wrinkles.

1294 **江山易改，本性難移**

jiāng shān yì gǎi, běn xìng nán yí

It's easier to change rivers and mountains than to change a person's character. (lit.)

What is bred in the bone will never come out of the flesh.

You cannot make a crab walk straight.

The child is father to the man.

The fox changes his skin but not his habits.

The leopard can't change its spots.

A crow is never the whiter for washing herself often.

Bred in the bone.

同 萬變不離其宗（2845）Once a knave and always a knave.

1295 **姜太公釣魚，願者上鈎**

jiāng tài gōng diào yú, yuàn zhě shàng gōu

The grand old man, Jiang, fishing, those who are willing will get hooked. (lit.)

If fools went not to the market, bad wares would not be sold.

The fish follow the bait.

Bite the hook.

1296 **將錯就錯** jiāng cuò jiù cuò

Let a mistake be a mistake. (lit.)

Make the best of a bad bargain.

Over shoes, over boots.

反 過則勿憚改（1004）It is never too late to mend.

源 釋普濟 · 五燈會元：“將錯就錯，西方極樂。”

1297 **將計就計** jiāng jì jiù jì

Let a plan as the plan. (lit.)

Turn to advantage an enemy's plot.

Beat someone at his own game.

Give Rowland for an Oliver.

同 請君入甕（2135）Give a person his own medicine.

1298 **將信將疑** jiāng xìn jiāng yí

Hesitating between doubt and belief. (lit.)

To be half in doubt.

Take with a grain of salt.

同 姑妄聽之（0931）Take the story for what it is worth.

反 深信不疑（2400）Feel it in one's bones.

源 李華 · 吊古戰場文：“人或有言，將信將疑。”

將欲取之，必先與之 1299
jiāng yù qǔ zhī, bì xiān yǔ zhī
In order to take it, one must first give something. (lit.)
Give one line enough.

同 欲擒先縱（3717）Give a thief enough rope and he'll hang himeself.
源 戰國策 · 魏策引周書：“將欲取之，必姑與之。”

將相頭上堪走馬，公侯肚裏好撐船 jiàng xiàng tóu shàng kān zǒu mǎ, gōng hóu dù lǐ hǎo chēng chuán 1300
One can run a horse on the head of a general or a prime minister, and to punt a boat on the belly of a duke or a marquis. (lit.)
Great gifts are from great men.
To take in good part.

反 心胸狹隘（3191）To be narrow-minded.

交班 jiāo bān 1301
Change shifts. (lit.)
Hand on the torch.

反 接班 Step into someone's shoes.

交流經驗 jiāo liú jīng yàn 1302
To exchange experiences. (lit.)
Compare notes.

交淺言深 jiāo qiǎn yán shēn 1303
Have deep (heart) talk with a slight acquaintance. (lit.)
Wear one's heart on one's sleeve.

同 一見如故（3403）Be hail-and-well-met with
源 後漢書：“交淺言深者，愚也。”

交頭接耳 jiāo tóu jiē ěr 1304
Join heads and whisper in each other's ears. (lit.)
To bill and coo.
Head to head.
Have a tête à tête with

源 水滸傳：“他那三四個交頭接耳說話。”

1305 交友滿天下，知心有幾人
jiāo yǒu mǎn tiān xià, zhī xīn yǒu jǐ rén
Friends made over the world, how many know one's heart. (lit.)
There is a scarcity of friendship, but not of friends.
Have but few friends, though many acquaintances.
Many kinsfolk and few friends.

1306 嬌生慣養 jiāo shēng guàn yǎng
Born in a well off family with soft upbringing. (lit.)
Nursed in cotton.
Born with a silver spoon in one's mouth.

同 養尊處優（3341）Lie on a bed of roses.
反 牛馬生活（1921）Lead a dog's life.

1307 驕兵必敗 jiāo bīng bì bài
Proud troops will certainly be defeated. (lit.)
Pride will have a fall.
Pride goes before, and shame follows after.

源 漢書："恃國家之大，矜人庶之眾，欲見威於敵者，謂之驕兵，兵驕者滅。"

1308 狡兔三窟 jiǎo tù sān kū
A cunning hare has three exits (to its burrow). (lit.)
A mouse that has but one hole is quickly taken.
Cunning as a fox.
A cat has nine lives.

源 戰國策・齊策："狡兔有三窟，僅得免其死耳。"

1309 狡兔死，走狗烹
jiǎo tù sǐ, zǒu gǒu pēng
(After) the cunning hare is killed, the running dog is to be cooked. (lit.)
Kick down the ladder.

同 飛鳥盡，良弓藏（0773）Once on shore, we pray no more.
源 史記・越世家："飛鳥盡，良弓藏，狡兔死，走狗烹。"

腳踏實地 jiǎo tà shí dì 1310

The feet stand on firm ground. (lit.)

Come down to bedrock.

Get down to brass tacks.

To be on firm ground.

同 務實（3040）Come down to earth.

反 好高騖遠（1042）Gaze at the moon and fall into the gutter.

源 宋史・劉甲傳：“甲嘗謂吾無他長，惟腳踏實地。”

絞盡腦汁 jiǎo jìn nǎo zhī 1311

Exhausted the juice of the brain. (lit.)

To rack one's brain.

Cudgel (rack) one's brain.

同 搜索枯腸（2646）Beat one's brain out.

反 飽食終日，無所用心（0085）A belly full of gluttony will never study willingly.

矯若游龍 jiǎo ruò yóu lóng 1312

As nimble as a floating dragon. (lit.)

As nimble as a squirrel.

同 生龍活虎（2415）Alive and kicking.

反 呆若木雞（0569）To be rooted to the spot.

教學相長 jiào xué xiāng zhǎng 1313

Teaching and learning grow together. (lit.)

Teaching others teaches one's self.

源 禮記・學記：“學然後知不足，教然後知困。知不足然後能自反也，知困然後能自強也，故曰教學相長也。”

接二連三 jiē èr lián sān 1314

Join the second and connect with the third. (lit.)

One after another.

In rapid succession.

同 紛至沓來（0791）Thick and fast.

接踵而至 jiē zhǒng ér zhì 1315

Following heels to arrive. (lit.)

Tread on the heels of

同 緊跟（1351）Follow hard after

反 姍姍來遲（2337）Arrive in an armchair.

源 戰國策・齊策：“若隨踵而至也，今子一朝而見七士，則士不亦眾乎。”

街談巷議 jiē tán xiàng yì 1316

Street talk and lane discussions. (lit.)

Wayside inn gossip.

The talk of the town.

同 道聽途説（0607）Hear something over the grapevine.

反 權威人士透露（2167）Straight from the horse's mouth.

源 漢書・藝文志：“小説家者流，蓋出於稗官，街談巷語，道聽途説者之所造也。”

揭穿內幕 jiē chuān nèi mù 1317

Uncover the inner curtain. (lit.)

Give the show away.

同 拆穿西洋鏡（0322）Take the mickey out of it.

1318 **結實耐用** jiē shí nài yòng
Tough and long-lasting. (lit.)
Things well fitted abide.

1319 **劫富濟貧** jié fù jì pín
Rob the rich and give to the poor. (lit.)
Steal the goose and give the giblets in alms.

1320 **劫數難逃** jié shù nán táo
Ill fate is difficult to escape. (lit.)
What must be must be.
No flying from fate.

反 化險為夷（1116）Fall on one's feet.

1321 **捷足先登** jié zú xiān dēng
Fast feet reach first. (lit.)
Beat someone to it.
Beat someone to the draw.

同 先到為君，後到為臣（3076）He that comes first to the hill may sit where he will.
反 姍姍來遲（2337）Arrive in an armchair.
源 史記："蒯通曰，秦失其鹿，天下共逐之，高材捷足者先得焉。"

1322 **結交須勝己，似我不如無**
jié jiāo xū shèng jǐ, sì wǒ bù rú wú
Friends made should be better than oneself, like oneself rather not to have. (lit.)
Keep good men company and you shall be of the number.

1323 **結結巴巴** jié jié bā bā
This is a phrase equivalent to "stuttering and muttering". (lit.)
Have stones in one's mouth.
Have a peppermint in one's speech.

同 期期艾艾（2032）Hem and haw.
反 滔滔不絕（2692）Talk nine words at once.

1324 **結局大團圓** jié jú dà tuán yuán
The ending is a big re-union. (lit.)
All is well that ends well.
All shall be well, Jack shall have Jill.

1325

節省開支 jié shěng kāi zhī

Cut down expenses. (lit.)

Pull (draw) in one's horns.

同 省吃儉用（2430）Pinch and scrape.

反 鋪張浪費（2011）Butter one's bread on both sides.

1326

節外生枝 jié wài shēng zhī

New branches arising from the nodes. (lit.)

Fly off at a tangent.

An off-shoot.

Hit a snag.

同 跑野馬（1956）To start a hare.

反 言歸正傳（3302）Return to our muttons.

源 朱熹．朱子語錄：“隨語生解，節上生枝，更讀萬卷書，亦無用處也。”

1327

節衣縮食 jié yī suō shí

To save clothing and reduce food. (lit.)

Pinch and scrape.

Trim one's sails.

To go on the skin.

Skin a flea for its hide.

Tighten one's belt.

Draw in one's horns.

同 勒緊褲帶（1585）Pull in one's belt.

反 大吃大喝（0508）To peg and quaff.

源 陸游詩：“節衣縮食勤耕桑。”

1328

竭盡全力 jié jìn quán lì

Exhaust one's full strength. (lit.)

Go all out.

Exert oneself to the utmost.

Strain every nerve.

Pull one's weight.

Do all in one's power.

Work one's fingers to the bone.

同 拼命幹（1982）To pound away.

反 磨洋工（1846）Lie on one's oars.

1329

竭盡所能 jié jìn suǒ néng

Exhaust one's ability. (lit.)

For all one is worth.

To the best of one's abilities.

With might and main.

Work up to the collar.

Lean over backwards.

同 有一分熱，發一分光（3677）Do one's utmost.

反 保留一手（0080）Reserve the master-blow.

源 禮記：“君子不盡人之歡，不竭人之忠。”

1330 竭澤而漁 jié zé ér yú
Drain dry the pool and catch the fish. (lit.)
Kill the goose that lays the golden eggs.
To exhaust the revenue.

源 呂氏春秋：“竭澤而漁，豈不獲得，而明年無魚。”

1331 潔身自好 jié shēn zì hào
Purify oneself for own good. (lit.)
Better be alone than in bad company.
Keep one's nose clean.

同 獨善其身（0680）Solitude is better than ill company.
反 隨波逐流（2653）Swim with the tide.

1332 解鈴還須繫鈴人
jiě líng hái xū jì líng rén
The one who unties the bells should be the one who has fastened them. (lit.)
It is better for the doer to undo what he has done.

源 指月錄：“法眼問眾，虎項金鈴，是誰解得，眾無對。清涼泰欽禪師適至，眼舉前語，曰，繫者解得。”

1333 介紹情況 jiè shào qíng kuàng
To introduce the situation. (lit.)
Put one in the picture.

1334 戒備森嚴 jiè bèi sēn yán
Under curfew and watch in a strict manner. (lit.)
Keep one's powder dry.

1335 借酒消愁 jiè jiǔ xiāo chóu
By means of wine to eliminate sad feelings. (lit.)
Drown one's sorrows (toubles).

1336 借債度日 jiè zhài dù rì
Pass the day by borrowing. (lit.)
Live on ticket.
Outrun the constable.
On the tick.
In the hole.
On the cuff.

今日之勞，勞於今日 1337
jīn rì zhī láo, láo yú jīn rì
To-day's work should be worked today. (lit.)
Never put off till tomorrow what may be done today.

同 勿失時機（3026）Take time by the forelock.
反 不急之務（0202）That can wait.

今夕吾軀歸故土，他朝君體也相同 jīn xī wú qū guī gù tǔ, tā zhāo jūn tǐ yě xiāng tóng 1338
Today my body returns to earth, other day your body would do the same. (lit.)
Death is the grand leveller.

今朝有酒今朝醉 1339
jīn zhāo yǒu jiǔ jīn zhāo zuì
Today have wine, today get drunk. (lit.)
Let us eat and drink, for tomorrow we shall die.
Better keep now than seek anon.

源 羅隱．自遣詩："今朝有酒今朝醉，明日愁來明日慮。"

斤斤計較 jīn jīn jì jiào 1340
Check the weight catty by catty. (lit.)
Look at both sides of a penny.
Strain at a gnat.
Skin a flint.

同 錙銖計較（3964）Chase eights and quarters.
反 滿不在乎（1740）Not to care a pin.

金睛火眼 jīn jīng huǒ yǎn 1341
Golden and fiery eye. (lit.)
Keep one's eyes skinned.
To be wide awake.
Lynx-eyed.

反 醉眼矇矓（4045）A sheet in the mind's eye.

金無赤金，人無完人 1342
jīn wú chì jīn, rén wú wán rén
There is no red gold, there is no perfect man. (lit.)
There are lees to every wine.
Every man has his faults.
Every bean has its black.
No wool is so white that a dyer cannot blacken it.

同 人非聖賢，孰能無過（2201）No one is without his faults.

1343 **金玉良言** jīn yù liáng yán

Gold, jade, and good words. (lit.)

Good advice is beyond price.

同 醍醐灌頂（2708）Give a person a rub of the thumb.

反 廢話（0779）Stuff and nonsense.

1344 **金玉其外** jīn yù qí wài

Gold and jade outwardly. (lit.)

To gild the pill.

On the surface only.

1345 **金玉其外，敗絮其中**

jīn yù qí wài, bài xù qí zhōng

Gold and jade outwardly but corrupted inwardly. (lit.)

A stuff shirt.

All that glitters is not gold.

Whited sepulchres, which indeed appear beautiful outward, but are within full of dead man's bones.

同 繡花枕頭Fair without and foul within.

源 劉基 · 誠意伯集 · 賣柑者言：“又何往而不金玉其外，敗絮其中也哉。”

1346 **津津樂道** jīn jīn lè dào

Talk with relish. (lit.)

To ride a hobby horse.

Everyone talks of what he loves.

反 不值一提（0283）Nothing to make a song about.

1347 **津津有味** jīn jīn yǒu wèi

Much juicy and tasty. (lit.)

Smack one's lips.

Lick one's chops.

With gusto (relish).

反 味同嚼蠟（2910）Dry as sawdust.

1348 **筋疲力竭** jīn pí lì jié

Muscles are weary and strength used up. (lit.)

To be worn (played, pumped) out.

To be dead beat.

More dead than alive.

Ready to drop.

The cord breaks at last by the weakest pull. (lit.)

Dead on one's feet.

Dog-tired.

Worn to a frazzle.

同 疲於奔命（1970）To be dead tired.

反 精力旺盛（1385）Full of beans.

僅以身免 jǐn yǐ shēn miǎn 1349
To escape with only one's body. (lit.)
Escape by the skin of one's teeth.

源 晉書・謝玄傳："難等相率北走，僅以身免。"

僅足糊口 jǐn zú hú kǒu 1350
Just enough to fill the mouth. (lit.)
Keep the wolf from the door.
Live within one's means.
Live from hand to mouth.

同 收支相抵（2545）Make both ends meet.
反 入不敷出（2284）Live above one's income.

緊跟 jǐn gēn 1351
Follow closely. (lit.)
Tread on the heels of
Follow hard after
Keep up with

同 亦步亦趨（3554）Dog one's steps.

緊急關頭 jǐn jí guān tóu 1352
Urgent and critical joint of events. (lit.)
In the thick of it.
Crucial juncture.
Critical moment.
When the chips are down.

錦標主義 jǐn biāo zhǔ yì 1353
Championism. (lit.)
Pot-hunting.

錦上添花 jǐn shàng tiān huā 1354
Add flowers to the embroidery. (lit.)
Gild the lily.
Put the tin hat on.
To crown all.

源 王安石詩："麗唱仍添錦上花。"

錦繡前程 jǐn xiù qián chéng 1355
Embroidered roads ahead. (lit.)
Have the ball before one.
With rosy prospects.
Glorious (Promising) future.

同 前程似錦（2073）Have a brilliant prospect.
反 窮途末路（2140）To be put to the pin of the collar.

1356 **錦衣美食** jǐn yī měi shí

Wear embroidered clothes and eat good food. (lit.)

Swim in luxury.

同 養尊處優（3341）Live in clover.
反 艱苦樸素（1272）To hog it.
源 宋史・李廌傳："廌雖山林，其文有錦衣玉食氣。"

1357 **謹訪扒手** jǐn fáng pá shǒu

Carefully prevent the pickpocket. (lit.)

Beware of pickpockets.

1358 **謹小慎微** jǐn xiǎo shèn wēi

Take care of small things. (lit.)

Dot one's i's and corss one's t's.

同 小心翼翼（3149）Mind one's P's and Q's.
反 大刀闊斧（0513）Go the whole hog.
源 荀子・大略："盡小者大，慎微者著。"

1359 **謹言慎行** jǐn yán shèn xíng

Careful in one's words and actions. (lit.)

Watch one's step.
Mind one's P's and Q's.
Say well, or be still.
Speak fitly, or be silent wisely.

同 小心戒慎（3148）Take heed is a good rede.
反 放蕩不羈（0757）Have one's fling.

1360 **近廚得食** jìn chú dé shí

Near the kitchen one gets (food) to eat. (lit.)

A baker's wife may bite of a bun, a brewer's wife may drink of a tun.

同 近官得力（1361）A friend in court makes the process short.

1361 **近官得力** jìn guān dé lì

Near the officials one gets strength (support). (lit.)

A friend in court makes the process short.

1362 **近水樓台先得月**

jìn shuǐ lóu tái xiān dé yuè

The pavilions near the water see the moon first. (lit.)

The parson always christens his own child first.

同 近廚得食（1360）A baker's wife may bite of a bun, a brewer's wife may drink of a tun.
反 遠水不救近火（3738）Water afar off quencheth not fire.
源 俞文豹・清夜錄："近水樓台先得月，向陽花木易為春。"

近在眼前 jìn zài yǎn qián 1363

Near in front of the eye. (lit.)

Right under one's nose.

同 近在咫尺（1364）Hard by.

反 鞭長莫及（0132）Out of reach.

近在咫尺 jìn zài zhǐ chǐ 1364

Hardly a foot near. (lit.)

Hard by.

Within calling distance.

Just round the corner.

Two whoops and a holler.

Near at hand.

反 天涯海角（2733）Ends of the earth.

源 蘇軾．杭州謝上表：“凜然威光，近在咫尺。”

近朱者赤，近墨者黑 1365

jìn zhū zhě chì, jìn mò zhě hēi

Contact with vermilion makes one red, with ink makes one black. (lit.)

Touch pitch, and you will be defiled.

He who lies down with dogs will rise with fleas.

Who keeps company with the wolf will learn to howl.

Keep not ill men company lest you increse the number.

同 染於蒼則蒼，染於黃則黃（2177）The finger that touches rouge will be red.

源 傅玄．太子少傅箴：“近朱者赤，近墨者黑。”

進退兩難 jìn tuì liǎng nán 1366

Go forward or retreat both difficult. (lit.)

In a dilemma.

Between the devil and the deep sea.

Get into a nice hobble.

同 進退維谷（1368）On the horns of a dilemma.

源 詩經：“人亦有言，進退維谷。”

進退失據 jìn tuì shī jù 1367

Both making an advance and retreat are difficult without a base. (lit.)

Between the devil and the deep sea.

1368 **進退維谷** jìn tuì wéi gǔ
One can's advance nor retreat in a dilemma. (lit.)
On the horns of a dilemma.
In a cleft stick.
In a scrape (fix).
Get into the hat.

同 前無去路，後有追兵（2082）Between the devil and the deep sea.
反 左右逢源（4050）It is good to have friends both in heaven and in hell.
源 詩經・大雅：“人亦有言，進退維谷。”

1369 **盡本份** jìn běn fèn
To do one's duty. (lit.)
Pull one's weight.
Do one's stint (whack).

反 推卸責任（2820）Pass the buck.

1370 **盡此一舉** jìn cǐ yì jǔ
All in this one move. (lit.)
Shoot one's bolt.

1371 **盡地主之誼** jìn dì zhǔ zhī yí
Give all the hospitality as the host of the place. (lit.)
Do the honours of the house.

同 作東道主（4064）Stand treat.
反 敬陪末座（1404）Sit below the salt.

1372 **儘管如此** jìn guǎn rú cǐ
In spite of all that. (lit.)
Be that as it may.
For all that.
In spite of
Nevertheless.

1373 **盡歡而散** jìn huān ér sàn
Disperse with full enjoyment. (lit.)
Merry meet, merry part.

源 南史：“盡歡共飲，迄暮而歸。”

1374 **盡善盡美** jìn shàn jìn měi
Most perfect and most beautiful. (lit.)
The pink of perfection.
Leaving nothing to be desired.
Tip-top.

同 十全十美（2461）All as it should be.
反 腐敗透頂（0835）Rotten to the core.
源 論語：“子謂韶，盡美矣，又盡善也。”

盡信書不如無書 1375
jìn xìn shū bù rú wú shū
Believing completely all books is not as good as no book. (lit.)
Better untaught than ill taught.

反 開卷有益（1470）A book that is shut is but a block.

盡忠職守 jìn zhōng zhí shǒu 1376
All one's loyalty to keep one's duty. (lit.)
When you are an anvil, hold you still; when you are a hammer, strike your fill.
Fulfil one's trust.
Do one's bit.
Keep up one's end.
Pull one's weight.

同 鞠躬盡瘁（1436）Burn oneself out.
反 開小差（1476）Desert one's colours.

噤若寒蟬 jìn ruò hán chán 1377
As quiet as a winter cicada. (lit.)
As close as wax.
Silent as the grave.
Mute as a fish.
Keep mum.

同 閉口不言（0119）Hold one's peace.
反 大發議論（0518）To enlarge one's self.
源 後漢書．杜密傳："劉勝位為大夫，見禮上賓，而知善不薦，聞惡無言，隱情惜己，自同寒蟬，此罪人也。"

經不起考驗 jīng bù qǐ kǎo yàn 1378
Can't stand the test. (lit.)
Weighed in the balance and found wanting.

反 經得起考驗（1379）To stand the test.

經得起考驗 jīng dé qǐ kǎo yàn 1379
Can stnad the test. (lit.)
Bear enquiry.
To stand the test.
Stand the gaff.

同 疾風知勁草（1219）Oaks may fall when reeds stand the storm.
反 經不起考驗（1378）Weighed in the balance and found wanting.

精兵簡政 jīng bīng jiǎn zhèng 1380
Better troops and simpler administration. (lit.)
Reduce to essentials.
I will keep no more cats than will catch mice.

反 人浮於事（2202）Too many cooks spoil the broth.

1381 **精彩之處** jīng cǎi zhī chù
The high lights of (lit.)
The beauty of it.

1382 **精誠團結** jīng chéng tuán jié
Unite with absolute sincerity. (lit.)
Hang (stick) together.
United as one.

反 四分五裂（2633）Fall apart.

1383 **精打細算** jīng dǎ xì suàn
Accurate and careful planning and calculating. (lit.)
Spare well and spend well.
Keep no more cats than will catch mice.
Take care of the pence and the pounds will take care of themselves.
Look at both sides of a penny.
Make every cent count.
On a shoestring.

同 該花就花，該省就省（0852）Spend not when you may save; spare not when you may spend.
反 鋪張浪費（2011）Butter one's bread on both sides.

1384 **精力充沛** jīng lì chōng pèi
Full of energy and strength. (lit.)
As strong as a horse.
Full of pep.

同 身壯力健（2395）Sound as a bell.
反 身心交困（2391）Burn the candle at both ends.

1385 **精力旺盛** jīng lì wàng shèng
Energy and strength are rich and abundant. (lit.)
As fit as a fiddle.
Full of beans.
Feel like a million.

反 筋疲力竭（1348）More dead than alive.

1386 **精明強幹** jīng míng qiáng gàn
Intelligent and capable. (lit.)
To be up to snuff.
There are no flies on him.
To be on the ball.

同 機靈果斷（1187）Have the presence of mind.
反 低能差勁（0632）Not worth one's salt.

精疲力竭 jīng pí lì jié 1387

Exhausted and strength used up. (lit.)

To be dead beat.
To be fagged (played) out.
Worn to a frazzle.
To be knocked up.
Ready to drop.

同 百舍重繭（0054）More dead than alive.
反 神采奕奕（2405）Full of pep.

精神飽滿 jīng shén bǎo mǎn 1388

Full of spirits. (lit.)

Full of vigour.
In full feather.

反 老油條（1578）A milk-sop.

精神不死 jīng shén bù sǐ 1389

One's spirit will not die. (lit.)

Absent in body, but present in spirit.
To be immortal.

同 永垂不朽（3612）Go down to posterity.

精神抖擻 jīng shén dǒu sǒu 1390

The spirit is being shaken up. (lit.)

Keep one's pecker up.
Get one's tail up.
Bestir oneself.

同 振作起來（3830）To brace up.
反 委靡不振（2903）In low spirits.
源 元曲選．單鞭奪槊：“你道是精神抖擻，又道是機謀通透。”

精神煥發 jīng shén huàn fā 1391

Spirit elated. (lit.)

As fresh as a daisy.

精神恍惚 jīng shén huǎng hū 1392

Spirit restless. (lit.)

Ill at ease.
One's mind wanders.

同 神不守舍（2404）Lose one's presence of mind.
反 全神貫注（2162）Focus one's attention on.

精神實質 jīng shén shí zhì 1393

The spirit and substance of. (lit.)

The long and the short of it.
The gist (essence) of it.
Not of the letter, but of the spirit.

1394 **精神奕奕** jīng shén yì yì

In great grand spirit. (lit.)

As fresh as paint.

In high spirits.

To be in the pink.

同 神采奕奕（2405）Fresh as a daisy.

反 沒精打采（1848）With the wind taken out of one's sails.

1395 **精神振奮** jīng shén zhèn fèn

The spirit is stimulated and excited. (lit.)

Keep up the spirits.

Feel on top of the world.

反 意氣消沉（3563）To be in the doldrums.

1396 **精衛填海** jīng wèi tián hǎi

Jing Wei (a bird like pheasant usually carries stones in its beak) fills the sea. (lit.)

Move heaven and earth.

源 博物志："炎帝女溺死，化精衛，常啣西山木石以填東海。"

1397 **精益求精** jīng yì qiú jīng

To seek from best to excellent. (lit.)

Though good be good, yet better is better.

Break one's own record.

Never contented.

同 百尺竿頭，更進一步（0048）Make further efforts.

反 不求上進（0242）Rest on one's laurels.

1398 **驚弓之鳥** jīng gōng zhī niǎo

A bird (wounded) is afraid of a bow. (lit.)

A burned child dreads the fire.

Once bitten, twice shy.

同 心有餘悸（3196）He has seen a wolf.

反 初生牛犢不畏虎（0427）They that know nothing fear nothing.

源 穀梁傳·成二年疏："敗軍之將不可以語勇，驚弦之鳥不可以應弓。"

1399 **驚惶失措** jīng huáng shī cuò

As frightened as to be at a loss. (lit.)

To be in a flat spin.

Stand aghast.

To be taken aback.

Frightened out of one's wits.

Shake in one's shoes.

Like ducks in a thunder-storm.

同 不知所措（0280）At a loss what to do.

反 不慌不忙（0201）Keep one's head.

1400 **驚恐萬分** jīng kǒng wàn fēn

Alarmed to the ten thousand degrees. (lit.)

One's heart skips a beat.

同 惶恐不安（1140）With one's heart going pit-pat.

反 泰山崩於前而目不瞬（2670）If the sky falls we shall catch larks.

驚天動地 jīng tiān dòng dì 1401

Startle the heaven and shake the earth. (lit.)

To startle the world.

World-shaking.

To move heaven and earth.

源 朱子語錄："聖人做事時，須要驚天動地。"

井井有條 jǐng jǐng yǒu tiáo 1402

Like the Chinese character, Jing, arranged in good order. (lit.)

In apple-pie order.

Keep everything ship-shape.

反 雜亂無章（3755）All in a muddle（mess）.

源 荀子．儒效："井井兮其有條理也。"

敬而遠之 jìng ér yuǎn zhī 1403

Respect but keep a distance apart. (lit.)

Keep one at a respectful distance.

The best remedy against an ill man is much ground between.

Prefer a person's room to his company.

Keep one at arm's length.

Give a wide berth to

同 避之則吉（0127）Steer clear of

反 依依不捨（3513）Can't tear onself away.

源 論語．雍也："敬鬼神而遠之。"

敬陪末座 jìng péi mò zuò 1404

Respectfully join the table but take the end-seat. (lit.)

Sit below the salt.

Take a back seat.

反 作東道主（4064）Stand treat.

敬謝不敏 jìng xiè bù mǐn 1405

Decline the invitation politely by admitting being incapable. (lit.)

Decline an offer.

Refuse one's invitation.

反 勉為其難（1806）Make the best of a bad bargain.

源 韓愈．寄盧仝詩："買羊沽酒謝不敏，偶逢明月曜桃李。"

靜處安身 jìng chǔ ān shēn 1406

In a quiet place to rest body and soul. (lit.)

Far from the madding crowd.

同 索居閒處（2666）Live in seclusion.

反 趁熱鬧 Climb on the bandwagon.

1407 **靜如處女** jìng rú chǔ nǚ
As quiet as a maiden. (lit.)
As quiet (gentle) as a lamb.

反 動如脱兔（0673）As fleet as (a) deer.

1408 **靜若辰星** jìng ruò chén xīng
As quiet as morning stars. (lit.)
As silent as the stars.

同 鴉雀無聲（3287）Silence reigns.
反 大吵大鬧（0507）Raise Cain.

1409 **迥然不同** jiǒng rán bù tóng
Absolutely not the same. (lit.)
That's a horse of another colour.
As different as chalk is from cheese.

同 霄壤之別（3131）A world of difference.
反 一模一樣（3428）As like as two peas in a pod.
源 張戒．歲寒堂詩話："文章今古，迥然不同。"

1410 **窘迫萬分** jiǒng pò wàn fēn
Pushed and pressed in ten thousand degrees. (lit.)
On one's beam ends.

同 處境困難（0429）Like a toad under a harrow.

1411 **九牛二虎之力** jiǔ niú èr hǔ zhī lì
The combined strength of nine oxen and two tigers. (lit.)
Strain every nerve.
Move heaven and earth to

同 全力以赴（2161）To go all out.
反 不費吹灰之力（0185）A lift of the finger.

1412 **九牛一毛** jiǔ niú yī máo
One hair from nine oxen. (lit.)
A drop in the bucket.

同 滄海一粟（0306）A drop in the ocean.
反 滿坑滿谷（1746）As thick as blackberries.
源 司馬遷．報任少卿書："假令僕伏法受誅，若九牛亡一毛，與螻蟻何以異。"

1413 **九泉之下** jiǔ quán zhī xià
Beneath the nine springs (nether world). (lit.)
In the nether world.
Beyond the veil.
Under the clods (sod).

同 入土為安（2288）Take an earth-bath.
源 阮瑀詩："冥冥九泉室，漫漫長夜台。"

九死一生 jiǔ sǐ yī shēng 1414

Nine dead, one alive. (lit.)

Have a close brush with death.

Have a close shave.

Bear a charmed life.

反 萬無一失（2856）Safe and sure.

源 離騷："亦余心之所善兮，雖九死其猶未悔。"

久別情疏 jiǔ bié qíng shū 1415

Long parting, affection thin. (lit.)

Long absent, soon forgotten.

Out of sight, out of mind.

Far from eye, far from heart.

Seldom seen, soon forgotten.

反 永誌不忘（3615）Keep the memory green.

久病新瘥 jiǔ bìng xīn chài 1416

After long illness, recently recovered. (lit.)

Up and about.

Take a fresh (new) lease of life.

To pull through.

On the mend.

同 恢復元氣（1147）To be on the mend.

久旱逢甘雨 jiǔ hàn féng gān yǔ 1417

After a long drought, to meet sweet rain. (lit.)

Feeling a sense of relief.

A sight for sore eyes.

反 屋漏更兼連夜雨（2943）It never rains but it pours.

源 容齋隨筆："久旱逢甘雨，他鄉遇故知，洞房花燭夜，金榜掛名時。"

久經風雨 jiǔ jīng fēng yǔ 1418

Long experience of wind and rain. (lit.)

To be weather-beaten.

To have weathered a storm.

同 曾經滄海（0317）To have sailed the seven seas.

反 初見世面（0424）Babes in the woods.

久經世故 jiǔ jīng shì gù 1419

Long experienced of life and world changes. (lit.)

Have seen the elephant.

同 老於世故（1579）Know every move on the board.

反 初出茅廬（0421）A raw recruit.

久住令人賤 jiǔ zhù lìng rén jiàn 1420

Long stay makes one cheap. (lit.)

To outstay (wear out) one's welcome.

A constant guest is never welcome.

同 但看三五日，相見不如初（0576）Fish and company stink in three days.

1421 **酒池肉林** jiǔ chí ròu lín
A lake of wine and woods of flesh. (lit.)
Beef and ale galore.

反 殘羹冷炙（0303）Crumbs from the table.

源 漢書・張騫傳："行賞賜，酒池肉林。"

1422 **酒逢知己千杯少**
jiǔ féng zhī jǐ qiān bēi shǎo
With wine meeting bosom friends, thousand cups are little. (lit.)
Old friends and old wine are best.
Old wine and an old friend are good provisions.
The company makes the feast.

1423 **酒過三巡** jiǔ guò sān xún
Wine is passed in three rounds. (lit.)
The first glass for thirst, the second for nourishment, the third for pleasure, and the fourth for madness.

1424 **酒囊飯袋** jiǔ náng fàn dài
A wine bag and a rice sack. (lit.)
Not worth one's salt.
A good-for-nothing.
Jack of straw.

同 飽食終日，無所用心（0085）A full belly neither fights nor flies well.

源 荊湘近事："馬殷好奢僭，諸王子僕從烜赫，文武之道，未嘗留意，時謂之酒囊飯袋。"

1425 **酒肉朋友** jiǔ ròu péng yǒu
Wine and meat friends. (lit.)
Cupboard love.
Fair-weather friends.
Trencher companions (friends).
Table friendship soon changes.
When good cheer is lacking, our friends will be packing.

同 交友滿天下，知心有幾人（1305）There is a scarcity of friendship, but not of friends.

反 患難之交（1133）A friend in need is a friend indeed.

1426 **酒色傷財** jiǔ sè shāng cái
Wine and women cost money. (lit.)
Wine and wenches empty men's purses.

咎由自取 jiù yóu zì qǔ 1427
Troubles that one makes himself. (lit.)
Asking for troubles.
Lie in the bed one has made.
To be hoisted with one's own petard.
Stew in one's own juice.

同 自取其咎（3990）Have oneself to blame.
源 尚書："自作孽。"

救人一命 jiù rén yī mìng 1428
Save one a life. (lit.)
Snatch a brand from a burning fire.

同 起死回生（2041）To bring one to.
反 殺人不眨眼（2325）Kill in cold blood.

救死扶傷 jiù sǐ fú shāng 1429
Save the one dying and help the injured. (lit.)
Rescue the perishing.
Care for the dying.

同 扶危濟困（0822）Help a lame dog over a stile.
反 荼毒生靈 Mow down like grass.
源 司馬遷．報任少卿書："所殺過當，虜救死扶傷不給。"

就我所知 jiù wǒ suǒ zhī 1430
According to what I know. (lit.)
To the best of my knowledge.
For my part.

舊調重彈 jiù diào chóng tán 1431
Old tune is played again. (lit.)
Sing the same old song.
Harp on the same (frayed) string.

同 陳詞濫調（0345）Flog the dead horse.

舊瓶新酒 jiù píng xīn jiǔ 1432
Old bottles containing new wine. (lit.)
New wine in old bottles.

舊事重提 jiù shì chóng tí 1433
An old matter is mentioned again. (lit.)
Dwell on it again.
Rake up the past.
Flog a dead horse.

同 翻老賬（0739）Rip up old sores.
反 既往不咎（1234）Let the dead bury the dead.

居安思危 jū ān sī wēi 1434
Living in peace, think of danger. (lit.)
The way to be safe is never to feel secure.

同 宜將有日思無日（3516）In fair weather prepare for foul.
源 左傳．襄十一年："居安思危，思則有備，有備無患。"

1435 居必擇鄰，交必良友
jū bì zé lín, jiāo bì liáng yǒu
One should choose his neighbours and make friends with good men only. (lit.)
Keep good men company and you shall be of the number.

1436 鞠躬盡瘁 jū gōng jìn cuì
Bow devotedly and exert all one's energy. (lit.)
Burn oneself out.
Die in harness.
Die with one's boots on.
Die in the last ditch.
Dedicate one's life to

同 盡忠職守（1376）Fulfil one's trust.
反 躺倒不幹（2690）To swing the lead.
源 諸葛亮．後出師表："鞠躬盡瘁，死而後已。"

1437 局勢扭轉 jú shì niǔ zhuǎn
The situation is turned around. (lit.)
The shoe is on the other foot.

1438 侷促不安 jú cù bù ān
Restrained and uneasy. (lit.)
On edge.
To be ill at ease.
Feel like a fish out of water.

同 心緒不寧（3192）Get out of bed on the wrong side.
反 泰然自若（2669）Feel at home.
源 漢書："侷促效轅下駒。"

1439 舉棋不定 jǔ qí bù dìng
Undecisive in making a move in playing chess. (lit.)
Let "I dare not" wait upon "I would".
Between hawk and buzzard.

同 猶疑不決（3642）Like one o'clock half struck.
反 當機立斷（0584）Take the bull by the horns.
源 左傳．襄二十五年："弈者舉棋不定，不勝其偶。"

1440 舉世無雙 jǔ shì wú shuāng
No double in the world. (lit.)
Second to none.
Without peer (parallel).

同 無與倫比（3004）Defy all comparison.
反 比比皆是（0113）Here and there and everywhere.
源 屈原．漁父："舉世皆濁我獨清。"

1441 舉手之勞 jǔ shǒu zhī láo
The effort of raising one's hand. (lit.)
A lift of the finger.
Turn a hand.

舉一反三 jǔ yī fǎn sān 1442

Raising one hints the other three. (lit.)

Read one's mind.

Know how to take a hint.

A word is enough to the wise.

Few words to the wise suffice.

源 論語．述而："舉一隅不以三隅反，則不復也。"

舉足輕重 jǔ zú qīng zhòng 1443

A step made by him light or heavy is (vitally) important. (lit.)

Play a key role in

Tip (Tilt, Turn) the scales.

Carry a big weight in

Hold the balance.

反 微不足道（2881）Nothing to speak of

源 漢書．竇融傳："權在將軍，舉足左右，便有輕重。"

句斟字酌 jù zhēn zì zhuó 1444

The sentence weighed and the word considered. (lit.)

Weigh one's words.

同 咬文嚼字（3353）To speak holiday.

反 信口雌黃（3206）Talk through one's hat.

拒人於千里之外 1445

jù rén yú qiān lǐ zhī wài

Keep others away beyond thousand miles. (lit.)

Keep at arm's length.

Give a wide berth to

A boiled shirt.

反 平易近人（1994）Easy to get along with

聚沙成塔 jù shā chéng tǎ 1446

Accumulation of sand becomes a tower. (lit.)

Many a mickle makes a muckle.

同 涓滴成河（1450）Every little helps.

源 法華經．方便品："乃至童子戲，聚沙為佛塔。"

聚訟紛紜 jù sòng fēn yún 1447

Assembled debate has various and confused opinions. (lit.)

So many men, so many minds.

Opinions are divided.

同 莫衷一是（1853）Agree like the clocks of London.

反 意見一致（3562）To see eye-to-eye with

1448 **據為己有** jù wéi jǐ yǒu
Seize it for one's possession. (lit.)
What's yours is mine, and what's mine's my own.

1449 **據我所知** jù wǒ suǒ zhī
In accordance with what I know. (lit.)
To my knowledge.
As far as I know.
For what I know.

1450 **涓滴成河** juān dī chéng hé
Continuous drippings and drops of water may form a river. (lit.)
Every little helps.

同 積少成多（1193）Many a little makes a mickle.

1451 **捲土重來** juǎn tǔ chóng lái
Raise up a cloud of dust and come back again. (lit.)
Make a new start.
Stage a comeback.
He that fights and runs away may live to fight another day.

同 東山再起（0666）Bob up like a cork.
反 一去不復返（3444）To be going for good and all.
源 杜牧．題烏江亭詩："江東子弟多才俊，捲土重來未可知。"

1452 **決不食言** jué bù shí yán
Definitely will not eat my words. (lit.)
Be as good as one's word.
His word is as good as his bond.

同 說一不二（2615）A bargain is a bargain.
反 說話不算數（2610）Eat one's words.

1453 **決定因素是人，不是武器**
jué dìng yīn sù shì rén, bú shì wǔ qì
The determining factor is man not weapon. (lit.)
All weapons of war cannot arm fear.

1454 **絕不稀罕** jué bù xī hǎn
It's not at all rare. (lit.)
Not the only fish in the sea.
Not the only pebble on the beach.

同 恆河沙數（1063）As numberless as the sands.
反 物罕為貴（3035）Precious things are not found in heaps.

絕處逢生 jué chù féng shēng 1455

To be alive in desperation. (lit.)

Have a close brush with death.

Escape by the skin of one's teeth.

A narrow escape.

A close shave.

Bear a charmed life.

同 虎口餘生（1089）To be snatched from the jaws of death.

反 死於非命（2632）Hop the twig.

攫為己有 jué wéi jǐ yǒu 1456

Grasp it for one's own possession. (lit.)

What's yours is mine, and what's mine's my own.

Sweep everything into one's net.

反 仗義疏財（3803）Be a good Samaritan.

君乘車，我戴笠，他日相逢下車揖；君擔簦，我跨馬，他日相逢為君下 1457

jūn chéng jū, wǒ dài lì, tā rì xiāng féng xià jū yī; jūn dān dèng, wǒ kuà mǎ, tā rì xiāng féng wèi jūn xià

You ride a carriage, I wear a straw hat, one day when we meet again, you come down the carriage and bow to me; you carry an (ancient) umbrella, I ride a horse, one day when we meet again, for you I dismount. (lit.)

Let not poverty part good company.

源 本條目原句出自《風土記》

君子安貧 jūn zǐ ān pín 1458

Gentlemen at ease with being poor. (lit.)

To glory in honest poverty.

Poverty is not a shame, but the being ashamed of it.

君子不立危牆之下 1459

jūn zǐ bú lì wēi qiáng zhī xià

Gentlemen would not stand below a collapsing wall. (lit.)

Never lean on a broken staff.

Rats desert a falling house.

1460 **君子不念舊惡** jūn zǐ bú niàn jiù è

Gentlemen do not remember old grudges. (lit.)

The noblest vengeance is to forgive.

同 既往不咎（1234）Forgive and forget.

反 永記血淚仇（3613）To nurse vengeance.

1461 **君子坦蕩蕩** jūn zǐ tǎn dàng dàng

Gentlemen frank and open. (lit.)

Open confession is good for the soul.

源 論語・述而："君子坦蕩蕩，小人長戚戚。"

1462 **君子之交淡如水**

jūn zǐ zhī jiāo dàn rú shuǐ

Gentlemen's friendship is as plain as water. (lit.)

A hedge between keeps friendship green.

Little intermeddling makes good friends.

Friends are like fiddle-strings, they must not be screwed too tight.

Good fences make good neighbours.

源 莊子・山木："君子之交淡如水，小人之交甘若醴。"

1463 **君子之交淡如水，小人之交甜如蜜** jūn zǐ zhī jiāo dàn rú shuǐ, xiǎo rén zhī jiāo tián rú mì

Gentlemen's friendship is as plain as water, mean man's friendship is as sweet as honey. (lit.)

Better be friends at a distance than neighbours and enemies.

K

開張大吉 kāi zhāng dà jí 1464

Grand opening great luck. (lit.)

Hang out one's shingle.

反 虧本倒閉（1531）Leave the key under the threshold.

源 古杭夢遊錄："其有趁賣早市者復起開張。"

開場白 kāi cháng bái 1465

Opening speech in an assembly. (lit.)

An opening speech.

開誠佈公 kāi chéng bù gōng 1466

Open and sincere pronounces justice. (lit.)

Wear one's heart on one's sleeve.

Put one's cards on the table.

Come into the open.

反 秘而不宣（1792）Keep one's own counsel.

源 三國志．蜀志．諸葛亮傳評："諸葛亮之為相國也，開誠心，佈公道。"

開倒車 kāi dào chē 1467

Start the car backward. (lit.)

To back-pedal.

反 一往無前（3469）Press forward.

開動腦筋 kāi dòng nǎo jīn 1468

Set the brain in action. (lit.)

Sharpen one's wits.

同 絞盡腦汁（1311）Cudgel one's brains.

反 飽食終日，無所用心（0085）Fat paunches make lean pates.

開個頭 kāi gè tóu 1469

Make a start. (lit.)

Set the ball rolling.

開卷有益 kāi juàn yǒu yì 1470

To open a book and derive some benefit from it. (lit.)

A book that is shut is but a block.

Ask counsel of the dead.

反 盡信書不如無書（1375）Better untaught than ill taught.

源 宋實錄："朕性喜讀書，頗得其趣，開卷有益，豈徒然也。"

1471 **開空頭支票** kāi kōng tóu zhī piào
Write an empty-account cheque. (lit.)
Good words without deeds are rushes and reeds.
You cackle often, but never lay an egg.

同 口惠而實不至（1505）He who gives fair words feeds you with an empty spoon.
反 坐言起行（4060）Say well is good, but do well is better.

1472 **開門紅** kāi mén hóng
Opening the door, red (triumph). (lit.)
The first blow is half the battle.
Off to a good start.

同 旗開得勝（2034）To start with a bang.
反 落手打三更（1721）Start off on the wrong foot.

1473 **開門見山** kāi mén jiàn shān
Opening the door, see the mountain. (lit.)
Come straight to the point.
Mince no matters.
Point-blank.

同 直言不諱（3874）Without reserve.
反 閃爍其詞（2341）Speak with one's tongue in one's cheek.
源 嚴羽 · 滄浪詩話 · 詩評："太白發句，謂之開門見山。"

1474 **開門揖盜** kāi mén yī dào
Opening the door, greet the thief. (lit.)
Ask for trouble.
At open doors dogs come in.
Opportunity makes the thief.

源 三國志 · 孫權傳："是猶開門而揖盜，未可以為仁也。"

1475 **開玩笑** kāi wán xiào
Making a joke. (lit.)
Playing a practical joke.
Pull a person's leg.

同 揶揄戲弄（3362）Make a hare of a person.
反 認認真真（2247）In sober earnest.

1476 **開小差** kāi xiǎo chāi
Start a little errand (run-away). (lit.)
Desert one's colours.
Looking for gape-seed.

反 埋頭苦幹（1735）Keep one's nose to the grindstone.

1477 **開足馬力** kāi zú mǎ lì
Start running in full horse-power. (lit.)
Do one's utmost (best).
For all one is worth.
At full speed (steam).
Try one's best.

同 不遺餘力（0265）Go to all lengths.
反 磨洋工（1846）Lie on one's oars.

侃侃而談 kǎn kǎn ér tán 1478
Talk with ease and confidence. (lit.)
A flow of eloquence.
Have a glib tongue.
Talk nineteen to the dozen.
Talk the bark off a tree.

同 大發議論（0518）To enlarge one's self.
反 沉默寡言（0342）Hold one's peace.
源 論語・鄉黨：“侃侃如也。”

看錯對象 kàn cuò duì xiàng 1479
See the wrong opposite side. (lit.)
Bark up the wrong tree.

看法一致 kàn fǎ yī zhì 1480
The way looking at it is in unison. (lit.)
See eye to eye.

同 英雄所見略同（3596）Great minds think alike.
反 意見分歧（3561）Opinions are divided.

看風使舵 kàn fēng shǐ duò 1481
Seeing how the wind blows, steer the boat. (lit.)
Go with the tide.
See how the wind blows.
Trim the sails.

同 順風轉舵（2601）To dance and sing all weathers.
源 陸游詩：“看風使帆第一籌，隨風倒柁更何憂。”

看佛面上 kàn fó miàn shàng 1482
For the buddha's face sake. (lit.)
For goodness sake.
For God's sake.

看清形勢 kàn qīng xíng shì 1483
See clearly the situation. (lit.)
See how the land lies.
See which way the cat jumps.

慷慨陳詞 kāng kǎi chén cí 1484
Present a talk in a generous way. (lit.)
Air one's views.
To enlarge oneself.
Talk the bark off the tree.

同 大鳴大放（0538）Stand up and be counted.
反 閉口不言（0119）Hold one's peace.

1485 慷慨解囊 kāng kǎi jiě náng
Generous in opening one's purse. (lit.)
Loose the purse strings.
Come down handsome.
Put one's hand in one's pocket.

同 仗義疏財（3803）Be a good Samaritan.
反 吝嗇小氣（1660）Cramp in the hand.

1486 慷慨就義 kāng kǎi jiù yì
Courageously to be executed for an ideal. (lit.)
Better a glorious death than a shameful life.
Die a martyr's death.

同 殺身成仁（2329）Lay down one's life.
反 見利忘義（1278）Honour and profit lie not in one sack.

1487 慷他人之慨 kāng tā rén zhī kǎi
To be generous with other people's things or money. (lit.)
Rob Peter to pay Paul.
Steal a goose and give the giblets in alms.

同 羊毛出在羊身上（3331）He does not lose his alms who gives it to his pig.

1488 糠裏榨油 kāng lǐ zhà yóu
To squeeze oil out of chaff. (lit.)
To squeeze blood out of stone.
Get blood from a turnip.

1489 靠邊站 kào biān zhàn
Stand aside. (lit.)
To be on the shelf.
Get the brush-off.
Step aside.
To be left high and dry.

1490 苛政猛於虎 kē zhèng měng yú hǔ
Harsh ruler is fiercer than a tiger. (lit.)
Rule with a rod of iron.

同 豺狼當道（0323）A lion in the path.
源 禮記：“苛政猛於虎。”

1491 可歌可泣 kě gē kě qì
How (it moves one) to sing and to weep. (lit.)
Set one in a melting mood.
Melt into tears.

同 感人肺腑（0868）Tug at one's heart-strings.

可見一斑 kě jiàn yì bān 1492

It can be seen only a spot. (lit.)

One may see day at a little hole.

同 管中窺豹（0976）You may know by a handful of the whole sack.

源 晉書．王獻之傳："此郎亦管中窺豹，時見一斑。"

可疑分子 kě yí fèn zǐ 1493

A doubtful element. (lit.)

A snake in the grass.

可以意會，不可以言傳 1494

kě yǐ yì huì, bù kě yǐ yán chuán

One can grasp the meaning but can not pass on in words. (lit.)

Beyond words.

同 不可言狀（0223）Beggar description.

渴時一滴如甘露，解後添杯不如無 kě shí yì dī rú gān lù, jiě hòu tiān bēi bù rú wú 1495

When thirsty one drop of water is like sweet dew, but after thirst is quenched an extra cup is not as good as without. (lit.)

A friend in need is a friend indeed.

克己奉公 kè jǐ fèng gōng 1496

Deny self to serve the public. (lit.)

Do one's bit.

Keep up one's end.

同 盡忠職守（1376）Fulfil one's trust.

反 尸位素餐（2444）Feast at the public crib.

源 後漢書．祭遵傳："遵為人廉約小心，克己奉公。"

克勤克儉kè qín kè jiǎn 1497

Able to be industrious and thrifty. (lit.)

Industry is fortune's right hand, and frugality her left.

反 好吃懶做（1041）Eat one's head off.

源 尚書．大禹謨："克勤於邦，克儉於家。"

刻不容緩 kè bù róng huǎn 1498

Even a moment cannot be delayed. (lit.)

Call for inmmediate attention.

Not a moment to lose.

Brook no delay.

同 事不宜遲（2510）The matter asks haste.

反 來日方長（1538）There's plenty of time yet.

1499 刻苦鍛煉 kè kǔ duàn liàn
Overcome hardship for drill and training. (lit.)
Go through the hoop.

同 磨礪以須（1844）Pull oneself through the mill.

1500 溘然長逝 kè rán cháng shì
Suddenly take the long leave (from life). (lit.)
Breathe one's last.
Pass away (into stillness).
To be no more.
To check out.
To breathe one's last.

同 與世長辭（3707）Go the way of all flesh.

1501 肯下功夫 kěn xià gōng fū
Willing to put down some hard work. (lit.)
Put one's back to it.

同 孜孜不倦（3961）Knuckle down to it.
反 懶骨頭（1545）Lazy bones.

1502 空中樓閣 kōng zhōng lóu gé
Towers in the air. (lit.)
Castles in the air.

同 海市蜃樓（1008）A fool's paradise.
源 李漁・閒情偶寄・結構第一："虛者，空中樓閣，隨意結構，無影無形之謂也。"

1503 口齒伶俐 kǒu chǐ líng lì
Mouth and teeth are smart. (lit.)
Have the gift of the gab.
Have a ready tongue.

同 能說會道（1892）A flannel mouth person.
反 結結巴巴（1323）Have stones in one's mouth.

1504 口服心服 kǒu fú xīn fú
Mouth and heart are convinced. (lit.)
Totally convinced.

1505 口惠而實不至 kǒu huì ér shí bú zhì
A verbal promise in fact is not kept. (lit.)
Fine (fair) words butter no parsnips.
He who gives fair words feeds you with an empty spoon.
Sympathy without relief is like mustard without beef.

反 說到做到（2606）Suit the action to the word.
源 禮記・表記："口惠而實不至，怨災及其身。"

Good words without deeds are rushes and reeds.
You cackle often, but never lay an egg.
The tune the old cow died of.

口蜜腹劍 kǒu mì fù jiàn 1506

A honey-mouth but a sword in the belly. (lit.)

A honey tongue, a heart of gall.
Bees that have honey in their mouths have stings in their tails.
To be nasty-nice.

同 笑裏藏刀（3151）Velvet paws hide sharp claws.

源 資治通鑑．唐紀："世謂李林甫口有蜜，腹有劍。"

口沫橫飛 kǒu mò héng fēi 1507

Saliva flies out (in all directions). (lit.)

Wag one's tongue (chin, jaws).
Talk one's head off.

口若懸河 kǒu ruò xuán hé 1508

(Words) flow from mouth like a torrent. (lit.)

Rattle on.
Talk nine words at once.

同 滔滔不絕（2692）Talk oneself out of breath.

反 期期艾艾（2032）Hem and haw.

源 劉義慶．世說新語．賞譽："郭子玄語議如懸河瀉水，注而不竭。"

口是心非 kǒu shì xīn fēi 1509

The mouth is right but the heart is false. (lit.)

Act the part of a do-gooder.
Speak with one's tongue in one's cheek.
Say one thing and mean another.
Play a double game.

同 言不由衷（3295）To be mealy-mouthed.

反 心口如一（3174）What the heart thinks the tongue speaks.

源 葛洪．抱朴子．微旨："若乃憎善好殺，口是心非，背向異辭，反戾直正……凡有一事，輒是一罪。"

口說不如身做 kǒu shuō bù rú shēn zuò 1510

Words are not as good as one's action. (lit.)

Say well is good, but do well is better.
Example is better than precept.

1511 口頭擁護 kǒu tóu yōng hù
Verbal support. (lit.)
Pay lip service.

反 鼎力支持（0659）Put one's hand to the plough.

1512 扣人心弦 kòu rén xīn xián
Pluck at one's heartstrings. (lit.)
Tug at one's heartstrings.

同 動人肺腑（0672）Come home to one's heart.

1513 哭喪着臉 kū sāng zhē liǎn
One looks like weeping as if in mourning. (lit.)
To sour one's cheeks.
Wear a long face.

反 笑破肚皮（3153）Burst one's sides with laughters.

1514 哭笑不得 kū xiào bù dé
Cannot cry nor laugh. (lit.)
Laugh out of the other side of one's mouth.

同 啼笑皆非（2707）What a cheek!

1515 枯木逢春 kū mù féng chūn
Dried-up wood meets the springs. (lit.)
Take a fresh lease of life.
To rise like the Phoenix.

同 久病新瘥（1416）Take a fresh lease of life.
反 無疾而終（2967）Sleep the final sleep.
源 釋道源 · 景德傳燈錄："問枯木逢春時如何。師曰，世間稀有。"

1516 枯燥無味 kū zào wú wèi
Dry and tasteless. (lit.)
As dry as dust.
Cut and dried.

同 索然無味（2667）Flat and insipid.
反 興致盎然（3226）Lick one's lips.

1517 苦不堪言 kǔ bù kān yán
The bitterness is inexpressible. (lit.)
As bitter as gall.

同 啞口吃黃連（3289）Swallow the leek.
反 快樂無邊（1525）To be in seventh heaven.

1518 苦恨年年壓金線，為他人作嫁衣裳 kǔ hèn nián nián yā jīn xiàn, wèi tā rén zuò jià yī sháng
Bitterly regret that every year one is pressed by golden thread, making wedding gowns for others. (lit.)
The cobbler's wife is the worst shod.

同 賣花姑娘插竹葉（1737）The ass that carries wine drinks water.
源 秦韜玉 · 貧女詩："苦恨年年壓金線，為他人作嫁衣裳。"

苦盡甘來 kǔ jìn gān lái 1519

When the bitter ends comes the sweet. (lit.)

After rain comes fair weather.
Take a turn for the better.
They that sow in tears shall reap in joy.
When things are at the worst they will mend.
Weeping may endure for a night, but joy cometh in the morning.
Pain past is pleasure.
Sadness and gladness succeed one another.

同 否極泰來（0819）The darkest hour is that before the dawn.
反 興盡悲來（3225）He who laughs on Friday will weep on Sunday.
源 元曲選·張國賓·合汗衫："這也是災消福長，苦盡甘來。"

苦苦哀求 kǔ kǔ āi qiú 1520

To implore bitterly and earnestly. (lit.)

On one's kness.

同 搖尾乞憐（3347）Grovel at the feet of

苦若黃連 kǔ ruò huáng lián 1521

As bitter as Huang Lian (a bitter Chinese herb). (lit.)

As bitter as wormwood.

同 千辛萬苦（2066）Toil and moil.

誇誇其談 kuā kuā qí tán 1522

To exaggerate his speech. (lit.)

Empty vessels make the most sound.
Sling the bull.
Throw the hatchet.
Shoot off one's mouth.
Empty talk.
They brag most who can do the least.
The greatest talkers are always the least doers.

同 信口開河（3207）Talk at random.
反 邊説邊幹（0131）No sooner said than done.

快刀斬亂麻 kuài dāo zhǎn luàn má 1523

Quick knife cuts off a tangle of hemp. (lit.)

Take drastic measures.
Cut the Gordian knot.
Get it over and done with.

同 乾脆利落（0863）To be clear-cut.
反 優柔寡斷（3628）To be neither off nor on.

1524 **快活神仙** kuài huó shén xiān

Happy angels. (lit.)

As jolly (merry) as a sandboy.

1525 **快樂無邊** kuài lè wú biān

Endless happiness. (lit.)

To be in seventh heaven.

I would not call the king my cousin.

同 其樂無窮（2021）Like a possum up a gum-tree.

反 苦不堪言（1517）As bitter as gall.

1526 **快人快語** kuài rén kuài yǔ

A quick man with quick words. (lit.)

Frank and outspoken.

同 心直口快（3199）Nearest the heart, nearest the mouth.

反 半吞半吐（0073）To mince matters.

1527 **快手快腳** kuài shǒu kuài jiǎo

Quick hands, quick feet. (lit.)

Draw the bow up to the ear.

Hand over fist.

同 迅速敏捷（3284）Hand over hand.

反 慢條斯理（1755）As slow as molasses in winter.

1528 **膾炙人口** kuài zhì rén kǒu

The roast meat tastes good to every mouth. (lit.)

Everyone speaks well of

To be in everyone's mouth.

Pass from mouth to mouth.

Enjoy great popularity.

同 家喻戶曉（1255）To be a household word.

源 唐音癸籤引埶圃擷餘："錢長信宜春句，於晴雪妙極形容，膾炙人口。"

1529 **寬大為懷** kuān dà wéi huái

Generous and broad-minded. (lit.)

Do the handsome towards one.

To be large-minded.

同 將相頭上堪走馬，公侯肚裏好撐船（1300）Great gifts are from great men.

反 心胸狹隘（3191）A little pot is soon hot.

1530 **寬限時日** kuān xiàn shí rì

To extend the limit for time and day. (lit.)

Days of grace.

1531 **虧本倒閉** kuī běn dǎo bì

Loss of capital and close down. (lit.)

Leave the key under the threshold.

虧空破產 kuī kōng pò chǎn 1532
Over-spending and bankruptcy. (lit.)
Gone through the sieve.
To go bust.

反 生意興隆（2421）Drive a roaring trade.

潰不成軍 kuì bù chéng jūn 1533
The soldiers turn deserters thus forming no army. (lit.)
To be put to rout.
To be utterly routed.
A crushing defeat.

反 得勝凱旋（0615）Come off with flying colours.

L

1534 拉關係 lā guān xì

Pull relation. (lit.)

To pull strings.
Scrape acquaintance with
Wire-pulling.
Pipe-laying.
Cotton up to
Grease the ways.

反 六親不認（1686）Cut loose from old ties.

1535 來而不往非禮也

lái ér bù wǎng fēi lǐ yě

Not to return a visit is impolite. (lit.)

Serve the same sauce.

源 禮記 · 曲禮上：“往而不來非禮也，來而不往亦非禮也。”

1536 來回往復 lái huí wǎng fù

Coming and returning repeatedly. (lit.)

Back and forth.
To and fro.
Backwards and forwards.

同 踱來踱去（0709）Walk the floor.

1537 來龍去脈 lái lóng qù mài

Comes the dragon and goes the track. (lit.)

The ins and outs of

1538 來日方長 lái rì fāng cháng

Coming days are yet long. (lit.)

No need to hurry.
There's plenty of time yet.
It can wait.
One of these days.
One of these days is none of these days.

反 急不可待（1208）To be bursting to do something.

源 朱子語錄：“勿謂今日不學而有來日。”

Tomorrow is another day.
A day to come shows longer than a year that's gone.
The time to come is no more than the time past.
What may be done at any time will be done at no time.

來如風雨，去似微塵 1539

lái rú fēng yǔ, qù sì wēi chén
Come as wind and rain, go like small dust. (lit.)
He who swells in prosperity will shrink in adversity.
Mischief comes by the pound and goes away by the ounce.
Misfortune comes on wings and departs on foot.

來說是非者，便是是非人 1540

lái shuō shì fēi zhě, biàn shì shì fēi rén
The one who comes to tell tales is the man of gossips. (lit.)
Who chatters to you will chatter of you.

來頭大 lái tóu dà 1541

Come as big head. (lit.)
He is the bishop's sister's son.

反 出身寒微（0411）Born in low water.

來者不拒 lái zhě bú jù 1542

All comers are not rejected. (lit.)
Take things as they come.
All is fish that comes to net.
All is grist that comes to my mill.

同 多多益善（0699）The more the better.
反 敬謝不敏（1405）Decline an offer.

來之不易 lái zhī bú yì 1543

It is not easy to come by. (lit.)
Hard to come by.

反 信手拈來（3208）Come in handy.

1544 蘭摧玉折 lán cuī yù zhé
The Epidendrum destroyed and the jade broken. (lit.)
Whom the gods love die young.

反 老而不死是為賊也（1564）He lives long that lives till all are weary of him.

源 世說新語：“寧為蘭摧玉折，不作蕭敷艾榮。”

1545 懶骨頭 lǎn gǔ tóu
Lazy bones. (lit.)
As lazy as Joe the marine who laid down his musket to sneeze.

同 衣來伸手，飯來張口（3506）Kitty Swerrock where she sat, come reach me this, come reach me that.

反 幹勁沖天（0874）To be a live wire.

1546 濫用職權 làn yòng zhí quán
Abuse one's official power. (lit.)
Abuse one's authority.
Strain one's right.

1547 爛醉如泥 làn zuì rú ní
Dead drunk lie earth. (lit.)
Go to bed in one's boots.

同 酩酊大醉（1833）As drunk as a fiddler.

反 神志清醒（2410）In one's sober senses.

1548 狼狽不堪 láng bèi bù kān
Wolf and (its) mongrel are in helpless distress. (lit.)
One shoe off and one shoe on.
All in a fluster.
In a pretty fix (tight corner).
Helter-skelter.
In an embarrassing situation (awkward predicament).
To be caught with one's pants down.

同 處境尷尬（0428）To be in a pretty pickle.

反 從容不迫（0457）Take things easy.

源 李密．陳情表：“臣之進退，實為狼狽。”

1549 狼狽為奸 láng bèi wéi jiān
Wolf and (its) mongrel banded together as traitors. (lit.)
Gang up with
Play into each other's hands.
In cahoots (collusion) with

同 朋比為奸（1906）Thick as thieves.

源 博物典彙：“狼前二足長，後二足短，狽前二足短，後二足長，狼無狽不立，狽無狼不行。”

狼吞虎嚥 láng tūn hǔ yàn 1550

Gobble like a wolf and swallow like a tiger. (lit.)

Eat like a horse.
Have a wolf in one's stomach.
Make a pig of oneself.
Eat one's head off.
Polish off a meal.
Make a beast of oneself.
Gobble up.
Garbage down.

同 大快朵頤（0536）Gorge oneself.
反 淺斟低酌（2086）Eat at pleasure, drink by measure.

浪子回頭金不換 làng zǐ huí tóu jīn bù huàn 1551

A prodigal son's return cannot be exchanged with gold. (lit.)

The return of the prodigal son.

牢記心頭 láo jì xīn tóu 1552

Remember firmly at heart. (lit.)

Take it to heart.
Knock into the head.

同 永誌不忘（3615）Keep the memory green.
反 水過鴨背（2590）Like water off a duck's back.

牢騷太盛防腸斷 1553

láo sāo tài shèng fáng cháng duàn

Too much grudging will cause breaking of intestine. (lit.)

Too too will in two.
A little pot is soon hot.

勞而無功 láo ér wú gōng 1554

One lays tasks without merits. (lit.)

Labour in vain.
Plow the sands.
Draw water with a sieve.
Go on a wild-goose chase.

同 白費氣力（0038）Beat the air.
反 練出功夫（1619）He that shoots oft shall at last hit the mark.
源 管子．形勢篇：“與不可，強不能，告不知，謂之勞而無功。”

勞累不堪 láo lèi bù kān 1555

Extremely tired from hard work. (lit.)

Crawl home on one's eye-brows.
To be dragged out.

同 百舍重繭（0054）To be dead beat.
反 精神充沛（1384）Full of pep.

1556 **勞燕分飛** láo yàn fēn fēi

Shrikes and swallows fly apart separately. (lit.)

Go separate ways.

Part company.

The best of friends must part.

源 古樂府・東飛伯勞歌："東飛伯勞西飛燕，黃姑織女時相見。"

1557 **勞逸結合** láo yì jié hé

Work and rest must go together. (lit.)

All work and no play makes Jack a dull boy.

Work while you work, play while you play, that's the way to be happy and gay.

Variety is the spice of life.

1558 **老病號** lǎo bìng hào

Always a sick man. (lit.)

To be on the sick list.

反 久病新瘥（1416）Take a fresh lease of life.

1559 **老成持重** lǎo chéng chí zhòng

Mature and prudent. (lit.)

To be dry behind the ears.

源 魏善伯・留侯論："而老成持重，坐靡歲月，終於無成者，不可勝數。"

1560 **老成練達** lǎo chéng liàn dá

Mature, refined, and farsighted. (lit.)

Know one's way about.

To have cut one's eyeteeth.

Know one's onions (stuff).

同 久經世故（1419）Have seen the elephant.

反 乳臭未乾（2283）One's mouth is full of pap.

1561 **老大難** lǎo dà nán

An old, big, and difficult fellow. (lit.)

A hard nut to crack.

Hot potato.

反 輕而易舉（2124）Mere child's play.

1562 **老當益壯** lǎo dāng yì zhuàng

The older one is, the stronger he will be. (lit.)

Live to a green old age.

To be hale and hearty.

There is fight in the old dog yet.

同 人老心不老，人窮志不窮（2208）Life begins at sixty.

源 後漢書・馬援傳："丈夫為志，窮當益堅，老當益壯。"

老調重彈 lǎo diào chóng tán 1563
Old tune is played again. (lit.)
Strike up the old tune.
Harp on the shopworn theme.

老而不死是為賊也 1564
lǎo ér bù sǐ shì wéi zéi yě
A man too old still living is a thief. (lit.)
He lives long that lives till all are weary of him.

反 年高德劭（1902）Old age is honourable.
源 論語．憲問："幼而不孫弟，長而無述焉，老而不死是為賊。"

老行尊 lǎo háng zūn 1565
The old senior in the trade. (lit.)
A know-how.

反 外行（2835）Not in one's beat.

老虎頭上捉虱子 lǎo hǔ tóu shàng zhuō shī zǐ 1566
Catching lice on a tiger's head. (lit.)
It is a bold mouse that nestles in the cat's ear.

老驥伏櫪 lǎo jì fú lì 1567
The old steed hidden in the stable. (lit.)
There is fight in the old dog yet.
The day is short and the work is long.
It is better to wear out than to rust out.

同 寶刀未老（0087）There's many a good tune played on an old fiddle.
反 少不更事（2366）As green as grass.
源 魏武帝集．步出夏門行："老驥伏櫪，志在千里，烈士暮年，壯心不已。"

老奸巨猾 lǎo jiān jù huá 1568
An old rogue and a big hypocrite. (lit.)
A wise old bird.
An old fox needs not to be taught tricks.
The fox may grow grey, but never good.
As slippery as an eel.
Know one point more than the devil.
As cunning as a fox.

反 年高德劭（1902）Old age is honourable.
源 資治通鑒．唐紀："雖老奸巨猾，無能逃其術者。"

1569 **老糠榨不出油** lǎo kāng zhà bú chū yóu

Cannot squeeze oil out of old chaffs. (lit.)

You cannot get water out of a stone.

1570 **老馬識途** lǎo mǎ shí tú

The old horse knows the way. (lit.)

An old dog for a hard road.
One who has been around.
An old ox makes a straight furrow.
If you wish for good advice, consult and old man.
They who live longest will see most.

同 駕輕就熟（1261）An old hand at the game.

源 韓非子・說林上：“乃放老馬而隨之，遂得道。”

1571 **老氣橫秋** lǎo qì héng qiū

The air of the aged claims importance. (lit.)

To be stricken in years.
A man of the world.
In the autumn of one's life.

反 精力旺盛（1385）Full of beans.

源 黃庭堅・山谷集：“老來忠義氣橫秋。”

1572 **老生常談** lǎo shēng cháng tán

An old scholar's common talk. (lit.)

Standing dish.
A tale twice told is cabbage twice sold.
Flog a dead horse.

反 奇談怪論（2025）A cock and bull story.

源 三國志・魏志・管輅傳：“此老生之常譚。”

1573 **老鼠跌落天平**

lǎo shǔ diē luò tiān píng

The rat falls down on a balance. (lit.)

Self-praise is no recommendation.

1574 **老鼠拉龜，無處下手**

lǎo shǔ lā guī, wú chù xià shǒu

A rat (trying) to pull a turtle does not know where to start. (lit.)

To catch a Tartar.

老態龍鍾 lǎo tài lóng zhōng 1575

An old man's manner shows senility. (lit.)

In one's dotage.

同 老朽昏聵（1577）To run to seed.

反 血氣方剛（3275）In the prime of youth.

老吾老以及人之老 1576

lǎo wú lǎo yǐ jí rén zhī lǎo

Respect the old members of my family and also those of other families. (lit.)

Charity begins at home.

同 推己及人（2816）Put oneself in another's shoes.

源 孟子："老吾老以及人之老，幼吾幼以及人之幼，天下可運於掌。"

老朽昏聵 lǎo xiǔ hūn kuì 1577

Old, mortal, dull and deaf. (lit.)

To run to seed.

Long in the tooth.

反 英姿煥發（3598）In one's vigorous youth.

源 鄭愚："欲役老朽之筋骸。"

老油條 lǎo yóu tiáo 1578

Old dough-strips. (lit.)

A milk-sop.

反 幹勁沖天（0874）To be a live wire.

老於世故 lǎo yú shì gù 1579

Long experience in life and the world. (lit.)

To be a man of the world.

Know every move on the board.

Know which way the wind blows.

同 閱歷其深（3748）Have seen much of the world.

反 初出茅廬（0421）A raw recruit.

老子天下第一 lǎo zi tiān xià dì yī 1580

Old dear me, the number one of the world. (lit.)

Look after Number One.

I love my friends well, but myself better.

同 唯我獨尊（2892）To be overweening.

反 甘拜下風（0860）Take a back seat.

樂不可支 lè bù kě zhī 1581

Happy with uncontrollable joy. (lit.)

Helpless with mirth.

To be tickled to death.

同 喜不自勝（3056）Beside oneself with joy.

反 悲不自勝（0096）Abandon oneself to grief.

源 後漢書·張堪傳："張公為政，樂不可支。"

1582 **樂極生悲** lè jí shēng bēi

Pleasure at its height often gives rise to sadness. (lit.)

He that talks much of his happiness summons grief.

Pleasure has a sting in its tail.

同 興盡悲來（3225）He who laughs on Friday will weep on Sunday.

反 苦盡甘來（1519）Pain past is pleasure.

源 史記：“酒極則亂，樂極則悲。”

1583 **樂善好施** lè shàn hào shī

Glad to do benevolence and fond of giving. (lit.)

Give with a free hand.

Free with one's money.

Come down handsome.

Be a good Samaritan.

反 見死不救（1280）Leave one in the lurch.

1584 **樂天知命** lè tiān zhī mìng

Accord with Providence and accept the fate. (lit.)

In the lap of the gods.

The world is his that enjoys it.

反 怨天尤人（3740）Everyone puts his faults on the times.

源 周易・繫辭上：“樂天知命，故不憂。”

1585 **勒緊褲帶** lēi jǐn kù dài

Tighten the trousers' belt. (lit.)

Tighten one's belt.

Pull in one's belt.

同 節衣縮食（1327）To go on the skin.

反 鋪張排場（2012）Do a thing in style.

1586 **雷打不動** léi dǎ bù dòng

Even thunder-stroke cannot move it. (lit.)

Take a firm hold.

同 安如磐石（0013）As firm as a rock.

1587 **雷厲風行** léi lì fēng xíng

Violence of thunder and swiftness of wind. (lit.)

Take drastic measures.

With great fanfare.

同 大刀闊斧（0513）Go the whole hog.

源 李漁・蜃中樓・獻壽：“大丈夫做事，雷厲風行。”

雷聲大，雨點小 1588
léi shēng dà, yǔ diǎn xiǎo
Big noise of thunder brings small drops of rain. (lit.)
Great cry and little wool.
Much bruit, little fruit.
The mountain has brought forth a mouse.

同 口惠而實不至（1505）You cackle often, but never lay an egg.
源 釋道源．景德傳燈錄："雷聲甚大，雨點全無。"

淚如泉湧 lèi rú quán yǒng 1589
Tears flowing like a dashing spring. (lit.)
Break into a passion of tears.
A deluge (flood) of tears.
Brimming with tears.
Burst into tears.

同 痛哭流涕（2780）Cry one's eyes out.
反 破涕為笑（2007）They that sow in tears shall reap in joy.

淚如雨下 lèi rú yǔ xià 1590
Tears trickling down like rain. (lit.)
To pipe one's eye.
Shed tears.

冷不提防 lěng bù dī fáng 1591
Too sudden to be on defence. (lit.)
Off one's guard.

冷嘲熱諷 lěng cháo rè fěng 1592
Cold sneer and hot sarcasm. (lit.)
Laugh to scorn.
Sneer and jeer at

冷酷無情 lěng kù wú qíng 1593
Cold, cruel and merciless. (lit.)
In cold blood.
As hard as nails.

同 冷若冰霜（1595）As cold as ice.
反 熱情洋溢（2187）Glow with enthusiasm.

冷酷心腸 lěng kù xīn cháng 1594
Cold, cruel heart (and intestines). (lit.)
Heart of marble.
As cold as a stone.

同 鐵石心腸（2750）Dead to all feeling.
反 熱血沸騰（2188）With heart afire.

1595 冷若冰霜 lěng ruò bīng shuāng
As cold as ice and frost. (lit.)
As cold as charity (ice).
An iceberg.

同 給以冷遇（0912）Give one the cold shoulder.
反 熱情洋溢（2187）Glow with enthusiasm.

1596 冷眼旁觀 lěng yǎn páng guān
A cold-eyed watch by the side. (lit.)
To be outside the ropes.
Treat with indifference.

同 袖手旁觀（3242）Look on with folded arms.
反 熱烈贊助（2185）Carry a torch for
源 元曲："常將冷眼觀螃蟹，看你橫行到幾時。"

1597 離羣索居 lí qún suǒ jū
Leave the crowd to live alone. (lit.)
Far from the madding crowd.
Keep oneself to oneself.
Plough one's lonely furrow.
Cut oneself off from the world.

同 退隱林下（2826）Go to grass.
反 趁熱鬧Jump on the bandwagon.
源 禮記·檀弓上："吾離羣而索居，亦已久矣。"

1598 離題萬丈 lí tí wàn zhàng
Ten thousand zhang (zhang=10 Chinese feet) off the topic. (lit.)
Beside the point.
Wide of the mark.
Lose the thread.
Fly off at a tangent.

同 文不對題（2921）Beside the mark.
反 一語到題 To come to the point.

1599 理所當然 lǐ suǒ dāng rán
The reason as it should be. (lit.)
As a matter of course.
It stands to reason.

同 天經地義（2714）It goes without saying.
反 毫無道理（1026）Without rhyme or reason.
源 文中子·魏相篇："非辯也，理當然耳。"

1600 禮多必詐 lǐ duō bì zhà
Too much politeness must be pretensions. (lit.)
Full of courtesy, full of craft.
Many kiss the hand they wish to cut off.

同 黃鼠狼給雞拜年（1143）When the fox preaches, beware the geese.

禮尚往來 lǐ shàng wǎng lái ◀1601
The customary act of giving and receiving. (lit.)
One good turn deserves another.
Give and take.
Kindness begets kindness.
Presents keep friendship warm.
He may freely receive courtesies that knows how to requite them.
Ka me, ka thee.

同 投桃報李（2793）Exchange of gifts.
反 雞犬之聲相聞，而老死不相往來（1202）Half the world knows not how the other half lives.
源 禮記·曲禮上："往而不來，非禮也，來而不往，亦非禮也。"

力不從心 lì bù cóng xīn ◀1602
The strength does not obey the heart. (lit.)
The spirit is willing, but the flesh is weak.
Beyond one's tether.

同 心有餘而力不足（3195）Bite off more than one can chew.
源 漢書·班超傳："如有卒暴，超之氣力不能從心。"

力不勝任 lì bù shēng rèn ◀1603
Ability not equal to the job. (lit.)
Beyond one.
Beyond one's power.
To be far below the mark.
Not cut out for.

反 勝任愉快（2442）Equal to the occasion.
源 易·繫辭："鼎折足，覆公餗，其形渥，凶，言不勝其任也。"

力竭聲嘶 lì jié shēng sī ◀1604
Strength exhausted, voice hoarse. (lit.)
Talk oneself hoarse.
Cry one's heart out.
Worn and husky.

力所能及 lì suǒ néng jí ◀1605
What one's strength can do. (lit.)
To the best of one's abilities.
To be on one's mettle.
To go great lengths.

力挽狂瀾 lì wǎn kuáng lán ◀1606
Fight against furious waves. (lit.)
Stem the tide.
Save the situation.

源 韓愈·進學解："障百川而東之，回狂瀾於既倒。"

1607 **利刀割肉創猶合，惡語傷人恨不消** lì dāo gē ròu chuāng yóu hé, è yǔ shāng rén hèn bù xiāo

The sharp knife cutting the flesh, the wound will heal; nasty words hurting people, the grudge will never disappear. (lit.)

Words cut more than swords.

An ill wound is cured, not an ill name.

1608 **利口不利腹** lì kǒu bú lì fù

Benefit one's mouth but not one's stomach. (lit.)

Good in the mouth and bad in the maw.

1609 **利令智昏** lì lìng zhì hūn

Profit makes wisdom blind. (lit.)

Wealth makes wit waver.

Greedy for money.

源 史記 · 平原君虞卿列傳："鄙諺曰，利令智昏。"

1610 **利如刀刃** lì rú dāo rèn

As sharp as a knife. (lit.)

As keen as razor.

1611 **利益均沾** lì yì jūn zhān

Sharing equal benefit. (lit.)

Share and share alike.

同 平分秋色（1988）Go fifty-fifty.

反 厚此薄彼（1076）Treat with partiality.

1612 **歷盡滄桑** lì jìn cāng sāng

Gone through great changes in life - mulbery field changed into sea. (lit.)

Through thick and thin.

Go through hell and high water.

同 久經風雨（1418）To have weathered a storm.

1613 **歷盡辛酸** lì jìn xīn suān

Have experienced all bitter and sour. (lit.)

Through the mill.

Through hell and high water.

同 曾經滄海（0317）Go through fire and water.

反 初見世面（0424）Babes in the woods.

歷歷在目 lì lì zài mù 1614

Every detail as if visualized in front of the eyes. (lit.)

A commanding view.
A bird's eye view.
A full view.
Fresh in one's mind.

同 一目了然（3429）Everybody can see that at a glance.
源 杜甫・歷歷詩："歷歷開元事，分明在眼前。"

歷史重演 lì shǐ chóng yǎn 1615

History repeats the show. (lit.)

History repeats itself.

反 破題兒第一遭（2006）Without precedent in history.

連打帶罵 lián dǎ dài mà 1616

Beating together with scolding. (lit.)

Add insult to injury.

連戰皆北 lián zhàn jiē běi 1617

Successive wars were defeated. (lit.)

To be beaten all hollow.

反 從勝利走向勝利（0463）Nothing succeeds like success.

廉潔清正 lián jié qīng zhèng 1618

Uncorrupted, clean and righteous. (lit.)

Have clean hands.

反 貪贓枉法（2676）Line one's purse.

練出功夫 liàn chū gōng fū 1619

Practice produces skill. (lit.)

He that shoots oft shall at last hit the mark.
The more you do, the more you may do.
Practice makes perfect.

反 白費氣力（0038）Beat the air.

良禽擇木而棲 liáng qín zé mù ér qī 1620

Good birds select tress to live on. (lit.)

Better be alone than in ill company.

良藥苦口利於病 1621

liáng yào kǔ kǒu lì yú bìng

Good medicine though bitter to the mouth is beneficial in curing a disease. (lit.)

Good medicine tastes bitter to the mouth.
Bitter pills may have wholesome effects.

源 家語："良藥苦口利於病，忠言逆耳利於行。"

1622 良莠不分 liáng yǒu bù fēn
Good and bad not be distinguished. (lit.)
Not know good from evil.

同 不辨菽麥（0174）Not know chalk from cheese.
反 判別真僞（1949）Know a hawk from a handsaw.

1623 梁上君子 liáng shàng jūn zǐ
A gentleman perched on a beam (of a house). (lit.)
Light-fingered gentry.
A cat burglar.

源 後漢書·陳寔傳："不善之人，未必本惡，習與性成，遂至於此，梁上君子是也。"

1624 兩敗俱傷 liǎng bài jù shāng
Both lose and all injured. (lit.)
Both suffer for it.
Fight like Kilkenny cats.
Quarrelling dogs come halting home.

源 戰國策："今兩虎爭人而鬥，小者必死，大者必傷。"

1625 兩鬢斑白 liǎng bìn bān bái
Both temples spotted white. (lit.)
Silver threads among the gold.

反 乳臭未乾（2283）Wet behind the ears.

1626 兩耳不聞窗外事
liǎng ěr bù wén chuāng wài shì
Both ears can't hear things outside the window. (lit.)
None so deaf as those who won't hear.
Turn a deaf ear to

同 專心致志（3938）With undivided attention.

1627 兩軍對壘 liǎng jūn duì lěi
Two armies are facing opposite. (lit.)
A pitched battle.

1628 兩碼事 liǎng mǎ shì
Two yard thing. (lit.)
That's another pair of shoes.
That's another cup of tea.
That's a horse of another colour.

同 風馬牛不相及（0802）As different as chalk is from cheese.
反 一而二，二而一（3387）One and the same thing.

1629 兩面派 liǎng miàn pài
A gang with two faces. (lit.)
Bear two faces in one hood.

同 兩面討好（1632）Sit on the hedge.

兩面三刀 liǎng miàn sān dāo 1630
Two faces and three knives. (lit.)
Run with the hound and hold with the hare.
Break my head and then give me plaster.
A double agent.
Have as many faces as the moon.

源 元曲選 · 李行道 · 灰闌記："豈知他有兩面三刀，向夫主廝搬調。"

兩面受敵 liǎng miàn shòu dí 1631
Meet enemies on both sides. (lit.)
Between two fires.

兩面討好 liǎng miàn tǎo hǎo 1632
Try to please both sides. (lit.)
Sit on the hedge.

同 騎牆派（2038）A fence-sitter.
反 一邊倒（3374）All on one side, like Bridgnorth election.

兩全其美 liǎng quán qí měi 1633
Make both respects complete. (lit.)
Make the best of both worlds.
It is good to have friends both in heaven and in hell.

源 晉書："忠孝之道，安得兩全。"

兩頭落空 liǎng tóu luò kōng 1634
Fall through at both ends. (lit.)
Fall between two stools.
If you run after two hares, you will catch neither.

反 一箭雙鵰（3404）Kill two birds with one stone.

兩廂情願 liǎng xiāng qíng yuàn 1635
Both parties are willing. (lit.)
With mutual consent.

兩袖清風 liǎng xiù qīng fēng 1636
Both sleeves hold pure air. (lit.)
To have clean hands.

亮相 liàng xiàng 1637
To show one's appearance. (lit.)
Cut a figure.

1638 **量力而行** liàng lì ér xíng

Act according to one's strength. (lit.)

Undertake no more than you can perform.

Raise no more spirits than you can conjure down.

Kindle not a fire that you cannot extinguish.

反 自不量力（3970）Bite off more than one can chew.

源 左傳．昭十年："力能則進，否則退，量力而行。"

1639 **量入為出** liàng rù wéi chū

Spend according to one's income. (lit.)

Make both ends meet.

Live within one's means.

Cut one's coat according to one's cloth.

反 寅吃卯糧（3583）Live above one's income.

源 禮記："以三十年之通制國用，量入以為出。"

1640 **聊勝於無** liáo shèng yú wú

It is better than nothing. (lit.)

A little is better than none.

Better small fish than empty dish.

Half a loaf is better than no bread.

Better half an egg than an empty shell.

One foot is better than two crutches.

Something is better than nothing.

A bad bush is better than an open field.

反 過猶不及（1003）Too much water drowned the miller.

源 陶淵明．和劉柴桑詩："慰情聊勝無。"

1641 **寥若晨星** liáo ruò chén xīng

As scarce as the morning stars. (lit.)

Few and far between.

同 屈指可數（2149）To be on the map.

反 恒河沙數（1063）As numberless as the sands.

源 韓愈．華山女詩："黃衣道士亦講說，座下寥落如明星。"

1642 **了此一生** liǎo cǐ yì shēng

Just to end this life. (lit.)

Shuffle off this mortal coil.

Go the way of all flesh.

同 自尋短見（4005）Make away with oneself.

了結塵緣 liǎo jié chén yuán
To finish the relation on this earthly world. (lit.)
Pay one's debt to nature.
Go to one's account.

同 與世長辭（3707）Pass away. 1643

了無瓜葛 liǎo wú guā gé
Without any entanglement, like a gourd and its stalk. (lit.)
Have nothing to do with
Have no bearing upon.

反 參與其事（0302）Have a finger in the pie. 1644

潦倒一生 liǎo dǎo yì shēng
Frustrated and down all one's life. (lit.)
To knock about.
Down and out.
Lead a dog's life.

同 參差不偶（0316）In a sorry plight. 1645
反 飛黃騰達（0771）Flourish like the Green bay-tree.

瞭如指掌 liǎo rú zhǐ zhǎng
As clear as the palm. (lit.)
As plain as a pikestaff.
As plain as the nose in one's face.

同 昭然若揭（3808）All too clear. 1646
反 如入五里霧中（2276）To be lost in the cloud.

料事如神 liào shì rú shén
Can foretell things like god. (lit.)
Have a long head.
Have great foresight.

1647

咧着嘴笑 liě zhe zuǐ xiào
The mouth breaks into a smile. (lit.)
Sport one's ivory.

同 露齒而笑（1704）Grin from ear to ear. 1648
反 哭喪着臉（1513）To sour one's cheeks.

烈士暮年，壯心不已
liè shì mù nián, zhuàng xīn bù yǐ
The martyrs at the eve of life still have a heart of courage. (lit.)
The day is short and the work is long.

同 人老心不老，人窮志不窮（2208）Life begins at sixty. 1649
源 原係魏武帝曹操詩句。

臨工 lín gōng
A temporary work. (lit.)
An odd-jobber.
Jack at a pinch.

1650

1651 **臨老學吹打** lín lǎo xué chuī dǎ

Getting old, one begins to learn to blow flute. (lit.)

An old dog will learn no new tricks.

1652 **臨難不懼** lín nàn bù jù

Not afraid of crisis. (lit.)

Look death in the face.

To affront death.

Grin and bear it.

同 從容就義（0458）Die a martyr's death.

反 無病呻吟（2949）Cry out before one is hurt.

1653 **臨難苟免** lín nàn gǒu miǎn

Shirk at the point of crisis. (lit.)

Save one's bacon.

同 死裏逃生（2627）Out of the jaws of death.

源 禮記："臨難毋苟免。"

1654 **臨深履薄** lín shēn lǚ báo

Approaching the brink of the abyss and treading on thin ice. (lit.)

Pick one's way (steps).

To tread upon eggs.

Keep on one's toes.

同 戰戰兢兢（3788）In a blue funk.

反 莽莽撞撞（1769）Like a bull in a china shop.

源 詩經．小雅．小旻："戰戰兢兢，如臨深淵，如履薄冰。"

1655 **臨堤走馬收轡晚，船到江心補漏遲** lín dī zǒu mǎ shōu jiāng wǎn, chuán dào jiāng xīn bǔ lòu chí

It is too late to hold the horse at the embankment; it is too late to mend the leaking boat in the middle of the river. (lit.)

It's too late to cast anchor when the ship's on the rocks.

It is too late to spare when the bottom is bare.

Never swop horses while crossing the stream.

源 本條目原句出自《牧羊記傳奇》

1656 **臨危不懼** lín wēi bù jù

Fearless in face of danger. (lit.)

If the sky falls, we shall catch larks.

Face the music.

同 勇猛過人（3617）Full of guts.

反 前怕狼，後怕虎（2077）Too much taking heed is loss.

臨崖勒馬 lín yá lè mǎ
To hold the horse on the brink of precipice. (lit.)
Pull oneself up.

源 名賢集："臨崖勒馬收韁晚，船到江心補漏遲。" 1657

臨淵羨魚，不如退而結網
lín yuān xiàn yú, bù rú tuì ér jié wǎng
Admiring the fish at the river one might as well return (home) to knit net. (lit.)
The end of fishing is not angling but catching.

源 漢書．董仲舒傳："古人有言，臨淵羨魚，不如退而結網。" 1658

臨陣退縮 lín zhèn tuì suō
To skulk when going to battle. (lit.)
Turn tail at the last moment.
Back down at the sight of the enemy.
Beat a retreat.
Willing to wound and yet afraid to strike.

同 畏縮不前（2912）Get cold feet.
反 挺身而出（2759）Stand in the gap. 1659

吝嗇小氣 lìn sè xiǎo qì
Stingy and narrow minded. (lit.)
Cramp in the hand.
Pinch pennies.

反 仗義疏財（3803）Come down handsome. 1660

伶仃孤苦 líng dīng gū kǔ
Lonely, desolate and bitter. (lit.)
His hat covers his family.

源 李密．陳情表："伶仃孤苦，至於成立。" 1661

玲瓏浮突 líng lóng fú tū
Carved openwork in bold relief. (lit.)
In bold relief. 1662

零分 líng fēn
Zero mark. (lit.)
A duck's egg. 1663

零零碎碎 líng líng suì suì
Fragments and fractions. (lit.)
Odds and ends.

反 一應俱全（3489）Root and branch. 1664

1665 **靈活處理** líng huó chǔ lǐ
Deal with matters promptly and lively. (lit.)
Stretch a point.
Make allowances.

同 隨機應變（2655）Stretch your legs according to your coverlet.
反 按老皇曆辦事（0020）Ride a method to death.

1666 **靈機一動** líng jī yī dòng
Hit a clever contrivance. (lit.)
Take a notion.
Have a brain wave.
Take it into one's head.
Have a brilliant inspiration.
Hit upon an idea.

反 冥頑不靈（1829）As stiff as a poker.

1667 **靈通界人士** líng tōng jiè rén shì
Well informative people. (lit.)
Those in the know.

同 消息靈通（3127）Have an ear to the ground.
反 蒙在鼓裏（1785）To be kept in the dark.

1668 **領導幹部** lǐng dǎo gàn bù
Leading cadres. (lit.)
The powers that be.
Those at the stern of public affairs.

反 小人物（3140）A small fry.

1669 **領會精神，別啃教條**
lǐng huì jīng shén, bié kěn jiào tiáo
Comprehand the basic spirit, don't swallow the dogmas. (lit.)
Not of the letter, but of the spirit.

反 生吞活剝（2420）Learn by rote.

1670 **另闢蹊徑**lìng pì xī jìng
To pioneer a new path. (lit.)
Take one's own line.

反 陳陳相因（0344）Follow the beaten track.

1671 **另起爐灶**lìng qǐ lú zào
Build another kitchen range. (lit.)
Start all over again.
Break fresh ground.
Strike out in another direction.

同 改弦更張（0855）Make a fresh start.
反 蕭規曹隨（3132）Take a leaf out of another's book.

另眼相看 lìng yǎn xiāng kàn 1672

To see with special eyes (attention). (lit.)

Regard with favour.

See in a new light.

同 士別三日，刮目相看（2493）Wanton kittens may make sober cats.

反 一視同仁（3457）When it rains it rains on all alike.

另有任務 lìng yǒu rèn wù 1673

Have another task to do. (lit.)

Have other fish to fry.

令人髮指 lìng rén fà zhǐ 1674

Make one's hair point (up). (lit.)

Drive one mad.

Make one's hair stand on end.

同 激起義憤（1183）Make one's blood boil.

源 史記．刺客列傳："士皆瞋目，髮盡上指冠。"

令人咋舌 lìng rén zhà shé 1675

Make one tongue-tied. (lit.)

Take one's breath away.

令人作嘔 lìng rén zuò ǒu 1676

Make one vomit. (lit.)

Make one sick.

Turn one's stomach.

源 晉書："中年以來傷於哀樂，與親友別，輒作數日惡。"（惡與嘔同）

溜之大吉 liū zhī dà jí 1677

Slip away with big luck. (lit.)

Give one the slip.

Make oneself scarce.

Take a powder.

Cut and run.

Turn on one's heels.

Seek safety in flight.

Show a clean pair of heels.

同 逃之夭夭（2696）Take flight.

反 突如其來（2805）Appear from nowhere.

流芳百世liú fāng bǎi shì 1678

Fragrant reputation pervailing hundred generations. (lit.)

Leave one's mark on history.

Have a niche in the temple of fame.

同 萬古流芳（2849）On the scroll of fame.

反 遺臭萬年（3523）The evil that men do lives after them.

源 世說新語："晉桓溫有大志，嘗撫枕歎曰，既不能流芳百世，不足復遺臭萬年耶。"

1679 流浪漢 liú làng hàn
A vagrant fellow. (lit.)
A bird of passage.

反 地頭蛇（0640）Cock on his own dunghill.
源 李白詩："感此瀟湘客，淒其流浪情。"

1680 流離失所 liú lí shī suǒ
Wander about, losing one's home. (lit.)
Here today and gone tomorrow.
Displaced person.

同 彳亍街頭（0381）Have got the key of the street.
源 白居易詩："骨肉流離道路中。"

1681 流連忘返 liú lián wàng fǎn
Fond of roaming and forget to return home. (lit.)
Held spellbound by
Can't tear oneself away.
Linger on.

反 溜之大吉（1677）Make oneself scarce.
源 孟子·梁惠王下："從流下而忘反謂之流，從流上而忘反謂之連。"

1682 流水不腐 liú shuǐ bù fǔ
Running water never stale. (lit.)
To keep busy is to keep fit.
Drawn wells have sweetest water.
Drawn wells are seldom dry.

源 雲笈七籤："流水不腐，戶樞不蠹，以其勞動不息也。"

1683 留得青山在，不怕沒柴燒
liú dé qīng shān zài, bù pà méi chái shāo
Keeping the green hill there, no fear of no firewood to burn. (lit.)
While there is life there is hope.
There is always life for the living.
Never say die.

1684 留有一手 liú yǒu yī shǒu
Still keeping one hand. (lit.)
Have a second string to one's bow.
Have a card up one's sleeve.

1685 留有餘地 liú yǒu yú dì
Leaving some spared ground. (lit.)
Leave room for
Leave some leeway.
Leave a door open.
Make allowance for
Tell not all you know, nor do all you can.

反 無迴旋之地（2965）Not room enough to swing a cat.

六親不認 liù qīn bú rèn 1686

Not being recognised by the six relations (father, mother, elder and younger brothers, (husband or) wife and son). (lit.)

Turn one's back on one's own flesh and blood.

Cut loose from old ties.

同 視如路人（2529）Cut one dead.

反 拉關係（1534）Scrape acquaintance with

源 老子·六親注：“父子兄弟夫婦也。”

六神無主 liù shén wú zhǔ 1687

The six gods have no resolution. (lit.)

To go to pieces.

To be all at sea.

同 魂飛魄散（1160）Like a hog in a squall.

反 心中有數（3201）Know one's own mind.

源 類函：“黃帝問玄女兵法，此為六神，為戰主也。”

隆冬時節 lóng dōng shí jié 1688

Bitter winter season. (lit.)

In the depth of winter.

源 漢書：“今水潦移於江南，迫隆冬至。”

隆重接待 lóng zhòng jiē dài 1689

Grand and dignified reception. (lit.)

Give royal reception.

Roll out the red carpet for

Make much of.

同 熱烈歡迎（2184）Give one three times three.

反 要理不理（3357）Leave one in the cold.

龍牀不如狗窩 lóng chuáng bù rú gǒu wō 1690

A dragon's bed is not as good as a dog's kennel. (lit.)

Every bird likes its own nest best.

Every bird thinks its own nest charming.

Home is home, be it ever so homely.

龍飛鳳舞 lóng fēi fèng wǔ 1691

Dragon flying and phoenix dancing. (lit.)

Write a fair hand.

Write a good fist.

同 筆走龍蛇（0116）Write with a flourish.

源 蘇軾·表忠觀碑：“天目之山，苕水出焉，龍飛鳳舞，萃於臨安。”

1692 **龍生龍，鳳生鳳**
lóng shēng lóng, fèng shēng fèng
Dragons give birth to dragons, phoenix to phoenix. (lit.)
Like father, like son.
Like begets like.
A chip of the old block.

同 有其父必有其子（3658）Like father, like son.
源 指月錄：“南陽慧忠國師云，龍生龍子，鳳生鳳兒。”

1693 **龍游淺水遭蝦戲**
lóng yóu qián shuǐ zāo xiā xì
Dragons swimming in shallow water may be attacked by shrimps. (lit.)
He came safe from the East Indies, and was drowned in the Thames.

同 虎落平陽被犬欺（1093）Hares may pull dead lions by the beard.

1694 **漏洞百出** lòu dòng bǎi chū
Leaking holes are hundreds. (lit.)
Full of loopholes.
Not to hold water.

同 破綻百出（2008）Show the cloven foot.
反 完美無缺（2840）The pink of perfection.

1695 **露出廬山真面目**
lòu chū lú shān zhēn miàn mù
Expose the true face of Lu-Shan (Mt. Lu). (lit.)
Show one's true colours.
Give oneself away.

反 喬裝打扮（2096）Sail under false colours.
源 蘇軾・題西林壁詩：“不識廬山真面目，只緣身在此山中。”

1696 **露出馬腳** lòu chū mǎ jiǎo
The horse's hoof is exposed. (lit.)
Let the cat out of the bag.
Heel of Achilles.
Give oneself away.
Show the cloven foot.

同 破綻百出（2008）Betray the cloven hoof.
反 文過飾非（2922）Gloss over faults.
源 元曲選・陳州糶米：“這一來只怕我們露出馬腳來了。”

1697 **露出苗頭** lòu chū miáo tóu
Expose the head of the seedling. (lit.)
Come to a head.
Shoot out buds.

同 方興未艾（0754）In the bud.

1698

廬山真面目 lú shān zhēn miàn mù

The true face of Lu-Shan (Mt. Lu). (lit.)

One's true self.

Come out in one's true colours.

反 喬裝打扮（2096）Sail under false colours.

源 蘇軾詩："不識廬山真面目，只緣身在此山中。"

1699

爐火純青 lú huǒ chún qīng

The stove fire is pure green. (lit.)

To have smelt the smell of fire.

Make oneself master of

1700

鹵莽從事 lǔ mǎng cóng shì

Carelessly and roughly doing things. (lit.)

Ride for a fall.

Rush headlong.

同 莽莽撞撞（1769）Like a bull in a china shop.

反 謹小慎微（1358）Dot one's i's and cross one's t's.

1701

魯莽滅裂 lǔ mǎng miè liè

Undertaking tasks roughly and rudely, causing breakage and destruction. (lit.)

As gruff as a bear.

Rush headlong.

Like a bull in a china shop.

同 莽莽撞撞（1769）Fly in the face of danger.

源 莊子．則陽："君為政焉勿魯莽，治民焉勿滅裂。"

1702

路遙知馬力 lù yáo zhī mǎ lì

When the journey is long one knows the strength of the horse. (lit.)

The good seaman is known in bad weather.

同 疾風知勁草（1219）Oaks may fall when reeds stand the storm.

源 元曲選．無名氏．爭報恩："可不道路遙知馬力，日久見人心。"

1703

戮力同心 lù lì tóng xīn

To unite strength and to have the same heart. (lit.)

To hang together.

Unite as one.

同 同心協力（2772）To pull together.

反 各行其是（0908）Have one's own way.

源 墨子，尚賢："聿求元聖，與之戮力同心，以治天下。"

1704

露齒而笑 lù chǐ ér xiào

Show the teeth and laugh. (lit.)

Sport one's ivory.

Grin from ear to ear.

反 痛哭流涕（2780）Cry one's eyes out.

1705 **屢試不爽** lǚ shì bù shuǎng
Satisfactory in repeated tests. (lit.)
Stand the test.
Without fail.

反 經不起考驗（1378）Weighed in the balance and found wanting.

1706 **律己律人** lǜ jǐ lǜ rén
Discipline oneself and others. (lit.)
The counsel you would have another keep, first keep thyself.
Through obedience learn to command.
He is not fit to command others that cannot command himself.

同 以身作則（3538）Set a good example for others.

1707 **亂蹦亂跳** luàn bèng luàn tiào
Leaping and jumping haphazardly. (lit.)
As crazy as a bedbug.

1708 **亂七八糟** luàn qī bā zāo
Seven in disorder and eight in a mess. (lit.)
At sixes and sevens.
All in a huddle.
Higgledy-piggledy.
A pretty kettle of fish.

同 一塌糊塗（3463）A devil of a mess.
反 有條不紊（3671）In apple-pie order.

1709 **亂説一通** luàn shuō yī tōng
Speak out recklessly. (lit.)
To fly a kite.
Talk nonsense.

反 引經據典（3584）Give chapter and verse.

1710 **亂作一團** luàn zuò yī tuán
Act recklessly in a mess. (lit.)
Go haywire.
It was hell broken loose.
All in a huddle.

反 步調一致（0292）To be in step.

1711 **淪落天涯** lún luò tiān yá
Sunk and down in life at the edge of heaven. (lit.)
To be down and out.
To knock about.

反 養尊處優（3341）Lie on a bed of roses.

輪休 lún xiū 1712

Take turn to rest. (lit.)

They also serve who only stand and wait.

羅通掃北 luó tōng sào běi 1713

Luo Tong (a famous warrior) swept to the north. (lit.)

Make a clean sweep of it.

洛陽紙貴 luò yáng zhǐ guì

Luo Yang's paper becomes expensive. (lit.)

A best seller.

源 晉書．文苑傳："左思賦三都，構思十年，豪貴之家，競相傳寫，洛陽為之紙貴。" 1714

絡繹不絕 luò yì bù jué

Coming to and fro uninterruptedly. (lit.)

In rapid succession.

An endless flow.

To be alive with.

同 川流不息（0433）A constant flow. 1715

源 後漢書．東海恭王強傳："數遣使者太醫令丞，方使道術，絡繹不絕。"

落草為寇 luò cǎo wéi kòu 1716

Go to the bush and become a bandit. (lit.)

Take to the road (heather).

落地生根 luò dì shēng gēn

Fallen (leaves) to the earth will take root. (lit.)

Strike root.

Take root.

同 安家落戶（0010）To settle down. 1717

落荒而逃 luò huāng ér táo

Run away to the wilderness. (lit.)

Jump the country.

Take to the wilderness.

同 投荒落草（2789）Take to the heather. 1718

1719 **落井下石** luò jǐng xià shí

Throw stones (on a person) trapped in a well. (lit.)

When a dog is drowning, everyone offers him a drink.

Take a mean advantage.

反 不為已甚（0253）Pour not water on a drowned mouse.

源 韓愈．柳宗元墓誌銘："落陷阱，不一引手救，反擠之，又下石焉者，皆是也。"

1720 **落入圈套** luò rù quān tào

Fall into a ring-like trap. (lit.)

Play into someone's hands.

Swallow the bait.

To be nicely left.

同 大上其當（0548）To be done brown.

反 衝破藩籬（0387）To break bounds.

1721 **落手打三更** luò shǒu dǎ sān gēng

To start with beating (drum and gong) for the third shift already. (lit.)

Start off on the wrong foot.

Begin at the wrong end.

To be off to a bad start.

反 一蹴而就（3383）At one stroke.

1722 **落湯雞** luò tāng jī

(Like) A chicken in the soup. (lit.)

As wet as a drowned rat (mouse).

Have not a dry thread on.

1723 **落葉歸根** luò yè guī gēn

Fallen leaves return to the roots. (lit.)

East or West, home is best.

To revert to its origin.

同 鳥倦飛而知還（1913）Home is the sailor, home from sea.

M

麻雀雖小，五臟俱全 1724
má què suī xiǎo, wǔ zàng jù quán
Sparrows though small have five viscera complete. (lit.)
There is life in a mussel, though it be little.

馬齒徒增 mǎ chǐ tú zēng 1725
The horse's teeth increase in length. (lit.)
Dog away one's time.
While away the time.
The insidious approach of age.

同 虛度年華（3243）Fritter away one's time.
反 一萬年太久，只爭朝夕（3467）Never put off till tomorrow what may be done today.
源 穀梁傳 · 僖二年："璧則猶是也，而馬齒加長矣。"

馬耳東風 mǎ ěr dōng fēng 1726
East wind (blowing past) a horse's ear. (lit.)
In at one ear and out at the other.

同 水過鴨背（2590）Like water off a duck's back.
反 側耳諦聽（0313）Strain one's ears.
源 蘇軾詩："何殊馬耳東風。"

馬後炮 mǎ hòu pào 1727
Cannon behind the horse. (lit.)
After meat, mustard.

反 先發制人（3078）Steal a march on one.

馬靠鞍裝，人靠衣裳 1728
mǎ kào ān zhuāng, rén kào yī shāng
A horse depends on saddle for decoration, man depends on his clothes. (lit.)
Fine feathers make fine birds.
The tailor makes the man.
The coat makes the man.

1729 **馬馬虎虎** mǎ mǎ hǔ hǔ

A Chinese slang somewhat equivalent to 'muddle through' in English. (lit.)

Rough and ready.

Fair to middling.

After a fashion.

同 敷衍塞責（0821）Huddle over one's duty.

反 認認真真（2247）In sober earnest.

1730 **馬屎憑官勢** mǎ shǐ píng guān shì

Even the horse manure (becomes important) because of the master's official authority. (lit.)

Great men's servants think themselves great.

The fly sat upon the axletree of the chariot wheel and said: What a dust do I raise!

同 仗勢欺人（3802）Pull rank on someone.

1731 **馬有失蹄** mǎ yǒu shī tí

Even a horse's hoof may slip. (lit.)

A horse stumbles that has four legs.

It's a good horse that never stumbles.

1732 **螞蟻啃骨頭** mǎ yǐ kěn gǔ tóu

Ants bite off a big piece of bone. (lit.)

Cut blocks with a razor.

同 細水長流（3062）A bit at a time.

反 大刀闊斧（0513）Go the whole hog.

1733 **罵不絕口** mà bù jué kǒu

Scolding (continuously) without stopping the mouth. (lit.)

Bite one's head off.

反 歌功頌德（0894）Chant the praises of

1734 **罵個狗血淋頭** mà gè gǒu xuè lín tóu

Such a scolding as if dog's blood pouring over the head. (lit.)

Blow one up sky high.

Call one for everything under the sun.

同 臭罵一頓（0400）To roast someone.

反 捧到天上（1962）Praise to the skies.

埋頭苦幹 máí tóu kǔ gàn 1735

Bury the head in hard work. (lit.)

Knuckle down to

Keep one's nose to the grindstone.

To peg away.

Sweat blood.

Work like a Trojan.

同 孜孜不倦（3961）Grind away at

反 吊兒郎當（0649）Gad about.

買櫝還珠 mǎi dú huán zhū 1736

Buy the casket and return a pearl. (lit.)

Grasp the shadow and let go the substance.

源 韓非子："鄭人買其櫝而還其珠。"

賣花姑娘插竹葉 mài huā gū niáng chā zhú yè 1737

The girls selling flowers wear bamboo leaves. (lit.)

Shoemakers' wives are worst shod.

The ass that carries wine drinks water.

賣花讚花香 mài huā zàn huā xiāng 1738

Those selling flowers praise their flowers fragrant. (lit.)

Every man praises his own wares.

Every cook praises her own broth.

Every potter boasts of his own pot.

There's nothing like leather.

瞞天過海 mán tiān guò hǎi 1739

Deceive the sky and cross the sea. (lit.)

Sail under false colours.

滿不在乎 mǎn bù zài hū 1740

Full but couldn't care. (lit.)

Snap one's fingers at

Not to care a fig (pin, hang, rush).

同 漠然置之（1855）Look on with unconcern.

反 斤斤計較（1340）Look at both sides of a penny.

1741 **滿腹經綸** mǎn fù jīng lún
The belly is full of classics. (lit.)
Well versed in
Give chapter and verse.
A walking dictionary.
Widely read.

同 博學多才（0169）Know a thing or two.
反 一竅不通（3440）All Greek to one.

1742 **滿腹妙計** mǎn fù miào jì
The belly is full of tricks. (lit.)
To be full of wrinkles (resources)

反 束手無策（2573）Throw up one's hands in despair.

1743 **滿懷醋意** mǎn huái cù yì
Full of sour thought (jealousy) in the bosom. (lit.)
To bite one's nails.

1744 **滿懷心腹事，盡在不言中**
mǎn huái xīn fù shì, jìn zài bù yán zhōng
Full of secrete thoughts in the bosom but all is not in what is said. (lit.)
More felt, least said.
I say little, but I think the more.

反 大鳴大放（0538）Stand up and be counted.

1745 **滿懷信心** mǎn huái xìn xīn
Full of confidence in the bosom. (lit.)
Feel like an ounce of uranium.
Sit on the top of the world.
Full of confidence.

同 胸有成竹（3233）Have an ace up one's sleeve.

1746 **滿坑滿谷** mǎn kēng mǎn gǔ
In full pit and full valley. (lit.)
As thick as blackberries.
As plentiful as blackberries.
Full of personage.

反 滄海一粟（0306）A drop in the ocean.
源 莊子・天運："在谷滿谷，在坑滿坑。"

1747 **滿臉通紅** mǎn liǎn tōng hóng
The whole face all red. (lit.)
To colour up.
Flush red all over.
As red as a beetroot.

反 面如土色（1805）As pale as death.

滿面春風 mǎn miàn chūn fēng 1748

The face full of spring breeze. (lit.)

To be all smiles.

Look like a million dollars.

同 笑容可掬（3154）A face wreathed in smiles.

源 杜甫詩："畫圖省識春風面。"

滿面紅光 mǎn miàn hóng guāng 1749

The whole face glowing pink. (lit.)

Glowing with health.

To be in the pink.

As sound as pippin.

反 面無人色（1806）As pale as a ghost.

滿腔熱情 mǎn qiāng rè qíng 1750

The heart is full of warm feelings. (lit.)

In the fullness of one's heart.

Filled with ardour.

With bells on.

同 熱情洋溢（2187）To glow with enthusiasm.

反 冷若冰霜（1595）As cold as charity.

滿身銅臭 mǎn shēn tóng chòu 1751

The whole body smells of copper. (lit.)

Wallow in money.

反 兩袖清風（1636）To have clean hands.

滿載而歸 mǎn zài ér guī 1752

Return home fully loaded. (lit.)

Make a fine haul.

Stuffed with

滿招損 mǎn zhāo sǔn 1753

Content can bring disadvantage. (lit.)

The last drop makes the cup run over.

Too much breaks the bag.

When the well is full, it will run over.

源 尚書 · 大禹謨："滿招損，謙受益。"

滿座傾倒 mǎn zuò qīng dǎo 1754

The whole audience fell with admiration. (lit.)

To carry the house.

To bring down the house.

同 哄堂大笑（1037）Set the room in a roar.

1755 **慢條斯理** màn tiáo sī lǐ

Slow and slack in dealing things. (lit.)

At a snail's pace.

As slow as molasses in winter.

Make two bites of a cherry.

同 從容不迫（0457）Take one's time.

反 急如星火（1213）In hot haste.

源 儒林外史：“怎的慢條斯理。”

1756 **漫不經心** màn bù jīng xīn

Hardly goes through the heart (mind). (lit.)

Totally unconcerned.

Devil-may-care.

Pay no heed to

同 毫不在意（1024）To make nothing of

反 全神貫注（2162）Focus one's attention on

1757 **漫天要價** màn tiān yào jià

Ask a price sky high. (lit.)

Quote sky-rocket prices.

同 向天索價（3120）Open one's mouth wide.

反 賤價而沽（1286）Go for a song.

1758 **忙不過來** máng bú guò lái

So busy that one can't even turn around. (lit.)

Have too many irons in the fire.

Have too much on one's plate.

To be up to the elbows.

Working against time.

同 分身乏術（0788）One can't be in two places at once.

反 逍遙自在（3129）Free and easy.

1759 **忙得不可開交** máng dé bù kě kāi jiāo

So busy that one can't get away from the involvement. (lit.)

To be up to one's ears in work.

To have one's hands full.

Not to have a moment one can call one's own.

To be rushed off one's feet.

反 閒得發慌（3091）Find time hang heavy on one's hands.

1760 **忙個不了** máng gè bù liǎo

No end of being busy. (lit.)

Busy as a bee in a treacle-pot.

To have eggs on the spit.

反 無事可為（2990）Have time hanging on one's hands.

忙個不停 máng gè bù tíng 1761

Cannot stop being busy. (lit.)

To be on the go.

On the fly.

To be on the hop.

同 疲於奔命（1970）Run off one's feet.

反 偷得浮生半日閒（2782）Let the grass grow under one's feet.

忙忙碌碌 máng máng lù lù 1762

Hurrying and bustling. (lit.)

Up and doing.

To be on the trot.

同 席不暇暖（3048）To be on the go.

反 無所事事（2996）Twiddle one's thumbs.

源 高駢詩："浮世忙忙蟻子羣。"／賈島詩："碌碌復碌碌。"

忙中有錯 máng zhōng yǒu cuò 1763

In a hurry one may make mistakes. (lit.)

Error is always in haste.

Haste trips over its own heels.

Haste makes waste.

同 欲速則不達（3719）More haste, less speed.

芒刺在背 máng cì zài bèi 1764

Having thorns on the back. (lit.)

A thorn in the flesh.

同 如坐針氈（2281）To be on pins and needles.

反 舒舒服服（2564）As snug as a bug in a rug.

源 漢書．霍光傳："漢宣帝見霍光，若有芒刺在背。"

盲目從事 máng mù cóng shì 1765

Blindly doing things. (lit.)

Go it blind.

A leap in the dark.

Put blind faith in

反 三思而後行（2312）Look before you leap.

盲拳打死老師傅 máng quán dǎ sǐ lǎo shī fù 1766

One's fist blindly hits the old master dead. (lit.)

The scholar may worst the master.

盲人騎瞎馬 máng rén qí xiā mǎ 1767

A blind man riding on a blind horse. (lit.)

Take a leap in the dark.

The blind leading the blind.

同 問道於盲（2932）If the blind lead the blind, both shall fall into the ditch.

源 劉義慶．世說新語："盲人騎瞎馬，夜半臨深池。"

1768 茫然無知 máng rán wú zhī

Confused and ignorant. (lit.)

To be at sea.

To be in the dark.

同 如入五里霧中（2276）To be in a fog.

反 心中有數（3201）Know it as well as a beggar knows his bag.

1769 莽莽撞撞 mǎng mǎng zhuàng zhuàng

Knock about roughly. (lit.)

Like a bull in a china shop.

To be harum-scarum.

To have eaten sauce.

Fly in the face of danger.

Fools rush in where angels fear to tread.

同 鹵莽從事（1700）Rush headlong.

反 小心從事（3147）Handle with kid glove.

1770 貓哭老鼠 māo kū lǎo shǔ

Like a cat weeping for a rat. (lit.)

Shed crocodile tears.

Carrion crows bewail the dead sheep and then eat them.

同 假仁假義（1257）A wolf in sheep's clothing.

1771 毛骨悚然 máo gǔ sǒng rán

Hair rising and bones feeling chilled. (lit.)

Make one's flesh creep.

Make one creep all over.

Make one's hair stand on end.

Get goose bumps.

同 不寒而慄（0199）Make one's teeth chatter.

1772 毛手毛腳 máo shǒu máo jiǎo

Hairy hands and hairy feet. (lit.)

One's fingers are all thumbs.

Have a hands like a foot.

Have two left hands.

Slip-shod.

1773 冒風險 mào fēng xiǎn

Risk the danger of storms. (lit.)

To be in the teeth of the wind.

Take one's chance.

Take a risk.

反 穩紮穩打（2931）Play safe.

冒失從事 mào shī cóng shì 1774
Risking loss in doing things. (lit.)
Buy a pig in a poke.
A leap in the dark.

同 莽莽撞撞（1769）Like a bull in a china shop.
反 三思而後行（2312）Measure thrice before you cut once.

眉飛色舞 méi fēi sè wǔ 1775
Eyebrows flying and countenance flashing. (lit.)
Beam with joy.

反 垂頭喪氣（0445）Down in the mouth.
源 官場現形記："王鄉紳一聽此言，不禁眉飛色舞。"

眉目傳情 méi mù chuán qíng 1776
To transmit speechless messages with eyes. (lit.)
Make eyes at
Cast sheep's eyes at
Leer one's eye at

眉頭一皺，計上心來 1777
méi tóu yī zhòu, jì shàng xīn lái
Eyebrow makes a wrinkle, an idea comes to the mind. (lit.)
Hit upon a bright idea.

同 靈機一動（1666）Have a brilliant inspiration.
反 無計可施（2968）At the end of one's rope.
源 紅樓夢："忽然眉頭一皺，計上心來。"

每況愈下 měi kuàng yù xià 1778
Every turn is getting worse. (lit.)
Go from bad to worse.
Go down drain.
Out of the parlour into the kitchen.
Out of the frying-pan into the fire.
To be on the wane.

同 一蟹不如一蟹（3479）From a smoke into smother.
反 蒸蒸日上（3837）Grow with each passing day.

美中不足 měi zhōng bù zú 1779
Beautiful yet incomplete. (lit.)
The peacock has fair feathers but foul feet.
There are lees to every wine.
There is no rose without a thorn.
There is no garden without its weeds.

反 十全十美（2461）The pink of perfection.

1780 **門當戶對** mén dāng hù duì

The doors of both sides are well matched. (lit.)

Marry with one's match.

源 元曲選．隔江鬥智："你把俺成婚作配何人氏，也則要門當戶對該如此。"

1781 **捫心自問** mén xīn zì wèn

Lay the hand on the heart (chest) and ask oneself. (lit.)

Examine one's own conscience.

Seach one's heart (soul).

1782 **悶悶不樂** mèn mèn bù lè

Depressed and unhappy. (lit.)

Eat one's heart out.

同 鬱鬱寡歡（3726）As melancholy as a cat.

反 心花怒放（3167）Burst with joy.

1783 **蒙混過關** méng hùn guò guān

To confuse and fool (people) so as to go through the customs. (lit.)

Sail under false colours.

Throw dust in the eyes of others.

1784 **蒙頭轉向** méng tóu zhuàn xiàng

Cover the head and turn direction.

Make one's brain reel.

Not know whether one is standing on one's head.

Not know which way to turn.

Lose one's bearings.

Make one's head swim.

To have quite lost one's head.

Go into a flat spin.

同 頭暈目眩（2801）Sick as a cat.

反 頭腦清醒（2798）Keep a level head.

1785 **蒙在鼓裏** méng zài gǔ lǐ

To be covered in a drum. (lit.)

To be kept in the dark.

同 一無所知（3475）Not to know beans about.

反 消息靈通（3127）Have an ear to the ground.

1786 **夢寐以求** mèng mèi yǐ qiú

Wishing it even in dreams and sleep. (lit.)

Hanker after

Long yearn for

同 望眼欲穿（2872）All agog.

迷了心竅 mí le xīn qiào 1787
Enchanting one's heart. (lit.)
Have a bee in one's bonnet.

反 頭腦清醒（2798）Keep one's head.

迷失方向 mí shī fāng xiàng 1788
Losing one's direction. (lit.)
Lose one's direction.
Lose oneself.

同 誤入歧途（3042）To have gone astray.
反 方向對頭（0753）On the right track.

彌天大謊 mí tiān dà huǎng 1789
Big lie that fills the sky. (lit.)
Eighteen-carat lie.
A lie with a latchet.
Cut out of whole cloth.
A lie laid on with a trowel.

米已成炊 mǐ yǐ chéng chuī 1790
The grains have been already cooked into rice. (lit.)
What's done can't be undone.
The die is cast.

同 事已臨頭（2517）To be in for it.

米珠薪桂 mǐ zhū xīn guì 1791
Rice like pearls and firewood like Cassia. (lit.)
Up corn, down horn.
In time of famine.

源 戰國策 · 楚策：“楚國之食貴於玉，薪貴於桂。”

秘而不宣 mì ér bù xuān 1792
Secrete and not to be announced. (lit.)
Between you and me and the post.
In strict confidence.
Keep one's own counsel.
To hush up.

反 一人傳十，十人傳百（3445）Pass from mouth to mouth.
源 三國志 · 魏志 · 董昭傳：“秘而不露，使權（孫權）得志，非計之上。”

綿裏藏針 mián lǐ cáng zhēn 1793
A needle hidden in the wool. (lit.)
The iron hand in the velvet glove.

源 趙松雪跋東坡書：“余書如綿裏鐵，觀此書，外柔內剛，真所謂綿裏鐵也。”

1794 勉奮從事 miǎn fèn cóng shì

Exert one's strength to do it. (lit.)

Get down to it.

Keep one's nose down to the grindstone.

Hit on all six.

Put one's own shoulder to the wheel.

Put one's back into it.

同 孜孜不倦（3961）To peg away.

反 敷衍塞責（0821）Huddle over one's duty.

1795 勉強撐持 miǎn qiǎng chēng chí

Reluctant to support it. (lit.)

To stick it out.

To shore (prop) up.

Keep one's end up.

Keep body and soul together.

1796 勉強將就 miǎn qiǎng jiāng jiù

Reluctant to give in to it. (lit.)

To stretch a point.

If you do not like it, you may lump it.

Like it or lump it.

Grin and bear it.

同 逆來順受（1898）What can't be cured must be endured.

1797 勉為其難 miǎn wéi qí nán

Try to overcome the difficulty. (lit.)

Make the best of a bad bargain.

Make a virtue of necessity.

Make a bold face on it.

反 知難而退（3856）To back out.

1798 面不改容 miàn bù gǎi róng

Without changing the facial expression. (lit.)

Not to bat an eye.

Without turning a hair.

Keep a straight face.

Face the music.

同 泰然自若（2669）With perfect composure.

反 大驚失色（0533）Jump out of one's skin.

1799 面斥不雅 miàn chì bù yǎ

Rebuke one to his face is not refined. (lit.)

Give a person a piece of one's mind.

To beard someone.

Haul over the coals.

同 當面申斥（0587）Comb a person's hair for him.

面紅耳赤 miàn hóng ěr chì 1800
Face and ears turn red. (lit.)
Turn red in the gills.
To colour up.
Flush with shame.
Blush with shyness.
One's ears burn.
As red as fire.
Blush as red as a peony.

同 滿臉通紅（1747）Flush red all over.

面面俱圓 miàn miàn jù yuán 1801
To be all round to all faces. (lit.)
He is a nose of wax.
Smooth and suave.
A man of the world.

同 八面玲瓏（0034）All things to all men.

面面相覷 miàn miàn xiāng qù 1802
Looking face to face. (lit.)
At a nonplus.
At a loss what to do.

源 李贄．焚書因記往事：“一旦有警，則面面相覷，絕無人色。”

面目全非 miàn mù quán fēi 1803
Face and eyes are completely different. (lit.)
Beyond recognition.
Put on a different look.

面皮三尺厚 miàn pí sān chǐ hòu 1804
The skin of the face three feet thick. (lit.)
Have plenty of cheek.
As bold as brass.

同 厚顏無恥（1078）Have the effrontery to
源 南史．卞彬傳：“徒有八尺圍，腹無一寸腸，面皮厚如許。”

面如土色 miàn rú tǔ sè 1805
The face has the colour of the earth. (lit.)
Turn pale. As pale as death.

同 顏色憔悴（3315）Peak and pine.
反 滿臉通紅（1747）To colour up.

面無人色 miàn wú rén sè 1806
A face with no human complexion. (lit.)
As white as a sheet.
As pale as a ghost.
Look ashen.
Pale around the gills.

同 面如土色（1085）Turn pale.
反 滿面紅光（1749）As sound as a pippin.
源 漢書．李廣傳：“廣為匈奴所敗，吏士皆無人色，廣意氣相若。”

1807 **滅他人志氣** miè tā rén zhì qì
Destroy other's ambition. (lit.)
Take the wind (gas) out of one.
Cut someone's comb.
Draw a person's eyeteeth.

同 打下他的威風（0501）Give one a dressing down.

1808 **民以食為天** mín yǐ shí wéi tiān
People regard food as heaven. (lit.)
Bread is the staff of life.
The way to a man's heart is through his stomach.
If it were not for the belly the back might wear gold.

同 衣食足而後知榮辱（3510）Well fed, well bred.
源 管子："王者以民為天，民以食為天。"

1809 **民脂民膏** mín zhī mín gāo
The fat and oil of the people. (lit.)
The fat of the land.

源 孟昶．戒石文："爾俸爾祿，民膏民脂。"

1810 **名不虛傳** míng bù xū chuán
The reputation is not falsely reputed. (lit.)
Live up to one's reputation.
Worthy of the name.

反 徒有虛名（2808）To be a figurehead.
源 北史："名下固無虛士也。"

1811 **名垂千古** míng chuí qiān gǔ
Leaving one's name for thousand ages. (lit.)
Their names liveth for evermore.

同 永垂不朽（3612）Go down to posterity.
反 身敗名裂（2381）Die like a dog.
源 蘇頲文："流譽千古。"

1812 **名垂竹帛** míng chuí zhú bó
Leaving one's name on bamboo and silk (used to be writing material). (lit.)
To be on the scroll of fame.

反 湮沒無聞（3293）Sink into oblivion.

1813 **名副其實** míng fù qí shí
One is in reality what the name shows. (lit.)
To be worthy of one's name.
In every sense of the word.

同 名不虛傳（1810）Live up to one's reputation.
反 虛有其名（3247）A rope of sand.

名列前茅 míng liè qián máo 1814

The name is listed in the front straw. (lit.)

Head the list.
Come to the fore.
Bear away the bell.
Carry everything before one.
Take the cake.

同 獨佔鰲頭（0681）Come out first.
反 倒數第一（0600）To bring up the rear.

名落孫山 míng luò sūn shān 1815

The name drops behind Sun-Shan (the last successful candidate). (lit.)

Get plucked.
Take a plough.
To be ploughed.
Flunk and exam.

反 獨佔鰲頭（0681）Carry off the palm.
源 范公偁．過庭錄：“孫山曰，解名盡處是孫山，賢郎更落孫山外。”

名譽掃地 míng yù sǎo dì 1816

One's reputation sweeping the floor. (lit.)

One's name is mud.
Fall into disgrace.

同 威信掃地（2880）Loss of prestige.
反 大名鼎鼎（0539）Of great renown.

名噪一時 míng zào yì shí 1817

One's name makes noise for a time. (lit.)

To rise to fame.
Make a noise in the world.

反 名譽掃地（1816）Fall into disgrace.
源 唐書：“即授太子正字，公卿邀請旁午，號神童，名震一時。”

明白事理 míng bái shì lǐ 1818

Understand matters and principles. (lit.)

Know a hawk from a handsaw.

同 通情達理（2762）Show good common sense.
反 不通情理（0251）Have no bowels.

明察秋毫 míng chá qiū háo 1819

Able to examine the tip of an autumn hair. (lit.)

Capable of keen perception.
See through a millstone.

同 歷歷在目（1614）A commanding view.
反 視而不見（2527）As blind as a bat.
源 孟子．梁惠王上：“明足以察秋毫之末。”

1820 **明火打劫** míng huǒ dǎ jié

To rob in daylight with weapons. (lit.)

House-breaking.

Daylight robbery.

反 偷偷摸摸（2784）On the sly.

1821 **明目張膽** míng mù zhāng dǎn

With opened eyes expose the gall (daring). (lit.)

To brazen it out.

Before one's very eyes.

Under one's very nose.

同 肆無忌憚（2641）To scruple at nothing.

反 暗中行事（0030）Under the rose.

源 唐書："丈夫當敢言地，須要明目張膽，以報天子，焉能碌碌保妻子耶。"

1822 **明槍易躲，暗箭難防**

míng qiāng yì duǒ, àn jiàn nán fáng

It is easy to escape from a gun visible; it is more difficult to take precaution of an arrow hidden. (lit.)

Better an open enemy than a false friend.

Better be stung by nettle than pricked by a rose.

1823 **明日復明日，萬事成蹉跎**

míng rì fù míng rì, wàn shì chéng cuō tuó

To-morrow and to-morrow again, ten thousand things would miss the chance. (lit.)

Never put off till tomorrow what may be done today.

1824 **明日黃花** míng rì huáng huā

A flower may turn yellow tomorrow. (lit.)

The day after the fair.

同 不合時宜（0200）Out of season.

反 當時得令（0590）Everything is good in it's season.

源 蘇軾．九日次韻王鞏詩："相逢不用忙歸去，明日黃花蝶也愁。"

1825 **明升暗降** míng shēng àn jiàng

Apparently promoted but actually demoted. (lit.)

Give one a bone to pick.

Kick one upstairs.

同 寓貶於褒（3720）A left-handed compliment.

明哲保身 míng zhé bǎo shēn 1826

Being understanding and philosophical, one can preserve himself (to survive). (lit.)

Think much, speak little, and write less.

A good name is sooner lost than won.

Be worldly wise and play safe.

Look to one's laurels.

反 置生死於度外（3901）Heedless of consequences.

源 詩經．大雅．烝民："既明且哲，以保其身。"

明知故犯 míng zhī gù fàn 1827

Knowing it well, one still commits the offence. (lit.)

Set the law at defiance.

Flout the rule intentionally.

明珠暗投 míng zhū àn tóu 1828

A bright pearl thrown into darkness. (lit.)

To hide one's light under a bushel.

Cast pearls before swine.

同 對牛彈琴（0690）It is lost labour to play a jig to an old cat.

源 史記．魯仲連鄒陽列傳："臣聞明月之珠，夜光之璧，以暗投人於道路，人無不按劍相眄者，何則，無因而至前也。"

冥頑不靈 míng wán bù líng 1829

Intrinsically stubborn and inactive. (lit.)

Ride the black donkey.

As stiff as a poker.

To be thickheaded.

同 固執如牛（0949）As obstinate as a mule.

反 隨機應變（2655）Rise to the emergency.

源 韓愈．祭鱷魚文："夫傲天子之命吏，不聽其言，不徙以避之，與冥頑不靈而為民物害者，皆可殺。"

銘誌不忘 míng zhì bù wàng 1830

To be engraved (in one's heart) and not to forget. (lit.)

Treasure up in one's memory.

同 牢記心頭（1552）Take it to heart.

反 水過鴨背（2590）Like water off a duck's back.

鳴鼓而攻之 míng gǔ ér gōng zhī 1831

To attack by beating drums. (lit.)

Beat a charge.

源 論語．先進："小子鳴鼓而攻之可也。"

鳴冤叫屈 míng yuān jiào qū 1832

Cry for injustice and vengeance. (lit.)

Plead not guilty.

反 投案自首（2785）Give oneself up.

1833 酩酊大醉 mǐng dǐng dà zuì

Drunk, intoxicated with strong spirit or liquor. (lit.)

Have a hangover.

As drunk as a fiddler (lord).

To be under the table.

Have a brick in one's hat.

Three sheets in the wind.

Drink like a fish.

同 爛醉如泥（1547）Go to bed in one's boots.

反 滴酒不沾（0636）Drink only with the duck.

源 白居易："歸鞍酩酊騎。"

1834 命不久矣 mìng bù jiǔ yǐ

Life will not be long now. (lit.)

One's days are numbered.

To be on one's last legs.

同 行將就木（3214）Have one foot in the grave.

反 老當益壯（1562）There is fight in the old dog yet.

1835 命數已盡 mìng shù yǐ jìn

Life number is at the end. (lit.)

One's hour has struck.

To go to one's account.

同 壽終正寢（2560）Die in one's own bed.

反 年年有今日，歲歲有今朝（1906）Many happy returns of the day.

1836 命途多舛 mìng tú duō chuǎn

Life path has many misfortunes. (lit.)

The times are out of joint.

To be down on one's luck.

源 王勃 · 滕王閣序："時運不齊，命途多舛。"

1837 命中注定 mìng zhōng zhù dìng

One's life is destined. (lit.)

He that is born to be hanged shall never be drowned.

As luck would have it.

同 人算不如天算（2222）An ounce of luck is better than a pound of wisdom.

反 人定勝天（2194）Everyone is the maker of his own fate.

1838 摸不着頭腦 mō bù zháo tóu nǎo

Cannot feel the head and brain. (lit.)

Can make neither head nor tail of

同 莫名其妙（1851）To be at sea.

反 一目了然（3429）Everybody can see that with half an eye.

1839 摸底 mō dǐ

Feel the bottom. (lit.)

Get the gauge of

Feel the pulse.

Size up.

Sound someone out.

摸門釘 mō mén dīng 1840

Feel the door nail. (lit.) (The door is closed, nobody is at home.)

Kiss the post.

同 撲了個空（2009）To be left holding the bag.

摸清形勢 mō qīng xíng shì 1841

Feel clear the situation. (lit.)

To know which way the wind blows.

See how the land lies.

反 盲目從事（1765）Put blind faith in

模棱兩可 mó léng liǎng kě 1842

Either blunt or sharp edge can do. (lit.)

Double talk.

Betwixt and between.

Answer like a Scot.

Cut both ways.

同 兩面討好（1632）Sit on the hedge.

反 一邊倒（3374）All on one side, like Bridgnorth election.

源 舊唐書．蘇味道傳："處事莫明斷，但模棱以持兩端可矣。"

磨刀霍霍向豬羊 1843

mó dāo huò huò xiàng zhū yáng

Sharpening the knife (with the sound, huo huo) and facing the pigs and goats. (lit.)

Kill the fatted calf.

源 木蘭詩："小弟聞姊來，磨刀霍霍向豬羊。"

磨礪以須 mó lì yǐ xū 1844

To grind weapon sharp in preparation. (lit.)

Go through the hoop.

Pull oneself through the mill.

Discipline oneself.

同 練出功夫（1619）He that shoots oft shall at last hit the mark.

源 左傳．昭十二年："磨礪以須，王出，吾刃將斬矣。"

摩拳擦掌 mó quán cā zhǎng 1845

Rub the fists and polish the palms. (lit.)

Poised to fight.

Roll up one's sleeves.

Eager for the fray.

To square off.

同 躍躍欲試（3750）Itch to have a go.

源 元曲選．爭報恩："那妮子舞旋旋摩拳擦掌，叫吖吖抻巷囉街。"

1846 **磨洋工** mó yáng gōng

Drag on the (office) work. (lit.)

Lie on one's oars.
To be a clock watcher.
Make two bites of a cherry.
Looking for gape-seed.
Lie down on the job.

同 躺倒不幹（2690）Sitdown strike.
反 加把勁（1240）Pull one's socks up.

1847 **末日來臨** mò rì lái lín

One's last day is coming. (lit.)

One's hour has come.

同 壽數已盡（2558）One's course is run.
反 方興未艾（0754）In the bud.

1848 **沒精打采** méi jīng dǎ cǎi

Dispirited and discouraged. (lit.)

Out of spirits.
In the dumps.
Out of heart.
With the wind taken out of one's sails.

同 委靡不振（2903）Get one's tail down.
反 精神奕奕（1394）As fresh as paint.
源 紅樓夢・第八十七回："賈寶玉滿肚疑團，沒精打采的歸至怡紅院中。"

1849 **莫測高深** mò cè gāo shēn

The height and depth cannot be fathomed. (lit.)

To be out of one's depth.

源 漢書・嚴延年傳："吏民莫能測其意深淺。"

1850 **莫道君行早，更有早行人**

mò dào jūn xíng zǎo, gèng yǒu zǎo xíng rén

Don't say you walk early, there are earlier walkers. (lit.)

The early bird catches the worm.

1851 **莫名其妙** mò míng qí miào

Cannot understand its mystery. (lit.)

Past comprehension.
To be at sea.
It's neither rhyme nor reason.
Can make neither head nor tail of

同 莫測高深（1849）To be out of one's depth.

莫逆之交 mò nì zhī jiāo 1852
An uninterrupted friendship. (lit.)
Get along well with each other.
A sworn friend.
A bosom friend.

同 管鮑之誼（0972）Damon and Pythias.
反 不共戴天之仇（0192）Deadly feud.
源 莊子．大宗師："三人相視而笑，莫逆於心，遂相與為友。"

莫衷一是 mò zhōng yī shì 1853
No agreement of one. (lit.)
Clash of views.
Agree like the clocks of London.

同 眾議紛紜（3925）So many men, so many minds.
反 看法一致（1480）See eye to eye.

漠不關心 mò bù guān xīn 1854
Of no concern in the heart. (lit.)
Not care a bit.
To fiddle while Rome is burning.
Not to care a hang (damn).
Devil-may-care.

同 毫不在意（1024）Not to give a damn.
反 多方照顧（0700）Heap favours upon.
源 韓愈："漠然不加喜戚於其心。"

漠然置之 mò rán zhì zhī 1855
Leave it without concern. (lit.)
Take it coolly.
Look on with unconcern.

同 滿不在乎（1740）Not to care a hang.
反 全神貫注（2162）Focus one's attention on

墨守成規 mò shǒu chéng guī 1856
To adhere to written law. (lit.)
To move in a rut.
Stick in the mud.
Follow the beaten track.

同 照章辦事（3820）Sign on the dotted line.
反 自出心裁（3972）Take the initiative.

默不作聲 mò bù zuò shēng 1857
Be silent without uttering a sound. (lit.)
As mute as a fish.
To pass over in silence.
Refrain from comment.
As dumb as a statue.

同 不吭一聲（0226）Not to breathe a syllable.
反 大叫大嚷（0532）Cry at the top of one's voice.

默默無聞 mò mò wú wén 1858
Perfectly silent, nothing is heard of. (lit.)
To be nobody.
To be no burner of navigable river.

同 湮沒無聞（3293）Sink into oblivion.
反 一鳴驚人（3426）Make a noise in the world.
源 法書要錄："書之為用，施於竹帛，千載不朽，猶愈沒沒而無聞。"

1859 **謀事在人，成事在天**
móu shì zài rén, chéng shì zài tiān
Planning a matter depends on the man, completing the matter depends on heaven. (lit.)
Man proposes, God disposes.
Man does what he can, and God what he will.
An ounce of luck is better than a pound of wisdom.

1860 **牡丹雖好，也要綠葉扶持**
mǔ dān suī hǎo, yě yào lǜ yè fú chí
Peony though good, yet needs green leaves to support it. (lit.)
The peacock has fair feather but foul feet.

1861 **木已成舟** mù yǐ chéng zhōu
The wood has already been made into a boat. (lit.)
It's no use crying over spilt milk.
What's done can't be undone.

同 米已成炊（1790）The die is cast.
反 初歸新婦，落地孩兒（0422）Train a tree when it is young.

1862 **目不交睫** mù bù jiāo jié
Eyes would not connect their lashes. (lit.)
To be wide awake.
To be all alert.

同 金睛火眼（1341）Keep one's eyes skinned.
反 昏昏欲睡（1159）Have a wink in one's eye.

1863 **目不忍睹** mù bù rěn dǔ
One's eye could not bear the scene. (lit.)
Cannot bear the sight of

1864 **目不識丁** mù bù shí dīng
The eye does not know the character 'Ding'. (lit.)
An illiterate.
Not to know A from a windmill.
Not to know B from a bull's foot.

同 胸無點墨（3232）A numskull.
反 博學多才（0169）Know a thing or two.
源 新唐書·張宏靖傳：“天下無事，爾輩挽兩石弓，不如識一丁字。”

目不轉睛 mù bù zhuǎn jīng 1865
The pupils do not even turn. (lit.)
Fix one's eyes on.
One's eyes are riveted on (glued to)
Keep one's best eye peeled.

目瞪口呆 mù dèng kǒu dāi 1866
Eyes wide open and mouth struck dumb. (lit.)
Struck dumb.
To be tongue-tied.
Lose one's tongue.
Looking for grape-seed.
Stunned and speechless.

同 瞠目結舌（0352）To be dumbfounded.
反 鼓如簧之舌（0944）Wag one's tongue.

目的已達 mù dì yǐ dá 1867
Having attained the aim. (lit.)
To carry one's point.

同 如願以償（2280）To have one's will.

目光炯炯 mù guāng jiǒng jiǒng 1868
Eyes are flashing. (lit.)
Keep one's eyes skinned.

同 金睛火眼（1341）To be wide awake.
反 醉眼矇矓（4045）A sheet in the mind's eye.

目光如豆 mù guāng rú dòu 1869
The eyesight is as big as a bean. (lit.)
See no further than one's nose.

同 鼠目寸光（2568）Have a narrow outlook on things.
反 大開眼界（0535）Broaden one's horizon.

目光遠大 mù guāng yuǎn dà 1870
The eyesight is far and wide. (lit.)
Show great foresight.
Have a great insight.

同 高瞻遠矚（0886）Have a second sight.
反 鼠目寸光（2568）Have a narrow outlook on things.

目空一切 mù kōng yī qiè 1871
Everything is nothing in his eye. (lit.)
View everyone with a scornful eye.
Turn a blind eye to
Have one's nose in the air.
As proud as a peacock.

同 唯我獨尊（2892）To be overweening.
反 妄自菲薄（2867）Make oneself too cheap.

1872 **幕後操縱** mù hòu cāo zòng
Control behind the curtain. (lit.)
Pull the strings.
Backstage manoeuvring.

同 身居幕後（2385）Keep in the background.
反 粉墨登場（0793）Appear before the footlights.

1873 **暮氣沉沉** mù qì chén chén
The atmosphere of the evening is heavy. (lit.)
Lack of spirit.
Lose one's grip.

同 老油條（1578）A milk-sop.
反 朝氣蓬勃（3813）Fresh as a daisy.
源 孫子："朝氣銳，晝氣惰，暮氣歸。"

N

1874 拿定主意 ná dìng zhǔ yì

Hold firmly the principle (idea). (lit.)

Put one's foot down.

Make up one's mind.

同 打定主意（0489）Take into one's head.

反 猶疑不決（3642）Like one o'clock half struck.

1875 拿手好戲 ná shǒu hǎo xì

A good hand at showing one's talent. (lit.)

A good show.

One's long suit.

A good hand at

1876 捺着性子 nà zhe xìng zi

Press down one's temper. (lit.)

Bottle up one's feelings.

同 忍得一時之氣，免得百日之憂（2242）Bite one's lips.

反 大發雷霆（0516）Explode with rage.

1877 南轅北轍 nán yuán běi zhé

Southern shafts (of a cart) and northern tracks. (lit.)

Look one way and row another.

Poles apart.

Diametrically opposite.

East is East and West is West.

同 背道而馳（0100）Run counter to

反 殊途同歸（2562）Extremes meet.

源 戰國策・魏策四：“南轅北轍，猶至楚而北行也。”

1878 難堪之事 nán kān zhī shì

An intolerable matter. (lit.)

A bitter pill for one to swallow.

1879 難能可貴 nán néng kě guì

Rarely possible and precious. (lit.)

Arouse admiration.

Hard to come by.

同 物罕為貴（3035）Precious things are not found in heaps.

反 賤如糞土（1288）As cheap as dirt.

源 蘇軾・荀卿論：“此三者，皆天下之所謂難能而可貴者也。”

1880 **難以忍受** nán yǐ rěn shòu
It is hard to endure. (lit.)
Stick in one's throat.
Have no patience with

同 是可忍，孰不可忍（2525）More than flesh and blood can bear.
反 忍得一時之氣，免得百日之憂（2242）Put up with

1881 **難以收拾** nán yǐ shōu shí
It is difficult to deal with. (lit.)
All the fat is in the fire.
Go haywire.

反 力挽狂瀾（1606）Save the situation.

1882 **難以形容** nán yǐ xíng róng
It is hard to describe. (lit.)
To beggar description.
Beyond description.

同 可以意會，不可以言傳（1494）Beyond words.
源 李純甫詩："千奇萬巧難形容。"

1883 **難以置信** nán yǐ zhì xìn
It is difficult to believe. (lit.)
To stagger belief.
It's a lot too thin.
Boggle the mind.
Beyond belief.

反 不容置疑（0244）Beyond all question.

1884 **難於啟齒** nán yú qǐ chǐ
Onerous to open one's mouth. (lit.)
Have a bone in one's throat.
Stick in the throat.

同 欲說還休（3718）To shut up shop.

1885 **囊空如洗** náng kōng rú xǐ
The purse is emptied as if it has been washed. (lit.)
Low in the pocket.
Quite clear out.
Dead broke.
Hard up.
Out of pocket.

同 不名一文（0232）Have not a penny to bless oneself with.

1886 **囊括一空** náng kuò yì kōng
Empty everything into one's bag. (lit.)
At one scoop.
Grand slam.

同 一掃而光（3450）Make a clean sweep of things.
反 留有餘地（1685）Leave some leeway.

囊螢映雪 náng yíng yìng xuě 1887

To bag the fire-flies and to reflect light from snow. (these were the ways by which two poor ancient Chinese scholars got the light for their study at night.) (lit.)

Burn the midnight oil.

反 日上三竿猶未起（2257）A sluggard makes his night till noon.

源 晉書："車胤夏月練囊盛數螢火以照書，以夜繼日焉。"／孫氏世錄："孫康家貧，嘗映雪讀書。"

腦滿腸肥 nǎo mǎn cháng féi 1888

The brain is full and the bowel fat. (lit.)

He is better fed than nurtured.

Fat like a pig.

Plump as a dumpling.

源 飲水辭："便是腦滿腸肥，尚難消受此荒煙落照。"

內行 nèi háng 1889

In the walk (of life). (lit.)

A know-how.

同 造詣甚深（3767）To be at home in

反 外行（2835）Not in one's beat.

內心慚疚 nèi xīn cán jiù 1890

Ashamed at heart. (lit.)

The prick of conscience.

同 於心有愧（3687）Have a guilty conscience.

反 恬不知恥（2741）Have the effrontery (face) to

能屈能伸 néng qū néng shēn 1891

Capable of bending and stretching. (lit.)

Stretch your legs according to your coverlet.

Fit in.

Do in Rome as the Romans do.

反 高不成，低不就（0877）He that will not stoop for a pin shall never be worth a pound.

能説會道 néng shuō huì dào 1892

Able to speak and know how to say it properly. (lit.)

Have the gift of the gab.

Have a glib tongue.

A flannel mouth person.

Have a ready tongue.

1893 **能者多勞** néng zhě duō láo

A capable man has always more work to do. (lit.)

Only an elephant can bear an elephant's load.

All lay loads on a willing horse.

反 獻醜不如藏拙（3102）Better hide one's ignorance.

源 莊子・列御寇："巧者勞而知者憂。"

1894 **泥菩薩過海** ní pú sà guò hǎi

A clay stature of god crosses the river. (lit.)

He that is fallen cannot help him that is down.

1895 **你吹我捧** nǐ chuī wǒ pěng

You blow and I lift. (lit.)

Scratch my back and I will scratch yours.

Claw me and I'll claw thee.

1896 **你的是我的，我的是我自己的**

nǐ de shì wǒ de, wǒ de shì wǒ zì jǐ de

Yours is mine, mine is my own. (lit.)

What's yours is mine, and what's mine's my own.

反 寧人負我，毋我負人（1915）Better suffer ill than do ill.

1897 **逆耳之言** nì ěr zhī yán

A speech that grates on the ears. (lit.)

A flea in one's ear.

反 甜言蜜語（2742）Give one a mouthful of moon-shine.

1898 **逆來順受** nì lái shùn shòu

Oppression comes, endure it. (lit.)

What can't be cured must be endured.

If you don't like it, you can lump it.

Grin and bear it.

Swallow one's pride.

Put up with it.

Take it lying down.

Make a virtue of necessity.

Make the best of it.

Take something in good part.

同 忍得一時之氣，免得百日之憂（2242）Bottle up one's feelings.

反 抵抗到底（0638）To be dead set against.

逆流而上 nì liú ér shàng 1899
Up against the stream. (lit.)
Strive against the stream.

同 知難而進（3855）Never shirk the hardest work.
反 順應潮流（2605）Go with the tide.

年代久遠 nián dài jiǔ yuǎn 1900
Of remote ages. (lit.)
In the year dot.
Time out of mind.

年方弱冠 nián fāng ruò guàn 1901
The age just reaches the (stage when an adult can wear) a cap. (lit.)
Arrive at majority.
Become of age.
To have cut one's eyeteeth.
To be past the spoon.

同 長大成人（3797）Out of one's teens.
反 耆艾之年（2027）To be advanced in years.

年高德劭 nián gāo dé shào 1902
High in years and greatly honoured for one's virtues. (lit.)
Old age is honourable.

反 老而不死，是為賊也（1564）He lives long that lives till all are weary of him.
源 法言·孝至：“年彌高而德彌卲者，是孔子之徒與。”

年紀老邁 nián jì lǎo mài 1903
The age is old and advance. (lit.)
Long in the tooth.
To be over the hill.

同 老氣橫秋（1571）To be stricken in years.
反 血氣方剛（3275）In one's raw youth.

年老昏聵 nián lǎo hūn guì 1904
Old age with blur vision and confusion of mind. (lit.)
In one's dotage.

反 身壯力健（2395）Sound as a bell.

年老閱歷深 nián lǎo yuè lì shēn 1905
The ages have deep reading experience. (lit.)
Those who live longest will see most.

同 老馬識途（1570）If you wish for good advice, consult an old man.
反 少不更事（2366）A green horn.

年年有今日，歲歲有今朝 1906
nián nián yǒu jīn rì, suì suì yǒu jīn zhāo
Every year there is today, every age there is this morning. (lit.)
Many happy returns of the day.

1907 年青時代 nián qīng shí dài
Young people times. (lit.)
In one's salad days.
Prime of life.

1908 年青一代 nián qīng yí dài
The young people generation. (lit.)
The rising generation.

同 新生力量（3205）New blood.

1909 年少老成 nián shào lǎo chéng
Young and mature. (lit.)
An old head on young shoulders.

同 返老還童（0749）In one's second childhood.

1910 年事已高 nián shì yǐ gāo
In senile age. (lit.)
Get along in years.
To be well on in life.

同 上了年紀（2357）Advanced in years.

1911 念念有如臨深日，心心常似過橋時 niàn niàn yǒu rú lín shēn rì, xīn xīn cháng sì guò qiáo shí
Always think that the "deep" days are coming, while the heart often is like at the time passing a bridge. (lit.)
The way to be safe is never to feel secure.

同 小心戒慎（3148）Take heed is a good rede.

1912 鳥愛其巢，人愛其家
niǎo ài qí cháo, rén ài qí jiā
Birds love their nests, men love their homes. (lit.)
Every bird likes its own nest.
East or west, home is best.

1913 鳥倦飛而知還
niǎo juàn fēi ér zhī huán
A bird tired of flying will know to return. (lit.)
Home is the sailor, home from sea.

反 杳如黃鶴（3352）To leave for good.

源 陶淵明 · 歸去來辭："雲無心以出岫，鳥倦飛而知還。"

寧欺白鬚公，莫欺蠢鈍兒 1914
nìng qī bái xū gōng, mò qī chǔn dùn ér
Rather fool a white bearded man, but not fool a stupid boy. (lit.)
Little pitchers have long ears.

寧人負我，毋我負人 1915
nìng rén fù wǒ, wú wǒ fù rén
Rather others trespass on me than I trespass on others. (lit.)
Better suffer ill than do ill.

反 你的是我的，我的是我自己的（1896）What's yours is mine, and what's mine's my own.

寧死不辱 nìng sǐ bù rǔ 1916
Rather to die than to be insulted. (lit.)
Take away my good name and take away my life.
Loss of honour is loss of life.

同 至死不屈（3890）Die game.
反 卑躬屈節（0095）Lick someone's shoes.

寧為雞口，不為牛後 1917
nìng wéi jī kǒu, bù wéi niú hòu
Rather be a chicken's mouth but not be a cow's tail. (lit.)
Better be the head of a dog than the tail of a lion.

反 不怕官，最怕管（0236）Better trust in God than in his saints.
源 戰國策．韓策："臣聞鄙語曰，寧為雞口，無為牛後。"

凝神細聽 níng shén xì tīng 1918
To concentrate and to listen attentively. (lit.)
Hang on the words (lips) of

同 側耳諦聽（0313）Strain one's ears.
反 掩耳不聞（3321）Turn a deaf ear to
源 莊子："用志不分，乃凝於神。"

牛不喝水，難按得牛頭低 1919
niú bù hē shuǐ, nán àn dé niú tóu dī
If a cow won't drink water, one cannot push its head down. (lit.)
You can take a horse to the water, but you can't make him drink.

反 俯首就範（0832）Knuckle down.

牛鬼蛇神 niú guǐ shé shén 1920
Cow-ghosts and snake-gods (freaks and monsters). (lit.)
Dregs of humanity.
The scum of society.

源 杜牧．李賀詩序："鯨呿鰲擲，牛鬼蛇神，不足為其虛幻荒誕也。"

1921 **牛馬生活** niú mǎ shēng huó
Life of cows and horses. (lit.)
Lead a dog's life.

反 錦衣美食（1356）Swim in luxury.

1922 **扭轉乾坤** niǔ zhuǎn qián kūn
Turn round the heaven and earth. (lit.)
Turn the tables (scales).

反 聽天由命（2756）Resigned to one's fate.
源 韓愈："躬自聽斷，旋乾轉坤。"

1923 **農村支援城市**
nóng cūn zhī yuán chéng shì
Farming villages support the cities. (lit.)
The chickens are the country's, but the city eats them.

1924 **濃裝艷抹** nóng zhuāng yàn mǒ
Heavily painted in make-up. (lit.)
As gaudy as a peacock.

1925 **弄巧成拙** nòng qiǎo chéng zhuō
Try to be clever but it shows stupidity. (lit.)
Ride one's horse to death.
Make a mess of things.

同 機關算盡太聰明（1185）To lose one's reckoning
源 黃庭堅・拙軒頌："弄巧成拙，為蛇添足。"

1926 **奴顏婢膝** nú yán bì xī
The face of a serf and the knees of a slave-girl. (lit.)
Lick somebody's boots.
Grovel in the dust.
Grovel at the feet of

同 阿諛諂媚（0712）Tickle one's ears.
反 趾高氣揚（3888）Ride the high horse.
源 抱朴子・交際篇："以奴顏婢膝者為曉解當世。"

1927 **努力從事** nǔ lì cóng shì
To do things with great effort. (lit.)
Put one's best foot forward.
Hold (keep) one's nose to the grindstone.

同 孜孜不倦（3961）Grind away at
反 躺倒不幹（2690）Sitdown strike.

怒不可遏 nù bù kě è 1928
One's rage cannot be stopped. (lit.)
To boil over.
To hit the roof.
Beside oneself with rage.
To be in a fume.

同 暴跳如雷（0092）In a towering rage.
反 心平氣和（3181）Compose oneself.

怒從心中起，惡向膽邊生 nù cóng xīn zhōng qǐ, è xiàng dǎn biān shēng 1929
Anger arises from the heart, wickedness goes towards the side of the gallbladder. (lit.)
Rouse one's bile.
Have one's gorge rise.
A fit of the spleen.

反 平心靜氣（1993）Keep one's temper.

怒髮衝冠 nù fà chōng guān 1930
In a fury hair lifts one's cap. (lit.)
Have one's dander up.
Bristle with anger.
To lose one's hair.
Mad as a hatter.
To be in a towering rage.
Flip one's lid.
Blow one's top.

同 令人髮指（1674）Make one's hair stand on end.
反 喜形於色（3060）A merry heart makes a cheerful countenance.
源 史記·藺相如傳："相如視秦王無意償趙城，因持璧卻立倚柱，怒髮衝冠。"

怒火中燒 nù huǒ zhōng shāo 1931
Angry fire is burning. (lit.)
Flare up.
All burnt up.
Burning with rage.
Take pepper in the nose.
A fit of the spleen.

同 七竅生煙（2016）Fuming with anger.

怒目而視 nù mù ér shì 1932
Looking with angry eye. (lit.)
Look daggers.

反 笑容可掬（3154）A face wreathed in smiles.

1933 怒氣沖沖 nù qì chōng chōng
In a great fury. (lit.)
Fuming with anger.
Vent one's anger.
Pour out the vials of one's wrath.

同 氣急敗壞（2045）To be worked up.
反 喜形於色（3060）Radiant with joy.

1934 怒形於色 nù xíng yú sè
Anger shows in one's face. (lit.)
One's blood is up.
Purple with rage.

反 心中好笑（3200）To laugh in one's sleeve.

1935 女為悅己者容 nǚ wèi yuè jǐ zhě róng
The girl who pleases one will be acceptable to him. (lit.)
Nightingales will not sing in a cage.

同 士為知己者用（2494）Respect a man, he will do the more.
源 司馬遷 · 報任少卿書："士為知己者用，女為悅己者容。"

偶一為之 ǒu yī wéi zhī 1936

Do it once a while. (lit.)

Once in a blue moon.

Once in a long while.

反 日以為常（2258）As regular as clockwork.

源 歐陽修 · 縱囚論："夫縱而來歸之而赦之，可偶一為之耳。"

嘔氣 ǒu qì 1937

Blow one's air out. (lit.)

Fret oneself to fiddle-strings.

Fret one's gizzard.

反 心情舒暢（3187）Get out of bed on the right side.

P

1938 **爬得越高，跌得越慘**

pá dé yuè gāo, diē dé yuè cǎn

The higher one climbs, the worse the fall. (lit.)

The higher up, the greater fall.

1939 **怕得要死** pà de yào sǐ

Frightened to death. (lit.)

Cowards die many times before their deaths.

同 嚇破了膽（3075）To be frightened out of one's wits.

反 臨危不懼（1656）If the sky falls, we shall catch larks.

1940 **拍馬屁** pāi mǎ pì

Pat the horse's buttock. (lit.)

Eat one's toads.
Lick one's boots.
Curry favour.
Give one the soft-soap.
Butter someone up.
Lay it on with a trowel.
Polish the apple.

同 吹吹捧捧（0440）Flatter grossly.

反 拂逆人意（0824）Go against the grain with one.

1941 **排長龍** pái cháng lóng

Line up in a long dragon. (lit.)

To queue (line) up.

同 僭隊（1285）Jump the queue.

1942 **排除萬難** pái chú wàn nán

Get rid of ten thousand difficulties. (lit.)

To hustle out of the way.
Sweep everything before one.

反 避難就易（0126）Where the hedge is lowest men leap over.

排難解紛 pái nàn jiě fēn 1943

Settle the difficulties and clear up misunderstanding. (lit.)

Make peace between

Bring to terms.

Pour oil on troubled waters.

同 息事寧人（3045）Patch up a quarrel.

反 挑撥離間（2743）Play off one against the other.

源 戰國策．趙策三：“所貴於天下之士者，為人排患釋難，解紛亂而無所取也。”

攀高峰 pān gāo fēng 1944

Climb up a peak. (lit.)

Scale the height.

同 百尺竿頭，更進一步（0048）Make further efforts.

攀龍附鳳 pān lóng fù fèng 1945

Mount the dragon and cling to the phoenix. (lit.)

Keep up with the Joneses.

To be a social climber.

同 趨炎附勢（2151）Hail the rising sun.

反 獨立自主（0678）Stand on one's own bottom.

源 後漢書：“望攀龍鱗，附鳳翼，以成其所志。”

盤點 pán diǎn 1946

Check and count. (lit.)

Take stock.

盤根錯節 pán gēn cuò jié 1947

Twisted roots and disorderly grown gnarls. (lit.)

There are wheels within wheels.

同 錯綜複雜（0485）The plot thickens.

反 瞭如指掌（1646）As plain as a pikestaff.

源 後漢書．虞詡傳：“不遇盤根錯節，何以別利器乎。”

盤根究底 pán gēn jiū dǐ 1948

To interrogate the root and investigate the matter to the bottom. (lit.)

Go to the root of

Get to the bottom of

同 尋根問底（3278）Get to the core of

判別真偽 pàn bié zhēn wěi 1949

Judging the difference between true and false. (lit.)

Know the difference between chalk and cheese.

Know a hawk from a handsaw.

Separate the wheat from the chaff.

同 分清是非（0786）Know the right from the wrong.

反 良莠不分（1622）Not know good from evil.

1950 **判若雲泥** pàn ruò yún ní
As different as cloud and mud. (lit.)
A world of difference.
As different as chalk is from cheese.

反 不相上下（0258）On a par with

1951 **旁觀者清** páng guān zhě qīng
The (mind) of the on-looker is lucid. (lit.)
Lookers-on see most of the game.
Lookers-on see more than the players.

反 當局者迷（0585）The darkest place is under the candle-stick.
源 新唐書．元行沖傳："當局者迷，旁觀必審。"

1952 **旁敲側擊** páng qiāo cè jī
To knock at one side and strike at the other. (lit.)
To sound out someone.
Beat about the bush.
In a roundabout way.

反 直截了當（3871）Give it to one straight.

1953 **拋頭露面** pāo tóu lù miàn
Toss the head and show the face. (lit.)
Come out into the open.
In the limelight.
Chuck one's weight about.

同 招搖過市（3806）Cut a dash.
反 隱姓埋名（3593）Live in the shadow.

1954 **拋磚引玉** pāo zhuān yǐn yù
Casting a brick to draw in a jade piece. (lit.)
Throw out a sprat (minnow) to catch a mackerel (whale).
Venture a small fish and catch a great one.

反 買櫝還珠（1736）Grasp the shadow and let go the substance.
源 釋道源．景德傳燈錄："比來拋磚引玉，卻引得個墼子。"

1955 **跑龍套** pǎo lóng tào
Run the dragon dance. (lit.)
Walk through a part.

反 執牛耳（3869）Take the lead.

1956 **跑野馬** pǎo yě mǎ
Run the wild horse. (lit.)
To start a hare.
Fly off at a tangent.
Get off the track.

反 言歸正傳（3302）Return to our muttons.

培育成材 péi yù chéng cái
To cultivate and accomplish talent. (lit.)
Lick into shape.

反 劏草除根（0326）Pluck up by the roots. 1957

賠了夫人又折兵
péi le fū rén yòu zhé bīng
Paid for the price of a lady and lost a number of soldiers. (lit.)
Throw the helve after the hatchet.
Throw good money after bad.

源 三國演義："周郎妙計安天下，賠了夫人又折兵。" 1958

賠禮道歉 péi lǐ dào qiàn
Pay respect and make an apology. (lit.)
Eat humble-pie.

同 負荊請罪（0842）To kiss the rod. 1959

朋比為奸 péng bǐ wéi jiān
To form a clique for corruption or treason. (lit.)
Play into each other's hands.
Gang up with
Thick as thieves.
In collusion with
To be hand and glove with.

同 狼狽為奸（1549）In cahoots with 1960
源 新唐書·李絳傳："趨利之人，常為朋比，同其私也。"

蓬頭垢面 péng tóu gòu miàn
With dishevelled hair and dirty face. (lit.)
Like a brick-broom in a fit.
Look as if one has been dragged through a hedge backwards.

反 瀟灑出塵（3133）Neat but not gaudy. 1961
源 魏書："君子整其衣冠，尊其瞻視，何必蓬頭垢面，然後為賢。"

捧到天上 pěng dào tiān shàng
Hold one up to the sky. (lit.)
Praise (Laud) to the skies.
Flatter up to the nines.

同 吹吹捧捧（0440）Lay it on with a trowel. 1962
反 罵個狗血淋頭（1734）Blow one up sky high.

捧腹大笑 pěng fù dà xiào
To hold the belly with laughter. (lit.)
Hold one's sides with laughter.
Convulsed with laughter.
Shake one's sides.

同 笑破肚皮（3153）Split one's sides. 1963
反 痛哭流涕（2780）Break into a passion of tears.
源 史記："司馬季主捧腹大笑。"

1964 碰得一鼻子灰 pèng dé yī bí zǐ huī

Get a hitting on the nose with ashes. (lit.)

To be sent off with a flea in one's ear.

Get a rebuff.

同 到處碰壁（0599）Driven from pillar to post.

反 無往不利（2997）To get it every way.

1965 批鬥 pī dòu

Criticize and strike against. (lit.)

Haul over the coals.

Call to account.

To sit on a person.

1966 批深揭透 pī shēn jiē tòu

Criticize deeply and expose clearly. (lit.)

Nail on the counter.

1967 披肝瀝膽 pī gān lì dǎn

Open the liver and empty the gall-bladder. (lit.)

To pledge loyalty.

Lay bare one's heart.

Unbosom oneself.

Make a clean breast of

Make no secret of

同 肺腑之言（0776）Speak one's conscience.

反 諱莫如深（1158）Breathe not a syllable.

源 司馬文正公集 · 上體要疏："雖訪問所不及，猶將披肝瀝膽，以效其區區之忠。"

1968 披堅執銳 pī jiān zhí ruì

Putting on hard (armour) and holding sharp (weapon). (lit.)

Take up arms.

Armed to all points.

Armed to the teeth.

同 全副武裝（2160）In full battle array.

源 戰國策："吾被堅執銳，赴強敵而死，此猶一卒也。"

1969 披荊斬棘 pī jīng zhǎn jí

Spread thorns and cut brambles. (lit.)

To blaze the trail.

源 後漢書 · 馮異傳："是吾起兵時主簿也，為吾披荊斬棘，定關中。"

1970 疲於奔命 pí yú bēn mìng

Weary as if one has run for his life. (lit.)

Drive oneself hard.

Run off one's feet.

To be dead tired.

同 筋疲力竭（1348）Ready to drop.

反 閒得發慌（3091）Find time hang heavy on one's hands.

源 左傳："吳於是伐巢取駕，克棘，入州來。楚罷於奔命。"

匹夫之勇 pǐ fū zhī yǒng 1971
Bravery of a common man. (lit.)
Brute courage.
Courage without discipline.

源 孟子："此匹夫之勇，敵一人者也。"

翩翩起舞 piān piān qǐ wǔ 1972
Elegantly rising to dance. (lit.)
Tread a measure.

胼手胝足 pián shǒu zhī zú 1973
Callosities on the hand and feet. (lit.)
Toil and moil.
Elbow grease.

同 拼命幹（1976）To pound away.
反 遊手好閒（3639）Fool away one's time.
源 荀子："手足胼胝。"

片言隻語 piàn yán zhī yǔ 1974
A few words and phrases. (lit.)
A very short note.
Bits and pieces.
Snatches of conversation.

源 元史："片言隻字，流傳人間，咸知寶重。"

飄飄欲仙 piāo piāo yù xiān 1975
Floating gracefully like a fairy. (lit.)
As light as a butterfly.
As slender as gossamer.

同 弱不禁風（2298）As weak as water.
反 大腹便便（0520）Beef to the heels.

拼命幹 pīn mìng gàn 1976
Dedicate one's life to hard work. (lit.)
To pound away.
To go all out.
Work one's fingers to the bone.
Do one's level best.

同 開足馬力（1477）At full steam.
反 躺倒不幹（2690）To swing the lead.

貧病交迫 pín bìng jiāo pò 1977
Pressed by both poverty and illness. (lit.)
His hair grows through his hood.
Poverty-striken and bedridden.

1978 **貧賤不能移** pín jiàn bù néng yí

Poverty cannot move one. (lit.)

Better be poor than wicked.

同 安貧樂道（0011）Poverty is not a shame but the being ashamed of it.

反 利令智昏（1609）Wealth makes wit waver.

1979 **貧賤夫妻百事哀**

pín jiàn fū qī bǎi shì āi

Poor husband and wife find hundred things miserable. (lit.)

When poverty (the wolf) comes in at the door, love flies (creeps) out of the window.

Bare walls make giddy housewives.

1980 **貧來親也疏** pín lái qīn yě shū

In poverty, few relatives will come. (lit.)

No one claims kindred with the poor.

Poverty parteth fellowship.

反 富在深山有遠親（0847）Everyone is kin to the rich men.

1981 **貧無立錐之地** pín wú lì zhuī zhī dì

So poor one has not a place of a pin to stand on. (lit.)

On one's uppers.

In rack and ruin.

As poor as lazarus.

源 漢書．食貨志："富者田連阡陌，貧者無立錐之地。"

1982 **牝雞司晨** pìn jī sī chén

The hen rules the morning. (lit.)

The wife wears the trousers.

The grey mare is the better horse.

同 河東獅吼（1053）Wear the breeches.

源 尚書．牧誓："古人有言曰，牝雞無晨，牝雞之晨，惟家之索。"

1983 **平安無事** píng ān wú shì

Peace, safe, and no problem. (lit.)

No news is good news.

All is well.

同 一帆風順（3391）It was roses all the way.

反 大難臨頭（0542）To be in hot waters.

源 西陽雜俎："每日報竹平安。"

1984 **平白無故** píng bái wú gù

Plain and white without reason. (lit.)

Without rhyme or reason.

Without provocation.

反 事起有因（2514）Where there's smoke there's fire.

平步青雲 píng bù qīng yún 1985
From the level step rise to the blue cloud (sky). (lit.)
Skyrocket to fame.
Hit the jackpot.
To have crept through the hawsehole.
Beat the top of the ladder (tree).
Come to the top over night.
Make a smashing hit.

同 飛黃騰達（0771）Rise in the world.
反 一落千丈（3420）To go to pot.
源 曹鄴詩："一旦公道開，青雲在平地。"

平淡無奇 píng dàn wú qí 1986
Plain and nothing strange. (lit.)
Nothing out of ordinary.
Nothing to write home about.

反 妙趣橫生 Enough to make a dog laugh.

平地一聲雷 píng dì yì shēng léi 1987
A thunderclap from the flatland. (lit.)
Take by surprise.
A bombshell.
A bolt out of the blue.

同 突如其來（2805）Appear from nowhere.
源 元曲選．馬致遠．薦福碑："都則為那平地一聲雷，今日對文武兩班齊。"

平分秋色 píng fēn qiū sè 1988
Share the brightness of autumn equally. (lit.)
On equal terms with
Share and share alike.
Go fifty-fifty.

同 二一添作五（0730）Go halves.
反 多吃多佔（0696）Take the lion share.
源 李樸．中秋詩："平分秋色一輪滿，長伴雲衢千里明。"

平平庸庸 píng píng yōng yōng 1989
Ordinary and common. (lit.)
Pass in a crowd in a push.

反 出類拔萃（0406）Tower above the rest.

平起平坐 píng qǐ píng zuò 1990
Rise and sit as equals. (lit.)
On an equal footing with
To rank with
Hank for hank
Rub shoulders with
At a round table there's no dispute of place.

同 不相伯仲（0257）On a par with

1991 **平生不作虧心事，半夜敲門也不驚** píng shēng bú zuò kuī xīn shì, bàn yè qiāo mén yě bù jīng

In ordinary life one does not do things against the conscience, one is not afraid of a knock at the door even at mid-night. (lit.)

A quiet conscience sleeps in thunder.
A good conscience is a soft pillow.
A clear conscience is a coat of mail.

反 作賊心虛（4075）He that lives ill, fear follows him.

1992 **平時不燒香，急時抱佛腳**

píng shí bù shāo xiāng, jí shí bào fó jiǎo

At normal time one does not burn incense, in an emergency one holds on Buddha's feet. (lit.)

Once on shore, we pray no more.
The danger past and God forgotten.

1993 **平心靜氣** píng xīn jìng qì

Calm mind and quiet breath. (lit.)

Keep one's temper.
Keep one's shirt on.
Collect oneself.
Cool as a cucumber.

同 心平氣和（3181）Compose oneself.

反 暴跳如雷（0092）Fly into a passion.

1994 **平易近人** píng yì jìn rén

Fair and easy going, one gets near to people. (lit.)

Have a taking way with one.
Easy to get along with.
To be well disposed.
Free and easy.
Have the common touch.

同 和藹可親（1048）As harmless as a dove.

反 拒人於千里之外（1445）Keep at arm's length.

源 史記．魯周公世家：“平易近民。”

1995 **評頭品足** píng tóu pǐn zú

Make comment on one from head to foot. (lit.)

Size one up.
Look a person up and down.
Pick one to pieces.
Try to find fault with

同 吹毛求疵（0441）Pick a hole in one's coat.

源 元史：“平居未嘗評品人物。”

萍水相逢 píng shuǐ xiāng féng 1996
The meeting of drifting duck-weeds by chance. (lit.)
Merry meet, merry part.
Strike up an acquaintance with

反 過訪不遇（0995）Kiss the post.
源 王勃："萍水相逢，盡是他鄉之客。"

萍蹤無定 píng zōng wú dìng 1997
The trail of duck-weed is uncertain. (lit.)
Here today and gone tomorrow.
Floating here and there.

反 安家落戶（0010）To settle down.

憑空捏造 píng kōng niē zào 1998
Based on nothing to fabricate. (lit.)
Trump up a story.
Out of thin air.
Sheer fabrication.

同 向壁虛構（3118）A cooked up story.
反 事不離實（2509）Facts are stubborn things.

頗具端倪 pō jù duān ní 1999
Having rather a (good) beginning. (lit.)
Come into shape.

同 有了眉目（3655）Begin to take shape.

潑婦罵街 pō fù mà jiē 2000
A shrew scolding in the street. (lit.)
A slanging match.
To bandy words.
Billingsgate.

潑冷水 pō lěng shuǐ 2001
Pour cold water on (lit.)
Throw cold water on
To be a wet blanket.

反 火上加油（1168）Pour oil on the flame.

迫不得已 pò bù dé yǐ 2002
Pressed to do with no alternative. (lit.)
It can't be helped.
Under duress.
Needs must when the devil drives.
Do something under protest.
Have no alternative but to

同 不由自主（0271）In spite of oneself.
源 漢書·王莽傳上："迫不得已然後受詔。"

2003 **破釜沉舟** pò fǔ chén zhōu

Smash the cauldron and sink the boat. (lit.)

Burn one's boats (bridges).

Go for broke.

同 背城借一（0099）Fight to the last ditch.

源 項羽："皆沉船，破釜甑。"

2004 **破鍋有爛灶，李大有張嫂**

pò guō yǒu làn zào, lǐ dà yǒu zhāng sǎo

The broken frying pan finds a worn-out stove, Li-Da meets woman, Zhang. (lit.)

Every Jack has his Jill.

同 無獨有偶（2957）Everything in the world has its counterpart.

2005 **破口大罵** pò kǒu dà mà

Open the mouth and shout abuses. (lit.)

Smite with one's tongue.

Cast in one's teeth.

Let loose a torrent of abuse.

Go off the deep end.

Jump down one's throat.

Hurl abuses.

Scream curses at

同 潑婦罵街（2000）To bandy words.

反 讚不絕口（3762）Lavish praises on

2006 **破題兒第一遭** pò tí ér dì yī zāo

Break the problem for the first time. (lit.)

Without precedent in history.

反 司空見慣（2618）Order of the day.

2007 **破涕為笑** pò tì wéi xiào

Break the tears into smile. (lit.)

They that sow in tears shall reap in joy.

Nothing dries sooner than a tear.

Sadness and gladness succeed each other.

反 樂極生悲（1582）He that talk much of his happiness summons grief.

源 劉琨・答盧諶書："時復相與舉觴對膝，破涕為笑。"

2008 **破綻百出** pò zhàn bǎi chū

Flaws come out by hundreds. (lit.)

Show the cloven foot.

Betray the cloven hoof.

同 漏洞百出（1694）Full of loopholes.

反 完美無缺（2840）Finished to the finger-nail.

源 方回："壞屋如敝衣，隨意補破綻。"

撲了個空 pū le gè kōng 2009

To rush on at nothing. (lit.)

To be left holding the bag (sack).

Draw a blank.

A fruitless errand.

同 過訪不遇（0995）Kiss the post.

鋪平道路 pū píng dào lù 2010

Pave the street and road flat. (lit.)

Pave the way.

鋪張浪費 pū zhāng làng fèi 2011

Spread out in extravagance. (lit.)

Butter one's bread on both sides.

同 恣意揮霍（4018）Throw money down the drain.

反 省吃儉用（2430）Pinch and scrape.

鋪張排場 pū zhāng pái chǎng 2012

Spread out in style. (lit.)

Make a splash.

Do a thing in style.

同 裝點門面（3945）Window dressing.

反 艱苦樸素（1272）To hog it.

普天之下 pǔ tiān zhī xià 2013

All under heaven. (lit.)

In all corners of the earth.

All the world over.

Under the scope of heaven.

反 彈丸之地（0580）Hole-in-the-wall.

源 詩經："普天之下，莫非王土。"

Q

2014 **七顛八倒** qī diān bā dǎo

Seven tumble and eight turn upside down. (lit.)

At sixes and sevens.

Heels over head.

Topsy-turvy.

反 直諒不阿（3872）As level as a die.

源 朱子語錄：“當商之末，七顛八倒，上下崩頽。”

2015 **七零八落** qī líng bā luò

Seven pieces and eight drops. (lit.)

To go rack and ruin.

2016 **七竅生煙** qī qiào shēng yān

The seven apertures (or cavities) (2 eyes, 2 ears, 2 nostrils and 1 mouth) spurting smoke. (lit.)

In great fury.

Fuming with anger.

同 怒火中燒（1931）Burning with rage.

反 平心靜氣（1993）Keep one's temper.

源 莊子：“人皆有七竅。”參閱3440

2017 **七上八下** qī shàng bā xià

Seven up and eight down. (lit.)

Cannot make up one's mind.

With one's heart going pitpat.

Drop off the hook.

To be greatly upset.

同 心慌意亂（3170）Fall into a flutter.

源 水滸傳：“那胡正卿心頭十五個吊桶打水，七上八下。”

2018 **七十二行** qī shí èr háng

Seventy two trades. (lit.)

All walks of life.

同 各行各業（0901）The butcher, the baker, the candle-stick maker.

2019 **漆黑一團** qī hēi yì tuán

Varnished black in one patch. (lit.)

As dark as night.

Pitch-dark.

反 光輝燦爛（0979）Dazzling to the eye.

其樂融融 qí lè róng róng 2020

The happiness is harmoniously complete. (lit.)

Happy as a lark.

Merry as a cricket.

As pleased as Punch.

Have a whale of a time.

同 喜不自勝（3056）Beside oneself with joy.

反 悲不自勝（0096）A bandon oneself to grief.

源 左傳：“大隧之中，其樂也融融。”

其樂無窮 qí lè wú qióng 2021

That happiness has no end. (lit.)

Like a possum up a gum-tree.

As happy as the day is long.

同 快樂無邊（1525）To be in seventh heaven.

反 苦不堪言（1517）As bitter as gall.

其貌不揚 qí mào bù yáng 2022

His appearance is undistinguished. (lit.)

As ugly as a scarecrow.

同 獐頭鼠目（3796）With a hangdog look.

反 一表人才（3375）Manners make the man.

源 全唐文．裴度．自題寫真贊：爾才不長，爾貌不揚。”

其身不正，雖令不從 2023

qí shēn bù zhèng, suī lìng bù cóng

He who is not righteous, though giving order is not obeyed. (lit.)

He is not fit to command others that cannot command himself.

He that cannot obey cannot command.

A cracked bell can never sound well.

源 論語．子路：“其身正，不令而行，其身不正，雖令不從。”

奇恥大辱 qí chǐ dà rǔ 2024

An unusual shame and a great insult. (lit.)

A big loss of face.

Burning (crying, galling) shame.

奇談怪論 qí tán guài lùn 2025

Strange talk and peculiar theory. (lit.)

A cock and bull story.

It's all moonshine.

同 齊東野語 A fishy story.

2026 **奇裝異服** qí zhuāng yì fú

Strange clothes and unusual dress. (lit.)

Fantastic garb.

Outlandish (exotic) costume.

2027 **耆艾之年** qí ài zhī nián

In the years of sixty and fifty respectively (qi=60 years of age and ai=50). (lit.)

To be advanced in years.

同 風燭殘年（0813）The lees of life.

2028 **歧路亡羊** qí lù wáng yáng

Astray goat gets lost at the cross-road. (lit.)

There are wheels within wheels.

同 錯綜複雜（0485）The plot thickens.

源 列子．說符："嘻，亡一羊何追者之眾，鄰人曰，多歧路。"

2029 **棋差一着** qí chā yī zhāo

His chess is a move behind. (lit.)

One false move may lose the game.

反 勝彼一籌（2439）One too many for a person.

2030 **棋逢敵手** qí féng dí shǒu

To meet a matched rival. (lit.)

Meet one's match.

When Greek meets Greek, then is the tug of war.

Nip and tuck.

A drawn game.

同 旗鼓相當（2033）A ding-dong fight.

反 小巫見大巫（3146）To be cast into the shade.

源 元曲選．百花亭："哎，高君也，咱兩個棋逢對手。"

2031 **棋高一着** qí gāo yī zhāo

His chess is one move ahead. (lit.)

To be one up on a person.

One too many for a person.

A stroke above.

反 不敢望其項背（0191）Not in the same street as

2032 **期期艾艾** qī qī ài ài

To talk like Qi-Qi and Ai-Ai (historical persons who stammered and stuttered). (lit.)

Hem and haw.

同 結結巴巴（1323）Have a peppermint in one's speech.

反 口若懸河（1508）Talk nine words at once.

源 源出鄧艾及周昌口吃故事，見《世說新語》及《史記》。

旗鼓相當 qí gǔ xiāng dāng 2033

To stand opposite to with flags and drums. (lit.)

A drawn game.
A Roland for an Oliver.
To be well-matched.
A ding-dong fight.
On a par with
Six of one and half a dozen of the other.

同 勢均力敵（2534）Evenly matched.
反 相形見絀（3113）Cast into the shade.
源 三國志．管輅傳注：“單子春曰，吾欲自與卿旗鼓相當。”

旗開得勝 qí kāi dé shèng 2034

When the flag is unfurled the victory is won. (lit.)

To start with a bang.
Get off to a flying start.
At one stroke.
Get off the ground.

同 開門紅（1472）The first blow is half the battle.
反 出師不利（0416）Step off on the wrong foot.

齊頭並進 qí tóu bìng jìn 2035

Heads together, march forward. (lit.)

Neck and neck.
On even board with
Have many irons in the fire.

同 並駕齊驅（0161）Keep abreast with
反 爭先恐後（3835）The devil takes the hindmost.

齊心協力 qí xīn xié lì 2036

Of one mind and united strength. (lit.)

With united effort.
To join forces.

同 羣策羣力（2173）Pool issues.
反 各人自掃門前雪（0904）Sweep before your own door.

騎虎難下 qí hǔ nán xià 2037

Difficult to dismount from the tiger's back. (lit.)

On the horns of a dilemma.
He who rides on a tiger can never dismount.
Hold a wolf by the ears.
Needs must when the devil drives.
To be up a tree.
Up a gum-tree.

同 欲罷不能（3714）To have a wolf by the ears.
源 隋書．獨孤皇后傳：“大事已然，騎虎之勢，必不得下。”

2038 **騎牆派** qí qiáng pài
Riding-on-a-wall type. (lit.)
A fence-sitter.

同 兩面討好（1632）Sit on the hedge.

2039 **乞漿得酒** qǐ jiāng dé jiǔ
To beg for broth one gets wine. (lit.)
Get more than one bargained for.
Fish for sprats and catch a herring.
To be overjoyed.

同 喜出望外（3057）To one's pleasant surprise.
反 偷雞不成蝕把米（2783）Many go out for wool and come home shorn.
源 朝野僉載："歲在申酉，求漿得酒。"

2040 **杞人憂天** qǐ rén yōu tiān
The man of Qi (a country name) worries about the fall of the sky. (lit.)
Meet trouble half-way.
Borrow trouble.

同 無病呻吟（2949）Cry out before one is hurt.
反 泰山崩於前而目不瞬（2670）If the sky falls we shall catch larks.
源 列子・天瑞："杞國有人，憂天崩墜，身無所寄。"

2041 **起死回生** qǐ sǐ huí shēng
Restoration of the dead to life. (lit.)
Come back to life.
Raise one from the dead.
To bring one to.
Bring one round (to).

同 救人一命（1428）Snatch a brand from a burning fire.
反 殺人不眨眼（2325）Kill in cold blood.
源 李開先・林沖寶劍記："吃緊的不識病名，休再提起死回生。"

2042 **豈能盡如人意** qǐ néng jìn rú rén yì
How can it all be as one wishes. (lit.)
It is hard to please all.

同 眾口難調（3917）No dish pleases all palates alike.

2043 **氣喘如牛** qì chuǎn rú niú
Heavy breathing like an ox. (lit.)
Out of breath.

同 氣急敗壞（2045）Gasping for breath.

2044 **氣得要命** qì de yào mìng
To be irritated to death. (lit.)
Mad as a hornet (wet hen).
Mad as hops.

同 氣急敗壞（2045）Get into wax.
反 心平氣和（3181）Keep cool.

2045 **氣急敗壞** qì jí bài huài
Quick temper ruins it. (lit.)
To be worked up.
Gasping for breath.
Get into wax.

反 心平氣和（3181）Keep cool.

氣派十足 qì pài shí zú 2046

The style is perfect. (lit.)

Stand upon one's dignity.

同 大擺架子（0505）Give oneself air.

反 平易近人（1994）Have a taking way with one.

氣味相投 qì wèi xiāng tóu 2047

(Persons of) the same smell (taste) are congenial to each other. (lit.)

Hit it off well.

Like draws to like.

Like will to like.

Birds of a feather flock together.

同 格格不入（0895）Out of keeping with

氣息奄奄 qì xī yǎn yǎn 2048

Gasping for breath. (lit.)

Dangerously ill.

Sinking fast.

At one's last gasp.

同 苟延殘喘（0928）Keep body and soul together.

反 生氣勃勃（2416）To be alive and kicking.

源 李密·陳情表："氣息奄奄，人命危淺。"

棄甲曳兵而走 qì jiǎ yè bīng ér zǒu 2049

Casting aside the armour and draging their weapons along. (lit.)

Run for one's life.

Beat a hasty retreat.

Run helter-skelter.

同 潰不成軍（1533）To be put to rout.

反 如入無人之境（2275）It was just a walk over.

源 孟子·梁惠王上："兵刃既接，棄甲曳兵而走。"

棄舊圖新 qì jiù tú xīn 2050

Throw away the old and plan for the new. (lit.)

Start afresh.

Start from a clean slate.

同 改弦更張（0855）Make a fresh start.

反 故態復萌（0951）Back in the old rut.

棄如敝屣 qì rú bì xǐ 2051

Like throwing away a pair of worn shoes. (lit.)

Discard as a squeezed lemon.

Cast aside like an old shoe.

Fling (throw) to the winds.

反 珍而藏之（3823）Lay it up in lavender.

源 孟子："猶棄敝屣也。"

2052 恰到好處 qià dào hǎo chù
It fits to nicely. (lit.)
Strike the right keynote.
To a turn.
Right on the beam.

反 差之毫釐，謬以千里（0320）There is but one step from the sublime to the ridiculous.

2053 恰恰相反 qià qià xiāng fǎn
Just the opposite. (lit.)
Just the other way round.
On the contrary.

同 適得其反（2539）Run counter to

2054 恰如其分 qià rú qí fèn
Exactly agreeing to his share. (lit.)
No more, no less.
Put the saddle on the right horse.
Suit to a T.

反 失之過甚（2448）Carry too far.

2055 千變萬化 qiān biàn wàn huà
Thousand changes and ten thousand variations. (lit.)
Vicissitudes of life.
The unexpected always happens.

反 食古不化（2467）Stick-in-the-mud.
源 列子："千變萬化，不可窮極。"

2056 千差萬別 qiān chā wàn bié
Thousand variations and ten thousand differences. (lit.)
As different as chalk is from cheese.
As like as a dock to a daisy.

反 一模一樣（3428）As like as two peas in a pod.
源 釋道源．景德傳燈錄："僧問，如何是無異底事，師曰，千差萬別。"

2057 千錘百煉 qiān chuí bǎi liàn
Thousand hammering and hundred refining. (lit.)
Steeled and tempered.
A good anvil does not fear the hammer.
Through the mill.
Gone through fire and water.

源 趙翼．甌北詩話："詩家好作奇句警語，必千錘百煉而後能成。"

千方百計 qiān fāng bǎi jì ◀2058
Thousand ways and hundred plans. (lit.)
By hook and by crook.
Explore every avenue.
Resort to every trick.
Leave no stone unturned.
In all manner of ways.
Try one's utmost.
Do everthing possible.

源 朱子語錄："譬如捉賊相似，須是著起精神，千方百計去趕捉他。"

千揀萬揀，揀了個爛燈盞 ◀2059
qiān jiǎn wàn jiǎn, jiǎn le gè làn dēng zhǎn
Choosing thousand and ten thousand times, eventually choose a broken lamp. (lit.)
A maiden with many wooers often chooses the worst.

千金散盡還復來 qiān jīn sàn jìn hái fù lái ◀2060
Thousand pieces of gold spent completely, they still will come back again. (lit.)
Give and spend, and God will send.
Give much to the poor doth increase a man's store.

千鈞一髮 qiān jūn yí fà ◀2061
Thirty thousand catties hung by a single hair. (lit.)
At the critical moment.
To hang by a thread.

源 韓愈．與孟尚書書："其危如一髮引千鈞。"

千里送鵝毛，物輕情意重 ◀2062
qiān lǐ sòng é máo, wù qīng qíng yì zhòng
A goose feather sent from thousand li (Chinese mile) a gift thought light, the affection is deep. (lit.)
A token of affection.
What is bought is cheaper than a gift.

源 邢俊臣詞："物輕人意重，千里送鵝毛。"

2063 **千里之堤，潰於蟻穴**
qiān lǐ zhī dī, kuì yú yǐ xué
Thousand li (Chinese mile) dike may collapse due to an ants' hole. (lit.)
A small leak will sink a great ship.
For want of a nail, the shoe is lost; for want of a shoe, the horse is lost; and for want of a horse, the rider is lost.

源 韓非子．喻老："千丈之堤，以螻蟻之穴潰，百尺之室，以突隙之煙焚。"

2064 **千里之行，始於足下**
qiān lǐ zhī xíng, shǐ yú zú xià
The walk of thousand li (Chinese mile) starts from this step. (lit.)
He who would climb the ladder must begin at the bottom.

源 老子："九層之台，起於纍土。千里之行，始於足下。"

2065 **千秋萬代** qiān qiū wàn dài
One thousand autumns and ten thousand generations. (lit.)
For ages.
In all the generations to come.
Throughout the ages.

同 世世代代（2499）From generation to generation.
源 江淹．恨賦："千秋萬世，為怨難勝。"

2066 **千辛萬苦** qiān xīn wàn kǔ
Thousand hardship and ten thousand bitterness. (lit.)
Undergo untold hardships.
Take great pains in
Suffer untold hardships.
Toil and moil.

同 歷盡辛酸（1613）Through hell and high water.
反 舒舒服服（2564）As snug as a bug in a rug.
源 李開先．林沖寶劍記："你我十載邊關，千辛萬苦。"

2067 **千載難逢** qiān zǎi nán féng
A rare chance in thousand years. (lit.)
It only happens once in a blue moon.
It chances in an hour that happens not in seven years.

反 司空見慣（2618）Order of the day.

2068 **千載一時** qiān zǎi yì shí
A time of a thousand years. (lit.)
The chance of a life time.
Now or never.
Chance for a lifetime.

同 大好時機（0527）High time.
源 文中子．關朗篇："千載一時，不可失也。"

千真萬確 qiān zhēn wàn què 2069

Thousand truth and ten thousand accuracy. (lit.)

Nothing but the truth.

As sure as eggs is eggs.

Sure as fate.

反 向壁虛構（3118）Sheer fabrication.

牽強附會 qiān qiǎng fù huì 2070

To present a false consent. (lit.)

To be too far-fetched.

牽着鼻子走 qiān zhe bí zǐ zǒu 2071

Walk one along by pulling his nose. (lit.)

Lead one by the nose.

同 頤指氣使（3522）Twist a person round one's fingers.

前車之鑒 qián chē zhī jiàn 2072

Take warning from the cart ahead. (lit.)

In doing we learn.

Learn wisdom by the follies of others.

Wise men learn by other men's mistakes.

同 前事不忘，後事之師（2080）Repent what's past, avoid what is to come.

源 賈誼·治安策："諺曰，前車覆，後車誡。"

前程似錦 qián chéng sì jǐn 2073

The future journey is like a brocade. (lit.)

To have the world before one.

To have the ball at one's feet.

Have a brilliant prospect.

同 錦繡前程（1355）Promising future.

反 日暮途窮（2256）Driven to the last extremity.

前功盡棄 qián gōng jìn qì 2074

All previous efforts are wasted. (lit.)

Go down the drain.

Have all the troubles for nothing.

All labour lost.

同 功虧一簣（0924）Look back from the plough.

反 練出功夫（1619）He that shoots oft shall at last hit the mark.

源 五代史補："今一旦反作脫空漢，前功盡棄，令公之心安乎。"

前後相符 qián hòu xiāng fú 2075

The front and back agree with each other. (lit.)

What's sauce for the goose is sauce for the gander.

2076 **前呼後擁** qián hū hòu yōng
(People) yelling in the front and pushing in the rear. (lit.)
With a long train of equipage.
Under escort.

反 形單影隻（3217）All alone.

2077 **前怕狼，後怕虎**
qián pà láng, hòu pà hǔ
Afraid of wolf at the front and also afraid of tiger at the back. (lit.)
Too much taking heed is loss.

同 畏首畏尾（2911）Full of misgivings.
反 敢作敢為（0867）Take one's courage in both hands.

2078 **前人栽樹，後人乘涼**
qián rén zāi shù, hòu rén chéng liáng
The forerunners planted the trees while the later men get cool in the shade. (lit.)
One man makes a chair, another man sits on it.

同 坐享其成（4059）Get something for nothing.

2079 **前人種樹後人收**
qián rén zhòng shù hòu rén shōu
The forerunners planted the trees, while the later men gather the fruits. (lit.)
Who plants a walnut tree expects not to eat the fruit.
One man sows and another reaps.

同 施恩莫望報（2451）Virtue is its own reward.

2080 **前事不忘，後事之師**
qián shì bú wàng, hòu shì zhī shī
The former events unforgotten may be teacher of later events. (lit.)
Repent what's past, avoid what is to come.
To day is yesterday's pupil.
He that would know what shall be must consider what has been.

反 一錯再錯（3385）Denying a fault doubles it.
源 戰國策 · 趙策一：“前事不忘，後事之師。”

前思後想 qián sī hòu xiǎng
To think before and after. (lit.)
Turn over in one's mind.
Chew the cud.
Weigh and consider.

同 仔細思量（3966）Consult one's pillow.

2081

前無去路，後有追兵
qián wú qù lù, hòu yǒu zhuī bīng
No road ahead can go but soldiers are chasing from behind. (lit.)
Between the devil and the deep sea.

同 上天無路，入地無門（2358）In a quandary.

2082

前因後果 qián yīn hòu guǒ
Antecedent and consequent. (lit.)
What brings about.
Cause and effect.

源 南齊書．高逸傳論：“今樹以前因，報以後果。”

2083

錢可通神 qián kě tōng shén
Money can move the gods. (lit.)
A golden key opens every door.

同 有錢能使鬼推磨（3659）Money makes the mare go.

源 張固．幽閒鼓吹：“錢十萬，可通神矣。”

2084

黔驢技窮 qián lǘ jì qióng
The trick of the Kwei Chow (a province of South West China) mule is used up. (lit.)
At the end of one's tether (rope).
At one's wit's end.

同 技止此耳（1229）All his goods in the window.

反 滿腹妙計（1742）To be full of wrinkles.

源 柳宗元．黔之驢：“驢不勝怒，蹄之，虎因喜，計曰，技止此耳。”

2085

淺斟低酌 qiǎn zhēn dī zhuó
Pour out little wine and eat slowly. (lit.)
Eat at pleasure, drink by measure.
To hob and nob.
Eat a bit before you drink.

同 細味品嘗（3063）Enjoy the full gusto of

反 狼吞虎嚥（1550）Have a wolf in one's stomach.

源 宋長編：“但能於銷金帳中，淺斟低唱，飲羊羔兒酒耳。”

2086

強弩之末 qiáng nǔ zhī mò
The strength of a spent arrow. (lit.)
On its last legs.
Worn to a frazzle.
A spent arrow.
On the decline.

同 大勢已去（0552）Come out of the little end of the horn.

反 方興未艾（0754）In the ascendant.

源 漢書．韓安國傳：“強弩之末，力不能入魯縞。”

2087

2088 強徵暴斂 qiáng zhēng bào liǎn
Fierce taxation and ruthless of (people's) money. (lit.)
Grind the faces of the poor.

2089 強中更有強中手，惡人自有惡人磨 qiáng zhōng gèng yǒu qiáng zhōng shǒu, è rén zì yǒu è rén mó
Among the strong there are still stronger hands, wicked people naturally have wicked people to grind them. (lit.)
Diamond cut diamond.

2090 牆有縫，壁有耳
qiáng yǒu fèng, bì yǒu ěr
Walls have cracks, partitions have ears. (lit.)
Walls (Pitchers) have ears.

同 若要人不知，除非己莫為（2296）There is a witness everywhere.

2091 強詞奪理 qiǎng cí duó lǐ
To force the argument and distort the reason. (lit.)
Without rhyme or reason.

反 以理服人（3531）Bring one to reason.
源 三國演義："座上一人忽曰，孔明所言，皆強詞奪理，均非正論，不必再言。"

2092 強迫命令 qiǎng pò mìng lìng
To compel orders. (lit.)
Shove (Ram) down one's throat.

同 瞎指揮（3068）Lead them a chase.
反 放任自流（0761）Let things drift.

2093 強人所難 qiǎng rén suǒ nán
Force one to do what he finds difficult. (lit.)
Put one to shame.
To force one's hand.

2094 敲骨吸髓 qiāo gǔ xī suǐ
Beat the bone and suck the marrow. (lit.)
Bleed someone white.

同 無情剝削（2985）To sweat a person.

敲起喪鐘 qiāo qǐ sāng zhōng 2095
To beat (up) the knell. (lit.)
To ring the knell.

喬裝打扮 qiáo zhuāng dǎ bàn 2096
Dressed up in disguise. (lit.)
Put up a front.
Sail under false colours.

反 剝去偽裝（0166）Cut someone down to size.

巧婦難為無米之炊 2097
qiǎo fù nán wéi wú mǐ zhī chuī
Even a resourceful housewife finds it difficult to prepare a meal without rice. (lit.)
Bare walls make giddy housewives.
You cannot make bricks without straw.
With empty hands men may no hawks lure.
What's a workman without his tools?

源 陸游．老學庵筆記："巧婦安能作無麵湯餅乎。"

巧舌如簧 qiǎo shé rú huáng 2098
Fine tongue like a reed organ (with a metallic tongue in it). (lit.)
Mealy mouthed.
Honey tongued.
To mouth one's words.
Talk glibly.

同 三寸不爛之舌（2303）Silver tongued.
反 張口結舌（3793）To be tongued-tied.
源 詩經．小雅．巧言："巧言如簧，顏之厚矣。"

悄然離去 qiǎo rán lí qù 2099
Left very quietly. (lit.)
Make oneself scarce.
Take French leave.

同 溜之大吉（1677）Give one the slip.

翹尾巴 qiào wěi bā 2100
Erecting the tail. (lit.)
Get one's tail up.
Be cocky.

反 俯首帖耳（0833）At one's beck and call.

2101 **切膚之痛** qiè fū zhī tòng

The pain of cutting one's skin. (lit.)

No one knows where the shoe pinches like the wearer.

Near is my shirt, but nearer is my skin.

2102 **鍥而不捨** qiè ér bù shě

Would not give up the engraving. (lit.)

Peg away at it.

Stick to it.

Firm and unyielding.

同 堅持到底（1265）Go through with it.

反 半途而廢（0072）Do things by halves.

源 荀子・勸學："鍥而捨之，朽木不折，鍥而不捨，金石可鏤。"

2103 **竊鈎者誅，竊國者侯**

qiè gōu zhě zhū, qiè guó zhě hóu

To steal a hook one gets death penalty but to usurp the country one may be rewarded a rank of peer. (lit.)

Strain at a gnat and swallow a camel.

Little thieves are hanged, but great ones escape.

源 莊子・胠篋："彼竊鈎者誅，竊國者為諸侯。"

2104 **竊竊私語** qiè qiè sī yǔ

To chat stealthily. (lit.)

Tete-a-tete.

Talk in whisper.

Under one's breath.

反 大聲疾呼（0549）Proclaim from the house-tops.

源 韓愈・順宗實錄："日引其黨屏人竊竊細語，謀奪宦者兵，以制四海之命。"

2105 **竊竊自喜** qiè qiè zì xǐ

Pleased with oneself privately. (lit.)

To hug oneself.

Pat oneself on the back.

同 洋洋自得（3333）To tread on air.

反 潸然淚下（2338）To pipe one's eyes.

2106 **親力親為** qīn lì qīn wéi

To put effort and do it oneself. (lit.)

If you want a thing done well, do it yourself.

同 事必躬親（2506）Better do it than wish it done.

反 假手於人（1258）Make a cat's paw of someone.

源 詩經："弗躬弗親。"

親密無間 qīn mì wú jiàn 2107
Very close without gap. (lit.)
Hit it off well.
On intimate terms with
Hand in hand (glove).
Those two are very thick.
As thick as thieves.
They cleave together like burrs.

反 冰炭不相容（0155）At loggerheads with one another.
源 漢書 · 蕭望之傳："蕭望之歷位將相，藉師傅之恩，可謂親暱無間。"

親朋戚友 qīn péng qī yǒu 2108
Relatives and friends. (lit.)
Kith and kin.

親自發動 qīn zì fā dòng 2109
To start the movement by oneself. (lit.)
Start the ball rolling.
On one's own initiative.

親自掛帥 qīn zì guà shuài 2110
Take up the commander-in-chief post by oneself. (lit.)
Take the lead.
Play first fiddle.

琴瑟之好 qín sè zhī hǎo 2111
The harmony of lute and psaltery. (lit.)
A good wife makes a good husband.

源 詩經："窈窕淑女，琴瑟友之。"

勤儉起家 qín jiǎn qǐ jiā 2112
Raising of the family by diligence and frugality. (lit.)
Industry is fortune's right hand, and frugality her left.
Industry will keep you from want.
Diligence is the mother of good luck.

同 富從升合起（0845）Little and offten fills the purse.
反 坐食山空（4056）Eat out of house and home.

2113 **勤勤力力，終須乞食；懶懶惰惰，高樓大座**
qín qín lì lì, zhōng xū qǐ shí; lǎn lǎn duò duò, gāo lóu dà zuò
Being diligent may end up in begging for food; being lazy may live in a tall and big mansion. (lit.)
One man sows and another reaps.
Desert and reward seldom keep company.

反 自己動手，豐衣足食（3982）In the sweat of thy face shalt thou eat bread.

2114 **青出於藍** qīng chū yú lán
Blue is extracted from the indigo. (lit.)
The scholar may excel the master.
Get ahead of

同 盲拳打死老師傅（1766）The scholar may worst the master.
反 不堪造就（0210）Ill beef never made good broth.
源 荀子・勸學："青取之於藍而青於藍。"

2115 **青黃不接** qīng huáng bù jiē
The green and yellow do not dovetail. (The green crops of this year will not be ripe before the yellow grains last year are exhausted.) (lit.)
A seasonal shortage.
Between hay and grass.

源 元典章・戶部・倉庫："即日正是青黃不接之際，各處物斛湧貴。"

2116 **青空一碧** qīng kōng yí bì
Blue heaven is a blue space. (lit.)
The blue expanse of heaven.

2117 **青史留名** qīng shǐ liú míng
To leave a name on the green bamboo slip of record. (lit.)
To be in the scroll of fame.

同 名垂千古（1811）Their names liveth for evermore.
反 湮沒無聞（3293）Sink into oblivion.

2118 **清澈可鑒** qīng chè kě jiàn
Clear and transparent that one can see (the bottom of the pool). (lit.)
As clear as crystal.

清規戒律 qīng guī jiè lǜ 2119
Clear rules and regulations. (lit.)
Rules and regulations.
Taboos and commandments.

源 釋門正統："百丈山懷海禪師始立天下禪林規式，謂之清規。"

蜻蜓點水 qīng tíng diǎn shuǐ 2120
The dragonfly touches the water. (lit.)
Skim over.
Touch lightly.

源 杜甫．曲江二："點水蜻蜓款款飛。"

傾耳細聽 qīng ěr xì tīng 2121
Bend the ear to listen carefully. (lit.)
To hang on a person's lips.
Lend an attentive ear to

同 豎起耳朵（2575）Prick up one's ears.
反 聽而不聞（2573）To hear as a hog in harvest.
源 禮記："傾耳而聽之，不可得而聞也。"

傾盆大雨 qīng pén dà yǔ 2122
The torrential rain like pouring from a basin. (lit.)
To rain cats and dogs.
To rain trams and omnibuses.
Rain buckets.

源 宋伯仁．雨中詩："終日翻盆雨，池亭晚更涼。"

傾吐衷情 qīng tǔ zhōng qíng 2123
Pour out the inner feelings. (lit.)
Get it off one's chest.
Unbosom oneself.
Open one's heart to
Lay one's heart bare.

同 披肝瀝膽（1967）Make a clean breast of
反 諱莫如深（1158）Keep one's own counsel.

輕而易舉 qīng ér yì jǔ 2124
Light and easy to lift. (lit.)
As easy as pie (pot).
Mere child's play.
Can do it on one's head.
Do something standing on one's head.
Duck soup.
As easy as anything.

同 不費吹灰之力（0185）There's nothing to it.
反 任務艱巨（2250）A herculean task.
源 詩經．大雅．烝民．朱熹注："言人皆言德甚輕而易舉，然人莫能舉也。"

2125 **輕舉妄動** qīng jǔ wàng dòng

Handle lightly and act blindly. (lit.)

Act on impulse.

To rush headlong.

A leap in the dark.

Neck and heels.

同 冒失從事（1774）Buy a pig in a poke.

反 如臨深淵，如履薄冰（2272）Tread as on eggs.

源 韓非子．解老："眾人之輕棄道理而易忘（妄）舉動者，不知其禍福之深大而道闊遠若是也。"

2126 **輕描淡寫** qīng miáo dàn xiě

A light sketch and simple writing. (lit.)

To skate over

Touch on lightly.

同 唱低調（0331）Play something down.

反 加鹽加醋（1244）Tell with unction.

2127 **輕如鵝毛** qīng rú é máo

As light as a goose feather. (lit.)

As light as feather.

反 燈芯扛成鐵（0625）On a long journey even a straw is heavy.

源 司馬遷．報任少卿書："人固有一死，或重於泰山，或輕於鴻毛。"

2128 **情不自禁** qíng bù zì jìn

Unable to suppress one's own emotion. (lit.)

Emotion gets the better of oneself.

Feel an irresistible impulse.

Feel impelled to

Can't refrain from

Can't help

2129 **情場失意** qíng chǎng shī yì

To be disappointed in realm of love. (lit.)

Fall out of love (with someone).

2130 **情急智生** qíng jí zhì shēng

An emergency sharpens one's wits. (lit.)

In a flash of inspiration.

Necessity is the mother of invention.

2131 **情況好轉** qíng kuàng hǎo zhuǎn

The circumstances have turned better. (lit.)

Turn the corner.

同 化險為夷（1116）To be out of the woods.

反 江河日下（1292）Go from bad to worse.

情人眼裏出西施 qíng rén yǎn lǐ chū xī shī 2132

In the lover's eye, there is Xi-Shi (name of the famous Chinese beauty in history). (lit.)

Beauty lies in lover's eyes.

The eye lets in love.

Beauty is in the eye of the beholder.

Every lover sees a thousand graces in the beloved object.

If Jack's in love, he's no judge of Jill's beauty.

情緒激昂 qíng xù jī áng 2133

The thread of emotion is high and excited. (lit.)

To be keyed up.

同 心情激動（3184）To be up in the boughs.

反 平心靜氣（1993）Cool as a cucumber.

晴天霹靂 qíng tiān pī lì 2134

The thunderclap from a blue sky. (lit.)

Catch one off guard.

A bolt from the blue.

It came absolutely out of the blue.

Out of the clear blue sky.

同 突如其來（2805）Appear from nowhere.

源 陸游詩："正如久蟄龍，青天飛霹靂。"

請君入甕 qǐng jūn rù wèng 2135

Please (you) step into the jar. (lit.)

Give a person his own (medicine).

Pay one back in his own coin.

同 以其人之道還治其人之身（3534）Pay back in kind.

源 資治通鑒："俊臣謂興曰，囚多不承，當為何法。興曰此甚易耳，取大甕，以炭四圍炙之，令囚入中，何事不承。俊臣乃索大甕，火圍如興法，因起謂興曰，有內狀推兄，請兄入此甕。"

慶祝一番 qìng zhù yī fān 2136

One big celebration. (lit.)

Kick up one's heels.

窮國與富國 qióng guó yǔ fù guó 2137

Poor countries and rich countries. (lit.)

The haves and the have-nots.

2138 **窮極無聊** qióng jí wú liáo

Extremely poor and nothing to do. (lit.)

To be on the hocks (hog).

源 費昶・思公子詩："虞卿亦何命，窮極若無聊。"

2139 **窮奢極欲** qióng shē jí yù

Unlimited extravagance and extreme lust. (lit.)

Live on the fat of the land.

Live at rack and manger.

Fast living.

同 糜爛生活 The primrose path.

反 淡泊明志（0578）Lead a stoical life.

源 漢書・谷永傳："窮奢極欲，沉湎荒淫。"

2140 **窮途沒路** qióng tú mò lù

No road ahead, the end of the path. (lit.)

At the end of one's rope.

To be put to the pin of the collar.

To be at bay.

On one's beam-ends.

同 山窮水盡（2334）To be on the rocks.

反 錦繡前程（1355）Have the ball before one.

2141 **窮相畢露** qióng xiàng bì lù

The awkward situation is completely exposed. (lit.)

Down (out) at heels.

Out at elbows.

反 衣服麗都（3502）Make a gallant show.

2142 **窮則變，變則通**

qióng zé biàn, biàn zé tōng

Poverty induces changes, changes may find a way out. (lit.)

Necessity is the mother of invention.

Want is the mother of industry.

同 置之死地而後生（3905）Despair gives courage to the coward.

源 周易・繫辭下："窮則變，變則通，通則久。"

2143 **秋風掃落葉** qiū fēng sǎo luò yè

Autumnal breeze sweeps the fallen leaves. (lit.)

Make a clean sweep.

Sweep everything before one.

同 囊括一空（1886）Grand slam.

源 三國志・魏志・辛毗傳："以明公之威，應困窮之敵，擊疲弊之寇，無異迅風之振秋葉矣。"

2144 **秋菊春桃** qiū jú chūn táo

Autumn chrysanthemum and Spring peach. (lit.)

Everything is good in its season.

求人不如求己 qiú rén bù rú qiú jǐ 2145
Asking others for help is not as good as asking oneself. (lit.)
Better do it than wish it done.
Better spare to have thine own than ask of other men.

同 事必躬親（2506）If you want a thing done well, do it yourself.
反 因人成事（3574）Come in through the cabin window.
源 貴耳集：“宋孝宗見觀音像，手持數珠，問何用，僧淨輝對曰，念觀世音菩薩。問自念則甚，對曰，求人不如求己。”

曲突徙薪 qū tū xǐ xīn 2146
To bend the chimney and remove the fuel. (lit.)
To guard against danger.
A stitch in time saves nine.
If you kill one flea in March, you kill a hundred.
Who repairs not his gutters repairs his whole house.

同 有備無患（3644）Forewarned is forearmed.
反 厝火積薪（0481）He lives unsafely that looks too near on things.
源 漢書．霍光傳：“曲突徙薪無恩澤，焦頭爛額為上客。”

曲意逢迎 qū yì féng yíng 2147
Distorting one's idea to please (someone). (lit.)
Curry favour with
Tickle a person's ear(s).
Insinuate oneself into another's favour.

反 嗤之以鼻（0378）Turn up one's nose at

屈打成招 qū dǎ chéng zhāo 2148
Use torture to extort a confession. (lit.)
Give one the third degree.
Grill a person.
Extort confession.

屈指可數 qū zhǐ kě shǔ 2149
Can be counted by bending fingers. (lit.)
A sprinkling.
A handful.
To be on the map.

同 寥若晨星（1641）Few and far between.
反 恒河沙數（1063）As numberless as the sands.
源 歐陽修．唐安公美政頌：“今文化之盛，其書屈指可數者，無三四人。”

2150 **區別對待** qū bié duì dài

Treat with discrimination. (lit.)

Make fish of one and flesh of another.

Make chalk of one and cheese of another.

同 厚此薄彼（1076）Treat with partiality.

反 一視同仁（3457）When it rains it rains on all alike.

2151 **趨炎附勢** qū yán fù shì

Follow the flame and join the influential. (lit.)

Hang on the skirts of

Hail the rising sun.

Come down on the right side of the fence.

同 攀龍附鳳（1945）Keep up with the Joneses.

源 宋史．李垂傳：“焉能趨炎附勢，看人眉睫，以冀推挽乎。”

2152 **取長補短** qǔ cháng bǔ duǎn

To adopt the long one to make up the short. (lit.)

A dwarf on a giant's shoulders sees further of the two.

源 孟子．滕文公上：“今滕，絕長補短，將五十里也。”

2153 **取而代之** qǔ ér dài zhī

Take it and replace (him). (lit.)

Elbow out someone.

Step into a person's shoes.

Fill a person's bonnet (shoes).

Put a person's nose out of joint.

Take the place of

Edge out someone.

源 史記．項羽本紀：“籍曰，彼可取而代之。”

2154 **取之不盡** qǔ zhī bù jìn

Take it without end. (lit.)

Know no limits.

There's as good fish in the sea as ever come out.

反 山窮水盡（2334）To be on the rocks.

2155 **取之無禁，用之不竭**

qǔ zhī wú jìn, yòng zhī bù jié

Take it without restriction and use it without being exhausted. (lit.)

The more the well is used, the more water it gives.

反 坐食山空（4056）Always taking out of a meal-tub, and never putting in, soon comes to the bottom.

源 蘇軾．前赤壁賦：“取之無禁，用之不竭。”

去惡從善 qù è cóng shàn 2156
Do away with evil and follow goodness. (lit.)
Eschew evil, and do good.
Wipe the slate clean.

同 改邪歸正（0856）To mend one's way.

去時終須去，再三留不住 2157
qù shí zhōng xū qù, zài sān liú bù zhù
Time to go one finally must go, even repeatedly three times, (you) can't keep him. (lit.)
The best of friends must part.

同 天下無不散之筵席（2729）The longest day must have an end.

全不知情 quán bù zhī qíng 2158
Completely ignorant of the situation. (lit.)
To be in the dark.

同 一無所知（3475）Not to know beans about
反 深知底細（2402）Know one（something） inside out.

全場喝彩 quán chăng hè căi 2159
The whole audience applauded. (lit.)
Bring down the house.

同 滿座傾倒（1754）To carry the house.

全副武裝 quán fù wŭ zhuāng 2160
Fully uniformed and armed. (lit.)
Armed to the teeth (to all points.)
In full battle array.
Under arms.

全力以赴 quán lì yĭ fù 2161
To meet with all the strength. (lit.)
To go all out.
Go at it hammer and tongs.
To work up to the collar.
Put the best foot (leg) forward (foremost).
Put one's shoulder to the wheel.
With might and main.

同 不遺餘力（0265）Tooth and nail.
反 袖手旁觀（3242）Stand by with folded arms.

2162 **全神貫注** quán shén guàn zhù
With all the energy to concentrate. (lit.)
Zero in on
Focus one's attention on
Concentrate upon
Sink one's teeth into

同 專心致志（3938）With undivided attention.
反 心不在焉（3160）To be wool-gathering.

2163 **全盛時期** quán shèng shí qī
The age of prime prosperity. (lit.)
Palmy days.
Heyday.

反 大勢已去（0552）Come out of the little end of the horn.

2164 **全心全意** quán xīn quán yì
Whole heart and whole will. (lit.)
Heart and soul.
Set one's mind on.

反 半心半意（0074）Half heart is no heart.

2165 **拳腳交加** quán jiǎo jiāo jiā
To strike and kick with fists and feet. (lit.)
Cuffs and kicks.

同 大打出手（0511）Come to blows.

2166 **權衡輕重** quán héng qīng zhòng
Weigh, light or heavy, in a balance. (To weigh which is less or more important). (lit.)
Strike a balance.

源 孟子："權而後知輕重。"

2167 **權威人士透露** quán wēi rén shì tòu lù
Leaked out by the authoritative people. (lit.)
Straight from the horse's mouth.

反 街談巷議（1316）Wayside inn gossip.

2168 **權宜行事** quán yí xíng shì
Do things with expediency. (lit.)
If you cannot have the best, make the best of what you have.

權宜之計 quán yí zhī jì

A plan of expediency. (lit.)

Makeshift device.

Stop-gap measure.

同 權宜行事（2168）If you cannot have the best, make the best of what you have.

源 後漢書："計日用之權宜。" 2169

卻之不恭 què zhī bù gōng

Refusing (an offer) is unrespectful. (lit.)

Favours unused are favours abused.

Never refuse a good offer.

Obedience is best of manners.

源 孟子："卻之卻之為不恭。" 2170

雀躍三百 què yuè sān bǎi

Hopping like sparrows for three hundred times. (lit.)

As cheerful as a lark.

To chirp up.

Leap with joy.

Jump for joy.

同 興高采烈（3224）Sitting on high cotton. 2171

反 怏怏不樂（3342）Have the blues.

源 莊子："鴻蒙拊髀，雀躍不絕。"

確鑿不移 què záo bù yí

Certain without doubt and can't be moved. (lit.)

You can kiss the book on that.

Beyond question.

同 千真萬確（2069）As sure as eggs is eggs. 2172

反 難以置信（1883）To stagger belief.

羣策羣力 qún cè qún lì

Collective planning and united effort. (lit.)

Join forces.

Pool issues.

Put our heads together.

同 戮力同心（1703）To hang together. 2173

反 各有打算（0909）The donkey means one thing, and the driver another.

源 楊雄．法言．重黎："漢屈羣策，羣策屈羣力。"

羣居終日，言不及義

qún jū zhōng rì, yán bù jí yì

When a group of people gather together all day, they make no worthy remarks. (lit.)

By doing nothing we learn to do ill.

Idle brains are the devil's workshop.

源 論語．衛靈公："羣居終日，言不及義，好行小惠，難矣哉。" 2174

2175 羣龍無首 qún lóng wú shǒu

A flock of dragons without a head. (lit.)

With no one in charge.

The mob has many heads but no brains.

同 烏合之眾（2944）Rag, tag and bobtail.

反 唯馬首是瞻（2889）Follow the lead.

源 周易．乾："見羣龍無首。"

R

燃眉之急 rán méi zhī jí

As urgent as if the eyebrows have caught fire. (lit.)

No time to be lost.

Pressing needs.

Not a moment to lose.

同 火燒眉毛（1169）Imminent danger.

反 不急之務（0202）That can wait.

源 五燈會元．蔣山法泉禪師："問，如何是急切一句，師曰，火燒眉毛。"

2176

染於蒼則蒼，染於黃則黃

rǎn yú cāng zé cāng, rǎn yú huáng zé huáng

Dyed in blue it becomes blue, dyed in yellow it becomes yellow. (lit.)

The finger that touches rouge will be red.

Touch pitch, and you will be defiled.

同 近朱者赤，近墨者黑（1365）He who lies down with dogs will rise with fleas.

反 出污泥而不染（0418）Lilies are whitest in a blackamoor's hand.

2177

惹火燒身 rě huǒ shāo shēn

Stir up a fire and burn oneself. (lit.)

He warms too near that burns.

2178

惹禍上身 rě huò shàng shēn

Get oneself into trouble. (lit.)

Wake a sleeping dog.

Stick one's neck out.

Put one's foot in it.

同 自找麻煩（4012）Invite trouble.

反 避之則吉（0127）To be out of harm's way.

2179

惹是生非 rě shì shēng fēi

Make trouble and provoke mischief. (lit.)

A storm in a tea-cup.

Trail one's coat.

Pick a quarrel.

Kick up a row.

Stir up trouble.

Make much ado about nothing.

Carry a chip on one's shoulder.

Put the cat among the pigeons.

同 無事生非（2992）Stir up mud.

反 息事寧人（3045）Pour oil on troubled waters.

2180

2181 熱鍋上的螞蟻 rè guō shàng de mǎ yǐ
Like an ant on a hot griddle.
Like a cat on hot bricks.
Like a hen on a hot griddle.
Like an ant on a hot pan.

同 惶惶不可終日（1139）To be on the rack.
反 優遊自在（3630）Free and easy.

2182 熱火朝天 rè huǒ cháo tiān
Hot flame heading skyward. (lit.)
Full of enthusiasm.
In full blast (swing).
At a high pitch.

同 風頭火勢（0808）Like a house on fire.
反 煙消雲散（3292）Vanish like smoke.

2183 熱淚盈眶 rè lèi yíng kuàng
Hot tears filling the eyes. (lit.)
Tears well up in one's eyes.
With eyes brimming with tears.

同 淚如泉湧（1589）Break into a passion of tears.
反 笑容可掬（3154）A face wreathed with smiles.

2184 熱烈歡迎 rè liè huān yíng
Warm and hearty welcome. (lit.)
Give one three times three.
Receive with open arms.

反 餉以閉門羹（3117）Leave one on the mat.

2185 熱烈贊助 rè liè zàn zhù
Warm and hearty praise and help. (lit.)
Carry a torch for
Lend oneself to
Give countenance to it.

同 鼎力支持（0659）Stand up for
反 潑冷水（2001）Throw cold water on

2186 熱門貨 rè mén huò
Hot (door) selling goods. (lit.)
Sell like hot cakes.
Good ware makes quick markets.
When ware is liked it is half sold.
Best seller.

2187 熱情洋溢 rè qíng yáng yì
Warm feelings overflow expressively. (lit.)
To glow with enthusiasm.

同 滿腔熱情（1750）Filled with ardour.
反 冷若冰霜（1595）As cold as charity.

2188 **熱血沸騰** rè xuè fèi téng
Hot blood is boiling. (lit.)
With heart afire.
Burning with righteous indignation.

反 冷酷心腸（1594）As cold as a stone.

2189 **人必先自愛而後人愛之**
rén bì xiān zì ài ér hòu rén ài zhī
A man must first love himself, then others will love him. (lit.)
Be a friend to thyself, and others will befriend thee.

2190 **人必先自侮而後人侮之**
rén bì xiān zì wǔ ér hòu rén wǔ zhī
A man must first have insulted himself, then others will insult him. (lit.)
Don't make yourself a mouse, or the cat will eat you.

2191 **人必先自重而後人重之** rén bì xiān zì zhòng ér hòu rén zhòng zhī
A man must first respect himself, then others will respect him. (lit.)
Respect yourself, or no one else will.
He that makes himself dirt the swine will tread on him.

2192 **人不可以貌相** rén bù kě yǐ mào xiàng
A man cannot be judged by his looks. (lit.)
Beauty is but skin-deep.
Never judge from appearances.
It is not the hood that makes the monk.

反 先敬羅衣後敬人（3082）Good clothes open all doors.

2193 **人不知，鬼不覺** rén bù zhī, guǐ bù jué
Not known by men, not perceived by ghosts. (lit.)
Behind one's back.
On the sly.
By stealth.
On tip-toe.

同 偷偷摸摸（2784）Up to some hangky-pangky.

源 元曲選．爭報恩：“恁做事可甚人不知鬼不覺。”

2194 人定勝天 rén dìng shèng tiān
With determination men conquer nature. (lit.)
Everyone is the maker of his own fate.

反 人算不如天算（2222）An ounce of luck is better than a pound of wisdom.

源 劉祁・歸潛志："天定能勝人，人定亦能勝天。"

2195 人多好做事 rén duō hǎo zuò shì
More people work better. (lit.)
Many hands make quick (light) work.

同 眾擎易舉（3920）Three helping one another bear the burden of six.

2196 人多勢眾 rén duō shì zhòng
More people more power. (lit.)
Their name is Legion.
There is safety in numbers.
Many hands make quick (light) work.

反 孤立無援（0936）To be left out in the cold.

2197 人多手腳亂 rén duō shǒu jiǎo luàn
More people more hands and feet causing confusion. (lit.)
The mob has many heads, but no brains.
Too many cooks spoil the broth.

2198 人多意見多 rén duō yì jiàn duō
More people more opinions. (lit.)
So many men, so many minds.

同 聚訟紛紜（1447）Opinions are divided.

反 異口同聲（3557）With one accord.

2199 人而無信，不知其可也
rén ér wú xìn, bù zhī qí kě yě
A man cannot be trusted, it is not known what he would do. (lit.)
He that has lost his credit is dead to the world.
He that once deceives is ever suspected.
A liar is not believed when he speaks the truth.
To cry wolf too often.
Honesty is the best policy.

反 殷實可靠（3580）Straight as a die.

源 本條目原句出自《論語・為政》

人非生而知之 2200

rén fēi shēng ér zhī zhī

A man is not born learned. (lit.)

No man is born wise or learned.

Wisdom is neither inheritance nor legacy.

源 論語．述而："我非生而知之者，好古敏以求之者也。"／韓愈．師說："人非生而知之者。"

人非聖賢，孰能無過 2201

rén fēi shèng xián, shú néng wú guò

Men are not all saints, how could they have no faults. (lit.)

No one is without his faults.

同 人誰無過（2221）Hs is lifeless that is faultless.

源 左傳．宣二年："人誰無過。"

人浮於事 rén fú yú shì 2202

People outnumber jobs available. (lit.)

Too many cooks spoil the broth.

To be over-staffed.

同 三個和尚沒水吃（2306）Everybody's business is nobody's business.

反 精兵簡政（1380）I will keep no more cats than will catch mice.

源 禮記．坊記："君子與其使食浮於人也，寧使人浮於食。"

人貴有自知之明 rén guì yǒu zì zhī zhī míng 2203

The value of a man is the wisdom of knowing himself. (lit.)

Know thyself.

He that has a head of wax must not walk in the sun.

人急造反，狗急跳牆 2204

rén jí zào fǎn, gǒu jí tiào qiáng

Men under pressure rebel, dogs under pressure jump over walls. (lit.)

Necessity knows no law.

Tread on a worm and it will turn.

人靠衣裳，佛靠金裝 2205

rén kào yī shāng, fó kào jīn zhuāng

Men depend on clothes, Buddha depends on gold ornaments. (lit.)

The tailor makes the man.

反 先敬羅衣後敬人（3082）Good clothes open all doors.

2206 **人靠衣裳，馬靠金鞍**
rén kào yī shāng, mǎ kào jīn ān
Men depend on clothes, horses depend on gold saddles. (lit.)
Fine feathers make fine birds.

2207 **人老精，鬼老靈**
rén lǎo jīng, guǐ lǎo líng
Old men wise, old ghosts haunting. (lit.)
Old birds are not caught with chaff.
It is lost labour to play a jig to an old cat.

同 老馬識途（1570）If you wish for good advice, consult an old man.
反 老朽昏聵（1577）To run to seed.

2208 **人老心不老，人窮志不窮**
rén lǎo xīn bù lǎo, rén qióng zhì bù qióng
A man may be old but his heart is not old, a man may be poor but his ambition is not. (lit.)
Enjoy a green old age.
Life begins at sixty

同 老驥伏櫪（1567）There is fight in the old dog yet.
反 吾老矣，無能為也矣（2945）Old bees yield no honey.

2209 **人面獸心** rén miàn shòu xīn
A human face but a beastly heart. (lit.)
A fox in lamb's skin.
A wolf in sheep's clothing.
A fair face may hide a foul heart.

同 衣冠禽獸（3505）It is not the coat that makes the gentleman.
源 漢書・匈奴傳贊："夷狄之人，貪而好利，披髮左衽，人面獸心。"

2210 **人怕出名豬怕壯**
rén pà chū míng zhū pà zhuàng
A man is afraid of being well known; a pig is afraid of being big and strong. (lit.)
Too much praise is a burden.
A good name is sooner lost than won.

源 紅樓夢・第八十三回："俗語兒説的，人怕出名豬怕壯。況且又是個虛名兒，經久還不知怎麼樣呢。"

2211 **人棄我取** rén qì wǒ qǔ
Others reject, I take. (lit.)
What one will not, another will.

源 史記・貨殖列傳："白圭樂觀時變，故人棄我取，人取我與。"

人去樓空 rén qù lóu kōng 2212
The man has gone and the tower is empty. (lit.)
The master absent and the house dead.

源 崔顥．黃鶴樓："昔人已乘黃鶴去，此地空餘黃鶴樓。"

人人為我 rén rén wèi wǒ 2213
Everyone for me. (lit.)
Every man for himself.
Look after Number One.
Every miller draws water to his own mill.

同 我字當頭（2938）I love my friends well but myself better.

人山人海 rén shān rén hǎi 2214
A mountain of people and a sea of humanity. (lit.)
A sea of faces.

人生何處不相逢 2215
rén shēng hé chù bù xiāng féng
In life, where don't people meet? (lit.)
Friends may meet, but mountains never greet.

反 送君千里，終須一別（2645）The best of friends must part.

人生如夢 rén shēng rú mèng 2216
Man's life is like a dream. (lit.)
Life is but a dream.

同 遊戲人間（3640）All the world is a stage.

人生如朝露 rén shēng rú zhāo lù 2217
Man's life is like the morning dew. (lit.)
Our life is but a span.
Man is a bubble.

同 人生如夢（2216）Life is but a dream.

源 漢書："人生如朝露，何自苦如此。"

人生似鳥同林宿，大限來時各自飛 rén shēng sì niǎo tóng lín sù, dà xiàn lái shí gè zì fēi 2218
Men live like birds in the same wood, when big troubles come, all fly their own ways. (lit.)
Near is my shirt, but nearer is my skin.

2219 **人生自古誰無死**
rén shēng zì gǔ shéi wú sǐ
Since the beginning of human life, who would not die. (lit.)
He that is once born, once must die.
We shall die all alike in our graves.
Death is the grand leveller.

同 有生必有死（3666）As a man lives, so shall he die.
反 永遠活在人心（3614）Though lost in sight, to memory dear.
源 文天祥・過伶仃洋詩："人生自古誰無死，留取丹心照汗青。"

2220 **人世艱難唯一死**
rén shì jiān nán wéi yì sǐ
The worst thing in life is only to die. (lit.)
A man can only die once.

2221 **人誰無過** rén shuí wú guò
Who has no fault? (lit.)
To err is human.
Every man has his faults.
He is lifeless that is faultless.
There are spots even on the sun.

2222 **人算不如天算**
rén suàn bù rú tiān suàn
Men's calulation is not as good as that of heaven. (lit.)
An ounce of luck is better than a pound of wisdom.

同 謀事在人，成事在天（1859）Man proposes, God disposes.
反 人定勝天（2194）Everyone is the maker of his own fate.

2223 **人太緊則無智** rén tài jǐn zé wú zhì
Men with too much tension lack wisdom. (lit.)
Wide will wear but tight will tear.
He that makes a thing too fine breaks it.
Follow not truth too near the heels, lest it dash out thy teeth.
He who follows truth too closely will have dirt kicked.

2224 **人太緊則無智，水太清則無魚**
rén tài jǐn zé wú zhì, shuǐ tài qīng zé wú yú
Men with too much tension lack

源 家語："水至清則無魚，人至察則無徒。"

wisdom. Water too clear gets no fish. (lit.)
Too much of one thing is good for nothing.

人同此心，心同此理 2225

rén tóng cǐ xīn, xīn tóng cǐ lǐ
Men have the same mind, minds have the same reason. (lit.)
All roads lead to Rome.

人望高處，水向低流 2226

rén wàng gāo chù, shuǐ xiàng dī liú
Men look up high, water flows down the stream. (lit.)
No priestling, small though he may be, but wishes someday Pope to be.

同 向上爬（3119）Climb the social ladder.

人為刀俎，我為魚肉 2227

rén wéi dāo zǔ, wǒ wéi yú ròu
Others are knife and chopping board, we are the fish and meat. (lit.)
Between the beetle and the block.
Between the hammer and the anvil.
At someone's mercy.

同 跳不出如來掌心（2745）At one's mercy.
反 操生殺之權（0307）Tread on the neck of
源 史記 · 項羽本紀："樊噲曰，人方為刀俎，我為魚肉。"

人微言輕 rén wēi yán qīng 2228

When one's position is lowly, his words are slighted. (lit.)
The reasons of the poor weigh not.
Poor men's reasons are not heard.
To kick the beam.
A small frog in a big pond.

同 炙手可熱（3893）At the zenith of one's power.
源 蘇軾 · 上執政乞度牒賑濟及因修廨宇書："蓋人微言輕，理自當耳。"

人無橫財不富 rén wú héng cái bú fù 2229

A man without windfall money can't get rich. (lit.)
Muck and money go together.
Much industry and little conscience make a man rich.
Every honest miller has a thumb of gold.

2230 **人無完人** rén wú wán rén

Man is no perfect man. (lit.)

Every man has his faults.

Every bean has its black.

No wool is so white that a dyer cannot blacken it.

同 人誰無過（2221）To err is human.

2231 **人無遠慮，必有近憂**

rén wú yuǎn lǜ, bì yǒu jìn yōu

A man has no worry for future must have near troubles. (lit.)

He lives unsafely that looks too near on things.

A danger foreseen is half avoided.

源 本條目原句出自《論語》

2232 **人心不同，有如其面**

rén xīn bù tóng, yǒu rú qí miàn

People's mind is as different as their faces. (lit.)

The mind is the man.

2233 **人心不足蛇吞象**

rén xīn bù zú shé tūn xiàng

A man with a discontented heart like that of Xiang (meaning elephant) is swallowed by a snake. (lit.) (a Chinese legend: Xiang who entering a snake's throat to reach its gall, stayed there too long to get more, was swallowed by the snake.)

No man ever thought his own too much.

同 貪得無厭（2672）As greedy as a wolf.

反 知足常足，終身不辱（3864）He is wise that knows when he is well enough.

源 羅洪先詩："人心不足蛇吞象，世事到頭螳捕蟬。"

2234 **人言可畏** rén yán kě wèi

Men's gossips are fearful. (lit.)

If all men say that thou art an ass, then bray.

What will Mr. Grundy say?

Fling dirt enough and some will stick.

We are all slaves of opinion.

Opinion rules the world.

反 笑罵由他笑罵，好官我自為之（3152）Hard words break no bones.

源 詩經 · 鄭風 · 將仲子："人之多言，亦可畏也。"

人以羣分 rén yǐ qún fēn 2235

Men are distinguished by his company. (lit.)

A man is known by the compay he keeps.

同 物以類聚（3083）Birds of a feather flock together.

源 周易．繫辭上：“方以類聚，物以羣分。”

人有霎時之禍福 2236

rén yǒu shà shí zhī huò fú

Man at any moment gets blessing or calamity. (lit.)

Today a man, tomorrow a mouse.

人有失手，馬有失蹄 2237

rén yǒu shī shǒu, mǎ yǒu shī tí

Man may make a slip of hand, horse a slip of hoof. (lit.)

A good marksman may miss.

反 萬無一失（2856）Safe and sure.

人云亦云 rén yún yì yún 2238

Say what other people say. (lit.)

Echo one's every word.

Pin one's faith upon another's sleeve.

Repeat like a parrot.

To say ditto.

同 隨聲附和（2656）To chime in.

反 別開生面（0143）Break fresh ground.

源 蔡松年．槽聲同彥高賦詩：“他日人云我亦云。”

人之常情 rén zhī cháng qíng 2239

Man's natural feeling. (lit.)

Fresh and blood.

It's human (nature).

源 江淹．雜體詩三十八首序：“貴遠賤近，人之常情。”

人之患在好為人師 2240

rén zhī huàn zài hào wéi rén shī

Man's weakness is liking to teach others. (lit.)

Never give advice unasked.

Come not to counsel uncalled.

源 孟子．離婁章：“人之患在好為人師。”

2241 仁者見仁，智者見智
rén zhě jiàn rén, zhì zhě jiàn zhì
A kind man sees kindness, a wise man sees wisdom. (lit.)
A matter of opinion.
Views vary from person to person.
Everything is as you take it.
Every man to his own taste.
Tastes differ.
Different things appeal to different people.

源 周易．繫辭上：“仁者見之謂之仁，知者見之謂之知。”

2242 忍得一時之氣，免得百日之憂
rěn dé yī shí zhī qì, miǎn dé bǎi rì zhī yōu
Can hold one's temper once, then can avoid trouble for hundred days. (lit.)
Bottle up one's feelings.
Put up with
Bite one's lips.

反 小不忍則亂大謀（3134）Anger and haste hinder good counsel.

2243 忍氣吞聲 rěn qì tūn shēng
Hold one's temper and swallow one's voice. (lit.)
Swallow the leek.
Swallow one's pride.
Eat dirt.
As patient as Job.

同 捺着性子（1876）Bottle up one's feelings.
反 大發雷霆（0516）Explode with rage.

2244 忍辱負重 rěn rǔ fù zhòng
To bear disgrace and a heavy burden. (lit.)
As patient as an ox.
Stoop to conquer.
Pocket an insult.
Eat boiled crow.
Bear with evil, and expect good.

同 卧薪嘗膽（2940）To nurse vengeance.
源 三國志．吳志．陸遜傳：“國家所以屈諸君使相承望者，以僕有尺寸可稱，能忍辱負重故也。”

2245 忍無可忍 rěn wú kě rěn
Can no longer bear it. (lit.)
Beyond one's endurance.
Patience runs out.
Even a worm will turn.
The last straw breaks the camel's back.

同 是可忍孰不可忍（2525）More than flesh and blood can bear.
反 百忍成金（0053）All good things come to those who wait.

忍一句，息一怒 rěn yí jù, xī yí nù 2246

Bear one sentence, stop an anger. (lit.)

Least said soonest mended.

A soft answer turneth away wrath.

認認真真 rèn rèn zhēn zhēn 2247

(Take it) seriously and earnestly. (lit.)

In sober earnest.

同 鄭重其事（3847）In all seriousness.

反 馬馬虎虎（1729）Fair to middling.

認賊作父 rèn zéi zuò fù 2248

Take a thief as one's father. (lit.)

Set a fox to keep one's geese.

反 相煎何太急（3107）The axe goes to the wood where it borrows its helve.

認真落實 rèn zhēn luò shí 2249

(Take it) seriously and genuinely. (lit.)

Make assurance doubly sure.

任務艱巨 rèn wù jiān jù 2250

One's duty is big and difficult. (lit.)

A herculean task.

A tall order.

An uphill job.

反 輕而易舉（2124）Mere child's play.

任意擺佈 rèn yì bǎi bù 2251

Push people around as one wishes. (lit.)

Twist one round one's finger.

任意踐踏 rèn yì jiàn tà 2252

Tread under foot as one wishes. (lit.)

Tread under foot.

日薄西山 rì bó xī shān 2253

The sun is approaching (setting) on the western hills. (lit.)

One's days are numbered.

The sands are running out.

Not to be long for this world.

Sinking fast.

同 行將就木（3214）On one's last legs.

源 李密 · 陳情表：“今劉日薄西山，氣息奄奄，人命危淺，朝不慮夕。”

2254 **日出而作，日入而息**
rì chū ér zuò, rì rù ér xī
Go to work at sunrise, to rest at sunset. (lit.)
Go to bed with the lamb, and rise with the lark.
Early to bed and early to rise.

同 早眠早起（3764）Keep early hours.
源 擊壤歌："日出而作，日入而息，鑿井而飲，耕田而食，帝力何有於我哉。"

2255 **日積月累** rì jī yuè lěi
Daily accumulating and monthly multiplying. (lit.)
Accumulated through the year.
Pile-up.
Keep some till more come.

同 銖積寸累（3932）Little and often fills the purse.
反 一擲千金（3497）Spend money like water.
源 顧炎武．日知錄．禁自宮："自是以後，日積月累，千百成羣，其為國之蠹害甚矣。"

2256 **日暮途窮** rì mù tú qióng
At sunset the road ended. (lit.)
At the end of one's tether (rope).
Driven to the last extremity.
On one's last legs.

反 前程似錦（2073）Have the ball at one's feet.
源 史記．伍子胥列傳："吾日暮途遠，吾故倒行而逆施之。"

2257 **日上三竿猶未起**
rì shàng sān gān yóu wèi qǐ
The sun is three rods high (8-9 a.m.) one still has not got up. (lit.)
A sluggard makes his night till noon.
Broad daylight.

反 坐以待旦（4062）Outwatch the Bear.
源 歲華紀麗．日上三竿注："古詩云，日上三竿風露消。"

2258 **日以為常** rì yǐ wéi cháng
Carry on daily as usual. (lit.)
As regular as clockwork.

同 十年如一日（2459）Go on in the same old rut.
反 偶一為之（1936）Once in a long while.

2259 **日益消瘦** rì yì xiāo shòu
Getting thinner everyday. (lit.)
Waste away.
Reduced to a skeleton.

同 骨瘦如柴（0942）As thin as a lath.
反 心廣體胖（3166）Laugh and grow fat.

2260 **日月如梭** rì yuè rú suō
Days and months (fleeting) like a weaver's shuttle. (lit.)
Time flies like an arrow.

反 寸陰若歲（0480）Time hangs heavy on one's hand.
源 宋．趙德璘．侯鯖錄："織烏，日也，往來如梭之織。"

戎馬出身 róng mǎ chū shēn 2261

Started from a soldier or a cavalier. (lit.)

Rise from the ranks.

容光煥發 róng guāng huàn fā 2262

One's appearance is radiant. (lit.)

Shine like a shittim barn door.

One's face brightens up.

One's face glows with health.

To be in the pink.

In radiant health.

同 滿面紅光（1749）Glowing with health.

反 面無人色（1802）As pale as a ghost.

融會貫通 róng huì guàn tōng 2263

To bring together and understand thoroughly. (lit.)

Have at one's finger-tips.

Know something inside out.

Have full comprehension.

同 心領神會（3178）To be on the beam.

反 一知半解（3495）Quarter flash and three parts foolish.

源 朱熹："舉一而反三，聞一而知十，乃學者用功之深，窮理之熟，然後能融會貫通，以至於此。"

融洽投契 róng qià tóu qì 2264

Harmoneously get on well (with each other). (lit.)

Hit it off well (with each other).

同 水乳交融（2593）To be finger and glove with another.

反 話不投機半句多（1119）It's ill talking between a full man and a fasting.

柔能克剛 róu néng kè gāng 2265

Softness can overcome hardness. (lit.)

A gentle hand may lead the elephant by a hair.

Soft and fair goes far.

源 左傳："商書曰，沈漸剛克，高明柔克。"

肉中刺 ròu zhōng cì 2266

Flesh thorn in it. (lit.)

A thorn in the flesh.

A pain in the neck.

同 眼中釘（3328）An eyesore.

如出一轍 rú chū yī zhé 2267

Like (wheels) following one track. (lit.)

Cast in the same mold.

Come from the same rut.

To run in the same groove.

反 迥然不同（1409）As different as chalk is from cheese.

源 宋·洪邁·容齋續筆·名將晚謬："此四人之過，如出一轍。"

2268 **如此等等** rú cǐ děng děng
Like this, etcetera (etc). (lit.)
And what not.
And all that.
And the like.

同 諸如此類（3933）And so on, and so forth.

2269 **如此這般** rú cǐ zhè bān
Like this and that. (lit.)
Thus and thus.

2270 **如火如荼** rú huǒ rú tú
Like fire and flowering rush. (lit.)
Crop up like mushrooms.
In full blast.
In full swing.

同 風頭火勢（0808）Like a house afire.
反 煙消雲散（3292）End in smoke.
源 國語・吳語："令萬人以為方陣，皆白裳，……望之如荼。左軍亦如之，皆赤裳，……望之如火。"

2271 **如膠似漆** rú jiāo sì qī
Like glue and varnish. (lit.)
Sticking together.
To be hand and glove with

同 親密無間（2107）They cleave together like burrs.
反 冰炭不相容（0155）At loggerheads with one another.
源 史記："感於心，合於行，親於膠漆。"

2272 **如臨深淵，如履薄冰**
rú lín shēn yuān, rú lǚ bó bīng
As on the edge of a deep gulf and tread on thin ice. (lit.)
On alert.
Tread as on eggs.

同 戰戰兢兢（3788）One the jig.
反 鹵莽從事（1700）Ride for a fall.
源 詩經・小雅："戰戰兢兢，如臨深淵，如履薄冰。"

2273 **如履薄冰** rú lǚ bó bīng
Like tread on thin ice. (lit.)
Skate on thin ice.
Tread as on eggs.

同 小心戒慎（3148）Take heed is a good rede.
反 莽莽撞撞（1769）Like a bull in a china shop.
源 成語來源見上一條目

2274 **如夢初醒** rú mèng chū xǐng
As if one were awaking from a dream. (lit.)
To wake up to
It dawns upon one.

同 恍然大悟（1144）See daylight.

如入無人之境 rú rù wú rén zhī jìng 2275

Like entering into a no man's land. (lit.)

Win in a walk.

It was just a walk over.

同 勢如破竹（2536）Sweep everything before one.

源 歐陽修・再論置兵御賊札子："入州入縣，如入無人之境。"

如入五里霧中 rú rù wǔ lǐ wù zhōng 2276

Like entering five li (Chinese mile) into the cloud. (lit.)

To be lost in the cloud.

To be in a fog.

To be tossed on an ocean of dubts.

同 丈二和尚，摸不着頭腦（3801）Can make neither head nor tail of

反 恍然大悟（1144）It dawned upon one.

如釋重負 rú shì zhòng fù 2277

Like releasing (one) from a heavy burden. (lit.)

Breathe easily (freely).

Lift a weight off one's mind.

It was good riddance.

Heave a sigh of relief.

源 穀梁傳・昭二十九年："昭公出奔，民如釋重負。"

如數家珍 rú shǔ jiā zhēn 2278

Like counting the family treasures. (lit.)

Know the inside out.

To have at one's fingers' tips (ends).

To cover the waterfront.

源 韓詩外傳："贈之不與家珍。"

如魚得水 rú yú dé shuǐ 2279

Like fish getting water. (lit.)

Feel oneself at home.

Like a duck to water.

To be in one's element.

同 優哉悠哉（3631）Free and easy.

反 涸轍之鮒（1054）A fish out of water.

源 三國志・蜀志・諸葛亮傳："孤（劉備自稱）之有孔明，猶魚之有水也。"

如願以償 rú yuàn yǐ cháng 2280

To have fulfilled one's wish. (lit.)

The prayer is answered.

Long looked for comes at last.

A dream comes true.

To have one's will.

Bring home the bacon.

同 正中下懷（3845）After one's own heart.

反 大失所望（0550）Fish for herring and catch a sprat.

源 黃庭堅："政當為公乞如願。"

2281 如坐針氈 rú zuò zhēn zhān
Like sitting on a carpet of standing pins. (lit.)
Sit on thorns.
To be on pins and needles.
To be on tenterhooks.
Lie on a bed of thorns.

同 坐立不安（4053）Sit on a bag of fleas.
反 舒舒服服（2564）As snug as a bug in a rug.
源 晉書．杜錫傳："置針著錫常所坐處氈中，刺之流血。"

2282 孺子可教 rú zǐ kě jiào
The lad can be taught. (lit.)
That's a good boy!

反 朽木不可雕（3241）He who is born a fool is never cured.
源 史記．留侯世家："孺子可教矣。"

2283 乳臭未乾 rǔ xiù wèi gān
The smell of milk is not yet dried. (lit.)
A greenhorn.
One's mouth is full of pap.
Wet behind the ears.

反 鬢髮斑白（0153）Silver threads among the gold.
源 漢書．高帝紀："王問魏大將誰，曰，柏直，王曰，是口尚乳臭，不能當吾韓信。"

2284 入不敷出 rù bù fū chū
The income does not meet the expenditure. (lit.)
Live above one's income.
Overrun the constable.

同 寅吃卯糧（3583）Live beyond one's means.
反 綽綽有餘（0453）Enough and to spare.

2285 入門休問榮枯事，但看容顏便得知 rù mén xiū wèn róng kū shì, dàn kàn róng yán biàn dé zhī
Entering the door don't ask about things good or bad, but looking at the face one would know. (lit.)
The face is the index of the mind.
A pitiful look asks enough.

2286 入木三分 rù mù sān fēn
To enter three tenths (of an inch) into the wood (writing characters with such forceful strokes that their imprints eat into the piece of wood). (lit.)
Give a vivid picture of
Cut to the quick.
Leave an indelible impression on

同 印象深刻（3595）Borne in upon one.
反 輕描淡寫（2126）Touch on lightly.
源 張懷瓘．書斷："晉王羲之書祝版，工人削之，筆入木三分。"

入人圈套 rù rén quān tào 2287

Get into someone's trap. (lit.)

Put one's neck into a noose.

反 衝破藩籬（0387）Kick over the traces.

入土為安 rù tǔ wéi ān 2288

Enter the earth to rest (after death). (lit.)

Pushing up the daisies.

Go to one's last home.

Sleep with one's fathers.

Take an earth-bath.

Grin at the daisy-roots.

Dust unto dust, and under dust to lie.

To be six feet under.

入鄉隨俗 rù xiāng suí sú 2289

Entering a village, follow the tradition of the village. (lit.)

Do in Rome as the Romans do.

To go native.

入芝蘭之室，久而不聞其香 2290

rù zhī lán zhī shì, jiǔ ér bù wén qí xiāng

Having entered a room with orchids for a long time one would not smell their fragrance. (lit.)

Good fortune is never good till it is lost.

Blessings are not valued till they are gone.

同 身在福中不知福（2393）Health is not valued till it is lost.

源 家語：“如入芝蘭之室，久而不聞其香。”

阮囊羞澀 ruǎn náng xiū sè 2291

Ruan (Fu, name of a historical person), his bag, shy and embarrassed. (lit.)

Not to have a bean.

同 囊空如洗（1885）Low in the pocket.

反 鄧通銅山（0631）Have money to burn.

源 宋．陰時夫．韻府羣玉：“阮孚持一皂囊，遊會稽。客問囊中何物。曰，但有一錢看囊，恐其羞澀。”

2292 **軟弱無能** ruǎn ruò wú néng

Weak and incapable. (lit.)

A milk-and-water sort of fellow.

As helpless as a babe.

As weak as a baby.

同 低能差勁（0632）Not worth one's salt.

反 勇猛過人（3617）Full of guts.

源 劉琨："咨余軟弱，弗克負荷。"

2293 **軟硬兼施** ruǎn yìng jiān shī

Double practice of the soft and the hard. (lit.)

The iron hand in the velvet glove.

Strong in action, gentle in method.

If the lion's skin cannot, the fox's shall.

同 恩威並施（0720）To temper justice with mercy.

2294 **瑞雪豐年** ruì xuě fēng nián

Auspicious snow (promises) good harvest year. (lit.)

A snow year, a rich year.

2295 **若無其事** ruò wú qí shì

As if there is no such thing. (lit.)

Calm and composed.

Cool as a cucumber.

As if nothing has happened.

同 行若無事（3215）With perfect composure.

反 煞有介事（2331）Fuss up and down.

2296 **若要人不知，除非己莫為**

ruò yào rén bù zhī, chú fēi jǐ mò wéi

If one does not want people to know, unless one does not do it. (lit.)

There is a witness everywhere.

What is done by night appears by day.

反 偷偷摸摸（2784）On the sly.

源 枚乘·上書諫吳王："欲人不聞，莫若不言，欲人不知，莫若不為。"

2297 **若有所思** ruò yǒu suǒ sī

As if having something to think. (lit.)

Lost in thought.

Look thoughtful.

同 遐思逸想（3070）Flight of fancy.

2298 **弱不禁風** ruò bù jīn fēng

So weak as to stand the wind. (lit.)

Weak as a child.

Fragile and tottering.

As weak as water.

反 身壯力健（2395）Sound as a bell.

源 陸游詩："白菡萏香初過雨，紅蜻蜓弱不禁風。"

弱肉強食 ruò ròu qiáng shí 2299

The weak is the prey of the strong. (lit.)

Jungle justice.

The weakest goes to the wall.

Survival of the fittest.

同 大魚吃小魚（0563）The little cannot be great unless he devours many.

源 韓愈 · 送浮屠文暢師序："弱之肉，強之食。"

S

2300 **撒手西歸** sā shǒu xī guī
To quit and return to the west. (lit.)
Go west.

同 西方極樂世界（3043）The sweet by-and-by.

2301 **塞翁失馬，焉知非福**
sài wēng shī mǎ, yān zhī fēi fú
The old man of the frontier lost his horse, how would one know it was not a blessing. (lit.)
A blessing in disguise.
Sometimes the best gain is to lose.
Sweet are the uses of adversity.

同 禍為福所倚（1179）Every cloud has a silver lining.
源 淮南子："塞上叟失馬，人皆弔之，叟曰，此何詎不為福。"

2302 **三步並作兩** sān bù bìng zuò liǎng
Three steps made into two. (lit.)
In seven league boots.
Walk with a rapid step.
Put one's best foot forward.

同 急不可待（1208）Leap over the hedge before one comes to the stile.
反 循序漸進（3281）Step by step.

2303 **三寸不爛之舌** sān cùn bú làn zhī shé
Three inches of unbreakable tongue. (lit.)
Silver tongued.

源 三國演義："憑三寸不爛之舌，說南北兩軍互相吞併。"

2304 **三番兩次** sān fān liǎng cì
Three turns and two times. (lit.)
Time and again.

同 一而再，再而三（3388）Over and over again.

2305 **三翻四覆** sān fān sì fù
Three times and four repetitions. (lit.)
Over and over again.

三個和尚沒水吃 sān gè hé shàng méi shuǐ chī 2306

Three monks together, no water to drink. (lit.)

Everybody's business is nobody's business.

Too many cooks spoil the broth.

三教九流 sān jiào jiǔ liú 2307

Three religions and nine schools of thoughts. (lit.) (i.e. Confucianism, Taoism, and Buddhism; the Confucians, the Taoists, the Yin-Yang, the Legalists, the Logicians, the Mohists, the Polittical Strategists, the Eclectics and the Agriculturists)

All walks of life.

源 三國演義："衡（禰衡）曰，天文地理，無一不通，三教九流，無所不曉。"

三句不離本行 sān jù bù lí běn háng 2308

In every three sentences, never leave one's own trade. (lit.)

Talk the same language.

Talk shop.

Pack-men speak of pack-saddles.

三人行必有我師，擇其善者而從之 sān rén xíng bì yǒu wǒ shī, zé qí shàn zhě ér cóng zhī 2309

Three men in a group, one must be my teacher and I can choose the good one to follow. (lit.)

Keep good men company and you shall be of the number.

源 論語・述而："三人行必有我師焉，擇其善者而從之，其不善者而改之。"

三三兩兩 sān sān liáng liǎng 2310

By twos and threes. (lit.)

A sprinkling of

In twos and threes.

源 晉・樂錄嬌女詩："魚行不獨自，三三兩兩俱。"

2311 三十六着，走為上着
sān shí liù zhāo, zǒu wéi shàng zhāo
Of thirty six ways, the best is to run away. (lit.)
Take flight.
Keep out of the way.
Give one the slip.
Give leg-bail.
Take to one's legs.

同 溜之大吉（1677）Seek safety in flight.
源 齊書・王敬則傳："檀公（檀道濟）三十六策，走為上計。"

2312 三思而後行 sān sī ér hòu xíng
After thinking thrice then act. (lit.)
Look before you leap.
Measure thrice before you cut once.
He thinks not well that thinks not again.
Second thoughts are best.
To sleep on a matter.

同 深思熟慮（2398）Turn it over in one's mind.
反 冒失從事（1774）Buy a pig in a poke.
源 論語・公冶長："季文子三思而後行，子聞之曰，再斯可矣。"

2313 三天打魚，兩天曬網
sān tiān dǎ yú, liǎng tiān shài wǎng
Three days of fishing followed by two days of net sunning. (lit.)
On and off.
By fits and starts.

同 或作或輟（1171）Off and on.
反 十年如一日（2459）Go on in the same old rut.

2314 三五成羣 sān wǔ chéng qún
Three and five form a crowd. (lit.)
Small gathering.
In small parties.
In groups.

同 三三兩兩（2310）In twos and threes.

2315 三緘其口 sān jiān qí kǒu
To close one's mouth thrice. (lit.)
Button up one's lip.
One's lips are sealed.
Hold one's peace.
To hush up.
To clam up.

同 守口如瓶（2551）As close as an oyster.
反 喋喋不休（0654）Talk the hind leg off a donkey.
源 家語："孔子觀周，入后稷之廟，有金人焉，三緘其口而銘其背曰，古之慎言人也。"

散工 sǎn gōng 2316
Part-time worker. (lit.)
An odd-jobber.

喪然若失 sàng rán ruò shī 2317
Feeling depressed and lost. (lit.)
To be left up a tree.
To be all adrift.

同 惘然若失（2866）Feel lost.
反 悠然自得（3623）Free and easy.

喪心病狂 sàng xīn bìng kuáng 2318
Lost the heart and so sick as to be crazy. (lit.)
Out of one's mind.
Go crazy.
Bereft of reason.

源 宋史・范如圭傳："公（秦檜）不喪心病狂，奈何為此。"

色即是空 sè jí shì kōng 2319
Colour and form are emptiness. (lit.)
Beauty is but skin-deep.

源 金剛般若波羅蜜經："色即是空，空即是色，受相行識，亦復如是。"

色厲內荏 sè lì nèi rěn 2320
Fierce looking but weak inside. (lit.)
Given to bluffing.
Many a one threatens while he quakes for fear.
Bullies are generally cowards.

同 外強中乾（2836）Put up a bold front.
源 論語・陽貨："色厲而內荏，譬諸小人，其猶穿窬之盜也歟。"

僧多粥少 sēng duō zhōu shǎo 2321
Many monks, little porridge. (lit.)
There are always more round pegs than square holes.
Not enough to go round.

同 杯水車薪（0094）A drop in the bucket.
反 綽綽有餘（0453）Enough and to spare.

僧敲月下門 sēng qiāo yuè xià mén 2322
The monk knocked the door under the moon. (lit.)
Weigh one's words.
To speak holiday.
Chop logic.

反 脱口而出（2829）Escape one' s lips.
源 唐詩紀事："賈島賦詩得'僧推月下門'之句，欲改推作敲。"

2323 **殺雞取卵** shā jī qǔ luǎn

Kill the hen to get eggs. (lit.)

Kill the goose that lays the golden eggs.

2324 **殺雞焉用牛刀** shā jī yān yòng niú dāo

To kill a chicken why use a knife that can kill a cow. (lit.)

Take not a musket to kill a butterfly.

Send not for a hatchet to break open an egg.

Never draw your dirk when a dunt will do.

Break not a butterfly on the wheel.

源 論語．陽貨："夫子莞爾而笑曰，殺雞焉用牛刀。"

2325 **殺人不眨眼** shā rén bù zhǎ yǎn

Kill people without blinking the eyes. (lit.)

Kill in cold blood.

反 起死回生（2041）To bring one to life.

源 五燈會元："汝不聞殺人不眨眼將軍乎。"

2326 **殺人放火** shā rén fàng huǒ

To slay men and set fire (upon houses). (lit.)

Fire and sword.

2327 **殺人如麻** shā rén rú má

Massacre men like (cutting) hemps. (lit.)

Mow down like grass.

Human slaughter.

源 李白．蜀道難詩："磨牙吮血，殺人如麻。"

2328 **殺人一萬，自損三千**

shā rén yī wàn, zì sǔn sān qiān

Killing ten thousand men (of other army), one will lose three thousand. (lit.)

The file grates other things, but rubs itself out too.

2329 **殺身成仁** shā shēn chéng rén

Sacrifice oneself to preserve one's virtue complete. (lit.)

Lay down one's life.

Die for a cause.

Die a martyr.

同 壯烈犧牲（3951）Die a glorious death.

反 身敗名裂（2381）Die like a dog.

源 論語．衛靈公："無求生以害人，有殺身以成仁。"

煞費苦心 shà fèi kǔ xīn 2330
Spend a lot on searchings of heart. (lit.)
Rack one's brain.
Make every effort.
Take great pains.
With much ado.

反 漠不關心（1854）Not to care a hang.

煞有介事 shà yǒu jiè shì 2331
As if there is a real thing. (lit.)
In dead earnest.
Make heavy weather of
Fuss up and down.
Busy as a hen with one chick.
As if in real earnest.

同 大驚小怪（0534）Much better of a wooden platter.
反 若無其事（2295）As if nothing has happened.

山重水覆疑無路，柳暗花明又一村 shān chóng shuǐ fù yí wú lù, liǔ àn huā míng yòu yì cūn 2332
Mountain after mountain (double) and river after river (repeating) as if there is no road; willows obscure flowers bright, there is another village. (lit.)
Every cloud has a silver lining.

源 陸游．遊西山詩："山重水覆疑無路，柳暗花明又一村。"

山間竹筍，嘴尖皮厚腹中空 shān jiān zhú sǔn, zuǐ jiān pí hòu fù zhōng kōng 2333
Among the hills, the bamboo shoots have pointed mouth-ends and thick skin but the inside is empty. (lit.)
The noisy drum has nothing in it but mere air.

同 不懂裝懂（0183）Assume a knowing air.

山窮水盡 shān qióng shuǐ jìn 2334
To the end of mountains and rivers. (lit.)
At the end of one's rope.
To be on the rocks.
At low water-mark.
Down to one's bottom dollar.

2335 **山雨欲來風滿樓**
shān yǔ yù lái fēng mǎn lóu
The wind sweeping the tower promises the coming of the mountain rain. (lit.)
A storm is brewing.
When the clouds are upon the hills, they'll come down by the mills.

源 許渾．咸陽城東樓詩："溪雲初起日沈閣，山雨欲來風滿樓。"

2336 **山中有直樹，世上無直人**
shān zhōng yǒu zhí shù, shì shàng wú zhí rén
There are upright trees in the mountain, there are no (absolute) upright man in the world. (lit.)
Good men are scarce.

2337 **姍姍來遲** shān shān lái chí
Come late with a lady-like gait. (lit.)
Kiss the hare's foot.
Arrive in an armchair.
At the eleventh hour.

反 爭先恐後（3835）The devil takes the hindmost.
源 漢書．外戚傳："立而望之，何姍姍其來遲。"

2338 **潸然淚下** shān rán lèi xià
A furtive tear stole down (the cheek). (lit.)
To pipe one's eyes.
Melt into tears.

同 淚如雨下（1590）Shed tears.
反 竊竊自喜（2105）To hug oneself.

2339 **羶極還是羊肉，舊極還是絲綢**
shān jí hái shì yáng ròu, jiù jí hái shì sī chóu
Although it has a strong smell, it is still mutton, although it is very old it is still silk. (lit.)
The moon is a moon still, whether it shine or not.
Little fish are sweet.

2340 **閃閃發光** shǎn shǎn fā guāng
Emitting shining light. (lit.)
As bright as silver.
Shining bright.

同 光彩奪目（0978）Dazzling to the eye.
反 黯然失色（0031）To be cast into the shade.

閃爍其詞 shǎn shuò qí cí 2341

His words flash as lightning. (lit.)

Beat about the bush.

Speak evasively.

Speak with one's tongue in one's cheek.

Make one boot serve either leg.

同 支吾其詞（3849）To hem and haw.

反 開門見山（1473）Come straight to the point.

扇風點火 shàn fēng diǎn huǒ 2342

Fan the wind and light the fire. (lit.)

Fan into a flame.

Blow the coals.

Stir up trouble.

反 釜底抽薪（0829）Take away fuel, take away flame.

善觀風色 shàn guān fēng sè 2343

Good at observing the wind and colours. (lit.)

Know which way the wind blows.

同 識時務者為俊傑（2481）Know the time of day.

善始善終 shàn shǐ shàn zhōng 2344

Good beginning and good ending. (lit.)

A good beginning makes a good ending.

Good to begin well, better to end well.

See a thing through.

同 貫徹始終（0977）Such beginning, such end.

源 莊子．大宗師："善妖善老，善始善終，人猶效之。"

善泳者溺 shàn yǒng zhě nì 2345

Good swimmer often drowned. (lit.)

Good swimmers at length are drowned.

善有善報 shàn yǒu shàn bào 2346

Goodness has a good recompense. (lit.)

Kindness like grain increase by sowing.

Sow good work and thou shalt reap gladness.

The charitable give out at the door and God puts in at the window.

同 厚德載福（1077）Virtue and happiness are mother and daughter.

反 惡有惡報（0716）Curses, like chickens, come home to roost.

2347 善有善報，惡有惡報，若然不報，時辰未到 shàn yǒu shàn bào, è yǒu è bào, ruò rán bú bào, shí chén wèi dào
Goodness has a good recompense, wickedness has a bad recompense, the time hasn't come. (lit.)
Justice has long arms.
The mills of God grind slowly.

同 天網恢恢，疏而不漏（2721）Heaven's vengeance is slow but sure.

2348 善於營謀 shàn yú yíng móu
Good at enterprising. (lit.)
Know on which side one's bread is buttered.
Play one's cards well.

反 自挖牆腳（4000）Quarrel with one's own bread and butter.

2349 善欲人見非真善 shàn yù rén jiàn fēi zhēn shàn
Goodness for others to see isn't real goodness. (lit.)
A good name keeps its luster in the dark.

反 惡恐人知，便是大惡（0714）Dissembled sin is double wickedness.

2350 擅作主張 shàn zuò zhǔ zhāng
To make presumptuous decision. (lit.)
Take the law into one's hands.
Reckon without one's host.

同 自作主張（4016）Take the bit in one's mouth.
反 有商有量（3664）Lay our heads together.

2351 傷盡腦筋 shāng jìn nǎo jīn
Working hard of the brain. (lit.)
Rack (cudgel) one's brain.
Beat one's brains out.

2352 傷人一語，利如刀割 shāng rén yī yǔ, lì rú dāo gē
Hurt one with a word, sharp like a knife cutting. (lit.)
The tongue is not steel, but it cuts.

同 惡語傷人恨不消（0717）Slander leaves a scar behind.

2353 傷心落淚 shāng xīn luò lèi
Broken heart and shedding tears. (lit.)
Cry one's heart out.

反 笑逐顏開（3155）Beam with joy.

上不沾天，下不着地 2354

shàng bù zhān tiān, xià bù zháo dì

Up cannot touch the sky, down cannot reach the earth. (lit.)

To be suspended in mid-air.

源 韓非子：“上不屬天，下不着地。”

上層社會 2355

shàng céng shè huì

The upper layer of society. (lit.)

The upper crust.

The top drawer.

同 頭面人物（2795）The upper ten thousand.

反 牛鬼蛇神（1920）The scum of society.

上得山多遇着虎 2356

shàng dé shān duō yù zhè hǔ

Going up the hill too often will meet a tiger. (lit.)

That fish will soon be caught that nibbles at every bait.

He that bites on every weed must need light on poison.

He that pryeth into every cloud may be stricken with a thunderbolt.

上了年紀 2357

shàng le nián jì

Getting on in age. (lit.)

To get on in years.

Advanced in years.

To turn grey.

同 年事已高（1910）To be well on in life.

反 乳臭未乾（2283）One's mouth is full of pap.

上天無路，入地無門 2358

shàng tiān wú lù, rù dì wú mén

To ascend to heaven, no road; to enter the earth, no door. (lit.)

In a quandary.

Between the devil and the deep sea.

End it or mend it.

同 走投無路（4030）Stand at bay.

源 本條目原句出自《宋．釋普濟．五燈會元》

上下交迫 2359

shàng xià jiāo pò

From above and below comes the pressure. (lit.)

Between the hammer and the anvil.

Between the beetle and the block.

2360 **上行下效** shàng xíng xià xiào

Superiors acting and inferiors imitating. (lit.)

Where the dam leaps over, the kid follows.

As the old cock crows, the young one learns.

源 意林・引崔寔・政論："上行下效，然謂之教。"

2361 **韶華已逝** sháo huá yǐ shì

The youth time has gone. (lit.)

Have had one's day.

The mill cannot grind with the water that is past.

同 光陰一去不復返（0985）Lost time is never found.

反 年方弱冠（1901）Arrive at majority.

2362 **少食多餐** shǎo shí duō cān

Eat little but more meals. (lit.)

Often and little eating makes a man fat.

2363 **少說話，多做事**

shǎo shuō huà, duō zuò shì

Talk less, work more. (lit.)

Least talk, most work.

2364 **少說為佳** shǎo shuō wéi jiā

Better to talk less. (lit.)

Few words are best.

Speech is silver, silence is gold.

No wisdom like silence.

Turn your tongue seven times before talking.

Talking comes by nature, silence by wisdom.

Even a fool, when he holdeth his peace, is counted wise.

He that hears much and speaks not at all, shall be welcome both in bower and in hall.

同 多言多敗（0706）Talk much and err much.

2365 **少走彎路** shǎo zǒu wān lù

Walk less the crooked roads. (lit.)

By the string rather than by the bow.

少不更事 shào bú gēng shì 2366

Too young to attend affairs. (lit.)

As green as grass.

Not dry behind the ears.

A green horn.

Born yesterday.

反 老成練達（1560）To have cut one's eyeteeth.

源 隋書．李雄傳："上謂雄曰，吾兒既少，更事未多。"

少年老成 shào nián lǎo chéng 2367

Mature young man. (lit.)

One is young but prudent.

Have an old head on young shoulders.

反 返老還童（0749）In one's second childhood.

少壯不努力，老大徒傷悲 2368

shào zhuàng bù nǔ lì, lǎo dà tú shāng bēi

One who doesn't work in the prime of life would only grieve when getting old. (lit.)

Rejoiced at in youth, repented in age.

Make the most of one's time.

If you lie upon roses when young, you'll lie upon thorns when old.

Reckless youth makes rueful age.

An idle youth, a needy age.

源 漢樂府．長歌行："百川東到海，何時復西歸，少壯不努力，老大徒傷悲。"

舌戰羣儒 shé zhàn qún rú 2369

Engage a tongue (verbal) warfare with the scholars. (lit.)

Good at repartee.

Have a ready tongue.

反 無言可對（3001）Come to a nonplus.

蛇吞象 shé tūn xiàng 2370

The snake swallowed the elephant. (lit.)

Catch a Tartar.

同 貪得無饜（2672）As greedy as a wolf.

捨本逐末 shě běn zhú mò 2371

Disregard the fundamental but see for the end. (lit.)

Stick at trifles.

Kill the goose that lay the golden eggs.

Penny wise, pound foolish.

源 晉書："農桑不修，遊食者多，皆由去本逐末故也。"

2372 **捨得一身剮** shě dé yì shēn guǎ

Dare to (risk) of a thousand cuts on one. (lit.)

To tempt the fates.

To tempt providence.

同 置生死於度外（3901）Take one's life in one's hands.

反 明哲保身（1826）Be worldly wise and play safe.

源 紅樓夢："俗語說，捨得一身剮，敢把皇帝拉下馬。

2373 **捨己為人** shě jǐ wèi rén

Sacrifice oneself for others. (lit.)

To bell the cat.

反 假公濟私（1256）To practise jobbery.

源 論語・先進・朱熹注："曾點之學……初無舍己為人之意。

2374 **捨近圖遠** shě jìn tú yuǎn

Ignore the nearer and scheme for farther away. (lit.)

Round the sun to meet the moon.

源 孫子・九地・杜牧注："迂其途，舍近即遠。"

2375 **捨生取義** shě shēng qǔ yì

Sacrifice one's life for righteousness. (lit.)

Die a martyr.

Lay down one's life.

Die for a cause.

同 從容就義（0458）Die a martyr's death.

反 明哲保身（1826）Be wordly wise and play safe.

源 孟子・告子上："生，亦我所欲也，義，亦我所欲也，二者不可得兼，舍生而取義者也。"

2376 **捨正道而不由** shě zhèng dào ér bù yóu

Deviate from following the right track. (lit.)

Leave the beaten track.

To go across country.

同 迂迴曲折（3685）Tortuous and devious.

反 循規蹈矩（3280）Toe the line.

源 孟子："舍其路而弗由，放其心而不知求，哀哉。"

2377 **射人先射馬，擒賊先擒王**

shè rén xiān shè mǎ, qín zéi xiān qín wáng

To shoot (down) a man, first shoot the horse; to catch the bandits, first catch the king (leader). (lit.)

He that would the daughter win must with the mother first begin.

源 杜甫・前出塞詩："射人先射馬，擒賊先擒王。"

2378 **設法把它想通** shè fá bǎ tā xiǎng tōng

Devise means and think clearly of it. (lit.)

Put that in your pipe and smoke it.

設身處地 shè shēn chǔ dì 2379

Put oneself in another's place. (lit.)

Put oneself in another's shoes.

Put oneself in the place of others.

To be in someone else's shoes.

源 禮記．中庸："體羣臣也。"朱熹注："體謂設以身，處其地而察以心也。"

申斥責罵 shēn chì zé mà 2380

Reprimanding, blaming and scolding. (lit.)

Call one to task.

Haul one over the coals.

Come down like a ton of bricks.

同 直斥不雅（3870）Give a person a piece of one's mind.

反 歌功頌德（0894）Chant the praises of

身敗名裂 shēn bài míng liè 2381

A personal defeat and reputation shattered. (lit.)

Shorn of one's glory.

Die like a dog.

Fall into disgrace.

To be under a cloud.

Come down in the world.

反 名噪一時（1817）To rise to fame.

源 辛稼軒．賀新郎詞："將軍百戰身名裂。"

身不由主 shēn bù yóu zhǔ 2382

Unable to control oneself. (lit.)

Couldn't help oneself.

The wagon must go whither the horses draw it.

同 不由自主（0271）In spite of oneself.

反 獨立自主（0678）Stand on one's feet.

身懷六甲 shēn huái liù jiǎ 2383

Her body was bosom with six "armours". (lit.)

In the family way.

Heavy with child.

In an interesting condition.

To be in trouble.

身教勝於言教 shēn jiào shèng yú yán jiào 2384

Teaching by examples is better than teaching by words. (lit.)

A good example is the best sermon.

Example is better than precept.

2385 **身居幕後** shēn jū mù hòu

Body (one) lives behind the curtain. (lit.)

Behind the scene.

Keep in the background.

同 幕後操縱（1872）Backstage manoeuvring.

2386 **身體發福** shēn tǐ fā fú

The body spreads blessings. (lit.)

Put on flesh.

Gain weight.

同 大腹便便（0520）Beef to the heels.

反 日益消瘦（2259）Reduced to a skeleton.

2387 **身體力行** shēn tǐ lì xíng

Personal practice with effort. (lit.)

Practise what one preaches.

Put into practice.

同 以身作則（3538）Set a good example for others.

反 言行不一（3309）Say one thing and do another.

源 淮南子 · 氾論訓："故聖人以身體之。" / 禮記 · 中庸："力行近乎仁。"

2388 **身體違和** shēn tǐ wéi hé

The body is against harmony. (lit.)

To be out of sorts.

To be under the weather.

反 身壯力健（2395）Sound as a bell.

2389 **身無長物** shēn wú cháng wù

With nothing valuable in one's possession. (lit.)

Have not a shirt to one's back.

反 腰纏萬貫（3344）Roll in wealth.

源 晉書 · 王恭傳："恭曰，吾平生無長物。"

2390 **身陷囹圄** shēn xiàn líng yǔ

Body (One) is trapped in a prison. (lit.)

Behind bolt and bar.

同 鐵窗風味（2748）Polish the king's iron with one's eyebrows.

反 逍遙法外（3128）To be at large.

2391 **身心交困** shēn xīn jiāo kùn

Both body and mind are tired. (lit.)

Burn the candle at both ends.

反 精力充沛（1384）Full of pep.

2392 **身在曹營心在漢**

shēn zài cáo yíng xīn zài hàn

The body is in the camp of Cao but the heart in Han. (lit.)

It is hard to sit in Rome and strive against the Pope.

同 心猿意馬（3197）Run with the hound and hold with the hare.

身在福中不知福 2393

shēn zài fú zhōng bù zhī fú

One living in blessings does not know it is a blessing. (lit.)

Blessings are not valued till they are gone.
Good fortune is never good till it is lost.
Health is not valued till sickness comes.
We never miss the water till the well runs dry.

身在鬼門關 shēn zài guǐ mén guān 2394

Body (One) is at the door of ghosts. (lit.)

To be at death's door.

同 末日來臨（1847）One's hour has come.

身壯力健 shēn zhuàng lì jiàn 2395

Body healthy and strong. (lit.)

As fit as a fiddle.
Sound as a bell.
In the pink.

反 弱不禁風（2298）As weak as water.

深藏若虛 shēn cáng ruò xū 2396

Embedded deeply as if it is empty. (lit.)

Still waters run deep.

反 高傲自大（0876）To be stuck up.
源 史記．老莊申韓列傳：“良賈深藏若虛，君子盛德，容貌若愚。”

深居簡出 shēn jū jiǎn chū 2397

Live in deep seclusion and rarely come out. (lit.)

Like a hermit.
Live in seclusion.
Keep oneself to oneself.

同 息交絕遊（3044）Retire into oneself.
反 拋頭露面（1953）Come out into the open.
源 秦觀．謝王學士書：“深居簡出，幾不與世人相通。”

深思熟慮 shēn sī shú lǜ 2398

Deep contemplation and ripe consideration. (lit.)

Ponder deeply over.
Put it through the meat grinder.
Turn it over in one's mind.
Take counsel of one's pillow.
Sleep on the matter.
Chew the cud.
Weigh and consider.

同 仔細思量（3966）sleep over it.
反 漫不經心（1756）Devil may care.
源 蘇軾．策別：“而其人亦得深思熟慮，周旋於其間。”

2399 **深惡痛絕** shēn wù tòng jué

To hate deeply and sever painfully. (lit.)

Wouldn't give one the time of day.

Harbour a bitter hatred for

同 恨之入骨（1062）Can eat one without salt.

2400 **深信不疑** shēn xìn bù yí

Deep in faith without doubt. (lit.)

Feel it in one's bones.

Totally convinced.

同 信以為真（3209）Swallow it hook, line and sinker.

反 頓起疑心（0692）To smell a rat.

2401 **深於世故** shēn yú shì gù

Deep in worldliness. (lit.)

Have seen much of the world.

Know which way the wind blows.

Know one's way about.

Know on which side one's bread is buttered.

Worldly wise.

同 歷盡滄桑（1612）Through thick and thin.

反 初出茅廬（0421）A new recruit.

2402 **深知底細** shēn zhī dǐ xì

Know deeply the bottom and details. (lit.)

To be in the know.

Know the length of a person's foot.

Know one (something) like a boot.

Know one inside out.

Know what's what.

Have (Get) a person's number.

同 洞悉內情（0671）To be in the swim.

反 全不知情（2158）To be in the dark.

2403 **深知其人** shēn zhī qí rén

Know deeply the man. (lit.)

Read one like a book.

Get a man taped.

同 深知底細（2402）Know one like a boot.

反 一面之交（3425）A bowing acquaintance.

2404 **神不守舍** shén bù shǒu shè

The spirit is out of the house. (lit.)

One's heart leaps into one's mouth.

Lose one's presence of mind.

To be harum-scarum.

Quite absent-minded.

同 心不在焉（3160）To be day-dreaming.

反 全神貫注（2162）Focus one's attention on

神采奕奕 shén cǎi yì yì 2405
The face appears full of life and spirit. (lit.)
Fresh as a daisy.
Full of pep (beans).
As fit as a fiddle.
Hale and hearty.
Look like a million dollars.

同 英姿煥發（3598）In one's vigorous youth.
反 沒精打采（1848）In the dumps.

神魂顛倒 shén hún diān dǎo 2406
One's soul and mind are upside-down. (lit.)
To fall for
To be infatuated.
Lose one's head.

同 墮入情網（0711）Lose one's heart to

神氣十足 shén qì shí zú 2407
The haughty air is completely enough. (lit.)
Full of oneself.
Puffed up with pride.
Put on side (grand airs).

同 架子十足（1259）Wear a high hat.
反 放下架子（0762）Lay off one's lid.

神槍手 shén qiāng shǒu 2408
Sharp shooter. (lit.)
A dead (crack) shot.
A sharpshooter.

神通廣大 shén tōng guǎng dà 2409
One's supernatural power is great and extensive. (lit.)
Have eyes in the back of one's head.

反 智窮才盡（3896）At one's wit's end.

神志清醒 shén zhì qīng xǐng 2410
The mind is clear and awake. (lit.)
In one's sober senses.
To be all there.

反 醉眼矇矓（4045）A sheet in the mind's eye.

慎重將事 shèn zhòng jiāng shì 2411
To do things with great care. (lit.)
Score twice before you cut once.
Handle with care.

同 鄭重其事（3847）In sober earnest.
反 馬馬虎虎（1729）Rough and ready.

2412 **生不逢時** shēng bù féng shí
Born untimely. (lit.)
Born before one's time.

反 時勢造英雄（2476）He is born in a good hour who gets a good name.
源 詩經・大雅・桑柔："我生不辰，逢此鞠凶。"

2413 **生動活潑** shēng dòng huó pō
Lively and vivacious. (lit.)
As brisk as a bee.

同 生氣勃勃（2416）To be alive and kicking.
反 死氣沉沉（2628）As dead as a doornail.

2414 **生老病死** shēng lǎo bìng sǐ
Life (birth), senility, sickness and death. (lit.)
The way of all flesh.

2415 **生龍活虎** shēng lóng huó hǔ
A lively dragon and an active tiger. (lit.)
Alive and kicking.
Look as if one has eaten live birds.
Brimming over with life.

同 蹦蹦跳跳（0109）Jump like parched peas.
反 呆若木雞（0569）To be rooted to the spot.

2416 **生氣勃勃** shēng qì bó bó
Full of life and breath. (lit.)
Full of vitality.
Full of vim and vigor.
Full of pep (life).
To be alive and kicking.

反 暮氣沉沉（1873）Lose one's grip.
源 鍾嶸詩品："袁嘏云，我詩有生氣，須人捉著，不爾便飛去。"

2417 **生死搏鬥** shēng sǐ bó dòu
Fight for life and death. (lit.)
Struggle for existence.
Life and death struggle.

同 作殊死戰（4072）Fight with a rope round one's neck.

2418 **生死攸關** shēng sǐ yōu guān
What life and death depend. (lit.)
A matter of life and death.

同 非同小可（0769）No small matter.
反 無關重要（2964）To be of little moment.

2419 **生死與共** shēng sǐ yǔ gòng
Life and death together. (lit.)
Share the same fate.
In weal or woe.
For better or for worse.

同 同生死，共命運（2770）Cast in one's lot with

生吞活剝 shēng tūn huó bō 2420

Swallow raw and skin alive. (lit.)

Learn by rote.

Copy blindly.

源 大唐新語 · 諧謔："張懷慶好偷名士詩文，人為之諺曰，活剝王昌齡，生吞郭正一。"

生意興隆 shēng yì xīng lóng 2421

The trade is prosperous. (lit.)

Drive a roaring trade.

With tail in the water.

Doing a land-office business.

同 貨如輪轉（1172）Small profits and quick returns.

反 虧本倒閉（1531）Leave the key under the threshold.

生於富貴之家 shēng yú fù guì zhī jiā 2422

Born in a wealthy family. (lit.)

Born with a silver spoon in one's mouth.

Come in hosed and shod.

同 養尊處優（3341）Live in clover.

反 出身寒微（0411）Rise from the gutter.

生張熟魏 shēng zhāng shú wèi 2423

Unfamiliar with Zhang and acquainted with Wei. (lit.)

Tom, Dick and Harry.

源 拊掌錄："君為北道生張八，我是西州熟魏三，莫怪尊前無笑語，半生半熟未相諳。"

聲價甚高 shēng jià shèn gāo 2424

A very high reputation. (lit.)

Of great celebrity.

同 名噪一時（1817）To rise to fame.

反 賤如糞土（1288）As cheap as dirt.

源 李白 · 與韓荊州書："一登龍門，則聲價十倍。"

聲名狼藉 shēng míng láng jí 2425

One's reputation is like wolf's. (lit.)

Earn oneself a bad name.

Fall into disgrace (discredit).

同 名譽掃地（1816）One's name is mud.

反 名噪一時（1817）To rise to fame.

源 史記 · 蒙恬列傳："惡聲狼藉，布於諸國。"

聲如洪鐘 shēng rú hóng zhōng 2426

One's voice is like a great bell. (lit.)

As clear as a bell.

聲色俱厲 shēng sè jù lì 2427

Harsh-voiced and severe-faced. (lit.)

An angry look in one's face.

To be short-spoken.

反 低聲下氣（0633）Pocket one's pride.

源 趙璘 · 因話錄 · 官部："上曰，韋溫，朕每欲用之，皆辭訴，又安用韋溫。聲色俱厲。"

2428 **聲嘶力竭** shēng sī lì jié

Become hoarse from shouting and exhausted. (lit.)

Worn and husky.

Talk one's self hoarse.

2429 **繩鋸木斷** shéng jù mù duàn

Rope can saw wood to pieces. (lit.)

Hair by hair you will pull out the horse's tail.

Feather by feather the goose is plucked.

同 水滴石穿（2588）Constant dropping wears away the stone.

源 羅大經．鶴林玉露：“繩鋸木斷，水滴石穿。”

2430 **省吃儉用** shěng chī jiǎn yòng

Reduce eating and spare using. (lit.)

Pinch and scrape.

同 節衣縮食（1327）Skin a flea for its hide.

反 鋪張浪費（2011）Butter one's bread on both sides.

2431 **省了草繩跑了牛**

shěng lè cǎo shéng pǎo lè niú

Saving the grass rope (string) has let the cow run away. (lit.)

Lose a ship for a halfpenny worth of tar.

2432 **盛極一時** shèng jí yī shí

Prosperity at its height for a time. (lit.)

Prevail for a time.

In full flourish.

In vogue.

To be all the rage.

2433 **盛氣凌人** shèng qì líng rén

Put up air and bully others. (lit.)

To lift up the horn.

Throw one's weight about.

To be overbearing.

同 仗勢欺人（3802）Pull rank on someone.

反 和藹可親（1048）Easy to get along with.

源 戰國策：“左師觸龍言願見太后，太后盛氣而胥之。”

2434 **盛情款待** shèng qíng kuǎn dài

Entertain with great favour. (lit.)

Do one proud.

Lavish hospitality on

Roll out the red carpet.

同 隆重接待（1689）Give royal reception.

反 給以冷遇（0912）Give one the cold shoulder.

盛衰榮辱 shèng shuāi róng rǔ 2435
Rise and fall; glory and shame. (lit.)
The ups and downs of life.
The vicissitudes of life.

同 成敗利鈍（0353）Hail, rain and shine.

盛筵難再 shèng yán nán zài 2436
It is difficult to have such a grand feast again. (lit.)
Opportunity seldom knocks twice.

源 王勃 · 滕王閣序：“勝地不常，盛筵難再。”

盛裝冠戴 shèng zhuāng guān dài 2437
Fully dressed and wearing a hat. (lit.)
Best bib and tucker.
In full fig (feather).
Dressed up to the nines.
Sunday best.

同 衣服麗都（3502）Doll oneself up.
反 衣不蔽體（3501）Not a rag to one ' s back.

勝敗兵家常事 2438
shèng bài bīng jiā cháng shì
Win or loss to soldiers is often happening. (lit.)
He that falls today may rise tomorrow.
He that fights and runs away may live to fight another day.

源 舊唐書 · 裴度傳：“一勝一敗，兵家常勢。”

勝彼一籌 shèng bǐ yī chóu 2439
Win him one stroke. (lit.)
Pip someone at the post.
Have an edge on one.
One too many for a person.
One stroke above.
Take the wind out of one's sails.
Go somebody one better.

同 棋高一着（2031）To be one up on a person.
反 相形見絀（3113）Pale beside another.

勝利在望 shèng lì zài wàng 2440
Victory can be hoped. (lit.)
Get on the home stretch.

同 前程似錦（2073）Have a brilliant prospect.
反 大勢已去（0552）The day is lost.

2441 **勝券在握** shèng quàn zài wò

The winning card is being held (in hand). (lit.)

Have the cards in one's own hand.

Have the game in one's hands.

同 穩操勝券（2930）Have an ace up one's sleeve.

反 不可收拾（0218）Got to pot.

2442 **勝任愉快** shèng rèn yú kuài

To fulfill one's duty happily. (lit.)

To hold a job down.

Equal to the occasion.

To be well qualified.

反 力不勝任（1603）Beyond one.

源 史記．酷吏列傳："當是之時，吏治若救湯揚沸，非武健嚴酷，惡能勝其任而愉快乎。"

2443 **屍骨未寒** shī gǔ wèi hán

Corpse's bones not yet cold. (lit.)

Hardly cold in the grave.

2444 **尸位素餐** shī wèi sù cān

One who impersonates the dead and consumes the sacrifices. (lit.)

A piece of deadwood.

Feast at the public crib.

Feed at the public trough.

反 枵腹從公（3121）Get all the kicks and none of the ha'pence.

源 漢書．朱雲傳："今朝廷大臣，上不能匡主，下亡（無）以益民，皆尸位素餐。"

2445 **失敗乃成功之母**

shī bài nǎi chéng gōng zhī mǔ

Failure is mother of success. (lit.)

Learn by experience.

Failure teaches success.

同 吃一塹，長一智（0376）Experience is the mother of wisdom.

2446 **失魂落魄** shī hún luò pò

Lost soul and fallen spirit. (lit.)

Drive one mad.

Stand aghast.

Scared out of one's wits.

Like a dying duck in a thunderstorm.

同 六神無主（1687）To be all at sea.

反 泰然自若（2669）Feel at home.

源 官場現形記："畢竟是賊人膽虛，終不免失魂落魄。"

失之東隅，收之桑榆 shī zhī dōng yú, shōu zhī sāng yú 2447

What is lost in the east is gained in Mulberry corner. (lit.)

Lose in hake but gain in herring.

What one loses on the swings, one gains on the roundabouts.

Get in the shire what one loses in the hundred.

反 賠了夫人又折兵（1958）Throw the helve after the hatchet.

源 後漢書．馮異傳："始雖垂翅回溪，終能奮翼澠池，可謂失之東隅，收之桑榆。"

失之過甚 shī zhī guò shèn 2448

To err on being too much. (lit.)

Carry too far.

同 過猶不及（1003）Overdone is worse than underdone.

失之交臂 shī zhī jiāo bì 2449

To lose even having touched one's arm. (lit.)

Come close to making one's acquaintance.

Slip through one's fingers.

Miss the bus.

See a pin and let it lie, you'll want a pin before you die.

反 十拿九穩（2457）Feel cork sure.

源 莊子．田子方："吾終身與汝交一臂而失之。"

施恩不望報 shī ēn bù wàng bào 2450

One does not expect gratitude by bestowing kindness. (lit.)

Cast one's bread upon the waters.

施恩莫望報 shī ēn mò wàng bào 2451

Bestowing kindness, don't expect reward. (lit.)

Virtue is its own reward.

施加壓力 shī jiā yā lì 2452

Give and add pressure. (lit.)

Put the screw on.

同 泰山壓頂（2671）Come down like a ton of bricks.

詩向會人吟 shī xiàng huì rén yín 2453

Recite poems to those who understand. (lit.)

When wits meet sparks fly out.

反 對牛彈琴（0690）Preach to deaf ears.

2454 **噓聲四起** shī shēng sì qǐ

Booing noise arises from four (directions). (lit.)

Hue and cry.

2455 **十個指頭有長短**

shí gè zhǐ tóu yǒu cháng duǎn

Ten fingers, some long, others short. (lit.)

One end is sure to be bone.

同 樹大有枯枝，族大有乞兒（2576）There are black sheep in every fold.

反 等量齊觀（0627）Six of one and half a dozen of the other.

2456 **十目所視，十手所指**

shí mù suǒ shì, shí shǒu suǒ zhǐ

Stared by ten eyes, pointed by ten fingers. (lit.)

Come under fire in every quarter.

The day has eyes and the night has ears.

Everybody points an accusing finger at

源 禮記．大學："曾子曰，十目所視，十手所指，其嚴乎。"

2457 **十拿九穩** shí ná jiǔ wěn

Ten things grasped nine assured. (lit.)

Ten to one.

Feel cork (pretty) sure.

To have taken for granted.

Have in the bag.

Safe bind, safe find.

With hands down.

源 阮大鋮．燕子箋："此是十拿九穩，必中的計策。"

2458 **十年成之不足，一旦壞之有餘**

shí nián chéng zhī bù zú, yí dàn huài zhī yǒu yú

Ten years is not enough to success but one day is more than enough to destroy. (lit.)

An hour may destroy what an age has been building.

It is easier to pull down than to build up.

Drive the swine through the hanks of yarns.

十年如一日 shí nián rú yī rì 2459
Ten years is like one day. (lit.)
As regular as clockwork.
Go on in the same old rut.

同 始終不渝（2483）Keep it up.
反 三天打魚，兩天曬網（2313）By fits and starts.

十年樹木，百年樹人 2460
shí nián shù mù, bǎi nián shù rén
Ten years to grow a tree, hundred years to educate a man. (lit.)
A skill is not acquired in a matter of days.
Rome was not built in a day.

源 管子 · 權修：“十年之計，莫如樹木。終身之計，莫如樹人。”

十全十美 shí quán shí měi 2461
Ten perfections and ten beauties. (lit.)
Done to perfection.
Leave nothing to be desired.
All as it should be.
The pink of perfection.

同 盡善盡美（1374）Tip-top.
反 美中不足（1779）The peacock has fair feathers but foul feet.

十萬火急 shí wàn huǒ jí 2462
Hundred thousand as fast as a fire. (lit.)
S. O. S.
In hot haste.
Not a moment to lose.

同 火燒眉毛（1169）Imminent danger.
反 慢條斯理（1755）At a snail's pace.

十有八九 shí yǒu bā jiǔ 2463
Eight or nine out of ten. (lit.)
Nine cases out of ten.
Ten to one.

石沉大海 shí chén dà hǎi 2464
A stone sunk in the big sea. (lit.)
Sink into oblivion.
Like a needle in a bundle of hay.

源 王實甫 · 西廂記：“他若是不來，似石沉大海。”

拾級而登 shí jí ér dēng 2465
Picking the steps in ascending. (lit.)
Step after step the ladder is ascended.

反 走下坡路（4031）On the down grade.
源 禮記：“拾級聚足，連步以上。”

2466 **拾人牙慧** shí rén yá huì
Pick another's tooth-wisdom (wits). (lit.)
Take a leaf out of another's book.

同 步人後塵（0293）Follow upon one's heels.
反 另闢蹊徑（1670）Take one's own line.
源 劉義慶・世説新語・文學："殷中軍（浩）云，康伯未得我牙後慧。"

2467 **食古不化** shí gǔ bù huà
Eat the ancient (ways) without digestion. (lit.)
Stick-in-the-mud.

反 改弦更張（0855）Start with a clean slate.
源 玉几山房畫外錄："定欲為古人而食古不化。"

2468 **食前方丈** shí qián fāng zhàng
A square zhang of food set before one. (1 fang zhang = 100 Chinese square feet) (lit.)
Eat like a king.
One's bread is buttered on both sides.
Live like fighting cocks.
Eat high on the hog.

同 鐘鳴鼎食（3915）Eat skylarks in a garret.
反 數米而炊（2571）Dine on potatoes and point.
源 孟子・盡心下："食前方丈，侍妾數百人。"

2469 **食言而肥** shí yán ér féi
Grow fat by eating one's words. (lit.)
Go back on one's word.
Break one's promise.

同 收回成命（2543）Eat one's words.
反 説話算數（2611）A man of his word.
源 左傳："是食言多矣，能無肥乎。"

2470 **食欲（慾）不振** shí yù bù zhèn
Appetite for food is not keen. (lit.)
Loss of appetite.
To be off one's feed.
Eat like a bird.

反 饞涎欲滴（0325）The mouth waters.

2471 **食指浩繁** shí zhǐ hào fán
Those waiting to eat are a big crowd. (lit.)
Have a large mouth but small girdle.
Eat one out of the house and home.

2472 **時不我待** shí bù wǒ dài
Time does not wait for me. (lit.)
Time marches on.
Time and tide wait for no man.

同 勿失時機（3026）Take fortune at the tide.

時乖命蹇 shí guāi mìng jiǎn 2473
Time is unfavourable and fate ill. (lit.)
A case of bad luck.
Born under an evil star.
The times are out of joint.

同 生不逢時（2412）Born before one's time.
源 元曲選．白仁甫．牆頭馬上："早是抱閑怨，時乖運蹇。"

時乎時乎不再來 2474
shí hū shí hū bù zài lái
Time, time will not come again. (lit.)
Lost time is never found.
Time past cannot be recalled.

同 光陰一去不復返（0985）One can't put the clock back.
源 漢書．蒯伍江息夫傳："時乎時，不再來。"

時來運轉 shí lái yùn zhuǎn 2475
When time comes, fortune turns. (lit.)
The turn of the tide.
Take a turn for the better.
Better luck next time.
The worse luck now, the better another time.

時勢造英雄 shí shì zào yīng xióng 2476
The trend of time makes one a hero. (lit.)
It is chance chiefly that makes heroes.
He is born in a good hour who gets a good name.

時運不齊 shí yùn bù qí 2477
The times are unpropitious. (lit.)
No butter will stick on his bread.
To be under a cloud.
In an evil hour.

反 一帆風順（3391）It's all plain sailing.
源 王勃．滕王閣序："時運不齊，命途多舛。"

實不相瞞 shí bù xiāng mán 2478
Not to deceive (you) really. (lit.)
To tell the truth.

2479 **實踐出真知** shí jiàn chū zhēn zhī
Practice produces true knowledge. (lit.)
Experience is the mother of wisdom.
In doing we learn.
The proof of the pudding is in the eating.
You never know till you have tried.
Take me on your back and you'll know what I weigh.

同 格物致知（0897）Sermons in stones.
源 宋史："真見實踐，深探聖城。"

2480 **實事求是** shí shì qiú shì
By verification of the facts to get at the truth. (lit.)
Down to earth.
Look fact in the face.

反 故弄玄虛（0950）The magician mutters, and knows not what he mutters.
源 漢書．河間獻王傳："河間獻王修學好古，實事求是。"

2481 **識時務者為俊傑**
shí shí wù zhě wéi jùn jié
Knowing the time and situation is a wise man. (lit.)
Know the time of day.

同 善觀風色（2343）Know which way the wind blows.
源 三國志："司馬德操曰，儒生俗士，豈識時務，識時務者，在乎俊傑。"

2482 **史無前例** shǐ wú qián lì
In history there was no previous case (like this). (lit.)
Unheard of.
Without precedent in history.

反 歷史重演（1615）History repeats itself.

2483 **始終不渝** shǐ zhōng bù yú
To be unchanged from beginning to end. (lit.)
Not to be shaken.
Dogged adherence.
Keep it up.
Stick to it.

同 堅持到底（1265）Hold out.
反 半途而廢（0072）Do things by halves.
源 晉書．謝安傳："安雖居朝寄，然東山之志，始末不渝，每形於言色。"

2484 **始作俑者** shǐ zuò yǒng zhě
Initiator of evil. (lit.)
The first to set a bad example.
Set a stone rolling.

源 孟子．梁惠王上："始作俑者，其無後乎。"

使人寒心 shǐ rén hán xīn
Make one's heart cold. (lit.)
Send a chill down one's spine.
Make one's blood run cold.

反 熱血沸騰（2188）With heart afire. 2485

使人難堪 shǐ rén nán kān
Make one embarrassed. (lit.)
Put one to the blush.
Set a person's teeth on edge.
Get under one's skin.

反 爽心快意（2586）Warm the cockles of one's heart. 2486

使人飄飄然 shǐ rén piāo piāo rán
Make one feel floating (in the air). (lit.)
Turn a person's head.

反 使人難堪（2486）Set a person's teeth on edge. 2487

使人心煩 shǐ rén xīn fán
Make one's heart worried. (lit.)
It gets on one's nerves.

2488

使人心碎 shǐ rén xīn suì
Make one's heart broken. (lit.)
Break one's heart.

2489

使人厭惡 shǐ rén yàn wù
Make one tired of it. (lit.)
Leave a bad taste in one's mouth.

同 討厭萬分（2699）Bored to death. 2490

使人語塞 shǐ rén yǔ sāi
Stop one talking. (lit.)
Jump down a person's throat.

同 駁得體無完膚（0170）Leave a person flat.
反 反唇相稽（0744）Give one a rolling for his all-over. 2491

使人乍舌 shǐ rén zhà shé
Make one protrude one's tongue (in surprise). (lit.)
Take one's breath away.

2492

2493 **士別三日，刮目相看**
shì bié sān rì, guā mù xiāng kàn
A scholar after departing for three days, one may need to clean one's eye to look at him. (lit.)
Naughty boys sometimes make good men.
Wanton kittens may make sober cats.
An ugly duckling.

同 非復吳下阿蒙（0765）The ugly duckling.
源 三國志・呂蒙傳注：“士別三日，即當刮目相待。”

2494 **士為知己者用** shì wèi zhī jǐ zhě yòng
A scholar works for those who know him. (lit.)
A friend in need is a friend indeed.
Respect a man, he will do the more.

同 女為悦己者容（1935）Nightingales will not sing in a cage.
源 司馬遷・報任少卿書：“士為知己者用，女為悦己者容。”

2495 **世道人心** shì dào rén xīn
The ways of the world and the heart of man. (lit.)
The way of the world.

2496 **世風日下，人心不古**
shì fēng rì xià, rén xīn bù gǔ
The normal standard of the world is going down every day, people's heart (thinking) is no more as that of old time. (lit.)
The more I see of men, the more I love dogs.

同 道德淪喪（0604）Go to the dogs.

2497 **世界末日** shì jiè mò rì
The world's doomsday. (lit.)
The crack of doom.

2498 **世上無難事，只怕有心人**
shì shàng wú nán shì, zhǐ pà yǒu xīn rén
There is no difficult matter in the world, only afraid of man having a heart (mind). (lit.)
Nothing is impossible to a willing heart.
Where there's a will there's a way.
It's dogged that does it.

同 事在人為（2520）Fortune favours the brave.
反 人算不如天算（2222）An ounce of luck is better than a pound of wisdom.

世世代代 shì shì dài dài 2499

From generation to generation and from age to age. (lit.)

From generation to generation.

同 千秋萬代（2065）Throughout the ages.

世事如棋局局新 shì shì rú qí jú jú xīn 2500

The world affairs are like playing chess, new in every game. (lit.)

The unexpected always happens.

世俗所云 shì sú suǒ yún 2501

A worldy saying. (lit.)

As the saying goes.

世外桃源 shì wài táo yuán 2502

A peach orchard beyond this world. (lit.)

Utopia.

A fool's paradise.

源 源出《陶潛．桃花源記》

世無英雄，遂使豎子成名 2503

shì wú yīng xióng, suì shǐ shù zǐ chéng míng

If there were no heroes in the world, then it would make fools become renowned. (lit.)

In the country of the blind the one-eyed man is king.

同 蜀中無大將，廖化作先鋒（2570）He will be a man among the geese when the gander is gone.

市儈氣 shì kuài qì 2504

The air of a market business man. (lit.)

Smell of the shop.

同 俗不可耐（2647）Vulgar in the extreme.

事倍功半 shì bèi gōng bàn 2505

Double the amount of work brings half the effect. (lit.)

For all one's efforts.

Be a fool for one's pains.

Make bricks without straw.

同 吃力不討好（0372）Bite on granite.

源 語本《孟子．公孫丑上》

2506 **事必躬親** shì bì gōng qīn

Attending respectfully the business personally. (lit.)

If you want a thing done well, do it yourself.

Better do it than wish it done.

同 求人不如求己（2145）Better spare to have thine own than ask of other men.

反 假手於人（1258）Make a cat's paw of someone.

2507 **事不得已** shì bù dé yǐ

Things can't be helped. (lit.)

It can't be helped.

If the mountain will not come to Mahomet, Mahomet must go to the mountain.

同 無可奈何（2975）What must be must be.

2508 **事不關己，高高掛起**

shì bù guān jǐ, gāo gāo guà qǐ

The matter that does not concern one can be hung up high. (lit.)

Dogs never go into mourning when a horse dies.

The stone that lies not in your way need not offend you.

It's none of my business.

I will neither meddle nor make.

Let the world wag.

同 各人自掃門前雪（0904）Let each tailor mend his own coat.

反 越俎代庖（3747）To be a back seat driver.

2509 **事不離實** shì bù lí shí

Facts will not leave the truth. (lit.)

Facts are stubborn things.

反 想入非非（3116）Build castles in the air.

2510 **事不宜遲** shì bù yí chí

The matter should not be delayed. (lit.)

There's no time to lose.

It brooks no delay.

The matter asks haste.

Not let the grass grow under one's feet.

Delays are dangerous.

同 勿失時機（3026）Now or never.

反 勿操之過急（3018）Draw not thy bow before thy arrow be fixed.

2511 **事出有因** shì chū yǒu yīn

Matter arising has a reason. (lit.)

There is no smoke without fire.

Everything must have a beginning.

同 無風不起浪（2960）There's no smoke without fire.

反 平白無故（1984）Without provocation.

事到臨頭 shì dào lín tóu 2512

When the matter comes to the head. (lit.)

When things come to a head.

If the worst comes to the worst.

事後諸葛亮 shì hòu zhū gě liàng 2513

After the event (it is easier) to be Zhu Ge-Liang (a very famous man in Chinese history). (lit.)

Prophesy after the event.

It is easy to be wise after the event.

If things were to be done twice, all would be wise.

After-wit is everybody's wit.

反 先知先覺（3089）Have a long head.

事起有因 shì qǐ yǒu yīn 2514

Matter derived from some reason. (lit.)

Every why has a wherefore.

There is good reason for it.

Where there's smoke there's fire.

反 平白無故（1984）Without rhyme or reason.

事實勝於雄辯 shì shí shèng yú xióng biàn 2515

Facts surpass sound arguments. (lit.)

Deeds (Actions) speak louder than words.

Truth needs not many words.

The effect speaks, the tongue needs not.

Deeds, not words.

Neither praise nor dispraise thyself; thy actions serve the turn.

事務紛繁 shì wù fēn fán 2516

Business affairs are numerous and complicated. (lit.)

Up to the ears in work.

Have one's hands full.

反 閒暇無事（3095）To be at a loose end.

事已臨頭 shì yǐ lín tóu 2517

The matter has already come to the head. (lit.)

The die is cast.

To be in for it.

同 臨堤走馬收韁晚，船到江心補漏遲（1655）It is too late to cast anchor when the ship's on the rock.

2518 **事有湊巧** shì yǒu còu qiǎo

Things may happen coincidentally. (lit.)

As luck (chance) would have it.

The long arm of coincidence.

2519 **事與願違** shì yǔ yuàn wéi

The fact contravenes the wish. (lit.)

To one's disappointment.

Fall short of one's expectation.

反 如願以償（2280）A dream comes true.

源 嵇康・幽憤詩："事與願違，遘茲淹留。"

2520 **事在人為** shì zài rén wéi

Things are done by man. (lit.)

Fortune favours the brave.

Where there's a will there's a way.

It's dogged that does it.

同 有志事竟成（3682）A wilful man will have his way.

反 人算不如天算（2222）An ounce of luck is better than a pound of wisdom.

2521 **恃才傲物** shì cái ào wù

Relying on one's ability slightens things. (lit.)

Look down upon others.

同 高傲自大（0876）To be stuck up.

反 虛懷若谷（3245）To humble oneself.

源 摭言："蕭穎士恃才傲物。"

2522 **拭目以待** shì mù yǐ dài

Wipe the eyes and be waiting. (lit.)

Wait and see.

It remains to be seen.

同 風物長宜放眼量（0810）See which way the cat jumps.

源 漢書："天下莫不拭目傾耳。"

2523 **是非之心** shì fēi zhī xīn

The heart to discern differences between right and wrong. (lit.)

Sense of justice.

源 孟子："是非之心，人皆有之。"

2524 **是非終日有，不聽自然無**

shì fēi zhōng rì yǒu, bù tīng zì rán wú

Whole day (always) there is right or wrong, if not listening there is naturally none. (lit.)

Were there no hearers, there would be no backbiters.

Ask no questions and you will be told no lies.

是可忍，孰不可忍

shì kě rěn, shú bù kě rěn

If this can be tolerated, what else can't be tolerated. (lit.)

More than flesh and blood can bear.

同 忍無可忍（2245）The last straw breaks the camel's back.

反 忍得一時之氣，免得百日之憂（2242）Bite one's lips.

源 論語 · 八佾："是可忍也，孰不可忍也。"

2525

逝者如斯 shì zhě rú sī

It passes away like this. (lit.)

Water over the dam.

Things past cannot be recalled.

The mill cannot grind with the water that is past.

源 論語："逝者如斯夫。"

2526

視而不見 shì ér bú jiàn

Look without seeing. (lit.)

Shut one's eyes to

As blind as a mole.

反 明察秋毫（1819）See through a millstone.

源 莊子 · 知北游："窅然空然，終日視之而不見，聽之而不聞。"

2527

視如敝屣 shì rú bì xǐ

Regard it as a pair of worn shoes. (lit.)

Wouldn't care a fig's end for

反 珍而藏之（3823）Lay it up in lavender.

2528

視如路人 shì rú lù rén

See one as a passer-by. (lit.)

Keep one at a distance.

Not on speaking terms.

Cut someone dead.

同 翻臉不認人（0740）Give one the go-by.

反 一見如故（3403）Be hail-fellow-well-met with

2529

視若無睹 shì ruò wú dǔ

Look as if not seeing. (lit.)

Look the other way.

Pay no heed to

There's none so blind as those who won't see.

Shut one's eyes against

Turn a blind eye to

同 隻眼開，隻眼閉（3865）Wink at small faults.

反 一覽無遺（3414）Have a commanding view.

2530

視死如歸 shì sǐ rú guī

Look at death as returning home. (lit.)

In defiance of death.

Give one's life for

Look death in the face.

同 從容就義（0458）Die a martyr's death.

源 韓非子："三軍若成陣，使士視死如歸。"

2531

2532 **勢不兩立** shì bù liǎng lì

Circumstances do not allow both stand together. (lit.)

Opposite as fire and water.

At daggers drawn.

Would not touch one with a barge pole (a pair of tongs).

同 不共戴天之仇（0192）Inveterate enemy.

反 通力合作（2761）To pull together.

源 三國志．周瑜傳："孤與老賊，勢不兩立。"

2533 **勢成騎虎** shì chéng qí hǔ

The situation is like mounting on a tiger. (lit.)

In an awkward position.

Needs must when the devil drives.

Up a gum-tree.

同 欲罷不能（3714）To have a wolf by the ears.

源 晉書．溫嶠傳："今之事勢，義無旋踵，騎猛獸安可下哉。"

2534 **勢均力敵** shì jūn lì dí

Power equals and strength matches that of the enemy. (lit.)

Balance of power.

Nip and tuck.

Diamond cut diamond.

When Greek meets Greek, then is the tug of war.

Evenly matched.

Tremble in the balance.

On a dead level with

A dead heat.

同 旗鼓相當（2033）A ding-dong fight.

反 小巫見大巫（3146）To be cast into the shade.

源 南史．劉穆之傳："劉，孟諸公，俱起布衣，共立大義……力敵勢均，終相吞咀。"

2535 **勢力範圍** shì lì fàn wéi

Within the limit of power. (lit.)

Sphere of influence.

2536 **勢如破竹** shì rú pò zhú

The situation is like splitting the bamboo. (lit.)

Like slicing cheese.

Sweep everything before one.

It was just a walk over.

Bowl over like ninepins.

To win in a canter.

Like a hot knife cutting through butter.

Win in a breeze.

同 秋風掃落葉（2143）Make a clean sweep.

反 到處碰壁（0599）Driven from pillar to post.

源 晉書．杜預傳："今兵威已振，譬如破竹，數節之後，皆迎刃而解。"

嗜殺成性 shì shā chéng xìng 2537

Fondness of killing becomes a habit. (lit.)

To be blood-thirsty.

同 草菅人命（0311）Kill like flies.

反 惻隱之心（0315）Milk of human kindness.

誓不干休 shì bù gān xiū 2538

Swear not to let it go. (lit.)

To go all lengths.

同 不到黃河心不死（0180）Hang on like grim death.

反 急流勇退（1211）A brave retreat is a brave exploit.

適得其反 shì dé qí fǎn 2539

Just get the opposite. (lit.)

Just the other way round.

Run counter to

The boot is on the other leg.

Just the reverse.

同 恰恰相反（2053）On the contrary.

反 不謀而合（0233）See eye to eye.

適可而止 shì kě ér zhǐ 2540

Go to and stop at a suitable place. (lit.)

Keep within proper limits.

Let (Leave) well alone.

Know where to stop.

More than enough is too much.

Stretch your arm no further than your sleeve will reach.

Stretch your legs according to your coverlet.

同 有分有寸（3646）Draw the line somewhere.

反 有過之而無不及（3648）Do a thing to a fault.

源 論語・鄉黨・朱熹注：“適可而止，毋貪心也。”

適者生存 shì zhě shēng cún 2541

The fittest can survive. (lit.)

Things well fitted abide.

Survival of the fittest.

噬臍莫及 shì qí mò jí 2542

Too late to bite one's naval. (lit.)

Repentance comes too late.

Things past cannot be recalled.

How can one bite his naval?

同 後悔莫及（1089）Lock the stable door after the horse is stolen.

反 亡羊補牢未為晚也（2861）It is never too late to mend.

源 左傳・莊六年：“若不早圖，後君噬臍，其及圖之乎。”

2543 **收回成命** shōu huí chéng mìng

To retract an order. (lit.)

To call back an order.

2544 **收斂起來** shōu liǎn qǐ lái

To gather up things. (lit.)

Draw in one's horns.

反 兇相畢露（3228）Bare one's fangs.

2545 **收支相抵** shōu zhī xiāng dǐ

Receipts and disbursements counter-balance. (lit.)

No gain, no loss.

Make both ends meet.

反 入不敷出（2284）Live above one's income.

2546 **手伸得很長** shǒu shēn dé hěn cháng

Hands can be stretched very long. (lit.)

Greedy folk have long arms.

2547 **手頭拮据** shǒu tóu jié jū

At hand hard up. (lit.)

In a tight squeeze.

To be hard up.

To be hard put to it.

On a shoe string.

同 左支右絀（4052）To be in a tight squeeze.

反 一擲千金（3497）Play ducks and drakes with one's money.

2548 **手無縛雞之力** shǒu wú fù jī zhī lì

One's hands have not the strength to tie up a chicken. (lit.)

Weak as a baby.

As weak as water.

源 元曲選 · 賺蒯通："那韓信手無縛雞之力。"

2549 **手舞足蹈** shǒu wǔ zú dǎo

Gesticulating with hands and treading with feet. (lit.)

Dance for joy.

Leap with joy.

源 詩經大序："永（詠）歌之不足，不知手之舞之，足之蹈之也。"

守財奴 shǒu cái nú 2550

Keeping money slave. (lit.)

A cheap skate.

A penny-pincher.

If money be not thy servant, it will be thy master.

As tight as a drum.

A close-fisted man.

反 揮金如土（1148）Spend money like water.

源 後漢書．馬援傳："凰殖貨財產，貴其能施賑也，否則守錢虜耳，乃盡散以班昆弟故舊。"

守口如瓶 shǒu kǒu rú píng 2551

Keep the mouth closed like a bottle. (lit.)

Put a lid on.

Not breathe a word about.

As close as an oyster.

To be a regular oyster.

Keep mum.

Clam up.

Wild horses would not drag it from one.

同 三緘其口（2315）One's lips are sealed.

反 洩漏機密（3156）Let the cat out of the bag.

源 周密．癸辛雜識："富鄭公有守口如瓶，防意如城之語。"

首當其衝 shǒu dāng qí chōng 2552

First one to bear the brunt. (lit.)

Exposed to danger.

Bear the brunt of

Throw oneself into the breach.

同 一馬當先（3421）To be in the lead.

反 避重就輕（0128）To ride off side issues.

源 漢書．五行志下之上："鄭當其衝，不能修德。"

受恩深處宜先退，得意濃時便好休 shòu ēn shēn chù yí xiān tuì, dé yì nóng shí biàn hǎo xiū 2553

When one is in deep gratitude, one must retreat, when one is doing well, one should retire. (lit.)

Leave a welcome behind you.

受命於危難之間 shòu mìng yú wēi nàn zhī jiān 2554

To receive orders during dangerous and difficult time. (lit.)

Gaze at the melody.

源 諸葛亮（孔明）．前出師表："受任於敗軍之際，奉命於危難之間。"

2555 受人擺佈 shòu rén bǎi bù

To be exploited by others. (lit.)

To be in leading strings.

Take something lying down.

同 身不由主（2382）The wagon must go whither the horse draw it.

反 爭取主動（3833）Take the initiative.

2556 受人利用 shòu rén lì yòng

To be pushed about by others. (lit.)

To be a cat's paw.

反 假手於人（1258）Make a cat's paw of someone.

2557 壽比南山 shòu bǐ nán shān

Live a life as long (old) as Mt. Nan (the southern mountains in Chinling Ridge remain). (lit.)

As old as the hills.

Have a good innings.

Many happy returns of the day.

同 壽同彭祖（2559）As old as Methuselah.

源 南史・齊豫章王嶷傳："嶷謂上曰，古來言願陛下壽比南山，或稱萬歲。"

2558 壽數已盡 shòu shù yǐ jìn

Age number is at the end. (lit.)

One's course is run.

One's time is come.

To be all over with one.

Slip off the hooks.

2559 壽同彭祖 shòu tóng péng zǔ

The longevity same as Peng-Zu (who was supposed to be eight hundred years old.) (lit.)

As old as Methuselah.

2560 壽終正寢 shòu zhōng zhèng qǐn

One's life ends on the bed. (lit.)

Sleep the final sleep.

Die in one's own bed.

Die a natural death.

反 死於非命（2632）Die in one's boots.

2561 瘦骨嶙峋 shòu gǔ lín xún

Thin and bony. (lit.)

As lean as a rake.

To be all skin and bone.

同 骨瘦如柴（0942）A mere bag of bones.

反 身體發福（2386）Put on flesh.

殊途同歸 shū tú tóng guī 2562

Different roads lead to the same destination. (lit.)

All roads lead to Rome.

Extremes meet.

同 百川歸海（0049）All rivers do what they can for the sea.

反 分道揚鑣（0783）To part company.

源 周易・繫辭下：“天下同歸而殊途，一致而百慮。”

書生氣味 shū shēng qì wèi 2563

The smell of a scholar. (lit.)

To be a book-worm.

To smell of the lamp.

舒舒服服 shū shū fú fú 2564

Comfortable, comfortable. (lit.)

As snug as a bug in a rug.

同 優哉悠哉（3631）At one's ease.

反 如坐針氈（2281）Lie on a bed of thorns.

疏不間親 shū bú jiàn qīn 2565

Distant relative may not come between near ones. (lit.)

Blood is thicker than water.

反 非我族類，其心必異（0770）The mice do not play with the cat's son.

熟能生巧 shú néng shēng qiǎo 2566

More practice produces skill. (lit.)

Experience counts.

Practice makes perfect.

同 功多藝熟（0923）He that shoots oft shall at last hit the mark.

熟視無睹 shú shì wú dǔ 2567

Look at for a long time but see nothing. (lit.)

Pay no attention.

Not to see right under one's nose.

Some men go through a forest and see no firewood.

Turn a blind eye to

同 隻眼開，隻眼閉（3865）Wink at small faults.

反 一目了然（3429）Everybody can see that at a glance.

源 劉伶・酒德頌：“靜聽不聞雷霆之聲，熟視不睹泰山之形。”

鼠目寸光 shǔ mù cùn guāng 2568

The eyes of a rat (see only) an inch of light. (lit.)

See no further than one's nose.

Have a narrow outlook on things.

Lack foresight.

反 目光遠大（1870）Show great foresight.

源 元好問詩：“鼠目求官空自忙。”

2569 **蜀犬吠日** shǔ quǎn fèi rì

Szechwan (west province in China) dogs bark at the sun (since the sun there seldom breaks through the thick cloud.) (lit.)

Make a fuss about trifles.

Much matter of a wooden platter.

Much cry and little wool.

Bay the moon.

同 煞有介事（2331）Fuss up and down.

源 韓愈文：“蜀中山高霧重，見日時少，每至日出，則羣犬疑而吠之。”

2570 **蜀中無大將，廖化作先鋒**

shǔ zhōng wú dà jiàng, liào huà zuò xiān fēng

The province of Shu (Szechwan) had no great general and made Liao-Hua the vanguard. (lit.)

He will be a man among the geese when the gander is gone.

In the country of the blind the one-eyed man is king.

2571 **數米而炊** shǔ mǐ ér chuī

Counting the number of rice grains to cook. (lit.)

Dine on potatoes and point.

Skin a flea for its hide and tallow.

Spare well and spend well.

同 稱薪而爨（0368）Pinch and scrape.

反 鐘鳴鼎食（3915）Eat skylarks in a garret.

源 淮南子：“量粟而舂，數米而炊，可以治家，而可以治國。”

2572 **曙光在前** shǔ guāng zài qián

Light of dawn is in front. (lit.)

The night is far spent, the day is at hand.

The darkest hour is that before the dawn.

同 勝利在望（2440）Get on the home stretch.

反 日暮途窮（2256）Driven to the last extremity.

2573 **束手無策** shù shǒu wú cè

Folding arms, find no way (to do something). (lit.)

At a loss what to do.

Find oneself in the mire.

Throw up one's hands in despair.

Not know which way to turn (jump).

同 一籌莫展（3381）To be at one's wit's end.

反 滿腹妙計（1742）To be full of wrinkles.

源 宋季三朝政要：“檜（秦檜）死而逆亮（金主完顏亮）南牧，孰不束手無策。”

束之高閣 shù zhī gāo gé 2574

Tie and put it on the high shelf. (lit.)

Hold up.

Lay aside.

Put on the shelf.

To be pigeon-holed.

源 晉書·庾翼傳："此輩宜束之高閣，俟天下太平，然後議其任耳。"

豎起耳朵 shù qǐ ěr duǒ 2575

Raise up the ears. (lit.)

Prick up one's ears.

Pin back one's ears.

Cock the ears.

同 側耳諦聽（0313）Strain one's ears.

反 兩耳不聞窗外事（1626）Turn a deaf ear to

樹大有枯枝，族大有乞兒 2576

shù dà yǒu kū zhī, zú dà yǒu qǐ ér

Big trees (usually) have rotten branches, big clans may have beggars. (lit.)

There are black sheep in every fold.

Shame in a kindred cannot be avoided.

同 十個指頭有長短（2455）One end is sure to be bone.

樹大招風 shù dà zhāo fēng 2577

Trees large attract wind. (lit.)

Tall trees catch much wind.

同 位高勢危（2908）High places have their precipices.

樹倒猢猻散 shù dǎo hú sūn sàn 2578

The trees fall and the monkeys scatter. (lit.)

Rats desert a falling house (sinking ship).

反 趨炎附勢（2151）Hail the rising sun.

源 曹詠事秦檜，檜死被貶，厲德斯致函詠，啟視之，乃樹倒猢猻散賦一首。見《宋·龐元英·談藪》

樹高千丈，葉落歸根 2579

shù gāo qiān zhàng, yè luò guī gēn

(Though) tall trees (may reach) a thousand zhang (10,000 Chinese feet), the fallen leaves will come back to the roots. (lit.)

East, west, home's best.

同 鳥倦飛而知還（1913）Home is the sailor, home from sea.

源 景德傳燈錄："葉落歸根，來時無口。"

2580 樹正何愁月影斜
shù zhèng hé chóu yuè yǐng xié
If the trees are straight, why worry the moon's shadow be crooked. (lit.)
If the staff be crooked, the shadow cannot be straight.

同 真金不怕紅爐火（3826）A good anvil does not fear the hammer.

2581 耍兩面派 shuǎ liǎng miàn pài
Play double-faced party. (lit.)
Cut both ways.
Play a double game.
Resort to double-dealing.
Carry fire in one hand and water in the other.

同 兩面三刀（1630）Break my head and then give me plaster.

2582 耍手段 shuǎ shǒu duàn
Play hand tricks. (lit.)
Pull a fast one on a person.
Pull a smart trick.
Play dirty tricks.

2583 雙管齊下 shuāng guǎn qí xià
Two brushes at the same time. (lit.)
Work along both lines.

2584 雙手贊成 shuāng shǒu zàn chéng
Agree with both hands. (lit.)
Thumbs up.
All for it.

反 提出異議（2704）Take exception to

2585 爽爽快快 shuǎng shuǎng kuài kuài
Very crisp and fast. (lit.)
Make it snappy.
With a good grace.

同 迅速敏捷（3284）Hand over fist.
反 費時失事（0778）Tarry-long brings little home.

2586 爽心快意 shuǎng xīn kuài yì
Pleasing the heart and happy idea. (lit.)
Warm the cockles of one's heart.
Do one's heart good.
Get a kick out of

同 心曠神怡（3175）In fine fettle.

誰人背後無人說，哪個人前不說人 2587

shuí rén bèi hòu wú rén shuō, nǎ gè rén qián bù shuō rén

Who has not one to talk about him behind his back, which one in front of people not talk about others. (lit.)

The absent are always in the wrong.

水滴石穿 shuǐ dī shí chuān 2588

Drips of water wear through a stone. (lit.)

By sheer strength of will.

Constant dripping of water wears away the stone.

Little strokes fell great oaks.

Hair and hair makes the man's head bare.

Drop by drop the sea is drained.

同 繩鋸木斷（2429）Feather by feather the goose is plucked.

源 漢書・枚乘傳："繩鋸木斷，水滴石穿。"

水鬼升城隍，得志便猖狂 2589

shuǐ guǐ shēng chéng huáng, dé zhì biàn chāng kuáng

When a water-devil is promoted to a city-god, getting his wish he becomes a dare-devil. (lit.)

Set a beggar on horseback and he will gallop (ride to the devil).

水過鴨背 shuǐ guò yā bèi 2590

Water over a duck's back. (lit.)

Like water off a duck's back.

Soon learnt, soon forgotten.

同 馬耳東風（1726）In at one ear and out at the other.

反 牢記心頭（1552）Knock into the head.

水落石出 shuǐ luò shí chū 2591

Stones peep out from the receding water. (lit.)

Brought to light.

Truth lies at the bottom of a well.

The truth will out.

To come out in the wash.

Murder is out.

同 真相大白（3828）Everything comes to light.

源 蘇軾・後赤壁賦："山高月小，水落石出。"

2592 **水能浮舟，亦能覆舟**

shuǐ néng fú zhōu, yì néng fù zhōu

Water can float a boat and can also turn over a boat. (lit.)

The fire which lights us at a distance will burn us when near.

The wind that blows out candles kindles the fire.

2593 **水乳交融** shuǐ rǔ jiāo róng

Water and milk mix well. (lit.)

To be hand (finger) and glove with another.

同 親密無間（2107）On intimate terms with

反 冰炭不相容（0155）At loggerheads with one another.

源 最勝五經："上下和穆，有如乳水。"

2594 **水深火熱** shuǐ shēn huǒ rè

Water deep and fire hot. (lit.)

Go through fire and water.

Get into hot water.

Hard in a clinch and no knife to cut the seizing.

To be in deep water.

源 孟子．梁惠王下："如水益深，如火益熱。"

2595 **水洩不通** shuǐ xiè bù tōng

Water cannot move in or out. (lit.)

Packed like sardines.

To be chock-a-block.

反 川流不息（0433）In rapid succession.

源 釋道源．景德傳燈錄："德山門下，水洩不通。"

2596 **水性楊花** shuǐ xìng yáng huā

Water disposition and Aspen flower (floating on a flowing stream and said of a woman). (lit.)

As changeable as the moon.

A woman's mind and winter wind change oft.

Unstable as water.

2597 **水中撈月** shuǐ zhōng lāo yuè

To fish the moon out of water. (lit.)

Grasp the shadow and let go the substance.

Crying for the moon.

Catch at the shadow and lose the substance.

源 黃庭堅．沁園春詞："鏡裏拈花，水中捉月，覷着無由得近伊。"

睡得正香 shuì dé zhèng xiāng 2598

Sleeping just fragranlty (sweelty). (lit.)

Dead to the world.

In the arms of Morpheus.

同 元龍高卧（3729）Sleep like a log.

反 輾轉反側（3779）Toss about all night.

吮癰舐痔 shǔn yōng shì zhì 2599

To lick ulcers and piles. (lit.)

Lick one's boots.

同 奴顏婢膝（1926）Grovel at the feet of

源 漢書．鄧通傳：“文帝嘗患癰，鄧通嘗為上嗽吮之。”

順風駛帆 shùn fēng shǐ fān 2600

To steer the sail with the wind. (lit.)

Go with the tide.

Hoist your sail when the wind is fair.

Trim the sails.

同 乘風破浪（0361）Brave the winds and waves.

順風轉舵 shùn fēng zhuǎn duò 2601

Steer round with the wind. (lit.)

To take advantage.

To dance and sing all weathers.

反 以不變應萬變（3524）Take a firm hold.

源 陸游詩：“相風使帆第一籌，隨風倒柁更何憂。”

順利進行 shùn lì jìn xíng 2602

To progress easily and favourably. (lit.)

To make headway.

反 停滯不前（2758）Get bogged down.

順手牽羊 shùn shǒu qiān yáng 2603

Lead away the sheep off hand. (lit.)

Make (Walk) away with

Walk (Make) off with

同 不問自取（0254）To make free with something.

順天者昌 shùn tiān zhě chāng 2604

He who obeys Heaven propers. (lit.)

If the mountain will not come to Mohammed, Mohammed must go to the mountain.

順應潮流 shùn yìng cháo liú 2605

To accord with the stream. (lit.)

To follow the fashion of the day.

Times change and we change with them.

Go with the tide.

同 隨大流（2654）Follow the trend.

反 逆流而上（1899）Strive against the stream.

2606 **說到做到** shuō dào zuò dào
Can do what is said. (lit.)
Live up to one's word.
Suit the action to the word.

同 言行一致（3310）Practise what you preach.
反 誇誇其談（1522）They brag most who can do the least.

2607 **說風涼話** shuō fēng liáng huà
Say windy and cool words. (lit.)
Ride a hobby.
An armchair critic.

2608 **說個沒完** shuō gè méi wán
There is no end of it to tell. (lit.)
Talk nineteen to the dozen.

同 滔滔不絕（2692）Talk a donkey's hind leg off.
反 張口結舌（3793）To be tongue-tied.

2609 **說過了頭** shuō guò le tóu
Words pass the point. (lit.)
Stretch (strain) a point.

同 言過其實（3303）Overshoot the mark.
反 輕描淡寫（2126）To skate over.

2610 **說話不算數** shuō huà bù suàn shù
Words said are not counted (at all). (lit.)
Go back on one's word.
Break (eat) one's words.

同 出爾反爾（0402）Play fast and loose.
反 誠實可靠（0364）To be on the square.

2611 **說話算數** shuō huà suàn shù
Words said are (definitely) counted. (lit.)
Live up to one's words.
To be as good as one's word.
Keep one's word.
Mean what one says.
A man of his word.
Mean business.

同 說一不二（2615）A bargain is a bargain.
反 食言而肥（2469）Go back on one's word.

2612 **說來話長** shuō lái huà cháng
It is a long account to tell. (lit.)
It's a long story (to tell).

2613 **說了就幹** shuō le jiù gàn
Having said it, just do it. (lit.)
No sooner said than done.

同 說到做到（2606）Live up to one' s word.
反 紙上談兵（3886）Talk hot air.

說時遲，那時快 2614
shuō shí chí, nà shí kuài
Slow in saying but time (has gone) fast. (lit.)
Before one can say Jack Robinson.
Before you can say knife.

同 轉瞬之間（3941）In the twinkling of an eye.

説一不二 shuō yī bù èr 2615
To say one and never (means) two. (lit.)
Mean business.
Mean what one says.
A bargain is a bargain.
A man of his word.

同 説話算數（2611）Keep one's word.
反 反覆無常（0746）Blow hot and cold.

説一套，做一套 2616
shuō yī tào, zuò yí tào
Say one set but do (another) one set. (lit.)
Say one thing and do another.
Fine words dress ill deeds.

同 好話説盡，壞事做盡（1037）The devil can cite Scripture for his purpose.
反 言行一致（3310）Suit the action to the word.

碩大無朋 shuò dà wú péng 2617
So great and no equal. (lit.)
Look as big as bull beef.

反 微不足道（2881）To be off the map.
源 詩經．唐風．椒聊："彼其之子，碩大無朋。"

司空見慣 sī kōng jiàn guàn 2618
Accustomed to seeing such things. (lit.)
Order of the day.
Par for the course.

同 比比皆是（0113）Right and left.
反 千戴難逢（2067）It only happens once in a blue moon.
源 劉禹錫詩："司空見慣渾閑事，斷盡蘇州刺史腸。"

私相授受 sī xiāng shòu shòu 2619
To give and receive secretly. (lit.)
Under the counter.

同 走後門（4025）Through backstairs influence.

思想開小差 sī xiǎng kāi xiǎo chāi 2620
The thought deserting (run wild). (lit.)
Let one's mind wander.
Lost in thought

同 心不在焉（3160）To be wool gathering.
反 全神貫注（2162）Focus one's attention on

2621 **思想狀態** sī xiǎng zhuàng tài
The state of thinking. (lit.)
Frame of mind.

2622 **撕開畫皮** sī kāi huà pí
Tear off the surface-coating of a picture. (lit.)
Take the gilt off the gingerbread.

同 剝去偽裝（0166）Cut someone down to size.
反 喬裝打扮（2096）Put up a front.

2623 **死不罷休** sǐ bú bà xiū
Death could not make one leave it. (lit.)
Hold on like grim death.

同 不到黃河心不死（0180）See Naples and then die.
反 知難而退（3856）To back out.

2624 **死不瞑目** sǐ bù míng mù
Die with eyes unshut. (lit.)
Not rest in peace.
To turn over in one's grave.

源 三國志．吳志．孫堅傳："今不夷汝三族，懸示四海，則吾死不瞑目。"

2625 **死胡同** sǐ hú tóng
A dead alley. (lit.)
A blind alley.

反 四通八達（2637）There are more ways to the wood than one.

2626 **死灰復燃** sǐ huī fù rán
Dead ashes ignite anew. (lit.)
Come to life again.
To rise like the Phoenix.
Flare up.
Stage a come back.

反 化為灰燼（1114）Reduced to ashes.
源 史記．韓長孺列傳："死灰獨不復燃乎。"

2627 **死裏逃生** sǐ lǐ táo shēng
A narrow escape from death. (lit.)
Out of the jaws of death.
Have a close brush with death.
Escape by the skin of one's teeth.
Have a narrow shave.
Get a fresh lease of life.

同 幸免於難（3222）Save one's bacon.
反 劫數難逃（1320）No flying from fate.

2628 **死氣沉沉** sǐ qì chén chén
The atmosphere is dead heavy. (lit.)
As dead as a doornail.

同 暮氣沉沉（1873）Lose one's grip.
反 生動活潑（2413）As brisk as a bee.

死生有命 sǐ shēng yǒu mìng 2629

Life and death are destined. (lit.)

Death when it comes will have no denial.

Every bullet has its billet.

源 孟子：“生死有命，富貴在天。”

死無對證 sǐ wú duì zhèng 2630

The dead can't be a witness. (lit.)

Dead men tell no tales.

反 鐵證如山（2752）Iron-clad evidence.

死硬派 sǐ yìng pài 2631

Die-hard clique. (lit.)

A die-hard.

反 風派（0804）A fence-sitter.

死於非命 sǐ yú fēi mìng 2632

To die an undestined death. (lit.)

Die in one's boots.

Hop the twig.

Come to an untimely end.

Die an unnatural death.

反 壽終正寢（2560）Sleep the final sleep.

四分五裂 sì fēn wǔ liè 2633

Four separated parts and five cracks. (lit.)

To be torn asunder.

Fall apart.

Break up.

反 團結一致（2814）To hang together.

源 漢書：“此四分五裂之國也。”

四海為家 sì hǎi wéi jiā 2634

Find a home within the four seas. (lit.)

Here today and gone tomorrow.

源 漢書 · 高帝紀：“天子以四海為家。”

四面八方 sì miàn bā fāng 2635

The four sides and eight directions. (lit.)

Here, there and everywhere.

Length and breadth.

Far and wide.

High and low.

In all directions.

Right and left.

Here and there.

源 釋道源 · 景德傳燈錄：“忽遇四面八方怎麼生。”

2636 四平八穩 sì píng bā wěn

Four flats and eight stabilities. (lit.)

As firm as a rock.

On the safe side.

On all fours.

Play safe.

Safe and sure.

反 鋌而走險（2760）Run a risk.

2637 四通八達 sì tōng bā dá

Communicating with four sides and reaching eight directions. (lit.)

Within easy reach.

There are more ways to the wood than one.

反 死胡同（2625）A blind alley.

源 子華子・晏子問黨："其途之所出，四通而八達。"

2638 四下埋伏 sì xià mái fú

To ambush on four sides. (lit.)

Lay an ambush.

2639 似是而非 sì shì ér fēi

Not such as it seems. (lit.)

Give a wrong impression.

Things are not what they are, but as they seem.

源 後漢書・章帝紀："夫俗吏矯飾外貌，似是而非。"

2640 伺機而動 sì jī ér dòng

Wait for an opportunity to act. (lit.)

Bide one's time.

Have an eye to the main chance.

2641 肆無忌憚 sì wú jì dàn

To act recklessly and fearlessly. (lit.)

In defiance of the law.

To scruple at nothing.

同 為所欲為（2894）To have one's own way.

反 投鼠忌器（2792）Burn not your house to rid the mouse.

源 禮記："小人而無忌。"

2642 鬆一口氣 sōng yī kǒu qì

To let a breath loose. (lit.)

A sigh of relief.

2643 聳入雲霄 sǒng rù yún xiāo

Towering into the clouds. (lit.)

Towering to the skies.

反 一落千丈（3420）Touch bottom.

送佛送到西天

sòng fó sòng dào xī tiān

Sending off a Buddha, send Him to reach Western Heaven. (lit.)

When you bow, bow low.

同 一不做，二不休（3378）What is worth doing at all is worth doing well. 2644

送君千里，終須一別

sòng jūn qiān lǐ, zhōng xū yī bié

Sending you off thousand miles, in the end (we) must part. (lit.)

The best of friends must part.

反 後會有期（1081）Till we meet again. 2645

搜索枯腸 sōu suǒ kū cháng

Search and get the decayed bowel. (lit.)

Rack (Cudgel) one's brains.

Beat one's brains out.

反 一揮而就（3399）Have a ready pen. 2646

源 宋 · 盧仝 · 謝孟諫議惠茶歌："三碗搜枯腸，唯有文章五千卷。"

俗不可耐 sú bù kě nài

Too vulgar to be tolerated. (lit.)

Disgustingly offensive.

To be in bad taste.

Vulgar in the extreme.

反 瀟灑出塵（3133）Neat but not gaudy. 2647

素昧平生 sù mèi píng shēng

Have never known (such person) in one's life. (lit.)

A total stranger.

Haven't had the pleasure of meeting one.

Not to know one from Adam.

反 深知底細（2402）Know the length of a person's foot. 2648

源 李商隱 · 贈田叟詩："交親得路昧平生。"

速戰速決 sù zhàn sù jué

A quick settlement through a quick battle. (lit.)

He that runs fast will not run long.

Get it over and done with.

Blitz tactics.

Make short work of

Launch a blitzkrieg.

反 穩紮穩打（2931）Slow but sure wins the race. 2649

2650 **訴苦** sù kǔ
To tell one's bitterness (complain). (lit.)
Air one's grievances.

同 大發牢騷（0515）Let off steam.
反 忍氣吞聲（2243）Swallow the leek.

2651 **訴諸武力** sù zhū wǔ lì
Appeal to force. (lit.)
Appeal to arms.
Resort to force.
Throw one's swords into the scale.

同 演全武行（3330）Fall to blows.
反 和平共處（1049）Peaceful co-existence.

2652 **隋珠彈雀** suí zhū tán què
To hit birds with jewels of Marquis Sui's. (lit.)
Not worth powder and shot.

同 得不償失（0609）The game is not worth the candle.
反 拋磚引玉（1954）Throw out a sprat to catch a mackerel.
源 莊子 · 讓王："以隋侯之珠，投千仞之雀，世必笑之。是何也，以其所用者重，所要者輕也。"

2653 **隨波逐流** suí bō zhú liú
Follow the waves and chase the current. (lit.)
Swim (Drift) with the tide.
Go with the stream.
Follow the crowd.

同 與世浮沉（3708）To drift with the stream.
反 獨善其身（0680）Better be alone than in ill company.
源 釋普濟 · 五燈會元："看風使舵，正是隨波逐流。"

2654 **隨大流** suí dà liú
Follow the big stream. (lit.)e.
Follow the crowd (trend).
Keep the common road and thou art safe.
There is safety in numbers.
Do as most men do and men will speak well of you.

同 隨波逐流（2653）Drift with the tide.
反 我行我素（2937）Take one's own cours

2655 **隨機應變** suí jī yìng biàn
Follow the change of opportunity accordingly. (lit.)
Act according to circumstances.
Rise to the emergency.
Cut your coat according to your cloth.
Stretch your legs according to your coverlet.
Play by ear.

同 見機行事（1277）Play it by ear.
反 冥頑不靈（1829）As stiff as a poker.
源 舊唐書 · 郭孝恪傳："孝恪進策太宗曰，……請固武牢，屯軍汜水，隨機應變，則易為克殄。"

隨聲附和 suí shēng fù hè 2656

To echo with the voice. (lit.)

Repeat like a parrot.

To chime in with

反 提出異議（2704）To take exception to

隨隨便便 suí suí biàn biàn 2657

At one's ease and convenience. (lit.)

To be easy going.

Free and easy.

反 認認真真（2247）In sober earnest.

隨心所欲 suí xīn suǒ yù 2658

Follow the wish of one's heart. (lit.)

At one's own sweet will.

Have it all one's own way.

At one's own discretion.

After one's own heart.

Do as one pleases.

同 如願以償（2280）To have one's will.

反 事與願違（2519）Fall short of one's expectation.

隨遇而安 suí yù ér ān 2659

To be at peace wherever one goes. (lit.)

Take things as you find them.

Being on sea, sail; being on land, settle.

Take the world as it is.

Able to sleep on a clothes-line.

Take what comes and be contented.

同 既來之，則安之（1233）Take things as they come.

反 見異思遷（1282）Grass is always greener on the other side of the hill.

源 清．劉獻廷．廣陽雜記："隨寓而安，斯真隱矣。"

歲歲年年人不同 suì suì nián nián rén bù tóng 2660

Years after years people are not the same. (lit.)

Times change and we change with them.

歲月不待人 suì yuè bú dài rén 2661

The months and years won't wait for men. (lit.)

Time and tide wait for no man.

損失殆盡 sǔn shī dài jìn 2662

The loss is completely finished. (lit.)

Bring haddock to paddock.

同 虧空破產（1532）Gone through the sieve.

反 一本萬利（3370）Light gains make heavy purses.

2663 **所費不貲** suǒ fèi bù zī

What has been spent is not little money. (lit.)

It has dipped into one's pocket.

Pay dear for one's whistle.

Pay through the nose.

反 惠而不費（1156）The cost is a mere fleabite.

2664 **所向披靡** suǒ xiàng pī mǐ

Wherever they went (the enemy) dispersed and collapsed. (lit.)

To carry all before one.

Nothing stands in one's way.

同 如入無人之境（2275）It was just a walk over.

反 潰不成軍（1533）To be put to rout.

源 漢書："漢軍皆披靡。"

2665 **所學非所用** suǒ xué fēi suǒ yòng

Whatever one learns is not what one uses. (lit.)

A round peg in a square hole.

同 不得其所（0181）Out of place.

2666 **索居閒處** suǒ jū xián chǔ

To live apart in leisure place. (lit.)

Live in seclusion.

Far from the madding crowd.

同 退隱林下（2826）Go to grass.

2667 **索然無味** suǒ rán wú wèi

Insipid and tasteless. (lit.)

As dull as ditch water.

Dry as sawdust.

Flat and insipid.

同 味如雞肋（2909）As dry as a bone.

反 津津有味（1347）Smack one's lips.

T

太平盛世 tài píng shèng shì
Peaceful and prosperous world. (lit.)
The piping times of peace.
Peace makes plenty.
Palmy days.

反 多事之秋（0704）In these eventful days. 2668

泰然自若 tài rán zì ruò
Calm and easy as before. (lit.)
At one's ease.
Take it calmly (easy).
Keep a level head.
Keep one's countenance.
Feel at home.
To be in one's element.
With perfect composure.

同 悠然自得（3623）To be carefree. 2669
反 侷促不安（1438）To be ill at ease.

泰山崩於前而目不瞬
tài shān bēng yú qián ér mù bù shùn
When the Mt. Tai avalanches in front, one's eyes do not even blink. (lit.)
If the sky falls we shall catch larks.

同 臨危不懼（1656）Face the music. 2670
反 畏首畏尾（2911）Too much taking heed is loss.

泰山壓頂 tài shān yā dǐng
Mt. Tai crushes the top. (lit.)
With the force of an avalanche.
Come down like a ton of bricks.

源 晉書．孫惠傳："烏獲摧冰，賁育拉朽，猛獸吞狐，泰山壓卵。" 2671

貪得無饜 tān dé wú yàn
Greed is never to be tired of. (lit.)
One's greed cannot be satisfied.
As greedy as a wolf.

同 我的就是我的，你的也是我的（2936）Heads I win, tails you lose. 2672
反 知足常足（3863）A contented mind is a perpetual feast.
源 左傳．昭二十八年："貪婪無厭。"

2673 **貪多務得** tān duō wù dé

The more one is greedy, the more one desires. (lit.)

The more one has, the more one desires.

As grasping as a miser.

同 貪得無饜（2672）As greedy as a wolf.

源 韓愈·進學解："貪多務得，細大不捐。"

2674 **貪他一斗米，失卻半年糧**

tān tā yī dǒu mǐ, shī què bàn nián liáng

Being greedy for one dou (Chinese unit for measuring volume) of rice, he lost half year's ration. (lit.)

Many go out for wool and come back shorn.

同 因小失大（3577）Lose a ship for a halfpenny worth of tar.

2675 **貪污腐化** tān wū fǔ huà

Being corrupt and rotten. (lit.)

Have an itching palm.

同 貪贓枉法（2676）Line one's purse.

反 廉潔清正（1618）Have clean hands.

2676 **貪贓枉法** tān zāng wǎng fǎ

Accept bribe and bend the law. (lit.)

Line one's purse (pocket).

Feather one's nest.

同 貪污腐化（2675）Have an itching palm.

反 廉潔清正（1618）Have clean hands.

2677 **談何容易** tán hé róng yì

How can it be easy to talk about. (lit.)

That's easier said than done.

Saying is one thing and doing another.

Sooner said than done.

反 輕而易舉（2124）As easy as pie.

源 漢書·東方朔傳："可乎哉，可乎哉，談何容易。"

2678 **談虎色變** tán hǔ sè biàn

Speaking of tiger makes one change colour. (lit.)

Grow pale with fear.

Have seen a wolf.

Once bitten, twice shy.

同 驚弓之鳥（1398）A burned child dreads the fire.

反 面不改容（1794）Keep a straight face.

源 歸有光·論三區水利賦役書："有光生長窮鄉談虎色變，安能默然而已。"

2679 **談情說愛** tán qíng shuō ài

Speaking of love. (lit.)

Bill and coo.

同 風流韻事（0801）Romantic affairs.

反 唇槍舌劍（0450）Speak daggers.

談天説地 tán tiān shuō dì 2680

Talk about heaven and earth. (lit.)

Talk of everything under the sun.

Shoot the breeze(bull).

曇花一現 tán huā yí xiàn 2681

The (rare) appearance of the night-blooming Cereus. (lit.)

Sudden glory soon goes out.

A wonder lasts but nine days.

A flash in the pan.

同 過眼煙雲（1002）Ephemeral grandeur.

源 妙法蓮華經．方便品第二："諸佛如來，時乃説之，如優曇缽花，時一現耳。"

罎罎罐罐 tán tán guàn guàn 2682

Pots and cans. (lit.)

Odds and ends.

Pots and pans.

坦白交代 tǎn bái jiāo dài 2683

Frankly hand over. (lit.)

Open confession is good for the soul.

To come clean.

Make a clean breast of it.

同 低頭認罪（0634）Plead guilty.

反 諱莫如深（1158）Keep one's own counsel.

忐忑不安 tǎn tè bù ān 2684

Nervous and uncomfortable. (lit.)

In a fidget.

Get hot under the collar.

To be high-strung.

To be on nettles.

Like a hen on a hot griddle.

同 心緒不寧（3192）Get out of bed on the wrong side.

反 泰然自若（2669）At one's ease.

探聽口實 tàn tīng kǒu shí 2685

To inquire and listen the truth by mouth. (lit.)

Throw out a feeler.

Pick someone's brains.

Worm out information.

Sound out someone.

Pick a person's brains.

2686 **探聽虛實** tàn tīng xū shí

To sound out if it is empty or solid. (lit.)

Throw out a feeler.

2687 **歎為觀止** tàn wéi guān zhǐ

To exclaim (with delight) seeing the (best) and stop here. (lit.)

Nothing can be better.

The pink of perfection.

同 登峰造極（0623）Reach the limit.

源 左傳．襄二十九年："觀止矣，若有他樂，吾不敢請已。"

2688 **堂堂正正** táng táng zhèng zhèng

Honourable and straight. (lit.)

With colours flying and band playing.

On the square.

Fair and square.

To be aboveboard.

同 光明磊落（0981）To be open and above-board.

反 偷偷摸摸（2784）On the sly.

源 孫子．軍爭："無要正正之旗，勿擊堂堂之陳（陣）。"

2689 **螳臂擋車** táng bì dǎng chē

Mantis tries to stop a cart with its feelers. (lit.)

To bell the cat.

Throw straw against the wind.

Kick against the pricks.

同 自不量力（3970）Bite off more than one can chew.

源 莊子．人間世："汝不知夫螳螂乎，怒其臂以當車轍，不知其不勝任也。"

2690 **躺倒不幹** táng dǎo bú gàn

To lie down and do nothing. (lit.)

To swing the lead.

Sitdown strike.

同 開小差（1476）Looking for gape-seed.

反 鞠躬盡瘁（1436）Burn oneself out.

2691 **叨陪末座** tāo péi mò zuò

To sit gratefully on the last seat. (lit.)

Sit below the salt.

Take a back seat.

同 甘拜下風（0860）Sit at a person's feet.

反 作東道主（4064）Stand treat.

2692 **滔滔不絕** tāo tāo bù jué

Like(water) rushing out endlessly. (lit.)

Talk oneself out of breath.

Talk nine words at once.

Talk a donkey's hind leg off.

Rattle off.

To talk against time.

同 絮絮不休（3253）To hold forth.

反 張口結舌（3793）To be tongue-tied.

源 王仁裕．開元天寶遺事："張九齡善談論，每與賓客議論經旨，滔滔不竭，如下阪走丸也。"

饕餮之徒 tāo tiè zhī tú 2693
A covetous and gluttonous person. (lit.)
A greedy fellow.
The Epicureans.

逃避現實 táo bì xiàn shí 2694
Escape from reality. (lit.)
Bury one's head in the sand.

逃避責任 táo bì zé rèn 2695
To evade one's duty. (lit.)
Dodge the column.
Slip the collar.
Hang aback.
Shirk responsibility.

同 開小差（1476）Desert one's colours.
反 勇挑重擔（3618）Bite off a big chunk.

逃之夭夭 táo zhī yāo yāo 2696
To have escaped. (lit.)
To be at large.
Slip away.
Take to one's heels.
Take flight.
Show a clean pair of heels.
Cut one's stick.
Cut and run.

同 溜之大吉（1677）Give one the slip.
源 詩經："有桃之夭夭。"

桃李無言，下自成蹊 2697
táo lǐ wú yán, xià zì chéng xī
Peaches and plums do not speak, but beaten tracks are formed below them. (lit.)
Good wine needs no bush.

同 有麝自然香（3665）A rose by any other name would smell as sweet.
源 漢書·李將軍列傳："諺曰，桃李不言，下自成蹊，此言雖小，可以喻大也。"

討價還價 tǎo jià huán jià 2698
To bargain for prices. (lit.)
Drive a bargain.

討厭萬分 tǎo yàn wàn fēn 2699
Tired of it ten thousand degrees. (lit.)
Bored to death.
To be browned off (with something.)

2700 **套取口供** tào qǔ kǒu gōng
Draw out the evidence from one's mouth. (lit.)
Draw a person out.
To pump someone.

2701 **特別健忘** tè bié jiàn wàng
Specially good at forgetting. (lit.)
Have a head like a sieve.

反 過目不忘（1000）Have a memory like an elephant.

2702 **特別賣力** tè bié mài lì
Specially sell one's effort. (lit.)
Lay oneself out.
Go out of one's way.

同 不遺餘力（0265）Go to all lengths.
反 開小差（1476）Looking for gape-seed.

2703 **騰雲架霧** téng yún jià wù
To mount the clouds and ride the mists. (lit.)
Travel through space.

2704 **提出異議** tí chū yì yì
Bring out different arguments. (lit.)
To take exception to
To call in question.
Raise objection.
Take the issue with

反 隨聲附和（2656）To chime in with

2705 **提高警惕** tí gāo jǐng tì
To lift high the warning and alert. (lit.)
Keep a sharp look-out.
To be on the alert.
Look sharp.

反 冷不提防（1591）Off one's guard.

2706 **提心吊膽** tí xīn diào dǎn
To lift the heart and hang the gall bladder. (lit.)
To pull up one's socks.
Have one's heart in one's mouth.
In a blue funk.
On pins and needles.
On tenterhooks.

同 七上八下（2017）Drop off the hook.
反 平生不作虧心事，半夜敲門也不驚（1991）A quiet conscience sleeps in thunder.

啼笑皆非 tí xiào jiē fēi
(One wouldn't know) either to cry or to laugh. (lit.)
Laugh on the wrong side of one's mouth.
What a cheek!

源 陳 · 樂昌公主 · 餞別自解："笑啼俱不敢，方信為人難。" 2707

醍醐灌頂 tí hú guàn dǐng
To pour cheese liquor over the head. (A Buddha phrase)(lit.)
Give a person a rub of the thumb.
To be enlightened.

源 顧況 · 華陽集 · 行路難詩："豈知灌頂有醍醐，能使清涼頭不熱。" 2708

體無完膚 tǐ wú wán fū
A body with no part of the skin left intact. (lit.)
With cuts and bruises.
Beaten black and blue.

源 段成式 · 酉陽雜俎："市里有三王子，力能揭巨石，遍身圖刺，體無完膚。" 2709

天方破曉 tiān fāng pò xiǎo
The sky begins to dawn. (lit.)
The break of day.
The crack of dawn.

同 東方發白（0662）The day is breaking.
反 夜幕低垂（3367）Under screen of night. 2710

天賦之才 tiān fù zhī cái
The talent, the fit of Heaven. (lit.)
To be cut out for
To be gifted with

同 得天獨厚（0617）Richly endowed by nature.
反 練出功夫（1619）Practice makes perfect. 2711

天各一方 tiān gè yī fāng
Each being in a different quarter of Heaven. (lit.)
Poles apart.
Poles asunder.

同 雞犬之聲相聞（1201）Within earshort.
源 蘇武詩："良友遠別離，各在天一方。" 2712

2713 **天將降大任於是（斯）人也，必先苦其心志，勞其筋骨**
tiān jiāng jiàng dà rèn yú shì rén yě, bì xiān kǔ qí xīn zhì, láo qí jīn gǔ
If Heaven is to bestow a great responsibility to a man, he must rack his brains and labour his bone and sinew. (lit.)
Storms make oaks take deeper roots.

2714 **天經地義** tiān jīng dì yì
The principles of Heaven and earth. (lit.)
A universal truth.
Matter of course
It goes without saying.

源 左傳 · 昭二十五年：“天之經也，地之義也。”

2715 **天南地北** tiān nán dì běi
Heaven south and earth north. (lit.)
As far apart as the Poles.
Poles apart.

同 相去十萬八千里（3111）A far cry from.
反 近在咫尺（1364）Just round the corner.
源 關漢卿 · 沉醉東風：“咫尺的天南地北，霎時間月缺花飛。”

2716 **天配良緣** tiān pèi liáng yuán
Good affinity matched by Heaven. (lit.)
Marriages are made in heaven.

同 赤繩繫足（0383）Marriage comes by destiny.

2717 **天生天養** tiān shēng tiān yǎng
Produced and norished by Heaven. (lit.)
God never sends mouths but he sends meat.

2718 **天生我才必有用**
tiān shēng wǒ cái bì yǒu yòng
Heaven gave me talent which must have use. (lit.)
All things in their being are good for something.
Everything is good for something.

反 朽木不可雕（3241）You cannot make a Mercury of every log.

天視自我民視，天聽自我民聽 源 語出《孟子》 2719
tiān shì zì wǒ mín shì, tiān tīng zì wǒ mín tīng
Heaven's view, the same as my people's view, Heaven's hearing, same as my people's hearing. (lit.)
The voice of the people is the voice of God.

天塌不下來 tiān tā bú xià lái 反 世界末日（2497）The crack of doom. 2720
The sky cannot fall down. (lit.)
It will be all the same a hundred years hence.

天網恢恢，疏而不漏 源 老子："天網恢恢，疏而不失。" 2721
tiān wǎng huī huī, shū ér bú lòu
Heaven's net is vast and thin but no leakage. (lit.)
Heaven's vengeance is slow but sure.
God's mill grinds slow but sure.
Justice has long arms.
Murder will out.

天無二日，民無二王 源 禮記："天無二日，土無二王。" 2722
tiān wú èr rì, mín wú èr wáng
Heaven hasn't two suns, people haven't two kings. (lit.)
No man can serve two masters.

天無絕人之路 tiān wú jué rén zhī lù 同 山重水覆疑無路，柳暗花明又一村（2332）Every cloud has a silver lining. 反 日暮途窮（2256）To be driven to the last extremity. 2723
Heaven never fails in giving a way to man. (lit.)
When one door shuts another opens.
God tempers the wind to the shorn lamb.

天下本無事，庸人自擾之 源 新唐書．陸象先傳："天下本無事，庸人擾之為煩耳。" 2724
tiān xià běn wú shì, yōng rén zì rǎo zhī
Under the Heaven nothing matters, but stupid people worry themselves. (lit.)
To bark at the moon.
Never trouble trouble till trouble troubles you.
Seek for a knot in a bulrush.

2725 **天下大亂** tiān xià dà luàn

Great confusion under the Heaven. (lit.)

In a state of turbulence.

Hell breaks loose.

反 太平盛世（2668）The piping times of peace.

2726 **天下大事，必作於細**

tiān xià dà shì, bì zuò yú xì

Great matter under the Heaven must start from the small. (lit.)

The thin end of the wedge is to be feared.

2727 **天下太平** tiān xià tài píng

Peace under the Heaven. (lit.)

All's right with the world.

同 太平盛世（2668）The piping times of peace.

反 戰火瀰漫（3786）Fire and sword.

源 呂氏春秋："天下太平，萬物安寧。"

2728 **天下烏鴉一般黑** tiān xià wū yā yì bān hēi

Under heaven all crows are equally black. (lit.)

The same holds true everywhere.

The world is much the same everywhere.

All tarred with the same brush.

2729 **天下無不散之筵席**

tiān xià wú bú sàn zhī yán xí

Under the Heaven there is no feast that does not disperse. (lit.)

Merry meet, merry part.

The longest day must have an end.

All good things come to an end.

Pleasant hours fly fast.

2730 **天下無難事，只怕有心人**

tiān xià wú nán shì, zhǐ pà yǒu xīn rén

Under the heaven no difficult thing especially if the man has the heart (for it). (lit.)

It's dogged that does it.

Where there's a will there's a way.

反 謀事在人，成事在天（1859）Man does what he can, and God what he will.

天下無完人 tiān xià wú wán rén 2731

Under the heaven no perfect man. (lit.)

No one is without his faults.

He is lifeless that is faultless.

同 金無赤金，人無完人（1342）Everyman has his faults.

天曉得 tiān xiǎo dé 2732

Heaven only knows. (lit.)

Heaven knows.

In the lap of the gods.

天涯海角 tiān yá hǎi jiǎo 2733

The horizon of Heaven and corners of the seas. (lit.)

Out-of-the-way places.

Ends of the earth.

The uttermost part of the earth.

反 近在咫尺（1364）Within calling distance.

源 游宦記聞："今之遠宦及遠服賈者，皆云天涯海角，蓋言遠也。"

天衣無縫 tiān yī wú fèng 2734

The dress of Heaven is seamless. (lit.)

Without a flaw.

Suit one down to the ground.

Fit like a glove.

Fit to a T.

同 十全十美（2461）The pink of perfection.

源 靈怪錄："有人冉冉自空而下，曰，吾織女也。徐視其衣，無縫。"

天有不測之風雲 2735

tiān yǒu bú cè zhī fēng yún

Heaven may produce unexpected wind and cloud. (lit.)

Though the sun shines, leave not your cloak at home.

A bolt out of the blue.

同 白雲蒼狗（0044）It is the unforseen that always happens.

天有不測之風雲，人有霎時之禍福 2736

tiān yǒu bú cè zhī fēng yún, rén yǒu shà shí zhī huò fú

Heaven may produce unexpected wind and cloud, men may have sudden happiness or calamity. (lit.)

It is the unforseen that always happens.

A bolt from the blue.

2737 天淵之別 tiān yuān zhī bié
The difference like between Heaven and bottom of the sea. (lit.)
A far cry from
As different as chalk is from cheese.

同 判若雲泥（1950）A world of difference.

2738 天造地設 tiān zào dì shè
Created by Heaven and put in place by earth. (lit.)
Made by nature.
Suit one down to the ground.
Suit to a T.

同 天衣無縫（2734）Fit like a glove.
反 格格不入（0895）Out of keeping with.
源 曹組賦："且山嶽之大，天造地設。"

2739 天真爛漫 tiān zhēn làn màn
Heavenly true and innocent. (lit.)
Simple and unaffected.
Wet behind the ears.
As innocent as a dove.

反 老於世故（1579）To be a man of the world.
源 吳禮部詩話．引龔開高馬小兒圖詩："天真爛漫好儀容。"

2740 天作孽猶可違，自作孽不可活
tiān zuò niè yóu kě wéi, zì zuò niè bù kě huó
If Heaven (wishes to punish one) for his sin, he may still do something, but if one sins oneself, he cannot live. (lit.)
If you leap into a well, Providence is not bound to fetch you out.
The evils we bring to ourselves are the hardest to bear.

源 孟子："天作孽猶可違，自作孽不可活，此之謂也。"

2741 恬不知恥 tián bù zhī chǐ
Not caring at all and not knowing shame. (lit.)
Thick-skinned.
Have the effrontery (face) to
Have no sense of shame.

同 厚顏無恥（1078）Have plenty of cheek.
反 於心有愧（3687）Have a guilty conscience.
源 馮贄．雲仙雜記："倪芳飲後，必有狂怪，恬然不恥。"

2742 甜言蜜語 tián yán mì yǔ
Sweet words and honeyed phrases. (lit.)
Pretty lies.
Give one a mouthful of moonshine.
Fine-sounding words.

源 宵光劍傳奇："甜言蜜語三冬煖，血污遊魂萬里沙。"

挑撥離間 tiāo bō lí jiàn 2743

Inciting and stirring up separation and driving a wedge between. (lit.)

Breed bad blood.

Stir the coals.

Sow dissension.

Play off one against the other.

Drive a wedge between

Set people at loggerheads.

Set people together by the ears.

同 惹事生非（2180）Stir up trouble.

反 排難解紛（1943）Pour oil on troubled waters.

挑三揀四 tiāo sān jiǎn sì 2744

Stir three and choose four. (lit.)

Pick and choose.

Be choosy.

反 飢不擇食（1196）Hunger finds no fault with the cookery.

跳不出如來掌心 2745

tiào bù chū rú lái zhǎng xīn

Cannot leap out of Ru-Lai's (the Buddha's) centre of his palm. (lit.)

Twist a person round one's little finger.

Under one's thumb.

At one's mercy.

同 受人擺佈（2555）To be in leading strings.

貼貼切切 tiē tiē qiè qiè 2746

Fitting closely and nicely. (lit.)

Fit like a glove.

同 天造地設（2738）Suit one down to the ground.

反 格格不入（0895）Out of keeping with

鐵杵磨成針 tiě chǔ mó chéng zhēn 2747

An iron pestle can be ground to a needle. (lit.)

Little strokes fell great oaks.

Hair by hair you will pull out the horse's tail.

Perseverance will prevail.

同 水滴石穿（2588）Constant dropping wears away the stone.

反 一曝十寒（3437）By fits and snatches.

源 源出李白少年時，遇老婦磨鐵杵作針，因發憤讀書。見《潛確類書》

鐵窗風味 tiě chuāng fēng wèi 2748

The manner and flavour (behind) an iron window. (lit.)

Polish the king's iron with one's eyebrows.

Behind bolt and bar.

2749 **鐵畫銀鉤** tiě huà yín gōu
Iron picture with silver hooks. (lit.)
Write a fair (good) hand.

同 筆走龍蛇（0116）To write with a flourish.
源 唐・歐陽詢・用筆論："徘徊俯仰，容與風流，剛則鐵畫，媚若銀鉤。"

2750 **鐵石心腸** tiě shí xīn cháng
Heart and bowels of iron and stone. (lit.)
Hard-boiled.
Heart of marble.
To be hardhearted.
Dead to all feelings.
As hard as a stone(nails).

同 無動於衷（2956）A heart insusceptible of pity.
源 皮日休賦序："余嘗慕宋廣平之為相，疑其鐵腸與石心，然睹其梅花賦，清便富艷，殊不類其為人。"

2751 **鐵樹開花** tiě shù kāi huā
When a Cycad blossoms. (lit.)
Beyond the bounds of possibility.
Pigs might fly.

源 錢謙益詩："吳儂莫向天南笑，鐵樹頻年已放花。"

2752 **鐵證如山** tiě zhèng rú shān
Iron-clad evidence(unchangeable) like a mountain. (lit.)
Iron-clad evidence.

反 死無對證（2630）Dead men tell no tales.

2753 **聽而不聞** tīng ér bù wén
Listen but do not hear. (lit.)
To hear as a hog in harvest.
None so deaf as those who won't hear.
As deaf as a post.

同 充耳不聞（0384）Turn a deaf ear to
反 言猶在耳（3311）Still ring in one's ears.
源 大學："聽而不聞。"參閱3160

2754 **聽其言而觀其行** tīng qí yán ér guān qí xíng
Listen to him but watch his behaviour. (lit.)
Handsome is as handsome does.
Of him that speaks ill consider the life more than the word.

2755 **聽其自然** tīng qí zì rán
Let things take their natural course. (lit.)
Let alone.
Live and let live.
Let things slide.
Give loose rein to something.

同 放任自流（0761）Let it run its course.

聽天由命 tīng tiān yóu mìng 2756
Let Heaven and fate decide. (lit.)
Man proposes and God disposes.
Submit to Providence.
Resigned to one's fate.
Trust to chance.
Leave things to chance.
In the lap of the gods.

同 坐以待斃（4061）A close mouth catches no flies.
反 人定勝天（2194）Everyone is the maker of his own fate.

停停打打 tíng tíng dá dǎ 2757
Stop and fight again. (lit.)
Off and on.
By fits and starts.

反 速戰速決（2649）Get it over and done with.

停滯不前 tíng zhì bù qián 2758
Stop, stagnate and not move forward. (lit.)
Get bogged down.
Mark time.
At a standstill.

同 不求上進（0242）Rest on one's laurels.
反 一往無前（3469）Press forward.

挺身而出 tǐng shēn ér chū 2759
To straighten one's body and come forward. (lit.)
Take the initiative.
Stand in the gap.
Stick up for
Gaze at the melody.

反 躲躲閃閃（0710）Wriggle like a cut snake.
源 元 · 王實甫，西廂記："小生挺身而出，作書與杜將軍。"

鋌而走險 tǐng ér zǒu xiǎn 2760
Forced to run a risk. (lit.)
Take chances.
Take a bear by the tooth.
Sail close to the wind.
Take a risk.
Run a risk.

反 明哲保身（1826）Be worldly wise and play safe.
源 左傳 · 文十七年："鋌而走險，急何能擇。"

通力合作 tōng lì hé zuò 2761
Cooperate with common effort. (lit.)
To pull together.
Play ball with someone.

同 羣策羣力（2173）Join forces.
反 各行其是（0908）Have one's own way.
源 論語朱注："通力合作，計畝均收。"

2762 **通情達理** tōng qíng dá lǐ

Understand the feeling and reach reason. (lit.)

Show good common sense.

Know what's what.

反 不通情理（0251）Have no bowels.

2763 **通融辦理** tōng róng bàn lǐ

Give some flexibility to deal with things. (lit.)

Stretch a point.

Make allowances.

反 毫不留情（1023）Pull no punches.

2764 **通宵達旦** tōng xiāo dá dàn

Throughout the night till dawn. (lit.)

From dusk to dawn.

All through the night.

The whole night through.

All night long.

Round-the-clock.

2765 **同病相憐** tóng bìng xiāng lián

Sufferers from the same illness show mutual sympathy. (lit.)

In the same boat.

Two in distress make trouble less.

Misery loves company.

Misery acquaints a man with strange bedfellows.

Company in distress makes sorrow less.

He that pities another remembers himself.

同 患難之交（1133）Foul weather friends.

反 漠不關心（1854）Devil-may-care.

源 吳越春秋・闔閭內傳："同病相憐，同憂相救。"

2766 **同牀異夢** tōng chuáng yì mèng

Share the same bed but have different dreams. (lit.)

Share the same work but not the same will.

A strange bedfellow.

An awkward bedfellow.

同 各有打算（0909）The donkey means one thing, and the driver another.

源 宋・陳亮・與朱元晦秘書書："同牀各做夢，周公且不能學得，何必一一論到孔明哉。"

同甘共苦 tóng gān gòng kǔ

2767

Sharing joy and sorrow together. (lit.)

Friendships multiply joys and divide griefs.

A sorrow shared is but half a trouble, but a joy that is shared is a joy made double.

In weal or woe.

同 有福同享，有禍同當（3647）For better or for worse.

反 有酒有肉多兄弟，急難何曾見一人（3651）In time of prosperity friends will be plenty; in time of adversity not one among twenty.

源 晉書．應詹傳："詹與分甘共苦，情若兄弟。"

同流合污 tóng liú hé wū

2768

Flow in the same stream and join with the vicious. (lit.)

Birds of a feather flock together.

Act in collusion with

Wallow in the mire with

Play into one another's hands.

同 朋比為奸（1960）Gang up with

反 潔身自好（1331）Better be alone than in bad company.

源 孟子．盡心下："同乎流俗，合乎污世。"

同明相照，同類相求

2769

tóng míng xiāng zhào, tóng lèi xiāng qiú

Same brightness illuminates each other, same kind helps each other. (lit.)

Like draws to like.

Birds of a feather flock together.

反 格格不入（0895）Out of keeping with.

源 周易．乾："同聲相連，同氣相求。"

同生死，共命運

2770

tóng shēng sǐ, gòng mìng yùn

Share the same fate, life and death. (lit.)

Cast in one's lot with

反 視如路人（2529）Cut someone dead.

同是天涯淪落人

2771

tóng shì tiān yá lún luò rén

Being also the wanderers in distress under the Heaven. (lit.)

Adversity makes strange bedfellows.

To be in the same box.

同 風雨同舟（0812）In the same boat.

源 白居易．琵琶行："同是天涯淪落人，相逢何必曾相識。"

2772 **同心協力** tóng xīn xié lì

Having the same heart make mutual effort. (lit.)

Make common cause.

Pull together.

Pool efforts.

Unite as one.

同 戮力同心（1703）To hang together.

反 各行其是（0908）Have one's own way.

源 三國演義："我三人結為兄弟，協力同心，然後可圖大事。"

2773 **同舟共濟** tóng zhōu gòng jì

Those in the same boat help one another. (lit.)

Company in distress makes sorrow less.

He that pities another remembers himself.

反 各自打算（0911）Strike out for oneself.

源 孫子・九地："夫吳人與越人相惡也，當其同舟而濟，遇風，其相救也，若左右手。"

2774 **童山濯濯** tóng shān zhuó zhuó

A bare hill with no plants. (lit.)

As bald as a coot.

Thin on top.

2775 **童顏鶴髮** tóng yán hè fà

With a lad's face and a crane's hair. (lit.).

In one's second childhood.

An old man is twice a child.

反 乳臭未乾（2283）One's mouth is full of pap.

2776 **銅皮鐵骨** tóng pí tiě gǔ

Brass skin and iron bones. (lit.)

A strong fellow.

As sound as a bell.

同 身壯力健（2395）As fit as a fiddle.

反 弱不禁風（2298）As weak as water.

2777 **捅馬蜂窩** tǒng mǎ fēng wō

Poke the hornet's nest. (lit.)

Stir up a nest of hornets.

Bring a nest of hornets about one's ears.

同 闖下彌天大禍（0439）All the fat is in the fire.

2778 **痛打一頓** tòng dǎ yī dùn

Get one beaten painfully. (lit.)

Dust a person's jacket.

Comb someone's head.

同 狠揍一頓（1061）Give a person socks.

痛改前非 tòng gǎi qián fēi 2779

Bitterly repent of former misdeeds. (lit.)

Make a fresh start.

Turn over a new leaf.

Mend one's way.

同 重新做人（0390）Start with a clean slate.
反 堅決不改（1268）To sit tight.

痛哭流涕 tòng kū liú tì 2780

To cry bitterly and shed tears. (lit.)

Break into a passion of tears.

Cry one's eyes out.

同 淚如泉湧（1589）Burst into tears.
反 笑到打滾（3150）To be helpless with mirth.
源 宋史："痛哭，流涕，極論天下事，今之賈誼也。"

痛下決心 tòng xià jué xīn 2781

Bitterly make a decision. (lit.)

To be dead set on

Set one's teeth.

Put one's foot down.

Where your will is ready, your feet are light.

反 躊躇不決（0397）Like one o'clock half struck.

偷得浮生半日閒 2782

tōu dé fú shēng bàn rì xián

Stealing half-day leisure from this floating (earthly) life. (lit.)

Let the grass grow under one's feet.

反 席不暇暖（3048）Not to have a moment one can call one's own.

偷雞不成蝕把米 tōu jī bù chéng shí bá mǐ 2783

Stealing a chicken unsuccessfully causes losing a handful of rice. (lit.)

Many go out for wool and come home shorn.

偷偷摸摸 tōu tōu mō mō 2784

Act stealthily. (lit.)

On the sly.

Up to some hangky-pangky.

Hole-and-corner.

同 暗中行事（0030）Under the rose.
反 光明磊落（0981）To be open and aboveboard.

投案自首 tóu àn zì shǒu 2785

Throw the case (to the police) and give oneself up. (lit.)

Give oneself up.

2786 **投鞭斷流** tóu biān duàn liú

Throw whips into the stream and stop its flowing. (lit.)

Their name is Legion.

同 人多勢眾（2196）There is safety in numbers.

源 晉書 · 苻堅載記："以吾之眾旅，投鞭於江，足斷其流。"

2787 **投敵叛變** tóu dí pàn biàn

Throw oneself to the enemy and revolt. (lit.)

Turn the cat in the pan.

反 忠心耿耿（3910）As true as the needle to the pole.

2788 **投河自盡** tóu hé zì jìn

Throw oneself to the river and commit suicide. (lit.)

Make a hole in the water.

同 自尋短見（4005）Make away with oneself.

2789 **投荒落草** tóu huāng luò cǎo

Run away to the wilderness (to hide) in the tall grasses. (lit.)

Take to the heather.

同 落草為寇（1716）Take to the road.

2790 **投機倒把** toú jī dǎo bǎ

Speculation and manipulation. (lit.)

Corner the market.

To be on the racket.

2791 **投其所好** tóu qí suǒ hào

To please one with what he likes. (lit.)

Suit one's fancy.

Scratch a person where he itches.

A drop of honey catches more flies than a hogshead of vinegar.

同 拍馬屁（1940）Butter someone up.

反 拂逆人意（0824）Rub one up the wrong way.

2792 **投鼠忌器** tóu shǔ jì qì

(One would not hit) the rat which has fallen into a precious vase. (lit.)

Burn not your house to rid the mouse.

Take not a musket to kill a butterfly.

反 百無禁忌（0058）To ride whip and spur.

源 漢書 · 賈誼傳："欲投鼠而忌器，此善諭也。"

投桃報李 tóu táo bào lǐ

Receive a peach and return a plum. (lit.)

Give and take.

Exchange of gifts.

Presents keep friendship warm.

One good turn deserves another.

同 禮尚往來（1601）He may freely receive courtesies that knows how to requite them. 2793

源 詩經．大雅．抑："投我以桃，報之以李。"

投閒置散 tóu xián zhì sǎn

Throw one to leisure and put to idleness. (lit.)

To be at a loose end.

Twiddle one's thumbs.

同 東遊西逛（0668）To moon about. 2794

反 忙忙碌碌（1762）As busy as a bee.

源 韓愈．進學解："投閒置散，乃分之宜。"

頭面人物 tóu miàn rén wù

Prominent figures. (lit.)

The upper ten thousand.

Big wigs.

Topnotch guys.

同 知名人士（3854）Man of great celebrity. 2795

反 無名小卒（2982）A mere nobody.

頭腦發熱 tóu nǎo fā rè

Head and brain get hot. (lit.)

To be over-anxious.

Go off the deep end (about)

Go overboard (for)

反 頭腦冷靜（2797）Have one's brain on ice. 2796

頭腦冷靜 tóu nǎo lěng jìng

Head and brain are cool and calm. (lit.)

Have one's brains on ice.

As cool as a cucumber.

反 頭腦發熱（2796）To be over-anxious. 2797

頭腦清醒 tóu nǎo qīng xǐng

Head and brain are clear and awake. (lit.)

To be all there.

Keep a level head.

Keep one's head.

反 六神無主（1687）To be all at sea. 2798

2799 頭頭是道 tóu tóu shì dào

The head and beginning are in proper way. (lit.)

To make headway.

Have the ball at one's feet.

Have the ball before one.

To be in the groove.

源 續傳燈錄 · 慧力洞源禪師："方知頭頭皆是道。"

2800 頭緒紛繁 tóu xù fēn fán

Threads of the head are numerous and complex. (lit.)

One can't see the wood for the trees.

2801 頭暈目眩 tóu yūn mù xuàn

Head giddy and eyes blurred. (lit.)

Sick as a cat.

同 蒙頭轉向（1784）Lose one's bearings.

2802 突飛猛進 tū fēi měng jìn

Sudden flying up to make great progress. (lit.)

In seven-league boots.

By leaps and bounds.

Make giant strides.

反 蝸牛上樹（2935）At a snail's pace.

2803 突擊隊 tū jī duì

Sudden attacking brigade. (lit.)

A striking force.

A shock brigade.

2804 突然襲擊 tū rán xí jī

Make a surprise attack. (lit.)

Swoop down upon

Take one by surprise.

Take one at a disadvantage.

A surprise attack.

同 攻其不備（0925）Take one napping.

反 鳴鼓而攻之（1831）Beat a charge.

2805 突如其來 tū rú qí lái

Come suddenly. (lit.)

Out of the blue.

A bolt from the blue.

Appear from nowhere.

Sally forth.

同 出乎意外（0404）Out of one's reckoning.

源 周易 · 離："突如其來。"

突兀不安 tū wù bù ān 2806
Suddenly feel uncomfortable. (lit.)
Get into a flap.
Get hot under the collar.

同 忐忑不安（2684）To be on nettles.
反 泰然自若（2669）At one's ease.

徒勞無功 tú láo wú gōng 2807
A vain labour without merit. (lit.)
A waste of effort.
A wild goose chase.
Shoe the goose.
Make ropes of sand.
Plow the sands and sow the waves.
Fruitless labour.
Beat one's head against a wall.

同 枉費心機（2865）To be a fool for one's pains.
反 練出功夫（1619）He that shoots oft shall at last hit the mark.

徒有虛名 tú yǒu xū míng 2808
Vainly possessing an empty name. (lit.)
What good can it do an ass to be called a lion?
To be a figurehead.

反 名副其實（1813）To be worthy of one's name.

土崩瓦解 tǔ bēng wá jiě 2809
Earth collapses and tiles disintegrate. (lit.)
Go to wreck (rack) and ruin.
Fall to pieces.
Fall apart.
Break up.
Go to pigs and whistle.
Collapse like a house of cards.

同 四分五裂（2633）To be torn asunder.
反 巍然屹立（2886）Firm as a rock.
源 史記・秦始皇本紀：“秦之積衰，天下土崩瓦解。”

土法上馬 tǔ fǎ shàng mǎ 2810
Native way to mount the horse. (lit.)
By rule of thumb.

吐露心情 tù lù xīn qíng 2811
Disclose one's feeling of the heart. (lit.)
Get something off one's chest.
Open one's heart (to)

同 傾吐衷情（2123）Unbosom oneself.
反 言不由衷（3295）To be mealy-mouthed.

2812 **兔起鶻落** tù qǐ hú luò

As the hare rises, the falcon swoops down. (lit.)

As swift as an arrow.

Draw the bow up to the ear.

Like a shot.

To dash off.

同 風馳電掣（0798）With lightning speed.

反 蝸牛上樹（2935）At a snail's pace.

源 郝經詩："兔起後鶻落，雲行溪水流。"

2813 **團結就是力量** tuán jié jiù shì lì liàng

Unity is strength. (lit.)

Union is strength.

Three helping one another bear the burden of six.

同 人多勢眾（2196）There is safety in numbers.

2814 **團結一致** tuán jié yí zhì

To cohere with united action. (lit.)

Hang together.

Act in unison.

同 齊心協力（2036）To join forces.

反 四分五裂（2633）To be torn asunder.

2815 **推波助瀾** tuī bō zhù lán

Help churning up waves and billows. (lit.)

Pour oil on the fire.

Add fuel to the flame.

Fan the fire.

Egg someone on.

同 火上加油（1168）Like a red rag to a bull.

反 息事寧人（3045）Take the monkey off one's back.

源 文中子．問易："真君建德之事，適足推波助瀾，縱風止燎爾。"

2816 **推己及人** tuī jǐ jí rén

Put oneself in the place of another. (lit.)

He that pities another remembers himself.

Put oneself in another's shoes.

同 老吾老以及人之老（1576）Charity begins at home.

反 人人為我（2213）Every man for himself.

源 論語．顏淵："己所不欲，勿施於人。"

2817 **推三阻四** tuī sān zǔ sì

Push away three and stop four. (lit.)

Make lame excuses.

A bad excuse is better than none.

反 勇挑重擔（3618）Bite off a big chunk.

源 荊釵傳傳奇："恁推三阻四，莫不是行濁言清。"

推食解衣 tuī shí jiě yī 2818

Cut down food and reduce clothing. (lit.)

Be a good Samaritan.

Give with a free hand.

Come down handsome.

同 濟弱扶傾（1237）Help a lame dog over a stile.

反 一毛不拔（3423）Not to part with the parings of one's nails.

源 史記："漢王解衣衣我，推食食我。"

推賢讓能 tuī xián ràng néng 2819

To cede to the worthy and yield to the able. (lit.)

Give place to your betters.

Let the best dog leap the stile first.

Let him who knows the instrument play upon it.

同 能者多勞（1893）Only an elephant can bear an elephant's load.

反 用人唯親（3621）Jobs for the boys.

源 尚書："推賢讓能。"

推卸責任 tuī xiè zé rèn 2820

To shirk responsibility. (lit.)

Pass the buck (baby).

Slip the collar.

Whip the devil round the stump.

同 逃避責任（2695）Dodge the column.

反 勇挑重擔（3618）Bite off a big chunk.

推心置腹 tuī xīn zhì fù 2821

Put someone at heart and belly. (lit.)

A heart to heart talk.

From the bottom of one's heart.

Take into confidence.

Let down one's hair.

Bare one's heart.

同 促膝談心（0472）Get knee to knee with one.

反 諱莫如深（1158）Keep one's own counsel.

源 後漢書 · 光武帝紀上："蕭王推赤心置人腹中，安得不投死乎。"

退避三舍 tuì bì sān shè 2822

Retreat to ninety li. (Chinese miles ; 30 Chinese miles = 1 she)(lit.)

Beat a retreat.

Fight shy of

同 避之則吉（0127）Give a wide berth to

反 勇往直前（3619）Forge ahead.

源 左傳 · 僖二十三年："其辟君三舍。"

退步思量事事難 2823

tuì bù sī liáng shì shì nán

Retreat and think, everything becomes difficult. (lit.)

Too much consulting confounds.

同 前怕狼，後怕虎（2077）Too much taking heed is loss.

2824 **退出舞台** tuì chū wǔ tái

To walk out of the dancing stage. (lit.)

Make one's exit.

反 粉墨登場（0793）Appear before the footlights.

2825 **退而思其次** tuì ér sī qí cì

Retreat and think of the second best. (lit.)

If you cannot have the best, make the best of what you have.

If we can't as we would, we must do as we can.

Of two evils choose the least (lesser).

Better the devil you know than the devil you don't know.

反 得寸進尺（0610）Give him an inch and he will take an ell.

2826 **退隱林下** tuì yǐn lín xià

Retire to the woods. (lit.)

Go to grass.

同 掛冠歸里（0959）Hang up one's axe.

反 大顯身手（0557）To try one's hand.

2827 **吞雲吐霧** tūn yún tù wù

Swallow cloud and blow mist. (lit.)

smoke like a chimney.

Blow a cloud.

Hit the gong.

源 梁書 · 沈約傳：“始吞雲而吐霧，終淩虛而倒景。”

2828 **屯積居奇** tún jī jū qí

Hoard up goods and take the advantage of their scare in the market. (lit.)

Hold one to something.

Corner the market.

源 史記：“奇貨可居也。”

2829 **脱口而出** tuō kǒu ér chū

Slip out of the mouth. (lit.)

Escape one's lips.

A slip of the tongue.

同 不假思索（0204）Say something off-hand.

反 咬文嚼字（3353）Talk like a book.

2830 **脱離羣眾** tuō lí qún zhòng

To free oneself from the people. (lit.)

Who does not mix with the crowd knows nothing.

同 離羣索居（1597）Keep oneself to oneself.

反 成羣結隊（0355）To muster in force.

脱穎而出 tuō yǐng ér chū 2831

The point of an awl sticking out (through a bag). (lit.)

To be head and shoulders taller.

Hit the head-line.

同 出人頭地（0410）Come to the fore.

反 平平庸庸（1989）Pass in a crowd in a push.

源 史記．平原君虞卿列傳：“使遂早得處囊中．乃脱穎而出。”

唾面自乾 tuò miàn zì gān 2832

To be spat to the face and let the saliva be dried by itself. (lit.)

Stomach an insult.

Pocket an affront.

同 忍氣吞聲（2243）Eat dirt.

源 大唐新語．容恕：“師德曰，人唾汝面，怒汝也，拭之是逆其意，止使自乾耳。”

W

2833 **挖空心思** wā kōng xīn sī

Dig deep and exhaust one's thinking. (lit.)

Rack(Cudgel) one's brains.

同 處心積慮（0430）After long deliberation.

反 不假思索（0204）Do（say）something off-hand.

2834 **歪曲篡改** wāi qū cuàn gǎi

Twist and illegally change (the document). (lit.)

To tamper with (the text).

Deliberate distortion.

反 一字不差（3499）Word for word.

2835 **外行** wài háng

Outside and not in the trade. (lit.)

A layman.

Not in one's beat.

反 老行尊（1565）A know-how.

2836 **外強中乾** wài qiáng zhōng gān

The outside is strong but the inside dried up (weak and fragile). (lit.)

On the surface only.

Rotten to the core.

Put up a bold front.

A paper tiger.

同 色厲內荏（2320）Bully are generally cowards.

源 左傳．僖十五年："張脈僨興，外強中乾。"

2837 **外圓內方** wài yuán nèi fāng

Round outside and square inside. (lit.)

A square peg in a round hole.

Strong in action, gentle in method.

An iron hand in a velvet glove.

同 軟硬兼施（2293）If the lion's skin cannot, the fox's shall.

剜肉補瘡 wān ròu bǔ chuāng 2838
Cut out a piece of flesh to mend a boil. (lit.)
Make one hole to stop up another.
The remedy is worse than the disease.

源 唐・聶夷中・傷田家詩："二月賣新絲，五月糶新穀，醫得眼前瘡，剜卻心頭肉。"

完成任務 wán chéng rèn wù 2839
Complete the mission. (lit.)
Keep one's end up.

同 大功告成（0523）Come off with honours.
反 功虧一簣（0924）Another course would have done it.

完美無缺 wán měi wú quē 2840
Perfection without blemish. (lit.)
Finished to the finger-nail.
The pink of perfection.

同 十全十美（2461）Leave nothing to be desired.
反 漏洞百出（1694）Full of loopholes.

玩火自焚 wán huǒ zì fén 2841
Play with fire and get oneself burned. (lit.)
Play with fire (edge tools).
It is ill jesting with edged tools.
He that mischief hatcheth mischief catcheth.
Put your finger into the fire, and they say it was your misfortune.

反 懲羹吹膾（0365）A burnt child dreads the fire.
源 左傳・隱四年："夫兵，猶火也，弗戢，將自焚也。"

玩世不恭 wán shì bù gōng 2842
Play with the world with no respect. (lit.)
Happy-go-lucky.
To be carefree.

紈袴子弟 wán kù zǐ dì 2843
Young fellow with fine silk breeches. (lit.)
A dandy.
Lounge lizard.
Gilded youth.

源 宋史・魯宗道傳："館閣育天下英才，豈紈袴子弟得以恩澤處耶。"

挽回局面 wǎn huí jú miàn 2844
Bring the situation back (to what it was). (lit.)
Save the situation.

同 力挽狂瀾（1606）Stem the tide.
反 不可收拾（0218）Go to pot.

2845 **萬變不離其宗** wàn biàn bù lí qí zōng
Ten thousand changes can't leave the origin. (lit.)
The fox changes his skin but not his habits.
Once a knave and always a knave.

同 江山易改，本性難移（1294）You cannot make a crab walk straight.

2846 **萬分差劲** wàn fēn chā jìn
Ten thousand times worse. (lit.)
Leave much to be desired.

2847 **萬古不變** wàn gǔ bú biàn
Unchanged for ten thousand years. (lit.)
It will be all the same a hundred years hence.

同 一成不變（3380）Hard and fast.
反 朝三暮四（3815）Chop and change.

2848 **萬古常青** wàn gǔ cháng qīng
Evergreen for ten thousand years. (lit.)
Ever new.
Their names liveth for evermore.
Keep someone's memory green.

同 永垂不朽（3612）Go down to posperity.

2849 **萬古流芳** wàn gǔ liú fāng
Leave a good name for ten thousand years. (lit.)
Leave one's mark on history.
On the scroll of fame.

反 遺臭萬年（3523）The evil that men do lives after them.

2850 **萬籟俱寂** wàn lài jù jì
Ten thousand sounds of nature are all quiet. (lit.)
In the dead of the night.
Silent as the grave.
You would have heard a pin drop.
As silent as the dead.
A dead silence.

同 鴉雀無聲（3287）Silence reigns.
反 震耳欲聾（3831）Split the ears.
源 唐 · 常建 · 題破山寺後禪院詩："萬籟此俱寂，唯聞鐘磬音。"

2851 **萬里無雲** wàn lǐ wú yún
Ten thousand miles no cloud. (lit.)
The blue expanse of heaven.

萬事大吉 wàn shì dà jí 2852

Ten thousand things great luck. (lit.)

All's well.

萬事俱備 wàn shì jù bèi 2853

Ten thousand things are all ready. (lit.)

Ready to the last gaiter button.

On one's toes.

To be all systems go.

同 準備就緒（3954）Get one's ducks in a row.

源 三國演義："萬事俱備，只欠東風。"

萬事起頭難 wàn shì qǐ tóu nán 2854

Ten thousand things are diffcult to start. (lit.)

All things are difficult before they are easy.

It is the first step which is troublesome.

The first blow is half the battle.

Well begun is half done.

Beware beginnings.

萬事如意 wàn shì rú yì 2855

Ten thousand things as one wishes. (lit.)

Everything is lovely and the goose hang high.

All as it should be.

All the world is oatmeal.

同 如願以償（2280）To have one's will.

反 大失所望（0550）Fish for a herring and catch a sprat.

萬無一失 wàn wú yì shī 2856

In ten thousand(trials) not a single failure. (lit.)

Foolproof.

Safe and sure.

Safe to win.

Under lock and key.

同 十拿九穩（2457）Feel cork sure.

反 損失殆盡（2262）Bring haddock to paddock.

萬選青錢 wàn xuǎn qīng qián 2857

From tens of thousand a green copper selected. (lit.)

The pick of the bunch.

源 唐書："張鷟登進士第，員半千數為公卿稱鷟文辭，猶青銅錢萬選萬中。"

2858 **萬應靈丹** wàn yìng líng dān

An effective pill for ten thousand ills. (lit.)

Panacea.

A cure-all.

反 心病還須心藥醫（3159）No herb will cure love.

2859 **萬丈高樓平地起**

wàn zhàng gāo lóu píng dì qǐ

Ten thousand zhang (10 feet in Chinese measurement) tall building starts from flat ground. (lit.)

A high building, a low foundation.

Great oaks from little acorns grow.

同 千里之行，始於足下（2064）He who would climb the ladder must begin at the bottom.

2860 **萬眾一心** wàn zhòng yì xīn

Ten thousand people are of one heart. (lit.)

United as one.

Of one mind.

同 眾志成城（3926）Unity is strength.

反 各有打算（0909）The donkey means one thing, and the driver another.

源 後漢書 · 朱勑傳：“萬人一心，猶不可當，況十萬乎。”

2861 **亡羊補牢，未為晚也**

wáng yáng bǔ láo, wèi wéi wǎn yě

Lost the sheep, mend the pen (now), it is not late. (lit.)

It is better late than never.

It is never too late to mend.

反 悔之晚矣（1155）Repentance comes too late.

源 戰國策 · 楚策四：“亡羊補牢，未為晚也。”

2862 **王顧左右而言他**

wáng gù zuǒ yòu ér yán tā

The emperor looking left and right, talks about other things. (lit.)

Turn the pigs into the clover.

To fob off.

同 避而不答（0124）To take the fifth.

源 孟子：“曰，四境之內不治，則如之何，王顧左右而言他。”

2863 **王婆賣瓜，自賣自誇**

wáng pó mài guā, zì mài zì kuā

The woman Wang while selling melon, boasted her goods. (lit.)

Every cook praises her own broth.

Nothing like leather.

同 賣花讚花香（1738）Every man praises his own wares.

往好處想 wǎng hǎo chù xiǎng 2864

Go to think of the good side. (lit.)

Look on the sunny (bright) side of things

反 作最壞打算（4076）If the worst comes to the worst.

枉費心機 wǎng fèi xīn jī 2865

To have wasted one's thought of the heart. (lit.)

To be a fool for one's pains.

Make a silk purse out of a sow's ear.

Go on a wild goose chase.

同 白費氣力（0038）Wash a blackamoor white.

源 元曲選・隔江鬥智："你使着這般科段，敢可也枉用心機。"

惘然若失 wǎng rán ruò shī 2866

Look blank as if lost. (lit.)

To be left up a tree.

To be all adrift.

To be at sea.

Feel lost.

反 悠然自得（3623）Free and easy.

源 後漢書・黃憲傳："同郡戴良，才高倨傲，而見憲未嘗不正容，及歸惘然若有失也。"

妄自菲薄 wàng zì fěi bó 2867

Underestimate oneself for no reason. (lit.)

A sense of inferiority.

Make oneself too cheap.

同 自暴自棄（3968）Stand in one's own light.

反 夜郎自大（3366）To be full of oneself.

源 諸葛亮・出師表："不宜妄自菲薄，引喻失義，以塞忠諫之路也。"

妄自尊大 wàng zì zūn dà 2868

Boast wildly of oneself. (lit.)

Full of conceit.

Think no small beer of oneself.

A fly on the coach wheel.

Grow too big for one's boots.

同 夜郎自大（3366）Every sprat nowadays calls itself herring.

反 自慚形穢（3971）Have an inferiority complex.

源 後漢書・馬援傳："子陽（公孫述字）井底蛙耳，而妄自尊大。"

忘恩負義 wàng ēn fù yì 2869

To be ungrateful and act contrary to justice. (lit.)

As soon as you have drunk, you turn your back on the spring.

源 元曲選・兒女團圓："他怎生忘恩負義。"

2870 望塵莫及 wàng chén mò jí

Having seen the dust (raised by the one ahead) but being unable to reach him. (lit.)

Not fit to hold a candle to one.

To be nowhere.

同 瞠乎其後（0351）Lag far behind.

反 遙遙領先（3349）Streets ahead of

源 南史："吳不解而退，琨追謝之，望塵不及矣。"

2871 望風披靡 wàng fēng pī mǐ

Watching the wind of the enemy(the soldiers) dispersed and collapsed. (lit.)

To flee pell-mell.

Beat a hasty retreat.

同 棄甲曳兵而走（2049）Run helter-skelter.

反 勇往直前（3619）Forge ahead.

源 司馬相如．上林賦："應風披靡，吐芳揚烈。"

2872 望眼欲穿 wàng yǎn yù chuān

The eyes look longingly (until) they are worn out. (lit.)

Look forward to

Hanker after

All agog.

同 望穿秋水 Hope against hope.

源 白居易．寄微之詩："白頭吟處變，青眼望中穿。"

2873 望洋興歎 wàng yáng xīng tàn

Looking over the ocean, one heaves a sigh. (lit.)

Feel helpless and powerless.

The fish that we did not catch is a very large one.

Distance lends enchantment to the view.

同 臨淵羨魚不如退而結網（1658）The end of fishing is not angling but catching.

源 莊子．秋水："於是焉，河伯始旋其面目，望洋向若而歎。"

2874 危急存亡 wēi jí cún wáng

An emergency of life and death. (lit.)

To be at stake.

反 太平盛世（2668）The piping times of peace.

2875 危急之際 wēi jí zhī jì

At a critical moment. (lit.)

At the eleventh hour.

2876 危在旦夕 wēi zài dàn xī

Impending danger at any moment. (lit.)

Hang on by the eyelids (one's eyelashes.)

Sword of Damocles.

同 火燒眉毛（1169）Imminent danger.

反 安如泰山（0014）Safe upon the solid rock.

源 三國志．吳志．太史慈傳："今管亥暴亂，北海（孔融）被圍，孤窮無援，危在旦夕。"

威風凜凜 wēi fēng lǐn lǐn 2877

One's power and authority are frightening. (lit.)

To be in a great state.

反 垂頭喪氣（0445）Hang one's head.

源 後漢書："明糾非法，宣振威風。"

威風掃地 wēi fēng sǎo dì 2878

One's powerful wind sweeps down to the ground. (lit.)

With one's tail between one's legs.

同 名譽掃地（1816）One's name is mud.

反 威風凜凜（2877）To be in a great state.

威武不屈 wēi wǔ bù qū 2879

Power and force can't bend (him). (lit.)

Refuse to yield.

Die in the last ditch.

Fall by the edge of the sword.

同 寧死不辱（1916）Take away my good name and take away my life.

反 俯首就範（0832）Give one's head for the washing.

源 孟子．滕文公下："威武不能屈。"

威信掃地 wēi xìn sǎo dì 2880

Authority and trust go down to the ground. (lit.)

Lose face.

A come down.

Loss of prestige.

同 名譽掃地（1816）Fall into disgrace.

微不足道 wēi bù zú dào 2881

So insignificant as to be not worth mentioning. (lit.)

Nothing to speak of

Not worth mentioning.

To be off the map.

同 不值一提（0283）Nothing to make a song about.

反 碩大無朋（2617）Look as big as bull beef.

微服出訪 wēi fú chū fǎng 2882

Go out visiting in plain clothes. (lit.)

Travel incognito.

反 前呼後擁（2076）With a long train of equipage.

微感不適 wēi gǎn bú shì 2883

Feeling slightly unwell. (lit.)

To feel off colour.

Out of sorts.

反 不可救藥（0213）Beyond remedy.

2884 **微乎其微** wēi hū qí wēi
How little of the little. (lit.)
A mere drop in the bucket.
Next to nothing.
One and none is all one.

同 滿坑滿谷（1746）As thick as blackberries.

2885 **微有醉意** wēi yǒu zuì yì
Having a little feeling of being drunk. (lit.)
Have an edge on.
To be half seas over.
To see double.
To be a sheet in the mind's eye.
Have a drop in one's eye.
Have a drop too much.

反 爛醉如泥（1547）Go to bed in one's boots.

2886 **巍然屹立** wēi rán yì lì
Stand impressively high like a mountain. (lit.)
Stand rock-firm.
Frim as a rock.
Towering majestically.
As steady as a rock.

同 雷打不動（1586）Take a firm hold.
反 搖搖欲墜（3348）Hang by a thread.

2887 **唯恐天下不亂** wéi kǒng tiān xià bú luàn
Only afraid the world not in chaos. (lit.)
Sow dragon's teeth.
To be eager for the fray.
Raise hell.

2888 **唯利是圖** wéi lì shì tú
Seeking profit only. (lit.)
Blinded by the love of gain.
To hog it.
Have an itching palm.
To be profit-seeking.

同 孜孜為利（3962）Chase eights and quarters.
源 左傳．成十三年：“余雖與晉出入，余唯利是視。”

2889 **唯馬首是瞻** wéi mǎ shǒu shì zhān
Only look to the head of the horse (ridden by the leader). (lit.)
Follow the lead.
Dance to one's whistle.

源 左傳．襄十四年：“荀偃令曰，雞鳴而駕，塞井夷竈，唯余馬首是瞻。”

唯命是從 wéi mìng shì cóng 2890
To obey entirely the order of. (lit.)
Do as one is told.
A yes-man.
At one's beck and call.
Under the thumb of
To be at one's service.
To be in a person's pocket.
To come to heel.
Jump through a hoop.
Do something at the drop of the hat.

同 百依百順（0061）Dance after someone's pipe.
反 我行我素（2937）Take one's own course.

唯命是聽 wéi mìng shì tīng 2891
Listen to order only. (lit.)
Dance to a person's pipe(tune)
Do one's bidding.

反 獨立自主（0678）To be on one's hook.

唯我獨尊 wéi wǒ dú zūn 2892
Only I alone the authority. (lit.)
Answer to no man.
I love my friends well, but myself better.
Look after Number One.
To be overweening.

同 我字當頭（2938）Every man for himself.
反 虛懷若谷（3245）To humble oneself.

為期不遠 wéi qī bù yuǎn 2893
Before long
In two shakes of a lamb's tail.
The appointed time will not be far. (fit.)

同 指日可待（3883）Be just around the corner.
反 遙遙無期（3350）One of these days is none of these days.

為所欲為 wéi suǒ yù wéi 2894
To do what one wishes. (lit.)
To have one's own way.

同 肆無忌憚（2641）To scruple at nothing.
反 瞻前顧後（3778）Take a look around.

為政不在多言 wéi zhèng bú zài duō yán 2895
In dealing politics one needs not speak much. (lit.)
Least talk, most work.

2896 **維持家計** wéi chí jiā jì
To support the family's finance. (lit.)
Keep the pot boiling.
Keep one's head above water.

同 為口奔馳（2915）To keep the wolf from the door.

2897 **維持現狀** wéi chí xiàn zhuàng
To maintain the present condition. (lit.)
To hold fast the status quo.
Keep the pot boiling.

2898 **維恭維謹** wéi gōng wéi jǐn
So respectful and so attentive. (lit.)
Cap in hand.
Bow and scrape.
Serve one hand and foot.

反 目空一切（1871）Have one's nose in the air.

2899 **維妙維肖** wéi miào wéi xiào
So wonderful and so alike. (lit.)
In bold relief.
True to life.
The very image of

同 栩栩如生（3251）A speaking likeness.
反 非驢非馬（0767）Neither fish nor fowl.

2900 **尾大不掉** wěi dà bú diào
The tail is too big to wag. (lit.)
Unequal to the situation.
The tail wags the dog.

源 左傳．昭十一年：“末大必折，尾大不掉。”

2901 **娓娓動聽** wěi wěi dòng tīng
Pleasing to the ear. (lit.)
Sweep one's audience along with one.
That is well spoken that is well taken.

2902 **委過於人** wěi guò yú rén
To lay the blame on others. (lit.)
Lay a fault a person's door.
Put the blame on someone.
Pass the buck.

反 代人受過（0571）To carry the can.
源 晉書：“委罪他人。”

委（萎）靡不振 wěi mǐ bú zhèn 2903

Cringed and dispirited. (lit.)

Get one's tail down.

Feel(Look)blue.

In low spirits.

Down in the dumps.

同 沒精打采（1848）With the wind taken out of one's sails.

反 精神抖擻（1390）Keep one's pecker up.

源 馬永卿輯．元城先生語錄：“至嘉佑末年，天下之事似乎舒緩，委靡不振。”

唯唯諾諾 wěi wěi nuò nuò 2904

Yes, yes, O.K, O.K. (lit.)

To be a yes-man.

Say ditto.

反 唱反調（0332）Whistle a different tune.

源 韓非子．八奸：“未命而唯唯，未使而諾諾。”

僞君子 wěi jūn zǐ 2905

A hypocrite. (lit.)

A whited sepulchre.

A wolf in sheep's clothing.

未吃五月粽，莫把寒衣送 2906

wèi chī wǔ yuè zòng, mò bǎ hán yī sòng

Having not eaten the May dumplings, don't send the winter clothings away. (lit.)

Cast never a clout till May is out.

未雨綢繆 wéi yǔ chóu móu 2907

Get prepared before it rains. (lit.)

Make hay while the sun shines.

Strike while the iron is hot.

Lay up against a rainy day.

In fair weather prepare for foul.

Though the sun shines, leave not your cloak at home.

同 防患未然（0755）Take precaution.

反 平時不燒香，急時抱佛腳（1992）Once on shore, we pray no more.

源 詩經．豳風．鴟鴞：“迨天之未陰雨，徹彼桑土，綢繆牖戶。”

位高勢危 wèi gāo shì wēi 2908

The higher the position the more dangerous the situation. (lit.)

He sits not sure who sits too high.

The highest branch is not the safest roost.

Uneasy lies the head that wears a crown.

High places have their precipices.

When the hop grows high it must have a pole.

同 人怕出名豬怕壯（2210）Too much praise is a burden.

2909 味如雞肋 wèi rú jī lèi
The taste is like chicken's ribs. (lit.)
As dry as a bone.

反 妙趣橫生 Enough to make a dog laugh.
源 三國志注："夫雞肋，棄之則可惜，食之則無所得。"

2910 味同嚼蠟 wèi tóng jiáo là
The taste is like chewing wax. (lit.)
Dry as sawdust.

同 索然無味（2667）As dull as ditch water.
反 津津有味（1347）Smack one's lips.
源 楞嚴經："當橫陳時，味如嚼蠟。"

2911 畏首畏尾 wèi shǒu wèi wěi
To fear, both head and tail. (lit.)
Too much taking heed is loss.
Full of misgivings.
Have cold feet.

同 膽小如鼠（0575）As timid as a mouse.
反 敢想敢幹（0865）To shoot one's wad.
源 左傳·文十七年："古人有言曰，畏首畏尾，身其餘幾。"

2912 畏縮不前 wèi suō bù qián
Cringing and not advancing. (lit.)
Flinch from.
Draw back.
Hang back.
Get cold feet.
Back out of
Show the white feather.
To chicken out.

反 一馬當先（3421）To be in the van.
源 宋·魏泰·東軒筆錄："及彈文彥博，則吳奎畏縮不前。"

2913 為叢驅雀 wèi cóng qū què
For the sake of the forest drive the birds away. (lit.)
To be hoisted with one's own petard.

源 孟子·離婁上："為叢驅雀者，鸇也，為湯武驅民者，桀與紂也。"

2914 為虎作倀 wèi hǔ zuò chāng
To act as an evil spirit to a tiger. (lit.)
Be an accomplice.
Hold a candle to the devil.

源 蘇軾·漁樵閑話："獵者曰，此倀鬼也，昔為虎食之人，既已鬼矣，遂為虎之役。"

2915 為口奔馳 wèi kǒu bēn chí
Running around for the mouth (for food to eat). (lit.)
To keep the wolf from the door.

同 維持家計（2896）Keep the pot boiling.

為人說項 wèi rén shuō xiàng 2916
Speak up for others. (lit.)
Put in a good word for

反 從中作梗（0469）Put a spoke in one's wheel.

為人作伐 wèi rén zuò fá 2917
Take steps (decision) for others. (lit.)
Act as a go-between.

同 穿針引線（0434）Act as a match-maker.

為人作嫁 wèi rén zuò jià 2918
(A girl) working on the bridal finery for another. (lit.)
To be a tool.
A wage slave.
Be in attendance on

反 坐享其成（4059）One beat the bush and another caught the hare.
源 秦韜王·貧女詩："苦恨年年壓金線，為他人作嫁衣裳。"

為淵驅魚 wéi yuān qū yú 2919
Helping the depth (a refuge for fish) to get rid of the fishes. (lit.)
Make a fool of oneself.
To fry in one's own grease.

源 孟子·離婁上："為淵驅魚者，獺也……為湯武驅民者，桀與紂也。"

溫柔敦厚 wēn róu dūn hòu 2920
Gentle and sincere. (lit.)
As harmless as a dove.
Have a taking way with one.
With a good grace.

同 和藹可親（1048）Easy to get along with.
反 專橫跋扈 Ride roughshod over.
源 語出《禮記·經解》

文不對題 wén bú duì tí 2921
The composition does not agree with the theme. (lit.)
Beside the point (mark).
To be wide of the mark.

同 離題萬丈（1598）Lose the thread.

文過飾非 wén guò shì fēi 2922
Whitewash a mistake and gloss over a fault. (lit.)
Gloss over faults.
Fine words dress ill deeds.
Varnishing hides a crack.
Speech was given to man to disguise his thoughts.
To whitewash something.

反 知錯認錯（3851）Confession is the first step to repentence.
源 唐·劉知幾·史通·惑經："庸儒末學，文過飾非。"

2923 **文人相輕** wén rén xiāng qīng
Men of letters despise one another. (lit.)
Two dogs over one bone seldom agree.
Two of a trade can never agree.

源 魏文帝．典論．論文："文人相輕，自古而然。"

2924 **文質彬彬** wén zhì bīn bīn
Cultured and refined. (lit.)
Manners make the man.

反 大老粗（0537）A rough diamond.
源 論語．擁也："文質彬彬，然後君子。"

2925 **聞雞起舞** wén jī qǐ wǔ
Hearing the cock's crow one rises to dance. (lit.)
Pull oneself together.

源 晉書．祖逖傳："中夜聞荒雞鳴，因起舞。"

2926 **聞一知十** wén yī zhī shí
Hearing one thing, know ten others. (lit.)
Read one's mind.
Few words to the wise suffice.

同 舉一反三（1442）A word is enough to the wise.
源 論語．公冶長："回也，聞一以知十，賜也，聞一以知二。"

2927 **聞者足戒** wén zhě zú jiè
Hearing of it is enough warning. (lit.)
Reproof never does a wise man harm.

反 笑罵由他笑罵，好官我自為之（3152）Hard words break no bones.

2928 **聞知風聲** wén zhī fēng shēng
Have heard and learned the wind and sound. (lit.)
Get wind of

同 消息靈通（3127）Have an ear to the ground.
反 一無所知（3475）To know no more than the man in the moon.

2929 **刎頸之交** wěn jǐng zhī jiāo
A cut-throat friendship. (lit.)
Damon and Pythias.

同 莫逆之交（1852）A sworn friend.
反 不共戴天之仇（0192）Deadly feud.
源 史記．廉頗藺相如列傳："卒相與歡，為刎頸之交。"

2930 **穩操勝券** wěn cāo shèng quàn
Safely holding the winning cards. (lit.)
Have the cards in one's own hand.
Have an ace up one's sleeve.
Hold all the trumps.

同 十拿九穩（2457）Feel cork sure.

穩紮穩打 wěn zhā wěn dǎ 2931

Tie securely and fight safely. (lit.)

Slow but sure wins the race.

Take no chances.

Play safe.

Play for safety.

Inch forward.

同 步步為營（0291）Pick one's steps.

反 速戰速決（2649）Get it over and done with.

問道於盲 wèn dào yú máng 2932

Ask a blind man the way. (lit.)

If the blind lead the blind, both shall fall into the ditch.

When a blind man flourishes the banner, woe be to those that follow him.

源 韓愈．問陳生書："是所謂借聽於聾，求道於盲。"

2933

問題複雜 wèn tí fù zá

The questions are complicated. (lit.)

The plot thickens.

There are wheels within wheels.

同 頭緒紛繁（2800）One can't see the wood for the trees.

2934

問心無愧 wèn xīn wú kuì

Asking one's heart, one has no shame. (lit.)

Have a clear conscience.

同 心安理得（3158）Have a easy conscience.

反 內心慚疚（1890）The prick of conscience.

蝸牛上樹 wō niú shàng shù 2935

As a snail climbing up a tree. (lit.)

At a snail's pace.

As slow as molasses winter.

同 慢條斯理（1755）Make two bites of a cherry.

反 疾如飛矢（1221）As swift an arrow.

我的就是我的，你的也是我的 2936

wǒ de jiù shì wǒ de, nǐ de yě shì wǒ de

Mine is mine, yours is also mine. (lit.)

Heads I win, tails you lose.

同 貪得無饜（2672）As greedy as a wolf.

我行我素 wǒ xíng wǒ sù 2937

I do what I normally believe. (lit.)

To be a law unto oneself.

Take one's own course.

Go one's own way.

Call one's soul one's own.

2938 我字當頭 wǒ zì dāng tóu

The word, I, comes first. (lit.)

Look after Number One.

Every man for himself.

I love my friends well, but myself better.

同 唯我獨尊（2892）To be overweening.

反 虛懷若谷（3245）Humble oneself.

2939 臥病牀笫 wò bìng chuáng zǐ

Being ill, one lies on a bed. (lit.)

To be laid up.

Keep to one's bed.

Confined to bed.

Take to one's bed.

反 恢復元氣（1147）To be on the mend.

2940 臥薪嘗膽 wò xīn cháng dǎn

Lie on firewood and taste the galls. (lit.)

Go through thick and thin.

To nurse vengeance.

同 刻苦鍛煉（1499）Go through the hoop.

源 蘇軾．擬孫權答曹操書："僕受遺以來，臥薪嘗膽。"

2941 握手言歡 wò shǒu yán huān

Shake hands and chat with pleasure. (lit.)

Come to terms.

To make it up.

Bury the hatchet.

同 言歸於好（3301）Heal the breach.

反 拳腳交加（2165）Cuff and kicks.

源 後漢書："馬援與公孫述少同里閈相善，以為既至當握手，如平生歡。"

2942 污衊誹謗 wū miè fěi bàng

Profanity and slander. (lit.)

Sling mud (dirt) at

同 欲加之罪，何患無詞（3716）Give a dog a bad name and hang him.

反 歌功頌德（0894）Chant the praises of

2943 屋漏更兼連夜雨

wū lòu gèng jiān lián yè yǔ

The roof of the house leaking plus successive nights of raining. (lit.)

It never rains but it pours.

同 禍不單行（1174）Misfortunes seldom come singly.

2944 烏合之眾 wū hé zhī zhòng

A crowd assembled like crows. (lit.)

Rag, tag and bobtail.

A scratched team.

The mob has many heads, but no brains.

反 百萬雄師（0056）Their name is Legion.

源 後漢書．耿弇傳："歸發突騎以轔烏合之眾，如摧枯拉腐耳。"

吾老矣，無能為也矣 2945
wú lǎo yǐ, wú néng wéi yě yǐ
I am old and can not do much now. (lit.)
Old bees yield no honey.
To run (go) to seed.

同 心有餘而力不足（3195）The spirit is willing, but the flesh is weak.
反 寶刀未老（0087）There's many a good tune played on an old fiddle.

吾生待明日，萬事成磋跎 2946
wú shēng dài míng rì, wàn shì chéng cuō tuó
If our life waits for tomorrow ten thousand things become missed. (lit.)
By the street of By and By one arrives at the house of Never.
Tomorrow comes never.

同 少壯不努力，老大徒傷悲（2368）Reckless youth makes rueful age.
反 一萬年太久，只爭朝夕（3467）Never put off till tomorrow what may be done today.

吳牛喘月 wú niú chuǎn yuè 2947
The buffaloes of the Wu State pant on seeing the moon. (lit.)
The scalded dog fears cold water.

同 驚弓之鳥（1398）A burned child dreads the fire.
反 初生之犢不畏虎（0427）They that know nothing fear nothing.
源 世說新語："臣如吳牛，見月而喘。"

無比興奮 wú bǐ xīng fèn 2948
Incomparable excitement. (lit.)
To be highly strung.
Great excitement.

同 心情激動（3184）To be up in the boughs.
反 沒精打采（1848）In the dumps.

無病呻吟 wú bìng shēn yín 2949
Groan without ailment. (lit.)
Full of grumbles.
Cry out before one is hurt.
The sea complains it wants water.
Make a fuss about nothing.

反 臨難不懼（1652）Look death in the face.
源 宋．辛棄疾．臨江仙詞："更歡須歎息，無病也呻吟。"

無本不生利 wú běn bù shēng lì 2950
Without capital profit will not grow. (lit.)
An empty hand is no lure for a hawk.
You must lose a fly to catch a trout.
If thou would reap money, sow money.

反 一本萬利（3370）Light gains make heavy purses.

2951 **無恥之尤** wú chǐ zhī yóu

Shameless to the extremes. (lit.)

Dead to all sense of shame.

As bold as brass.

Lost to decency (shame).

同 恬不知恥（2741）Have no sense of shame.

反 內心慚疚（1890）The prick of conscience.

2952 **無出其右** wú chū qí yòu

No one on his right. (lit.) (the first one on a winning list starts at the right.)

To be second to none.

同 無與倫比（3004）Have no equal.

源 史記・田叔傳："漢廷諸臣，無能出其右者。"

2953 **無黨無派** wú dǎng wú pài

Belong to no party and no gang. (lit.)

A free-lance.

A non-partisan.

2954 **無的放矢** wú dì fàng shǐ

Shooting arrows aimlessly. (lit.)

Shoot at rovers.

Draw a bow at a venture.

To talk without thinking is to shoot without aiming.

2955 **無地自容** wú dì zì róng

Not a place to stand on. (lit.)

To be put out of countenance.

To be nowhere.

反 出人頭地（0410）Come to the fore.

源 三國志・魏志・管寧傳："夙宵戰怖，無地自厝。"

2956 **無動於中** wú dòng yú zhōng

Cannot move one's heart (centre of a man). (lit.)

Not turn a hair.

A heart insusceptible of pity.

As hard as nail.

同 毫不動容（1020）Keep one's hair on.

反 心情激動（3184）To be up in the boughs.

2957 **無獨有偶** wú dú yǒu ǒu

Not a single one but in pair. (lit.)

Everything in the world has its counterpart.

反 舉世無雙（1440）Without peer.

無惡不作 wú è bú zuò 2958
No wicked thing that one does not do. (lit.)
Up to every evil.

同 無所不為（2993）Stop at nothing.
反 從善如流（0462）If the counsel be good, no matter who gave it.

無法無天 wú fǎ wú tiān 2959
No law and no heaven. (lit.)
Flagrant offenses.
Lawless as a town-bull.
In defiance of law.
To run riot.

同 知法犯法（3852）Set the law at defiance.
反 循規蹈矩（3280）Toe the line.

無風不起浪 wú fēng bù qǐ làng 2960
Without wind there arise no waves. (lit.)
There's no smoke without fire.
Where there is smoke there is fire.

同 事起有因（2514）Every why has a wherefore.

無隔宿之糧 wú gé sù zhī liáng 2961
No food left overnight. (lit.)
To live from hand to mouth.

反 食前方丈（2468）One's bread is buttered on both sides.

無關宏旨 wú guān hóng zhǐ 2962
Not concerning the big purposes. (lit.)
To be neither here nor there.
It matters little.

無官一身輕 wú guān yì shēn qīng 2963
Not being an official one feels light. (lit.)
Out of office, out of danger.
Far from court, far from care.

同 如釋重負（2277）Lift a weight off one's hand.
反 兼職過多（1263）Have too many irons in the fire.
源 蘇軾・賀子由生第四孫詩："無官一身輕，有子萬事足。"

無關重要 wú guān zhòng yào 2964
No concern of importance. (lit.)
That cuts no ice.
To be of little moment.

同 不足介意（0288）Of no consequence.
反 關鍵所在（0967）There's the rub（snag）.

無迴旋之地 wú huí xuán zhī dì 2965
No ground to turn around. (lit.)
Not room enough to swing a cat.

反 留有餘地（1685）Leave room for

2966 **無稽之談** wú jī zhī tán
An unfounded talk. (lit.)
Sheer nonsense.
A fishy story.
A tale of tub.
A cock and bull story.

同 放葫蘆 Pitch a yarn.
源 尚書·大禹謨："無稽之言勿聽。"

2967 **無疾而終** wú jí ér zhōng
Life ends without sickness. (lit.)
Sleep the final sleep.
Die a natural death.

同 壽終正寢（2560）Die in one's own bed
反 久病新瘥（1416）Take a fresh lease of life.

2968 **無計可施** wú jì kě shī
No plan to be executed. (lit.)
At the end of one's rope.
Up the creek without a paddle.

同 一籌莫展（3381）To be at one's wit's end.
反 足智多謀（4033）Fruitful of expedients.
源 三國演義："賊臣董卓，將欲篡位，朝中文武，無計可施。"

2969 **無濟於事** wú jì yú shì
Not helping matters. (lit.)
To be of little avail.

反 頂事（0658）Serve the purpose（turn）.

2970 **無家可歸** wú jiā kě guī
No home one can return. (lit.)
To have got the key of the street.

同 流離失所（1680）Here today and gone tomorrow.

2971 **無價之寶** wú jià zhī bǎo
Priceless treasure. (lit.)
Not to be had for love or money.

反 分文不值（0790）Not worth a rap（dump, stitch）.
源 周曇詩："寶劍能稱無價寶，行心更貴不欺心。"

2972 **無可比擬** wú kě bǐ nǐ
Cannot be compared. (lit.)
Beyond comparison.
cannot hold a candle to

同 不可企及（0214）Beyond one's reach.

2973 **無可非議** wú kě fēi yì
Cannot be criticised. (lit.)
There are no flies on him.
Beyond reproach.

反 漏洞百出（1694）Not to hold water.

無可救藥 wú kě jiù yào 2974
Cannot be saved by medicine. (lit.)
Past praying for
Beyond remedy.
There is no medicine against death.
There is no redemption from hell.

同 病入膏肓（0164）Too far gone.
反 起死回生（2041）To bring one to.

無可奈何 wú kě nài hé 2975
Cannot be helped. (lit.)
Have no alternative.
There is no help for it.
What must be must be.
Dogs gnaw bones because they can not swallow them.

同 無選擇餘地（3000）Having no alternative.
源 史記・周本紀：“太史伯陽曰，禍成矣，無可奈何。”

無可爭辯 wú kě zhēng biàn 2976
Can't be disputed. (lit.)
Cannot be argued.
Beyond dispute.

反 聚訟紛紜（1447）Opinions are divided.

無可置疑 wú kě zhì yí 2977
It can't be doubted. (lit.)
Leave no room for doubt.

同 毫無疑義（1031）A moral certainty.

無孔不入 wú kǒng bú rù 2978
Leave no opening not entered. (lit.)
Stop at nothing.
By hook or by crook.

源 蘇軾：“如水銀瀉地，無孔不入。”

無理取鬧 wú lǐ qǔ nào 2979
Kick up a row for no reason. (lit.)
Make a scene.
Pick up a quarrel with
Find fault with a fat goose.
To fly in the face of

反 以理服人（3531）Bring one to reason.
源 韓愈・答柳柳州食蝦蟆詩：“鳴聲相呼和，無理只取鬧。”

無論如何 wú lùn rú hé 2980
No matter how. (lit.)
At all events.
At any rate.
In any circumstances.

2981 無面目見江東父老
wú miàn mù jiàn jiāng dōng fù lǎo
No face and eye to see the elders at east of the river. (lit.)
To fly from the face of men.

2982 無名小卒 wú míng xiǎo zú
A petty soldier of no repute. (lit.)
A mere nobody.
A small potato.

同 小人物（3140）A small fry
反 當權派（0589）The powers that be.
源 論語：“蕩蕩乎民無能名焉。”

2983 無能為力 wú néng wéi lì
No ability to give strength. (lit.)
Beyond one's depth.

2984 無奇不有 wú qí bù yǒu
Nothing strange that one has not got. (lit.)
Pigs might fly.

2985 無情剝削 wú qíng bō xuē
Exploitation without feelings. (lit.)
Grind the faces of the poor.
To sweat a person.

2986 無任敬佩 wú rèn jìng pèi
Boundless respect and admiration. (lit.)
Take off one's hat to
To think no end of
Stand in awe of (to)
Lost in admiration.

同 五體投地（3014）Hold a person in high esteem.
反 嗤之以鼻（0378）Turn up one's nose at

2987 無傷大雅 wú shāng dà yǎ
No harm to elegance. (lit.)
Nothing worth speaking of.
It doesn't matter much.

同 無關宏旨（2962）It matters little.

2988 無聲狗，咬死人
wú shēng gǒu, yǎo sǐ rén
Noiseless dog bites one to death. (lit.)
Dumb dogs are dangerous.

無事不登三寶殿 2989
wú shì bù dēng sān bǎo diàn
If nothing one would not ascend the three precious thrones(in a temple). (lit.)
Have an axe to grind.

反 串門（0438）Go jagging.

無事可為 wú shì kě wéi 2990
Nothing one can do. (lit.)
Have time hanging on one's hands.

同 投閒置散（2794）To be at a loose end.
反 忙得不可開交（1759）To be up to one's ears in work.

無事忙 wú shì máng 2991
Busy for nothing. (lit.)
Make much ado about nothing.
A great harvest of a little corn

無事生非 wú shì shēng fēi 2992
Make trouble out of nothing. (lit.)
Make mountains out of molehills.
Stir up mud.
Kick up a row.
Put the cat among the pigeons (canaries).

反 息事寧人（3045）Pour oil troubled waters.

無所不為 wú suǒ bù wéi 2993
Nothing that one has not done (to do all the bad things). (lit.)
Go to any limit.
Up to every evil.
Stop at nothing.

同 作惡多端（4065）Up to all sorts of evils.
反 安分守己（0009）Know one's distance.
源 三國志・吳志・張溫傳："揆其奸心，無所不為。"

無所不用其極 wú suǒ bú yòng qí jí 2994
Nothing not going to the extreme. (lit.)
Go to the extreme.
Leave no stone unturned.
Stick at nothing.

反 有分有寸（3646）Know where to draw a line.
源 禮記・大學："是故君子，無所不用其極。"

無所適從 wú suǒ shì cóng 2995
Not knowing which way to follow. (lit.)
At a loss what to do.
Torn between.
Not knowing which way to turn.

同 惘然若失（2866）Feel lost.
反 心中有數（3201）Know one's own mind.
源 宋・姚寬・西溪叢語："源殊派異，無所適從。"

2996 無所事事 wú suǒ shì shì
Having nothing to do. (lit.)
At a loose end.
Twiddle one's thumbs.

同 閒暇無事（3095）Kick one's heel.
反 忙忙碌碌（1762）As busy as a bee.

2997 無往不利 wú wǎng bú lì
No going without profit. (lit.)
To get it every way.

同 從勝利走向勝利（0463）Nothing succeeds like success.
反 到處碰壁（0599）Driven from pillar to post.

2998 無微不至 wú wēi bú zhì
Never come short in the smallest detail. (lit.)
Show every concern.
Wait on one hand and foot.

同 大獻殷勤（0558）Dance attendance on
反 要理不理（3357）Leave one in the cold.

2999 無懈可擊 wú xiè kě jī
No weak point can be attacked. (lit.)
Have to fault to find with

同 完美無缺（2840）The pink of perfection.
反 破綻百出（2008）Show the cloven foot.
源 孫子・曹操注："擊其懈怠，出其空虛。"

3000 無選擇餘地 wú xuǎn zé yú dì
No ground left to choose. (lit.)
Where bad's the best, bad must be the choice.
Hobson's choice.
Having no alternative.

同 無可奈何（2975）What must be must be.

3001 無言可對 wú yán kě duì
Nothing to say in reply. (lit.)
Come to a nonplus.

同 啞口無言（3290）Be rendered speechless.
反 駁得體無完膚（0170）Have a person on toast.

3002 無業游民 wú yè yóu mín
A wanderer with no job. (lit.)
Inspector of pavements.

同 二流子（0728）A lay-about.

3003 無憂無慮 wú yōu wú lǜ
Nothing to worry about and care for. (lit.)
Happy-go-lucky.
To be carefree.
Free from care.

同 高枕無憂（0888）A good conscience is a soft pillow.
反 憂心忡忡（3625）To be on the rack.

無與倫比 wú yǔ lún bǐ 3004

Nothing to compare with. (lit.)

Second to none.

Defy all comparison.

Without parallel (peer).

Have no equal.

反 倒數第一（0600）Bring up the rear.

源 韓愈 · 論佛骨表：“數千年以來，未有倫比。”

無債一身輕 wú zhài yì shēn qīng 3005

No debt, whole body is light. (lit.)

Out of debt, out of danger.

反 負債纍纍（0844）Over head and ears in debt.

無中生有 wú zhōng shēng yǒu 3006

Begetting something out of nothing. (lit.)

A pure invention.

Sheer fabrication.

Made out of thin air.

同 向壁虛構（3118）Trump up a story.

反 鐵證如山（2752）Iron-clad evidence.

源 老子：“天下萬物生於有，有生於無。”

無足輕重 wú zú qīng zhòng 3007

Not enough to affect whether light or heavy. (lit.)

Not to matter a farthing.

同 無關重要（2964）To be of little moment.

反 舉足輕重（1443）To tilt the scales.

五彩繽紛 wǔ cǎi bīn fēn 3008

Five-coloured ribbons fluttering. (lit.)

A riot of colour.

As gaudy as a peacock.

反 黑漆一團（1059）As black as pitch.

五穀豐登 wǔ gǔ fēng dēng 3009

The five grains fully rising (in the graneries). (lit.)

A bumper harvest.

五花八門 wǔ huā bā mén 3010

Five flowers and eight doors. (lit.)

A hodgepodge.

Of every description.

源 清 · 張潮 · 虞初新志：“如平沙萬幕，八門五花。”

3011 **五日京兆** wǔ rì jīng zhào

To be in official authority for only five days. (lit.)

Short term of office.

Hang on by one's eyelashes.

同 曇花一現（2681）Sudden glory soon goes out.

源 漢書．張敞傳："五日京兆耳，安能復案事。"

3012 **五十步笑百步** wǔ shí bù xiào bǎi bù

One (drawing back from enemy) fifty paces laughs at another back hundred paces. (lit.)

An inch in a miss is as good as an ell.

A miss is as good as a mile.

A failure by however little is still a failure.

The pot calls the kettle black.

One ass nicknames another "Long ears".

源 孟子．梁惠王上："棄甲曳兵而走，或百步而後止，或五十步而後止。以五十步笑百步，則何如。"

3013 **五十而知天命** wǔ shí ér zhī tiān mìng

At fifty one should know Heaven's will. (lit.)

Life is half spent before we know what it is.

There needs a long time to know the world's pulse.

源 論語："五十而知天命。"

3014 **五體投地** wǔ tǐ tóu dì

Five members of the body (head, hands and knees) touching the ground. (lit.)

Take one's hat to

On all fours.

Throw oneself at someone's feet.

Hold a person in high esteem.

Fall on one's knees.

同 甘拜下風（0860）Sit at a person's feet.

反 鼻子朝天（0112）Cock up the nose.

源 楞嚴經："五體投地，長跪合掌，而白佛言。"

3015 **舞文弄墨** wǔ wén nòng mò

Dance with writing and play with ink. (lit.)

Chuck out ink.

Play on words.

Chop logic.

Phrase-mongering.

源 隋書．王充傳："明習法律而舞弄文物，高下其心。"

勿半途而廢 wù bàn tú ér fèi 3016
Don't give up half way. (lit.)
Never do things by halves.
Seek till you find, and you'll not lose your labour.

同 一氣呵成（3438）At a stretch.

勿避重就輕 wù bì zhòng jiù qīng 3017
Don't avoid the heavy (important) and take up the light. (lit.)
Never shirk the hardest work.

同 勇挑重擔（3618）Bite off a big chunk.

勿操之過急 wù cāo zhī guò jí 3018
Don't work in too great haste. (lit.)
Never cross a bridge till you come to it.
Draw not thy bow before thy arrow be fixed.
Easy does it.

同 三思而後行（2312）Look before you leap.
反 急如星火（1213）In hot haste.

勿打草驚蛇 wù dǎ cǎo jīng shé 3019
Don't beat the grass to frighten the snakes. (lit.)
Wake not a sleeping lion.
Let sleeping dogs lie.

勿蹈前轍 wù dǎo qián zhé 3020
Don't step on tracks of previous carriages. (lit.)
Repent what's past, avoid what is to come.

同 前車之鑒（2072）Learn wisdom by the follies of others.
反 一錯再錯（3385）Two wrongs don't make a right.

勿多管閒事 wù dūo guǎn xián shì 3021
Do not mind (other's people's) business. (lit.)
Enquire not what's in another's pot.

勿費唇舌 wù fèi chún shé 3022
Don't waste lips and tongue. (lit.)
Keep your breath to cool your porridge.

反 叨叨嘮嘮（0596）To chew the rag.

3023 勿好高騖遠 wù hào gāo wù yuǎn
Don't expect only something high and far above (like a bird). (lit.)
Hew not too high lest the chips fall in thine eye.

同 實事求是（2480）Look fact in the face.

3024 勿臨渴掘井 wù lín kě jué jǐng
Don't (wait) till you are thirsty then dig the well. (lit.)
Have not thy cloak to make when it begins to rain.

同 有備無患（3644）Forewarned is forearmed.

3025 勿落井下石 wù luò jǐng xià shí
Don't drop stones into the well (when someone has fallen there). (lit.)
Never hit a man when he is down.
Pour not water on a drowning mouse.

3026 勿失時機 wù shī shí jī
Do not miss the opportunity. (lit.)
Catch the tide.
Take fortune at the tide.
Now or never.
Take time by the forelock.
Hoist sail when the wind is fair.
Lose an hour in the morning and you'll be all day hunting for it.

同 趁機行事（0347）Make hay while the sun shines.
反 失之交臂（2449）Slip through one's fingers.

3027 勿為明日慮 wù wèi míng rì lǜ
Do not worry about tomorrow. (lit.)
Leave tomorrow till tomorrow.

同 今朝有酒今朝醉（1339）Let us eat and drink, for tomorrow we shall die.
反 人無遠慮，必有近憂（2231）He lives unsafely that looks too near on things.

3028 勿誤農時 wù wù nóng shí
Don't miss farming time (season). (lit.)
Make hay while the sun shines.
They must hunger in winter that will not work in summer.

勿小題大做 wù xiǎo tí dà zuò 3029
Don't make a small problem big. (lit.)
Take not a musket to kill a butterfly.

勿削足就履 wù xuē zú jiù lǚ 3030
Don't trim your feet to fit the shoes. (lit.)
Better cut the shoe than pinch the foot.

勿以貌取人 wù yǐ mào qǔ rén 3031
Don't judge one by his look. (lit.)
Judge not according to the appearance.
The cowl does not make the monk.
All that glitters is not gold.
Things are seldom what they seem.
You cannot know wine by the barrel.

反 先敬羅衣後敬人（3082）A smart coat is a good letter of introduction.
源 史記．仲尼弟子列傳："孔子曰，吾以貌取人，失之子羽。"

勿因人廢言 wù yīn rén fèi yán 3032
Do not abolish his words because of the man. (lit.)
Truth may sometimes come out of the devil's mouth.

勿錙銖計較 wù zī zhū jì jiào 3033
Don't be calculating over Zi and Zhu (small units of gold and silver used in ancient Chinese exchange). (lit.)
Never grudge a penny for a penny-worth.

反 一毛不拔（3423）Not to part with the parings of one's nails.

勿自尋煩惱 wù zì xún fán nǎo 3034
Don't look for your own trouble. (lit.)
Never trouble trouble till trouble troubles you.
When sorrow is asleep wake it not.
Never meet trouble half-way.

反 自討苦吃（3998）Make a rod for one's own back.

3035 **物罕為貴** wù hǎn wéi guì

Things rare are more precious. (lit.)

The worth of a thing is best known by the want of it.

Precious things are not found in heaps.

We never know the worth of water till the well is dry.

3036 **物極必反** wù jí bì fǎn

When things have come to the extreme they will certainly reverse. (lit.)

Extreme right is extreme wrong.

Extremes meet.

Too much good fortune is bad fortune.

A flow will have an ebb.

The tide never goes out so far but it always comes in again.

源 鶡冠子・環流：“物極則反，命曰環流。”

3037 **物盡其利** wù jìn qí lì

Things are fully utilized. (lit.)

Make the most of a thing.

Turn to good account.

All is grist that comes to one's mill.

3038 **物以類聚** wù yǐ lèi jù

Things of the same kind get together. (lit.)

Birds of a feather flock together.

Like draws to like.

同 人以羣分（2235）A man is known by the company he keeps.

源 周易・繫辭：“方以類聚，物以羣分。”

3039 **物質享受** wù zhì xiǎng shòu

Material enjoyment. (lit.)

Creature (material) comforts.

The loaves and fishes.

3040 **務實** wù shí

Get down to facts. (lit.)

Get down to brass tacks.

Descend to particulars.

Come down to earth.

同 實事求是（2480）Look fact in the face.

反 務虛（3041）Air one's views.

務虛 wù xū

Attend to empty (talks). (lit.)

Air one's views.

同 大發議論（0518）To enlarge oneself.

反 務實（3040）Come down to earth.

3041

誤入歧途 wù rù qí tú

Mistakely enter the wrong way. (lit.)

To have gone astray.

Drift off course.

Get lost.

同 迷失方向（1788）Lose one's bearings.

3042

X

3043 西方極樂世界 xī fāng jí lè shì jiè

The Western happiest world. (lit.)

The sweet by-and-by.

同 九泉之下（1413）In the nether world.

3044 息交絕遊 xī jiāo jué yóu

Stop social contact and cease moving about. (lit.)

Shake off the dust from one's feet.

Retire into onself.

同 深居簡出（2397）Live in seclusion.

反 串門（0438）Go jagging.

源 陶潛．歸去來辭："請息交以絕遊。"

3045 息事寧人 xī shì níng rén

Settle the matter and pacify the people concerned. (lit.)

Pour oil on troubled waters.

Take the monkey off one's back.

Patch up a quarrel.

反 惹事生非（2180）Kick up a row.

源 後漢書．章帝紀："其令有司，罪非殊死，且勿案驗，……冀以息事寧人。"

3046 稀稀落落 xī xī luò luò

Sparse and scattered. (lit.)

Few and far between.

反 擠作一團（1227）Packed like sardines.

3047 熙熙攘攘 xī xī rǎng rǎng

Coming and going of a noisy crowd. (lit.)

Hustle and bustle.

Bustling with activity.

同 絡繹不絕（1715）An endless flow.

源 史記．貨殖列傳："天下熙熙，皆為利來，天下攘攘，皆為利往。"

3048 席不暇暖 xí bù xiá nuǎn

(Sitting) not long enough to warm the mat. (lit.)

To be in a great hurry.

To be on the go.

Not to have a moment one can call one's own.

反 偷得浮生半日閒（2782）Let the grass grow under one's feet.

源 韓愈："孔席不暇暖，而墨突不得黔。"

習慣成自然 xí guàn chéng zì rán

Habit becomes natural. (lit.)

Habit is a second nature.

Custom makes all things easy.

Once a use, for ever a custom.

源 漢書："少成若天性，習慣成自然。" 3049

習以為常 xí yǐ wéi cháng

Practice becomes habitual. (lit.)

Get into the way of

Get into one's stride.

An old dog cannot alter his way of barking.

Custom reconciles us to everything.

Get used to it as a skinned eel.

源 宋 · 釋道原 · 景德傳燈錄："獅洞獠民畏鬼神，多淫祀，殺牛釃酒，習以為常。" 3050

習與性成 xí yǔ xìng chéng

Practice becomes second nature. (lit.)

Once a knave and ever a knave.

Bred in the bone.

源 尚書："茲乃不義，習與性成。" 3051

襲人故智 xí rén gù zhì

Copy others' old tricks (wisdom). (lit.)

Take a leaf out of another's book.

同 步人後塵（0293）Tread in one's footsteps.

反 自出心裁（3972）Do a thing off one's own bat. 3052

洗耳恭聽 xǐ ěr gōng tīng

To cleanse one's ears and listen respectfully. (lit.)

Prick up one's ears.

To be all ears.

Strain one's ears.

反 充耳不聞（0384）Turn a deaf ear to

源 單刀會傳奇："請君侯試說一遍，下官洗耳恭聽。" 3053

洗手不幹 xǐ shǒu bú gàn

Wash one's hand and have nothing more to do with. (lit.)

Fed up with

Wash one's hands of a business.

To be through with

反 參與其事（0302）Have a finger in the pie. 3054

3055 **洗心革面** xǐ xīn gé miàn

Purify the heart and amend the face. (lit.)

Mend one's way.

Turn over a new leaf.

反 堅決不改（1268）To sit tight.

源 周易．繫辭上：“聖人以此洗心。” 周易．革：“君子豹變，小人革面。”

3056 **喜不自勝** xǐ bú zì shèng

Excited and happy beyond control. (lit.)

Beside oneself with joy.

Happy as a lark.

Merry as a cricket.

同 樂不可支（1581）Helpless with mirth.

反 悲不自勝（0096）Be overcome with grief.

3057 **喜出望外** xǐ chū wàng wài

Joy comes unexpectedly. (lit.)

Go into rapture.

Beyond expectation.

To one's pleasant surprise.

Get more than one bargained for

To be overjoyed.

同 乞漿得酒（2039）Fish for sprats and catch a herring.

源 蘇軾．與李之儀書：“辱書尤數，喜出望外。”

3058 **喜怒無常** xǐ nù wú cháng

Inconsistant in joy and anger. (lit.)

Go into hysterics.

同 東邊日出西邊雨（0660）The devil is beating his wife with a shoulder of mutton.

反 不動聲色（0184）Keep a straight face.

源 呂氏春秋：“喜怒無處，言談日易。”

3059 **喜氣洋洋** xǐ qì yáng yáng

The face overflows with happy expression. (lit.)

Beam with joy.

Light up with pleasure.

同 其樂融融（2020）Merry as a cricket.

反 怒氣沖沖（1933）Vent one's anger.

3060 **喜形於色** xǐ xíng yú sè

An expression of delight in one's face. (lit.)

Put on a smiling face.

Radiant with joy.

A merry heart makes a cheerful countenance.

反 愁眉苦臉（0396）Pull a long face.

源 宋．孫光憲．北夢瑣言：“見其喜形於色，駐馬懇詰。”

系出名門 xì chū míng mén 3061
One came from a well-known door (family). (lit.)
To be of gentle birth.

反 出身寒微（0411）Born with a wooden spoon in one's mouth.

細水長流 xì shuǐ cháng liú 3062
Small streams flow long. (lit.)
A bit at a time.
Little by little and bit by bit.

源 清．翟灝．通俗編．地理："譬如小水長流，則能穿石。"

細味品嘗 xì wèi pǐn cháng 3063
To taste attentively and appreciate the quality. (lit.)
Enjoy the full gusto of

同 淺斟低酌（2086）Eat at pleasure, drink by measure.
反 狼吞虎嚥（1550）Have a wolf in one's stomach.

繫以縲絏 xì yǐ léi xiè 3064
To tie up with ropes. (applied to prisoner) (lit.)
Put in irons.
Put in a strait waistcoat.

瞎猜一頓 xiā cāi yí dùn 3065
Blindly make a random guess. (lit.)
Hazard a conjecture.
A shot in the dark.
Take a random shot at.

瞎搞一通 xiā gǎo yì tōng 3066
To play blindly in every way. (lit.)
Monkey (Mess) about.

瞎說 xiā shuō 3067
Talk blindly (nonsense). (lit.)
Talk rubblish.
All my eye.

同 信口雌黃（3206）Talk though one's head.
反 言之成理（3313）It stands to reason.

瞎指揮 xiā zhǐ huī 3068
Direct blindly. (lit.)
Lead someone a dance.
Lead them a chase.

同 指手劃腳（3884）Boss people about.

3069 **狹路相逢** xiá lù xiāng féng

Meeting in a narrow path. (lit.)

When Greek meets Greek, then is the tug of war.

反 風雨故人來（0811）A friend in need is a friend indeed.

源 古樂府．相逢行："相逢狹路間，道隘不容車。"

3070 **遐思逸想** xiá sī yì xiǎng

Fancy thoughts and thinking astray. (lit.)

Flight of fancy.

同 想入非非（3116）Build castles in the air.

反 事不離實（2509）Facts are stubborn things.

3071 **下定決心** xià dìng jué xīn

To make definite decision. (lit.)

Put one's foot down.

Set one's face to

To be set on

同 義無反顧（3568）With colours nailed to the mast.

反 猶疑不決（3642）Like one o'clock half-struck.

3072 **下逐客令** xià zhú kè lìng

Order to dismiss a visitor. (lit.)

Show someone the door.

Turn one out head and shoulders.

Send one into the middle of next week.

Send one about one's business.

反 倒屣相迎（0601）Give one three times three.

源 史記．秦始皇紀："秦大索逐客，李斯上書說，乃止逐客令。"

3073 **夏行冬令** xià xíng dōng lìng

The summer has the winter weather. (lit.)

As seasonable as snow in summer.

同 不合時宜（0200）Out of season.

3074 **嚇了一跳** xià le yí tiào

Jump up with fright. (lit.)

Jump out of one's skin.

One's heart leaps into one's mouth (throat).

3075 **嚇破了膽** xià pò le dǎn

Frightened to break his gall. (lit.)

To be frightened out of one's wits.

To have cold feet.

Jump out of one's skin.

反 臨危不懼（1656）If the sky falls, we shall catch larks.

先到為君，後到為臣 3076
xiān dào wéi jūn, hòu dào wéi chén
First arrival becomes king, later arrival becomes the courtier. (lit.)
He that comes first to the hill may sit where he will.

先到先得 xiān dào xiān dé 3077
First arrival gets first. (lit.)
First come, first served.
The early bird catches the first worm.

先發制人 xiān fā zhì rén 3078
Overcome one by acting first. (lit.)
To anticipate the enemy.
Steal a march on one.
Get the jump (drop) on one.
Catch the ball before the bound.
Steal one's thunder.
Take the wind out of one's sails.

同 先下手為強（3085）Forestall the enemy.
源 漢書．項籍傳："先發制人，後發制於人。"

先付後吃 xiān fù hòu chī 3079
First pay and eat afterwards. (lit.)
Pay beforehand is never well served.

先獲我心 xiān huò wǒ xīn 3080
First get my heart. (lit.)
Prepossess one favourably.

先進工作者 xiān jìn gōng zuò zhě 3081
Progressive workers. (lit.)
Salt of the earth.
A leading light.

先敬羅衣後敬人 3082
xiān jìng luó yī hòu jìng rén
First respect the good clothes and then respect the man. (lit.)
A smart coat is a good letter of introduction.
Good clothes open all doors.

同 人靠衣裳，佛靠金裝（2205）The tailor makes the man.
反 勿以貌取人（3031）Judge not according to the appearance.

3083 **先苦後甜** xiān kǔ hòu tián

First bitter, later sweet. (lit.)

No sweet without sweat.

No gain without pain.

That which was bitter to endure may be sweet to remember.

同 否極泰來（0819）They that sow in tears shall reap in joy.

反 興盡悲來（3225）He who laughs on Friday will weep on Sunday.

3084 **先禮後兵** xiān lǐ hòu bīng

Courtesy first and war later. (lit.)

Dogs bark before they bite.

源 三國演義：“劉備遠來求援，先禮後兵，主公當用好言答之。”

3085 **先下手為強** xiān xià shǒu wéi qiáng

The one who first hit with his hand is stronger. (lit.)

Better strike the first blow.

Forestall the enemy.

同 先發制人（3078）Steal one's thunder.

源 關漢卿 · 單刀赴會：“我想來先下手的為強。”

3086 **先小人，後君子** xiān xiǎo rén, hòu jūn zǐ

First be a little fellow and afterwards a gentleman. (lit.)

Beat one to it.

Be just before you are generous.

3087 **先斬後奏** xiān zhǎn hòu zòu

First cut (the head) and then report to the (emperor). (lit.)

Do something over a person's head.

源 漢書 · 申屠嘉傳：“吾悔不先斬錯乃請之。”

3088 **先正己而後正人**

xiān zhèng jǐ ér hòu zhèng rén

First put oneself right and then correct others. (lit.)

He that cannot obey cannot command.

They who live in a glass-house should not throw stones.

Know your own faults before blaming others for theirs.

He that mocks a cripple ought to be whole.

Who laughs at crooked men should walk very straight.

同 以身作則（3538）Set a good example for others.

先知先覺 xiān zhī xiān jué 3089

Man of foresight and vision. (=wise man) (lit.)

Have a long head.

同 料事如神（1647）Have great foresight.

反 事後諸葛亮（2513）It is easy to be wise after the event.

先知先覺，後知後覺 3090

xiān zhī xiān jué, hòu zhī hòu jué

Man of foresight and vision, (=wise man), and the later followers. (lit.)

What the fool does in the end, the wise man does at the beginning.

源 孟子・萬章上：“使先知覺後知，使先覺覺後覺也。”

閒得發慌 xián de fā huāng 3091

Frightfully bored to fever with too much time. (lit.)

Find time hang heavy on one's hands.

反 忙得不可開交（1759）To be up to one's ears in work.

閒極無聊 xián jí wú liáo 3092

Extremely idle and without resources. (lit.)

Twiddle one's thumbs.

Bored to death.

同 閒得發慌（3091）Find time hang heavy on one's hands.

反 忙個不了（1760）To have eggs on the spit.

閒人免進 xián rén miǎn jìn 3093

Stranger, not allowed to enter. (lit.)

No admittance.

閒時不燒香，急時抱佛腳 3094

xián shí bù shāo xiāng, jí shí bào fó jiǎo

At leisure, not to burn incense, at urgency to embrace Buddha's feet. (lit.)

The devil sick would be a monk.

閒暇無事 xián xiá wú shì 3095

At leisure, no business. (lit.)

To be at a loose end.

Kick one's heels.

Twiddle one's thumbs.

同 偷得浮生半日閒（2782）Let the grass grow under one's feet.

反 忙忙碌碌（1762）As busy as a bee.

3096 **險些兒** xiǎn xiē ér
What a danger. (lit.)
Within an ace of.

同 間不容髮（1284）By a hair's breadth.

3097 **顯而易見** xiǎn ér yì jiàn
Obvious enough and easy to see. (lit.)
As plain as a pikestaff.
Leap to the eye.
In bold relief.
He that runs may read.
Stick out a mile.

同 洞若觀火（0670）Clear as noonday.
反 莫測高深（1849）To be out of one's depth.

3098 **現出廬山真面目**
xiàn chū lú shān zhēn miàn mù
Has shown the real face of the Mt. Lu.(lit.)
Come out in one's true colours.

反 喬裝打扮（2096）Sail under false colours.

3099 **現金交易** xiàn jīn jiāo yì
Cash transaction. (lit.)
Touch pot, touch money.
No penny, no paternoster.
Pay on the nail.

3100 **現身說法** xiàn shēn shuō fǎ
Setting a personal example in speaking of the principles (of Buddhism). (lit.)
A good example is the best sermon.
An ounce of practice is worth a pound of preaching.

同 以身作則（3538）Set a good example for others.
源 楞嚴經："我於彼前，皆現其身，而為說法，令其成就。"

3101 **陷入困境** xiàn rù kùn jìng
Sinking in difficult condition. (lit.)
Get into a scrape.
Like a toad under a harrow.
To be up a tree.
To be in the soup.
Come to a pretty pass.

同 水深火熱（2594）Get into hot water.
反 渡過難關（0686）Tide over difficulties.

獻醜不如藏拙 3102

xiàn chǒu bù rú cáng zhuō

Showing off one's ugliness is not as good as hiding one's ignorance. (lit.)

Better hide one's diminished head.

Better hide one's ignorance.

反 出洋相（0420）To make an ass of oneself.

相安無事 xiāng ān wú shì 3103

Live together in peace without trouble. (lit.)

Get along fairly well.

To be on speaking terms.

Live in peace.

同 和平共處（1049）Peaceful co-existence.

反 大打出手（0511）Come to blows.

源 宋．鄧牧．伯牙琴．吏道："古者君民間相安無事。"

相當被動 xiāng dāng bèi dòng 3104

Considerably passive. (lit.)

To be in the cart.

同 不由自主（0271）In spite of oneself.

反 自動自覺（3976）Of one's own free will.

相輔相成 xiāng fǔ xiāng chéng 3105

Mutual assistance for mutual success.(lit.)

Complement (supplement) each other.

相互交往 xiāng hù jiāo wǎng 3106

Exchange visit with each other. (lit.)

Rub elbows (shoulders).

同 禮尚往來（1601）Give and take.

反 敬而遠之（1403）Keep one at arm's length.

相煎何太急 xiāng jiān hé tài jí 3107

Why fry one another so furiously. (lit.)

The axe goes to the wood where it borrows its helve.

同 自相殘殺（4004）Cut one another's throat.

反 惺惺惜惺惺（3211）Crows do not pick crow's eyes.

源 曹植詩："煮豆持作羹，漉菽以為汁，萁在釜下燃，豆在釜中泣，本是同根生，相煎何太急。"

3108 **相見好，同住難**
xiāng jiàn hǎo, tóng zhù nán
Seeing each other is good, living together is difficult. (lit.)
Familiarity breeds contempt.
Better be friends at a distance than neighbours and enemies.
The fire which lights us at a distance will burn us when near.

同 久住令人賤（1420）Wear out one's welcome.

3109 **相見恨晚** xiāng jiàn hèn wǎn
To have met each other regretfully late. (lit.)
Short acquaintance brings repentence.

源 漢書．第五倫傳："後臨去，握倫臂曰，恨相知晚。"

3110 **相去不遠** xiāng qù bù yuǎn
Not far away from here. (lit.)
At a stone's throw.
Just round the corner.
At close quarters.

同 近在咫尺（1364）Within calling distance.
反 天南地北（2715）As far apart as the poles.

3111 **相去十萬八千里**
xiāng qù shí wàn bā qiān lǐ
It is hundred and eight thousand li (Chinese mile) from here. (lit.)
As wide as the poles asunder.
Poles apart.
A far cry from

同 風馬牛不相及（0802）As different as chalk is from cheese.
反 近在咫尺（1364）Within calling distance.

3112 **相提並論** xiāng tí bìng lùn
Bring two things together in the discussion. (lit.)
Lumped together.
Put in the same class.
Place on a par.

反 不可同日而語（0219）Not to be mentioned in the same breath.
源 史記．魏其武安侯列傳："相提而論。"

相形見絀 xiāng xíng jiàn chù 3113
Comparison shows the inferior. (lit.)
Can't sustain comparison with.
Cast into the shade.
Pale beside another (by comparison).
Make one shrink small.
Take the shine out of
To be outshone.

同 小巫見大巫（3146）The moon is not seen where the sun shines.

詳情細節 xiáng qíng xì jié 3114
Detailed report with small items. (lit.)
The ins and outs.

反 簡而言之（1276）In a nutshell.

想當然 xiǎng dāng rán 3115
To think it is so. (lit.)
To take for granted.

源 後漢書．孔融傳："融與操書，稱武王伐紂，以妲己賜周公。操問出何經典。對曰，以今度之，想當然耳。"

想入非非 xiǎng rù fēi fēi 3116
To think of something fanciful. (lit.)
Imagine things.
Build castles in the air (Spain).
Have a bee in one's bonnet.
Go off into wild flights of fancy.
To be in the clouds.
Show him an egg, and instantly the whole air is full of feathers.

同 異想天開（3559）Cry for the moon.
反 腳踏實地（1310）Come down to bedrock.
源 楞嚴經："如存不存，若盡不盡，如是一類，名非想非非想處。"

餉以閉門羹 xiǎng yǐ bì mén gēng 3117
Treat one with the closed door (soup).
Leave one on the mat.
Sport one's oak.

同 閉門謝客（0120）Not at home.
反 倒屣相迎（0601）Give one three times three.
源 馮贄．雲仙雜記："待客有差別，最下者不相見，以閉門羹待之。"

向壁虛構 xiàng bì xū gòu 3118
Facing the wall to fabricate (a story). (lit.)
Trump up a story.
Sheer fabrication.
A cooked up story.

同 憑空揑造（1998）Out of thin air.
反 事不離實（2509）Facts are stubborn things.
源 說文解字序："詭更正文，鄉（向）壁虛造不可知之書。"

3119 **向上爬** xiàng shàng pá

To climb upward. (lit.)

To sweat on promotion.

Climb the social ladder.

反 掛冠歸里（0959）To bow out.

3120 **向天索價** xiàng tiān suǒ jià

Ask for a sky-high price. (lit.)

Open one's mouth wide.

同 漫天要價（1757）Quote sky-rocket prices.

反 賤價而沽（1286）Go for a song.

3121 **枵腹從公** xiāo fù cóng gōng

To attend office with an empty belly. (lit.)

Get all the kicks and none of the ha'pence.

More kicks than halfpence.

反 尸位素餐（2444）Feast at the public crib.

源 范成大："寶玩何曾救枵腹。"

3122 **削尖腦袋** xiāo jiān nǎo dài

Sharpen one's head. (lit.)

To worm oneself into

3123 **消愁解悶** xiāo chóu jiě mèn

Get rid of worry and release the gloom. (lit.)

Chase one's gloom away.

3124 **消除分歧** xiāo chú fēn qí

Eliminate the differences. (lit.)

Sink (iron out) differences.

同 排難解紛（1943）Pour oil on troubled waters.

反 挑撥離間（2743）Sow dissension.

3125 **消磨時光** xiāo mó shí guāng

Melt away time and day. (lit.)

While away the time.

Kill time.

反 分秒必爭（0785）Every minute counts.

3126 **消聲匿跡** xiāo shēng nì jì

Dissipate voice and hide footprints. (lit.)

Make oneself scarce.

同 杳如黃鶴（3352）Nowhere to be found.

反 拋頭露面（1953）Come out into the open.

消息靈通 xiāo xī líng tōng 3127

News from a well-informed source. (lit.)

Well-informed.

Have an ear to the ground.

To be in the know.

同 聞知風聲（2928）Get wind of

反 孤陋寡聞（0937）Who does not mix with the crowd knows nothing.

源 晉書："陸機語犬曰，我家絕無書信，汝能齎書取消息否。"

逍遙法外 xiāo yáo fǎ wài 3128

To wander about, being out of law. (lit.)

To be at large.

To go scot-free.

反 身陷囹圄（2390）Behind bolt and bar.

逍遙自在 xiāo yáo zì zài 3129

To wander about freely and happily. (lit.)

To be carefree.

Free and easy.

同 優哉悠哉（3631）At one's ease.

反 疲於奔命（1970）Run off one's feet.

源 五燈會元："二十四臘，逍遙自在，逢人則喜，見佛不拜。"

銷聲匿跡 xiāo shēng nì jì 3130

Make no voice and hide oneself. (lit.)

Make oneself scarce.

Drop out of sight.

同 湮沒無聞（3293）Sink into oblivion.

反 一鳴驚人（3426）Make a noise in the world.

源 宋·孫光憲·北夢瑣言："銷聲匿跡，惟恐人知。"

霄壤之別 xiāo rǎng zhī bié 3131

The difference is like between Heaven and earth. (lit.)

A world of difference.

As different as chalk is from cheese.

同 迥然不同（1409）That's a horse of another colour.

反 一模一樣（3428）Cast in the same mold.

源 抱朴子·內篇·論仙："其為不同，已有天壤之覺（較）。"

蕭規曹隨 xiāo guī cáo suí 3132

Prime minister Xiao (of West Han dynasty) made plans which were followed by his successor, Prime minister Cao. (lit.)

Go on in the same old rut.

Take a leaf out of another's book.

Follow in the footsteps (tracks).

同 依樣畫葫蘆（3512）Play the sedulous ape.

反 另起爐灶（1671）Break fresh ground.

源 揚雄·法言："蕭也規，曹也隨。"

3133 **瀟灑出塵** xiāo sǎ chū chén
Light-hearted and out of the earthly crowd. (lit.)
Neat but not gaudy.

反 俗不可耐（2647）Vulgar in the extreme.
源 孔稚圭・北山移文："耿介拔俗之標，瀟灑出塵之想。"

3134 **小不忍則亂大謀**
xiǎo bù rěn zé luàn dà móu
Being unable to endure little things will upset big plans. (lit.)
Anger and haste hinder good counsel.

源 語出《論語・衛靈公》

3135 **小懲大誡** xiǎo chéng dà jiè
Petty punishment warns against great crime. (lit.)
A stumble may prevent a fall.

源 周易・繫辭下："小懲而大誡，此小人之福也。"

3136 **小廣播** xiǎo guǎng bō
Little broadcast (lit.)
Small talk.

反 大吹大擂（0510）A flourish of trumpets.

3137 **小裏小氣** xiǎo lǐ xiǎo qì
Small capacity and narrow-minded. (lit.)
A little pot is soon hot.

反 將相頭上堪走馬，公侯肚裏好撐船（1300）Great gifts are from great men.

3138 **小人得志便猖狂**
xiǎo rén dé zhì biàn chāng kuáng
When little man gets power, he becomes a dare-devil. (lit.)
Set a beggar on horseback and he'll ride to the devil.

3139 **小人無大志** xiǎo rén wú dà zhì
Little man has no ambition. (lit.)
Little things amuse little minds.

3140 **小人物** xiǎo rén wù
Little man thing. (lit.)
A cog in the machine.
A small fry (potato).
Little frog in a big pond.

反 當權派（0589）The powers that be.

小時偷雞，大時偷牛 3141

xiǎo shí tōu jī, dà shí tōu niú

Little time (when young) steals chickens, big time (when older) steals cows. (lit.)

He that steals an egg will steal an ox.

小時偷針，大時偷金 3142

xiǎo shí tōu zhēn, dà shí tōu jīn

Little time (when young) one steals pins, big time (when older) steals gold. (lit.)

Show me a liar, and I'll show you a thief.

小事精明，大事糊塗 3143

xiǎo shì jīng míng, dà shì hú tú

In small matter bright and clear, in great matter foolish. (lit.)

Penny wise, pound foolish.

Strain at a gnat and swallow a camel.

同 揀了芝麻，丟了西瓜（1274）Spare at the spigot and spill at the bung.

小題大做 xiǎo tí dà zuò 3144

Make a issue on a small theme. (lit.)

Make a mountain out of a molehill.

A tempest in a teapot.

A storm in a teacup.

Break a butterfly on a wheel.

Fuss about trifles.

Great cry and little wool.

同 張大其詞（3790）Draw the long bow.

反 大題小做（0554）The mountain has brought forth a mouse.

小頭頭 xiǎo tóu tóu 3145

Little head. (lit.)

Chief muck of the crib.

Big frog in a small pond.

Cock of the walk.

小巫見大巫 xiǎo wū jiàn dà wū 3146

A small witch sees a giant witch. (lit.)

Not measure up to.

The moon is not seen where the sun shines.

To be cast into the shade.

同 相形見絀（3113）Cast into the shade.

源 莊子．逸篇：“小巫見大巫，拔茅而棄，此其所以終身弗如。”

3147 小心從事 xiǎo xīn cóng shì
Little heart to attend duties. (lit.)
Handle with kid gloves.

同 一絲不茍（3460）Dot one's i's and cross one's t's.
反 草草了事（0310）To huddle through.

3148 小心戒慎 xiǎo xīn jiè shèn
Little heart, careful guard. (lit.)
Take heed is a good rede.
On one's guard.

同 鄭重其事（3847）In all seriousness.
反 鹵莽從事（1700）Rush headlong.

3149 小心翼翼 xiǎo xīn yì yì
Little heart with respect and care. (lit.)
Very gingerly.
Pay minute attention.
Mind one's P's and Q's.

反 莽莽撞撞（1769）Like a bull in a china shop.
源 詩經・大雅・文王："維此文王，小心翼翼。"

3150 笑到打滾 xiào dào dǎ gǔn
Laugh till one rolling. (lit.)
In stitches.
To be helpless with mirth.
To be tickled to death.
Laugh one's head off.

反 痛哭流涕（2780）Cry one's eyes out.

3151 笑裏藏刀 xiào lǐ cáng dāo
Dagger hidden in the smile. (lit.)
Velvet paws hide sharp claws.
Feline amenities.
Stab one in the back.
To be nasty-nice.

同 口蜜腹劍（1506）A honey tongue, a heart of gall.
反 心地光明（3162）Have one's heart in the right place.
源 水滸傳："林沖道，這是笑裏藏刀，言清行濁的人。"

3152 笑罵由他笑罵，好官我自為之
xiào mà yóu tā xiào mà, hǎo guān wǒ zì wéi zhī
Let him laugh and curse, I myself will be a good official. (lit.)
Hard words break no bones.

反 聞者足戒（2927）Reproof never does a wise man harm.
源 語出《宋史》

3153 笑破肚皮 xiào pò dù pí
Splitting the belly with laughter. (lit.)
Burst one's sides with laughters.
Split one's sides.

反 哭喪着臉（1513）To sour one's cheeks.

笑容可掬 xiào róng kě jū 3154

One's smile can be plucked like (flowers). (lit.)

A face wreathed in smiles.

Beaming with joy.

同 滿面春風（1748）To be all smiles.

反 怒目而視（1932）Look daggers.

源 清・蒲松齡・聊齋誌異："容華絕代，笑容可掬。"

笑逐顏開 xiào zhú yán kāi 3155

One's face breaks into a smile. (lit.)

Beam with joy.

Be all smiles.

Be wreathed in smiles.

反 愁眉不展（0395）Mope about.

洩漏機密 xiè lòu jī mì 3156

Divulge the secret plot. (lit.)

Let the cat out of the bag.

Spill the beans.

Give oneself away.

Give the game away.

Tell tales out of school.

反 守口如瓶（2551）Keep mum.

邂逅相遇 xiè hòu xiāng yù 3157

Meet unexpectedly. (lit.)

Chance upon someone.

Run into someone.

Come across a person.

Bump into someone.

同 萍水相逢（1996）Merry meet, merry part.

源 詩經・鄭風・野有蔓草："邂逅相遇，適我願兮。"

心安理得 xīn ān lǐ dé 3158

Heart at ease and the principle is maintained. (lit.)

Have an easy conscience.

Feel justified.

Have the peace of mind.

同 問心無愧（2934）Have a clear conscience.

反 內心慚疚（1890）The prick of conscience.

源 論語："則心安而德全矣。"

心病還須心藥醫 xīn bìng hái xū xīn yào yī 3159

Heart trouble needs heart medicine to cure. (lit.)

No herb will cure love.

Like cures like.

Where love is in the case, the doctor is an ass.

3160 **心不在焉** xī bú zài yān

The heart is not here. (lit.)

Out to lunch.

To be wool gathering.

To be day-dreaming.

To be absent minded.

A brown study.

Jump the track.

同 神不守舍（2404）Lose one's presence of mind.

反 全神貫注（2162）Focus one's attention on.

源 禮記．大學："心不在焉，視而不見，聽而不聞，食而不知其味。"

3161 **心存芥蒂** xīn cún jiè dì

A knot exists in the heart. (lit.)

Have a straw to break with one.

反 推心置腹（2821）A heart to heart talk.

3162 **心地光明** xīn dì guāng míng

The heart's floor is bright and clear. (lit.)

Have one's heart in the right place.

反 心懷鬼胎（3169）Have an ulterior purpose.

3163 **心煩技癢** xīn fán jì yǎng

The heart is itching to show one's skill. (lit.)

Itch to have a go.

同 躍躍欲試（3750）Have an itch to

源 文選．潘岳．射雉賦："徒心煩而技癢。"

3164 **心煩意亂** xīn fán yì luàn

Heart troubled and mind confused. (lit.)

Tied up with knots.

Drop off the hooks.

Greatly upset.

同 心緒不寧（3192）Get out of the bed on the wrong side.

源 楚辭．卜居："心煩意亂，不知所從。"

3165 **心甘情願** xīn gān qíng yuàn

Heart contented and willing. (lit.)

With good cheer.

Of one's own accord.

On one's own initiative or free will.

3166 **心廣體胖** xīn guǎng tǐ pàng

When one's heart is broad, his body grows fat. (lit.)

Laugh and grow fat.

反 瘦骨嶙峋（2561）As lean as a rake.

源 禮記．大學："富潤屋，德潤身，人廣體胖。"

心花怒放 xīn huā nù fàng 3167

Flower of the heart in full bloom. (lit.)

Burst with joy.

One's heart sings with joy.

To be in one's glory.

反 悶悶不樂（1782）Eat one's heart out.

源 梁·簡文帝："心花成樹，共轉六塵。"

心懷惡意 xīn huái è yì 3168

The heart bears malice. (lit.)

Bear someone malice.

反 與人為善（3704）Think well of all men.

心懷鬼胎 xīn huái guǐ tāi 3169

The heart harbours ghost's embryo. (lit.)

Have an ulterior purpose.

反 胸懷坦蕩（3231）Lay one's heart bare.

心慌意亂 xīn huāng yì luàn 3170

Heart scared and mind confused. (lit.)

With one's heart going pitpat.

Have one's heart in one's mouth.

Fall into a flutter.

Lose one's head.

同 慌慌張張（1137）In a flurry.

反 勇敢果斷（3616）Take the bull by the horn.

心灰意冷 xīn huī yì lěng 3171

Heart turns ashes and mind cold. (lit.)

To lose heart.

Down in the bushes.

In the dumps.

In black despair.

反 得意洋洋（0621）In high feather.

心驚膽戰 xīn jīng dǎn zhàn 3172

Heart startled and gall bladder trembling. (lit.)

Tremble (shake) like a leaf.

Tremble with fear.

To be panic stricken.

Get cold feet.

Have one's heart in one's mouth.

Push the panic button.

Send a chill down one's spine.

同 不寒而慄（0199）Make one's teeth chatter.

3173 **心驚肉跳** xīn jīng ròu tiào

Heart startled and flesh jumping. (lit.)

Shudder with horror.

Shiver with fright.

Make one's flesh creep.

源 快心編："疑慮悽惶，心飛肉跳。"

3174 **心口如一** xīn kǒu rú yī

Heart and mouth are like one. (lit.)

What the heart thinks the tongue speaks.

Mean what one says.

Practice what one preaches.

同 由衷之言（3636）From the bottom of one's heart.

反 口是心非（1509）Speak with one's tongue in one's cheek.

3175 **心曠神怡** xīn kuàng shén yí

The heart is broad and the spirit delighted. (lit.)

In fine fettle.

Feel on top of the world.

Get out of bed on the right side.

In good spirit.

源 宋・范仲淹・岳陽樓記："心曠神怡，寵辱皆忘。"

3176 **心勞日拙** xīn láo rì zhuō

The heart is laboured and getting worse day by day. (lit.)

To be a fool for one's pains.

To find a mare's nest.

同 枉費心機（2865）Make a silk purse out of a sow's ear.

反 得心應手（0618）As clay in the hands of the potter.

源 尚書・周官："作德心逸日休，作偽心勞日拙。"

3177 **心力交瘁** xīn lì jiāo cuì

Both the heart and strength are exhausted. (lit.)

Burn the candle at both ends.

Dead beat.

源 梁書："吾年時朽暮，心力稍殫。"

3178 **心領神會** xīn lǐng shén huì

The heart receives and the spirit understands. (lit.)

To be on the beam.

Have a thorough grasp.

源 明・李東陽・懷麓堂詩話："苟非心領神會，雖日提耳而教之，無益也。"

心亂如麻 xīn luàn rú má 3179
The heart is confused like entangled hemp. (lit.)
To be in a state (a stew).
Greatly upset.
Out of one's mind.

心滿意足 xīn mǎn yì zú 3180
Heart and mind are fully satisfied. (lit.)
Pat oneself on the back.
To one's heart's content.
After one's own heart.
Rest on one's laurels.
Warm the cockles of one's heart.
Look like the cat that ate (swallowed) the canary.

同 如願以償（2280）To have one's will.

心平氣和 xīn píng qì hé 3181
The heart is calm and spirit peaceful. (lit.)
Keep cool.
Compose oneself.
Cool as a cucumber.

同 平心靜氣（1993）Keep one's shirt on.
反 怒氣沖沖（1933）Fuming with anger.
源 蘇軾．菜羹賦："先生心平而氣和，故雖老而體胖。"

心情沉重 xīn qíng chén zhòng 3182
The feeling of the heart sinks heavily. (lit.)
One's heart sinks.

反 心情舒暢（3187）Get out of bed on the right side.

心情低落 xīn qíng dī luò 3183
Feeling of the heart drops low. (lit.)
Down in the mouth.
To be a peg too low.
Have one's heart in one's boots.

同 意氣消沉（3563）To be in the doldrum.
反 精神振奮（1395）Feeling on top of the world.

心情激動 xīn qíng jī dòng 3184
The heart's feeling is excited. (lit.)
Have a lump in one's throat.
To be up in the boughs.
To be in a lather.

反 無動於衷（2956）Not turn a hair.

3185 **心情焦躁** xīn qíng jiāo zào

The heart feels anxious and impatient. (lit.)

Ill at ease.

Hot and bothered.

To be in a stew.

同 坐立不安（4053）Have ants in one's pants.

反 處之泰然（0431）Take it coolly.

3186 **心情緊張** xīn qíng jǐn zhāng

To be keyed up.

All het up.

The heart feels tense.

反 悠然自得（3623）Free and easy.

3187 **心情舒暢** xīn qíng shū chàng

The heart feels cheerful. (lit.)

As happy as a sand-boy.

Get out of bed on the right side.

同 心曠神怡（3175）Feel on top of the world.

反 嘔氣（1937）Fret one's gizzard.

3188 **心如刀割** xīn rú dāo gē

The heart is like being cut by a knife. (lit.)

Cut one to the heart.

Make one's heart bleed.

The iron entered into his soul.

3189 **心神不定** xīn shén bú dìng

Both the heart and spirit are unsettled. (lit.)

Have a bee in one's bonnet.

To have the fidgets.

同 精神恍惚（1392）One's mind wanders.

源 獨異志："李廣夜夢一人曰，我心神也，君役我太苦。"

3190 **心生一計** xīn shēng yí jì

The heart bears a plan. (lit.)

Hit upon an idea.

An idea strikes one.

同 靈機一動（1666）Have a brilliant inspiration.

反 一籌莫展（3381）At one's wit's end.

3191 **心胸狹隘** xīn xiōng xiá ài

The heart and chest (mind) are narrow. (lit.)

To be narrow-minded.

A little pot is soon hot.

反 胸懷坦蕩（3231）As open as day.

心緒不寧 xīn xù bù níng

The state of the heart is not at ease. (lit.)

Get out of bed on the wrong side.

In a flutter.

同 忐忑不安（2684）Like a hen on a hot griddle.

反 心安理得（3158）Have an easy conscience.

3192

心血來潮 xīn xuè lái cháo

The tide of the blood rises from the heart. (lit.)

On the impulse of the moment.

同 倉猝之間（0304）On the spur of the moment.

反 蓄謀已久（3254）Done in cold blood.

3193

心有成見 xīn yǒu chéng jiàn

The heart has prejudice. (lit.)

Look through blue glasses.

Look through coloured spectacles.

3194

心有餘而力不足

xīn yǒu yú ér lì bù zú

Plenty of heart but not enough strength. (lit.)

The spirit is willing, but the flesh is weak.

Old bees yield no honey.

Bite off more than one can chew.

同 力不從心（1602）Beyond one's tether.

反 餘勇可賈（3696）Enough and to spare.

3195

心有餘悸 xīn yǒu yú jì

The heart still has fear. (lit.)

A burned child dreads the fire.

Once bitten, twice sky.

He has seen a wolf.

反 毫無顧慮（1027）Make no scruple of

3196

心猿意馬 xīn yuán yì mǎ

While his heart means a gibbon, he thinks of a horse. (lit.)

Run with the hound and hold with the hare.

Carry fire in one hand and water in the other.

源 參同契注：“心猿不定，意馬四馳。”

3197

心照不宣 xīn zhào bù xuān

It is understood at heart but not expressed. (lit.)

Between you and me and the post.

源 潘岳．夏侯常侍誄：“心照神交，唯我與子。”

3198

3199 心直口快 xīn zhí kǒu kuài
Heart straight and mouth quick. (lit.)
Nearest the heart, nearest the mouth.
What the heart thinks the tongue speaks.
Frank and out-spoken.

同 知無不言，言無不盡（3861）Lay one's heart bare.
反 支吾其詞（3849）To hum and haw.
源 元曲選・張國賓・羅李郎："哥哥是心直口快射糧軍。"

3200 心中好笑 xīn zhōng hǎo xiào
Good laugh at heart. (lit.)
To laugh in one's sleeve.
Laugh in one's beard.

反 怒形於色（1934）Purple with rage.

3201 心中有數 xīn zhōng yǒu shù
There is calculation at heart. (lit.)
Know what's what.
Know one's own mind.
Know it as well as a beggar knows his bag.

同 胸有成竹（3233）Know the ropes.
反 一籌莫展（3381）To be at one's wit's end.

3202 欣喜若狂 xīn xǐ ruò kuáng
Mad with joy and happiness. (lit.)
Leap with joy.
Go into raptures.
Franctic (mad, wild) with joy.
To be on cloud nine.

同 雀躍三百（2171）Jump for joy.
反 悲痛欲絕（0098）Torn with grief.

3203 欣欣向榮 xīn xīn xiàng róng
Joyous and prosperous. (lit.)
Flourish like the green bay-tree.

同 雨後春筍（3700）Spring up like mushrooms.
源 陶潛・歸去來辭："木欣欣以向榮，泉涓涓而始流。"

3204 新官上任三把火
xīn guān shàng rèn sān bǎ huǒ
New official being appointed has three bundles of fire. (lit.)
A new broom sweeps clean.

3205 新生力量 xīn shēng lì liàng
New life strength. (lit.)
New blood.

同 年青一代（1908）The rising generation.

信口雌黃 xìn kǒu cí huáng 3206

Talk as freely as one can daub yellow ocher (on paper). (lit.)

Talk through one's hat.

Speak through the back of one's neck.

With a tongue too long for one's teeth.

Talk glibly.

同 大放厥詞（0519）To let oneself loose.

反 引經據典（3584）Speak by the book.

源 晉．孫盛．晉陽秋：“王衍能言，於意有不安者，輒更易之，時號口中雌黃。”

信口開河 xìn kǒu kāi hé 3207

Speak freely like a flowing river. (lit.)

Speak off the top of one's head.

Shoot off one's mouth.

To talk without thinking is to shoot without aiming.

Talk at random.

反 守口如瓶（2551）As close as an oyster.

源 元曲選．爭報恩：“那妮子一尺水翻騰做一丈波，怎當他只留支刺，信口開河。”

信手拈來 xìn shǒu niān lái 3208

Writing out with a free hand. (lit.)

Come in handy.

反 來之不易（1543）Hard to come by.

源 苕溪漁隱．詩眼：“此詩如禪家所謂信手拈來，頭頭是道者。”

信以為真 xìn yǐ wéi zhēn 3209

Believe it to be true. (lit.)

Swallow it hook, line and sinker.

反 難以置信（1883）To stagger belief.

星火燎原 xīng huǒ liáo yuán 3210

A spark of fire may burn a prairie. (lit.)

Little chips light great fire.

源 書經．盤庚上：“若火之燎於原，不可向邇。”

惺惺惜惺惺 xīng xīng xī xīng xīng 3211

Wise men pity wise men. (lit.)

Crows do not pick crow's eyes.

Dog does not eat dog.

同 官官相護（0963）The devil is kind to his own.

反 自相殘殺（4004）Cut one another' s throats.

源 王實甫．西廂記：“方信道，惺惺自古惜惺惺。”

興奮異常 xīng fèn yì cháng 3212

To be unusually excited. (lit.)

To be highly excited.

反 沒精打采（1848）To be in the dumps.

3213 **興師問罪** xīng shī wèn zuì

To raise the army to condemn the enemy. (lit.)

Bring someone to book.

Have a bone to pick with one.

反 負荊請罪（0842）To kiss the rod.

3214 **行將就木** xíng jiāng jiù mù

One is going soon into the wood (coffin). (lit.)

Have one foot in the grave.

On one's last legs.

At death's door.

The old man's staff is a knocker at death's door.

同 日薄西山（2253）Sinking fast.

反 方興未艾（0754）In the bud.

源 左傳・僖二十三年："公子重耳謂季隗曰，待我二十五年不來而後嫁。季隗曰：我二十五年矣，又如是而嫁，則就木焉，請待子。"

3215 **行若無事** xíng ruò wú shì

Act as if nothing has happened. (lit.)

As if nothing has happened.

With perfect composure.

3216 **行屍走肉** xíng shī zǒu ròu

A walking corpse and running flesh. (lit.)

Idle men are dead all their life long.

To be dead alive.

A piece of dead wood.

同 酒囊飯袋（1424）Jack of straw.

源 王嘉・拾遺記："好學雖死若存，不學者雖存，行屍走肉耳。"

3217 **形單影隻** xíng dān yǐng zhī

One figure, single shadow. (lit.)

All alone.

His hat covers his family.

A confirmed bachelor.

An old maid.

All by oneself.

同 孤雲野鶴（0938）Keep oneself to oneself.

反 魚貫而出（3690）In Indian file.

源 韓愈・祭十二郎文："兩世一身，形單影隻。"

3218 **形跡可疑** xíng jì kě yí

One's trace arouses suspicion. (lit.)

To smell a rat.

Suspicious looking .

源 陶潛詩："真想初在襟，誰為形跡拘。"

形勢大變 xíng shì dà biàn
The situation greatly changed. (lit.)
The tide turns.

同 扭轉乾坤（1922）Turn the tables（scales）. 3219

形勢大好 xíng shì dà hǎo
The situation is very good. (lit.)
The goose hangs high.

反 大勢已去（0552）The field is lost. 3220

幸福無邊 xìng fú wú biān
The blessing is limitless. (lit.)
As happy as the day is long.
Happy as a clam at high tide.
To be in clover (seven heaven).
One's cup runs over.

同 其樂無窮（2021）Like a possum up a gum-tree. 3221
反 苦不堪言（1517）As bitter as gall.

幸免於難 xìng miǎn yú nàn
Luckily avoided the disaster. (lit.)
Have a narrow shave.
Save one's bacon.

同 死裏逃生（2627）Out of the jaws of death. 3222
反 死於非命（2632）Die an unnatural death.

幸災樂禍 xìng zāi lè huò
Feeling lucky oneself but pleased in the calamity of another. (lit.)
Gloat over the ruin of another.
When a dog is drowning,everyone offers him drink.

源 左傳："背施無親，幸災不仁樂禍也。" 3223

興高采烈 xìng gāo cǎi liè
To be in high glee and spirit. (lit.)
To be on top of the world.
Leap with joy.
Dance with joy.
Sitting on high cotton.

同 欣喜若狂（3202）Go into rapture. 3224
反 鬱鬱寡歡（3726）Out of spirits.
源 文心雕龍："叔夜俊俠，故興高而采烈。"

興盡悲來 xìng jìn bēi lái
Joy ends and sadness comes. (lit.)
He who laughs on Friday will weep on Sunday.
Sadness and gladness succeed each other.

同 樂極生悲（1582）Pleasure has a sting in its tail. 3225
反 否極泰來（0819）They that sow in tears shall reap in joy.
源 王勃・滕王閣序："興盡悲來，識盈虛之有數。"

3226 **興致盎然** xìng zhì àng rán
Overflow with joy. (lit.)
With gusto.
Lick one's lips.

同 津津有味（1347）With relish.

3227 **興致勃勃** xìng zhì bó bó
Enthusiasm with full excitement. (lit.)
Bubbling with enthusiasm.
To be keen on.
To be in high feather.

3228 **兇相畢露** xiōng xiàng bì lù
Ferocious appearance shows itself at last. (lit.)
Bare one's fangs.
Show one's horns (claws).

3229 **洶湧澎湃** xiōng yǒng péng pài
Rushing of water and roaring of waves. (lit.)
Rise in a surging tide.
Rolling and billowing.
Choppy waves.

反 一潭死水（3464）Like stagnant water.
源 司馬相如 · 上林賦："沸乎暴怒，洶湧澎湃。"

3230 **胸懷大志** xiōng huái dà zhì
The bosom harbours a big ambition. (lit.)
To fly high.

反 小人無大志（3139）Little things amuse little minds.

3231 **胸懷坦蕩** xiōng huái tǎn dàng
The bosom harbours frankness. (lit.)
As open as the day.
Lay one's heart bare.

反 心胸狹隘（3191）To be narrow-minded.

3232 **胸無點墨** xiōng wú diǎn mò
Not a drop of ink (knowledge) in one's chest (mind). (lit.)
A numskull.
Not to know A from a windmill.

同 目不識丁（1864）Not to know B from a bull's foot.
反 滿腹經綸（1741）To give chapter and verse.

胸有成竹 xiōng yǒu chéng zhú 3233

In the chest (mind) there is a bamboo (an image which must have been in the painter's mind when he is to paint the bamboo). (lit.)

Have an ace up one's sleeve.

Have more than one string to one's bow.

Know the ropes.

同 心中有數（3201）Know one's own mind.

反 一籌莫展（3381）To be at one's wit's end.

源 晁補之・雞肋集："與可畫竹時，胸中有成竹。"參閱0357

雄才大略 xióng cái dà lüè 3234

A brave talent and great strategist. (lit.)

Full of shifts and devices.

反 小人無大志（3139）Little things amuse little minds.

源 漢書・武帝紀贊："如武帝之雄才大略。"

休戚相關 xiū qī xiāng guān 3235

Mutual concern in joy and sorrow. (lit.)

Stand together through thick and thin.

To be in the same boat.

Throw in one's lot with

源 元曲選・石君寶・曲江池："全無一點休戚相關之意。"

休戚與共 xiū qī yǔ gòng 3236

Sharing joy and sorrow. (lit.)

In weal or woe.

Two in distress make trouble less.

Share the same fate.

同 同甘共苦（2767）For better or for worse.

源 晉書・王導傳："吾與元規（庾亮）休戚是同。"

休爭閒氣，日又平西 3237

xiū zhēng xián qì, rì yòu píng xī

Do not fight leisure breath (triffle) (for) the sun is setting again. (lit.)

A soft answer turneth away wrath.

Least said, soonest mended.

同 息事寧人（3045）Pour oil on troubled waters.

源 志林："吾輩不肖，方傍人門戶，何暇爭閒氣耶。"

修修補補 xiū xiū bǔ bǔ 3238

To make do and mend.

Improving and mending.

羞羞答答 xiū xiū dā dā 3239

Bashful and shy. (lit.)

Feel like thirty cents.

One's ears burn.

同 滿臉通紅（1747）Flush red all over.

反 厚顏無恥（1078）Have plenty of cheek.

源 王實甫・西廂記："羞人答答的，怎生去。"

3240 羞與噲伍 xiū yǔ kuài wǔ

Shameful to be in company with vulgar persons. (lit.)

Not to touch one with a barge pole.

Prefer a person's room to his company.

Your room is better than your company.

同 避之則吉（0127）The best remedy against an ill man is much ground between.

反 稱兄道弟（0350）Call cousins with

源 史記・淮陰侯列傳："（韓）信常過樊將軍噲，噲跪拜迎送，言稱臣，曰大王乃肯臨臣。信出門笑曰，生乃與噲等為伍。"

3241 朽木不可雕 xiǔ mù bù kě diāo

A decayed piece of wood can't be carved. (lit.)

You cannot make a Mercury out of every log.

No man can make a good coat with bad cloth.

Of a pig's tail you can never make a good shaft.

He who is born a fool is never cured.

同 不堪造就（0210）Ill beef never made good broth.

反 天生我才必有用（2718）Everything is good for something.

源 論語・公冶長："子曰，朽木不可雕也，糞土之牆不可杇也。"

3242 袖手旁觀 xiù shǒu páng guān

Folding hands in the sleeves and looking on. (lit.)

Stand by (Look on) with folded arms.

Stand aloof.

Sitting on the fence.

Leave one to sink or swim.

同 冷眼旁觀（1596）To be outside the ropes.

反 全力以赴（2161）Put one's shoulder to the wheel.

源 韓愈・祭柳子厚文："巧匠旁觀，縮手袖間。"

3243 虛度年華 xū dù nián huá

To fritter away the youthful years. (lit.)

Fritter (Dog) away one's time.

While away the time.

反 焚膏繼晷（0792）Burn the midnight oil.

源 王炎詩："不應令節亦虛度，特為萸菊觴新醪。"

3244 虛度時光 xū dù shí guāng

To fritter away time and light. (lit.)

Twiddle one's thumbs.

Kick one's heels.

同 消磨時光（3125）Kill time.

反 分秒必爭（0785）Every minute counts.

虛懷若谷 xū huái ruò gǔ

Empty the bosom like a valley. (lit.)

Still waters run deep.

To humble oneself.

Keep an open mind.

Free from prejudice.

同 大智若愚（0568）No man can play the fool so well as the wise man.

反 高傲自大（0876）To be stuck up.

源 老子：“曠兮其若谷。” 3245

虛有其表 xū yǒu qí biǎo

Empty but a mere show. (lit.)

More poke than pudding.

A stuff shirt.

All is not gold that glitters.

More sauce than pig.

More squeak than wool.

A camourflage.

同 金玉其外，敗絮其中（1345）Whited sepulchres, which indeed appear beautiful outward, but are within full of dead man's bones.

反 名副其實（1813）To be worthy of the name.

源 鄭處誨．明皇雜錄：“嵩既退，上擲其草於地曰，虛有其表耳。” 3246

虛有其名 xū yǒu qí míng

Having an empty name. (lit.)

A rope of sand.

In name only.

反 名不虛傳（1810）Live up to one's reputation. 3247

虛與委蛇 xū yǔ wēi yí

Pretending to be amiable and agreeable (but off like a snake). (lit.)

Stall for time.

Handle with kid gloves.

源 莊子．應帝王：“吾與之虛而委蛇。” 3248

虛張聲勢 xū zhāng shēng shì

Pretending to have a lot of noise and strength. (lit.)

His bark is worse than his bite.

Barking dogs seldom bite.

Empty vessels make the most noise.

Show a bold front.

Cut a fat hog.

Be swashbuckling.

反 不動聲色（0184）Set one's face like a flint.

源 韓愈．論淮西事宜狀：“然皆暗弱，自保無暇，虛張聲勢，則必有之。” 3249

3250 噓寒問暖 xū hán wèn nuǎn

Breathe the warmth to dispel the cold and ask if one feels warmer. (lit.)

With kindest regards to

Present one's compliments to

Inquire after someone's health.

Give one's best regards to

Show every concern.

3251 栩栩如生 xǔ xǔ rú shēng

Look as if alive. (lit.)

A speaking likeness.

True to life.

源 莊子 · 齊物論："昔者莊周夢為胡蝶，栩栩然胡蝶也。"

3252 旭日東升 xù rì dōng shēng

The sun rising from the east at day break. (lit.)

The morning sun rises in the east.

同 東方發白（0662）The day is breaking.

反 日薄西山（2253）Sinking fast.

3253 絮絮不休 xù xù bù xiū

A ceaseless chattering. (lit.)

Talk the bark off a tree.

Hold a person by the button.

To hold forth.

同 話匣子（1121）A chatter-box.

反 三緘其口（2315）Button up one's lip.

源 兩抄摘腴："休休絮絮，我自明朝歸去。"

3254 蓄謀已久 xù móu yǐ jiǔ

Harbour such a plan for a long time. (lit.)

Done in cold blood.

Long premeditated.

同 處心積慮（0430）After long deliberation.

反 心血來潮（3193）On the impulse of the moment.

3255 喧賓奪主 xuān bīn duó zhǔ

The noisy guest seizes the place of his host. (lit.)

The sauce was better than the fish.

The tail wags the dog.

Steal the show from

To be a back seat driver.

喧聲震天 xuān shēng zhèn tiān 3256

The roaring sound shakes the Heaven. (lit.)

Raise the roof.

反 萬籟俱寂（2850）Silent as the grave.

玄之又玄 xuán zhī yòu xuán 3257

Abstruse, profound and mysterious. (lit.)

Explaining what is unknown by what is still more unknown.

同 莫測高深（1849）To be out of one's depth.

反 彰明較著（3795）As clear as day.

源 老子：“玄之又玄，眾妙之門。”

旋得旋失 xuán dé xuán shī 3258

To lose it soon after it is obtained. (lit.)

Easy come, easy go.

懸而不決 xuán ér bù jué 3259

Hanging without decision. (lit.)

Leave a matter (in the air).

To have a matter at a loose end.

反 當機立斷（0584）Take the bull by the horns.

懸而未決 xuán ér wèi jué 3260

Hanging not yet decided. (lit.)

Hang in the balance (wind).

Left in the air.

To be at stake.

懸樑刺股 xuán liáng cì gǔ 3261

Tie the head to the beam and prick the thigh with an awl. (lit.)(stories of two famous scholars using such ways to wake themselves up from dossing during studying.)

Go through the hoop.

源 戰國策．秦策：“（蘇秦）讀書欲睡，引錐自刺其股。”太平御覽：“孫敬好學，晨夕不休，及至睡眠疲寢，以繩繫頭，懸屋梁。”

選賢任能 xuǎn xián rèn néng 3262

Select men with good character and employ the able. (lit.)

Let him who knows the instrument play upon it.

反 用人唯親（3621）Jobs for the boys.

源 禮記：“大道之行也，天下為公，選賢與能，講信修睦。”

3263 炫玉賈石 xuàn yù gǔ shí
To show off jade but selling stone. (lit.)
Cry up wine and sell vinegar.

同 以假亂真（3530）Foist a thing off on one.
反 貨真價實（1173）Worth its weight in gold.
源 揚子．法言："炫玉賈石者，其狙詐乎。"

3264 削足適履 xuē zú shì lǚ
Trim the foot to fit the shoe. (lit.)
You take more care of your shoe than your foot.

源 淮南子．說林訓："夫所以養而害所養，譬猶削足而適履，殺頭而便冠。"

3265 學非所用 xué fēi suǒ yòng
Not using what one has learned. (lit.)
A round peg in a square hole.

3266 學富五車 xué fù wǔ chē
Knowledge and learning as rich as five carts of books. (lit.)
A walking dictionary.
A book worm.

同 博學多才（0169）Know a thing or two.
源 莊子．天下："惠施多方，其書五車。"

3267 學如逆水行舟
xué rú nì shuǐ xíng zhōu
Learning is like sailing a boat against current. (lit.)
There is no royal road to learning.

同 不進則退（0206）Not to advance is to go back.

3268 學無止境 xué wú zhǐ jìng
There is no stopping limit for learning. (lit.)
Live and learn.

同 活到老，學到老（1164）Never too old to learn.

3269 學以致用 xué yǐ zhì yòng
To learn so as to make use of it. (lit.)
Put into practice.

反 學非所用（3265）A round peg in a square hole.

3270 雪泥鴻爪 xuě ní hóng zhuǎ
Swan's foot prints found on ice and mud. (lit.)
Footprints on the sand of time.

源 蘇軾詩："人生到處知何似，應似飛鴻踏雪泥。泥上偶然留指爪，鴻飛那復計東西。"

雪上加霜 xuě shàng jiā shuāng 3271
Frost added to snow. (lit.)
One misfortune comes on the neck of another.
Troubles never come singly.

同 禍不單行（1174）It never rains but it pours.
源 景德傳燈錄："伊禪謂大陽和尚雪上更加霜。"

雪中送炭 xuě zhōng sòng tàn 3272
Send charcoal during a snowfall. (lit.)
Help a lame dog over a stile.
A friend in need is a friend indeed.

源 宋・范成大・大雪送炭與芥隱詩："不是雪中須送炭，聊裝風景要詩來。"

血本無歸 xuè běn wú guī 3273
No return of blood-capital (hardearned). (lit.)
Sell one's hens on a rainy day.

同 虧空破產（1532）To go bust.
反 一本萬利（3370）Light gains make heavy purses.

血海深仇 xuè hǎi shēn chóu 3274
Deep feud of the blood sea. (lit.)
A blood feud.
Deadly feud.

同 不共戴天之仇（0192）Inveterate enemy.
反 莫逆之交（1852）A bosom friend.

血氣方剛 xuè qì fāng gāng 3275
Blood and strength are just at the vigorous stage. (lit.)
Full of vim and vigour.
In one's raw youth.
In the prime of youth.
To be in the green.
In one's salad days.

反 老氣橫秋（1571）To be stricken in years.
源 論語・季氏："及其壯也，血氣方剛，戒之在鬥。"

血肉相連 xuè ròu xiāng lián 3276
Linked together as flesh and blood. (lit.)
Ties of blood.
Flesh and blood.
Flesh of the flesh.

反 非我族類，其心必異（0770）The mice do not play with the cat's son.

血債要用血來償 3277
xuè zhài yào yòng xuè lái cháng
Blood debt must use blood to repay. (lit.)
Blood will have blood.

同 以眼還眼，以牙還牙（3543）An eye for an eye; a tooth for a tooth.

3278 尋根問底 xún gēn wèn dǐ

Look for the root and enquire into the bottom. (lit.)

Pry into.

Press the question.

Go to the root of

Get to the bottom (core) of

同 追根究底（3952）Go down to rock bottom.

反 漠不關心（1854）Not care a damn.

源 紅樓夢：“似你這樣尋根問底，便是刻舟求劍，膠柱鼓瑟了。”

3279 尋歡作樂 xún huān zuò lè

To seek pleasure and to make fun. (lit.)

Go on a spree.

反 自討苦吃（3998）Make a rod for one's own back.

3280 循規蹈矩 xún guī dǎo jǔ

Follow the compass and step into the square. (lit.)

Toe the line (mark).

Walk the chalk.

Follow the beaten track.

反 無法無天（2959）Lawless as a town-bull.

源 紅樓夢：“看的你們是三四代老媽媽，最是循規蹈矩。”

3281 循序漸進 xún xù jiàn jìn

Follow in proper order and advance gradually. (lit.)

Step by step.

Advance by small degrees.

Inch forward.

By stages.

同 由淺入深（3635）Learn to walk before you run.

反 僭隊（1285）Jump the queue.

源 語出《論語・憲問・朱熹注》

3282 馴如羔羊 xùn rú gāo yáng

As tame as a lamb. (lit.)

As harmless as a kitten.

As meek (gentle) as a lamb.

Harmless as doves.

3283 迅雷不及掩耳 xùn léi bù jí yǎn ěr

Thunder so fast, no time to plug one's ears. (lit.)

It came absolutely out of the blue.

As swift as lightning.

Before you could say Jack Robinson.

反 慢條斯理（1755）As slow as molasses in winter.

源 六韜・軍勢：“疾雷不及掩耳，迅電不及瞑目。”

迅速敏捷 xùn sù mǐn jié 3284

Swift and nimble. (lit.)

Hand over fist.

Hand over hand.

反 毛手毛腳（1772）One's fingers are all thumbs.

徇私枉法 xùn sī wǎng fǎ 3285

Indulging private wishes, abuse the law. (lit.)

As a man is friended, so the law is ended.

訓斥一番 xùn chì yì fān 3286

Give a lecture and a good scolding. (lit.)

Take one to task.

Give one the length of one's tongue.

Y

3287 **鴉雀無聲** yā què wú shēng

Crows and other birds make no noise. (lit.)

You would have heard a pin drop.

As silent as the grave.

Silence reigns.

A dead silence.

同 萬籟俱寂（2850）As silent as the dead.

反 震耳欲聾（3831）Split the ears.

源 蘇軾詩："天風吹雨入闌干，烏鵲無聲夜向闌。"

3288 **衙門八字開，有理無錢莫進來**

yá mén bā zì kāi, yǒu lǐ wú qián mò jìn lái

The gate of the official bureau opens like the Chinese character 'eight', having reason but no money, don't come in. (lit.)

Possession is nine-tenths of the law.

Possession is eleven points of the law, and they say there are but twelve.

3289 **啞口吃黃連** yǎ kǒu chī huáng lián

Dumb-mouth eating Huang Lian. (lit.) (A very bitter Chinese herb)

Swallow the leek.

同 苦不堪言（1517）As bitter as gall.

反 訴苦（2650）Air one's grievances.

3290 **啞口無言** yǎ kǒu wú yán

Dumb mouth and speechless. (lit.)

Come to a nonplus.

Be rendered speechless.

同 瞠目結舌（0352）Stare tongue-tied.

反 滔滔不絕（2692）Talk nine words at once.

3291 **啞然失笑** yǎ rán shī xiào

Laughing out without saying anything. (lit.)

Burst out laughing.

Can't help laughing.

Chuckle to oneself.

反 勃然大怒（0168）Fly into a rage.

源 列子 · 周穆王："同行者啞然大笑。"

煙消雲散 yān xiāo yún sàn 3292
The smoke disappears and the cloud disperses. (lit.)
Gone with the wind.
End in smoke.
Vanish like smoke.
Vanish into thin air.

同 化為烏有（1115）To come to naught.
反 風頭火勢（0808）Like a house afire.

湮沒無聞 yān mò wú wén 3293
Lost and unheard of. (lit.)
Clean forgotten.
Sink into oblivion.

同 默默無聞（1858）To be no burner of navigable river.
反 大名鼎鼎（0539）Of great renown.

言必信，行必果 3294
yán bì xìn, xíng bì guǒ
Words must be trustworthy and action must be fruitful. (lit.)
Say well is good, but do well is better.

源 語出《論語 · 子路》

言不由衷 yán bù yóu zhōng 3295
Words spoken not from the heart. (lit.)
Not tell the truth.
To be mealy-mouthed.

反 吐露心情（2811）Get something off one's chest.
源 左傳 · 隱三年：“言不由衷。”

言出不行 yán chū bù xíng 3296
Speak without action. (lit.)
You cackle often, but never lay an egg.

同 説話不算數（2610）Break one's words.
反 説了就幹（2613）No sooner said than done.

言傳不如身教 3297
yán chuán bù rú shēn jiào
Preaching by words is not as good as personal example by action. (lit.)
Example is better than precept.
An ounce of practice is worth a pound of preaching.

同 現身説法（3100）A good example is the best sermon.

言多必敗 yán duō bì bài 3298
Too much talk must fail. (lit.)
He that talks much errs much.

反 多吃飯，少開口（0697）Save one's breath to cool one's porridge.

3299 **言多必妄** yán duō bì wàng
Talk much lie much. (lit.)
He that talks much lies much.

3300 **言多語失皆因酒** yán duō yǔ shī jiē yīn jiǔ
Talkative and saying the wrong things, all due to drinking wine. (lit.)
When the wine sinks, words swim.
When the wine is in, the wit is out.

3301 **言歸於好** yán guī yú hǎo
Say sorry and return to good terms. (lit.)
Patch up a quarrel.
Heal the breach.
Bury the hatchet.

同 握手言歡（2941）To make it up.
反 勢不兩立（2532）At daggers drawn.
源 左傳・僖九年：“凡我同盟之人，既盟之後，言歸於好。”

3302 **言歸正傳** yán guī zhèng zhuàn
Words return to the original story. (lit.)
Return to our muttons.
Come back to brass tacks.

反 跑野馬（1956）Fly off at a tangent.

3303 **言過其實** yán guò qí shí
Overstate the facts. (lit.)
To make a mountain out of a mole hill.
Overshoot oneself (the mark).
Draw the long bow.
Stretch the truth.
Paint the devil blacker than he is.
The lion is not so fierce as he is painted.

同 過甚其詞（1001）The devil is not so black as he is painted.
反 輕描淡寫（2126）To skate over
源 三國志・馬良傳：“馬謖言過其實，不能大用。”

3304 **言簡意賅** yán jiǎn yì gāi
Simple words but embracing idea. (lit.)
Precise and to the point.
Brevity is the soul of wit.
Speak little and to the purpose.
To hit it off.
To be sparing of words.
Short and sweet.

反 叨叨嘮嘮（0596）To chew the rag.

言人人殊 yán rén rén shū
Different men say different words. (lit.)
So many men, so many minds.
Opinions are divided.

同 莫衷一是（1853）Agree like the clocks of London.
反 異口同聲（3557）Be of one voice.
源 漢書・曹參傳："齊故諸儒以百數，言人人殊，參未知所定。" 3305

言聽計從 yán tīng jì cóng
Listen to one's words and follow his plan. (lit.)
To have a person's ear.
At one's beck and call.
To go all out on a person.
Dance after one's whistle.
Come to heel.

同 百依百順（0061）Have a nose of wax.
源 蘇軾・古史："言聽計從，致君於王伯（霸）矣。" 3306

言外之意 yán wài zhī yì
Meaning outside the words. (lit.)
Understatement.
Implied meaning.
Read between the lines.

源 宋・葉夢得・石林詩話："七言難於氣象雄渾，句中有力而紆余，不失言外之意。" 3307

言為心聲 yán wéi xīn shēng
Words are the voice of the heart. (lit.)
Speech is the picture of the mind.
What the heart thinks the tongue speaks.
When the heart is afire some sparks will fly out at the mouth.
Nearest the heart, nearest the mouth.

源 揚雄・法言・問神："言，心聲也。書，心畫也。" 3308

言行不一 yán xíng bù yī
Words and deeds are not the same. (lit.)
Say one thing and do another.

反 說到做到（2606）Live up to one's word.
源 逸周書・官人："言行不類，終始相悖。" 3309

言行一致 yán xíng yí zhì
Words and action in accord. (lit.)
Suit the action to the word.
Practise what you preach.
As good as one's word.
Mean what one says.

同 坐言起行（4060）Say well is good, but do well is better.
反 說一套做一套（2616）Say one thing and do another. 3310

3311 **言猶在耳** yán yóu zài ěr
His words are still in one's ears. (lit.)
Fresh in one's mind.
Still ring in one's ears.

反 左耳入，右耳出（4046）In at one ear and out at the other.
源 左傳．文七年："今君雖終，言猶在耳。"

3312 **言者無罪，聞者足戒**
yán zhě wú zuì, wén zhě zú jiè
Speaker has no crime, the listener has enough warning. (lit.)
Though the speaker be a fool, let the hearer be wise.
If the shoe fits, wear it.

源 詩經大序："言之者無罪，聞之者足以戒。"

3313 **言之成理** yán zhī chéng lǐ
Speak with reasons. (lit.)
It stands to reason.
To hold water.
Make sense.

反 一派胡言（3433）Broad nonsense.
源 荀子．非十二子篇："然而其持之有故，其言之成理，足以欺惑愚眾。"

3314 **言之無物** yán zhī wú wù
There is nothing in the speech. (lit.)
Hollow words.
Empty talk.
A deluge of words and a drop of sense.

反 話中有話（1122）There's a catch in one's words.

3315 **顏色憔悴** yán sè qiáo cuì
Colour of the face fading. (lit.)
Peak and pine.

反 容光煥發（2262）Shine like a shittim barn door.
源 戰國策："顏色憔悴。"

3316 **嚴加懲處** yán jiā chéng chǔ
Severe punishment. (lit.)
Throw the book at
Put it across one.
To be for the high jump.
To have a person's hide.

反 從輕發落（0461）Let one off lightly.

3317 **嚴峻考驗** yán jùn kǎo yàn
Severe test. (lit.)
The acid test.

嚴肅認真 yán sù rèn zhēn 3318
Dignified and serious. (lit.)
As grave (sober) as a judge.
As keen as mustard.

同 慎重將事（2411）Score twice before you cut once.
反 吊兒郎當（0649）Gad about.

嚴陣以待 yán zhèn yǐ dài 3319
Waiting with tense array. (lit.)
Poised for action.
In battle array.

同 摩拳擦掌（1845）Roll up one's sleeves.
反 冷不提防（1591）Off one's guard.

奄奄一息 yǎn yǎn yì xī 3320
There is only a little breath. (lit.)
At one's last gasp.
To be sinking fast.

反 蒸蒸日上（3837）Grow with each passing day.
源 李密・陳情表：“氣息奄奄，人命危殆。”

掩耳不聞 yǎn ěr bù wén 3321
Covering the ears and not listening. (lit.)
Turn a deaf ear to

反 凝神細聽（1918）Hang on the words of

掩人耳目 yǎn rén ěr mù 3322
Covering one's ears and eyes. (lit.)
Draw the wool over one's eyes.
Throw dust into one's eyes.
Hoodwink others.

同 蒙混過關（1783）Sail under false colours.
反 拆穿西洋鏡（0322）Take the mickey out of it.

眼觀六路，耳聽八方 3323
yǎn guān liù lù, ěr tīng bā fāng
The eyes see six roads, the ears hear eight directions. (lit.)
On the look out.
On the alert.

同 金睛火眼（1341）To be wide awake.
反 昏昏欲睡（1159）Gather straws.

眼光遠大 yǎn guāng yuǎn dà 3324
One's eye looks far and wide. (lit.)
Farsightedness.
Have a great foresight.

同 風物長宜放眼量（0810）Wait and see.
反 目光如豆（1869）no further than one's nose.

眼闊肚窄 yǎn kuò dù zhǎi 3325
The eye is wide but the belly narrow. (lit.)
Bite off more than one can chew.
The eye is bigger than the belly.

3326 **眼露兇光** yǎn lù xiōng guāng

Eyes show fierce light. (lit.)

Have eyes like a ferret.

同 兇相畢露（3228）Bare one's fangs.

反 和藹可親（1048）With good grace.

3327 **眼明手快** yǎn míng shǒu kuài

Sharp-eyed and nimble-handed. (lit.)

Full of alert.

Sleight of hand.

With one's eyes peeled..

反 毛手毛腳（1772）Have a hand like a foot

3328 **眼中釘** yǎn zhōng dīng

A nail in the eye. (lit.)

An eyesore.

A thorn in the eye.

同 肉中刺（2266）A pain in the neck.

反 掌上明珠（3798）The apple of one's eye.

源 馮贄．雲仙雜記："趙在禮在宋州所為不法……一日制下，移鎮永興，百姓相賀曰，眼中釘拔郤矣。"

3329 **偃旗息鼓** yǎn qí xī gǔ

Put away the flag and silence the drum. (lit.)

Lie low.

Draw in one's horns.

反 大張旗鼓（0566）With great fanfare.

源 三國志．趙雲傳注："雲陷敵還，更大開門，偃旗息鼓，曹軍疑有伏兵，引去。"

3330 **演全武行** yǎn quán wǔ háng

Play the full fighting act. (lit.)

Come (Fall) to blows.

同 訴諸武力（2651）Resort to force.

反 相安無事（3103）Get along fairly well.

3331 **羊毛出在羊身上**

yáng máo chū zài yáng shēn shàng

Sheep's wool comes out of sheep's body. (lit.)

He does not lose his alms who gives it to his pig.

3332 **羊質虎皮** yáng zhì hǔ pí

A sheep dressed in a tiger's skin. (lit.)

A bully is always a coward.

同 色厲內荏（2320）Many a one threatens while he quakes for fear.

源 揚雄．法言．吾子："羊質虎皮，見草而悅，見豺而戰，忘其皮之虎也。"

洋洋自得 yáng yáng zì dé 3333

Greatly self-satisfied. (lit.)

To tread on air.

To be very pleased with oneself.

同 沾沾自喜（3777）Hug one's self.

反 垂頭喪氣（0445）Hang one's head.

揚長而去 yáng cháng ér qù 3334

To swagger and walk away. (lit.)

To light out.

Take a powder.

Make oneself scarce.

Fly the coop.

To beat it.

同 掉頭不顧（0650）Never to look back.

反 突如其來（2805）Appear from nowhere.

陽奉陰違 yáng fèng yīn wéi 3335

To obey openly and infringe secretly. (lit.)

Pay lip service only.

同 當面是人，背後是鬼（0588）Who flatters me to my face will speak ill of me behind my back.

反 表裏如一（0137）What the heart thinks the tongue speaks.

仰人鼻息 yǎng rén bí xī 3336

Look to one's nose breathing. (lit.)

Live on the charity of

To be under one's thumb.

To be led by the nose.

Consult one's pleasure.

At somebody's mercy.

反 頤指氣使（3522）Get someone by the short hairs.

源 後漢書．袁紹傳："袁紹孤客窮軍，仰我鼻息。"

養兵千日，用在一朝 3337

yǎng bīng qiān rì, yòng zài yì zhāo

Feed the soldiers thousand days, use them for one day. (lit.)

Keep a thing seven years and you will find a use for it.

養不教父之過，教不嚴師之惰 3338

yǎng bú jiào fù zhī guò, jiào bù yán shī zhī duò

Rearing (a child) without teaching him is father's fault, teaching without strictness is teacher's laziness. (lit.)

One father is more than a hundred schoolmasters.

源 原句出自"訓蒙三字經"一書。

3339 **養虎遺患** yǎng hǔ yí huàn

Rearing a tiger to cause trouble. (lit.)

Cherish a serpent in one's bosom.

Warm a snake in one's bosom.

Bring up a raven and it will peck out your eyes.

同 引狼入室（3585）Set a fox to keep the geese.

反 防患未然（0755）Crush in the egg.

源 史記．項羽紀：“不如因其機而遂取之。今釋弗擊，此所謂養虎自遺患也。”

3340 **養精蓄銳** yǎng jīng xù ruì

To nourish the spirit and save vigour. (lit.)

Conserve one's strength.

Freshen up.

Pull one's self together.

Recharge one's mental batteries.

反 挫其銳氣（0482）Take the wind out of one's sails.

3341 **養尊處優** yǎng zūn chǔ yōu

Provide oneself a comfortable place. (lit.)

Live high off the hog.

Lie on a bed of roses.

Live in clover.

In the lap of luxury.

Up to the high-water mark.

Live like a lord.

Live the life of Rily.

To be on velvet.

同 嬌生慣養（1306）Nursed in cotton.

反 潦倒一生（1056）Down and out.

3342 **怏怏不樂** yàng yàng bú lè

To be disconsolate and unhappy. (lit.)

Have the blues.

Out of spirits.

同 鬱鬱寡歡（3726）As melancholy as a cat.

反 喜形於色（3060）Radiant with joy.

3343 **樣樣都抓，等於不抓**

yàng yàng dōu zhuā, děng yú bù zhuā

Grasping everything equals to grasping nothing. (lit.)

Grasp all, lose all.

A little of everything is nothing in the main.

反 執簡馭繁（3868）Take care of the pence and the pounds will take care of themselves.

腰纏萬貫 yāo chán wàn guàn 3344

To tie ten thousand of strings of cash around the waist. (lit.)

Roll in wealth.

同 家財萬貫（1247）Have money to burn.

反 囊空如洗（1885）Dead broke.

源 明．陶宗儀．説郛．商芸小説：“腰纏十萬貫，騎鶴上揚州。”

搖唇鼓舌 yáo chún gǔ shé 3345

Shake the lips and wag the tongue. (lit.)

Wag one's tongue.

同 巧舌如簧（2098）Talk glibly.

反 三緘其口（2315）Button up one's lip.

源 莊子．盜跖：“搖唇鼓舌，擅生是非。”

搖錢樹 yáo qián shù 3346

The tree shaken (yield) money. (lit.)

A golden thumb.

A milch cow.

The goose that lays the golden eggs.

搖尾乞憐 yáo wěi qǐ lián 3347

Wag the tail and beg for pity. (lit.)

Play up to

Curry favour with

Grovel in the dust.

Grovel at the feet of

反 不屑一顧（0260）Snap one's fingers at

源 韓愈：“若俛首帖耳，搖尾乞憐者，非我之志也。”

搖搖欲墜 yáo yáo yù zhuì 3348

Shaking as if one is going to fall. (lit.)

Hang by a thread.

Hang on by one's eyelids (eyelashes).

Tremble in the balance.

同 危在旦夕（2876）Sword of Damocles.

反 巍然屹立（2886）Stand rock-firm.

源 淮南子．兵略訓：“推其搖搖。”

遙遙領先 yáo yáo lǐng xiān 3349

Leading ahead in future. (lit.)

Streets ahead of

To be in the van.

同 一馬當先（3421）To be in the lead.

反 瞠乎其後（0351）Lag far behind.

遙遙無期 yáo yáo wú qī 3350

In very distant future without no definite date. (lit.)

One of these days in none of these days.

What may be done at any time will be done at no time.

Till the cows come home.

反 指日可待（3883）Before long.

3351 **謠言滿天飛** yáo yán mǎn tiān fēi
Rumours flying all over the sky. (lit.)
Rumour is a great traveller.

同 蜚短流長（0774）Shoot a paper-bolt.

3352 **杳如黃鶴** yǎo rú huáng hè
Gone as the yellow crane. (lit.)
To leave for good.
Nowhere to be found.

同 一去不復返（3444）Gone forever.
反 捲土重來（1451）Stage a comeback.
源 崔顥．黃鶴樓詩："黃鶴一去不復返，白雲千載空悠悠。"

3353 **咬文嚼字** yǎo wén jiáo zì
To chew letters and gnaw words. (lit.)
To be pedantic.
Use flowery words.
To speak holiday.
To have swallowed the dictionary.
Talk like a book.
Chop logic.

同 句斟字酌（1444）Weigh one's words.
反 信口開河（3207）Shoot off one's mouth.
源 元曲選．殺狗勸夫："使不的你咬文嚼字。"

3354 **咬牙切齒** yǎo yá qiè chǐ
Grind one's teeth. (lit.)
File one's teeth.
Gnash one's teeth in anger.

同 恨之入骨（1062）Hate one's guts.
源 元曲選．勘頭巾："為甚事咬牙切齒，唬的犯罪人面色如金紙。"

3355 **窈窕淑女，君子好逑**
yǎo tiǎo shū nǚ, jūn zǐ hào qiú
Modest, retiring yound ladies are sorted by gentlemen. (lit.)
She that is born a beauty is half married.

源《詩經．關雎》句

3356 **要把顛倒了的顛倒過來**
yào bǎ diān dǎo le de diān dǎo guò lái
Must put the upside down position to upside down again. (i.e. upright position) (lit.)
The boot is on the other leg.

3357 **要理不理** yào lǐ bù lǐ
Want to bother without bothering. (lit.)
Leave one in the cold.
Give one the cold shoulder.
To be standoffish.

反 多方照顧（0700）Heap favours upon

要相信羣眾 yào xiāng xìn qún zhòng 3358
Must trust the masses. (lit.)
It must be true that all men say.

反 人言可畏（2234）What will Mr. Grundy say?

要言不煩 yào yán bù fán 3359
Essential words are not numerous. (lit.)
In a nutshell.
It boils down to this.
To be terse and pithy.

同 言簡意賅（3304）Brevity is the soul of wit.
反 説個沒完（2608）Talk nineteen to the dozen.
源 世説新語："管公明曰，善易者不論易也，何平叔含笑曰，可謂要言不煩。"

要有分寸 yào yǒu fēn cùn 3360
Must have the measurement of an inch and its fractions. (lit.)
Draw the line somewhere.

反 百無禁忌（0058）To ride whip and spur.

耀武揚威 yào wǔ yáng wēi 3361
To shine force and display power. (lit.)
Bluff and bluster.
Brandish one's sword.
Swagger about.
Sabre-rattling.

同 大張旗鼓（0566）With great fanfare.
源 元曲選．無名氏．謝金吾三："他也會斬將搴旗，耀武揚威，普天下哪一個不識的他是楊無敵。"

揶揄戲弄 yé yú xì nòng 3362
Tease and ridicule. (lit.)
Hold one up to ridicule.
Make a hare of a person.
Pull a person's leg.

野火燒不盡，春風吹又生 3363
yě huǒ shāo bù jìn, chūn fēng chuī yòu shēng
Wild fire burns no end, spring wind blows it alive again. (lit.)
Weeds want no sowing.
Ill weeds grow apace.

源 白居易詩："野火燒不盡，春風吹又生。"

3364 **野心勃勃** yě xīn bó bó

One's savage heart is suddenly issuing forth. (lit.)

Ruthlessly ambitious.
To level at the moon.
To fly at high game.
The sky is one's limit.
Burn with ambition.
Hitch one's wagon to a star.

反 當一天和尚撞一天鐘（0593）Come day, go day, God send Sunday.

3365 **夜長夢多** yè cháng mèng duō

Long night and numerous dreams. (lit.)

There's many a slip between the cup and the lip.

同 事不宜遲（2510）Delays are dangerous.

源 清・呂留良："薦舉事近復紛紜，夜長夢多，恐將來有意外，奈何。"

3366 **夜郎自大** yè láng zì dà

The self-importance of Ye-Lang (name of an ancient chieftain). (lit.)

A humble-bee in a cow-turd thinks himself a king.
To be too long for one's boots.
To be full of oneself.
Every sprat nowadays calls itself a herring.

同 自高自大（3978）Think no small beer of oneself.

反 妄自菲薄（2867）Make oneself too cheap.

源 漢使至夜郎，夜郎侯問漢與夜郎孰大。見《漢書・西南夷傳》

3367 **夜幕低垂** yè mù dī chuí

The night screen has hung down. (lit.)

Under screen of night.
At dusk.

同 更深人靜（0914）In the dead of night.

反 光天化日（0983）In broad daylight.

3368 **一敗塗地** yī bài tú dì

A defeat stains the earth. (lit.)

Down to the ground.
Lick the dust.
To land with a thud.
Down and out.
Knocked into a cocked hat.
Get the worst of it.
To be left at the post.
To come off crabs.

同 潰不成軍（1533）To be put to rout.

反 所向披靡（2664）To carry all before one.

源 史記・高祖本紀："天下方擾，諸侯並起，今置將不善，一敗塗地。"

一輩子 yī bèi zǐ
A life time. (lit.)
In a life time.
In a month of Sundays.

反 轉瞬之間（3941）In the twinkling of an eye. 3369

一本萬利 yī běn wàn lì
With one capital to gain ten thousand interest. (lit.)
Light gains make heavy purses.
Make a scoop.
Reap a fat profit.

反 血本無歸（3273）Sell one's hens on a rainy day. 3370

一本正經 yī běn zhèng jīng 3371
One book of seriousness. (lit.)
Look as if butter wouldn't melt in one's mouth.
Speak like a book.
Goody-goody.
Have a serious look.
Put on a solemn look.
Nice Nelly (Nellie).

一筆勾銷 yī bǐ gōu xiāo
Cancelled with one stroke of the pen. (lit.)
All annulled.
Cancel out.
Write off at a stroke.
Get even with

源 宋史：“范十二丈一筆勾去，焉知一家哭矣。” 3372

一臂之助 yī bì zhī zhù
With the help of one's arm. (lit.)
Lend a hand.
Give a lift.
Give a leg up.
Throw in one's weight.

反 袖手旁觀（3242）Look on with folded arms. 3373

一邊倒 yī biān dǎo
Fall on one side. (lit.)
All on one side, like Bridgnorth election.

反 不偏不倚（0237）Sit on the rail. 3374

3375 一表人才 yī biǎo rén cái

To appear a talented person. (lit.)

Manners make the man.

A commanding presence.

An imposing figure.

反 大老粗（0537）A rough diamond.

3376 一波未平，一波又起

yī bō wèi píng, yī bō yòu qǐ

One wave not yet flattened, another rises again. (lit.)

Wave after wave.

Hit one snag after another.

It never rains but it pours.

A run of bad luck.

同 禍不單行（1174）Misfortunes seldom come singly.

反 一帆風順（3391）It's all plain sailing.

源 姜夔 · 白石道人詩說："波瀾開闔，如在江湖中，一波未平，一波已作。"

3377 一步一個腳印 yī bù yí gè jiǎo yìn

One step, one foot print. (lit.)

Step by step.

3378 一不做，二不休 yī bù zuò, èr bù xiū

First you don't do anything (once you have started doing it), second don't stop. (lit.)

What is worth doing at all is worth doing well.

In for a penny, in for a pound.

As well be hanged for a sheep as a lamb.

Over shoes, over boots.

Go the whole hog.

源 水滸傳："一不做，二不休，眾好漢相助着晁某，直殺盡江州軍。"

3379 一塵不染 yī chén bù rǎn

Unstained by a speck of dust. (lit.)

Spick and span.

Dust free.

同 玉潔冰清（3713）As chaste as ice.

源 易本義："聖人具三者之德，而無一塵之累。"

3380 一成不變 yī chéng bú biàn

Once completed it cannot be changed. (lit.)

Hard and fast.

同 原封不動（3730）Keep intact.

反 變幻莫測（0135）The unexpected always happens.

源 禮記 · 王制："刑者型也，型者成也，一成而不可變。"

一籌莫展 yī chóu mò zhǎn 3381

Not a single plan has been designed. (lit.)

To be at one's wit's end.

同 黔驢技窮（2085）At the end of one's tether.

反 心生一計（3190）Hit upon an idea.

源 宋史・蔡幼學傳："多士盈庭而一籌不吐。"

一觸即發 yī chù jí fā 3382

One touch, it goes off. (lit.)

Touch-and-go.

Reach a breaking point.

Explode at a touch.

一蹴而就 yī cù ér jiù 3383

One kick, it is done. (lit.)

At one stroke.

Succeed overnight.

Take something all in one stride.

To start with a bang.

同 旗開得勝（2034）Get off to a flying start.

反 功敗垂成（0922）A slip betwixt the cup and the lip.

源 宋・蘇洵・上田樞密書："天下之學者，孰不欲一蹴而造聖人之域。"

一寸光陰一寸金 3384

yī cùn guāng yīn yī cùn jīn

One inch of light-dark (time), one inch of gold. (lit.)

Time is money.

There is nothing more precious than time.

Make the best of one's time.

一錯再錯 yī cuò zài cuò 3385

One mistake after another. (lit.)

Denying a fault doubles it.

Two wrongs don't make a right.

一刀兩斷 yī dāo liǎng duàn 3386

One knife cuts it into two. (lit.)

Sever at one blow.

Split up.

Break with.

Be (have) done with a person.

Make a clean break with.

源 朱子語錄："克己者，是從根源上一刀兩斷，便斬絕了。"

3387 **一而二，二而一** yī ér èr, èr ér yī

One to two, two to one. (lit.)

One and the same thing.

同 兩碼事（1628）That's another cup of tea.

3388 **一而再，再而三** yī ér zài, zài ér sān

Once again, and again thrice. (lit.)

Over and over again.

Time and again.

Time after time.

同 繼續不斷（1239）For ever more.

源 尚書 · 多方："至於再，至於三。"

3389 **一法立，一弊生** yī fǎ lì, yī bì shēng

One law is made, an disadvantage arises. (lit.)

Every law has a loophole.

The more laws, the more offenders.

3390 **一髮千鈞** yī fà qiān jūn

A thousand Jun (weight of 30 catties) hung by a hair. (lit.)

Hang by a thread.

At moment of danger.

同 危在旦夕（2876）Hang on by the eyelids.

源 韓愈 · 與孟尚書書："其危如一髮引千鈞。"

3391 **一帆風順** yī fān fēng shùn

One sails with the wind smoothly. (lit.)

It's all plain sailing.

Sail before the wind.

It was roses all the way.

Without a hitch.

Godspeed! everything goes well.

反 命途多舛（1836）The times are out of joint.

3392 **一分為二** yī fēn wéi èr

One divides into two. (lit.)

There are two sides to every question.

Every may-be has a may-not-be.

3393 **一竿到底** yī gān dào dǐ

One pole to the bottom. (lit.)

To see a thing through.

同 貫徹始終（0977）Such beginning, such end.

反 半途而廢（0072）Do things by halves.

一個巴掌拍不響 3394
yī gè bā zhǎng pāi bù xiǎng
Clapping with one hand makes no noise. (lit.)
It takes two to make a quarrel.
A soft answer turneth away wrath.

一個蘿蔔一個坑 yī gè luó bó yī gè kēng 3395
One turnip, one cavity (in the ground). (lit.)
A place for everything, and everything in its place.

一鼓作氣 yī gǔ zuò qì 3396
To rouse the spirit with the beat of the drum. (lit.)
Come to the scratch.
Make a vigorous effort.

源 左傳．莊十年：“夫戰，勇氣也，一鼓作氣，再而衰，三而竭。”

一哄而散 yī hōng ér sàn 3397
Dispersed in an uproar. (lit.)
To flee helter-skelter.

同 作鳥獸散（4071）To flee pell-mell.
反 魚貫而出（3690）In Indian file.

一呼百應 yī hū bǎi yìng 3398
A call draws response from hundred persons. (said of a rich influential man.) (lit.)
One barking dog sets all the streets a-barking.
Chime in with.

源 元曲選．舉案齊眉：“堂上一呼，階下百諾。”

一揮而就 yī huī ér jiù 3399
One stroke (of the pen) to finish it. (lit.)
To dash off
Have a ready pen.

反 搜索枯腸（2646）Cudgel one's brains.
源 宋史．文天祥傳：“其言萬餘，不為稿，一揮而成。”

一記耳光 yī jì ěr guāng 3400
A box on the ear. (lit.)
A slap in the face.

3401 **一家飽暖百家愁** yī jiā bǎo nuǎn bǎi jiā chóu

One family being well-fed and warm, hundred families in misery. (lit.)

It may be fun to you, but it is death to the frogs.

The pleasures of the mighty are the tears of the poor.

3402 **一家不知一家事** yī jiā bù zhī yī jiā shì

One family does not know another's affairs. (lit.)

On half the world does not know how the other half lives.

3403 **一見如故** yī jiàn rú gù

One glance, like old friends. (lit.)

Be hail-fellow-well-met with

Hit it off right away.

反 翻臉不認人（0740）Cut one dead.

源 宋．張洎．賈氏譚錄：“吳人顧況西遊長安，鄴侯一見如故。”

3404 **一箭雙鵰** yī jiàn shuāng diāo

One arrow, two big birds. (lit.)

Kill two birds with one stone (shaft).

同 一舉兩得（3408）To cut both ways.

源 唐書：“高駢見二鵰並飛，駢曰，我且貴，當中之。一發貫二鵰焉。”

3405 **一見鍾情** yī jiàn zhōng qíng

One glance, deep in love. (lit.)

Love at first sight.

Take an instant fancy to

3406 **一將功成萬骨枯**

yī jiàng gōng chéng wàn gǔ kū

A general's success (in war), ten thousand bones rot. (lit.)

What millions died that Caesar might be great.

3407 **一舉成名** yī jǔ chéng míng

Make a name for oneself at one try. (lit.)

Make a name for oneself.

Make a mark in the world.

To rise to fame.

To come into one's own

Rocket to fame.

Become famous overnight.

反 身敗名裂（2381）Fall into disgrace.

源 韓愈．竇公墓誌銘：“公一舉成名而東。”

一舉兩得 yī jǔ liǎng dé 3408

To acquire two by one lift. (lit.)

Kill two flies with one slap.

Stop two gaps with one bush.

Catch two pigeons with one bean.

To cut both ways.

反 兩頭落空（1634）Fall between two stools.

源 東觀漢記．耿弇傳：“所謂一舉而兩得者也。”

一蹶不振 yī jué bù zhèn 3409

Having slipped down, one could not get up again. (lit.)

Meet one's Waterloo.

Land with a thud.

Come a cropper.

Fall flat.

同 一敗塗地（3368）Lick the dust.

反 再接再厲（3759）Redouble one's effort.

源 說苑．談叢：“一蹶之故，卻足不行。”

一決雌雄 yī jué cí xióng 3410

To decide who is the male and female. (lit.)

To fight it out.

Have a showdown with

源 史記．項羽本紀：“願與漢王挑戰決雌雄。”

一顆紅心，兩種準備 3411

yī kē hóng xīn, liǎng zhǒng zhǔn bèi

To have a red heart, two kinds of preparation. (lit.)

Hope for the best and prepare for the worst.

一刻千金 yī kè qiān jīn 3412

One moment, thousand gold (referring to the happiness of nuptial evening). (lit.)

Every mimute counts.

Time is money.

Lost time is never found again.

源 蘇軾．春夜詩：“春宵一刻值千金。”

一口咬定 yī kǒu yǎo dìng 3413

One bite, it is fixed. (lit.)

Stick to one's guns.

Stick to what one says.

反 出爾反爾（0402）Go back to one's word.

3414 **一覽無遺** yī lǎn wú yí

One full view, nothing left. (lit.)

In full view.

To have a commanding view.

Command a bird's eye view.

Nothing escapes a glance.

同 瞭如指掌（1646）As plain as the nose in one's face.

源 世說新語："若使阡陌條暢，則一覽而盡。"

3415 **一攬子** yī lǎn zǐ

A whole bundle (of rubbish). (lit.)

Lock, stock and barrel.

Bag and baggage.

同 一應俱全（3489）Root and branch.

3416 **一了百了** yī liǎo bǎi liǎo

One finished, hundred (all) are finished. (lit.)

Once and for all.

Get it over and done with.

反 繼續不斷（1239）On and on.

3417 **一溜煙** yī liū yān

Gone like a (streak) of smoke. (lit.)

Go like the wind.

Take a powder.

同 不翼而飛（0268）Vanish from sight.

反 突如其來（2805）Appear from nowhere.

3418 **一路貨色** yī lù huò sè

All the same goods and colour. (lit.)

All tarred with the same brush.

Cast in the same mold.

Of the same kidney.

It's six of one and half a dozen of the other.

3419 **一路平安** yī lù píng ān

All the way safe. (lit.)

Fare thee well!

God speed!

Bon voyage!

同 一帆風順（3391）It's all plain sailing.

反 一波未平，一波又起（3376）Hit one snag after another.

3420 **一落千丈** yī luò qiān zhàng

One fall of thousand zhang. (1 zhang = 10 Chinese feet) (lit.)

To go to pot.

To touch bottom.

A total failure.

同 江河日下（1292）Go down drain.

反 飛黃騰達（0771）His star was in the ascendant.

源 韓愈．聽穎師彈琴詩："躋攀分寸不可上，失勢一落千丈強。"

一馬當先 yī mǎ dāng xiān 3421
One horse in the lead. (lit.)
To be in the van (lead).
Break a path.
Show the way.

同 遙遙領先（3349）Streets ahead of
反 畏縮不前（2912）Back out of

一碼事 yī mǎ shì 3422
A yard matter. (lit.)
One and the same thing.

反 兩碼事（1628）That's another pair of shoes.

一毛不拔 yī máo bù bá 3423
Let not a single hair be plucked. (lit.)
Not to part with the parings of one's nails.
As close as a clam.
As tight as a drum.
Be close-fisted.
Utterly stingy.

同 吝嗇小氣（1660）Cramp in the hand.
反 仗義疏財（3803）Come down handsome.
源 孟子・盡心上："揚子取為我，拔一毛而利天下，不為也。"

一面之詞 yī miàn zhī cí 3424
One-sided words. (lit.)
A one-sided story.

一面之交 yī miàn zhī jiāo 3425
Acquaintance after one face (meeting). (lit.)
A bowing acquainatance.

反 管鮑之誼（0972）Damon and Pythias.
源 袁宏・三國名臣序贊："徒以一面之交，定臧否之決。"

一鳴驚人 yī míng jīng rén 3426
To startle (people) with one crow. (lit.)
Come as a bombshell.
Make a noise in the world.
To startle the world.

反 默默無聞（1858）To be a nobody.
源 史記・滑稽列傳："此鳥不飛則已，一飛沖天，不鳴則已，一鳴驚人。"

一命嗚呼 yī mìng wū hū 3427
Kick the bucket.
To peg out.
With one's feet foremost.
Turn up one's toes.
To snuff it.
One life sadly gone.

3428 一模一樣 yī mú yī yàng
One and the same. (lit.)
A spitting image.
There is nothing to choose between them.
As like as two peas in a pod.
Cast in the same mold.
The very image of
The very spit of
Without a shade of difference.

反 迴然不同（1409）As different as chalk is from cheese.

3429 一目了然 yī mù liǎo rán
To perceive at a glance. (lit.)
Everbody can see that at a glance (with half an eye).
He that runs may read.
Leap to the eye.

同 一望而知（3471）One glance was enough.

3430 一年到頭 yī nián dào tóu
One year to end (head). (lit.)
All the year round.

3431 一年之計在於春
yī nián zhī jì zài yú chūn
A year's plan is in the spring. (lit.)
April and May are the key of the year.

源 南朝．梁．蕭繹．纂要："一年之計在於春，一日之計在於晨。"

3432 一諾千金 yī nuò qiān jīn
A promise worth thousand gold. (lit.)
Words as good as gold.
The promise of a man of faith.
To be as good as one's word.

反 人而無信，不知其可也（2199）He that has lost his credit is dead to the world.
源 史記．季布欒布列傳："得黃金百斤，不如得季布一諾。"

3433 一派胡言 yī pài hú yán
A lot of nonsense. (lit.)
Broad nonsense.

同 亂說一通（1707）To fly a kite.
反 言之成理（3313）It stands to reason.

一貧如洗 yī pín rú xǐ ◀3434
So poor as if one has been washed. (lit.)
As poor as a church mouse.
Be down and out.
Be hard up.
On one's uppers.
One's hair grows through one's hood.

同 不名一文（0323）Have not a penny to bless oneself with.
反 腰纏萬貫（3344）Roll in wealth.

一抔之土未乾 yī póu zhī tǔ wèi gān ◀3435
The earth of a grave is not yet dried. (lit.)
Hardly cold in the grave.

源 駱賓王．討武曌檄："一抔之土未乾，六尺之孤何托。"

一僕不事二主 yī pú bú shì èr zhǔ ◀3436
A servant does not serve two masters. (lit.)
No man can serve two masters.
Masters two will not do.

一曝十寒 yī pù shí hán ◀3437
One day of sunning followed by ten days of cooling. (lit.)
By fits and snatches (starts).

反 堅持不懈（1264）Peg away at it.
源 孟子．告子上："雖有天下易生之物也，一日暴之，十日寒之，未有能生者也。"

一氣呵成 yī qì hē chéng ◀3438
To accomplish with one breath. (lit.)
At a breath (stretch).
At one sitting.

同 貫徹始終（0977）Such beginning, such end.
反 或作或輟（1171）Off and on.
源 清．李漁．閒情偶寄．賓白："亦皆一氣呵成，無有斷續。"

一錢不值 yī qián bù zhí ◀3439
Not worth a copper. (lit.)
Not worth a farthing.
Not worth a fig.

同 賤如糞土（1288）As cheap as dirt.
反 無價之寶（2971）Not to be had for love or money.
源 史記．魏其武安侯列傳："生平毀程不識不值一錢。"

一竅不通 yī qiào bù tōng ◀3440
Not one cavity open. (lit.) (The seven cavities: eyes, ears mouth and nostrils are the channels of intelligence).
All Greek to one.
A babe in the woods.
A total greenhorn.

反 滿腹經綸（1741）To give chapter and verse.
源 呂氏春秋注："紂心不通，安於為惡，若其一竅通，則比干不殺矣。"

3441 一切完蛋 yī qiè wán dàn

All is finished and zero (= 0 which looks like an egg). (lit.)

The game is up.

The jig is up.

All is up.

3442 一清二楚 yī qīng èr chǔ

One plain, two clear. (lit.)

As plain as the nose on one's face.

As clear as day.

As clear as crystal.

同 毫不含糊（1021）Make no bones of

反 糊裏糊塗（1088）To be in a muddle.

3443 一丘之貉 yī qiū zhī hé

Badgers of the same mound. (lit.)

All tarred with the same brush.

Cut from the same cloth.

源 漢書．楊惲傳："古與今，如一丘之貉。"

3444 一去不復返 yī qù bú fù fǎn

Once gone, never return. (lit.)

Gone with the wind.

To be going for good and all.

Gone forever.

Have left for good.

同 杳如黃鶴（3352）Nowhere to be found.

反 捲土重來（1451）Stage a comeback.

源 崔顥．黃鶴樓詩："黃鶴一去不復返。"

3445 一人傳十，十人傳百

yī rén chuán shí, shí rén chuán bǎi

Spread (news) from one person to ten and from ten to hundred. (lit.)

Pass from mouth to mouth.

Flow from lip to lip.

同 不脛而走（0208）Spread like wildfire.

反 不可為外人道（0222）Between you, me and the gatepost.

源 宋．陶谷．清異錄："一傳十，十傳百，展轉無窮，故號義疾。"

3446 一人傳虛，萬人傳實

yī rén chuán xū, wàn rén chuán shí

One person may spread false, ten thousand people will spread the truth. (lit.)

Fling dirt enough and some will stick.

源 語出《釋道源．景德傳燈錄．東禪契納禪師》

一人計短，二人計長 3447
yī rén jì duǎn, èr rén jì cháng
One person's plan short, two persons' long. (lit.)
Two heads are better than one.
Four eyes see more than two.

同 集思廣益（1224）In the multitude of counsellors there is safety.

一日三秋 yī rì sān qiū 3448
One day is like three autumns. (lit.)
It seems ages.
Time hangs heavy on one's hand.
An eternity.

源 詩經．王風．采葛：“彼采蕭兮，一日不見，如三秋兮。”

一如既往 yī rú jì wǎng 3449
The same as the past. (lit.)
Just like the days of yore.
To be left intact.

同 依然如故（3511）Everything in the garden is rosy once more.
反 面目全非（1799）Beyond recognition.

一掃而光 yī sǎo ér guāng 3450
One sweep to clean. (lit.)
Make a clean sweep of things.
Completely wipe out.
Snapped up.

一身兒女債，半世老婆奴 3451
yī shēn ér nǚ zhài, bàn shì lǎo pó nú
A man owes his sons and daughters debt, half life slaves for his wife. (lit.)
Wife and children are bills of charges.

一身清白 yī shēn qīng bái 3452
One body clean and white. (lit.)
To have clean hands.
Live a clean life.

一身是膽 yī shēn shì dǎn 3453
One body is all galls. (lit.)
With plenty of guts.
As bold as a lion.

反 膽小如鼠（0575）As timid as a mouse.
源 三國志．蜀志．趙雲傳：“子龍一身都是膽也。”

3454 **一生一世** yī shēng yí shì
One life, one generation. (lit.)
From the cradle to the grave.

同 一輩子（3369）In a life time.

3455 **一失足成千古恨** yī shī zú chéng qiān gǔ hèn
One misstep may become an eternal regret. (lit.)
One wrong step may bring a great fall.
One false move may lose the game.
Do wrong once and you'll never hear the end of it.

3456 **一時之興** yī shí zhī xìng
Spur of the moment. (lit.)
On the impulse (spur) of the moment.

反 蓄謀已久（3254）Done in cold blood.

3457 **一視同仁** yī shì tóng rén
Seeing everyone the same. (lit.)
When it rains it rains on all alike.
The sun shines upon all alike.
The sea has fish for every man.
Not to make chalk of one and cheese of another.
Without discrimination.

同 等量齊觀（0627）Put on a par.
反 區別對待（2150）Make fish of one and flesh of another.
源 韓愈・原人："一視而同仁。"

3458 **一事無成** yī shì wú chéng
Without a single accomplishment. (lit.)
Have nothing to show for it.
Not a thing accomplished.
All ended in smoke.

反 從勝利走向勝利（0463）Nothing succeeds like success.
源 白居易・除夜寄微之詩："鬢毛不覺白毿毿，一事無成百不堪。"

3459 **一說曹操，曹操就到**
yī shuō cáo cāo, cáo cāo jiù dào
One mention of Cao-Cao (a famous war-lord in Chinese history in the period of Three Kingdoms), he'll arrive. (lit.)
Talk of the devil, and he'll appear.
Mention the wolf's name is to see the same.
Speak of the angels, and you will hear their wings.
Think of the devil, and he is looking over your shoulder.
Talk of the devil, and he's sure to come.

一絲不苟 yī sī bù gǒu 3460

Not careless even with a thread. (lit.)

Dot one's i's and cross one's t's.

Take care of the pence and the pounds will take care of themselves.

同 認認真真（2247）In sober earnest.

反 隨隨便便（2657）Free and easy.

一絲不掛 yī sī bú guà 3461

Not even hanging with a silk thread (on one's body). (lit.)

With not a stitch on.

In nature's garb.

In birthday clothes.

In the buff.

In the raw.

反 盛裝冠戴（2437）In full fig (feather).

源 宋・楊萬里詩："放閘老翁殊耐冷，一絲不掛下冰灘。"

一死了之 yī sǐ liǎo zhī 3462

To finish with one's death. (lit.)

Death pay all debts.

同 了此一生（1642）Go the way of all flesh.

一塌糊塗 yī tā hú tú 3463

The whole bed in disorder. (lit.)

A pretty kettle of fish.

A devil of a mess.

同 亂七八糟（1708）At sixes and sevens.

反 有條不紊（3671）In apple-pie order.

一潭死水 yī tán sǐ shuǐ 3464

A deep pool of stagnant water. (lit.)

Like stagnant water.

反 洶湧澎湃（3229）Rise in a surging tide.

一天到晚 yī tiān dào wǎn 3465

A day (from dawn) to night. (lit.)

Day in, day out.

All the day long.

一條臭魚弄腥一鍋湯 3466

yī tiáo chòu yú nòng xīng yì guō tāng

One smelly fish makes a pan of soup fishy. (lit.)

One ill weed mars a whole pot of pottage.

A fly in the ointment.

3467 一萬年太久，只爭朝夕
yī wàn nián tài jiǔ, zhǐ zhēng zhāo xī
Ten thousand years may seem too long, but the difference may be a morning and an evening. (lit.)
Never put off till tomorrow what may be done today.

反 來日方長（1538）There's plenty of time yet.

3468 一網打盡 yī wǎng dǎ jìn
Capture all in one net. (lit.)
Sweep everything into one's net.
Make a clean sweep.

源 宋 · 魏泰 · 東軒筆錄："聊為相公一網打盡。"

3469 一往無前 yī wǎng wú qián
To go ahead with nothing in front. (lit.)
Press forward.
Never to look back.
Carry all before one.
Never to look behind one.

同 勇往直前（3619）Forge ahead.
反 開倒車（1467）To back-pedal.

3470 一往直前 yī wǎng zhí qián
To go straight forward. (lit.)
Follow one's nose.
Make a bee-line.
As the crow flies.

反 拐彎抹角（0961）In a roundabout way.

3471 一望而知 yī wàng ér zhī
To know at one glance. (lit.)
One glance was enough.

3472 一無是處 yī wú shì chù
Nothing is right or good. (lit.)
Good for nothing.
Good-for-naught.

3473 一無所長 yī wú suǒ cháng
Having not one special ability. (lit.)
A rolling stone gathers no moss.
Jack of all trades and master of none.

反 多才多藝（0694）To be all-round.

一無所有 yī wú suǒ yǒu
Without a single thing. (lit.)
Not a shirt to one's name.
Nothing in the world.
As poor as Lazarus.

同 一貧如洗（3434）As poor as a church mouse.
源 敦煌變文集・盧山遠公話："如水中之月，空里之風，萬法皆無，一無所有，此即名為無形。" 3474

一無所知 yī wú suǒ zhī
To know no more than the man in the moon about it.
To be in the dark.
Not to know beans about
To be no wiser (none the wiser).
To know neither buff nor style.
To know not a thing.

同 茫然無知（1768）To be at sea.
反 消息靈通（3127）To be in the know. 3475

一息尚存 yī xī shàng cún
One last breath is still present. (lit.)
At one's last gasp.
While there is life.

源 朱熹・朱子全書・論語："一息尚存，此志不容少懈，可謂遠矣。" 3476

一線希望 yī xiàn xī wàng
A thread of hope. (lit.)
A gleam (ray) of hope. 3477

一笑置之 yī xiào zhì zhī
Leave it with a laugh. (lit.)
Dismiss with a laugh.
Laugh it off.
Carry off with a laugh.
Laugh out of court.

源 宋・楊萬里・觀水歎詩："出處未可必，一笑姑置之。" 3478

一蟹不如一蟹 yī xiè bù rú yí xiè
One crab is not as good as the other. (lit.)
From smoke into smother.
Go from bad to worse.

同 每況愈下（1778）Out of the parlour into the kitchen.
源 清・翟灝・通俗編引聖宋掇遺："真所謂一蟹不如一蟹也。" 3479

一心一意 yī xīn yí yì
One heart, one mind. (lit.)
With undivided attention.
Heart and soul.

同 專心致志（3938）Set one's heart on.
反 漠不關心（1854）Not to care a hang.
源 書經："予有臣三千，惟一心。" 3480

3481 **一言蔽之** yī yán bì zhī

One word covers it. (lit.)

Briefly speaking.

Make a long story short.

In a nutshell.

同 簡而言之（1276）It boils down to this.

源 論語："詩三百，一言以蔽之，曰，思無邪。"

3482 **一言不發** yī yán bù fā

Not one word is spoken. (lit.)

Hold one's peace (tongue).

As mum as a mouse.

同 閉口不言（0119）Not to breathe a syllable.

反 絮絮不休（3253）Talk the bark off a tree.

3483 **一言既出，駟馬難追**

yī yán jì chū, sì mǎ nán zhuī

A word once spoken, four horses cannot recall. (lit.)

A word spoken is past recalling.

When the word is out, it belongs to another.

源 宋．歐陽修．筆說："俗云，一言出口，駟馬難追。"

3484 **一言難盡** yī yán nán jìn

Hard to finish by one word. (lit.)

Can't be put in a few words.

It is a long story.

源 元曲選．虎頭牌："我一言難盡，來探望你這歹孩兒，索是遠路風塵。"

3485 **一言堂** yī yán táng

One speaking hall. (lit.)

The voice of one man is the voice of no one.

The eternal talker neither hears nor learns.

To lay down the law.

3486 **一言為定** yī yán wéi dìng

One word can decide it. (lit.)

A bargain is a bargain.

You can take my word for it.

3487 **一眼三關** yī yǎn sān guān

One eye watches three. (lit.)

Keep one's eyes peeled (skinned).

Have one's eyes about one.

To be all eyes.

同 金睛火眼（1341）Keep one's eyes skinned.

反 視而不見（2527）As blind as a bat.

一意孤行 yī yì gū xíng 3488

To act alone with one mind. (lit.)

Take the law into one's hand.

Go one's own way.

Take the bit in one's mouth (teeth).

同 一言堂（3485）Lay down the law.

反 集思廣益（1224）Lay our heads together.

源 史記．張湯列傳："絕知友賓客之請，孤立行一意而已。"

一應俱全 yī yìng jù quán 3489

Everything is complete. (lit.)

Root and branch.

反 零零碎碎（1664）Odds and ends.

一語道破 yī yǔ dào pò 3490

One word speaks through the truth. (lit.)

To strike home.

Hit the nail right on the head.

同 一針見血（3494）Sting to the quick.

一語到題 yī yǔ dào tí 3491

One say reaches the point. (lit.)

To come to the point.

Hit the bull's eye.

同 開門見山（1473）Mince no matters.

反 閃爍其詞（2341）Speak with one's tongue in one's cheek.

一朝被蛇咬，三年怕井繩 3492

yī zhāo bèi shé yǎo, sān nián pà jǐng shéng

One day bitten by a snake, three years still afraid of rope of the well. (lit.)

Once bitten, twice shy.

The burnt child dreads the fire.

同 心有餘悸（3196）He has seen a wolf.

反 初生之犢不畏虎（0427）They that know nothing fear nothing.

一朝之計在於晨 yī zhāo zhī jì zài yú chén 3493

The plan of the day is made in the morning. (lit.)

An hour in the morning is worth two in the evening.

一針見血 yī zhēn jiàn xiě 3494

One needle, see blood. (lit.)

Put one's finger on.

String to the quick.

Hit the right nail on the head.

Touch one on the raw.

3495 一知半解 yī zhī bàn jiě

Knowing one, understand half. (lit.)

Have only a smattering of

Quarter flash and three parts foolish.

Holding the eel of science by the tail.

A little learning is a dangerous thing.

Tyro and smatterer.

反 造詣甚深（3767）To be at home in

源 宋・嚴羽・滄浪詩話：“有透徹之悟，有但得一知半解之悟。”

3496 一紙空文 yī zhǐ kōng wén

A sheet of empty statement. (lit.)

A scrap of paper.

A mere formality.

3497 一擲千金 yī zhì qiān jīn

One fling thousand gold. (lit.)

Play ducks and drakes with one's money.

Spend money like water.

同 大肆揮霍（0553）Buy a white horse.

反 錙銖計較（3964）Look at both sides of a penny.

源 高適詩：“一擲千金都是膽，家徒四壁不知貧。”

3498 一專多能 yī zhuān duō néng

Specialised in one and talented in many. (lit.)

Know something of everything and everything of something.

反 一無所長（3473）A rolling stone gathers no moss.

3499 一字不差 yī zì bù chā

Not one word wrong. (lit.)

Word for word.

To the letter.

反 歪曲篡改（2834）To tamper with（the text）.

3500 衣鉢相傳 yī bō xiāng chuán

To inhert priestly robe. (lit.)

One's mantle falls on another.

同 交班（1301）Hand on the torch.

源 金・王若虛・滹南遺老集：“門徒親黨以衣鉢相傳。”

3501 衣不蔽體 yī bù bì tǐ

The garments do not cover the body. (lit.)

Not a rag to one's back.

反 盛裝冠戴（2437）In full feather.

衣服麗都 yī fú lì dū 3502
The clothes beautiful and elegant. (lit.)
Doll oneself up.
Make a gallant show.
Got up like a dog's dinner.

源 戰國策："妻子衣服麗都。"

衣冠不整 yī guān bù zhěng 3503
Dressed untidily. (lit.)
In one's shirt-sleeves.

反 盛裝冠戴（2437）In full fig.

衣冠楚楚 yī guān chǔ chǔ 3504
One is brightly dressed. (lit.)
Well groomed.
Dressed up to the ninety nines.
To dress within an inch of one's life.
In full feather (fig).

同 盛裝冠戴（2437）In full fig.
反 衣衫襤褸（3507）To be out at elbows.
源 詩經·曹風·蜉蝣："衣裳楚楚。"

衣冠禽獸 yī guān qín shòu 3505
A dressed-up fowl and beast. (lit.)
A wolf in sheep's clothing.
It is not the coat that makes the gentleman.

同 人面獸心（2209）A fair face may hide a foul heart.

衣來伸手，飯來張口 3506
yī lái shēn shǒu, fàn lái zhāng kǒu
Clothes come stretch out the hand, rice comes open the mouth. (lit.)
Kitty Swerrock where she sat, come reach me this, come reach me that.

反 自己動手，豐衣足食（3982）He that will eat the kernel must crack the nut.

衣衫襤褸 yī shān lán lǚ 3507
The clothes shabby and ragged. (lit.)
Out at elbows.
Down at the heels.

同 鶉衣百結（0451）To be threadbare.

衣食足而後禮義興 3508
yī shí zú ér hòu lǐ yì xīng
Only after clothes and food are enough, righteous principles prosper. (lit.)
Meat is much, but manners is more.

3509 衣食足而後知禮義 yī shí zú ér hòu zhī lǐ yì

Only after clothes and food are enough, one knows righteousness. (lit.)

Sharp stomachs make short graces.

3510 衣食足而後知榮辱

yī shí zú ér hòu zhī róng rǔ

Only after clothes and food are enough, one knows honour and shame. (lit.)

Well fed, well bred.

The belly hates a long sermon.

An empty sack cannot stand upright.

同 民以食為天（1808）Bread is the staff of life.

3511 依然如故 yī rán rú gù

To remain unchanged as before. (lit.)

Everything in the garden is rosy once more.

同 原封不動（3730）To be left intact.

反 面目全非（1799）Beyond recognition.

3512 依樣畫葫蘆 yī yàng huà hú lú

Sketch the gourd in the same pattern. (lit.)

A carbon copy.

Play the sedulous ape.

A copy cat.

同 襲人故智（3052）Take a leaf out of another's book.

反 自出心裁（3972）Out of one's own head.

源 續湘山野錄："堪笑翰林陶學士，年年依樣畫葫蘆。"

3513 依依不捨 yī yī bù shě

Unwilling to part from. (lit.)

Leave one with regret.

Can't tear oneself away.

反 避之則吉（0127）Steer clear of

源 楚辭："戀戀兮依依。"

3514 醫得病，醫不得命

yī dé bìng, yī bù dé mìng

Medicine can cure diseases but cannot cure life. (lit.)

God heals and the doctor takes the fee.

If the doctor cures, the sun sees it; but if he kills, the earth hides it.

3515 夷為廢墟 yí wéi fèi xū

To demolish into ruins. (lit.)

To lay waste.

宜將有日思無日 3516
yí jiāng yǒu rì sī wú rì
One ought to use the days having (plenty) to think of days having nothing. (lit.)
In fair weather prepare for foul.

同 積穀防饑（1189）Lay up against a rainy day.

宜將有日思無日，莫把無時作有時 3517
yí jiāng yǒu rì sī wú rì, mò bǎ wú shí zuò yǒu shí
One ought to use the days having plenty to think of days having nothing and not to consider time of nothing as time of plenty. (lit.)
Better spare at brim than at bottom.

移山倒海 yí shān dǎo hǎi 3518
Move the mountains and turn over the sea. (lit.)
Move heaven and earth.

貽笑大方 yí xiào dà fāng 3519
Make a laughing stock of the gentility. (lit.)
Expose oneself to ridicule.
Make an ass of oneself.
Cut a sorry figure.
Make a laughing stock of oneself.

同 有失體統（3669）Drop a brick.
源 莊子・秋水：“吾長見笑於大方之家。”

疑神疑鬼 yí shén yí guǐ 3520
Suspicious of gods and ghosts. (lit.)
Take every bush for a bugbear.
Harbour suspicions.

同 頓起疑心（0692）To smell a rat.
反 信以為真（3209）Swallow it hook, line and sinker.

疑信參半 yí xìn cān bàn 3521
Being half in belief and half in doubt. (lit.)
Half in doubt.

同 姑妄聽之（0931）Take with a grain of salt.
反 深信不疑（2400）Feel it in one's bones.

3522 **頤指氣使** yí zhǐ qì shǐ

To give order by moving the cheek. (lit.)

With a haughty air.

Twist a person round one's little finger.

Have a person under one's girdle.

Get someone by the short hairs.

To boss about.

同 招之即來，揮之即去（3807）At one's beck and call.

反 唯命是從（2890）To be at one's service.

源 漢書．貢禹傳：“家富勢足，目指氣使。”

3523 **遺臭萬年** yí chòu wàn nián

To leave a nasty smell for ten thousand years. (lit.)

The evil that men do lives after them.

同 身敗名裂（2381）Die like a dog.

反 流芳百世（1678）Have a niche in the temple of fame.

源 世說新語：“晉桓溫有大志，嘗撫枕歎曰，既不能流芳百世，不足復遺臭萬年耶。”

3524 **以不變應萬變**

yǐ bú biàn yìng wàn biàn

With unchanged situation face ten thousand changes. (lit.)

Play possum.

Quietness is best.

Better sit still than rise and fall.

When in doubt, do nowt.

Take a firm hold.

反 見機行事（1277）Play it by ear.

3525 **以德報怨** yǐ dé bào yuàn

To recompense hatred with kindness. (lit.)

Return good for evil.

Heap coals of fire on a person's head.

反 恩將仇報（0719）Bite the hand that feeds one.

源 論語．憲問：“以德報怨，何如。”

3526 **以毒攻毒** yǐ dú gōng dú

With poison to attack poison. (lit.)

Give tit for tat.

Set a rogue to catch a rogue.

Like cures like.

同 以夷制夷（3544）An old poacher makes the best keeper.

源 明．陶宗儀．輟耕錄：“骨咄犀，蛇角也，其性至毒，而能解毒，蓋以毒攻毒也。”

3527 **以寡敵眾** yǐ guǎ dí zhòng

Few fight against masses. (lit.)

To fight against odds.

反 投鞭斷流（2786）Their name is Legion.

以和為貴 yǐ hé wéi guì 3528
To consider peace precious. (lit.)
A bad compromise is better than a good lawsuit.
反 爭一日之長短（3836）Wrangle for an ass's shadow.

以己度人 yǐ jǐ duó rén 3529
Measure others by oneself. (lit.)
Measure another's corn by one's own bushel.
Measure another's foot by your own last.

以假亂真 yǐ jiǎ luàn zhēn 3530
Use false to confuse truth. (lit.)
Foist a thing off on one.
同 掛羊頭賣狗肉（0960）Cry up wine and sell vinegar.
反 貨真價實（1173）Worth its weight in gold.

以理服人 yǐ lǐ fú rén 3531
Persuade others with reason. (lit.)
Bring around.
Bring one to reason.
Drive home one's point.
反 強詞奪理（2091）Without rhyme or reason.

以禮相待 yǐ lǐ xiāng dài 3532
Treat each other with courtesy. (lit.)
Give and take.
反 劍拔弩張（1289）At sword's points with each other.

以卵擊石 yǐ luǎn jī shí 3533
Use eggs to hit stones. (lit.)
Throw a straw against the wind.
Run one's head against a stone wall.
Whether the pitcher strikes the stone, or the stone the pitcher, it is bad for the pitcher.
同 螳臂擋車（2689）Kick against the pricks.
源 墨子・貴義：“以其言非吾言者，是猶以卵投石也。”

以其人之道還治其人之身 3534
yǐ qí rén zhī dào huán zhì qí rén zhī shēn
Return and practice one's way upon himself. (lit.)
Pay one back in his own coin.
Give one some of his own medicine.
Pay back in kind.

3535 **以人之長補己之短**
yǐ rén zhī cháng bǔ jǐ zhī duǎn
Use others' long (good points) to mend one's own shortcomings. (lit.)
A dwarf on a giant's shoulders sees further of the two.

3536 **以柔制剛** yǐ róu zhì gāng
Use gentleness to subjugate hardness. (lit.)
Willows are weak yet they bind other wood.
Soft and fair goes far.

3537 **以身殉職** yǐ shēn xùn zhí
Sacrifice one's life for duty. (lit.)
To die in harness.

同 鞠躬盡瘁（1436）Die in the last ditch.

3538 **以身作則** yǐ shēn zuò zé
Use oneself as an example. (lit.)
Practice what you preach.
Set a good example for others.

同 身教勝於言教（2384）Example is better than precept.
反 好話說盡，壞事做盡（1037）The devil can cite Scripture for his purpose.

3539 **以恕己之心恕人** yǐ shù jǐ zhī xīn shù rén
With the heart forgiving oneself forgive others. (lit.)
Forget others' faults by remembering your own.

3540 **以天下為己任** yǐ tiān xià wéi jǐ rèn
Take the world as one's own business. (lit.)
Have the weight of the world on one's shoulders.

同 勇挑重擔（3618）Bite off a big chunk.
反 事不關己，高高掛起（2508）I'll neither meddle nor make.

3541 **以退為進** yǐ tuì wéi jìn
Retreat in order to go forward. (lit.)
We must recoil a little, to the end we may leap the better.
Retreat a few paces in order to get a better leap.

源 語出《漢・楊雄・法言》

以小人之心度君子之腹 3542
yǐ xiǎo rén zhī xīn duó jūn zǐ zhī fù
A mean person with his mind to measure a gentleman's belly. (lit.)
A rogue always suspects deceit.

同 以己度人（3529）Measure another's corn by one's own bushel.
源 世說新語："可謂以小人之慮，度君子之心。"

以眼還眼，以牙還牙 3543
yǐ yǎn huán yǎn, yǐ yá huán yá
To return eye with eye, return tooth with tooth. (lit.)
Pay one back in his own coin.
An eye for an eye; a tooth for a tooth.
Return like for like.
Tit for tat.
Give as good as one gets (takes).

同 針鋒相對（3824）Measure for measure.

以夷制夷 yǐ yí zhì yí 3544
Use barbarous people to subjugate barbarous people. (lit.)
Set a thief (rogue) to catch a thief (rogue).
An old poacher makes the best keeper.
Play both ends against the middle.

同 強中更有強中手，惡人自有惡人磨（2089）Diamond cut diamond.
源 王安石・梅侍讀碑銘："兵法所謂以夷攻夷。"

以怨報德 yǐ yuàn bào dé 3545
To compense kindness with hatred. (lit.)
Bite the hand that feeds one.
Return evil for good.
The axe goes to the wood where it borrowed its helve.
Save a thief from the gallows and he will cut your throat.

反 以德報怨（3525）Return good for evil.

以責人之心責己 yǐ zé rén zhī xīn zé jǐ 3546
With the heart blaming others blame oneself. (lit.)
Those who live in glass houses should not throw stones.

3547 **以責人之心責己，以恕己之心恕人**
yǐ zé rén zhī xīn zé jǐ, yǐ shù jǐ zhī xīn shù rén
With the heart blaming others blame oneself, with the heart forgiving oneself forgive others. (lit.)
Pardon all but thyself.
Forgive any sooner than thyself.

3548 **以直報怨** yǐ zhí bào yuàn
To recompense hatred with righteousness. (lit.)
To get even with
To pay home.
Serve one with the same sauce.
Return like for like.

源 論語．憲問："以直報怨，以德報德。"

3549 **以珠彈雀** yǐ zhū tán què
Use pearls to strike birds. (lit.)
The game is not worth the candle.
Not worth powder and shot.

同 得不償失（0609）Give a lark to catch a kite.
反 拋磚引玉（1954）Throw out a sprat to catch a whale.
源 莊子．讓王："以隋侯之珠，彈千仞之雀，世必笑之。"

3550 **以子之矛攻子之盾**
yǐ zǐ zhī máo gōng zǐ zhī dùn
Direct one's spear against one's own shield. (lit.)
Turn a person's battery against himself.
Beat one with his own staff.

同 以其人之道，還治其人之身（3534）Give one some of his own medicine.
源 韓非子："以子之矛，攻子之盾何如。"

3551 **倚老賣老** yǐ lǎo mài lǎo
Pride oneself's old age and "sell" his seniority. (lit.)
Set great store by one's age.
To come the old soldier over one.
Talk to one like a Dutch uncle.

源 元曲選．謝金吾："則管裏倚老賣老，口裏嘮嘮叨叨的說個不了。"

3552 **倚馬可待** yǐ mǎ kě dài
Leaning on a horse one can wait. (lit.)
In two shakes of a lamb's tail.

同 指日可待（3883）Before long.
反 望眼欲穿（2872）All agog.
源 李白．與韓荊州書："請日試萬言，倚馬可待。"

衣錦夜行 yī jǐn yè xíng 3553

Wearing embroidered robes, one strolls by night. (lit.)

Hide one's light under a bushel.

反 家醜外揚（1250）Wash one's dirty linen in public.

源 史記及漢書 · 項籍傳：“富貴不歸故鄉，如衣繡（錦）夜行。”

亦步亦趨 yì bù yì qū 3554

Step for step, stride for stride. (lit.)

Follow in the wake (tail) of another.

Follow suit.

Dog one's steps.

Dance to someone's music.

Play the sedulous ape.

Copy in every way.

同 緊跟（1351）Follow hard after.

源 莊子 · 田子方：“夫子步亦步，趨亦趨。”

易放難收 yì fàng nán shōu 3555

Easy to relax but difficult to hold back. (lit.)

Scatter with one hand, gather with two.

Raise no more spirits than you can conjure down.

Fire is a good servant but a bad master.

易如反掌 yì rú fǎn zhǎng 3556

As easy as turning over the palm of the hand. (lit.)

As easy as winking (shelling peas).

As easy as pie.

As easy as rolling off a log.

Mere child's play.

I would do it before breakfast.

As easy as A B C.

同 輕而易舉（2124）Can do it on one's head.

反 老大難（1561）A hard nut to crack.

源 枚乘 · 上書諫吳王：“變所欲為，易於反掌，安如泰山。”

異口同聲 yì kǒu tóng shēng 3557

Different mouths with the same voice. (lit.)

With one accord.

Be of one voice.

In chorus.

反 莫衷一是（1853）Agree like the clocks of London.

源 宋書 · 庾炳之傳：“今之事跡，異口同音。”

3558 異途同歸 yì tú tóng guī
Taking different routes, return together. (lit.)
All roads lead to Rome.
There are more ways to the wood than one.

同 百川歸海（0049）All rivers do what they can for the sea.
反 分道揚鑣（0783）Go separate ways.
源 淮南子："五帝三王，異路同歸。"

3559 異想天開 yì xiǎng tiān kāi
Fanciful wish, the Heaven would open. (lit.)
Cry for the moon.
Have one's head full of bees.
Flight of fancy.
Wishful thinking.
Farfetched.

同 想入非非（3116）Build castles in the air.
反 實事求是（2480）Look fact in the face.

3560 逸趣橫生 yì qù héng shēng
Leisured interest comes from every side. (lit.)
As good as a play.
Enough to make a dog laugh.

同 興致盎然（3226）With gusto.
反 枯燥無味（1516）As dry as dust.

3561 意見分歧 yì jiàn fēn qí
To be divided in opinions. (lit.)
Cannot draw horses together.
Opinions are divided.

同 莫衷一是（1853）Agree like the clocks of London.
反 英雄所見略同（3596）Great minds think alike.

3562 意見一致 yì jiàn yí zhì
Opinions agree as one. (lit.)
To see eye-to-eye with
To be of one mind.

反 議論紛紜（3925）So many men, so many minds.

3563 意氣消沉 yì qì xiāo chén
To be low spirit and depressed. (lit.)
Have one's heart in one's boots.
Down in the mouth.
To be in the doldrums.

同 心情低落（3183）To be a peg too low.
反 精神抖擻（1390）Keep one's pecker up.

3564 意氣用事 yì qì yòng shì
To act according to sentiment. (lit.)
Act on impulse.
For sentimental reasons.
Carried away by

源 史記："意氣揚揚，甚自得也。"

意味深長 yì wèi shēn cháng 3565

Idea and taste are deep and lengthy (profound). (lit.)

To express volumes.

源 杜牧詩："始覺空門意味長。"

義不容辭 yì bù róng cí 3566

Duty should not be shirked. (lit.)

To be incumbent upon one.

Make a virtue of necessity.

Under a moral obligation.

同 責無旁貸（3768）To be duty-bound.

反 多一事不如少一事（0707）Leave well alone.

源 三國演義："使玄德同力拒曹，……玄德既為東吳之婿，亦義不容辭。"

義憤填膺 yì fèn tián yīng 3567

Righteous indignation fills one's breast. (lit.)

It makes one's blood boil.

One's blood boils with indignation.

Filled with resentment.

義無反顧 yì wú fǎn gù 3568

Righteousness will not look back. (lit.)

With colours nailed to the mast.

Burn one's bridges.

Neck or nothing.

Go all lengths.

Go to a thing bald-headed.

To the bitter end.

Heedless of consequences.

同 捨得一身剮（2372）To tempt providence.

源 司馬相如．喻巴蜀檄："義不反顧，計不旋踵。"

義務勞動 yì wù láo dòng 3569

Voluntary labour. (lit.)

Labour of love.

同 枵腹從公（3121）Get all the kicks and none of the ha'pence.

反 尸位素餐（2444）Feast at the public crib.

義正辭嚴 yì zhèng cí yán 3570

Righteous principles and stern phrases. (lit.)

Express one's righteous indignation.

In no uncertain terms.

3571 **億萬斯年** yì wàn sī nián

Numerous years and innumerable ages. (lit.)

Forever and ever.

For all time.

同 千秋萬代（2065）Throughout the ages.

反 轉瞬之間（3941）In the twinkling of an eye.

源 宋・歐陽文忠集・祝壽文："千八百國，咸歸至治之風，億萬斯年，共祝無疆之壽。"

3572 **憶苦思甜** yì kǔ sī tián

Recalling the bitter (experience), think of the sweet (things to come). (lit.)

Misfortunes tell us what fortune is.

3573 **因妒生忌** yīn dù shēng jì

Fear because of jealousy. (lit.)

Look through green glasses.

3574 **因人成事** yīn rén chéng shì

Create a post for a particular person. (lit.)

Come in through the cabin window.

同 走後門（4025）Through backstairs influence.

反 獨自謀生（0682）Paddle one's own canoe.

源 史記・平原君虞卿列傳："公等碌碌，所謂因人成事者也。"

3575 **因時制宜** yīn shí zhì yí

Do what is suitable to the occasion. (lit.)

Hoist sail when the wind is fair.

源 晉書・劉頌傳："所遇不同，故當因時制宜，以盡事適今。"

3576 **因勢利導** yīn shì lì dǎo

To be guided by the advantage of the situation. (lit.)

Turn the occasion into account.

源 史記・孫子吳起列傳："善戰者因其勢而利導之。"

3577 **因小失大** yīn xiǎo shī dà

Suffer a big loss for a little gain. (lit.)

Lose a ship for a halfpenny worth of tar.

同 貪他一斗米，失卻半年糧（2674）Many go out for wool and come back shorn.

源 呂氏春秋："達子請金齊王以賞軍，齊王怒不給……及戰大敗……此貪於小利以失大利者也。"

3578 **因循慣例** yīn xún guàn lì

To fall in with habit and rule. (lit.)

Be as regular as clockwork.

同 陳陳相因（0344）Ride a method to death.

反 自出心裁（3972）Take the initiative.

因循守舊 yīn xún shǒu jiù 3579
For keeping the old (custom). (lit.)
Follow the beaten track.
Stick-in-the-mud.

反 墨守成規（1856）To move in a rut.

殷實可靠 yīn shí kě kào 3580
Honest and reliable. (lit.)
Straight as a die.
There are no flies on him.

反 人而無信，不知其可也（2199）He that once deceives is ever suspected.

陰謀敗露 yīn móu bài lù 3581
A dark plan fails and is exposed. (lit.)
The murder is out.

陰謀詭計 yīn móu guǐ jì 3582
A dark plan and a crafty scheme. (lit.)
Sharp practice.
Hatch a plot.
Intrigues and plots.
Underhand scheme.
Dirty tricks.

反 打開天窗說亮話（0490）Place one's cards on the table.

源 史記："陳平曰，我多陰謀，是道家之所禁。"

寅吃卯糧 yín chī mǎo liáng 3583
At the hour of Yin (5-6 a.m.) eat the food of Mao (7-8 a.m.). (lit.)
Outrun the constable.
Live beyond one's means.
Live above one's income.
Who more than he is worth to spend, he maketh a rope his life to end.

同 饔飧不繼（3609）Can hardly make both ends meet.

反 積穀防饑（1189）Lay up against a rainy day.

引經據典 yǐn jīng jù diǎn 3584
Quote from classics and canons. (lit.)
Give chapter and verse.
Speak by the book.

反 胡說八道（1086）Talk through one's hat.

引狼入室 yǐn láng rù shì 3585
Let a wolf into the house. (lit.)
Set a fox to keep the geese.
Play with fire.

3586 引領以待 yǐn lǐng yǐ dài
Stretch out the neck and wait. (lit.)
To be all agog for (to)
Look forward to
Crane one's neck to see.

同 望眼欲穿（2872）Hanker after.
源 孟子：“如有不嗜殺人者，則天下之民，皆引領而望之矣。”

3587 引入歧途 yǐn rù qí tú
Leading one astray. (lit.)
Lead one up the garden path.
To lead astray.
Put one off the scent.

3588 引以為榮 yǐn yǐ wéi róng
To be considered as an honour. (lit.)
To plume oneself on

3589 引以自豪 yǐn yǐ zì háo
Consider it to be one's pride. (lit.)
To pride oneself on

反 獻醜不如藏拙（3102）Better hide one's diminished head.

3590 飲酒作樂 yǐn jiǔ zuò lè
Drink and be merry. (lit.)
Wet one's whistle.

3591 飲鴆止渴 yǐn zhèn zhǐ kě
To drink poison to quench thirst. (lit.)
The remedy is worse than the disease.

源 後漢書 · 霍諝傳：“譬猶療饑於附子，止渴於鴆毒，未入腸胃，已絕咽喉，豈可為哉。”

3592 隱己之美 yǐn jǐ zhī měi
Hide one's own beauty. (lit.)
Hide one's light (candle) under a bushel.

同 不露才華（0228）Hide one's talent under a bushel.
反 自我吹噓（4001）Sing one's own praise.

3593 隱姓埋名 yǐn xìng mái míng
Conceal one's real name. (lit.)
Live in the shadow.
Live like a hermit.

反 沽名釣譽（0930）Fish for compliments.
源 元曲選 · 誤入桃源：“不事王侯，不求聞達，隱姓埋名。”

3594 隱約其辭 yǐn yuē qí cí
Hesitating to speak out. (lit.)
Mince one's words.
Say it vaguely.

同 閃爍其詞（2341）Speak with one's tongue in one's cheek.

印象深刻 yìn xiàng shēn kè
The impression is deeply engraved. (lit.)
Hit one between the eyes.
Borne in upon one.

同 入木三分（2286）Leave an indelible impression on

3595

英雄所見略同
yīng xióng suǒ jiàn lüè tóng
Heroes' views are about the same. (lit.)
Share the same view.
Great minds think alike.
Great wits jump.
See eye to eye.

同 意見一致（3562）To be of one mind.
反 意見分歧（3561）Opinions are divided.
源 三國志．蜀志．龐統傳："天下智謀之士，所見略同耳。"

3596

英雄無用武之地
yīng xióng wú yòng wǔ zhī dì
A hero has no ground to use his weapon. (lit.)
What's the good of a sun-dial in the shade?
A square peg in a round hole.

同 懷才不遇（1123）Have soul above buttons.
反 天生我才必有用（2718）All things in their being are good for something.
源 三國志："今操破荊州，威震四海，英雄無用武之地。"

3597

英姿煥發 yīng zī huàn fā
Hero's gesture shows off exuberantly. (lit.)
In one's vigorous youth.
In the flesh of youth.

反 老態龍鍾（1575）In one's dotage.

3598

迎風招展 yíng fēng zhāo zhǎn
Facing the wind to wave and unfurl. (lit.)
Flutter in the breeze.

同 飄飄欲仙（1975）As light as a butterfly.

3599

迎刃而解 yíng rèn ér jiě
Splitting as it meets the edge of a knife. (lit.)
Cut the Gordian knot.
Solve itself.

源 晉書．杜預傳："今兵威已振，譬如破竹，數節之後，皆迎刃而解，無復着手處也。"

3600

迎頭趕上 yíng tóu gǎn shàng
Facing the head (lead) catch up with. (lit.)
Make up for leeway.
To catch up with
To overtake one.

同 不甘後人（0189）Not to be outdone.
反 姍姍來遲（2337）Kiss the hare's foot.

3601

3602 **迎頭痛擊** yíng tóu tòng jī
Give a painful blow to the head. (lit.)
Deal a telling blow.
Give a great wallop.
Receive a direct hit.

同 當頭一棒（0592）Deal a head-on blow.

3603 **硬着頭皮幹到底**
yìng zhe tóu pí gàn dào dǐ
Thickening the head skin, do it to the end. (lit.)
Brazen it out.
Face it out.
Face the music.

同 知不可為而為之（3850）To square the circle.
反 急流勇退（1211）A brave retreat is a brave exploit.

3604 **應對如流** yìng duì rú liú
A flow of words in reply. (lit.)
Quick on the trigger.
Have a ready tongue.
Know all the answers.
Good at repartee.

反 張口結舌（3793）At a loss for words.
源 南史，徐勉傳："坐客充滿，應對如流。"

3605 **應付自如** yìng fù zì rú
Cope with the situation as one likes. (lit.)
Equal to every situation.
Have a ready wit.
Take care of everything.

同 縱橫捭闔（4023）Wheel and deal.

3606 **應接不暇** yìng jiē bù xiá
No time to attend to it. (lit.)
Have too many irons in the fire.
Have one's hand full.
Up to one's ears in work.

同 分身乏術（0788）One can't be in two places at once.
源 世說新語．言語："從山陰道上行，山川相映發，使人應接不暇。"

3607 **應聲蟲** yìng shēng chóng
At call worm. (lit.)
A yes-man.

同 人云亦云（2238）Repeat like a parrot.
源 文昌雜錄："淮西士人楊勔，得應聲蟲病，劉伯時教以讀《本草》至雷丸，不復應，服之而愈。"

3608 **應運而生** yìng yùn ér shēng
One is born at the right fate. (lit.)
There is a time for all things.

饔飧不繼 yōng sūn bú jì 3609

Breakfast and supper not to continue. (lit.)

Live from hand to mouth.

Can hardly make both ends meet.

反 食前方丈（2468）Live like fighting cocks.

庸人自擾 yōng rén zì rǎo 3610

Stupid people disturb themselves. (lit.)

Much ado about nothing.

Shearing of hogs.

The devil rides on a fiddlestick.

Borrow trouble.

Fret over nothing.

同 自找麻煩（4012）Invite trouble.

源 唐書．陸象先傳："天下本無事，庸人自擾之。"

庸中佼佼 yōng zhōng jiǎo jiǎo 3611

The beauty amongst the commonplace (lit.)

A Triton among the minnows.

A giant among dwarfs.

同 鶴立雞羣（1056）Stand head and shoulders above others.

源 後漢書．劉盆子傳："卿所謂鐵中錚錚，庸中佼佼者也。"

永垂不朽 yǒng chuí bù xiǔ 3612

The (spirit) is immortal. (lit.)

Go down to posterity.

One's memory will always live.

同 萬古長青（2848）Their names liveth for evermore.

永記血淚仇 yǒng jì xuè lèi chóu 3613

Always remember the vengeance of blood and tears. (lit.)

To nurse vengeance.

反 不念舊惡（0235）Let bygones be bygones.

永遠活在人心中 3614

yǒng yuǎn huó zài rén xīn zhōng

Forever living in people's heart. (lit.)

Though lost in sight, to memory dear.

永誌不忘 yǒng zhì bú wàng 3615

Permenant record is not forgotten. (lit.)

Keep the memory green

同 記憶猶新（1231）Fresh in the memory.

反 久別情疏（1415）Out of sight, out of mind.

3616 **勇敢果斷** yǒng gǎn guǒ duàn
Bravery decides the result. (lit.)
Take the bull by the horns.
Take the wolf by the ears
Grasp the nettle.

同 快刀斬亂麻（1523）Cut the Gordian knot.
反 優柔寡斷（3628）To be shilly-shally.

3617 **勇猛過人** yǒng měng guò rén
One's valour surpasses others. (lit.)
Full of guts.

反 膽小如鼠（0575）Afraid of one's own shadow.

3618 **勇挑重擔** yǒng tiāo zhòng dàn
Bravely carry the heavy load. (lit.)
Bite off a big chunk.
Carry the ball.

同 自告奮勇（3979）Take upon oneself.
反 推卸責任（2820）Pass the buck.

3619 **勇往直前** yǒng wǎng zhí qián
Bravely go straight ahead. (lit.)
Forge ahead.
Go well up to the bridle.

同 一往無前（3469）Press forward.
反 臨陣退縮（1659）Turn tail at the last moment.

3620 **用腦過度** yòng nǎo guò dù
Use the brain too much. (lit.)
Overtax the brains.

同 絞盡腦汁（1311）Rack one's brains.
反 飽食終日，無所用心（0085）A belly full of gluttony will never study willingly.

3621 **用人唯親** yòng rén wéi qīn
Employ people who should be the close relatives. (lit.)
Jobs for the boys.

反 選賢任能（3262）Let him who knows the instrument play upon it.

3622 **用心計較般般錯，退步思量事事難** yòng xīn jì jiào bān bān cuò, tuì bù sī liáng shì shì nán
Calculating by heart, all goes wrong, retreat and think, everything is difficult. (lit.)
Too much taking heed is loss.
Too much consulting confounds.
The more wit, the less courage.
He who hesitates is lost.

悠然自得 yōu rán zì dé 3623

Leisurely and pleased with oneself. (lit.)

To be carefree.

Free and easy.

同 自由自在（4009）As free as the air.

反 惘然若失（2866）To be left up a tree.

憂能傷人 yōu néng shāng rén 3624

Worry can hurt one. (lit.)

Care killed the cat.

憂心忡忡 yōu xīn chōng chōng 3625

Worried heart greatly disturbed. (lit.)

Afflicted with worry.

To have kittens.

To be on the rack.

同 惶惶不可終日（1139）To be kept in suspense.

反 無憂無慮（3003）Happy-go-lucky.

源 詩經・召南・草蟲："未見君子，憂心忡忡。"

憂心如焚 yōu xīn rú fén 3626

Worried as if one's heart burning. (lit.)

Like a hen on a hot griddle.

源 詩經・小雅・節南山："憂心如惔。"（惔，焚燒）

憂鬱寡歡 yōu yù guǎ huān 3627

Worried and seldom happy. (lit.)

As melancholy as a cat.

反 喜氣洋洋（3059）Radiant with joy.

優柔寡斷 yōu róu guǎ duàn 3628

Hesitant and lacking determination. (lit.)

To be shilly-shally.

To be neither off nor on.

同 躊躇不決（0397）Like one o'clock half struck.

反 快刀斬亂麻（1523）Cut the Gordian knot.

源 韓非子・亡征："緩心而無成，柔茹而寡斷。"

優勝劣敗 yōu shèng liè bài 3629

The superior wins and the inferior loses. (lit.)

Survival of the fittest.

同 弱肉強食（2299）Jungle justice.

優遊自在 yōu yóu zì zài 3630

Free, leisurely and comfortable. (lit.)

Free and easy.

同 舒舒服服（2564）As snug as a bug in a rug.

反 如坐針氈（2281）To be on pins and needles.

3631 **優哉悠哉** yōu zāi yōu zāi

Free and easy with leisure. (lit.)

At one's ease.

Free and easy.

同 無憂無慮（3003）To be carefree.

反 心情焦躁（3185）Hot and bother.

源 詩經．小雅．采菽：“優哉游哉，亦是戾矣。”

3632 **尤有進者** yóu yǒu jìn zhě

It is still more significant that. (lit.)

What's more.

In addition.

Into the bargain.

3633 **由儉入奢易，由奢入儉難**

yóu jiǎn rù shē yì, yóu shē rù jiǎn nán

From thriftiness into luxury is easy but from luxury into thriftiness is difficult. (lit.)

Riches come better after poverty than poverty after riches.

3634 **由來已久** yóu lái yǐ jiǔ

The cause is of long origin. (lit.)

Of a long standing.

Time honoured.

Deep-seated.

同 冰凍三尺，非一日之寒（0154）Ill habits gather by unseen degrees.

3635 **由淺入深** yóu qiǎn rù shēn

From shallow to profound. (lit.)

Learn to walk before you run.

同 循序漸進（3281）By stages.

3636 **由衷之言** yóu zhōng zhī yán

Words spoken from the heart. (lit.)

From the bottom of one's heart.

同 肺腑之言（0776）Speak one's conscience.

反 口是心非（1509）Say one thing and mean another.

3637 **油嘴滑舌** yóu zuǐ huá shé

Oily mouth and slippery tongue. (lit.)

Suave-spoken.

Oil one's tongue.

Have a well-oiled tongue.

反 結結巴巴（1323）Have stones in one's mouth.

遊山玩水 yóu shān wán shuǐ 3638
To roam in hills and play with water. (lit.)
On a pleasure trip.
Go sight-seeing.

源 景德傳燈錄："問如何是學人自己，師曰，遊山玩水去。"

遊手好閒 yóu shǒu hào xián 3639
A loafer loves idleness. (lit.)
Keep one's hands in one's pockets.
Lounge around.
Fool away one's time.
Do a mike.

同 吊兒郎當（0649）Gad about.
反 事務紛繁（2516）Up to the ears in work.
源 晉書："鄉無游手，邑不廢時。"

遊戲人間 yóu xì rén jiān 3640
To wander and play among the people. (lit.)
All the world is a stage.

同 人生如夢（2216）Life is but a dream.
源 世説新語補："世傳端明（蘇軾）已歸道山，今尚遊戲人間邪。"

遊遊逛逛 yóu yóu guàng guàng 3641
Lounging and wandering. (lit.)
To knock about.
On the loaf.

猶疑不決 yóu yí bù jué 3642
Hesitant and undecisive. (lit.)
To be capricious.
Like one o'clock half struck.
Between hawk and buzzard.
To shilly-shally.
In two minds about something.

同 優柔寡斷（3628）To be neither off nor on.
反 快刀斬亂麻（1523）Cut the Gordian knot.
源 戰國策·趙策："平原君猶豫未有所決。"

友誼賽 yǒu yì sài 3643
A friendly match. (lit.)
A round with gloves.

有備無患 yǒu bèi wú huàn 3644
Having preparedness, there is no harm. (lit.)
Have a second string to one's bow.
Though the sun shines, leave not your cloak at home.
Forewarned is forearmed.

源 左傳·襄十一年："居安思危，思則有備，有備無患。"

3645 有發言權 yǒu fā yán quán

Having the right to speak. (lit.)

Have one's say.

反 人微言輕（2228）Poor men's reasons are not heard.

3646 有分有寸 yǒu fēn yǒu cùn

Having fractions and inches. (lit.)

Know where to draw a line.

Draw the line somewhere.

Know one's distance.

3647 有福同享，有禍同當

yǒu fú tóng xiǎng, yǒu huò tóng dāng

Having blessing to share and having calamity to face together. (lit.)

For better or for worse.

Friendships multiply joys and divide griefs.

Throw in one's lot with

同 休戚與共（3236）In weal or woe.

反 有酒有肉多兄弟，急難何曾見一人（3651）In time of prosperity friends will be plenty; in time of adversity not one among twenty.

3648 有過之而無不及

yǒu guò zhī ér wú bù jí

There is only surpassing but nothing inferior. (lit.)

Go too far.

To err on the safe side.

Do a thing to a fault.

By a long chalk.

Overshoot the mark.

3649 有季常癖 yǒu jì cháng pì

Having the kink (of fear of wife) of Ji Chang. (lit.)

To be henpecked.

3650 有酒有肉多兄弟

yǒu jiǔ yǒu ròu duō xiōng dì

Having wine and meat, many brothers. (lit.)

Rich folk have many friends.

He that hath a full purse never wanted a friend.

同 富在深山有遠親（0847）Everyone is kin to the rich man.

有酒有肉多兄弟，急難何曾見一人 yǒu jiǔ yǒu ròu duō xiōng dì, jí nán hé céng jiàn yī rén 3651

Having wine and meat, many brothers; in an emergency can one person hardly be seen. (lit.)

In time of prosperity friends will be plenty; in time of adversity not one among twenty.

Prosperity makes friends, adversity tries them.

Table friendship soon changes.

Many friends, few helpers.

同 交友滿天下，知心有幾人（1305）There is a scarcity of friendship, but not of friends.

反 患難之交（1133）A friend in need is a friend indeed.

有口皆碑 yǒu kǒu jiē bēi 3652

Where there are mouths, there are one's memorial tablets. (lit.)

Everyone has a word of praise for.

Win universal praise.

To be a household word.

源 釋普濟．五燈會元："勸君不用鐫頑石，路上行人口似碑。"

有口難言 yǒu kǒu nán yán 3653

Having mouth but difficult to say. (lit.)

One's tongue fails one.

源 蘇軾．醉醒者詩："有道難行不如醉，有口難言不如睡。"

有禮走遍天下 yǒu lǐ zǒu biàn tiān xià 3654

Having courtesy one can run round under the sky (the world). (lit.)

All doors open to courtesy.

有了眉目 yǒu liǎo méi mù 3655

Beginning to have eyebrows. (lit.)

Begin to take shape.

Have made some headway.

To be under way.

同 露出苗頭（1697）Come to a head.

有名無實 yǒu míng wú shí 3656

Having a name but no reality. (lit.)

A rope of sand.

In name but not in deed.

In name only.

同 徒有虛名（2808）What good can it do an ass to be called a lion?

反 名不虛傳（1810）Worthy of the name.

源 國語．晉語："宣子曰，吾有卿之名而無其實。"

3657 **有目共睹** yǒu mù gòng dǔ

All those who have eye can see. (lit.)

It is for all the world to see.
As clear as daylight.
One would be blind not to see.
Dazzling to the eye.
Stick out a mile.
There is a witness everywhere.

3658 **有其父必有其子** yǒu qí fù bì yǒu qí zǐ

Having such a father must have such a son. (lit.)

Like father, like son.
A chip of the old block.

同 龍生龍，鳳生鳳（1692）Like begets like.

3659 **有錢能使鬼推磨**

yǒu qián néng shǐ guǐ tuī mò

Having money one can make even a ghost push a grinder. (lit.)

Money makes the mare go.
Wage will get a page.
Money talks.
Have green power.

同 錢可通神（2084）A golden key opens every door.

反 衙門八字開，有理無錢莫進來（3288）Possession is nine-tenths of the law.

3660 **有情人終成眷屬**

yǒu qíng rén zhōng chéng juàn shǔ

Having lovers, they eventually make a family. (lit.)

All shall be well, Jack shall have Jill.

同 破鍋有爛灶，李大有張嫂（2004）Every Jack has his Jill.

反 終身不嫁（3914）Lead apes in hell.

3661 **有強權，無公理**

yǒu qiáng quán, wú gōng lǐ

Having strong power, without righteousness. (lit.)

Might is right.
Providence is always on the side of great battalions.

有人掛冠歸故里，有人臨夜趕科場 yǒu rén guà guān guī gù lǐ, yǒu rén lín yè gǎn kē chǎng 3662

Someones hang up the official hat and return native home; someones at night rush to Examination Hall. (lit.)

The world is a ladder for some to go up and some down.

The world is a staircase, some are going up and some are going down.

同 宦海浮沉（1130）Ups and downs of life.

有人見，沒人見，一個樣 3663

yǒu rén jiàn, méi rén jiàn, yí gè yàng

Whether being seen or not being seen, one acts the same. (lit.)

Do on the hill as you would do in the hall.

反 當面是人，背後是鬼（0588）Who flatters me to my face will speak ill of me behind my back.

有商有量 yǒu shāng yǒu liáng 3664

There are consultations. (lit.)

Lay our heads together.

同 集思廣益（1224）In the multitude of counsellors there is safety.

反 擅作主張（2350）Take the laws into one's hands.

有麝自然香 yǒu shè zì rán xiāng 3665

Having musk there is naturally fragrance. (lit.)

Good wine needs no bush.

A rose by any other name would smell as sweet.

有生必有死 yǒu shēng bì yǒu sǐ 3666

There is life, there must be death. (lit.)

He that is once born, once must die.

As a man lives, so shall he die.

Dying is as natural as living.

同 人生自古誰無死（2219）We shall die all alike in our graves.

有失身分 yǒu shī shēn fèn 3667

Having lost one's status. (lit.)

To lose caste.

3668 **有失體面** yǒu shī tǐ miàn

Having lost one's face. (lit.)

Lose face.

Beneath one's dignity.

反 顧全顏面（0957）Keep up appearances.

3669 **有失體統** yǒu shī tǐ tǒng

Having lost dignity. (lit.)

Drop a brick.

Put one's foot into it.

反 氣派十足（2046）Stand upon one's dignity.

3670 **有始無終** yǒu shǐ wú zhōng

Have a beginning but no end. (lit.)

Left unfulfilled.

Do things by halves.

同 半途而廢（0072）Drop by the wayside.

反 一氣呵成（3438）At a stretch.

源 詩經："靡不有初，鮮克有終。"

3671 **有條不紊** yǒu tiáo bù wěn

They are in lines and not confused. (lit.)

In trim.

In apple-pie order.

Keep ship-shape.

反 亂七八糟（1708）At sixes and sevens.

源 尚書・盤庚上："若網在綱，有條不紊。"

3672 **有頭無尾** yǒu tóu wú wěi

Having a head but no tail. (lit.)

Leave a job half done.

Do things by halves.

反 善始善終（2344）See a thing through.

源 朱子全書："若是有頭無尾底人。"

3673 **有先見之明** yǒu xiān jiàn zhī míng

Having the brightness of foresight. (lit.)

Have a long head.

Have foresight.

反 事後諸葛亮（2513）It is easy to be wise after the event.

源 後漢書・楊彪傳："愧無日磾先見之明。"

3674 **有幸有不幸** yǒu xìng yǒu bú xìng

Some have luck but some have no luck. (lit.)

It is an ill wind that blows nobody good.

Some have hap, some stick in the gap.

3675 **有眼不識泰山** yǒu yǎn bù shí tài shān

Having eyes without knowing Tai Shan (famous mountain in Shan Tung Province). (lit.)

He is very blind that cannot see the sun.

有眼無珠 yǒu yǎn wú zhū ◀3676

Having eyes without pupils. (lit.)

As blind as a bat.

Wanting in judgement.

同 視而不見（2527）As blind as a mole.

反 明察秋毫（1819）See through a millstone.

有一分熱，發一分光 ◀3677

yǒu yī fēn rè, fā yī fēn guāng

Having one part of heat, produce one part of light. (lit.)

Do oneself justice.

Put one's best foot forward.

Do one's utmost.

同 各盡所能（0902）When you are an anvil, hold you still; when you are a hammer, strike your fill.

有一利必有一弊 yǒu yī lì bì yǒu yí bì ◀3678

Where there is an advantage, there must be a disadvantage. (lit.)

Nothing is perfect.

If you would enjoy the fire, you must put up with the smoke.

There is no fire without some smoke.

No rose without a thorn.

No garden without its weeds.

Bees that have honey in their mouths have stings in their tails.

The same knife cuts bread and fingers.

The wind that blows out candles kindles the fire.

有勇無謀 yǒu yǒng wú móu ◀3679

Having courage but no plan. (lit.)

Courageous but not resourceful.

Have more guts than brains.

反 用心計較般般錯，退步思量事事難（3662）The more wit, the less courage.

源 三國演義："曹操曰，吾料呂布有勇無謀，不足慮也。"

有冤報冤，有仇報仇 ◀3680

yǒu yuān bào yuān, yǒu chóu bào chóu

If there are grievances, revenge, if there are animosities, take vengeance. (lit.)

Where vice is, vengeance follows.

Measure for measure.

同 永記血淚仇（3613）To nurse vengeance.

3681 **有朝一日** yǒu zhāo yī rì

Perhaps there is such a day. (lit.)

One of these days.

One of these days is better than none of these days.

同 為期不遠（2893）Before long.

3682 **有志事竟成** yǒu zhì shì jìng chéng

One who has ambition will succeed. (lit.)

Where there's a will there's a way.

It's dogged that does it.

A wilful man will have his way.

同 世上無難事，只怕有心人（2498）Nothing is impossible to a willing heart.

反 謀事在人，成事在天（1859）Man proposes, God disposes.

源 後漢書·耿弇傳："有志者事竟成也。"

3683 **又要馬兒好，又要馬兒不吃草**

yòu yào mǎ ér hǎo, yòu yào mǎ ér bù chī cǎo

Want a horse good but also want the horse eat no grass. (lit.)

You can't eat your cake and have it.

You can't have it both ways.

You cannot sell the cow and drink the milk.

3684 **幼吾幼以及人之幼**

yòu wú yòu yǐ jí rén zhī yòu

Protect my youngs and also other people's youngs. (lit.)

Charity begins at home.

同 推己及人（2816）Put oneself in another's shoes.

源 孟子："老吾老以及人之老，幼吾幼以及人之幼，天下可運於掌。"

3685 **迂迴曲折** yū huí qū zhé

Winding (as a river) and crooked (as a path). (lit.)

Twists and turns.

Tortuous and devious.

同 拐彎抹角（0961）In a round-about way.

反 一往直前（3470）Make a bee-line.

3686 **於事無補** yú shì wú bǔ

No means to save the situation. (lit.)

To be of little avail.

3687 **於心有愧** yú xīn yǒu kuì

Ashamed in the heart. (lit.)

To have on one's conscience.

Have a guilty (bad) conscience.

同 內心慚疚（1890）The prick of conscience.

反 恬不知恥（2141）Have the effrontery （face） to

予取予攜 yú qǔ yú xié
To take and to carry away. (lit.)
Make free with

源 左傳："楚文王謂申侯曰，惟我知女（汝，下仝），女專利而不厭，予取予求，不女疵瑕也。" 3688

魚傳尺素 yú chuán chǐ sù
The fish passes a foot of message (written on a foot of cloth). (lit.)
Drop one a line.

源 古詩："客從遠方來，遺我雙鯉魚，呼童烹鯉魚，中有尺素書。" 3689

魚貫而出 yú guàn ér chū
Coming out in succession as a shoal of fish. (lit.)
In Indian file.
One behind the other.
One following another.

同 成羣結隊（0355）To muster in force. 3690
源 三國志："將士皆攀木緣崖，魚貫而進。"

魚米之鄉 yú mǐ zhī xiāng
A village (full) of fish and rice. (lit.)
Flowing with milk and honey.
A land of plenty.

源 王逢詩："魚米駢登橘柚垂。" 3691

魚目混珠 yú mù hùn zhū
Mix up fish-eyes with pearls. (lit.)
Foist on
All is not gold that glitters.

同 以假亂真（3530）Foist a thing off on one. 3692
源 漢．魏伯陽．參同契："魚目豈為珠，蓬蒿不成檟。"

愚不可及 yú bù kě jí
Can't be as stupid as that. (lit.)
No fool like an old fool.
More know Tom Fool than Tom Fool knows.

同 蠢如鹿豕（0452）As stupid as a donkey. 3693
反 足智多謀（4033）Fruitful of expedients.
源 論語．公冶長："其知可及也，其愚不可及也。"

愚昧無知 yú mèi wú zhī
Stupid and ignorant. (lit.)
Simple minded.
Not to know a hawk from a handsaw.
Not to know A from a windmill.

同 目不識丁（1864）Not to know B from a bull's foot. 3694
反 博學多才（0169）Know what's what.

3695 **愚者千慮，必有一得**
yú zhě qiān lǜ, bì yǒu yī dé
Even a fool who may have thousand troubles must have one accomplishment. (lit.)
A fool may give a wise man counsel.

反 智者千慮，必有一失（3898）No man is wise at all times.
源 晏子春秋．內篇雜下：“愚人千慮，必有一得。”

3696 **餘勇可賈** yú yǒng kě gǔ
Remaining bravery can still be used. (lit.)
Full of beans.
Enough and to spare.

源 左傳．成二年：“欲勇者鼓余餘勇。”

3697 **予人方便，自己方便**
yǔ rén fāng biàn, zì jǐ fāng biàn
Giving convenience to others is to give oneself convenience. (lit.)
Live and let live.
The hand that gives gathers.

3698 **予人可乘之機** yǔ rén kě chéng zhī jī
Give others opportunity to take. (lit.)
Lay oneself open to
A bad padlock invites a picklock.
Play into one's hands.

3699 **雨過天晴** yǔ guò tiān qíng
The rain having passed, the sky clears up. (lit.)
Change for the better.
After rain comes fine weather.
After rain comes sunshine.
The worst is over.

反 山雨欲來風滿樓（2335）When the clouds are upon the hills they'll come down by the mills.
源 謝在杭文海披沙記：“雨過天青雲破處，這般顏色做將來。”

3700 **雨後春筍** yǔ hòu chūn sǔn
Bamboo shoots sprout after a spring rain. (lit.)
Shoot up.
Spring up like mushrooms.

同 欣欣向榮（3203）Flourish like the green bay-tree.

與虎謀皮 yǔ hǔ móu pí 3701

Negotiate with a tiger for its skin. (lit.)

Make a futile effort.

Ask a kite for a feather.

源 太平御覽 · 符子："欲為千金之裘而與狐謀其皮。"

與君一夕話，勝讀十年書 3702

yǔ jūn yī xī huà, shèng dú shí nián shū

Talking with you for one night is better than reading books for ten years. (lit.)

Sweet discourse makes short days and nights.

反 話不投機半句多（1119）It's ill talking between a full man and a fasting.

與人不睦 yǔ rén bú mù 3703

Unfriendly with others. (lit.)

To be on the outs with one.

At loggerheads with

反 親密無間（2107）They cleave together like burrs.

與人為善 yǔ rén wéi shàn 3704

To do good deeds to others. (lit.)

Good intentions toward one.

Think well of all men.

反 心懷惡意（3168）To bear someone malice.

源 孟子 · 公孫丑上："是與人為善者也。"

與日俱增 yǔ rì jù zēng 3705

Increasing with days. (lit.)

Ever-increasing.

Growing with time.

Grow with each passing day.

同 蒸蒸日上（3837）On the up and up.

與生俱來 yǔ shēng jù lái 3706

To come with birth. (lit.)

Bred in the bone.

In the blood.

與世長辭 yǔ shì cháng cí 3707

Ever long leave from the world. (lit.)

Go the way of all flesh.

Join the great majority.

To be gathered to one's fathers.

Pass away.

同 溘然長逝（1500）To be no more.

3708 **與世浮沉** yǔ shì fú chén

To sink or float with the world. (lit.)

To drift with the stream.

同 隨波逐流（2653）Swim with the tide.

反 獨善其身（0680）Better be alone than in ill company.

源 史記："豈若卑論儕俗，與世沉浮，而取榮名哉。"

3709 **與世隔絕** yǔ shì gé jué

Separate completely with the world. (lit.)

Keep oneself to oneself.

All by oneself.

3710 **與世無爭** yǔ shì wú zhēng

Not in competition with the world. (lit.)

At peace with all men.

On good terms (footing) with the world.

反 爭一日之長短（3836）Wrangle for an ass's shadow.

3711 **與眾不同** yǔ zhòng bù tóng

Unlike the masses. (lit.)

To be a class by itself.

Out of the common run.

Out of the ordinary.

同 別開生面（0143）Break fresh ground.

反 平平庸庸（1989）Pass in a crowd in a push.

3712 **玉不琢不成器，人不學不知理**

yù bù zhuó bù chéng qì, rén bù xué bù zhī lǐ

Jade if not carved would not become an article; if men do not study they would not know reasoning. (lit.)

The best horse needs breaking, and the aptest child needs teaching.

源 禮記 · 學記："玉不琢不成器，人不學不知道。"

3713 **玉潔冰清** yù jié bīng qīng

As clean as jade and clear as ice. (lit.)

As chaste as ice.

同 一塵不染（3379）Spick and span.

源 晉書 · 賀循傳："冰清玉潔，行為俗表。"

3714 **欲罷不能** yù bà bù néng

Wishing to stop but unable to do so. (lit.)

To have a wolf by the ears.

同 勢成騎虎（2533）Needs must when the devil drives.

反 洗手不幹（3054）Wash one's hands of a business.

源 論語 · 子罕："欲罷不能。"

欲蓋彌彰 yù gài mí zhāng

3715

Wanting the conceal (an affair) but it would spread more openly. (lit.)

Give oneself away.

Though a lie be well dressed it is ever overcome.

源 左傳．昭三十一年："或求名而不得，或欲蓋而名章。"

欲加之罪，何患無詞 yù jiā zhī zuì, hé huàn wú cí

3716

Wanting to impose a crime to one, there is no fear of shortage of words. (lit.)

Give a dog a bad name and hang him.

He that would hang his dog gives out first that he is mad.

If you want a pretence to whip a dog, say that he ate the frying pan.

There is no wool so white but a dyer can make it black.

A stick is quickly found to beat a dog with.

源 左傳．僖十年："不有廢也，君何以興，欲加之罪，其無辭乎。"

欲擒先縱 yù qín xiān zòng

3717

If we want to catch someone, let him get away first. (lit.)

Give someone line enough.

Allow someone more latitude.

Give a thief enough rope and he'll hang himself.

Play cat and mouse with.

欲説還休 yù shuō hái xiū

3718

Wanting to say something but stop doing so. (lit.)

To shut up shop.

同 難於啟齒（1884）Stick in the throat.

反 暢所欲言（0333）Speak one's mind.

源 辛棄疾詞："如今識盡愁滋味，欲説還休，欲説還休，卻道天涼好個秋。"

欲速則不達 yù sù zé bù dá

3719

Wanting to be quick one cannot attain. (lit.)

More haste, less speed.

Haste trips over its own heels.

Haste makes waste.

The shortest way round is the longest way home.

同 忙中有錯（1763）Error is always in haste.

反 穩紮穩打（2931）Slow but sure wins the race.

源 論語．子路："無欲速，無見小利，欲速則不達，見小利則大事不成。"

3720 寓貶於褒 yù biǎn yú bāo

To reprimand in praise. (lit.)

A left-handed compliment.

Damn with faint praise.

同 明升暗降（1825）Kick one upstairs.

3721 遇飲酒時須飲酒，得高歌處且高歌

yù yǐn jiǔ shí xū yǐn jiǔ, dé gāo gē chù qiě gāo gē

While there is wine, drink; while you can sing loudly, sing. (lit.)

When you are an anvil, hold you still; when you are a hammer, strike your fill.

3722 愈陷愈深 yù xiàn yù shēn

Fallen into a trap deeper and deeper. (lit.)

Out of the frying pan into the fire.

反 回頭是岸（1149）It is never too late to mend.

3723 慾壑難填 yù hè nán tián

The cavity of lust is hard to fill up. (lit.)

The more you have, the more you want.

Avarice knows no bounds.

同 貪得無饜（2672）As greedy as a wolf.

反 知足常足（3863）A contented mind is a perpetual feast.

3724 鷸蚌相持，漁人得利

yù bàng xiāng chí, yú rén dé lì

The snip and mussel grip each other, the fishman gets the benefit. (lit.)

Two dogs fight for a bone, and a third runs away with it.

源 戰國策：“蚌方出曝而鷸啄其肉，蚌合而鉗其喙。兩者不肯相舍，漁者得而並禽之。”

3725 鬱鬱不樂 yù yù bú lè

Grieving and unhappy. (lit.)

In the blues.

同 悶悶不樂（1782）Eat one's heart out.

反 爽心快意（2586）Warm the cockles of one's heart.

3726 鬱鬱寡歡 yù yù guǎ huān

Grieving with little joy. (lit.)

Out of spirits.

As melancholy as a cat.

反 興高采烈（3224）Dance for joy.

3727 冤家宜解不宜結 yuān jiā yí jiě bù yí jié

Enmity should be untied and should not be tied. (lit.)

A bad compromise is better than a good lawsuit.

冤哉枉也 yuān zāi wǎng yě 3728

Injustice and slanderous. (lit.)

What an outrageous fabrication!

Suffer injustice.

反 昭雪平反（3809）Redress a wrong.

元龍高卧 yuán lóng gāo wò 3729

Yuan Long sleeps on a high pillow. (lit.)

Sleep like a top (log).

In a sound sleep.

Dead to the world.

同 高枕而卧（0887）Sleep upon both ears.

源 黃庭堅詩：“今年貧到骨，豪氣似元龍。”

原封不動 yuán fēng bù dòng 3730

The whole intact and not been moved. (lit.)

Keep (to be left) intact.

To be in its intergrity.

同 依然如故（3511）Everything in the garden is rosy once more.

反 面目全非（1799）Beyond recognition.

源 元曲選．救孝子：“我可也原封不動，送還你罷。”

原來如此 yuán lái rú cǐ 3731

Originally it is like this. (lit.)

So that's how it is!

So that accounts for the milk in the coconut!

原形畢露 yuán xíng bì lù 3732

One's original form was eventually revealed. (lit.)

Put one's cards on the table.

Show the cloven foot (hoof).

Show one's horns.

Come out in one's true colours.

Have feet of clay.

同 兇相畢露（3228）Bare one's fangs.

反 喬裝打扮（2096）Sail under false colours.

圓滑周旋 yuán huá zhōu xuán 3733

Round, smooth, and spinning around. (lit.)

Handle with kid gloves.

Smooth and suave.

A man of the world.

同 縱橫捭闔（4023）Wheel and deal.

3734 **緣木求魚** yuán mù qiú yú

Climb up a tree in search of fish. (lit.)

To fish in the air.

Wring water from a flint.

Milk the bull.

Seek a hare in a hen's nest.

反 十拿九穩（2457）Feel cork sure.

源 孟子．梁惠王上："猶緣木而求魚也。"

3735 **緣慳一面** yuán qiān yí miàn

Lacking of affinity to have a meeting. (lit.)

Haven't had the pleasure of meeting one.

同 素昧平生（2648）Not to know one from Adam.

3736 **遠親不如近鄰** yuǎn qīn bù rú jìn lín

A relative far away is not as good as a neighbour. (lit.)

Better is a neighbour that is near than a brother far off.

We can live without our friends, but not without our neighbours.

反 疏不間親（2565）Blood is thicker than water.

3737 **遠涉重洋** yuǎn shè chóng yáng

To have waded far through seas and oceans. (lit.)

Cross the seven seas.

反 深居簡出（2397）Live is seclusion.

3738 **遠水不救近火**

yuǎn shuǐ bú jiù jìn huǒ

Distant water cannot save (put out) a near fire. (lit.)

Almost too late to do anything.

Water afar off quencheth not fire.

反 近水樓台先得月（1362）The parson always christens his own child first.

源 韓非子．說林上："失火而取水於海，海水雖多，火必不滅矣，遠水不救近火也。"

3739 **遠走高飛** yuǎn zǒu gāo fēi

Run far away and soar high up. (lit.)

Cannot be traced.

Clear out.

Flee as a bird.

Take a powder.

Never to look back.

源 後漢書．卓茂傳："汝獨不欲修之，寧能高飛遠走，不在人間邪。"

怨天尤人 yuàn tiān yóu rén 3740

Repine at Heaven and lay blame upon others. (lit.)

Complain of one's lot.

Everyone puts his faults on the times.

Say the devil's paternoster.

A bad workman always blames his tools.

反 樂天知命（1584）The world is his that enjoys it.

源 論語・憲問："不怨天，不尤人。"

願假天年，成此大業 3741

yuàn jiǎ tiān nián, chéng cǐ dà yè

Wishing Heaven to bestow (more) years so as to complete this big enterprise. (lit.)

The day is short and the work is long.

Live on borrowed time.

願天保祐 yuàn tiān bǎo yòu 3742

Wishing Heaven's protection. (lit.)

Keep one's fingers crossed.

願執巾櫛 yuàn zhí jīn zhì 3743

Willing to serve with the towel and comb. (lit.)

Set her cat at

Make a dead set at

Throw oneself at the head of

反 終身不嫁（3914）Lead apes in hell.

源 左傳："寡君之使婢子侍執巾櫛。"

月是故鄉明 yuè shì gù xiāng míng 3744

The moon in home village is brighter. (lit.)

Dry bread at home is better than roast meat abroad.

East or West, home is best.

There's no place like home.

同 在家千日好（3756）The smoke of a man's own house is better than the fire of another.

反 本地薑不辣（0105）A prophet is not without honour, save in his own country and his own house.

源 杜甫詩："露從今夜白，月是故鄉明。"

月下老人 yuè xià lǎo rén 3745

The old man in the moonlight. (lit.)

Act as a go-between.

A match-maker.

源 續幽怪錄："韋固旅次宋城南店，有老人向月檢書，固問何書，曰天下之婚牘耳。"

3746 **月有暗晴圓缺**
yuè yǒu àn qíng yuán quē
The moon may be dim, bright, full or wane. (lit.)
Wax and wane.

源 蘇軾詞："人有悲歡離合，月有陰晴圓缺，此事古難全。"

3747 **越俎代庖** yuè zǔ dài páo
Taking over the chopping board, replace the cook. (lit.)
To be a back seat driver.

同 喧賓奪主（3255）Steal the show from

反 事不關己，高高掛起（2508）Dogs never go into mourning when a horse dies.

源 莊子．逍遙遊："庖人雖不治庖，尸祝不越樽俎而代之。"

3748 **閱歷甚深** yuè lì shèn shēn
Very deep in experience. (lit.)
The black ox has trod on his foot.
Have seen much of the world.
Know every move on the board.

同 老於世故（1579）To be a man of the world.

反 初出茅廬（0421）A raw recruit.

3749 **躍然紙上** yuè rán zhǐ shàng
Leaping on the paper. (lit.)
Vivid with life.
True to life.
Leap to the eye.

同 栩栩如生（3251）A speaking likeness.

3750 **躍躍欲試** yuè yuè yù shì
Merrily wanting to try. (lit.)
Loaded for bear.
As keen as mustard.
Have an itch to
Itch to have a go.

3751 **芸芸眾生** yún yún zhòng shēng
All the living beings. (lit.)
All flesh.
All the world and his wife.
The multitude.

源 老子："夫物芸芸。"

允執厥中 yǔn zhí jué zhōng 3752

Rightly or justly keep the (golden) mean. (lit.)

Follow the golden mean.

運用自如 yùn yòng zì rú 3753

Apply freely as one wishes. (lit.)

At one's finger tips.

Z

3754 **砸個稀巴爛** zá gè xī bā làn

Crush it into tiny broken pieces. (lit.)

Make mincemeat of

同 徹底粉碎（0337）Smash to smithereens.

反 修修補補（3238）To make do and mend.

3755 **雜亂無章** zá luàn wú zhāng

All mixed up without system. (lit.)

Higgledy-piggledy.

All in a muddle (mess).

同 亂七八糟（1706）At sixes and sevens.

反 有條不紊（3671）In apple-pie order.

源 韓愈・送孟東野序：“其為言也，雜亂而無章。”

3756 **在家千日好** zài jiā qiān rì hǎo

At home thousand days are good. (lit.)

There's no place like home.

East or West, home is best.

Dry bread at home is better than roast meat abroad.

The smoke of a man's own house is better than the fire of another.

反 本地薑不辣（0105）A prophet is not without honour, save in his own country and his own house.

3757 **在家千日好，出外半朝難**

zài jiā qiān rì hǎo, chū wài bàn zhāo nán

At home thousand days are good, going away half-day is difficult. (lit.)

Far from home is near to harm.

Talk of camps but stay at home.

3758 **在哪裏受屈，就在哪裏平反**

zài nǎ li shòu qū, jiù zài nǎ li píng fǎn

Where one was bent down is where one should get back his own level. (lit.)

Seek your salve where you get your sore.

再接再厲 zài jiē zài lì 3759
Making repeated efforts. (lit.)
Redouble one's efforts.
Make unremitting efforts.

同 百尺竿頭，更進一步（0048）Make further efforts.
反 一蹶不振（3409）Fall flat.
源 韓愈・鬥雞聯句："一噴一醒然，再接再礪乃。"

再思可矣 zài sī kě yǐ 3760
Repeated thinking can be right. (lit.)
Second thoughts are best.

反 心血來潮（3193）On the impulse of the moment.
源 論語・公冶長："季文子三思而後行，子聞之曰，再斯可矣。"

暫且按下不提 zàn qiě àn xià bù tí 3761
Temporarily leave it and not to mention. (lit.)
To leave it at that.

反 言歸正傳（3302）Return to our muttons.

讚不絕口 zàn bù jué kǒu 3762
Praising without stopping mouth. (lit.)
Lavish praises on
To lay it on thick.
Sing the praises of
Rave about.

同 歌功頌德（0894）Chant the praises of
反 罵個狗血淋頭（1734）Blow one up sky high.

葬身魚腹 zàng shēn yú fù 3763
To be burried in the maws of fishes. (lit.)
Feed the fishes.
Take one's last drink.

早眠早起 zǎo mián zǎo qǐ 3764
Early to sleep and early to rise. (lit.)
Early to bed and early to rise.
Keep early (good, regular) hours.

同 日出而作，日入而息（2254）Go to bed with the lamb, and rise with the lark.
反 日上三竿猶未起（2257）A sluggard makes his night till noon.

早晚時價不同 zǎo wǎn shí jià bù tóng 3765
The current values of (things) are not the same in the evening as in the morning. (lit.)
Butter is gold in the morning, silver at noon, and lead at night.

3766 **早知今日，何必當初**
zǎo zhī jīn rì, hé bì dāng chū
If only this day had been known, why must have been the beginning? (lit.)
Repentance is good, but innocence is better.

3767 **造詣甚深** zào yì shèn shēn
The attainment of learning is very profound. (lit.)
Have at the tips of one's fingers.
To be at home in
To be a past master.
Of great attainments.

同 內行（1889）A know-how.
反 一知半解（3495）Have only a smattering of

3768 **責無旁貸** zé wú páng dài
There is no shirking of responsibility. (lit.)
Can't pass the buck.
To be duty-bound.
With bounden duty.

同 義不容辭（3566）Make a virtue of necessity.
反 事不關己，高高掛起（2508）It's none of my business.

3769 **賊喊捉賊** zéi hǎn zhuō zéi
Thieves call out "catch the thief". (lit.)
Satan reproves sin.

3770 **賊眉賊眼** zéi méi zéi yǎn
Having eyebrows and eyes of a thief. (lit.)
Have the brand of a villian in one's looks.
He that winks with one eye and looks with the other I will not trust him though he were my brother.

同 獐頭鼠目（3796）With a hangdog look.
反 道貌岸然（0606）To look as if butter would not melt in one's mouth.

3771 **賊去關門** zéi qù guān mén
After the thieves have gone, the door is closed. (lit.)
Lock the stable door after the horse is stolen.

同 後悔莫及（1080）Repentance comes too late.
反 財不可露眼（0297）He that shows his purse longs to be rid of it.
源 釋道源．景德傳燈錄：“賊去後關門。”

賊頭賊腦 zéi tóu zéi nǎo 3772

Having a thief's head and brain. (lit.)

With a hang-gallows look.

A hangdog look.

反 一表人才（3375）Manners make the man.

賊性難改 zéi xìng nán gǎi 3773

It is hard to change a thief's nature. (lit.)

Once a knave and ever a knave.

同 故態復萌（0951）At one's little games again.

反 洗心革面（3055）Turn over a new leaf.

乍暖還寒 zhà nuǎn huán hán 3774

Suddenly getting warm and then cold. (lit.)

Soon hot, soon cold.

宅心仁厚 zhái xīn rén hòu 3775

Dwelling in the heart are kindness and sincerity. (lit.)

Have one's heart in the right place.

反 心懷惡意（3168）Bear someone malice.

源 書經："宅心知訓。"

債台高築 zhài tái gāo zhù 3776

Building a high tower of debts. (lit.)

Run up bills.

Up to the ears in debt.

To be involved in debt.

To be debt-ridden.

同 負債纍纍（0844）Over head and ears in debt.

反 無債一身輕（3005）Out of debt, out of danger.

源 諸侯王表序："有逃責（債）之台。"指周赧王負債，避居宮中高台故事。

沾沾自喜 zhān zhān zì xǐ 3777

Very happy with oneself. (lit.)

Hug one's self.

Pat oneself on the back.

Lick one's chops.

反 怏怏不樂（3342）Have the blues.

源 史記·魏其侯竇英傳："魏其者，沾沾自喜，多易，難以為相。"

瞻前顧後 zhān qián gù hòu 3778

Looking the front and watching the back. (lit.)

Take a look around.

Look about

Look round the corner.

反 肆無忌憚（2641）To scruple at nothing.

源 楚辭："瞻前顧後兮，相觀民之計極。"

3779 **輾轉反側** zhǎn zhuǎn fǎn cè
Toss and turn about (in bed). (lit.)
Toss about all night.

反 高枕而卧（0887）To be able to sleep on a clothes line.
源 詩經・關雎："悠哉悠哉，輾轉反側。"

3780 **佔上風** zhàn shàng fēng
Get the upper wind. (lit.)
Get the upper hand.
Have the inside track.
Gain the wind of
Have the weather gage of
Get (Have) the edge on one.

反 甘拜下風（0860）Play second fiddle.

3781 **站不住腳** zhàn bú zhù jiǎo
Unable to stand on one's feet. (lit.)
Have not a leg to stand on.

反 巍然屹立（2886）Stand rock-firm.

3782 **站錯隊** zhàn cuò duì
Stand in the wrong queue. (lit.)
To be in the wrong box.

3783 **站得住腳** zhàn dé zhù jiǎo
Able to stand on one's feet. (lit.)
Hold one's own.
Hold one's ground.
Hold water.

反 駁得體無完膚（0170）Cut the ground from under someone's feet.

3784 **站穩立場** zhàn wěn lì chǎng
Stand firmly on one's ground. (lit.)
Stand one's ground.
Take a firm stand.

同 堅持原則（1266）Stick to one's guns.
反 朝秦暮楚（3814）Play fast and loose.

3785 **戰鬥到底** zhàn dòu dào dǐ
Fight to the (bitter) end. (lit.)
Fight back to the ropes.
Die in the last ditch.

同 抵抗到底（0638）To be dead set against
反 棄甲曳兵而走（2049）Run helter-skelter.

3786 **戰火彌漫** zhàn huǒ mí màn
The war fire is spreading. (lit.)
Fire and sword.

反 太平盛世（2668）The piping times of peace.

戰死沙場 zhàn sǐ shā chǎng 3787
Die in battle sand field. (lit.)
Bite the dust.
Fall by the edge of the sword.

戰戰兢兢 zhàn zhàn jīng jīng 3788
Trembling with fear. (lit.)
Shake in one's shoes.
To be on thin ice.
On the jig.
In a blue funk.
Very gingerly.

同 臨深履薄（1654）To tread upon eggs.
源 詩經．小雅．小旻："戰戰兢兢，如臨深淵，如履薄冰。"

戰爭與和平 zhàn zhēng yǔ hé píng 3789
War and peace. (lit.)
Arms and gown.

張大其詞 zhāng dà qí cí 3790
Exaggerating one's words. (lit.)
To go beyond the truth.
Make a great fuss about.
Draw the long bow.
Sling the hatchet.

同 言過其實（3303）Paint the devil blacker than he is.
反 輕描淡寫（2126）Touch on lightly.
源 韓愈．送楊少尹序："太史氏又能張大其事，為傳繼二疏蹤跡否。"

張冠李戴 zhāng guān lǐ dài 3791
Zhang's hat is worn by Li. (lit.)
An impostor.
The boot is on the other leg.

源 明．田藝蘅．留青日記："有人作賦云，物各有主，貌貴相宜，竊張公之帽也，假李老而戴之。"

張惶失措 zhāng huáng shī cuò 3792
Frightened and lost control (of oneself). (lit.)
Lose one's head.
At a loss what to do.
Scared out of one's wits.

同 不知所措（0280）Stand at gaze.
反 不慌不忙（0201）At one's ease.

張口結舌 zhāng kǒu jié shé 3793
Open the mouth and tongue-tied. (lit.)
Left speechless.
To be tongue-tied.
Lose one's tongue.
At a loss for words.
Gape with astonishment.

同 無言可對（3001）Come to a nonplus.
反 口若懸河（1508）Talk nine words at once.
源 晉．陸機．謝平原內史表："鉗口結舌，不敢上訴所天。"

3794 **張牙舞爪** zhāng yá wǔ zhǎo

Bare one's fangs and brandish the claws. (lit.)

Bare one's fangs.

Show one's claws (teeth).

同 劍拔弩張（1289）At daggers drawn.

反 不露鋒芒（0229）Draw in one's horns.

源 敦煌變文集 · 孔子項托相問書："魚生三日游於江湖，龍生三日張牙舞爪。"

3795 **彰明較著** zhāng míng jiào zhù

Distinguished, and clearly illuminated (cases) in comparison. (lit.)

As clear as day.

As clear as the nose on one's face.

As plain as a pikestaff.

同 顯而易見（3097）In bold relief.

反 玄之又玄（3257）Explaining what is unknown by what is still more unknown.

源 史記 · 伯夷列傳："此其尤大彰明較著者也。"

3796 **獐頭鼠目** zhāng tóu shǔ mù

Like the head of a roebuck and the eyes of a rat. (lit.)

With a hangdog look.

Have the brand of a villian in one's look.

同 賊眉賊眼（3770）He that winks with one eye and looks with the other I will not trust him though he were my brother.

反 一表人才（3375）Manners make the man.

源 舊唐書 · 李揆傳："龍章鳳姿士不見用，麞頭鼠目子乃求官耶。"

3797 **長大成人** zhǎng dà chéng rén

Grow up to become a man. (lit.)

To be of age.

Out of one's teens.

同 年方弱冠（1901）Arrive at majority.

3798 **掌上明珠** zhǎng shàng míng zhū

A bright pearl in the palm. (lit.)

Set on the pedestal.

The apple of one's eyes.

反 眼中釘（3328）A thorn in the eye.

源 晉 · 傅玄 · 短歌行："昔君視我，如掌中珠，何意一朝，棄我溝渠。"

3799 **掌聲如雷** zhǎng shēng rú léi

The noise of clapping hands like thunders. (lit.)

Thunders of applause.

To bring the house down.

同 全場喝彩（2159）Bring down the house.

反 喝倒彩（1055）Make cat calls.

掌握情況 zhǎng wò qíng kuàng

To hold and control the situation. (lit.)

To get the picture.

反 不得要領（0182）Not get the gist. 3800

丈二和尚，摸不着頭腦

zhàng èr hé shàng, mō bù zháo tóu nǎo

Of a twelve-foot monk (stature) one cannot touch the head. (lit.)

Can make neither head nor tail of

同 莫名其妙（1851）To be at sea. 3801

仗勢欺人 zhàng shì qī rén

Leaning on one's power bully others. (lit.)

Pull rank on someone.

Throw one's weight about.

同 盛氣凌人（2433）Throw one's weight about. 3802

源 明・李開先・林沖寶劍記："賊子無知，仗勢欺人敢妄為。"

仗義疏財 zhàng yì shū cái

Relying on righteousness and generous with money. (lit.)

Come down handsome.

Tip the brads.

Be a good Samaritan.

A do-gooder.

同 扶危濟困（0822）Help a lame dog over a stile. 3803

反 一毛不拔（3423）As tight as a drum.

源 水滸傳傳奇："宋公明他扶危濟困隱功曹，晁保正他疏財仗義豪。"

招兵買馬 zhāo bīng mǎi mǎ

Recruit and buy horses. (lit.)

Beat up for recruits.

To beef up

Muster up a force.

Raise an army.

源 明・無名氏・白免記："到了鄭州，岳節度使在那裏招兵買馬。" 3804

招降納叛 zhāo xiáng nà pàn 3805

Receive the surrenders and accept the rebels. (lit.)

Rope one in.

招搖過市 zhāo yáo guò shì

Flaunting through the streets. (lit.)

Cut a dash.

Seek the limelight.

Show off.

同 拋頭露面（1953）Come out into the open. 3806

源 史記・孔子世家："靈公與夫人同車……使孔子為次乘，招搖市過之。"

3807 **招之即來，揮之即去**
zhāo zhī jí lái, huī zhī jí qù
To be called, one comes immediately, to be waved away, one goes at once. (lit.)
At one's beck and call.
Speak when you're spoken to; come when you're called.

同 頤指氣使（3522）Get someone by the short hairs.

3808 **昭然若揭** zhāo rán ruò jiē
As clear as if the cover is taken off. (lit.)
Stare one in the face.
As clear as the sun in noonday.
All too clear.

同 顯而易見（3097）In bold relief.
源 莊子・達生："昭昭乎若揭日月而行也。"

3809 **昭雪平反** zhāo xuě píng fǎn
As white as snow when a wrong has been turned right. (lit.)
Right the wrong.
Exonerate one from blame.
Redress a wrong.

反 含垢茹辱（1013）Pocket an insult.

3810 **朝不保夕** zhāo bù bǎo xī
The morning cannot guarantee (the safety) of the evening. (lit.)
Live from hand to mouth.
None knows what will happen to him before sunset.
Hang by a thread.
Can't keep the wolf from the door.
Dangerously ill.
Touch and go.

同 危在旦夕（2876）Hang on by the eyelids.
源 李密・陳情表："人命危淺，朝不慮夕。"

3811 **朝令夕改** zhāo lìng xī gǎi
An order given in the morning is changed in the evening. (lit.)
The law is not the same at morning and night.

同 出爾反爾（0402）Go back on one's word.
反 貫徹始終（0977）Carry through to the end.
源 漢書・食貨志上：急政暴虐，賦斂不時，朝令而夕改。"

朝起紅雲不過未，晚起紅雲曬裂地 zhāo qǐ hóng yún bú guò wèi, wǎn qǐ hóng yún shài liè dì 3812

Red clouds rise in the morning will not last till early afternoon; red clouds rise in the night the sunshine will crack the earth. (lit.)

Red sky at night, shepherd's delight; red sky in the morning, shepherd's warning.

朝氣蓬勃 zhāo qì péng bó 3813

The air of the dawn issues forth sharply. (lit.)

Brim over with high spirit.

Fresh as a daisy.

Full of vigour and vitality.

Look as if one has come out of a bandbox.

同 英姿煥發（3598）In one's vigorous youth.

反 暮氣沉沉（1873）Lose one's grip.

源 孫子．軍事："是故朝氣鋭，晝氣惰，暮氣歸。"

朝秦暮楚 zhāo qín mù chǔ 3814

Morning Qin State, evening Chu State. (lit.)

Play fast and loose.

Blow hot and cold.

In a switch of loyalties.

反 忠心耿耿（3910）As true as the dial to the sun.

源 宋．晁補之．北渚亭賦："托生理於四方，固朝秦而暮楚。"

朝三暮四 zhāo sān mù sì 3815

Say three in the morning and four in the evening. (lit.)

Chop and change.

In two minds about.

同 反覆無常（0746）Blow hot and cold.

源 莊子．齊物論："狙公賦芧曰，朝三而暮四。眾狙皆起而怒。俄而曰，然則朝四而暮三，眾狙皆悦。"

朝為座上客，暮作階下囚 3816

zhāo wéi zuò shàng kè, mù zuò jiē xià qiú

In the morning as guest on high seat, in the evening becoming a prisoner down at court yard. (lit.)

Today a man, tomorrow a mouse.

3817 **找着竅門** zhǎo zháo qiào mén
Having found doors and openings. (lit.)
Get the hand of it.
Know the ropes.

反 不得要領（0182）Miss the point.

3818 **照本宣科** zhào běn xuān kē
According to the book make the announcement. (lit.)
Speak by the book (card).

3819 **照價賠償** zhào jià péi cháng
According to the price make the compensation. (lit.)
Make good the damage.

3820 **照章辦事** zhào zhāng bàn shì
According to the ordinance manage the business. (lit.)
Sign on the dotted line.

反 通融辦理（2763）Stretch the point.

3821 **折衷妥協** zhé zhōng tuǒ xié
Settle together eclectically. (lit.)
Meet one halfway.
Strike the happy medium.

3822 **這人不簡單** zhè rén bù jiǎn dān
This person is not simple. (lit.)
Not as green as his cabbage-looking.

3823 **珍而藏之** zhēn ér cáng zhī
Treasure should be collected and stored. (lit.)
Lay it up in lavender.

反 棄如敝屣（2051）Cast aside like an old shoe.

3824 **針鋒相對** zhēn fēng xiāng duì
The sharp points of needles are facing each other. (lit.)
Give tit for tat.
Measure for measure.
A Roland for an Oliver.
Measure swords.

同 以眼還眼，以牙還牙（3543）An eye for an eye; a tooth for a tooth.

反 互忍互讓（1095）Live and let live.

源 景德傳燈錄：“夫一切問答，如針鋒相投，無纖毫參差。”

真材實料 zhēn cái shí liào 3825
Genuine material and real substance. (lit.)
Worth its weight in gold.

反 金玉其外，敗絮其中（1345）All is not gold that glitters.

真金不怕紅爐火 3826
zhēn jīn bú pà hóng lú huǒ
Genuine gold is not afraid of red stove fire. (lit.)
Truth fears no colours.
The anvil fears no blows.
True blue will never stain.
A good anvil does not fear the hammer.
Proved in the fires of
With sterling qualities.

同 樹正何愁月影斜（2580）If the staff be crooked, the shadow cannot be straight.

真理還須實踐來檢驗 3827
zhēn lǐ hái xū shí jiàn lái jiǎn yàn
Truth still needs practice to test out.
The proof of the pudding is in the eating.
Prove all things; hold fast that which is good.
Deem the best till the truth is tried out.

同 實踐出真知（2479）Experience is the mother of wisdom.

真相大白 zhēn xiàng dà bái 3828
The true situation is all clear. (lit.)
Everything comes to light.
The truth will out.
The scales fall from one's eyes.

同 水落石出（2591）Truth lies at the bottom of a well.

反 蒙在鼓裏（1785）To be in the dark.

枕戈待旦 zhěn gē dài dàn 3829
Sleeping with weapon for a pillow and waiting for dawn. (lit.)
Keep one's powder dry.
To be on the alert.
To be up in arms.
In full battle array.

源 晉書．劉琨傳：“吾枕戈待旦，志梟逆虜。”

3830 **振作起來** zhèn zuò qǐ lái
Shake oneself up and arouse into action. (lit.)
Gird up one's loins.
To brace up.
Pull oneself together.

反 意氣消沉（3563）To be in the doldrums.

3831 **震耳欲聾** zhèn ěr yù lóng
Shocking the ear to deaf. (lit.)
As loud as thunder.
Enough to wake the dead.
Split the ears.

反 鴉雀無聲（3287）As silent as the grave.

3832 **爭取時間** zhēng qǔ shí jiān
Fighting to get time. (lit.)
Play for time.

3833 **爭取主動** zhēng qǔ zhǔ dòng
Fight for the first move. (lit.)
Take the initiative.

反 受人擺佈（2555）To be in leading strings.

3834 **爭生競存** zhēng shēng jìng cún
Fight for survival and struggle for existence. (lit.)
Self-preservation is the first law of nature.
Struggle for existence.

同 生死搏鬥（2417）Life and death struggle.
反 自尋短見（4005）Make away with oneself.

3835 **爭先恐後** zhēng xiān kǒng hòu
Fight for the first lest one should fall behind. (lit.)
The devil takes the hindmost.

反 姍姍來遲（2337）Arrive in an arm chair.
源 江南野話：“相對雖無語，爭先各有心。”

3836 **爭一日之長短**
zhēng yí rì zhī cháng duǎn
Fight for one day's long and short (difference). (lit.)
Wrangle for an ass's shadow.

反 與世無爭（3710）On good terms with the world.

蒸蒸日上 zhēng zhēng rì shàng 3837
Going up and up every day. (lit.)
Grow with each passing day.
On the up and up.
Show increasing prosperity.

同 欣欣向榮（3203）Flourish like the green bay-tree.
反 一落千丈（3420）To go to pot.

癥結所在 zhēng jié suǒ zài 3838
Where the knot in the bowels lies. (lit.)
The name of the game.
The crux of the matter.
Where the problem lies.

同 關鍵所在（0967）There's the rub.
源 史記："扁鵲治疾，能盡見藏癥結。"

整裝待發 zhěng zhuāng dài fā 3839
Pack the baggages and wait to start (a journey). (lit.)
Pull one's freight.

正大光明 zhèng dà guāng míng 3840
Upright and bright-minded. (lit.)
Play fair and square.
To be above-board.

同 光明磊落（0981）Clear as crystal.
反 暗中行事（0030）On the sly.

正反兩面 zhèng fǎn liǎng miàn 3841
The right and opposite, two sides. (lit.)
The pros and cons.
The ayes and noes.
Every medal has its reverse (two sides).

正酣之際 zhèng hān zhī jì 3842
Right at the moment of sound sleep. (lit.)
In the thick of

正合時宜 zhèng hé shí yí 3843
At the right and suitable time or moment. (lit.)
In the nick of time.

同 大好時機（0527）High time.
反 不合時宜（0200）Out of season.

3844 正面教育為主
zhèng miàn jiào yù wéi zhǔ
The positive education is the main principle. (lit.)
Praise Peter, but don't find fault with Paul.

反 懲一儆百（0367）He that chastiseth one amendeth many.

3845 正中下懷 zhèng zhòng xià huái
Exactly what is in my mind. (lit.)
After one's own heart.
To one's liking.

同 先獲我心（3080）Prepossess one favourably.
反 討厭萬分（2699）Bored to death.

3846 正中要害 zhèng zhòng yào hài
Hitting the fatal point. (lit.)
To strike home.

同 觸到痛處（0432）Cut to the quick.
反 不着邊際（0285）It's neither here nor there.

3847 鄭重其事 zhèng zhòng qí shì
Take the matter seriously. (lit.)
To mean business.
In sober earnest.
In all seriousness.
Make a point of doing a thing.

同 慎重將事（2411）Score twice before you cut once.
反 等閒視之（0628）Take things lightly.

3848 支離破碎 zhī lí pò suì
Torn apart and broken. (lit.)
Torn to pieces.
In shreds.
Rip apart.

反 完美無缺（2840）Finished to the finger-nail.
源 莊子："夫支離其身者，猶足以養其身，終其天年。"

3849 支吾其詞 zhī wú qí cí
Prevaricate one's statement. (lit.)
To hem and haw.
To hum and ha.
Speak with one's tongue in one's cheek.
To falter one's words.

同 含糊其詞（1014）Beat about the bush.
反 心直口快（3199）Nearest the heart, nearest the mouth.
源 史記："諸將皆慴伏，無敢枝梧。"

3850 知不可為而為之
zhī bù kě wéi ér wéi zhī
Knowing it can not be done, one does it. (lit.)
To square the circle.

同 硬着頭皮幹到底（3603）Brazen it out.
反 知難而退（3856）To back out.
源 論語・憲問："是知其不可而為之者與。"

知錯認錯 zhī cuò rèn cuò

Knowing the faults one confesses them. (lit.)

Confession is the first step to repentance.

Never have disgrace through life.

反 文過飾非（2922）Gloss over faults. 3851

知法犯法 zhī fǎ fàn fǎ

Knowing the law, one transgresses the law. (lit.)

Set the law at defiance.

同 無法無天（2959）Lawless as a town-bull. 3852

反 執法守法（3867）Magistrates are to obey as well as execute laws.

知己知彼 zhī jǐ zhī bǐ

Knowing oneself, one knows others. (lit.)

A thief knows a thief as a wolf knows a wolf.

源 孫子："知彼知己，百戰不殆。" 3853

知名人士 zhī míng rén shì

Well-known persons. (lit.)

Man of mark (great celebrity).

反 無名小卒（2982）A mere nobody. 3854

知難而進 zhī nán ér jìn

Knowing the difficulty, one still goes ahead. (lit.)

Never shirk the hardest work.

Grasp the thistle firmly.

Face the music.

Face it out.

同 勇挑重擔（3618）Bite off a big chunk. 3855

反 打退堂鼓（0499）Beat a retreat.

知難而退 zhī nán ér tuì

Realizing the difficulty one withdraws. (lit.)

To back out.

To cut a loss.

Shrink back.

反 勉為其難（1797）Make the best of a bad bargain. 3856

源 左傳："見可而進，知難而退。"

知其為人 zhī qí wéi rén

Knowing the kind of such person. (lit.)

Know the length of one's foot.

同 深知底細（2402）Know one inside out. 3857

3858 **知其心意** zhī qí xīn yì

Knowing the idea in his heart. (lit.)

Read one's mind.

反 知人口面不知心（3859）A fair face may hide a foul heart.

3859 **知人口面不知心**

zhī rén kǒu miàn bù zhī xīn

Knowing a man's mouth and face, one does not know his heart. (lit.)

A fair face may hide a foul heart.

You cannot know wine by the barrel.

同 人不可以貌相（2192）Never judge from appearances.

反 深知底細（2402）Know someone inside out.

3860 **知識寶庫** zhī shí bǎo kù

The treasury of knowledge. (lit.)

A mine of information.

3861 **知無不言，言無不盡**

zhī wú bù yán, yán wú bù jìn

Not fail to tell all that one knows and to tell all without reserve. (lit.)

Lay one's heart bare.

Unbosom oneself.

Tell the truth and the whole truth.

同 暢所欲言（0333）Open one's budget.

反 見事莫説，問事不知（1279）Keep your mouth shut and your eyes open.

源 蘇軾："是以知無不言，言無不行，其所欲用，雖其親愛可也。"

3862 **知之為知之，不知為不知，是知也** zhī zhī wéi zhī zhī, bù zhī wéi bù zhī, shì zhī yě

Knowing it say knowing it, not knowing it say not knowing it, that is real knowledge. (lit.)

He knows most that knows he knows little.

源 論語 · 學而："子曰，由，誨女知之乎，知之為知之，不知為不知，是知也。"

3863 **知足常足** zhī zú cháng zú

Knowing having enough, one will always have enough. (lit.)

A contented mind is a perpetual feast.

Content is the philosopher's stone that turns all it touches into gold.

Enough is as good as a feast.

More than enough is too much.

Leave well alone.

He is rich that has few wants.

反 貪得無饜（2672）As greedy as a wolf.

知足常足，終身不辱

zhī zú cháng zú, zhōng shēn bù rǔ

Knowing having enough, one will always have enough; never have disgrace through life. (lit.)

He is wise that knows when he is well enough.

The greatest wealth is contentment with a little.

Enough is better than too much.

源 漢書 · 疏廣傳："吾聞知足不辱，知止不殆。" 3864

隻眼開，隻眼閉

zhī yǎn kāi, zhī yǎn bì

Open one eye and close one eye. (lit.)

Wink at small faults.

反 追根究底（3952）Get down to rock bottom. 3865

隻字不提 zhī zì bù tí

Mention not a word. (lit.)

Say neither buff nor baff.

Say neither muff nor mum.

Keep it dark.

反 反覆叮嚀（0745）To rub in. 3866

執法守法 zhí fǎ shǒu fǎ

To execute and uphold the law. (lit.)

Magistrates are to obey as well as execute laws.

反 監守自盜（1271）The friar preached against stealing and had a goose in his sleeve. 3867

執簡馭繁 zhí jiǎn yù fán

Hold the simple ones to control the complex. (lit.)

Take care of the pence and the pounds will take care of themselves.

反 老鼠拉龜，無處下手（1574）To catch a Tartar. 3868

執牛耳 zhí niú ěr

Hold the bull's ear.

Rule the roast.

Take the lead.

Play first fiddle.

同 大權在握（0546）Take the rein into one's hand.

反 跑龍套（1955）Walk through a part.

源 左傳："諸侯盟，誰執牛耳。" 3869

3870 **直斥不雅** zhí chì bù yǎ

To reprimand without refinement. (lit.)

Throw in a person's face.
Straight from the shoulder.
Cast in one's teeth.
Take one to task.
Give a person a piece of one's mind.
Tell someone where to get off.

同 當面申斥（0587）Comb a person's hair for him.

3871 **直截了當** zhí jié liǎo dàng

Straight forward and finished with. (lit.)

Give it to one straight.
Come straight to the point.
By the string rather than by the bow.
Point-blank.

同 乾脆利落（0863）To be clear-cut.
反 拐彎抹角（0961）In a roundabout way.

3872 **直諒不阿** zhí liàng bù ē

Straight and understanding without bias. (lit.)

As level as a die.

3873 **直抒己見** zhí shū jǐ jiàn

Give one's own opinion candily. (lit.)

Speak one's mind.

同 慷慨陳詞（1484）Air one's views.
反 半吞半吐（0073）To mince matters.

3874 **直言不諱** zhí yán bú huì

Speak straight without concealment. (lit.)

From the bottom of one's heart.
Speak one's mind.
Call a spade a spade.
Speak the truth and shame the devil.
Own up readily.
Without reserve.
Straight from the shoulder.

同 開門見山（1473）Come straight to the point.
反 半吞半吐（0073）To mince matters.
源 左傳疏：“至於制作經典，則直言不諱。”

3875 **直言賈禍** zhí yán gǔ huò

Plain speaking invites trouble. (lit.)

The tongue talks at the head's cost.

反 明哲保身（1826）Think much, speak little, and write less.
源 左傳．成十五年：“子好直言，必及於難。”

只見其一，不見其二 3876
zhǐ jiàn qí yī, bú jiàn qí èr
Only seeing one (side) and not the two. (lit.)
A one-sided view.

只見樹木，不見森林 3877
zhǐ jiàn shù mù, bú jiàn sēn lín
Only seeing the trees but not forest. (lit.)
One can't see the wood for the trees.

反 觀微知著（0970）A straw will show which way the wind blows.

只可意會，不可言傳 3878
zhǐ kě yì huì, bù kě yán chuán
Only can be comprehanded but cannot be expressed in words. (lit.)
To beggar (defy) description.

源 清．劉大櫆．論文偶記："凡行文……可以意會，而不可以言傳。"

只要功夫深，鐵杵磨成針 zhǐ yào gōng fū shēn, tiě chǔ mó chéng zhēn 3879
Only need deep hard work, (even) iron rods can be ground to needles. (lit.)
Feather by feather the goose is plucked.
Little strokes fell great oaks.
Hair by hair you will pull out the horse's tail.

同 有志事竟成（3682）Where there's a will there's a way.
源 來源見 2747

只知責人，不知責己 3880
zhǐ zhī zé rén, bù zhī zé jǐ
Only know to blame others but know not to blame oneself. (lit.)
See a mote in another's eye.

反 以恕己之心恕人（3593）Forget others' faults by remembering your own.

指鹿為馬 zhǐ lù wéi mǎ 3881
Pointing to a deer as a horse. (lit.)
Talk black into white.
Swear black is white.

反 丁是丁，卯是卯（0655）Call a spade a spade.
源 史記："趙高持鹿獻於二世曰，馬也。"

指名道姓 zhǐ míng dào xìng 3882
To point the name and mention the surname. (lit.)
Call by name.

3883 **指日可待** zhǐ rì kě dài

Point to the day and wait for it. (lit.)

Before long.

Be just around the corner.

同 為期不遠（2893）In two shakes of a lamb's tail.

反 遙遙無期（3350）One of these days is none of these days.

3884 **指手劃腳** zhǐ shǒu huà jiǎo

Point with fingers and draw with feet. (lit.)

To lord it over.

Be a back seat driver.

Boss people about.

Come the old soldier over one.

Dictate to others.

同 發號施令（0733）Lay down the law.

反 言聽計從（3306）At one's beck and call.

3885 **指天立誓** zhǐ tiān lì shì

Pointing to the sky, one swears. (lit.)

Call heaven to witness.

Take bread and salt.

源 韓愈．柳子厚墓誌銘："指天日涕泣，誓生死不相背負。"

3886 **紙上談兵** Zhǐ shàng tán bīng

Speak of soldiers on paper. (lit.)

Talk hot air.

反 實事求是（2480）Look fact in the face.

源 劉三吾詩："朝野猶誇紙上兵。"

3887 **紙醉金迷** zhǐ zuì jīn mí

Fascinated with the glitter of tinsel. (lit.)

Given to merry making.

Gaming, women and wine, while they laugh they make men pine.

源 陶谷．清異錄："歸語人曰，此室暫憇，令人金迷紙醉。"

3888 **趾高氣揚** zhǐ gāo qì yáng

Toes high and putting on air. (lit.)

Ride the high horse.

In high snuff.

Give oneself airs.

To strut about.

Hoity-toity.

同 高視闊步（0883）Prance about.

反 垂頭喪氣（0445）Hang one's head.

源 左傳．桓十三年："莫敖必敗，舉趾高，心不固矣。"

3889 **至親骨肉** zhì qīn gǔ ròu

Nearest relatives, flesh and bone. (lit.)

One's own flesh and blood.

至死不屈 zhì sǐ bù qū 3890
One would not yield till death. (lit.)
Die game.

同 寧死不辱（1916）Take away my good name and take away my life.
反 俯首就範（0832）Give one's head for the washing.

志大才疏 zhì dà cái shū 3891
Great ambition, little ability. (lit.)
Zeal without knowledge is fire without light.
A runaway horse.

同 好高騖遠（1042）Hitch one's wagon to a star.
源 後漢書．孔融傳："融負其高氣，志在靖難，而才疏意廣，迄無成功。"

志在必得 zhì zài bì dé 3892
To aim at getting (success). (lit.)
Neck or nothing.

炙手可熱 zhì shǒu kě rè 3893
To put one's hand on someone and feel the heat. (lit.)
At the zenith of one's power.
In the palm of one's hand.
High and mighty.

同 大權在握（0546）Take the rein into one's hand.
反 人微言輕（2228）Poor men's reasons are not heard.
源 唐．語林："會昌中語曰，鄭楊段薛，炙手可熱。"

致命打擊 zhì mìng dǎ jī 3894
A blow that causes death. (lit.)
A nail in one's coffin.
A fatal (mortal, deadly) blow.

同 擊中要害（1195）Hit one where it hurts.

智囊團 zhì náng tuán 3895
A group of knowledge bag. (lit.)
Brain trust.

智窮才盡 zhì qióng cái jìn 3896
Knowledge and ability utterly exhausted. (lit.)
At one's wit's end.
At the end of one's rope.

同 江郎才盡（1293）At the end of one's tether.
反 滿腹妙計（1742）To be full of wrinkles.

3897 **智取為上** zhì qǔ wéi shàng
To take by wisdom is the best. (lit.)
The Trojan horse.
One good head is better than a hundred strong arms.
Contrivance is better than force.

同 攻心為上（0926）Scare a bird is not the way to catch it.

3898 **智者千慮，必有一失**
zhì zhě qiān lǜ, bì yǒu yī shī
A wise man thinking over matters thousand times must have a fault. (lit.)
No man is wise at all times.
Even Homer sometimes nods.
The wisest make mistakes.

同 人有失手，馬有失蹄（2237）A good marksman may miss.
反 愚者千慮，必有一得（3695）A fool may give a wise man counsel.
源 晏子春秋．內篇雜下：“聖人千慮，必有一失，愚人千慮，必有一得。”

3899 **置若罔聞** zhì ruò wǎng wén
Act as if one has not heard of it. (lit.)
Turn a deaf ear to

同 充耳不聞（0384）None so deaf as those who won't hear.
反 言猶在耳（3311）Still ring in one's ears.

3900 **置身事外** zhì shēn shì wài
Keep oneself out of the affair. (lit.)
Fold one's arms.
Stand aloof.
To hold off.

同 作壁上觀（4063）Sit upon the fence.
反 插上一手（0321）Have a finger in the pie.

3901 **置生死於度外** zhì shēng sǐ yú dù wài
Leave life and death out of consideration. (lit.)
Heedless (regardless) of consequences.
Take one's life in one's hands.
Throw caution to the wind.

同 捨得一身剮（2372）To tempt providence.
反 明哲保身（1826）Be worldly wise and play safe.

3902 **置之不理** zhì zhī bù lǐ
Put it aside and disregard it. (lit.)
Shut one's eyes to
Leave it alone.
Not care a fig.

同 漠然置之（1855）Look on with unconcern.
反 追根究底（3952）Get down to rock bottom.

3903 **置之度外** zhì zhī dù wài
Leave it out of consideration. (lit.)
Leave something out of account.
Have no regard for

源 後漢書：“光武……謂諸將曰，當置此兩子度外。”

置之腦後 zhì zhī nǎo hòu
Put it at the back of the brain. (lit.)
Banish from thought.
Consign to oblivion.
Put out of one's head.
Think no more of (it).

反 仔細思量（3966）Consult one's pillow. 3904

置之死地而後生
zhì zhī sǐ dì ér hòu shēng
Put one to the state of death and he may survive. (lit.)
Despair gives courage to a coward.

同 窮則變，變則通（2142）Want is the mother of industry. 3905
源 孫子："投之亡地然後存，陷之死地然後生。"

質而言之 zhì ér yán zhī
Primarily speaking. (lit.)
The long and the short of it.

同 一言蔽之（3481）In a nutshell. 3906

中飽私囊 zhōng bǎo sī náng
To fill personal pocket full. (lit.)
Line one's pocket.
Feather one's nest.

同 貪污腐化（2675）Have an itching palm. 3907
反 廉潔清正（1618）With clean hands.

中流換馬 zhōng liú huàn mǎ 3908
Exchange horses in midstream. (lit.)
Swap horses in midstream.

中庸之道 zhōng yōng zhī dào
The doctrine of the golden mean. (lit.)
The golden mean.
Steer a middle course.
Safety lies in the middle course.
Moderation in all things.

同 允執厥中（3752）Follow the golden mean. 3909
反 無所不用其極（2994）Stick at nothing.

忠心耿耿 zhōng xīn gěng gěng
Firmly faithful. (lit.)
As true as the needle to the pole.
As true as the dial to the sun.
As true as flint (steel, touch).
True to one's salt.

同 誠實可靠（0364）To be on the square. 3910
反 背信棄義（0102）Play one false.

3911 忠言逆耳 zhōng yán nì ěr
Sincere advice offends the ear. (lit.)
The sting of a reproach is the truth of it.
Good advice hurts.

源 家語："良藥苦口利於病，忠言逆耳利於行。"

3912 忠忠直直，終須乞食
zhōng zhōng zhí zhí, zhōng xū qǐ shí
Being honest and straight, one may in the end have to beg for food. (lit.)
The properer man, the worse luck.

3913 終成泡影 zhōng chéng pào yǐng
In the end it becomes bubbles. (lit.)
Vanish like bubble.

同 化為烏有（1115）To come to naught.
反 如願以償（2280）A dream comes true.

3914 終身不嫁 zhōng shēn bù jià
For the whole life, she remains unmarried. (lit.)
Lead apes in hell.

3915 鐘鳴鼎食 zhōng míng dǐng shí
The bell tolled and rice cooked in cauldrons (for a big and rich family). (lit.)
Eat skylarks in a garret.
Lie at rack and manger.
Live like fighting cocks.
High eating.
Eat high on the hog.

源 張衡．西京賦："擊鐘鼎食，連騎相過。"

3916 重賞之下，必有勇夫
zhòng shǎng zhī xià, bì yǒu yǒng fū
By heavy reward, there must be brave men. (lit.)
A good paymaster never wants workmen.
Wage will get a page.

同 有錢能使鬼推磨（3659）Money makes the mare go.

3917 眾口難調 zhòng kǒu nán tiáo
It is difficult to suit all mouths. (lit.)
No dish pleases all palates alike.
It is hard to please all.

源 歐陽修．歸田錄："補仲山之袞，雖曲盡於巧心，和傳說之羹，實難調於眾口。"

眾口鑠金 zhòng kǒu shuò jīn 3918

Mouths of the people can fuse gold. (lit.)

If all men say that thou art an ass, then bray.

同 人言可畏（2234）Opinion rules the world.

源 國語．周語下："眾心成城，眾口鑠金。"

眾目睽睽 zhòng mù kuí kuí 3919

Under the watchful eyes of people. (lit.)

There is a witness everywhere.

同 有目共睹（3657）One would be blind not to see.

反 人不知，鬼不覺（2193）On the sly.

源 韓愈："萬目睽睽。"

眾擎易舉 zhòng qíng yì jǔ 3920

It is easy to lift with all hands. (lit.)

Three helping one another bear the burden of six.

同 人多好做事（2195）Many hands make light work.

眾人皆濁我獨清，眾人皆醉我獨醒 zhòng rén jiē zhuó wǒ dú qīng, zhòng rén jiē zuì wǒ dú xǐng 3921

All people are confused, only I am clear; all people are drunk, only I am awake. (lit.)

Better be alone than in bad company.

同 獨善其身（0680）Solitude is better than ill company.

反 隨大流（2654）Follow the crowd.

源 史記．屈原傳："舉世混濁而我獨清，眾人皆醉而我獨醒。"

眾人拾柴火焰高 zhòng rén shí chái huǒ yàn gāo 3922

Many people collecting firewood will make the flame of a fire high. (lit.)

Many hands make quick (light) work.

反 三個和尚沒水吃（2306）Too many cooks spoil the broth.

眾矢之的 zhòng shǐ zhī dì 3923

The aim of all arrows. (lit.)

A target of attack.

A clay pigeon.

A marked man.

Come under attack.

同 十目所視，十手所指（2456）Everybody points an accusing finger at

眾所周知 zhòng suǒ zhōu zhī 3924

It is generally known by all. (lit.)

As is generally known.

同 家喻戶曉（1255）Pass from mouth to mouth.

3925 眾議紛紜 zhòng yì fēn yún

People's opinions differ greatly. (lit.)

So many men, so many minds.

同 莫衷一是（1853）Agree like the clocks of London.

反 異口同聲（3557）With one accord.

3926 眾志成城 zhòng zhì chéng chéng

Unanimity of will makes a (fenced) city. (lit.)

Union (unity) is strength.

Make a united effort.

反 獨木不成林（0679）One flower makes no garland.

源 國語・周語下：“眾心成城，眾口鑠金。”

3927 種瓜得瓜，種豆得豆

zhòng guā dé guā, zhòng dòu dé dòu

Having planted melon, get melon, having planted beans, get beans. (lit.)

As a man sows, so he shall reap.

If thou would reap money, sow money.

同 前因後果（2083）Cause and effect.

源 涅槃經：“種瓜得瓜，種李得李。”

3928 周而復始 zhōu ér fù shǐ

Make a round and start from the beginning again. (lit.)

The tide never goes out so far but it always comes in again.

Ever recurring.

Every flow must have its ebb.

源 淮南子・兵略訓：“象日月之運行，……終而復始，明而復晦。”

3929 晝伏夜動 zhòu fú yè dòng

To lie by day and move by night. (lit.)

Sit up by moonshine and lie abed in sunshine.

同 通宵達旦（2764）All through the night.

3930 晝夜不息 zhòu yè bù xī

To work day and night incessantly. (lit.)

Day and night.

Round the clock.

By night and day.

反 日上三竿猶未起（2257）A sluggard makes his night till noon.

朱門酒肉臭，路有凍死骨
zhū mén jiǔ ròu chòu, lù yǒu dòng sǐ gǔ
Wine and meat behind the red door smelled foul (doors of the nobles used to be painted vermilion red) while on the road there were frozen dead bones. (lit.)
The pleasures of the mighty are the tears of the poor.

源 杜甫詠懷五百字詩：“朱門酒肉臭，路有凍死骨。” 3931

銖積寸累 zhū jī cùn lěi
To accumulate coin by coin and increase inch by inch. (lit.)
Every little makes a mickle.
Penny and penny laid up will be many.
Little and often fills the purse.money.

同 日積月累（2255）Keep some till more come. 3932
反 一擲千金（3497）Play ducks and drakes with one's money.
源 蘇軾．裙靴銘：“寒女之絲，銖積寸累。”

諸如此類 zhū rú cǐ lèi
Something of that kind. (lit.)
And the like.
And what not.
And so on and so forth.

同 如此等等（2268）And all that. 3933
源 晉書．劉頌傳：“諸如此類，亦不得已已。”

矚目皆是 zhǔ mù jiē shì
All eyes can see. (lit.)
Right and left.
Here and there and everywhere.

同 俯拾即是（0831）High and low. 3934
反 物罕為貴（3035）Precious things are not found in heaps.

助紂為虐 zhù zhòu wéi nüè
To help 'Zhou' to do evil. (lit.) (Zhou was an infamous tyrant causing the downfall of Shang Dynasty).
Hold a candle to the devil.

源 史記：“此所謂助桀為虐。” 3935

築室道謀 zhù shì dào móu
To build a house and ask opinion from others. (lit.)
He that builds by the wayside has many masters.
Too much consulting confounds.

源 詩經．小雅．小旻：“如彼築室於道謀，是用不潰於成。” 3936

3937 鑄成大錯 zhù chéng dà cuò

To cast a great mistake. (lit.)

Put one's foot in it.

源 蘇軾詩："不知幾州鐵，鑄此一大錯。"

3938 專心致志 zhuān xīn zhì zhì

To devote one's heart and mind to (lit.)

Set one's heart on

Devote oneself to

With undivided attention.

Wrapped up in

同 兩耳不聞窗外事（1626）Turn a deaf ear to

源 孟子．告子上："不專心致志，則不得也。"

3939 轉敗為勝 zhuǎn bài wéi shèng

Turn from defeat to victory. (lit.)

Pull out of the fire.

Snatch a victory out of defeat.

Turn the tables on

Save the day.

源 史記："其為政也，善因禍而為福，轉敗而為功。"

3940 轉念之間 zhuǎn niàn zhī jiān

In a time of sudden change of thought. (lit.)

As quick as thought.

3941 轉瞬之間 zhuǎn shùn zhī jiān

In the time of twinkling of an eye. (lit.)

In the twinkling of an eye.

In half a jiffy.

In less than no time.

In two twos.

Like one o'clock.

同 說時遲，那時快（2614）Before you can say knife.

源 北史．魏太武紀："帝雅長聽察，轉瞬之間，下無以措其姦隱。"

3942 轉彎抹角 zhuǎn wān mò jiǎo

Turning round a corner. (lit.)

In a round-about way.

Beat about the bush.

3943 轉移視線 zhuǎn yí shì xiàn

Changing the direction of sight. (lit.)

Draw a red herring across the path.

Divert one's attention.

莊稼漢 zhuāng jià hàn — 3944
Farm-house man. (lit.)
Son of the soil.

反 紈袴子弟（2843）Gilded youth.

裝點門面 zhuāng diǎn mén miàn — 3945
To decorate the (front) door and house. (lit.)
Keep up appearances.
Window dressing.
Put up a front.
Put one's best foot forward.

裝瘋賣傻 zhuāng fēng mài shǎ — 3946
Pretending mad and selling fool. (lit.)
Act like a clown.
Play possum.
It's all false pretence.
Play the fool.

反 一本正經（3371）Look as if butter wouldn't melt in one's mouth.

裝鬼臉 zhuāng guǐ liǎn — 3947
Make a ghost face. (lit.)
Mop and mow.

裝聾作啞 zhuāng lóng zuò yǎ — 3948
Feigning deaf and dumb. (lit.)
Masters should be sometimes blind and sometimes deaf.
Feign ignorance.

同 隻眼開，隻眼閉（3865）Wink at small faults.
源 元曲選．馬致遠．青衫淚："可怎生裝聾作啞。"

裝模作樣 zhuāng mú zuò yàng — 3949
Pretending to act this and that. (lit.)
To strike an attitude.
To be in borrowed plumes.
To make believe.

反 拆穿西洋鏡（0322）Take the mickey out of it.

裝腔作勢 zhuāng qiāng zuò shì — 3950
Making a falsetto voice, act grand. (lit.)
Put on airs.
Give oneself airs.
Strike a pose.
Put on an act.
Go through the motions of

同 擺架子（0065）Put on side.

3951 **壯烈犧牲** zhuàng liè xī shēng
Sacrifice one's life bravely and gloriously. (lit.)
Die a glorious (martyr's) death.

同 殺身成仁（2329）Lay down one's life.

3952 **追根究底** zhuī gēn jiū dǐ
Get to the root and find the bottom. (lit.)
Get down to rock bottom.
Run to earth.

同 尋根問底（3278）Get to the root of
反 隻眼開，隻眼閉（3865）Wink at small faults.

3953 **惴惴不安** zhuì zhuì bù ān
To be anxious and uneasy. (lit.)
In a fidget.
Ill at ease.
To be on tenterhooks.

同 心緒不寧（3192）Get out of bed on the wrong side.
反 泰然自若（2669）At one's ease.
源 詩經・秦風・黃鳥："臨其穴，惴惴其栗。"

3954 **準備就緒** zhǔn bèi jiù xù
Well prepared. (lit.)
Get one's ducks in a row.
Ready to the last gaiter button.

3955 **準備兩手** zhǔn bèi liǎng shǒu
Preparing two hands. (lit.)
Have a second string to one's bow.

同 作兩手準備（4070）Hope for the best and prepare for the worst.
反 孤注一擲（0939）Bet one's bottom dollar on.

3956 **準備萬一** zhǔn bèi wàn yī
Prepared for one in ten thousand. (lit.)
Keep one's powder dry.

同 防患未然（0755）Take precaution.

3957 **卓爾不羣** zhuō ěr bù qún
Eminent and not with groups. (lit.)
Out of the common run.
To be head and shoulders above (taller).
Come to the fore.
Carry everything before one.

同 鶴立雞羣（1056）A triton among the minnows.
反 平平庸庸（1989）Pass in a crowd in a push.
源 漢書・河間獻王傳贊："夫惟大雅，卓爾不羣。"

3958 **捉襟見肘** zhuō jīn jiàn zhǒu
Tightening the lapel of the jacket, one exposed the elbow. (lit.)
Unable to make both ends meet.
Out at elbows.

源 莊子・讓王："曾子居衛，十年不製衣，正冠纓絕，捉衿而肘見。"

捉迷藏 zhuō mí cáng 3959

To catch the hiding. (lit.)

Hide and seek.

Blindman's buff.

源 元稹詩："憶得雙文籠月下，小樓前後捉迷藏。"

着先鞭 zhuó xiān biān 3960

To make the first whip. (lit.)

Jump (Beat) the gun.

同 先發制人（3078）Steal a march on one.

反 馬後炮（1272）After meat, mustard.

源 晉書．劉琨傳："吾枕戈待旦，志梟逆虜，常恐祖生先吾着鞭。"

孜孜不倦 zī zī bú juàn 3961

Work diligently and tirelessly. (lit.)

With tireless energy.

To peg away.

Grind away at

Knuckle down to it.

Keep the cart on the wheels.

Keep one's nose to the grindstone.

Knock oneself out.

同 埋頭苦幹（1735）Work like a Trojan.

反 遊手好閒（3639）Fool away one's time.

源 後漢書．魯丕傳："丕性沈深好學，孶孶不倦。"

孜孜為利 zī zī wèi lì 3962

Work tirelessly for profit. (lit.)

Chase eights and quarters.

Have an itching palm.

同 唯利是圖（2888）To be profit-seeking.

趑趄不前 zī jū bù qián 3963

Hobble along without going forward. (lit.)

At a standstill.

Hang back.

Rooted to the spot.

同 停滯不前（2758）Get bogged down.

反 勇往直前（3619）Forge ahead.

源 韓愈："足將進而趑趄。"

錙銖計較 zī zhū jì jiào 3964

Look after the trifling accounts. (lit.)

Chase eights and quarters.

Look at both sides of a penny.

Skin a flint.

同 斤斤計較（1340）Strain at a gnat.

反 一擲千金（3497）Play ducks and drakes with one's money.

源 禮記："雖分圍如錙銖。"

3965 **子是中山狼，得志便猖狂**
zǐ shì zhōng shān láng, dé zhì biàn chāng kuáng
His son is the wolf in the mountain, when getting power, he will be wicked. (lit.)
Save a thief from the gallows and he will cut your throat.

源 紅樓夢："子係中山狼，得志便猖狂。"

3966 **仔細思量** zǐ xì sī liáng
Carefully think and weigh. (lit.)
Consult one's pillow.
Listen to oneself.
Sleep over it.
Put on one's thinking cap.

同 深思熟慮（2398）Sleep on the matter.
反 不假思索（0204）Do（Say）something off-hand.

3967 **字裏行間** zì lǐ háng jiān
Among the words and between the lines. (lit.)
Read between the lines.

3968 **自暴自棄** zì bào zì qì
To expose and throw oneself away. (lit.)
Ruin oneself.
Abandon oneself to despair.
Cut one's own throat.
Stand in one's own light.

反 發憤圖強（0732）Shake oneself together.
源 孟子．離婁上："自暴者，不可與有言也。自棄者，不可與有為也。"

3969 **自不待言** zì bú dài yán
Naturally need not wait to be said. (lit.)
It goes without saying.
Needless to say.
Not to speak of

同 不在話下（0273）To be taken for granted.

3970 **自不量力** zì bú liàng lì
Not measuring one's own strength. (lit.)
Go out of one's depth.
Overreach oneself.
Bite off more than one can chew.

同 螳臂擋車（2689）Throw straw against the wind.
反 量力而行（1638）Kindle not a fire that you cannot extinguish.

自慚形穢 zì cán xíng huì 3971
To be ashamed of oneself's poor shape. (lit.)
Hang one's head.
To feel like two cents.
He that has a great nose thinks everybody is speaking of it.
Have an inferiority complex.
Not fit to hold a candle to one.
Have a sense of inferiority.

源 世説新語．容止："晉王濟見衛玠，歎曰，珠玉在側，覺我形穢。"

自出心裁 zì chū xīn cái 3972
Out of one's own heart and mind. (lit.)
Take the initiative.
Do a thing off one's own bat.
Out of one's own head.

反 依樣畫葫蘆（3512）Play the sedulous ape.
源 清．袁枚．復家實堂："古文有十弊……不自出心裁，五弊也。"

自吹自擂 zì chuī zì léi 3973
Blow one's own trumpet and beat the drum. (lit.)
Blow one's own trumpet (horn).
Self-praise is no recommendation.
Crack oneself up.

同 自我吹嘘（4001）Sing one's own praise.

自得其樂 zì dé qí lè 3974
Enjoy himself. (lit.)
He is happy that thinks himself so.
Take delight in
Get a kick out of
The world is his that enjoys it.

反 自尋煩惱（4006）To fret one's gizzard.
源 明．陶宗儀．輟耕錄："雌雄和鳴，自得其樂。"

自頂至踵 zì dǐng zhì zhǒng 3975
From top to heel. (lit.)
From top to toe.

源 任昉文："自頂至踵，功歸造化。"

自動自覺 zì dòng zì jué 3976
Self motivated and self-conscious. (lit.)
Of one's own accord.
On one's own initiative.
Of one's own free will.

反 冥頑不靈（1829）As stiff as a poker.

3977 **自奉甚薄** zì fèng shèn báo

To treat oneself very meanly. (lit.)

Practise self-denial.

Live on simple fare.

同 淡泊明志（0578）Lead a stoical life.

反 多吃多佔（0696）Take the lion's share.

源 説苑：“其政平，其吏不苛，其賦斂節，其自奉薄。”

3978 **自高自大** zì gāo zì dà

Self-exalted and self-important. (lit.)

Think no small beer of oneself.

Too big for one's boots.

As vain as a peacock.

Have a high opinion of oneself.

同 夜郎自大（3366）A humble-bee in a cow-turd thinks himself a king.

反 虛懷若谷（3245）Humble oneself.

3979 **自告奮勇** zì gào fèn yǒng

To volunteer one's undaunted service. (lit.)

To bell the cat.

Take upon oneself.

Accept the challenge.

Bravely offer.

3980 **自古以來** zì gǔ yǐ lái

From ancient times till now. (lit.)

From time out of mind.

From time immemorial.

3981 **自顧不暇** zì gù bù xiá

Having not enough time to look after one's affair. (lit.)

Unable to fend for oneself.

He that is fallen cannot help him that is down.

源 晉書．劉曜載記：“彼方憂自固，何暇來耶。”

3982 **自己動手，豐衣足食**

zì jǐ dòng shǒu, fēng yī zú shí

Using one's own hand, plenty of clothes and enough food. (lit.)

He that would eat the nut must first crack the shell.

He that will eat the kernel must crack the nut.

In the sweat of thy face shalt thou eat bread.

He that would have the fruit must climb the tree.

同 自食其力（3994）Shift for oneself.

反 衣來伸手，飯來張口（3506）Kitty Swerrock where she sat, come reach me this, come reach me that.

自力更生 zì lì gēng shēng
Regeneration by one's own effort. (lit.)
Stand on one's own feet.
Pull oneself up by the footstraps.

同 發憤圖強（0732）Shake oneself together. 3983
反 寄人籬下（1236）To eat out of one's hand.

自賣自誇 zì mài zì kuā
Advertise and boast oneself. (lit.)
Every man praises his own wares.
There's nothing like leather.

同 自吹自擂（3973）Blow one's own trumpet. 3984
反 有麝自然香（3665）Good wine needs no bush.

自鳴得意 zì míng dé yì
Sing one's own praises. (lit.)
Like a dog with two tails.
Cry roast meat.
Pat oneself on the back.
To crow over
To be corned with oneself.
Preen oneself.

反 大喊倒霉（0526）Get it in the neck. 3985

自命不凡 zì mìng bù fán
Fancy oneself to be uncommon. (lit.)
Think one is the whole cheese.
Think something of oneself.
To be full of oneself.
Pique oneself on
Everyone can keep house better than her mother, till she tries.

同 自命清高 Holier-than-thou 3986
反 妄自菲薄（2867）Make oneself too cheap.

自欺欺人 zì qī qī rén
Deceive oneself and others. (lit.)
The magician mutters, and knows not what he mutters.
Liars begin by imposing upon others, but end by deceiving themselves.

源 大學：“所謂誠其意者，毋自欺也。” 3987

3988 **自強不息** zì qiáng bù xī

Strengthen oneself incessantly. (lit.)

Shake oneself together.

Brace up.

Stand on one's feet.

Work one's way up.

Buck one's ideas up.

同 奮發有為（0795）Rouse oneself to action.

反 自暴自棄（3968）Abandon oneself to despair.

源 周易・乾："天行健，君子以自強不息。"

3989 **自取滅亡** zì qǔ miè wáng

Bring destruction upon oneself. (lit.)

Invite self destruction.

Court one's own doom.

Pull down one's house about one's ears.

Head for ruin.

Cut one's own throat.

反 自力更生（3983）Stand on one's own feet.

源 陰符經下："沉水入火，自取滅亡。"

3990 **自取其咎** zì qǔ qí jiù

To bring the trouble to oneself and get blame for. (lit.)

Have oneself to blame.

Make a rod for one's own back.

Fry in one's own grease.

Stew in one's own juice.

同 咎由自取（1427）To be hoisted with one's own petard.

源 莊子："咸其自取，怒者其誰耶。"

3991 **自身難保** zì shēn nán bǎo

Difficult to protect oneself. (lit.)

He that is fallen cannot help him that is down.

3992 **自生自滅** zì shēng zì miè

Self-regeneration and self-destruction. (lit.)

Abandon one to one's own fate.

Many things grow in the garden that were never sown there.

Weeds want no sowing.

源 元稹詩："心火自生還自滅。"

3993 **自食其果** zì shí qí guǒ

Eat the (bitter) fruit of one's own making. (lit.)

Stew in one's own juice.

As you brew, so you must drink.

Fry in one's own grease.

同 自作自受（4017）As you make your bed, so you must lie on it.

自食其力 zì shí qí lì 3994

To eat by one's own exertion. (lit.)

Earn one's own bread.
Shift for oneself.
Cut one's own grass.
Paddle one's own canoe.
Hoe one's own row.

反 借債度日（1336）Live on ticket.
源 太平經："各自衣食其力。"

自始至終 zì shǐ zhì zhōng 3995

From start to finish. (lit.)

From beginning to end.
From alpha to omega.
From the egg to the apples.
From start to finish.

同 從頭到尾（0464）From first to last.

自視甚高 zì shì shèn gāo 3996

To see oneself very high. (lit.)

Think one's penny silver.
To be on good terms with oneself.

同 自命不凡（3986）Think someone of oneself.
反 自慚形穢（3971）Have an inferiority complex.

自私自利 zì sī zì lì 3997

To seek private and personal advantage. (lit.)

To be self-seeking.
Play one's own hand.
In one's own interest.
To hog it.

反 捨己為人（2373）To bell the cat.

自討苦吃 zì tǎo kǔ chī 3998

One asks to eat bitterness. (lit.)

Ask for trouble.
Ask for it (trouble).
Stick out one's neck.
Make a rod for one's own back.

同 自找麻煩（4012）Wake a sleeping dog.

自投羅網 zì tóu luó wǎng 3999

Fall into one's own trap. (lit.)

Put one's neck into a noose.

4000 自挖牆腳 zì wā qiáng jiǎo
Dig the foot of one's own wall. (lit.)
Quarrel with one's own bread and butter.
Cut the bough one is standing on.
Cry stinking fish.
He's cooked his goose.

同 自作孽，不可活（4015）The evils we bring on ourselves are the hardest to bear.

4001 自我吹噓 zì wǒ chuī xū
To bluff for oneself. (lit.)
Self-advertise.
Sing one's own praise.
Plume oneself on

同 王婆賣瓜，自賣自誇（2863）Every cook praises her own broth.

4002 自我反省 zì wǒ fǎn xǐng
Self reflection. (lit.)
Examine one's own conscience.

同 捫心自問（1781）Search one's soul.

4003 自我陶醉 zì wǒ táo zuì
Intoxicated with oneself. (lit.)
Each bird loves to hear himself sing.
As the fool thinks, so the bell chinks.
Congratulate oneself on
In one's glory.
Licks one's chops.

4004 自相殘殺 zì xiāng cán shā
Kill each other ruthlessly. (lit.)
Cut one another's throats.

源 晉書 · 石季龍載記下：“季龍十三子，五人為冉閔所殺，八人自相殘害。”

4005 自尋短見 zì xún duǎn jiàn
To find short sight oneself. (lit.)
Lay hands on oneself.
Shut one's light off.
Make away with oneself.

同 了此一生（1642）Snuffle off this mortal coil.

4006 自尋煩惱 zì xún fán nǎo
To find trouble for oneself. (lit.)
To fret one's gizzard.

反 自得其樂（3974）He is happy that thinks himself so.

自言自語 zì yán zì yǔ 4007
Talk to oneself. (lit.)
Utter a soliloquy.
To think aloud.
Mutter to oneself.

自以為是 zì yǐ wéi shì 4008
Consider oneself right. (lit.)
Too sure of oneself.
Self-opinionated.

同 剛愎自用（0875）Reckon without one's host.
反 不恥下問（0171）Bow down thy ear.
源 荀子．榮辱：“凡鬥者必自以為是，而以人為非也。”

自由自在 zì yóu zì zài 4009
To be free and comfortable. (lit.)
In a state of bliss.
As free as (the) air.
As free as a bird.

同 舒舒服服（2564）As snug as a bug in a rug.
反 侷促不安（1438）To be ill at ease.
源 景德傳燈錄：“問牛頭未見四祖時如何，師曰，自由自在，問先後如何，師曰，自由自在。”

自怨自艾 zì yuàn zì yì 4010
Blame and hate oneself. (lit.)
Full of self-reproach.
Kick oneself.
Cry over spilt milk.
Stew in one's own juice.

反 自鳴得意（3985）Preen oneself.
源 孟子．萬章上：“太甲自怨自艾。”

自朝至暮 zì zhāo zhì mù 4011
From morning till evening. (lit.)
From dawn till dusk.

同 晝夜不息（3930）Round the clock.

自找麻煩 zì zhǎo má fán 4012
Seeking trouble for oneself. (lit.)
Wake a sleeping dog.
Invite trouble.
Ask for it (trouble).

同 自討苦吃（3998）Make a rod for one's own back.

自助即天助 zì zhù jí tiān zhù 4013
Heaven's help means help oneself. (lit.)
God (Heaven) helps those who help themselves.

4014 **自作孽** zì zuò niè
To do evil by self. (lit.)
Make a rod for one's own back.

4015 **自作孽，不可活** zì zuò niè, bù kě huó
Doing evil by self, one may not live. (lit.)
Drive a nail in one's coffin.
Stand in one's own light.
The evils we bring on ourselves are the hardest to bear.

源 書經："天作孽，猶可違，自作孽，不可逭。"

4016 **自作主張** zì zuò zhǔ zhāng
Make one's own opinion. (lit.)
Take the bit in one's mouth (teeth).

同 擅作主張（2350）Take the law into one's hands.
反 有商有量（3664）Lay our heads together.

4017 **自作自受** zì zuò zì shòu
Bear the consequences of one's own deeds. (lit.)
Suffer for what one does.
One must drink as one brews.
He that handles thorns shall prick his fingers.
As you make your bed, so you must lie on it.
Fry in one's own grease.
Serve one right.

同 作繭自縛（4068）Caught in one's own trap.
源 釋普濟·五燈會元："僧問金山穎，一百二十斤鐵枷，教阿誰擔，穎曰，自作自受。"

4018 **恣意揮霍** zì yì huī huò
Carefreely spendthrift. (lit.)
To blue one's money.
Bring one's noble to nine pence.
Money burns a hole in his pocket.
Throw money down the drain.

同 一擲千金（3497）Spend money like water.
反 省吃儉用（2430）Pinch and scrape.

4019 **綜合分析** zōng hé fēn xī
A general analysis. (lit.)
Put two and two together.
Taking one thing with another.

總而言之 zǒng ér yán zhī 4020
To say it in general. (lit.)
By and large.
All and all.
On the whole.
In brief.
To make a long story short.

同 一言蔽之（3481）In a nutshell.
源 漢書．高帝紀．顏師古注："鄉邑之人老及長者，父兄之行少及幼者，子弟之黨，故總而言之。"

總角之交 zǒng jiǎo zhī jiāo 4021
Tuft of hair friendship (from children). (lit.)
Old pals.
Great chums.
One's beddies.

反 點頭朋友（0648）A nodding acquaintance.
源 詩經："總角丱兮。"

總結起來 zǒng jié qǐ lái 4022
In all conclusion. (lit.)
The long and short of it is that.
In summing up.

縱橫捭闔 zòng héng bǎi hé 4023
Vertical, horizontal, open and close. (lit.)
Wheel and deal.

同 應付自如（3605）Equal to the situation.

走錯門路 zǒu cuò mén lù 4024
Run to the wrong door and road (entrance). (lit.)
Bark up the wrong tree.
Drive one's pig to the pretty market.

走後門 zǒu hòu mén 4025
Run to back door. (lit.)
Through backstairs influence.
Do something under the counter.
Pull strings (wires).

同 捨正道而不由（2376）Leave the beaten track.

走捷徑 zǒu jié jìng 4026
Run short cut. (lit.)
Take the shortest cut.
By the string rather than by the bow.
Cut corners.

反 迂迴曲折（3685）Twists and turns.

4027 **走馬看花** zǒu mǎ kàn huā

Looking at the flowers from the back of a galloping horse. (lit.)

Hit the high spots.

Go sight-seeing.

A brief fleeting look.

反 流連忘返（1681）Can't tear oneself away.

源 孟郊詩："春風得意馬蹄疾，一日看遍長安花。"

4028 **走內線** zǒu nèi xiàn

Run internal lines. (lit.)

To pull strings.

Through backstairs influence.

4029 **走入歧途** zǒu rù qí tú

Run into wrong route. (lit.)

To go astray.

Go out of the right path.

同 迷失方向（1788）Lose one's bearings.

反 方向對頭（0753）On the right tack.

4030 **走投無路** zǒu tóu wú lù

Running to the end of the road. (lit.)

In a tight spot.

Stand at bay.

To be driven to the wall.

同 到處碰壁（0599）Driven from pillar to post.

反 左右逢源（4050）It is good to have friends both in heaven and in hell.

源 元曲選．楊顯之．瀟湘雨："淋的我走投無路。"

4031 **走下坡路** zǒu xià pō lù

Run down the hill slope. (lit.)

On the decline.

On the down grade.

Go farther and fare worse.

Jump from the frying pan into the fire.

Go into a tailspin.

同 江河日下（1292）Go from bad to worse.

反 拾級而登（2465）Step after step the ladder is ascended.

4032 **走運** zǒu yùn

Run into luck. (lit.)

Hit the jackpot.

同 紅到發紫（1074）At the zenith of one's power.

4033 **足智多謀** zú zhì duō móu

Sufficient wisdom and many plans. (lit.)

Fruitful of expedients.

Have plenty of brains.

同 精明強幹（1386）To be up to snuff.

反 愚不可及（3693）No fool like an old fool.

源 元曲選．連環計："此人足智多謀，可與共事。"

族大有乞兒 zú dà yǒu qǐ ér 4034
There may be beggars in any big clans. (lit.)
There are black sheep in every fold.
Shame in a kindred cannot be avoided.
同 十個指頭有長短（2455）One end is sure to be bone.

鑽牛角尖 zuān niú jiǎo jiān 4035
Drill into the bull horn's tip. (lit.)
Look at the needle point of things.
Number the streaks of the tulip.
Split hairs (straws).
同 明察秋毫之末，而不見輿薪 Can't see the wood for the trees.
反 從大處着眼（0460）Have an eye to the main chance.

最後定案 zuì hòu dìng àn 4036
The case is finally decided. (lit.)
Set the seal on.

最後攤牌 zuì hòu tān pái 4037
Final laying down the cards. (lit.)
Show-down.
Put one's cards on the table.

最後掙扎 zuì hòu zhēng zhá 4038
The final struggle. (lit.)
Clutch at a straw.
A last-ditch struggle.
In one's death throes.

罪惡昭彰 zuì è zhāo zhāng 4039
Flagrant crimes. (lit.)
Crying sin.
Besetting sin.
Heinous crime.

罪有應得 zuì yǒu yīng dé 4040
His crime deserve what he got. (lit.)
It serves one right.
反 冤哉枉也（3728）What an outrageous fabrication!

罪責難逃 zuì zé nán táo 4041
It is difficult to escape debt of crime. (lit.)
Every sin brings its punishment with it.
One can't get away with it.
同 天網恢恢，疏而不漏（2721）Justice has long arms.
反 逍遙法外（3128）To be at large.

4042 醉後吐真言 zuì hòu tǔ zhēn yán
When drunk, speak the true words. (lit.)
What soberness conceals drunkenness reveals.
Truth lies at the bottom of the decanter.
In wine there is truth.

4043 醉生夢死 zuì shēng mèng sǐ
To live drunk and die dreaming. (lit.)
Go on the binge (a spree).
Dream one's life away.
Live on the cross.

同 行屍走肉（3216）To be dead alive.
反 奮發有為（0795）Rouse oneself to action.
源 程子語錄："雖高才明智，膠於見聞，醉生夢死，不自覺也。"

4044 醉翁之意不在酒
zuì wēng zhī yì bú zài jiǔ
The intention of a drunkard lies not on the wine (but on other purposes). (lit.)
Many kiss the child for the nurse's sake.
With ulterior motives.

源 歐陽修·醉翁亭記："醉翁之意不在酒，在乎山水之間也。"

4045 醉眼朦朧 zuì yǎn méng lóng
Drunken eyes are blur. (lit.)
A sheet in the mind's eye.
Three sheets in the wind.
See pink elephants.

反 金睛火眼（1341）Keep one's eyes skinned.

4046 左耳入，右耳出 zuǒ ěr rù, yòu ěr chū
Entering the left ear, out the right ear. (lit.)
Water over the duck's back.
In at one ear and out at the other.

同 水過鴨背（2590）Like water off a duck's back.
反 言猶在耳（3311）Still ring in one's ears.

4047 左鄰右里 zuǒ lín yòu lǐ
With neighbours both on the left and right. (lit.)
One's next-door neighbours.

4048 左偏右袒 zuǒ piān yòu tǎn
Leaning to the left and protecting the right. (lit.)
Make fish of one and flesh of another.

同 厚此薄彼（1076）Make chalk of one and cheese of the other.
反 一視同仁（3457）The sun shines upon all alike.

左思右想 zuǒ sī yòu xiǎng
Thinking of the left and pondering over the right. (lit.)
Turn over in one's mind.

同 仔細思量（3966）Consult one's pillow. 4049

左右逢源 zuǒ yòu féng yuán
To meet and receive left and right. (lit.)
Everything goes well.
It is good to have friends both in heaven and in hell.

同 八面玲瓏（0034）All things to all men. 4050
反 進退維谷（1368）On the horns of a dilemma.
源 孟子 · 離婁下：“資之深，則取之左右逢其原。”

左右為難 zuǒ yòu wéi nán
Difficulties on both the left and right. (lit.)
Torn between.
In a plight.
Between Scylla and Charybdis.
Driven from pillar to post.

同 進退維谷（1368）In a cleft stick. 4051

左支右絀 zuǒ zhī yòu chù
Paying on the left and deficient on the right. (lit.)
Can't make both ends meet.
To be in a tight squeeze.

同 手頭拮据（2547）To be hard up. 4052
反 一擲千金（3497）Spend money like water.
源 清 · 紀昀 · 閱微草堂筆記：“左支右絀，困不可忍。”

坐立不安 zuò lì bù ān
Uneasy in sitting and standing. (lit.)
Give one the fidgets.
Sit on a bag of fleas.
Have ants in one's pants.

同 忐忑不安（2684）In a fidget. 4053
反 高枕無憂（0888）A good conscience is a soft pillow.

坐山觀虎鬥 zuò shān guān hǔ dòu
Sitting on a hill, watch tigers at fight. (lit.)
Look on with folded arms.

同 作壁上觀（4063）Sit upon the fence. 4054
反 插上一手（0321）Have a hand in
源 源出《史記 · 張儀列傳》卞莊子欲刺虎，兩虎鬥，大者傷，小者死，莊子從傷者而刺之，一舉果有雙虎之功。

坐失良機 zuò shī liáng jī
While sitting, one loses a good opportunity. (lit.)
Miss the boat.
Slip through one's fingers.

同 失之交臂（2449）Miss the bus. 4055
反 見機行事（1277）Make hay while the sun shines.

4056 坐食山空 zuò shí shān kōng

Sitting and eating can empty the hill. (lit.)

Dig one's grave with one's teeth.

Eat out of house and home.

Always taking out of a meal-tub, and never putting in, soon comes to the bottom.

反 勤儉起家（2112）Industry is fortune's right hand and frugality her left.

源 京本通俗小說．錯斬崔寧："坐吃山空，立吃地陷。"

4057 坐視不救 zuò shì bú jiù

Sitting and watching without saving one (from danger). (lit.)

Stand by with folded arms.

Not lift a finger.

同 見死不救（1280）Leave one in the lurch.

4058 坐臥不寧 zuò wò bù níng

Uneasy in both sitting and lying down. (lit.)

Ill at ease.

On pins ans needles.

同 惴惴不安（3953）In a fidget.

反 悠然自得（3623）Free and easy.

4059 坐享其成 zuò xiǎng qí chéng

Sitting down to enjoy the success (the fruit). (lit.)

One beat the bush and another caught the hare.

Get something for nothing.

Unearned income.

同 衣來伸手，飯來張口（3506）Kitty Swerrock where she sat, come reach me this, come reach me that.

反 為人作嫁（2918）Be in attendance on

源 孟子："千歲之日至，可坐而致也。"

4060 坐言起行 zuò yán qǐ xíng

To say when sitting and act while rising. (lit.)

Say well is good, but do well is better.

同 說到做到（2606）Live up to one's words.

反 誇誇其談（1522）The greatest talkers are always the least doers.

源 荀子．性惡："故坐而言之，起而可設，張而可施行。"

4061 坐以待斃 zuò yǐ dài bì

Sitting down wait for death. (lit.)

A close mouth catches no flies.

反 積穀防饑（1189）Lay up against a rainy day.

源 清．朱佐朝．後漁家樂傳奇："何必坐以待斃。"

坐以待旦 zuò yǐ dài dàn 4062
Sitting down wait for the dawn. (lit.)
Outwatch the Bear.

同 通宵達旦（2764）All through the night.
反 日上三竿猶未起（2257）A sluggard makes his night till noon.
源 三國志．吳志．孫權傳：“思齊先代，坐而待旦。”

作壁上觀 zuò bì shàng guān 4063
Sitting on the wall, look on. (lit.)
Sit upon the fence.
Stand aloof.

同 袖手旁觀（3242）Look on with folded arms.
反 插上一手（0321）Have a finger in the pie.
源 漢書：“及楚擊秦，諸侯皆從壁上觀。”

作東道主 zuò dōng dào zhǔ 4064
To act as a host standing treat. (lit.)
Do the honours.
Stand treat.

同 盡地主之誼（1371）Do the honours of the house.
反 敬陪末座（1404）Sit below the salt.
源 左傳．僖三十年：“若舍鄭以為東道主，行李之往來，共其乏困，君亦無所害。”

作惡多端 zuò è duō duān 4065
To commit all kinds of evils and crimes. (lit.)
Every sort of vice.
Up to all sorts of evils.

同 無所不為（2993）Go to any limit.
反 積善多福（1191）A good deed is never lost.

作法自斃 zuò fǎ zì bì 4066
To work a plan and kill oneself. (lit.)
To fry in one's own grease.
Curses come home to roost.

作和事老 zuò hé shì lǎo 4067
To be an old peace maker. (lit.)
Heal the breach.

同 排難解紛（1943）Pour oil on troubled waters.
反 挑撥離間（2743）Sow dissension.

作繭自縛 zuò jiǎn zì fù 4068
Forming a cocoon and tying round oneself. (lit.)
Sow the wind and reap the whirlwind.
Caught in one's own trap.
Fry in one's own grease.
Hoist with one's own petard.

同 自作自受（4017）One must drink as one brews.
反 衝破藩籬（0387）To break bounds.
源 傳燈錄：“志公坐禪，如蠶吐絲自縛。”

4069 **作困獸鬥** zuò kùn shòu dòu

Struggle like cornered animal. (lit.)
Turn to bay.
Fight with one's back to the wall.
To be at bay.

源 左傳 · 宣公十二年："困獸猶鬥，況國相乎。"

4070 **作兩手準備** zuò liǎng shǒu zhǔn bèi

Make preparation with two hands. (lit.)
Hope for the best and prepare for the worst.
Have two strings to one's bow.

反 孤注一擲（0939）Bet one's bottom dollar on.

4071 **作鳥獸散** zuò niǎo shòu sàn

Disperse like the birds and animals. (lit.)
To flee helter-skelter (pell-mell).

反 蜂擁而至（0814）Swarm like bees.
源 漢書 · 李陵傳："今無兵復戰，天明坐受縛矣，各鳥獸散，猶有得脱歸報天子者。"

4072 **作殊死戰** zuò shū sǐ zhàn

To fight a death struggle. (lit.)
Fight with a rope round one's neck.
Fight tooth and nail.

同 生死搏鬥（2417）Life and death struggle.
反 臨陣退縮（1659）Turn tail at the last moment.
源 史記："軍皆殊死戰。"

4073 **作威作福** zuò wēi zuò fú

To act as if one has a lot of power and blessing. (lit.)
Lord it over.
Throw one's weight about.
Push people around.

同 專橫跋扈 Play the bully.
反 畢恭畢敬（0121）Cap in hand.
源 尚書 · 洪範："惟辟作福，惟辟作威。……臣無有作福作威。"

4074 **作揖打拱** zuò yī dǎ gǒng

To make a bow and salute with folded hands. (lit.)
Bow and scrape.

反 拳腳交加（2165）Cuffs and kicks.

4075 **作賊心虛** zuò zéi xīn xū

Being a thief, he is timid at heart. (lit.)
Have a guilty conscience.
He that lives ill, fear follows him.
He that commits a fault thinks everyone speaks of it.
A bully is always a coward.

反 平生不作虧心事，半夜敲門也不驚（1991）A quiet conscience sleeps in thunder.
源 宋 · 悟明 · 聯燈會要："卻顧侍者云，適來有人看方丈麼，侍者云有，師云，作賊人心虛。"

作最壞打算 zuò zuì huài dǎ suàn 4076
Prepared for the worst. (lit.)
Come what may.
If the worst comes to the worst.

同 過分樂觀（0996）Count one's chickens before they are hatched.

做思想工作 zuò sī xiǎng gōng zuò 4077
Thought-molding work. (lit.)
To bring to reason.
Brain-washing.

鑿壁偷光 zuò bì tōu guāng 4078
To steal the light by knocking through the wall. (lit.)
Burn the midnight oil.

源 西京雜記：“匡衡勤學而無燭，鄰舍有燭而不逮，衡乃穿壁引其光，以書映光而讀之。”

鑿井而飲，耕田而食 4079
zuò jǐng ér yǐn, gēng tián ér shí
To sink a well for drink (of water) and plough the fields for food. (lit.)
No gain without pain.
By the sweat of one's brow.

同 自己動手，豐衣足食（3982）In the sweat of thy face shalt thou eat bread.
源 齊書：“鑿飲耕食，自幸唐年。”
又參閱2254

英文索引
English Index

A

B

C

D

E

F

G

H

I

J

K

L

M

N

O

P

Q

R

S

T

U

V

W

Y

Z

附錄 Appendices

漢語拼音方案

Scheme for the Chinese Phonetic Alphabet

一 字母表

字母：	Aa	Bb	Cc	Dd	Ee	Ff	Gg
名稱：	ㄚ	ㄅㄝ	ㄘㄝ	ㄉㄝ	ㄜ	ㄝㄈ	ㄍㄝ
	Hh	Ii	ji	Kk	Ll	Mm	Nn
	ㄏㄚ	ㄧ	ㄐㄧㄝ	ㄎㄝ	ㄝㄌ	ㄝㄇ	ㄋㄝ
	Oo	Pp	Qq	Rr	Ss	Tt	
	ㄛ	ㄆㄝ	ㄑㄧㄡ	ㄚㄦ	ㄝㄙ	ㄊㄝ	
	Uu	Vv	Ww	Xx	Yy	Zz	
	ㄨ	ㄪㄝ	ㄨㄚ	ㄒㄧ	ㄧㄚ	ㄗㄝ	

V 只用來拼寫外來語、少數民族語言和方言。字母的手寫體依照拉丁字母的一般書寫習慣。

二 聲母表

b	p	m	f	d	t	n	l
ㄅ玻	ㄆ坡	ㄇ摸	ㄈ佛	ㄉ得	ㄊ特	ㄋ訥	ㄌ勒
g	k	h			j	q	x
ㄍ哥	ㄎ科	ㄏ喝			ㄐ基	ㄑ欺	ㄒ希
zh	ch	sh	r		z	c	s
ㄓ知	ㄔ蚩	ㄕ詩	ㄖ日		ㄗ資	ㄘ雌	ㄙ思

在給漢字注音的時候，為了使拼式簡短，zh ch sh 可以省作 ẑ ĉ ŝ。

三　韻母表

	i 丨　衣	u ㄨ　烏	ü ㄩ　迂
a ㄚ　啊	ia 丨ㄚ　呀	ua ㄨㄚ　蛙	
o ㄛ　喔		uo ㄨㄛ　窩	
e ㄜ　鵝	ie 丨ㄝ　耶		üe ㄩㄝ　約
ai ㄞ　哀		uai ㄨㄞ　歪	
ei ㄟ　欸		uei ㄨㄟ　威	
ao ㄠ　熬	iao 丨ㄠ　腰		
ou ㄡ　歐	iou 丨ㄡ　憂		
an ㄢ　安	ian 丨ㄢ　煙	uan ㄨㄢ　彎	üan ㄩㄢ　冤
en ㄣ　恩	in 丨ㄣ　因	uen ㄨㄣ　溫	ün ㄩㄣ　暈
ang ㄤ　昂	iang 丨ㄤ　央	uang ㄨㄤ　汪	
eng ㄥ　亨的韻母	ing 丨ㄥ　英	ueng ㄨㄥ　翁	
ong （ㄨㄥ）轟的韻母	iong ㄩㄥ　雍		

（1）“知、蚩、詩、日、資、雌、思”等七個音節的韻母用 i，即：知、蚩、詩、日、資、雌、思等字拼作 zhi，chi，shi，ri，zi，ci，si。

（2）韻母ㄦ寫成 er，用做韻尾的時候寫成 r。例如：“兒童”拼作 ertong，“花兒”拼作 huar。

（3）韻母ㄝ單用的時候寫 ê。

（4）i 行的韻母，前面沒有聲母的時候，寫成：yi（衣），ya（呀），ye（耶），yao（腰），you（憂），yan（煙），yin（因），yang（央），ying（英），yong（雍）。

u 行的韻母，前面沒有聲母的時候，寫成：wu（烏），wa（蛙），wo（窩），wai（歪），wei（威），wan（彎），wen（溫），wang（汪），weng（翁）。

ü 行的韻母，前面沒有聲母的時候，寫成：yu（迂），yue（約），yuan（冤），yun（暈）；ü 上兩點省略。

ü 行的韻母跟聲母 j，q，x 拼的時候，寫成：ju（居），qu（區），xu（虛），ü 上兩點也省略；但是跟聲母 n，l 拼的時候，仍然寫成：nü（女），lü（呂）。

（5）iou，uei，uen 前面加聲母的時候，寫成：iu，ui，un。例如 niu（牛），gui（歸），lun（論）。

（6）在給漢字注音的時候，為了使拼式簡短，ng 可以省作 ŋ。

四　聲調符號

陰平	陽平	上聲	去聲
ˉ	ˊ	ˇ	ˋ

聲調符號標在音節的主要母音上，輕聲不標。例如：

媽 mā	麻 má	馬 mǎ	罵 mà	嗎 ma
（陰平）	（陽平）	（上聲）	（去聲）	（輕聲）

五　隔音符號

a，o，e 開頭的音節連接在其他音節後面的時候，如果音節的界限發生混淆，用隔音符號（'）隔開，例如：pi'ao（皮襖）。

標準漢語拼音與 Wade 氏漢字拼音對照表

Standard Hanyu Pinyin Versus Wade Romanization

聲母		韻母			
標準	Wade 氏	標準	Wade 氏	標準	Wade 氏
b	p	a	a	u	u, wu
p	p‘	o	o	ua	ua, wa
m	m	e (ê)	ê, o	uo	uo, wo
f	f	ai	ai	uai	uai, wai
d	t‘	ei	ei	uei (ui)	ui, wei
t	t	ao	ao	uan	uan, wan
n	n	ou	ou	uen (un)	un, wên
l	l	an	an	uang	uang, wang
g	k	en	en	ueng	wêng
k	k‘	ang	ang	ü	ü, yü
h	h	eng	eng	üe	üeh, yüeh
j	ch	ong	ung	üan	üan, üen, yüen
q	ch‘	i	i, ih	ün	ün, yün
x	hs	ia	ia, yia		
zh (ẑ)	ch	ie	ieh, yeh		
ch (ĉ)	ch‘	iao	iao, yao		
sh (ŝ)	sh	iou (iu)	iu, yu		
r	j	ian	ien, yen		
z	ts, tz	in	in, yin		
c	ts‘, tz‘	iang	iang		
s	s, ss, sz	ing	ing, ying		
		iong	iung, yung		

簡化字檢字表

Simplified Versions of Chinese Characters

説　明

一、为了便利读者检查已经公布推行的简化字，我们根据《简化字总表》第二版编了这本简化字表。

二、本检字分三个表：A. 从简体查繁体；B. 从繁体查简体；C. 从拼音查汉字。

三、A 表和 B 表是按汉字笔数排列的，同笔数的字以横、竖、撇、点、折为序。

四、C 表是按汉语拼音字母的顺序排列的，一字异读的互见，一音异调的只列一调。

五、凡《简化字总表》规定可作偏旁用的简化字，都用＊号标在字前，以便同不标＊号的，即不作偏旁用的简化字区别开来。

六、《简化字总表》第二表中的 14 个简化偏旁：讠〔言〕、饣〔食〕、𠃓〔昜〕、纟〔糸〕、収〔臤〕、𫇧〔𤇾〕、𠂉〔臨〕、只〔戠〕、钅〔金〕、𭕄〔𦥯〕、𠬤〔睪〕、𢀖〔巠〕、亦〔䜌〕、呙〔咼〕，一般不能独立成字，本检字没有收录。

七、凡《简化字总表》中附有注释的字，都用数码标在字后，注释统一排在 C 表的后面。

八、除了 A，B，C 三表外，本检字还附有异体字整理表中 39 个习惯被看作简化字的选用字和已经更改的生僻地名用字。

附　錄

以下 39 个字是从《第一批异体字整理表》摘录出来的。这些字习惯被看作简化字，附此以便检查。括弧里的字是停止使用的异体字。

呆〔獃騃〕	挂〔掛〕	昆〔崑崐〕	猫〔貓〕	席〔蓆〕	涌〔湧〕	占〔佔〕
布〔佈〕	哄〔閧鬨〕	捆〔綑〕	栖〔棲〕	凶〔兇〕	岳〔嶽〕	周〔週〕
痴〔癡〕	迹〔跡蹟〕	泪〔淚〕	弃〔棄〕	绣〔繡〕	韵〔韻〕	注〔註〕
床〔牀〕	秸〔稭〕	厘〔釐〕	升〔陞昇〕	锈〔鏽〕	灾〔災〕	
唇〔脣〕	杰〔傑〕①	麻〔蔴〕	笋〔筍〕	岩〔巖〕	札〔劄箚〕	
雇〔僱〕	巨〔鉅〕	脉〔脈〕	它〔牠〕	异〔異〕	扎〔紥紮〕	

注　释

①蚕：上从天，不从夭。②缠：右从廛，不从厘。③尝：不是賞的简化字。賞的简化字是赏（见 shang）。④长：四笔。笔顺是：丿 𠂉 𠂒 长。⑤在迭和叠意义可能混淆时，叠仍用叠。⑥四川省酆都县已改丰都县。姓酆的酆不简化作邦。⑦答覆、反覆的覆简化作复，覆盖、颠覆仍用覆。⑧乾坤、乾隆的乾读 qián（前），不简化。⑨不作坯。坯是砖坯的坯，读 pī（批），坏坯二字不可互混。⑩作多解的夥不简化。⑪系带子的系读 jì（计）。⑫将、浆、桨、奖、酱：右上角从夕，不从夂或爫。⑬藉口、凭藉的藉简化作借，慰藉、狼藉等的藉仍用藉。⑭鬥字头的字，一般也写作門字头，如鬧、鬮、鬩写作閙、鬮、閲。因此，这些鬥字头的字可简化作门字头。但鬥争的鬥应简作斗（见 dou）。⑮壳：几上没有一小横。⑯类：下从大，不从犬。⑰丽：七笔。上边一横，不作两小横。⑱临：左从一短竖一长竖，不从刂。⑲岭：不作岺，免与岑混。⑳马：三笔。笔顺是：㇆马马。上部向左稍斜，左上角开口，末笔作左偏旁时改作平挑。㉑卖：从十从买，上不从士或土。㉒读 me 轻声。读 yāo（夭）的么应作幺（么本字）。吆应作吆。麼读 mó（摩）时不简化，如幺麼小丑。㉓黾：从口从电。㉔鸟：五笔。㉕作门屏之间解的宁（古字罕用）读 zhù（柱）。为避免此宁字与寧的简化字混淆，原读 zhù 的宁作𡧖。㉖区：不作区。㉗前仆后继的仆读 pū（扑）。㉘庆：从大，不从犬。㉙赏：不可误作尝。尝是嘗的简化字（见 chang）。㉚古人南宫适、洪适的适（古字罕用）读 kuò（括）。此适字本作𨓈，为了避免混淆，可恢复本字𨓈。㉛中药苍术、白术的术读 zhú（竹）。㉜肃：中间一竖下面的两边从八，下半中间不从米。㉝条：上从夂，三笔，不从夊。㉞厅：从厂，不从广。㉟袜：从末，不从未。㊱乌：四笔。㊲无：四笔。上从二，不可误作旡。㊳恐吓的吓读 hè（赫）。㊴纤维的纤读 xiān（先）。㊵县：七笔。上从且。㊶在象和像意义可能混淆时，像仍用像。㊷写：上从冖，不从宀。㊸压：六笔。土的右旁有一点。㊹尧：六笔。右上角无点，不可误作尧。㊺叶韵的叶读 xié（协）。㊻义：从乂（读 yì）加点，不可误作叉（读 chā）。㊼在余和馀意义可能混淆时，馀仍用馀。㊽喘吁吁，长吁短叹的吁读 xū（虚）。㊾在折和摺意义可能混淆时，摺仍用摺。㊿宫商角徵羽的徵读 zhǐ（止），不简化。(51)庄：六笔。土的右旁无点。

A. 从简体查繁体

2笔

厂〔廠〕
卜〔蔔〕
儿〔兒〕
*几〔幾〕
了〔瞭〕

3笔

干〔乾〕⑧
〔幹〕
亏〔虧〕
才〔纔〕
*万〔萬〕
*与〔與〕
千〔韆〕
亿〔億〕
个〔個〕
么〔麼〕㉒
*广〔廣〕
*门〔門〕
*义〔義〕㊻
卫〔衛〕
飞〔飛〕
习〔習〕
*马〔馬〕⑳
*乡〔鄉〕

4笔

【一】
*丰〔豐〕⑥
开〔開〕
*无〔無〕㊲
*韦〔韋〕
*专〔專〕
*云〔雲〕
*艺〔藝〕
厅〔廳〕㉞
*历〔歷〕
〔曆〕
*区〔區〕㉘
*车〔車〕

【丨】
*冈〔岡〕
*贝〔貝〕
*见〔見〕

【丿】
*气〔氣〕
*长〔長〕④
仆〔僕〕㉗
币〔幣〕
*从〔從〕
*仑〔侖〕
*仓〔倉〕
*风〔風〕
仅〔僅〕
凤〔鳳〕
*乌〔烏〕㊱

【丶】
闩〔閂〕
*为〔為〕
斗〔鬥〕
忆〔憶〕
订〔訂〕
计〔計〕
讣〔訃〕
认〔認〕
讥〔譏〕

【乛】
丑〔醜〕
*队〔隊〕
办〔辦〕
邓〔鄧〕
劝〔勸〕
*双〔雙〕
书〔書〕

5笔

【一】
击〔擊〕
*戋〔戔〕
扑〔撲〕
*节〔節〕
术〔術〕㉛
*龙〔龍〕
厉〔厲〕
灭〔滅〕
*东〔東〕
轧〔軋〕

【丨】
*卢〔盧〕
*业〔業〕
旧〔舊〕
帅〔帥〕
*归〔歸〕
叶〔葉〕㊺
号〔號〕
电〔電〕
只〔隻〕
〔祇〕
叽〔嘰〕
叹〔嘆〕

【丿】
们〔們〕
仪〔儀〕
丛〔叢〕
*尔〔爾〕
*乐〔樂〕
处〔處〕
冬〔鼕〕
*鸟〔鳥〕㉔
务〔務〕
*刍〔芻〕
饥〔饑〕

【丶】
邝〔鄺〕
冯〔馮〕
闪〔閃〕
兰〔蘭〕
*汇〔匯〕
〔彙〕
头〔頭〕
汉〔漢〕
*宁〔寧〕㉕
讦〔訐〕
讧〔訌〕
讨〔討〕
*写〔寫〕㊷
让〔讓〕
礼〔禮〕
讪〔訕〕
讫〔訖〕
训〔訓〕
议〔議〕
讯〔訊〕
记〔記〕

【乛】
辽〔遼〕
*边〔邊〕
出〔齣〕
*发〔發〕
〔髮〕
*圣〔聖〕
*对〔對〕
台〔臺〕
〔檯〕
〔颱〕
纠〔糾〕
驭〔馭〕
丝〔絲〕

6笔

【一】
玑〔璣〕
*动〔動〕
*执〔執〕
巩〔鞏〕
圹〔壙〕
扩〔擴〕
扪〔捫〕
扫〔掃〕
扬〔揚〕
场〔場〕
*亚〔亞〕
芗〔薌〕
朴〔樸〕
机〔機〕
权〔權〕
*过〔過〕
协〔協〕
*压〔壓〕㊸
厌〔厭〕
厍〔厙〕
*页〔頁〕
夸〔誇〕
夺〔奪〕
*达〔達〕
*夹〔夾〕
轨〔軌〕
*尧〔堯〕㊹
划〔劃〕
迈〔邁〕
*毕〔畢〕

【丨】
贞〔貞〕
*师〔師〕
*当〔當〕
〔噹〕
尘〔塵〕
吁〔籲〕㊽
吓〔嚇〕㊳
*虫〔蟲〕
曲〔麯〕
团〔團〕
〔糰〕
吗〔嗎〕
屿〔嶼〕
*岁〔歲〕
回〔迴〕
*岂〔豈〕
则〔則〕
刚〔剛〕
网〔網〕

【丿】
钆〔釓〕
钇〔釔〕
朱〔硃〕
*迁〔遷〕
*乔〔喬〕
伟〔偉〕
传〔傳〕
伛〔傴〕
优〔優〕
伤〔傷〕
伥〔倀〕
价〔價〕
伦〔倫〕
伧〔傖〕
*华〔華〕
伙〔夥〕⑩
伪〔偽〕
向〔嚮〕
后〔後〕
*会〔會〕
*杀〔殺〕
合〔閤〕
众〔眾〕
爷〔爺〕
伞〔傘〕
创〔創〕
杂〔雜〕
负〔負〕
犷〔獷〕
犸〔獁〕
凫〔鳧〕
邬〔鄔〕
饦〔飥〕
饧〔餳〕

【丶】
壮〔壯〕
冲〔衝〕
妆〔妝〕
庄〔莊〕(51)
庆〔慶〕㉘
*刘〔劉〕
*齐〔齊〕
*产〔產〕
闭〔閉〕
问〔問〕
闯〔闖〕
关〔關〕
灯〔燈〕
汤〔湯〕
忏〔懺〕
兴〔興〕
讲〔講〕
讳〔諱〕
讴〔謳〕
军〔軍〕
讵〔詎〕
讶〔訝〕
讷〔訥〕
许〔許〕
讹〔訛〕
䜣〔訢〕
论〔論〕
讻〔訩〕
讼〔訟〕
讽〔諷〕
*农〔農〕
设〔設〕
访〔訪〕
诀〔訣〕

【乛】
*寻〔尋〕
*尽〔盡〕
〔儘〕
导〔導〕
*孙〔孫〕
阵〔陣〕
阳〔陽〕
阶〔階〕
*阴〔陰〕
妇〔婦〕
妈〔媽〕
戏〔戲〕
观〔觀〕
欢〔歡〕
*买〔買〕
纡〔紆〕
红〔紅〕
纣〔紂〕
驮〔馱〕
纤〔縴〕
〔纖〕㊴
纥〔紇〕
驯〔馴〕
纨〔紈〕
约〔約〕
级〔級〕
纩〔纊〕
纪〔紀〕
驰〔馳〕
纫〔紉〕

7笔

【一】
*寿〔壽〕
*麦〔麥〕
玛〔瑪〕
*进〔進〕
远〔遠〕
违〔違〕
韧〔韌〕
刬〔剗〕
运〔運〕
抚〔撫〕
坛〔壇〕
〔罎〕
抟〔摶〕
坏〔壞〕⑨
抠〔摳〕
坜〔壢〕
扰〔擾〕

坝〔壩〕 贡〔貢〕 㧑〔撝〕 折〔摺〕㊾ 抡〔掄〕 抢〔搶〕 坞〔塢〕 坟〔墳〕 护〔護〕 *壳〔殼〕⑮ 块〔塊〕 声〔聲〕 报〔報〕 拟〔擬〕 㧐〔擻〕 芜〔蕪〕 苇〔葦〕 芸〔蕓〕 苈〔藶〕 苋〔莧〕 苁〔蓯〕 苍〔蒼〕 *严〔嚴〕 芦〔蘆〕 劳〔勞〕 克〔剋〕 苏〔蘇〕 〔囌〕 极〔極〕 杨〔楊〕 *两〔兩〕 *丽〔麗〕⑰ 医〔醫〕 励〔勵〕 还〔還〕 矶〔磯〕 奁〔奩〕 歼〔殲〕 *来〔來〕 欤〔歟〕 轩〔軒〕

连〔連〕 轫〔軔〕

【丨】

*卤〔鹵〕 〔滷〕 邺〔鄴〕 坚〔堅〕 *时〔時〕 呒〔嘸〕 县〔縣〕 里〔裏〕 呓〔囈〕 呕〔嘔〕 园〔園〕 呖〔嚦〕 旷〔曠〕 围〔圍〕 吨〔噸〕 旸〔暘〕 邮〔郵〕 困〔睏〕 员〔員〕 呗〔唄〕 听〔聽〕 呛〔嗆〕 呜〔嗚〕 别〔彆〕 财〔財〕 囵〔圇〕 觃〔覎〕 帏〔幃〕 岖〔嶇〕 岗〔崗〕 岘〔峴〕 帐〔帳〕 岚〔嵐〕

【丿】

针〔針〕 钉〔釘〕 钊〔釗〕 钋〔釙〕 钌〔釕〕 乱〔亂〕 体〔體〕 佣〔傭〕 㑇〔㑳〕 彻〔徹〕 余〔餘〕㊼ *佥〔僉〕 谷〔穀〕 邻〔鄰〕 肠〔腸〕 *龟〔龜〕 *犹〔猶〕 狈〔狽〕 鸠〔鳩〕 *条〔條〕㉝ 岛〔島〕 邹〔鄒〕 饨〔飩〕 饩〔餼〕 饪〔飪〕 饫〔飫〕 饬〔飭〕 饭〔飯〕 饮〔飲〕 系〔係〕 〔繫〕⑪

【丶】

冻〔凍〕 状〔狀〕 亩〔畝〕 庑〔廡〕 库〔庫〕 疖〔癤〕 疗〔療〕 应〔應〕 这〔這〕 庐〔廬〕 闰〔閏〕 闱〔闈〕 闲〔閑〕 间〔間〕 闵〔閔〕 闷〔悶〕 灿〔燦〕 灶〔竈〕 炀〔煬〕 沣〔灃〕 沤〔漚〕 沥〔瀝〕 沦〔淪〕 沧〔滄〕 沨〔渢〕 沟〔溝〕 沩〔溈〕 沪〔滬〕 沈〔瀋〕 怃〔憮〕 怀〔懷〕 怄〔慪〕 忧〔憂〕 忾〔愾〕 怅〔悵〕 怆〔愴〕 *穷〔窮〕 证〔證〕 诂〔詁〕 诃〔訶〕 启〔啟〕 评〔評〕 补〔補〕 诅〔詛〕 识〔識〕 诇〔詗〕 诈〔詐〕 诉〔訴〕 诊〔診〕 诋〔詆〕 诌〔謅〕 词〔詞〕 诎〔詘〕 诏〔詔〕 译〔譯〕 诒〔詒〕

【𠃍】

*灵〔靈〕 层〔層〕 迟〔遲〕 张〔張〕 际〔際〕 陆〔陸〕 陇〔隴〕 陈〔陳〕 坠〔墜〕 陉〔陘〕 妪〔嫗〕 妩〔嫵〕 妫〔媯〕 刭〔剄〕 劲〔勁〕 鸡〔雞〕 纬〔緯〕 纭〔紜〕 驱〔驅〕 纯〔純〕 纰〔紕〕 纱〔紗〕 纲〔綱〕 纳〔納〕 纴〔紝〕 驳〔駁〕 纵〔縱〕 纶〔綸〕 纷〔紛〕 纸〔紙〕 纹〔紋〕 纺〔紡〕 驴〔驢〕 纼〔紖〕 纽〔紐〕 纾〔紓〕

8笔

【一】

玮〔瑋〕 环〔環〕 责〔責〕 现〔現〕 表〔錶〕 玱〔瑲〕 规〔規〕 匦〔匭〕 拢〔攏〕 拣〔揀〕 垆〔壚〕 担〔擔〕 顶〔頂〕 拥〔擁〕 势〔勢〕 拦〔攔〕 㧟〔擓〕 拧〔擰〕 拨〔撥〕 择〔擇〕 茏〔蘢〕 苹〔蘋〕 茑〔蔦〕 范〔範〕 茔〔塋〕 茕〔煢〕 茎〔莖〕 枢〔樞〕 枥〔櫪〕 柜〔櫃〕 㭎〔棡〕 枧〔梘〕 枨〔棖〕 板〔闆〕 枞〔樅〕 松〔鬆〕 枪〔槍〕 枫〔楓〕 构〔構〕 丧〔喪〕 *画〔畫〕 枣〔棗〕 *卖〔賣〕㉑ 郁〔鬱〕 矾〔礬〕 矿〔礦〕 砀〔碭〕 码〔碼〕 厕〔廁〕 奋〔奮〕 态〔態〕 瓯〔甌〕 欧〔歐〕 殴〔毆〕 垄〔壟〕 郏〔郟〕 轰〔轟〕 顷〔頃〕 转〔轉〕 轭〔軛〕 斩〔斬〕 轮〔輪〕 软〔軟〕 鸢〔鳶〕

【丨】

*齿〔齒〕 *虏〔虜〕 肾〔腎〕 贤〔賢〕 昙〔曇〕 *国〔國〕 畅〔暢〕 咙〔嚨〕 虮〔蟣〕 *黾〔黽〕㉓ 鸣〔鳴〕 咛〔嚀〕 咝〔噝〕 *罗〔羅〕 〔囉〕 岽〔崬〕 岿〔巋〕 帜〔幟〕 岭〔嶺〕⑲ 刿〔劌〕 剀〔剴〕 凯〔凱〕 峄〔嶧〕 败〔敗〕 账〔賬〕 贩〔販〕 贬〔貶〕 贮〔貯〕 图〔圖〕 购〔購〕

【丿】

钍〔釷〕 钎〔釺〕 钏〔釧〕 钐〔釤〕 钓〔釣〕 钒〔釩〕 钔〔鍆〕 钕〔釹〕 钖〔鍚〕 钗〔釵〕 制〔製〕 迭〔疊〕⑤ 刮〔颳〕 侠〔俠〕 侥〔僥〕 侦〔偵〕 侧〔側〕 凭〔憑〕 侨〔僑〕 侩〔儈〕 货〔貨〕 侪〔儕〕 侬〔儂〕 *质〔質〕 征〔徵〕㊿ 径〔徑〕 舍〔捨〕 刽〔劊〕 郐〔鄶〕 怂〔慫〕 籴〔糴〕 觅〔覓〕 贪〔貪〕 贫〔貧〕 戗〔戧〕 肤〔膚〕 䏝〔膞〕 肿〔腫〕 胀〔脹〕 肮〔骯〕 胁〔脅〕 迩〔邇〕 *鱼〔魚〕 狞〔獰〕 *备〔備〕 枭〔梟〕 饯〔餞〕 饰〔飾〕 饱〔飽〕 饲〔飼〕 饳〔飿〕 饴〔飴〕

【丶】

变〔變〕 庞〔龐〕 庙〔廟〕 疟〔瘧〕 疠〔癘〕 疡〔瘍〕 剂〔劑〕 废〔廢〕 闸〔閘〕 闹〔鬧〕⑭ *郑〔鄭〕 卷〔捲〕 *单〔單〕 炜〔煒〕

炝〔熗〕
炉〔爐〕
浅〔淺〕
泷〔瀧〕
泸〔瀘〕
泺〔濼〕
泞〔濘〕
泻〔瀉〕
泼〔潑〕
泽〔澤〕
泾〔涇〕
怜〔憐〕
㤘〔㥮〕
怿〔懌〕
峃〔嶨〕
学〔學〕
宝〔寶〕
宠〔寵〕
*审〔審〕
帘〔簾〕
实〔實〕
诓〔誆〕
诔〔誄〕
试〔試〕
诖〔詿〕
诗〔詩〕
诘〔詰〕
诙〔詼〕
诚〔誠〕
郓〔鄆〕
衬〔襯〕
祎〔禕〕
视〔視〕
诛〔誅〕
话〔話〕
诞〔誕〕
诟〔詬〕
诠〔詮〕
诡〔詭〕
询〔詢〕
诣〔詣〕

诤〔諍〕
该〔該〕
详〔詳〕
诧〔詫〕
诨〔諢〕
诩〔詡〕

【㇕】

*肃〔肅〕㉜
隶〔隸〕
*录〔錄〕
弥〔彌〕
〔瀰〕
陕〔陝〕
驽〔駑〕
驾〔駕〕
*参〔參〕
艰〔艱〕
线〔線〕
绀〔紺〕
绁〔紲〕
绂〔紱〕
练〔練〕
组〔組〕
驵〔駔〕
绅〔紳〕
䌷〔紬〕
细〔細〕
驶〔駛〕
驸〔駙〕
驷〔駟〕
驹〔駒〕
终〔終〕
织〔織〕
驺〔騶〕
绉〔縐〕
驻〔駐〕
绊〔絆〕
驼〔駝〕
绋〔紼〕
绌〔絀〕
绍〔紹〕

驿〔驛〕
绎〔繹〕
经〔經〕
骀〔駘〕
绐〔紿〕
贯〔貫〕

9笔

【一】

贰〔貳〕
帮〔幫〕
珑〔瓏〕
顸〔頇〕
韨〔韍〕
垭〔埡〕
挜〔掗〕
挝〔撾〕
项〔項〕
挞〔撻〕
挟〔挾〕
挠〔撓〕
赵〔趙〕
贲〔賁〕
挡〔擋〕
垲〔塏〕
挢〔撟〕
垫〔墊〕
挤〔擠〕
挥〔揮〕
挦〔撏〕
*荐〔薦〕
荚〔莢〕
贳〔貰〕
荛〔蕘〕
荜〔蓽〕
*带〔帶〕
茧〔繭〕
荞〔蕎〕
荟〔薈〕
荠〔薺〕
荡〔蕩〕
垩〔堊〕
荣〔榮〕
荤〔葷〕
荥〔滎〕
荦〔犖〕
荧〔熒〕
荨〔蕁〕
胡〔鬍〕
荩〔藎〕
荪〔蓀〕
荫〔蔭〕
荬〔蕒〕
荭〔葒〕
荮〔葤〕
药〔藥〕
标〔標〕
栈〔棧〕
栉〔櫛〕
栊〔櫳〕
栋〔棟〕
栌〔櫨〕
栎〔櫟〕
栏〔欄〕
柠〔檸〕
柽〔檉〕
树〔樹〕
䴓〔鳾〕
郦〔酈〕
咸〔鹹〕
砖〔磚〕
砗〔硨〕
砚〔硯〕
砜〔碸〕
面〔麵〕
牵〔牽〕
鸥〔鷗〕
䶮〔龑〕
残〔殘〕
殇〔殤〕
轱〔軲〕
轲〔軻〕
轳〔轤〕
轴〔軸〕
轶〔軼〕
轷〔軤〕
轸〔軫〕
轹〔轢〕
轺〔軺〕
轻〔輕〕
鸦〔鴉〕
虿〔蠆〕

【丨】

战〔戰〕
觇〔覘〕
点〔點〕
临〔臨〕⑱
览〔覽〕
竖〔豎〕
*尝〔嘗〕③
眍〔瞘〕
昽〔曨〕
哑〔啞〕
显〔顯〕
哒〔噠〕
哓〔嘵〕
哔〔嗶〕
贵〔貴〕
虾〔蝦〕
蚁〔蟻〕
蚂〔螞〕
虽〔雖〕
骂〔罵〕
哕〔噦〕
剐〔剮〕
郧〔鄖〕
勋〔勛〕
哗〔嘩〕
响〔響〕
哙〔噲〕
哝〔噥〕
哟〔喲〕
峡〔峽〕
峣〔嶢〕
帧〔幀〕
罚〔罰〕
峤〔嶠〕
贱〔賤〕
贴〔貼〕
贶〔貺〕
贻〔貽〕

【丿】

钘〔鈃〕
钙〔鈣〕
钚〔鈈〕
钛〔鈦〕
𫓧〔釾〕
钝〔鈍〕
钞〔鈔〕
钟〔鐘〕
〔鍾〕
钡〔鋇〕
钢〔鋼〕
钠〔鈉〕
钥〔鑰〕
钦〔欽〕
钧〔鈞〕
钤〔鈐〕
钨〔鎢〕
钩〔鈎〕
钪〔鈧〕
钫〔鈁〕
钬〔鈥〕
钭〔鈄〕
钮〔鈕〕
钯〔鈀〕
毡〔氈〕
氢〔氫〕
选〔選〕
适〔適〕㉚
种〔種〕
秋〔鞦〕
复〔復〕
〔複〕
〔覆〕⑦
笃〔篤〕
俦〔儔〕
俨〔儼〕
俩〔倆〕
俪〔儷〕
贷〔貸〕
顺〔順〕
俭〔儉〕
剑〔劍〕
鸧〔鶬〕
须〔須〕
〔鬚〕
胧〔朧〕
胨〔腖〕
胪〔臚〕
胆〔膽〕
胜〔勝〕
胫〔脛〕
鸨〔鴇〕
狭〔狹〕
狮〔獅〕
独〔獨〕
狯〔獪〕
狱〔獄〕
狲〔猻〕
贸〔貿〕
饵〔餌〕
饶〔饒〕
蚀〔蝕〕
饷〔餉〕
饸〔餄〕
饹〔餎〕
饺〔餃〕
饻〔餏〕
饼〔餅〕

【丶】

峦〔巒〕
弯〔彎〕
孪〔孿〕
娈〔孌〕
*将〔將〕⑫
奖〔獎〕⑫
疬〔癧〕
疮〔瘡〕
疯〔瘋〕
*亲〔親〕
飒〔颯〕
闺〔閨〕
闻〔聞〕
闼〔闥〕
闽〔閩〕
闾〔閭〕
闿〔闓〕
阀〔閥〕
阁〔閣〕
阐〔闡〕
阂〔閡〕
养〔養〕
姜〔薑〕
类〔類〕⑯
*娄〔婁〕
总〔總〕
炼〔煉〕
炽〔熾〕
烁〔爍〕
烂〔爛〕
烃〔烴〕
洼〔窪〕
洁〔潔〕
洒〔灑〕
㳠〔澾〕
浃〔浹〕
浇〔澆〕
浈〔湞〕
浉〔溮〕
浊〔濁〕
测〔測〕
浍〔澮〕
浏〔瀏〕
济〔濟〕
浐〔滻〕
浑〔渾〕
浒〔滸〕
浓〔濃〕
浔〔潯〕
浕〔濜〕
恸〔慟〕
恹〔懨〕
恺〔愷〕
恻〔惻〕
恼〔惱〕
恽〔惲〕
*举〔舉〕
觉〔覺〕
宪〔憲〕
窃〔竊〕
诫〔誡〕
诬〔誣〕
语〔語〕
袄〔襖〕
诮〔誚〕
祢〔禰〕
误〔誤〕
诰〔誥〕
诱〔誘〕
诲〔誨〕
诳〔誑〕
鸩〔鴆〕
说〔說〕
诵〔誦〕
诶〔誒〕

【㇕】

垦〔墾〕
昼〔晝〕
费〔費〕
逊〔遜〕
陨〔隕〕
险〔險〕
贺〔賀〕
怼〔懟〕
垒〔壘〕
娅〔婭〕

娆〔嬈〕
娇〔嬌〕
绑〔綁〕
绒〔絨〕
结〔結〕
绔〔絝〕
骁〔驍〕
绕〔繞〕
绖〔絰〕
骄〔驕〕
骅〔驊〕
绘〔繪〕
骆〔駱〕
骈〔駢〕
绞〔絞〕
骇〔駭〕
统〔統〕
绗〔絎〕
给〔給〕
绚〔絢〕
绛〔絳〕
络〔絡〕
绝〔絕〕

10笔

【一】

艳〔艷〕
顼〔頊〕
珲〔琿〕
蚕〔蠶〕①
顽〔頑〕
盏〔盞〕
捞〔撈〕
载〔載〕
赶〔趕〕
盐〔鹽〕
埘〔塒〕
损〔損〕
埙〔塤〕
埚〔堝〕
捡〔撿〕
贽〔贄〕
挚〔摯〕
热〔熱〕
捣〔搗〕
壶〔壺〕
*聂〔聶〕
莱〔萊〕
莲〔蓮〕
莳〔蒔〕
莴〔萵〕
获〔獲〕
〔穫〕
莸〔蕕〕
恶〔惡〕
〔噁〕
䓖〔藭〕
莹〔瑩〕
莺〔鶯〕
鸪〔鴣〕
莼〔蒓〕
桡〔橈〕
桢〔楨〕
档〔檔〕
桤〔榿〕
桥〔橋〕
桦〔樺〕
桧〔檜〕
桩〔樁〕
样〔樣〕
贾〔賈〕
逦〔邐〕
砺〔礪〕
砾〔礫〕
础〔礎〕
砻〔礱〕
顾〔顧〕
轼〔軾〕
轾〔輊〕
轿〔轎〕
辂〔輅〕
较〔較〕
鸫〔鶇〕
顿〔頓〕
趸〔躉〕
毙〔斃〕
致〔緻〕

【丨】

龀〔齔〕
鸬〔鸕〕
*虑〔慮〕
*监〔監〕
紧〔緊〕
*党〔黨〕
唛〔嘜〕
晒〔曬〕
晓〔曉〕
唝〔嗊〕
唠〔嘮〕
鸭〔鴨〕
唡〔啢〕
晔〔曄〕
晕〔暈〕
鸮〔鴞〕
唢〔嗩〕
㖞〔喎〕
蚬〔蜆〕
鸯〔鴦〕
崂〔嶗〕
崃〔崍〕
*罢〔罷〕
圆〔圓〕
觊〔覬〕
贼〔賊〕
贿〔賄〕
赂〔賂〕
赃〔贜〕
赅〔賅〕
赆〔贐〕

【丿】

钰〔鈺〕
钱〔錢〕
钲〔鉦〕
钳〔鉗〕
钴〔鈷〕
钵〔鉢〕
钶〔鈳〕
钷〔鉕〕
钹〔鈸〕
钺〔鉞〕
钻〔鑽〕
钼〔鉬〕
钽〔鉭〕
钾〔鉀〕
铀〔鈾〕
钿〔鈿〕
铁〔鐵〕
铂〔鉑〕
铃〔鈴〕
铄〔鑠〕
铅〔鉛〕
铆〔鉚〕
铈〔鈰〕
铉〔鉉〕
铊〔鉈〕
铋〔鉍〕
铌〔鈮〕
铍〔鈹〕
䥽〔鏺〕
铎〔鐸〕
氩〔氬〕
牺〔犧〕
敌〔敵〕
积〔積〕
称〔稱〕
笕〔筧〕
*笔〔筆〕
债〔債〕
借〔藉〕⑬
倾〔傾〕
赁〔賃〕
颀〔頎〕
徕〔徠〕
舰〔艦〕
舱〔艙〕
耸〔聳〕
*爱〔愛〕
鸰〔鴒〕
颁〔頒〕
颂〔頌〕
脍〔膾〕
脏〔臟〕
〔髒〕
脐〔臍〕
脑〔腦〕
胶〔膠〕
脓〔膿〕
鸱〔鴟〕
玺〔璽〕
鱽〔魛〕
鸲〔鴝〕
猃〔獫〕
鸵〔鴕〕
袅〔裊〕
鸳〔鴛〕
皱〔皺〕
饽〔餑〕
饿〔餓〕
馁〔餒〕

【丶】

栾〔欒〕
挛〔攣〕
恋〔戀〕
桨〔槳〕⑫
浆〔漿〕⑫
症〔癥〕
痈〔癰〕
斋〔齋〕
痉〔痙〕
准〔準〕
*离〔離〕
颃〔頏〕
资〔資〕
竞〔競〕
阃〔閫〕
阄〔鬮〕
阉〔閹〕⑭
阅〔閱〕
阆〔閬〕
郸〔鄲〕
烦〔煩〕
烧〔燒〕
烛〔燭〕
烨〔燁〕
烩〔燴〕
烬〔燼〕
递〔遞〕
涛〔濤〕
涝〔澇〕
涞〔淶〕
涟〔漣〕
涠〔潿〕
涢〔溳〕
涡〔渦〕
涂〔塗〕
涤〔滌〕
润〔潤〕
涧〔澗〕
涨〔漲〕
烫〔燙〕
涩〔澀〕
悭〔慳〕
悯〔憫〕
宽〔寬〕
家〔傢〕
*宾〔賓〕
窍〔竅〕
窎〔窵〕
请〔請〕
诸〔諸〕
诹〔諏〕
诺〔諾〕
诼〔諑〕
读〔讀〕
诽〔誹〕
袜〔襪〕㉟
祯〔禎〕
课〔課〕
诿〔諉〕
谀〔諛〕
谁〔誰〕
谂〔諗〕
调〔調〕
谄〔諂〕
谅〔諒〕
谆〔諄〕
谇〔誶〕
谈〔談〕
谊〔誼〕
谉〔讅〕

【乛】

恳〔懇〕
剧〔劇〕
娲〔媧〕
娴〔嫻〕
*难〔難〕
预〔預〕
绠〔綆〕
骊〔驪〕
绡〔綃〕
骋〔騁〕
绢〔絹〕
绣〔繡〕
验〔驗〕
绥〔綏〕
绦〔縧〕
继〔繼〕
绨〔綈〕
骎〔駸〕
骏〔駿〕
鸶〔鷥〕

11笔

【一】

焘〔燾〕
琎〔璡〕
琏〔璉〕
琐〔瑣〕
麸〔麩〕
掳〔擄〕
掴〔摑〕
鸷〔鷙〕
掷〔擲〕
掸〔撣〕
壶〔壼〕
悫〔慤〕
据〔據〕
掺〔摻〕
掼〔摜〕
职〔職〕
聍〔聹〕
萚〔蘀〕
勚〔勩〕
萝〔蘿〕
萤〔螢〕
营〔營〕
萦〔縈〕
萧〔蕭〕
萨〔薩〕
梦〔夢〕
觋〔覡〕
检〔檢〕
棂〔欞〕
*啬〔嗇〕
匮〔匱〕
酝〔醖〕
厣〔厴〕
硕〔碩〕
硖〔硤〕
硗〔磽〕
硙〔磑〕
硚〔礄〕
鸸〔鴯〕
聋〔聾〕
龚〔龔〕
袭〔襲〕
䴕〔鴷〕
殒〔殞〕
殓〔殮〕
赉〔賚〕
辄〔輒〕
辅〔輔〕
辆〔輛〕
堑〔塹〕

【丨】

颅〔顱〕
啧〔嘖〕
悬〔懸〕
啭〔囀〕
跃〔躍〕
啮〔嚙〕
跄〔蹌〕
蛎〔蠣〕
蛊〔蠱〕
蛏〔蟶〕
累〔纍〕
啸〔嘯〕
帻〔幘〕
崭〔嶄〕
逻〔邏〕
帼〔幗〕
赈〔賑〕
婴〔嬰〕
赊〔賒〕

【丿】

铏〔鉶〕
铸〔鑄〕
铑〔銠〕
铒〔鉺〕
铓〔鋩〕
铕〔銪〕
铗〔鋏〕
铙〔鐃〕
铛〔鐺〕
铝〔鋁〕
铜〔銅〕
铞〔銱〕
铟〔銦〕
铠〔鎧〕

铡〔鍘〕
铢〔銖〕
铣〔銑〕
铥〔銩〕
铤〔鋌〕
铧〔鏵〕
铨〔銓〕
铩〔鎩〕
铪〔鉿〕
铫〔銚〕
铭〔銘〕
铬〔鉻〕
铮〔錚〕
铯〔銫〕
铰〔鉸〕
铱〔銥〕
铲〔鏟〕
铳〔銃〕
铵〔銨〕
银〔銀〕
铷〔銣〕
矫〔矯〕
鸹〔鴰〕
秽〔穢〕
笺〔箋〕
笼〔籠〕
笾〔籩〕
偾〔僨〕
鸺〔鵂〕
偿〔償〕
偻〔僂〕
躯〔軀〕
皑〔皚〕
衅〔釁〕
鸻〔鴴〕
衔〔銜〕
舻〔艫〕
盘〔盤〕
鸼〔鵃〕
龛〔龕〕
鸽〔鴿〕
敛〔斂〕
领〔領〕
脶〔腡〕
脸〔臉〕
象〔像〕㊶
猎〔獵〕
猡〔玀〕
猕〔獼〕
馃〔餜〕
馄〔餛〕
馅〔餡〕
馆〔館〕

【丶】

鸾〔鸞〕
庼〔廎〕
痒〔癢〕
䴔〔鵁〕
旋〔鏇〕
阈〔閾〕
阉〔閹〕
阊〔閶〕
阅〔閲〕⑭
阌〔閿〕
阍〔閽〕
阎〔閻〕
阏〔閼〕
阐〔闡〕
羟〔羥〕
盖〔蓋〕
粝〔糲〕
*断〔斷〕
兽〔獸〕
焖〔燜〕
渍〔漬〕
鸿〔鴻〕
渎〔瀆〕
渐〔漸〕
渑〔澠〕
渊〔淵〕
渔〔漁〕
淀〔澱〕
渗〔滲〕
惬〔愜〕
惭〔慚〕
惧〔懼〕
惊〔驚〕
惮〔憚〕
惨〔慘〕
惯〔慣〕
祷〔禱〕
谌〔諶〕
谋〔謀〕
谍〔諜〕
谎〔謊〕
谏〔諫〕
皲〔皸〕
谐〔諧〕
谑〔謔〕
裆〔襠〕
祸〔禍〕
谒〔謁〕
谓〔謂〕
谔〔諤〕
谕〔諭〕
谖〔諼〕
谗〔讒〕
谘〔諮〕
谙〔諳〕
谚〔諺〕
谛〔諦〕
谜〔謎〕
谝〔諞〕
谞〔諝〕

【乛】

弹〔彈〕
堕〔墮〕
随〔隨〕
粜〔糶〕
*隐〔隱〕
婳〔嫿〕
婵〔嬋〕
婶〔嬸〕
颇〔頗〕
颈〔頸〕
绩〔績〕
绪〔緒〕
绫〔綾〕
骐〔騏〕
续〔續〕
绮〔綺〕
骑〔騎〕
绯〔緋〕
绰〔綽〕
骒〔騍〕
绲〔緄〕
绳〔繩〕
骓〔騅〕
维〔維〕
绵〔綿〕
绶〔綬〕
绷〔繃〕
绸〔綢〕
绺〔綹〕
绻〔綣〕
综〔綜〕
绽〔綻〕
绾〔綰〕
绿〔綠〕
骖〔驂〕
缀〔綴〕
缁〔緇〕

12 笔

【一】

靓〔靚〕
琼〔瓊〕
辇〔輦〕
鼋〔黿〕
趋〔趨〕
揽〔攬〕
颉〔頡〕
揿〔撳〕
搀〔攙〕
蛰〔蟄〕
絷〔縶〕
搁〔擱〕
搂〔摟〕
搅〔攪〕
联〔聯〕
蒇〔蕆〕
蒉〔蕢〕
蒋〔蔣〕
蒌〔蔞〕
韩〔韓〕
椟〔櫝〕
椤〔欏〕
赍〔賫〕
椭〔橢〕
鹁〔鵓〕
鹂〔鸝〕
觌〔覿〕
硷〔鹼〕
确〔確〕
詟〔讋〕
殚〔殫〕
颊〔頰〕
雳〔靂〕
辊〔輥〕
辋〔輞〕
椠〔槧〕
暂〔暫〕
辍〔輟〕
辎〔輜〕
翘〔翹〕

【丨】

辈〔輩〕
凿〔鑿〕
辉〔輝〕
赏〔賞〕㉙
睐〔睞〕
睑〔瞼〕
喷〔噴〕
畴〔疇〕
践〔踐〕
遗〔遺〕
蛱〔蛺〕
蛲〔蟯〕
蛳〔螄〕
蛴〔蠐〕
鹃〔鵑〕
喽〔嘍〕
嵘〔嶸〕
嵚〔嶔〕
嵝〔嶁〕
赋〔賦〕
𧹑〔䝼〕
赌〔賭〕
赎〔贖〕
赐〔賜〕
赒〔賙〕
赔〔賠〕
赕〔賧〕

【丿】

铸〔鑄〕
铹〔鐒〕
铺〔鋪〕
铼〔錸〕
铽〔鋱〕
链〔鏈〕
铿〔鏗〕
销〔銷〕
锁〔鎖〕
锃〔鋥〕
锄〔鋤〕
锂〔鋰〕
锅〔鍋〕
锆〔鋯〕
锇〔鋨〕
锈〔鏽〕
锉〔銼〕
锋〔鋒〕
锌〔鋅〕
锎〔鐦〕
锏〔鐧〕
锐〔鋭〕
锑〔銻〕
锒〔鋃〕
锓〔鋟〕
锔〔鋦〕
锕〔錒〕
犊〔犢〕
鹄〔鵠〕
鹅〔鵝〕
颋〔頲〕
筑〔築〕
筚〔篳〕
筛〔篩〕
牍〔牘〕
傥〔儻〕
傧〔儐〕
储〔儲〕
傩〔儺〕
惩〔懲〕
御〔禦〕
颌〔頜〕
释〔釋〕
鹆〔鵒〕
腊〔臘〕
腘〔膕〕
鱿〔魷〕
鲁〔魯〕
鲂〔魴〕
颍〔潁〕
飓〔颶〕
觞〔觴〕
惫〔憊〕
馇〔餷〕
馈〔饋〕
馉〔餶〕
馊〔餿〕
馋〔饞〕

【丶】

亵〔褻〕
装〔裝〕
蛮〔蠻〕
湾〔灣〕
谟〔謨〕
裢〔褳〕
裣〔襝〕
裤〔褲〕
裥〔襇〕
禅〔禪〕
谠〔讜〕
谡〔謖〕
谢〔謝〕
谣〔謠〕
谤〔謗〕
谥〔謚〕
谦〔謙〕
谧〔謐〕

【乛】

*属〔屬〕
屡〔屢〕
骘〔騭〕
巯〔巰〕
毵〔毿〕
翚〔翬〕
骛〔騖〕
缂〔緙〕
缃〔緗〕
缄〔緘〕
脔〔臠〕
痨〔癆〕
痫〔癇〕
赓〔賡〕
颏〔頦〕
鹇〔鷳〕
阑〔闌〕
阒〔闃〕
阔〔闊〕
阕〔闋〕
粪〔糞〕
鹈〔鵜〕
*窜〔竄〕
窝〔窩〕
喾〔嚳〕
愤〔憤〕
愦〔憒〕
滞〔滯〕
湿〔濕〕
溃〔潰〕
溅〔濺〕
缅〔緬〕
缆〔纜〕
缇〔緹〕
缈〔緲〕
缉〔緝〕
缊〔緼〕
缌〔緦〕
缎〔緞〕
缑〔緱〕
缓〔緩〕
缒〔縋〕
缔〔締〕
缕〔縷〕
骗〔騙〕
编〔編〕
缗〔緡〕
骚〔騷〕
缘〔緣〕
飨〔饗〕

13 笔

【一】

耢〔耮〕
鹉〔鵡〕
䴖〔鶄〕
韫〔韞〕
骜〔驁〕
摄〔攝〕
摅〔攄〕
摆〔擺〕
〔襬〕
赪〔赬〕
摈〔擯〕
毂〔轂〕
摊〔攤〕
鹊〔鵲〕

蓝〔藍〕
蓦〔驀〕
鹋〔鶓〕
蓟〔薊〕
蒙〔矇〕
〔濛〕
〔懞〕
颐〔頤〕
*献〔獻〕
蓣〔蕷〕
榄〔欖〕
榇〔櫬〕
榈〔櫚〕
楼〔樓〕
榉〔櫸〕
赖〔賴〕
碛〔磧〕
碍〔礙〕
碜〔磣〕
鹌〔鵪〕
尴〔尷〕
殨〔殨〕
雾〔霧〕
辏〔輳〕
辐〔輻〕
辑〔輯〕
输〔輸〕
【丨】
频〔頻〕
龃〔齟〕
龄〔齡〕
龅〔齙〕
龆〔齠〕
鉴〔鑒〕
韪〔韙〕
嗫〔囁〕
跷〔蹺〕
跸〔蹕〕
跻〔躋〕
跹〔躚〕
蜗〔蝸〕
嗳〔噯〕
赗〔賵〕
【丿】
锗〔鍺〕
错〔錯〕
锘〔鍩〕
锚〔錨〕
锛〔錛〕
锝〔鍀〕
锞〔錁〕
锟〔錕〕
锡〔錫〕
锢〔錮〕
锣〔鑼〕
锤〔錘〕
锥〔錐〕
锦〔錦〕
锧〔鑕〕
锨〔鍁〕
锫〔錇〕
锭〔錠〕
键〔鍵〕
锯〔鋸〕
锰〔錳〕
锱〔錙〕
辞〔辭〕
颓〔頹〕
穇〔穇〕
筹〔籌〕
签〔簽〕
〔籤〕
简〔簡〕
觎〔覦〕
颔〔頷〕
腻〔膩〕
鹏〔鵬〕
腾〔騰〕
鲅〔鮁〕
鲆〔鮃〕
鲇〔鮎〕
鲈〔鱸〕
鲊〔鮓〕
稣〔穌〕
鲋〔鮒〕
鲫〔鯽〕
鲍〔鮑〕
鲏〔鮍〕
鲐〔鮐〕
颖〔穎〕
鸽〔鴿〕
飔〔颸〕
飕〔颼〕
触〔觸〕
雏〔雛〕
馎〔餺〕
馍〔饃〕
馏〔餾〕
馐〔饈〕
【、】
酱〔醬〕⑫
鹑〔鶉〕
瘅〔癉〕
瘆〔瘮〕
鹒〔鶊〕
阖〔闔〕
阗〔闐〕
阙〔闕〕
誊〔謄〕
粮〔糧〕
数〔數〕
滟〔灧〕
滠〔灄〕
满〔滿〕
滤〔濾〕
滥〔濫〕
滗〔潷〕
滦〔灤〕
漓〔灕〕
滨〔濱〕
滩〔灘〕
滪〔澦〕
慑〔懾〕
誉〔譽〕
鲎〔鱟〕
骞〔騫〕
寝〔寢〕
窥〔窺〕
窦〔竇〕
谨〔謹〕
谩〔謾〕
谪〔謫〕
谫〔譾〕
谬〔謬〕
【乛】
辟〔闢〕
嫒〔嬡〕
嫔〔嬪〕
缙〔縉〕
缜〔縝〕
缚〔縛〕
缛〔縟〕
辔〔轡〕
缝〔縫〕
骝〔騮〕
缞〔縗〕
缟〔縞〕
缠〔纏〕②
缡〔縭〕
缢〔縊〕
缣〔縑〕
缤〔繽〕
骗〔騙〕

14 笔

【一】
瑷〔璦〕
赘〔贅〕
觏〔覯〕
韬〔韜〕
叆〔靉〕
墙〔牆〕
撄〔攖〕
蔷〔薔〕
蔑〔衊〕
蔹〔蘞〕
蔺〔藺〕
蔼〔藹〕
鹕〔鶘〕
槚〔檟〕
槛〔檻〕
槟〔檳〕
槠〔櫧〕
酽〔釅〕
丽〔麗〕
酿〔釀〕
霁〔霽〕
愿〔願〕
殡〔殯〕
辕〔轅〕
辖〔轄〕
辗〔輾〕
【丨】
龇〔齜〕
龈〔齦〕
䴗〔鶪〕
颗〔顆〕
瞜〔瞜〕
暧〔曖〕
鹖〔鶡〕
踌〔躊〕
踊〔踴〕
蜡〔蠟〕
蝈〔蟈〕
蝇〔蠅〕
蝉〔蟬〕
鹗〔鶚〕
嘤〔嚶〕
罴〔羆〕
赙〔賻〕
罂〔罌〕
赚〔賺〕
鹘〔鶻〕
【丿】
锲〔鍥〕
锴〔鍇〕
锶〔鍶〕
锷〔鍔〕
锹〔鍬〕
锸〔鍤〕
锻〔鍛〕
锼〔鎪〕
锾〔鍰〕
锵〔鏘〕
锿〔鎄〕
镀〔鍍〕
镁〔鎂〕
镂〔鏤〕
镃〔鎡〕
镄〔鐨〕
镅〔鎇〕
鹙〔鶖〕
稳〔穩〕
箦〔簀〕
箧〔篋〕
箨〔籜〕
箩〔籮〕
箪〔簞〕
箓〔籙〕
箫〔簫〕
舆〔輿〕
膑〔臏〕
鲑〔鮭〕
鲒〔鮚〕
鲔〔鮪〕
鲖〔鮦〕
鲗〔鰂〕
鲙〔鱠〕
鲚〔鱭〕
鲛〔鮫〕
鲜〔鮮〕
鲟〔鱘〕
飗〔飀〕
馑〔饉〕
馒〔饅〕
【、】
銮〔鑾〕
瘗〔瘞〕
瘘〔瘻〕
阚〔闞〕
羞〔羞〕
鲞〔鯗〕
糁〔糝〕
鹚〔鷀〕
潇〔瀟〕
潋〔瀲〕
潍〔濰〕
赛〔賽〕
窭〔窶〕
谭〔譚〕
谮〔譖〕
禯〔禯〕
褛〔褸〕
谯〔譙〕
谰〔讕〕
谱〔譜〕
谲〔譎〕
【乛】
鹛〔鶥〕
嫱〔嬙〕
鹜〔鶩〕
缥〔縹〕
骠〔驃〕
缦〔縵〕
骡〔騾〕
缧〔縲〕
缨〔纓〕
骢〔驄〕
缩〔縮〕
缪〔繆〕
缫〔繅〕

15 笔

【一】
耧〔耬〕
璎〔瓔〕
叇〔靆〕
撵〔攆〕
撷〔擷〕
撺〔攛〕
聩〔聵〕
聪〔聰〕
觐〔覲〕
鞑〔韃〕
鞒〔鞽〕
蕲〔蘄〕
赜〔賾〕
蕴〔藴〕
樯〔檣〕
樱〔櫻〕
飘〔飄〕
靥〔靨〕
魇〔魘〕
餍〔饜〕
霉〔黴〕
辘〔轆〕
【丨】
龉〔齬〕
龊〔齪〕
觑〔覷〕
瞒〔瞞〕
题〔題〕
颙〔顒〕
踬〔躓〕
踯〔躑〕
蝾〔蠑〕
蝼〔螻〕
噜〔嚕〕
嘱〔囑〕
颛〔顓〕
【丿】
镊〔鑷〕
镇〔鎮〕
镉〔鎘〕
镋〔钂〕
镌〔鎸〕
镍〔鎳〕
镎〔鎿〕
镏〔鎦〕
镐〔鎬〕
镑〔鎊〕
镒〔鎰〕
镓〔鎵〕
镔〔鑌〕
镉〔鎘〕
篑〔簣〕
篓〔簍〕
䴘〔鷉〕
鹡〔鶺〕
鹞〔鷂〕
鲠〔鯁〕
鲡〔鱺〕
鲢〔鰱〕
鲣〔鰹〕
鲥〔鰣〕
鲤〔鯉〕
鲦〔鰷〕
鲧〔鯀〕
鲩〔鯇〕
鲫〔鯽〕
馓〔饊〕
馔〔饌〕
【、】
瘪〔癟〕
瘫〔癱〕
齑〔齏〕
颜〔顔〕
鹣〔鶼〕
鲨〔鯊〕
澜〔瀾〕
额〔額〕
谳〔讞〕
褴〔襤〕
谴〔譴〕
鹤〔鶴〕
谵〔譫〕
【乛】
屦〔屨〕
缬〔纈〕

缭〔繚〕
缮〔繕〕
缯〔繒〕

16 笔

【一】

𦓈〔䎱〕
擞〔擻〕
颞〔顳〕
颟〔顢〕
薮〔藪〕
颠〔顛〕
橹〔櫓〕
橼〔櫞〕
鹥〔鷖〕
赝〔贗〕
飙〔飆〕
豮〔豶〕
錾〔鏨〕
辙〔轍〕
辚〔轔〕

【丨】

鹾〔鹺〕
螨〔蟎〕
鹦〔鸚〕
赠〔贈〕

【丿】

锗〔鍺〕
镙〔鏍〕
镗〔鏜〕
镘〔鏝〕
镚〔鏰〕
镛〔鏞〕
镜〔鏡〕
镝〔鏑〕
镞〔鏃〕
氇〔氌〕
赞〔贊〕
穑〔穡〕
篮〔籃〕
篱〔籬〕
魉〔魎〕
鲭〔鯖〕
鲮〔鯪〕
鲰〔鯫〕
鲱〔鯡〕
鲲〔鯤〕
鲳〔鯧〕
鲵〔鯢〕
鲶〔鯰〕
鲷〔鯛〕
鲸〔鯨〕
鲻〔鯔〕
獭〔獺〕

【丶】

鹧〔鷓〕
瘿〔癭〕
瘾〔癮〕
斓〔斕〕
辩〔辯〕
濑〔瀨〕
濒〔瀕〕
懒〔懶〕
黉〔黌〕

【乛】

鹨〔鷚〕
颡〔顙〕
缰〔繮〕
缱〔繾〕
缲〔繰〕
缳〔繯〕
缴〔繳〕

17 笔

【一】

藓〔蘚〕
鹩〔鷯〕

【丨】

龋〔齲〕
龌〔齷〕
瞩〔矚〕
蹒〔蹣〕
蹑〔躡〕
蟏〔蠨〕
㘚〔囒〕
羁〔羈〕
赡〔贍〕

【丿】

镢〔鐝〕
镣〔鐐〕
镤〔鏷〕
镥〔鑥〕
镦〔鐓〕
镧〔鑭〕
𬭉〔鐥〕
镨〔鐠〕
镡〔鐔〕
镪〔鏹〕
镫〔鐙〕
龂〔齗〕
鹪〔鷦〕
䲠〔鰆〕
鲽〔鰈〕
鲙〔鱠〕
鳃〔鰓〕
鳁〔鰮〕
鳄〔鱷〕
鳅〔鰍〕
鳆〔鰒〕
鳇〔鰉〕
鳉〔鱂〕
鳊〔鯿〕

【丶】

鹫〔鷲〕
辫〔辮〕
赢〔贏〕
懑〔懣〕

【乛】

鹬〔鷸〕
骤〔驟〕

18 笔

【一】

鳌〔鰲〕
鞯〔韉〕
黡〔黶〕

【丨】

歔〔歔〕
颢〔顥〕
鹭〔鷺〕
嚣〔囂〕
髅〔髏〕

【丿】

镬〔鑊〕
镭〔鐳〕
镮〔鐶〕
镯〔鐲〕
镰〔鐮〕
镱〔鐿〕
雠〔讎〕
䲢〔䲢〕
鳍〔鰭〕
鳎〔鰨〕
鳏〔鰥〕
鳑〔鰟〕
鳒〔鰜〕

【丶】

鹯〔鸇〕
鹰〔鷹〕
癞〔癩〕
辗〔輾〕
谳〔讞〕

【乛】

䴘〔鷉〕

19 笔

【一】

攒〔攢〕
霭〔靄〕

【丨】

鳖〔鱉〕
蹿〔躥〕
巅〔巔〕
髋〔髖〕
髌〔髕〕

【丿】

镲〔鑔〕
籁〔籟〕
鳘〔鰵〕
鳓〔鰳〕
鳔〔鰾〕
鳕〔鱈〕
鳗〔鰻〕
鳙〔鱅〕
鳛〔鰼〕

【丶】

颤〔顫〕
癣〔癬〕
谶〔讖〕

【乛】

骥〔驥〕
缵〔纘〕

20 笔

【一】

瓒〔瓚〕
鬓〔鬢〕
颥〔顬〕

【丨】

鼍〔鼉〕
黩〔黷〕

【丿】

镳〔鑣〕
镴〔鑞〕
臜〔臢〕
鳜〔鱖〕
鳝〔鱔〕
鳞〔鱗〕
鳟〔鱒〕

【乛】

骧〔驤〕

21 笔

颦〔顰〕
躏〔躪〕
鳢〔鱧〕
鳣〔鱣〕
癫〔癲〕
赣〔贛〕
灏〔灝〕

22 笔

鹳〔鸛〕
镶〔鑲〕

23 笔

趱〔趲〕
颧〔顴〕
躜〔躦〕

25 笔

䦆〔钁〕
馕〔饢〕
戆〔戇〕

B. 从繁体查简体

7笔
*〔車〕车
*〔夾〕夹
*〔貝〕贝
*〔見〕见
〔壯〕壮
〔妝〕妆

8笔
【一】
*〔長〕长④
*〔亞〕亚
〔軋〕轧
*〔東〕东
*〔兩〕两
〔協〕协
*〔來〕来
*〔戔〕戋
【丨】
*〔門〕门
*〔岡〕冈
【丿】
*〔侖〕仑
〔兒〕儿
【乛】
〔狀〕状
〔糾〕纠

9笔
【一】
〔剋〕克
〔軌〕轨
〔厙〕厍
*〔頁〕页
〔郟〕郏
〔剄〕刭
〔勁〕劲
【丨】
〔貞〕贞
〔則〕则
〔閂〕闩
〔迴〕回
【丿】
〔俠〕侠
〔係〕系
〔鳧〕凫
〔帥〕帅
〔後〕后
〔釓〕钆
〔釔〕钇
〔負〕负
*〔風〕风
【丶】
〔訂〕订
〔計〕计
〔訃〕讣
*〔為〕为
〔軍〕军
〔祗〕只
【乛】
〔陣〕阵
*〔韋〕韦
〔陝〕陕
〔陘〕陉
〔飛〕飞
〔紆〕纡
〔紅〕红
〔紂〕纣
〔紈〕纨
〔級〕级
〔約〕约
〔紇〕纥
〔紀〕纪
〔紉〕纫

10笔
【一】
*〔馬〕马⑳
〔挾〕挟
〔貢〕贡
*〔華〕华
〔莢〕荚
〔莖〕茎
〔莧〕苋
〔莊〕庄(51)
〔軒〕轩
〔連〕连
〔軔〕轫
〔劃〕划
【丨】
〔鬥〕斗
*〔時〕时
*〔畢〕毕
〔財〕财
〔覎〕觃
〔閃〕闪
〔唄〕呗
〔員〕员
*〔豈〕岂
〔峽〕峡
〔峴〕岘
〔剛〕刚
〔剮〕剐
【丿】
*〔氣〕气
〔郵〕邮
〔倀〕伥
〔倆〕俩
*〔條〕条㉝
〔們〕们
〔個〕个
〔倫〕伦
〔隻〕只
〔島〕岛
*〔烏〕乌㊱
*〔師〕师
〔徑〕径
〔釘〕钉
〔針〕针
〔釗〕钊
〔釙〕钋
〔釕〕钌
*〔殺〕杀
*〔倉〕仓
〔脅〕胁
〔狹〕狭
〔狽〕狈
*〔芻〕刍
【丶】
〔訐〕讦
〔訌〕讧
〔討〕讨
〔訕〕讪
〔訖〕讫
〔訓〕训
〔這〕这
〔訊〕讯
〔記〕记
〔凍〕冻
〔畝〕亩
〔庫〕库
〔浹〕浃
〔涇〕泾
【乛】
〔書〕书
〔陸〕陆
〔陳〕陈
*〔孫〕孙
*〔陰〕阴
〔務〕务
〔紜〕纭
〔純〕纯
〔紕〕纰
〔紗〕纱
〔納〕纳
〔紝〕纴
〔紛〕纷
〔紙〕纸
〔紋〕纹
〔紡〕纺
〔紖〕纼
〔紐〕纽
〔紓〕纾

11笔
【一】
〔責〕责
〔現〕现
〔匭〕匦
〔規〕规
*〔殼〕壳⑮
〔埡〕垭
〔掗〕挜
〔捨〕舍
〔捫〕扪
〔掆〕㧏
〔頂〕顶
〔掄〕抡
*〔執〕执
〔捲〕卷
〔掃〕扫
〔堊〕垩
〔萊〕莱
〔萵〕莴
〔乾〕干⑧
〔梘〕枧
〔軛〕轭
〔斬〕斩
〔軟〕软
*〔專〕专
*〔區〕区㉖
〔堅〕坚
*〔帶〕带
〔廁〕厕
〔硃〕朱
*〔麥〕麦
〔頃〕顷
【丨】
*〔鹵〕卤
〔處〕处
〔敗〕败
〔販〕贩
〔貶〕贬
〔啞〕哑
〔閉〕闭
〔問〕问
*〔婁〕娄
〔啢〕唡
*〔國〕国
〔帳〕帐
〔崬〕岽
〔崍〕崃
〔眾〕众
〔崗〕岗
〔圇〕囵
【丿】
〔氫〕氢
*〔動〕动
〔偵〕侦
〔側〕侧
〔貨〕货
*〔進〕进
〔偽〕伪
〔梟〕枭
*〔鳥〕鸟㉔
〔偉〕伟
〔徠〕徕
〔術〕术㉛
*〔從〕从
〔釷〕钍
〔釺〕钎
〔釧〕钏
〔釤〕钐
〔釣〕钓
〔釩〕钒
〔釹〕钕
〔釵〕钗
〔貪〕贪
〔覓〕觅
〔飥〕饦
〔貧〕贫
〔脛〕胫
*〔魚〕鱼
【丶】
〔詎〕讵
〔訝〕讶
〔訥〕讷
〔許〕许
〔訛〕讹
〔訢〕䜣
〔訩〕讻
〔訟〕讼
〔設〕设
〔訪〕访
〔訣〕诀
*〔產〕产
〔牽〕牵
〔烴〕烃
〔淶〕涞
〔淺〕浅
〔淪〕沦
〔悵〕怅
〔鄆〕郓
〔啟〕启
〔視〕视
【乛】
*〔將〕将⑫
〔晝〕昼
〔張〕张
〔階〕阶
〔陽〕阳
*〔隊〕队
〔婭〕娅
〔婦〕妇
〔習〕习
*〔參〕参
〔紺〕绀
〔紲〕绁
〔紱〕绂
〔組〕组
〔紳〕绅
〔紬〕䌷
〔細〕细
〔終〕终
〔絆〕绊
〔紼〕绋
〔絀〕绌
〔紹〕绍
〔紿〕绐
〔貫〕贯
*〔鄉〕乡

12笔
【一】
〔貳〕贰
〔預〕预
*〔堯〕尧㊹
〔揀〕拣
〔馭〕驭
〔項〕项
〔賁〕贲
〔場〕场
〔揚〕扬
〔塢〕坞
〔塊〕块
*〔達〕达
〔報〕报
〔揮〕挥
〔壺〕壶
〔惡〕恶
〔葉〕叶㊺
〔貰〕贳
〔萵〕莴
*〔萬〕万
〔葷〕荤
〔喪〕丧
〔葦〕苇
〔葒〕荭
〔葤〕荮
〔棖〕枨
〔棟〕栋
〔棧〕栈
〔棡〕㭎

〔極〕极
〔軲〕轱
〔軻〕轲
〔軸〕轴
〔軼〕轶
〔軤〕轷
〔軫〕轸
〔軺〕轺
*〔畫〕画
〔腎〕肾
〔棗〕枣
〔硨〕砗
〔硤〕硖
〔硯〕砚
〔殘〕残
*〔雲〕云
【丨】
〔覘〕觇
〔睏〕困
〔貼〕贴
〔貺〕贶
〔貯〕贮
〔貽〕贻
〔閏〕闰
〔開〕开
〔閑〕闲
〔間〕间
〔閔〕闵
〔悶〕闷
〔貴〕贵
*〔過〕过
〔鄖〕郧
〔勛〕勋
〔喎〕㖞
*〔單〕单
〔喲〕哟
*〔買〕买
〔剴〕剀
〔凱〕凯
〔幀〕帧
〔嵐〕岚

〔幃〕帏
〔圍〕围
【丿】
*〔無〕无㊲
〔氫〕氢
*〔喬〕乔
*〔筆〕笔
*〔備〕备
〔貸〕贷
〔順〕顺
〔傖〕伧
〔㑳〕㑇
〔傢〕家
〔鄔〕邬
〔復〕复
〔須〕须
〔鈃〕钘
〔鈣〕钙
〔鈃〕钘
〔鈈〕钚
〔鈦〕钛
〔釾〕釾
〔鈍〕钝
〔鈔〕钞
〔鈉〕钠
〔鈴〕铃
〔欽〕钦
〔鈞〕钧
〔鈎〕钩
〔鈧〕钪
〔鈁〕钫
〔鈥〕钬
〔鈄〕钭
〔鈕〕钮
〔鈀〕钯
〔傘〕伞
〔爺〕爷
〔創〕创
〔飩〕饨
〔飪〕饪
〔飫〕饫

〔飭〕饬
〔飯〕饭
〔飲〕饮
〔脹〕胀
〔腖〕胨
〔勝〕胜
*〔猶〕犹
〔貿〕贸
〔鄒〕邹
【丶】
〔詁〕诂
〔訶〕诃
〔評〕评
〔詛〕诅
〔詗〕诇
〔詐〕诈
〔訴〕诉
〔診〕诊
〔詆〕诋
〔詞〕词
〔詘〕诎
〔詔〕诏
〔詒〕诒
〔馮〕冯
〔廁〕厕
〔痙〕痉
〔勞〕劳
〔湞〕浈
〔測〕测
〔湯〕汤
〔渦〕涡
〔淵〕渊
〔渢〕沨
〔渾〕浑
〔溈〕沩
〔愜〕惬
〔惻〕恻
〔惲〕恽
〔惱〕恼
〔運〕运
〔補〕补

【乛】
*〔尋〕寻
〔費〕费
〔違〕违
〔韌〕韧
〔隕〕陨
〔賀〕贺
*〔發〕发
〔綁〕绑
〔絨〕绒
〔結〕结
〔絝〕绔
〔絰〕绖
〔絎〕绗
〔給〕给
〔絢〕绚
〔絳〕绛
〔絡〕络
〔絞〕绞
〔統〕统
〔絕〕绝
〔絲〕丝
*〔幾〕几

13笔

【一】
〔頊〕顼
〔琿〕珲
〔瑋〕玮
〔頑〕顽
〔載〕载
〔馱〕驮
〔馴〕驯
〔馳〕驰
〔塒〕埘
〔塤〕埙
〔損〕损
〔遠〕远
〔塏〕垲
〔勢〕势
〔搶〕抢

〔搗〕捣
〔塢〕坞
〔壺〕壶
*〔聖〕圣
〔蓋〕盖
〔蓮〕莲
〔蒔〕莳
〔蓽〕荜
〔夢〕梦
〔蒼〕苍
〔幹〕干
〔蓀〕荪
〔蔭〕荫
〔蒓〕莼
〔楨〕桢
〔楊〕杨
*〔嗇〕啬
〔楓〕枫
〔軾〕轼
〔輊〕轾
〔輅〕辂
〔較〕较
〔賈〕贾
*〔匯〕汇
〔電〕电
〔頓〕顿
〔盞〕盏
【丨】
*〔歲〕岁
*〔虜〕虏
*〔業〕业
*〔當〕当
〔睞〕睐
〔賊〕贼
〔賄〕贿
〔賂〕赂
〔賅〕赅
〔嗎〕吗
〔嘩〕哗
〔嗊〕唝
〔暘〕旸

〔閘〕闸
*〔黽〕黾㉓
〔暈〕晕
〔號〕号
〔園〕园
〔蛺〕蛱
〔蜆〕蚬
*〔農〕农
〔嗩〕唢
〔嗶〕哔
〔鳴〕鸣
〔嗆〕呛
〔圓〕圆
〔骯〕肮
【丿】
〔筧〕笕
*〔節〕节
*〔與〕与
〔債〕债
〔僅〕仅
〔傳〕传
〔傴〕伛
〔傾〕倾
〔僂〕偻
〔賃〕赁
〔傷〕伤
〔傭〕佣
〔裊〕袅
〔頎〕颀
〔鈺〕钰
〔鉦〕钲
〔鉗〕钳
〔鈷〕钴
〔鉢〕钵
〔鉅〕钜
〔鈳〕钶
〔鈸〕钹
〔鉞〕钺
〔鉬〕钼
〔鉭〕钽
〔鉀〕钾

〔鈾〕铀
〔鈿〕钿
〔鉑〕铂
〔鈴〕铃
〔鉛〕铅
〔鉚〕铆
〔鈰〕铈
〔鉉〕铉
〔鉈〕铊
〔鉍〕铋
〔鈮〕铌
〔鈹〕铍
*〔僉〕佥
*〔會〕会
〔亂〕乱
*〔愛〕爱
〔飾〕饰
〔飽〕饱
〔飼〕饲
〔飿〕饳
〔飴〕饴
〔頒〕颁
〔頌〕颂
〔腸〕肠
〔腡〕脶
〔腫〕肿
〔腦〕脑
〔魛〕鱽
〔像〕象㊶
〔獁〕犸
〔鳩〕鸠
〔獅〕狮
〔猻〕狲
【丶】
〔誆〕诓
〔誄〕诔
〔試〕试
〔詿〕诖
〔詩〕诗
〔詰〕诘
〔誇〕夸

〔詼〕诙
〔誠〕诚
〔誅〕诛
〔話〕话
〔誕〕诞
〔詬〕诟
〔詮〕诠
〔詭〕诡
〔詢〕询
〔詣〕诣
〔諍〕诤
〔該〕该
〔詳〕详
〔詫〕诧
〔詡〕诩
〔裏〕里
〔準〕准
〔頏〕颃
〔資〕资
〔羥〕羟
*〔義〕义㊻
〔煉〕炼
〔煩〕烦
〔煬〕炀
〔塋〕茔
〔煢〕茕
〔煒〕炜
〔遞〕递
〔溝〕沟
〔漣〕涟
〔滅〕灭
〔溳〕涢
〔滌〕涤
〔溮〕浉
〔塗〕涂
〔滄〕沧
〔愷〕恺
〔愾〕忾
〔愴〕怆
〔㥮〕㤘
〔禎〕祯

〔禍〕祸
〔禕〕祎
【乛】
*〔肅〕肃㉜
〔裝〕装
〔遜〕逊
〔際〕际
〔媽〕妈
〔預〕预
〔綆〕绠
〔經〕经
〔綃〕绡
〔絹〕绢
〔綉〕绣
〔綈〕绨
〔彙〕汇

14笔

【一】
〔瑪〕玛
〔璉〕琏
〔瑣〕琐
〔瑲〕玱
〔駁〕驳
〔摶〕抟
〔摳〕抠
〔趙〕赵
〔趕〕赶
〔摟〕搂
〔摑〕掴
〔臺〕台
〔墊〕垫
*〔壽〕寿
〔摺〕折㊾
〔摻〕掺
〔摜〕掼
〔勩〕勚
〔蔞〕蒌
〔蔦〕茑
〔蓯〕苁
〔蔔〕卜

〔蔣〕蒋
〔薌〕芗
〔構〕构
〔樺〕桦
〔榿〕桤
〔覡〕觋
〔槍〕枪
〔輒〕辄
〔輔〕辅
〔輕〕轻
〔塹〕堑
〔匱〕匮
*〔監〕监
〔緊〕紧
〔厲〕厉
*〔厭〕厌
〔碩〕硕
〔碭〕砀
〔碸〕砜
〔奩〕奁
*〔爾〕尔
〔奪〕夺
〔殞〕殒
〔鳶〕鸢
〔巰〕巯

【丨】

*〔對〕对
〔幣〕币
〔彆〕别
*〔嘗〕尝③
〔嘖〕啧
〔曄〕晔
〔夥〕伙⑩
〔賑〕赈
〔賒〕赊
〔嘆〕叹
〔暢〕畅
〔嘜〕唛
〔閨〕闺
〔聞〕闻
〔閩〕闽
〔閭〕闾
〔閥〕阀
〔閤〕合
〔閣〕阁
〔閘〕闸
〔閡〕阂
〔嘔〕呕
〔團〕团
〔嘍〕喽
〔鄲〕郸
〔鳴〕鸣
〔幘〕帻
〔嶄〕崭
〔嶇〕岖
〔罰〕罚
〔嶁〕嵝
〔幗〕帼
〔圖〕图

【丿】

〔製〕制
〔種〕种
〔稱〕称
〔箋〕笺
〔僥〕侥
〔僨〕偾
〔僕〕仆㉗
〔僑〕侨
〔銜〕衔
〔鉶〕铏
〔銬〕铐
〔銠〕铑
〔鉺〕铒
〔鋩〕铓
〔銪〕铕
〔銅〕铜
〔銱〕铞
〔銦〕铟
〔銖〕铢
〔銑〕铣
〔銩〕铥
〔鋌〕铤
〔銓〕铨
〔鉿〕铪
〔銚〕铫
〔銘〕铭
〔鉻〕铬
〔銫〕铯
〔鉸〕铰
〔銥〕铱
〔銃〕铳
〔銨〕铵
〔銀〕银
〔銣〕铷
〔戧〕戗
〔餌〕饵
〔蝕〕蚀
〔餉〕饷
〔餄〕饸
〔餎〕饹
〔餃〕饺
〔餏〕饻
〔餅〕饼
〔領〕领
〔鳳〕凤
〔颱〕台
〔獄〕狱

【丶】

〔誡〕诫
〔誣〕诬
〔語〕语
〔誚〕诮
〔誤〕误
〔誥〕诰
〔誘〕诱
〔誨〕诲
〔誑〕诳
〔說〕说
〔認〕认
〔誦〕诵
〔誒〕诶
*〔廣〕广
〔麼〕么㉒
〔廎〕庼
〔瘧〕疟
〔瘍〕疡
〔瘋〕疯
〔塵〕尘
〔颯〕飒
〔適〕适㉚
*〔齊〕齐
〔養〕养
〔鄰〕邻
*〔鄭〕郑
〔燁〕烨
〔熗〕炝
〔榮〕荣
〔滎〕荥
〔犖〕荦
〔熒〕荧
〔漬〕渍
〔漢〕汉
〔滿〕满
〔漸〕渐
〔漚〕沤
〔滯〕滞
〔滷〕卤
〔漊〕溇
〔漁〕渔
〔滸〕浒
〔滻〕浐
〔滬〕沪
〔漲〕涨
〔滲〕渗
〔慚〕惭
〔慪〕怄
〔慳〕悭
〔慟〕恸
〔慘〕惨
〔慣〕惯
〔寬〕宽
*〔賓〕宾
〔窩〕窝
〔窪〕洼
*〔寧〕宁㉕
〔寢〕寝
〔實〕实
〔皸〕皲
〔複〕复

【乛】

〔劃〕划
*〔盡〕尽
〔屢〕屡
〔獎〕奖⑫
〔墮〕堕
〔隨〕随
〔韍〕韨
〔墜〕坠
〔嫗〕妪
〔頗〕颇
〔態〕态
〔鄧〕邓
〔緒〕绪
〔綾〕绫
〔綺〕绮
〔緋〕绯
〔綽〕绰
〔緄〕绲
〔綱〕纲
〔網〕网
〔維〕维
〔綿〕绵
〔綸〕纶
〔綬〕绶
〔綳〕绷
〔綢〕绸
〔綹〕绺
〔綣〕绻
〔綜〕综
〔綻〕绽
〔綰〕绾
〔綠〕绿
〔綴〕缀
〔緇〕缁

15笔

【一】

〔鬧〕闹⑭
〔璡〕琎
〔靚〕靓
〔輦〕辇
〔髮〕发
〔撓〕挠
〔墳〕坟
〔撻〕挞
〔駔〕驵
〔駛〕驶
〔駟〕驷
〔駙〕驸
〔駒〕驹
〔駐〕驻
〔駝〕驼
〔駘〕骀
〔撲〕扑
〔頡〕颉
〔撣〕掸
〔撾〕挝
*〔賣〕卖㉑
〔撫〕抚
〔撟〕挢
〔撳〕揿
〔熱〕热
〔鞏〕巩
〔摯〕挚
〔撈〕捞
〔穀〕谷
〔慤〕悫
〔撏〕挦
〔撥〕拨
〔蕘〕荛
〔蕆〕蒇
〔蕓〕芸
〔邁〕迈
〔蕢〕蒉
〔蕒〕荬
〔蕪〕芜
〔蕎〕荞
〔蕕〕莸
〔蕩〕荡
〔蕁〕荨
〔樁〕桩
〔樞〕枢
〔標〕标
〔樓〕楼
〔樅〕枞
〔麩〕麸
〔賫〕赍
〔樣〕样
〔橢〕椭
〔豎〕竖
〔輛〕辆
〔輥〕辊
〔輞〕辋
〔槧〕椠
〔暫〕暂
〔輪〕轮
〔輟〕辍
〔輜〕辎
〔甌〕瓯
〔歐〕欧
〔毆〕殴
〔賢〕贤
*〔遷〕迁
〔鴇〕鸨
〔憂〕忧
〔碼〕码
〔磑〕硙
〔確〕确
〔賚〕赉
〔遼〕辽
〔殤〕殇
〔鴉〕鸦

【丨】

〔輩〕辈
〔劌〕刿
*〔齒〕齿
〔劇〕剧
〔膚〕肤
*〔慮〕虑
〔鄴〕邺
〔輝〕辉
〔賞〕赏㉘
〔賦〕赋
〔䝼〕䞍
〔賬〕账
〔賭〕赌
〔賤〕贱
〔賜〕赐
〔賙〕赒
〔賠〕赔
〔賧〕赕
〔曉〕晓
〔噴〕喷
〔噠〕哒
〔噁〕恶
〔閫〕阃
〔閬〕阆
〔閱〕阅
〔閬〕阆
〔數〕数
〔踐〕践
〔遺〕遗
〔蝦〕虾
〔蝸〕蜗
〔嘸〕呒
〔嘮〕唠
〔噝〕咝
〔嘰〕叽
〔嶢〕峣
〔罵〕骂
*〔罷〕罢
〔嶠〕峤
〔嶔〕嵚
〔幟〕帜
〔嶗〕崂

【丿】

〔頲〕颋
〔篋〕箧
〔範〕范
〔價〕价
〔儂〕侬
〔儉〕俭
〔儈〕侩
〔億〕亿
〔儀〕仪
〔皚〕皑
*〔樂〕乐
*〔質〕质
〔徵〕征㊿
〔衝〕冲
〔慫〕怂
〔徹〕彻
〔衛〕卫
〔鋪〕铺
〔鋏〕铗
〔鋱〕铽
〔銷〕销
〔鋥〕锃
〔鋰〕锂
〔鋇〕钡
〔鋤〕锄
〔鋁〕铝
〔鋯〕锆
〔鋨〕锇
〔銼〕锉
〔鋒〕锋
〔鋅〕锌
〔鋭〕锐
〔銻〕锑
〔鋃〕锒
〔鋟〕锓
〔錒〕锕
〔鋦〕锔
〔頜〕颌
〔劍〕剑
〔劊〕刽
〔鄶〕郐
〔餑〕饽
〔餓〕饿

〔餘〕余㊼
〔餕〕馂
〔膞〕䏝
〔膕〕腘
〔膠〕胶
〔鴇〕鸨
〔魷〕鱿
〔魯〕鲁
〔魴〕鲂
〔潁〕颍
〔颳〕刮
*〔劉〕刘
〔皺〕皱

【丶】

〔請〕请
〔諸〕诸
〔諏〕诹
〔諾〕诺
〔諑〕诼
〔誹〕诽
〔課〕课
〔諉〕诿
〔諛〕谀
〔誰〕谁
〔論〕论
〔諗〕谂
〔調〕调
〔諂〕谄
〔諒〕谅
〔諄〕谆
〔誶〕谇
〔談〕谈
〔誼〕谊
〔廟〕庙
〔廠〕厂
〔廡〕庑
〔瘞〕瘗
〔瘡〕疮
〔賡〕赓
〔慶〕庆㉘
〔廢〕废
〔敵〕敌
〔頦〕颏
〔導〕导
〔瑩〕莹
〔潔〕洁
〔澆〕浇
〔澾〕汏
〔潤〕润
〔澗〕涧
〔潰〕溃
〔潿〕涠
〔滻〕浐
〔澇〕涝
〔潯〕浔
〔潑〕泼
〔憤〕愤
〔憫〕悯
〔憒〕愦
〔憚〕惮
〔憮〕怃
〔憐〕怜
*〔寫〕写㊷
*〔審〕审
*〔窮〕穷
〔褳〕裢
〔褲〕裤
〔鴆〕鸩

【乛】

〔遲〕迟
〔層〕层
〔彈〕弹
〔選〕选
〔槳〕桨⑫
〔漿〕浆⑫
〔險〕险
〔嬈〕娆
〔嫻〕娴
〔駕〕驾
〔嬋〕婵
〔嫵〕妩
〔嬌〕娇
〔嫿〕婳
〔駑〕驽
〔翬〕翚
〔毿〕毵
〔緙〕缂
〔緗〕缃
〔練〕练
〔緘〕缄
〔緬〕缅
〔緹〕缇
〔緲〕缈
〔緝〕缉
〔緦〕缌
〔緞〕缎
〔緱〕缑
〔縋〕缒
〔線〕线
〔緩〕缓
〔締〕缔
〔編〕编
〔緡〕缗
〔緯〕纬
〔緣〕缘

16笔

【一】

〔璣〕玑
〔駱〕骆
〔駭〕骇
〔駢〕骈
〔擓〕㧟
〔擄〕掳
〔擋〕挡
〔擇〕择
〔赬〕赪
〔撿〕捡
〔擔〕担
〔壇〕坛
〔擁〕拥
〔據〕据
〔薔〕蔷
〔薑〕姜
〔薈〕荟
〔薊〕蓟
*〔薦〕荐
〔蕭〕萧
〔頤〕颐
〔鴣〕鸪
〔薩〕萨
〔蕢〕蒉
〔橈〕桡
〔樹〕树
〔樸〕朴
〔橋〕桥
〔機〕机
〔輳〕辏
〔輻〕辐
〔輯〕辑
〔輸〕输
〔賴〕赖
〔頭〕头
〔醞〕酝
〔醜〕丑
〔勵〕励
〔磧〕碛
〔磚〕砖
〔磣〕碜
*〔歷〕历
〔曆〕历
〔奮〕奋
〔頰〕颊
〔殨〕㱮
〔殫〕殚
〔頸〕颈

【丨】

〔頻〕频
*〔盧〕卢
〔曉〕晓
〔瞞〕瞒
〔縣〕县㊵
〔瞘〕眍
〔瞜〕䁖
〔瞷〕瞯
〔鴨〕鸭
〔閾〕阈
〔閹〕阉
〔閶〕阊
〔閿〕阌
〔閽〕阍
〔閻〕阎
〔閼〕阏
〔曇〕昙
〔噸〕吨
〔鴞〕鸮
〔噦〕哕
〔踴〕踊
〔螞〕蚂
〔螄〕蛳
〔噹〕当
〔噥〕哝
〔戰〕战
〔噲〕哙
〔鴦〕鸯
〔噯〕嗳
〔嘯〕啸
〔還〕还
〔嶧〕峄
〔嶼〕屿

【丿】

〔積〕积
〔頹〕颓
〔穇〕䅟
〔篤〕笃
〔築〕筑
〔篳〕筚
〔篩〕筛
*〔舉〕举
〔興〕兴
〔嚳〕喾
〔學〕学
〔儔〕俦
〔憊〕惫
〔儕〕侪
〔儐〕傧
〔儘〕尽
〔鴕〕鸵
〔艙〕舱
〔錶〕表
〔鍺〕锗
〔錯〕错
〔鍩〕锘
〔錨〕锚
〔錛〕锛
〔錸〕铼
〔錢〕钱
〔鍀〕锝
〔錁〕锞
〔錕〕锟
〔鍆〕钔
〔錫〕锡
〔錮〕锢
〔鋼〕钢
〔錘〕锤
〔錐〕锥
〔錦〕锦
〔鍁〕锨
〔錚〕铮
〔錇〕锫
〔錠〕锭
〔鍵〕键
*〔錄〕录
〔鋸〕锯
〔錳〕锰
〔錙〕锱
〔覦〕觎
〔墾〕垦
〔餞〕饯
〔餜〕馃
〔餛〕馄
〔餡〕馅
〔館〕馆
〔頷〕颔
〔鴒〕鸰
〔膩〕腻
〔鴟〕鸱
〔鮁〕鲅
〔鮃〕鲆
〔鮎〕鲇
〔鮓〕鲊
〔穌〕稣
〔鮒〕鲋
〔鮣〕䲟
〔鮑〕鲍
〔鮍〕鲏
〔鮐〕鲐
〔鴝〕鸲
〔獲〕获
〔穎〕颖
〔獨〕独
〔獫〕猃
〔獪〕狯
〔鴛〕鸳

【丶】

〔謀〕谋
〔諶〕谌
〔諜〕谍
〔謊〕谎
〔諫〕谏
〔諧〕谐
〔謔〕谑
〔謁〕谒
〔謂〕谓
〔諤〕谔
〔諭〕谕
〔諼〕谖
〔諷〕讽
〔諮〕谘
〔諳〕谙
〔諺〕谚
〔諦〕谛
〔謎〕谜
〔諢〕诨
〔諞〕谝
〔諱〕讳
〔諝〕谞
〔憑〕凭
〔鄺〕邝
〔瘻〕瘘
〔瘮〕瘆
*〔親〕亲
〔辦〕办
*〔龍〕龙
〔劑〕剂
〔燒〕烧
〔燜〕焖
〔熾〕炽
〔螢〕萤
〔營〕营
〔縈〕萦
〔燈〕灯
〔濛〕蒙
〔燙〕烫
〔澠〕渑
〔濃〕浓
〔澤〕泽
〔濁〕浊
〔澮〕浍
〔澱〕淀
〔澦〕滪
〔懞〕蒙
〔懌〕怿
〔憶〕忆
〔憲〕宪
〔窺〕窥
〔窶〕窭
〔窵〕窎
〔褸〕褛
〔禪〕禅

【乛】

*〔隱〕隐
〔嬙〕嫱
〔嬡〕嫒
〔縉〕缙
〔縝〕缜
〔縛〕缚
〔縟〕缛
〔緻〕致
〔縧〕绦
〔縫〕缝
〔縐〕绉
〔縗〕缞
〔縞〕缟
〔縭〕缡
〔縑〕缣
〔縊〕缢

17笔

【一】

〔耬〕耧
〔環〕环
〔贅〕赘
〔璦〕瑷
〔覯〕觏
〔黿〕鼋
〔幫〕帮
〔騁〕骋
〔駸〕骎
〔駿〕骏
〔趨〕趋
〔擱〕搁
〔擬〕拟
〔擴〕扩
〔壙〕圹
〔擠〕挤
〔蟄〕蛰
〔縶〕絷
〔擲〕掷
〔擯〕摈
〔擰〕拧
〔轂〕毂
〔聲〕声
〔藉〕借⑬
〔聰〕聪
〔聯〕联
〔艱〕艰
〔藍〕蓝
〔舊〕旧

〔薺〕荠
〔藎〕荩
〔韓〕韩
〔隸〕隶
〔檉〕柽
〔檣〕樯
〔檟〕槚
〔檔〕档
〔櫛〕栉
〔檢〕检
〔檜〕桧
〔麯〕曲
〔轅〕辕
〔轄〕辖
〔輾〕辗
〔擊〕击
〔臨〕临⑱
〔磽〕硗
〔壓〕压㊸
〔礄〕硚
〔磯〕矶
〔鴯〕鸸
〔邇〕迩
〔尷〕尴
〔鴷〕䴕
〔殮〕殓
【丨】
〔齔〕龀
〔戲〕戏
〔虧〕亏
〔斃〕毙
〔瞭〕了
〔顆〕颗
〔購〕购
〔賻〕赙
〔嬰〕婴
〔賺〕赚
〔嚇〕吓㊳
〔闌〕阑
〔闃〕阒
〔闆〕板
〔闊〕阔
〔闈〕闱
〔闋〕阕
〔曖〕暧
〔蹕〕跸
〔蹌〕跄
〔蟎〕螨
〔螻〕蝼
〔蟈〕蝈
〔雖〕虽
〔嚀〕咛
〔覬〕觊
〔嶺〕岭⑲
〔嶸〕嵘
〔點〕点
【丿】
〔矯〕矫
〔鴰〕鸹
〔簀〕箦
〔簍〕篓
〔輿〕舆
〔歟〕欤
〔鵂〕鸺
〔優〕优
〔償〕偿
〔儲〕储
〔魎〕魉
〔鴴〕鸻
〔禦〕御
〔聳〕耸
〔鵃〕鸼
〔鍥〕锲
〔鍇〕锴
〔鍘〕铡
〔鍚〕钖
〔鍶〕锶
〔鍋〕锅
〔鍔〕锷
〔鍤〕锸
〔鍾〕钟
〔鍛〕锻
〔鎪〕锼
〔鍬〕锹
〔鍰〕锾
〔鍄〕𫟹
〔鍍〕镀
〔鎂〕镁
〔鎡〕镃
〔鎇〕镅
〔懇〕恳
〔餷〕馇
〔餳〕饧
〔餿〕馊
〔斂〕敛
〔鴿〕鸽
〔膿〕脓
〔臉〕脸
〔膾〕脍
〔膽〕胆
〔謄〕誊
〔鮭〕鲑
〔鮚〕鲒
〔鮪〕鲔
〔鮦〕鲖
〔鮫〕鲛
〔鮮〕鲜
〔颶〕飓
〔獷〕犷
〔獰〕狞
【丶】
〔講〕讲
〔謨〕谟
〔謖〕谡
〔謝〕谢
〔謠〕谣
〔謅〕诌
〔謗〕谤
〔謚〕谥
〔謙〕谦
〔謐〕谧
〔褻〕亵
〔氈〕毡
〔應〕应
〔癘〕疠
〔療〕疗
〔癇〕痫
〔癉〕瘅
〔癆〕痨
〔鵁〕䴔
〔齋〕斋
〔鮝〕鲞
〔鮺〕鲝
〔糞〕粪
〔糝〕糁
〔燦〕灿
〔燭〕烛
〔燴〕烩
〔鴻〕鸿
〔濤〕涛
〔濫〕滥
〔濕〕湿
〔濟〕济
〔濱〕滨
〔濘〕泞
〔濜〕浕
〔澀〕涩
〔濰〕潍
〔懨〕恹
〔賽〕赛
〔襇〕裥
〔襀〕䙊
〔襖〕袄
〔禮〕礼
【乛】
〔屨〕屦
〔彌〕弥
〔牆〕墙
〔嬪〕嫔
〔績〕绩
〔縹〕缥
〔縷〕缕
〔縵〕缦
〔縲〕缧
〔總〕总
〔縱〕纵
〔縴〕纤
〔縮〕缩
〔繆〕缪
〔繅〕缫
〔嚮〕向

18笔

【一】
〔耮〕耢
〔鬩〕阋⑭
〔瓊〕琼
〔攆〕撵
〔鬆〕松
〔翹〕翘
〔擷〕撷
〔擾〕扰
〔騏〕骐
〔騎〕骑
〔騍〕骒
〔騅〕骓
〔攄〕摅
〔擻〕擞
〔鼕〕冬
〔擺〕摆
〔贄〕贽
〔燾〕焘
*〔聶〕聂
〔聵〕聩
〔職〕职
*〔藝〕艺
〔覲〕觐
〔鞦〕秋
〔藪〕薮
〔蠆〕虿
〔繭〕茧
〔藥〕药
〔藭〕䓖
〔賾〕赜
〔檯〕台
〔櫃〕柜
〔檻〕槛
〔檳〕槟
〔檸〕柠
〔鵓〕鹁
〔轉〕转
〔轆〕辘
〔覆〕复⑦
〔醫〕医
〔礎〕础
〔殯〕殡
〔霧〕雾
【丨】
*〔豐〕丰⑥
〔覷〕觑
〔懟〕怼
〔叢〕丛
〔矇〕蒙
〔題〕题
〔韙〕韪
〔瞼〕睑
〔闖〕闯
〔闔〕阖
〔闐〕阗
〔闓〕闿
〔闕〕阙
〔顒〕颙
〔曠〕旷
〔蹣〕蹒
〔嚙〕啮
〔壘〕垒
〔蟯〕蛲
*〔蟲〕虫
〔蟬〕蝉
〔蟣〕虮
〔鵑〕鹃
〔嚕〕噜
〔顓〕颛
【丿】
〔鵠〕鹄
〔鵝〕鹅
〔穫〕获
〔穡〕穑
〔穢〕秽
〔簡〕简
〔簣〕篑
〔簞〕箪
*〔雙〕双
〔軀〕躯
*〔邊〕边
*〔歸〕归
〔鏵〕铧
〔鎮〕镇
〔鏈〕链
〔鎘〕镉
〔鎖〕锁
〔鎧〕铠
〔鎸〕镌
〔鎳〕镍
〔鎢〕钨
〔鎩〕铩
〔鎿〕镎
〔鎦〕镏
〔鎬〕镐
〔鎊〕镑
〔鎰〕镒
〔鎵〕镓
〔鍽〕𫔀
〔鵮〕鹐
〔饃〕馍
〔餺〕馎
〔餶〕馉
〔餼〕饩
〔餾〕馏
〔饈〕馐
〔雞〕鸡
〔臍〕脐
〔臏〕膑
*〔龜〕龟
〔鯁〕鲠
〔鯉〕鲤
〔鯀〕鲧
〔鯇〕鲩
〔鯽〕鲫
〔颸〕飔
〔颼〕飕
〔觴〕觞
〔獵〕猎
〔雛〕雏
【丶】
〔謹〕谨
〔謳〕讴
〔謾〕谩
〔謫〕谪
〔謭〕谫
〔謬〕谬
〔癤〕疖
〔雜〕杂
*〔離〕离
〔顏〕颜
〔糧〕粮
〔燼〕烬
〔鵜〕鹈
〔瀆〕渎
〔瀈〕瀈
〔濾〕滤
〔鯊〕鲨
〔濺〕溅
〔瀏〕浏
〔濼〕泺
〔瀉〕泻
〔瀋〕沈
*〔竄〕窜
〔竅〕窍
〔額〕额
〔禰〕祢
〔襠〕裆
〔襝〕裣
〔禱〕祷
【乛】
〔醬〕酱⑫
〔隴〕陇
〔嬸〕婶
〔繞〕绕
〔繚〕缭
〔織〕织
〔繕〕缮
〔繒〕缯
*〔斷〕断

19笔

【一】
〔鵡〕鹉
〔鶄〕䴖
〔鬍〕胡
〔騙〕骗
〔壢〕坜
〔壚〕垆
〔壞〕坏⑨
〔攏〕拢
〔籜〕箨
*〔難〕难
〔鵲〕鹊
〔藶〕苈
〔蘋〕苹
〔蘆〕芦
〔鶘〕鹕
〔藺〕蔺
〔躉〕趸
〔蘄〕蕲
〔勸〕劝
〔蘇〕苏
〔藹〕蔼
〔蘢〕茏
〔顛〕颠
〔蘊〕蕴
〔櫝〕椟
〔櫟〕栎
〔櫓〕橹
〔櫧〕槠
〔櫚〕榈
〔櫞〕橼
〔轎〕轿
〔鏨〕錾

〔轍〕辙
〔轔〕辚
〔繫〕系⑪
〔鶇〕鸫
*〔麗〕丽⑰
〔厴〕厣
〔礪〕砺
〔礙〕碍
〔礦〕矿
〔贗〕赝
〔願〕愿
〔鵪〕鹌
〔璽〕玺
〔豶〕豮
【丨】
〔贈〕赠
〔闞〕阚
〔關〕关
〔嚦〕呖
〔疇〕畴
〔蹺〕跷
〔蟶〕蛏
〔蠅〕蝇
〔蟻〕蚁
*〔嚴〕严
〔獸〕兽
〔嚨〕咙
〔羆〕罴
*〔羅〕罗
【丿】
〔氌〕氇
〔犢〕犊
〔贊〕赞
〔穩〕稳
〔簽〕签
〔簾〕帘
〔簫〕箫
〔牘〕牍
〔懲〕惩
〔鐯〕锗
〔鏗〕铿
〔鏢〕镖
〔鏜〕镗
〔鏤〕镂
〔鏝〕镘
〔鏰〕镚
〔鏞〕镛
〔鏡〕镜
〔鏟〕铲
〔鏑〕镝
〔鏃〕镞
〔鏇〕旋
〔鏘〕锵
〔鏹〕镪
〔辭〕辞
〔饉〕馑
〔饅〕馒
〔鵬〕鹏
〔臘〕腊
〔鯖〕鲭
〔鯪〕鲮
〔鯫〕鲰
〔鯡〕鲱
〔鯤〕鲲
〔鯧〕鲳
〔鯢〕鲵
〔鯰〕鲶
〔鯛〕鲷
〔鯨〕鲸
〔鯔〕鲻
〔獺〕獭
〔鵮〕鹐
〔飀〕飗
【丶】
〔譚〕谭
〔譖〕谮
〔譙〕谯
〔識〕识
〔譜〕谱
〔證〕证
〔譎〕谲
〔譏〕讥
〔鶉〕鹑
〔廬〕庐
〔癟〕瘪
〔癢〕痒
〔龐〕庞
〔壟〕垄
〔鶊〕鹒
〔類〕类⑯
〔爍〕烁
〔瀟〕潇
〔瀨〕濑
〔瀝〕沥
〔瀕〕濒
〔瀘〕泸
〔瀧〕泷
〔懶〕懒
〔懷〕怀
〔寵〕宠
〔襪〕袜㉟
〔襤〕褴
【乛】
〔韜〕韬
〔韞〕韫
〔騭〕骘
〔騖〕骛
〔顙〕颡
〔繮〕缰
〔繩〕绳
〔繾〕缱
〔繰〕缲
〔繹〕绎
〔繯〕缳
〔繳〕缴
〔繪〕绘
〔繡〕绣

20笔

【一】
〔瓏〕珑
〔驁〕骜
〔驊〕骅
〔騮〕骝
〔騶〕驺
〔騸〕骟
〔騷〕骚
〔攖〕撄
〔攔〕拦
〔攙〕搀
〔聹〕聍
〔顢〕颟
〔驀〕蓦
〔蘭〕兰
〔蘞〕蔹
〔蘚〕藓
〔鶘〕鹕
〔飄〕飘
〔櫪〕枥
〔櫨〕栌
〔櫸〕榉
〔礬〕矾
〔麵〕面
〔櫬〕榇
〔櫳〕栊
〔礫〕砾
【丨】
〔鹹〕咸
〔鹺〕鹾
〔齟〕龃
〔齡〕龄
〔齣〕出
〔齙〕龅
〔齠〕龆
*〔獻〕献
*〔黨〕党
〔懸〕悬
〔鶪〕䴗
〔罌〕罂
〔贍〕赡
〔闥〕闼
〔闡〕阐
〔鶡〕鹖
〔曨〕昽
〔蠣〕蛎
〔蠐〕蛴
〔蠑〕蝾
〔嚶〕嘤
〔鶚〕鹗
〔髏〕髅
〔鶻〕鹘
【丿】
〔犧〕牺
〔鶖〕鹙
〔籌〕筹
〔籃〕篮
〔譽〕誉
〔覺〕觉
〔嚳〕喾
〔衊〕蔑
〔艦〕舰
〔鐃〕铙
〔鐝〕镢
〔鐐〕镣
〔鏷〕镤
〔鐦〕锎
〔鐧〕锏
〔鐓〕镦
〔鐘〕钟
〔鐥〕𫔍
〔鐠〕镨
〔鐒〕铹
〔鐨〕镄
〔鐙〕镫
〔鏺〕钹
〔釋〕释
〔饒〕饶
〔饊〕馓
〔饋〕馈
〔饌〕馔
〔饑〕饥
〔臚〕胪
〔朧〕胧
〔騰〕腾
〔鰆〕䲠
〔鰈〕鲽
〔鰂〕鲗
〔鰛〕鳁
〔鰓〕鳃
〔鰐〕鳄
〔鰍〕鳅
〔鰒〕鳆
〔鰉〕鳇
〔鰌〕䲡
〔鯿〕鳊
〔獼〕猕
〔觸〕触
【丶】
〔護〕护
〔譴〕谴
〔譯〕译
〔譫〕谵
〔議〕议
〔癥〕症
〔辮〕辫
〔龑〕䶮
〔競〕竞
〔贏〕赢
〔糲〕粝
〔糰〕团
〔鷀〕鹚
〔爐〕炉
〔瀾〕澜
〔瀲〕潋
〔瀰〕弥
〔懺〕忏
〔寶〕宝
〔騫〕骞
〔竇〕窦
〔襬〕摆
【乛】
〔鶥〕鹛
〔鶩〕鹜
〔纊〕纩
〔繽〕缤
〔繼〕继
〔饗〕飨
〔響〕响

21笔

【一】
〔䎱〕䎬
〔瓔〕璎
〔鼇〕鳌
〔攝〕摄
〔騾〕骡
〔驅〕驱
〔驃〕骠
〔驄〕骢
〔驂〕骖
〔㩳〕𢶤
〔攛〕撺
〔韃〕鞑
〔鞽〕鞒
〔歡〕欢
〔權〕权
〔櫻〕樱
〔欄〕栏
〔轟〕轰
〔覽〕览
〔酈〕郦
〔飆〕飙
〔殲〕歼
【丨】
〔齜〕龇
〔齦〕龈
〔[illegible]〕[illegible]
〔贐〕赆
〔囁〕嗫
〔囈〕呓
〔闢〕辟
〔囀〕啭
〔顥〕颢
〔躊〕踌
〔躋〕跻
〔躑〕踯
〔躍〕跃
〔纍〕累
〔蠟〕蜡
〔囂〕嚣
〔巋〕岿
【丿】
〔儺〕傩
〔儷〕俪
〔儼〕俨
〔鷉〕䴘
〔鐵〕铁
〔鑊〕镬
〔鐳〕镭
〔鐺〕铛
〔鐸〕铎
〔鐶〕镮
〔鐲〕镯
〔鐮〕镰
〔鐿〕镱
〔鏽〕锈
〔鶺〕鹡
〔鷂〕鹞
〔鶬〕鸧
〔臟〕脏
〔臢〕臜
〔鰭〕鳍
〔鰱〕鲢
〔鰣〕鲥
〔鰨〕鳎
〔鰥〕鳏
〔鰷〕鲦
〔鰟〕鳑
〔鰜〕鳒
【丶】
〔癩〕癞
〔癧〕疬
〔癮〕瘾
〔斕〕斓
〔辯〕辩
〔礱〕砻
〔鶼〕鹣
〔爛〕烂
〔鶯〕莺
〔灄〕滠
〔灃〕沣
〔灕〕漓
〔懾〕慑
〔懼〕惧
〔竈〕灶
〔顧〕顾
〔襯〕衬
〔鶴〕鹤
【乛】
*〔屬〕属
〔纈〕缬
〔續〕续
〔纏〕缠②

22笔

【一】
〔鬚〕须
〔驍〕骁
〔驕〕骄
〔攤〕摊
〔覿〕觌
〔攢〕攒
〔鷙〕鸷
〔聽〕听
〔蘿〕萝
〔驚〕惊
〔轢〕轹
〔鷗〕鸥
〔鑒〕鉴
〔邐〕逦
〔鷖〕鹥
〔霽〕霁
【丨】
〔齬〕龉
〔齪〕龊
〔鱉〕鳖
〔贖〕赎
〔躚〕跹
〔躓〕踬

〔疊〕迭⑤
〔蠨〕蟏
〔囌〕苏
〔囉〕罗
〔囒〕嘫
〔轣〕轣
〔巔〕巅
〔邏〕逻
〔髒〕脏
【丿】
〔罎〕坛
〔籜〕箨
〔籟〕籁
〔籙〕箓
〔籠〕笼
〔鰲〕鳌
〔儻〕傥
〔艫〕舻
〔鑄〕铸
〔鑌〕镔
〔鑔〕镲
〔龕〕龛
〔糴〕籴
〔鰳〕鳓
〔鰹〕鲣
〔鰾〕鳔
〔鱈〕鳕
〔鰻〕鳗
〔鱅〕鳙
〔鰼〕鳛
〔玀〕猡
【丶】
〔讀〕读
〔讅〕谉
〔巒〕峦
〔彎〕弯
〔孿〕孪
〔孌〕娈
〔顫〕颤
〔鷓〕鹧
〔癭〕瘿

〔癬〕癣
〔聾〕聋
〔龔〕龚
〔襲〕袭
〔灘〕滩
〔灑〕洒
〔竊〕窃
【乛】
〔鷚〕鹨
〔轡〕辔

23笔
【一】
〔瓚〕瓒
〔驛〕驿
〔驗〕验
〔攪〕搅
〔欏〕椤
〔轤〕轳
〔靨〕靥
〔魘〕魇
〔饜〕餍
〔鷯〕鹩
〔靆〕叇
〔顬〕颥
【丨】
〔曬〕晒
〔鷴〕鹇
〔顯〕显
〔蠱〕蛊
〔髖〕髋
〔體〕体
【丿】
〔籤〕签
〔讎〕雠
〔鷦〕鹪
〔黴〕霉
〔鑠〕铄
〔鑕〕锧
〔鑥〕镥
〔鑣〕镳
〔鑞〕镴

〔臢〕臜
〔鱖〕鳜
〔鱔〕鳝
〔鱗〕鳞
〔鱒〕鳟
〔鱘〕鲟
【丶】
〔讌〕䜩
〔欒〕栾
〔攣〕挛
〔變〕变
〔戀〕恋
〔鷲〕鹫
〔癰〕痈
〔齏〕齑
〔讋〕詟
【乛】
〔鷸〕鹬
〔纓〕缨
〔纖〕纤㊴
〔纔〕才
〔鸞〕鸶

24笔
【一】
〔鬢〕鬓
〔攬〕揽
〔驟〕骤
〔壩〕坝
〔韆〕千
〔觀〕观
〔鹽〕盐
〔釀〕酿
〔靂〕雳
*〔靈〕灵
〔靄〕霭
〔蠶〕蚕①
【丨】
〔艷〕艳
〔顰〕颦
〔齲〕龋

〔齷〕龌
〔鹼〕硷
〔臟〕脏
〔鷺〕鹭
〔髕〕髌
〔鬢〕鬓
〔矚〕瞩
〔羈〕羁
【丿】
〔籩〕笾
〔籬〕篱
〔籪〕簖
〔黌〕黉
〔鱟〕鲎
〔鱧〕鳢
〔鱠〕鲙
〔鱣〕鳣
【丶】
〔讕〕谰
〔讖〕谶
〔讒〕谗
〔讓〕让
〔鸇〕鹯
〔鷹〕鹰
〔癱〕瘫
〔癲〕癫
〔贛〕赣
〔灝〕灏
【乛】
〔鸊〕䴙

25笔
【一】
〔韉〕鞯
〔欖〕榄
〔靉〕叆
【丨】
〔顱〕颅
〔躡〕蹑
〔躥〕蹿
〔鼉〕鼍

【丿】
〔籮〕箩
〔鑭〕镧
〔鑰〕钥
〔鑲〕镶
〔饞〕馋
〔鱨〕鲿
〔鱭〕鲚
【丶】
〔蠻〕蛮
〔臠〕脔
〔廳〕厅㉞
〔灣〕湾
【乛】
〔糶〕粜
〔纘〕缵

26笔
【一】
〔驥〕骥
〔驢〕驴
〔趲〕趱
〔顴〕颧
〔黶〕黡
〔釃〕酾
〔釅〕酽
【丨】
〔矚〕瞩
〔躪〕躏
〔躦〕躜
【丿】
〔釁〕衅
〔鑷〕镊
〔鑹〕镩
【丶】
〔灤〕滦

27笔
【一】
〔鬮〕阄⑭
〔驤〕骧

〔顳〕颞
【丨】
〔鸕〕鸬
〔黷〕黩
【丿】
〔鑼〕锣
〔鑽〕钻
〔鱸〕鲈
【丶】
〔讞〕谳
〔讜〕谠
〔鑾〕銮
〔灩〕滟
【乛】
〔纜〕缆

28笔
〔鸛〕鹳
〔欞〕棂
〔鑿〕凿
〔鸚〕鹦
〔钂〕锐
〔钁〕镢
〔戇〕戆

29笔
〔驪〕骊
〔鬱〕郁

30笔
〔鸝〕鹂
〔饢〕馕
〔鱺〕鲡
〔鸞〕鸾

32笔
〔籲〕吁㊽

C. 從拼音查漢字

A
a
锕〔錒〕
ai
锿〔鎄〕
皑〔皚〕
霭〔靄〕
蔼〔藹〕
*爱〔愛〕
叆〔靉〕
瑷〔璦〕
嗳〔噯〕
暧〔曖〕
嫒〔嬡〕
碍〔礙〕
an
谙〔諳〕
鹌〔鵪〕
铵〔銨〕
ang
肮〔骯〕
ao
鳌〔鰲〕
骜〔驁〕
袄〔襖〕
B
ba
鲅〔鮁〕
钯〔鈀〕
坝〔壩〕
*罢〔罷〕
罴〔羆〕
bai
摆〔擺〕
〔襬〕
败〔敗〕
ban
颁〔頒〕
板〔闆〕
绊〔絆〕
办〔辦〕
bang
帮〔幫〕
绑〔綁〕
谤〔謗〕
镑〔鎊〕
bao
龅〔齙〕
宝〔寶〕
饱〔飽〕
鸨〔鴇〕
报〔報〕
鲍〔鮑〕
bei
惫〔憊〕
辈〔輩〕
*贝〔貝〕
钡〔鋇〕
狈〔狽〕
*备〔備〕
呗〔唄〕
ben
锛〔錛〕
贲〔賁〕
beng
绷〔繃〕
镚〔鏰〕
bi
*笔〔筆〕
铋〔鉍〕
贲〔賁〕
*毕〔畢〕
哔〔嗶〕
筚〔篳〕
荜〔蓽〕
跸〔蹕〕
滗〔潷〕
币〔幣〕
闭〔閉〕
毙〔斃〕
bian
鳊〔鯿〕
编〔編〕
*边〔邊〕
笾〔籩〕
贬〔貶〕
辩〔辯〕
辫〔辮〕
变〔變〕
biao
镳〔鑣〕
标〔標〕
骠〔驃〕
镖〔鏢〕
飙〔飆〕
表〔錶〕
鳔〔鰾〕
bie
鳖〔鱉〕
瘪〔癟〕
别〔彆〕
bin
*宾〔賓〕
滨〔濱〕
槟〔檳〕
傧〔儐〕
缤〔繽〕
镔〔鑌〕
濒〔瀕〕
鬓〔鬢〕
摈〔擯〕
殡〔殯〕
膑〔臏〕
髌〔髕〕
bing
槟〔檳〕
饼〔餅〕
bo
饽〔餑〕
钵〔鉢〕
拨〔撥〕
鹁〔鵓〕
馎〔餺〕
钹〔鈸〕
驳〔駁〕
铂〔鉑〕
卜〔蔔〕
bu
补〔補〕
钚〔鈈〕
C
cai
才〔纔〕
财〔財〕
can
*参〔參〕
骖〔驂〕
蚕〔蠶〕①
惭〔慚〕
残〔殘〕
惨〔慘〕
穇〔穇〕
灿〔燦〕
cang
*仓〔倉〕
沧〔滄〕
苍〔蒼〕
伧〔傖〕
鸧〔鶬〕
舱〔艙〕
ce
测〔測〕
恻〔惻〕
厕〔廁〕
侧〔側〕
cen
*参〔參〕
ceng
层〔層〕
cha
馇〔餷〕
锸〔鍤〕
镲〔鑔〕
诧〔詫〕
chai
钗〔釵〕
侪〔儕〕
虿〔蠆〕
chan
搀〔攙〕
掺〔摻〕
缠〔纏〕②
禅〔禪〕
蝉〔蟬〕
婵〔嬋〕
谗〔讒〕
馋〔饞〕
*产〔產〕
浐〔滻〕
铲〔鏟〕
蒇〔蕆〕
阐〔闡〕
骣〔驏〕
谄〔諂〕
颤〔顫〕
忏〔懺〕
刬〔剗〕
chang
伥〔倀〕
阊〔閶〕
鲳〔鯧〕
*尝〔嘗〕③
偿〔償〕
鲿〔鱨〕
*长〔長〕④
肠〔腸〕
场〔場〕
厂〔廠〕
怅〔悵〕
畅〔暢〕
chao
钞〔鈔〕
che
*车〔車〕
砗〔硨〕
彻〔徹〕
chen
谌〔諶〕
尘〔塵〕
陈〔陳〕
碜〔磣〕
榇〔櫬〕
衬〔襯〕
谶〔讖〕
称〔稱〕
龀〔齔〕
cheng
柽〔檉〕
蛏〔蟶〕
铛〔鐺〕
赪〔赬〕
称〔稱〕
枨〔棖〕
诚〔誠〕
惩〔懲〕
骋〔騁〕
chi
鸱〔鴟〕
迟〔遲〕
驰〔馳〕
*齿〔齒〕
炽〔熾〕
饬〔飭〕
chong
冲〔衝〕
*虫〔蟲〕
宠〔寵〕
铳〔銃〕
chou
䌷〔紬〕
畴〔疇〕
筹〔籌〕
踌〔躊〕
俦〔儔〕
雠〔讎〕
绸〔綢〕
丑〔醜〕
chu
出〔齣〕
锄〔鋤〕
*刍〔芻〕
雏〔雛〕
储〔儲〕
础〔礎〕
处〔處〕
绌〔絀〕
触〔觸〕
chuai
[illegible]
chuan
传〔傳〕
钏〔釧〕
chuang
疮〔瘡〕
闯〔闖〕
怆〔愴〕
创〔創〕
chui
锤〔錘〕
chun
䲠〔鰆〕
鹑〔鶉〕
纯〔純〕
莼〔蒓〕
chuo
绰〔綽〕
龊〔齪〕
辍〔輟〕
ci
鹚〔鷀〕
辞〔辭〕
词〔詞〕
赐〔賜〕
cong
聪〔聰〕
骢〔驄〕
枞〔樅〕
苁〔蓯〕
*从〔從〕
丛〔叢〕
cou
辏〔輳〕
cuan
撺〔攛〕
蹿〔躥〕
镩〔鑹〕
攒〔攢〕
*窜〔竄〕
cui
缞〔縗〕
cuo
鹾〔鹺〕
错〔錯〕
锉〔銼〕
D
da
*达〔達〕
哒〔噠〕
鞑〔韃〕
dai
贷〔貸〕
绐〔紿〕
*带〔帶〕
叇〔靆〕
dan
*单〔單〕
担〔擔〕
殚〔殫〕
箪〔簞〕
郸〔鄲〕
掸〔撣〕
胆〔膽〕
赕〔賧〕
惮〔憚〕

瘅〔癉〕
弹〔彈〕
诞〔誕〕
dang
裆〔襠〕
铛〔鐺〕
*当〔當〕
〔噹〕
*党〔黨〕
谠〔讜〕
挡〔擋〕
档〔檔〕
砀〔碭〕
荡〔蕩〕
dao
鱽〔魛〕
祷〔禱〕
岛〔島〕
捣〔搗〕
导〔導〕
de
锝〔鍀〕
deng
灯〔燈〕
镫〔鐙〕
邓〔鄧〕
di
镝〔鏑〕
觌〔覿〕
籴〔糴〕
敌〔敵〕
涤〔滌〕
诋〔詆〕
谛〔諦〕
缔〔締〕
递〔遞〕
dian
颠〔顛〕
癫〔癲〕
巅〔巔〕
点〔點〕
淀〔澱〕
垫〔墊〕
电〔電〕
钿〔鈿〕
diao
鲷〔鯛〕
铫〔銚〕
铞〔銱〕
窎〔窵〕
钓〔釣〕
调〔調〕
die
谍〔諜〕
鲽〔鰈〕
绖〔絰〕
迭〔疊〕⑤
ding
钉〔釘〕
顶〔頂〕
订〔訂〕
锭〔錠〕
diu
铥〔銩〕
dong
*东〔東〕
鸫〔鶇〕
岽〔崬〕
冬〔鼕〕
*动〔動〕
冻〔凍〕
栋〔棟〕
胨〔腖〕
dou
钭〔鈄〕
斗〔鬥〕
窦〔竇〕
du
读〔讀〕
渎〔瀆〕
椟〔櫝〕
黩〔黷〕
犊〔犢〕
牍〔牘〕
独〔獨〕
赌〔賭〕
笃〔篤〕
镀〔鍍〕
duan
*断〔斷〕
锻〔鍛〕
缎〔緞〕
簖〔籪〕
dui
怼〔懟〕
*对〔對〕
*队〔隊〕
dun
吨〔噸〕
镦〔鐓〕
趸〔躉〕
钝〔鈍〕
顿〔頓〕
duo
夺〔奪〕
铎〔鐸〕
驮〔馱〕
堕〔墮〕
饳〔飿〕
E
e
额〔額〕
锇〔鋨〕
鹅〔鵝〕
讹〔訛〕
恶〔惡〕
〔噁〕
垩〔堊〕
轭〔軛〕
谔〔諤〕
鹗〔鶚〕
鳄〔鱷〕
锷〔鍔〕
饿〔餓〕
ê
诶〔誒〕
er
儿〔兒〕
鸸〔鴯〕
饵〔餌〕
铒〔鉺〕
*尔〔爾〕
迩〔邇〕
贰〔貳〕
F
fa
*发〔發〕
〔髮〕
罚〔罰〕
阀〔閥〕
fan
烦〔煩〕
矾〔礬〕
钒〔釩〕
贩〔販〕
饭〔飯〕
范〔範〕
fang
钫〔鈁〕
鲂〔魴〕
访〔訪〕
纺〔紡〕
fei
绯〔緋〕
鲱〔鯡〕
飞〔飛〕
诽〔誹〕
废〔廢〕
费〔費〕
镄〔鐨〕
fen
纷〔紛〕
坟〔墳〕
豮〔豶〕
粪〔糞〕
愤〔憤〕
偾〔僨〕
奋〔奮〕
feng
*丰〔豐〕⑥
沣〔灃〕
锋〔鋒〕
*风〔風〕
沨〔渢〕
疯〔瘋〕
枫〔楓〕
砜〔碸〕
冯〔馮〕
缝〔縫〕
讽〔諷〕
凤〔鳳〕
赗〔賵〕
fu
麸〔麩〕
肤〔膚〕
辐〔輻〕
韨〔韍〕
绂〔紱〕
凫〔鳧〕
绋〔紼〕
辅〔輔〕
抚〔撫〕
赋〔賦〕
赙〔賻〕
缚〔縛〕
讣〔訃〕
复〔復〕
〔複〕
〔覆〕⑦
鳆〔鰒〕
驸〔駙〕
鲋〔鮒〕
负〔負〕
妇〔婦〕
G
ga
钆〔釓〕
gai
该〔該〕
赅〔賅〕
盖〔蓋〕
钙〔鈣〕
gan
干〔乾〕⑧
〔幹〕
尴〔尷〕
赶〔趕〕
赣〔贛〕
绀〔紺〕
gang
*冈〔岡〕
刚〔剛〕
㭎〔棡〕
纲〔綱〕
钢〔鋼〕
㧏〔掆〕
岗〔崗〕
gao
镐〔鎬〕
缟〔縞〕
诰〔誥〕
锆〔鋯〕
ge
鸽〔鴿〕
搁〔擱〕
镉〔鎘〕
颌〔頜〕
阁〔閣〕
个〔個〕
铬〔鉻〕
gei
给〔給〕
geng
赓〔賡〕
鹒〔鶊〕
鲠〔鯁〕
绠〔綆〕
gong
龚〔龔〕
巩〔鞏〕
贡〔貢〕
唝〔嗊〕
gou
缑〔緱〕
沟〔溝〕
钩〔鉤〕
觏〔覯〕
诟〔詬〕
构〔構〕
购〔購〕
gu
轱〔軲〕
鸪〔鴣〕
诂〔詁〕
钴〔鈷〕
贾〔賈〕
蛊〔蠱〕
毂〔轂〕
馉〔餶〕
鹘〔鶻〕
谷〔穀〕
鹄〔鵠〕
顾〔顧〕
锢〔錮〕
gua
刮〔颳〕
鸹〔鴰〕
剐〔剮〕
诖〔詿〕
guan
关〔關〕
纶〔綸〕
鳏〔鰥〕
观〔觀〕
馆〔館〕
鹳〔鸛〕
贯〔貫〕
惯〔慣〕
掼〔摜〕
guang
*广〔廣〕
犷〔獷〕
gui
妫〔媯〕
沩〔溈〕
规〔規〕
鲑〔鮭〕
闺〔閨〕
*归〔歸〕
*龟〔龜〕
轨〔軌〕
匦〔匭〕
诡〔詭〕
鳜〔鱖〕
柜〔櫃〕
贵〔貴〕
刿〔劌〕
桧〔檜〕
刽〔劊〕
gun
辊〔輥〕
绲〔緄〕
鲧〔鯀〕
guo
涡〔渦〕
埚〔堝〕
锅〔鍋〕
蝈〔蟈〕
*国〔國〕
掴〔摑〕
帼〔幗〕
馃〔餜〕
腘〔膕〕
*过〔過〕
H
ha
铪〔鉿〕
hai
还〔還〕
骇〔駭〕
han
顸〔頇〕
韩〔韓〕
阚〔闞〕
㘎〔㘚〕
汉〔漢〕
颔〔頷〕
hang
绗〔絎〕
颃〔頏〕
hao
颢〔顥〕
灏〔灝〕
号〔號〕
he
诃〔訶〕
阂〔閡〕
阖〔闔〕
鹖〔鶡〕
颌〔頜〕
饸〔餄〕
合〔閤〕
纥〔紇〕
鹤〔鶴〕
贺〔賀〕
吓〔嚇〕
heng
鸻〔鴴〕
hong
轰〔轟〕
黉〔黌〕
鸿〔鴻〕
红〔紅〕
荭〔葒〕
讧〔訌〕
hou
后〔後〕
鲎〔鱟〕
hu

轷〔軤〕
壶〔壺〕
胡〔鬍〕
鹕〔鶘〕
鹄〔鵠〕
鹘〔鶻〕
浒〔滸〕
沪〔滬〕
护〔護〕
hua
*华〔華〕
骅〔驊〕
哗〔嘩〕
铧〔鏵〕
*画〔畫〕
婳〔嫿〕
划〔劃〕
桦〔樺〕
话〔話〕
huai
怀〔懷〕
坏〔壞〕⑨
huan
欢〔歡〕
还〔還〕
环〔環〕
缳〔繯〕
镮〔鐶〕
锾〔鍰〕
缓〔緩〕
鲩〔鯇〕
huang
鳇〔鰉〕
谎〔謊〕
hui
挥〔揮〕
辉〔輝〕
翚〔翬〕
诙〔詼〕
回〔迴〕
*汇〔匯〕
〔彙〕
贿〔賄〕
秽〔穢〕
*会〔會〕
烩〔燴〕
荟〔薈〕
绘〔繪〕
诲〔誨〕
㱮〔殨〕
讳〔諱〕
hun
荤〔葷〕
阍〔閽〕
浑〔渾〕
珲〔琿〕
馄〔餛〕
诨〔諢〕
huo
钬〔鈥〕
伙〔夥〕⑩
镬〔鑊〕
获〔獲〕
〔穫〕
祸〔禍〕
货〔貨〕
J
ji
齑〔齏〕
跻〔躋〕
击〔擊〕
赍〔賫〕
缉〔緝〕
积〔積〕
羁〔羈〕
机〔機〕
饥〔饑〕
讥〔譏〕
玑〔璣〕
矶〔磯〕
叽〔嘰〕
鸡〔雞〕
鹡〔鶺〕
辑〔輯〕
极〔極〕
级〔級〕
挤〔擠〕
给〔給〕
*几〔幾〕
虮〔蟣〕
济〔濟〕
霁〔霽〕
荠〔薺〕
剂〔劑〕
鲚〔鱭〕
际〔際〕
绩〔績〕
计〔計〕
系〔繫〕⑪
骥〔驥〕
觊〔覬〕
蓟〔薊〕
鲫〔鯽〕
记〔記〕
纪〔紀〕
继〔繼〕
jia
家〔傢〕
镓〔鎵〕
*夹〔夾〕
浃〔浹〕
颊〔頰〕
荚〔莢〕
蛱〔蛺〕
铗〔鋏〕
郏〔郟〕
贾〔賈〕
槚〔檟〕
钾〔鉀〕
价〔價〕
驾〔駕〕
jian
鹣〔鶼〕
鳒〔鰜〕
缣〔縑〕
*戋〔戔〕
笺〔箋〕
坚〔堅〕
鲣〔鰹〕
缄〔緘〕
鞯〔韉〕
*监〔監〕
歼〔殲〕
艰〔艱〕
间〔間〕
谫〔譾〕
硷〔鹼〕
拣〔揀〕
笕〔筧〕
茧〔繭〕
检〔檢〕
捡〔撿〕
睑〔瞼〕
俭〔儉〕
裥〔襇〕
简〔簡〕
谏〔諫〕
渐〔漸〕
槛〔檻〕
贱〔賤〕
溅〔濺〕
践〔踐〕
饯〔餞〕
*荐〔薦〕
鉴〔鑒〕
*见〔見〕
枧〔梘〕
舰〔艦〕
剑〔劍〕
键〔鍵〕
涧〔澗〕
锏〔鐧〕
jiang
姜〔薑〕
*将〔將〕⑫
浆〔漿〕⑫
缰〔繮〕
讲〔講〕
桨〔槳〕⑫
奖〔獎〕⑫
蒋〔蔣〕
酱〔醬〕⑫
绛〔絳〕
jiao
胶〔膠〕
鲛〔鮫〕
䴔〔鵁〕
浇〔澆〕
骄〔驕〕
娇〔嬌〕
鹪〔鷦〕
饺〔餃〕
铰〔鉸〕
绞〔絞〕
侥〔僥〕
矫〔矯〕
搅〔攪〕
缴〔繳〕
觉〔覺〕
较〔較〕
轿〔轎〕
挢〔撟〕
峤〔嶠〕
jie
阶〔階〕
疖〔癤〕
讦〔訐〕
洁〔潔〕
诘〔詰〕
撷〔擷〕
颉〔頡〕
结〔結〕
鲒〔鮚〕
*节〔節〕
借〔藉〕⑬
诫〔誡〕
jin
谨〔謹〕
馑〔饉〕
觐〔覲〕
紧〔緊〕
锦〔錦〕
仅〔僅〕
劲〔勁〕
*进〔進〕
琎〔璡〕
缙〔縉〕
*尽〔盡〕
〔儘〕
浕〔濜〕
荩〔藎〕
赆〔贐〕
烬〔燼〕
jing
惊〔驚〕
鲸〔鯨〕
䴖〔鶄〕
泾〔涇〕
茎〔莖〕
经〔經〕
颈〔頸〕
刭〔剄〕
镜〔鏡〕
竞〔競〕
痉〔痙〕
劲〔勁〕
胫〔脛〕
径〔徑〕
靓〔靚〕
jiu
纠〔糾〕
鸠〔鳩〕
阄〔鬮〕⑭
鹫〔鷲〕
旧〔舊〕
ju
*车〔車〕
驹〔駒〕
鸲〔鴝〕
锔〔鋦〕
*举〔舉〕
龃〔齟〕
榉〔櫸〕
讵〔詎〕
惧〔懼〕
飓〔颶〕
窭〔窶〕
屦〔屨〕
据〔據〕
剧〔劇〕
锯〔鋸〕
juan
鹃〔鵑〕
镌〔鎸〕
卷〔捲〕
绢〔絹〕
jue
觉〔覺〕
镢〔鐝〕
䦆〔钁〕
谲〔譎〕
诀〔訣〕
绝〔絶〕
jun
军〔軍〕
皲〔皸〕
钧〔鈞〕
骏〔駿〕
K
kai
开〔開〕
锎〔鐦〕
恺〔愷〕
垲〔塏〕
剀〔剴〕
铠〔鎧〕
凯〔凱〕
闿〔闓〕
锴〔鍇〕
忾〔愾〕
kan
龛〔龕〕
槛〔檻〕
kang
钪〔鈧〕
kao
铐〔銬〕
ke
颏〔頦〕
轲〔軻〕
钶〔鈳〕
颗〔顆〕
*壳〔殼〕⑮
缂〔緙〕
克〔剋〕
课〔課〕
骒〔騍〕
锞〔錁〕
ken
恳〔懇〕
垦〔墾〕
keng
铿〔鏗〕
kou
抠〔摳〕
眍〔瞘〕
ku
库〔庫〕
裤〔褲〕
绔〔絝〕
喾〔嚳〕
kua
夸〔誇〕
kuai
㧟〔擓〕
*会〔會〕
浍〔澮〕
哙〔噲〕
郐〔鄶〕
侩〔儈〕
脍〔膾〕
鲙〔鱠〕
狯〔獪〕
块〔塊〕
kuan
宽〔寬〕
髋〔髖〕
kuang
诓〔誆〕
诳〔誑〕
矿〔礦〕
圹〔壙〕
旷〔曠〕
纩〔纊〕
邝〔鄺〕
贶〔貺〕
kui
窥〔窺〕
亏〔虧〕
岿〔巋〕
溃〔潰〕
𫌀〔䙡〕
愦〔憒〕
聩〔聵〕
匮〔匱〕
蒉〔蕢〕
馈〔饋〕
篑〔簣〕
kun
鲲〔鯤〕
锟〔錕〕
壸〔壼〕
阃〔閫〕
困〔睏〕
kuo
阔〔闊〕
扩〔擴〕
L
la

蜡〔蠟〕
腊〔臘〕
镴〔鑞〕

lai

*来〔來〕
涞〔淶〕
莱〔萊〕
崃〔崍〕
铼〔錸〕
徕〔徠〕
赖〔賴〕
濑〔瀨〕
癞〔癩〕
籁〔籟〕
睐〔睞〕
赉〔賚〕

lan

兰〔蘭〕
栏〔欄〕
拦〔攔〕
阑〔闌〕
澜〔瀾〕
谰〔讕〕
斓〔斕〕
镧〔鑭〕
褴〔襤〕
蓝〔藍〕
篮〔籃〕
岚〔嵐〕
懒〔懶〕
览〔覽〕
榄〔欖〕
揽〔攬〕
缆〔纜〕
烂〔爛〕
滥〔濫〕

lang

锒〔鋃〕
阆〔閬〕

lao

捞〔撈〕
劳〔勞〕
崂〔嶗〕
痨〔癆〕
铹〔鐒〕
铑〔銠〕
涝〔澇〕
唠〔嘮〕
耢〔耮〕

le

鳓〔鰳〕
*乐〔樂〕
饹〔餎〕

lei

镭〔鐳〕
累〔纍〕
缧〔縲〕
诔〔誄〕
垒〔壘〕
类〔類〕⑯

li

*离〔離〕
漓〔灕〕
篱〔籬〕
缡〔縭〕
骊〔驪〕
鹂〔鸝〕
鲡〔鱺〕
礼〔禮〕
逦〔邐〕
里〔裏〕
锂〔鋰〕
鲤〔鯉〕
鳢〔鱧〕
*丽〔麗〕⑰
俪〔儷〕
郦〔酈〕
厉〔厲〕
励〔勵〕
砾〔礫〕
*历〔歷〕
〔曆〕
沥〔瀝〕
坜〔壢〕
疬〔癧〕
雳〔靂〕
枥〔櫪〕
苈〔藶〕
呖〔嚦〕
疠〔癘〕
粝〔糲〕
砺〔礪〕
蛎〔蠣〕
栎〔櫟〕
轹〔轢〕
隶〔隸〕

lia

俩〔倆〕

lian

帘〔簾〕
镰〔鐮〕
联〔聯〕
连〔連〕
涟〔漣〕
莲〔蓮〕
鲢〔鰱〕
琏〔璉〕
奁〔奩〕
怜〔憐〕
敛〔斂〕
蔹〔蘞〕
脸〔臉〕
恋〔戀〕
链〔鏈〕
炼〔煉〕
练〔練〕
潋〔瀲〕
殓〔殮〕
裣〔襝〕
裢〔褳〕

liang

粮〔糧〕
*两〔兩〕
俩〔倆〕
唡〔啢〕
魉〔魎〕
谅〔諒〕
辆〔輛〕

liao

鹩〔鷯〕
缭〔繚〕
疗〔療〕
辽〔遼〕
了〔瞭〕
钌〔釕〕
镣〔鐐〕

lie

猎〔獵〕
䴕〔鴷〕

lin

辚〔轔〕
鳞〔鱗〕
临〔臨〕⑱
邻〔鄰〕
蔺〔藺〕
躏〔躪〕
赁〔賃〕

ling

鲮〔鯪〕
绫〔綾〕
龄〔齡〕
铃〔鈴〕
鸰〔鴒〕
*灵〔靈〕
棂〔欞〕
领〔領〕
岭〔嶺〕⑲

liu

飗〔飀〕
*刘〔劉〕
浏〔瀏〕
骝〔騮〕
镏〔鎦〕
绺〔綹〕
馏〔餾〕
鹨〔鷚〕
陆〔陸〕

long

*龙〔龍〕
泷〔瀧〕
珑〔瓏〕
聋〔聾〕
栊〔櫳〕
砻〔礱〕
笼〔籠〕
茏〔蘢〕
咙〔嚨〕
昽〔曨〕
胧〔朧〕
垄〔壟〕
拢〔攏〕
陇〔隴〕

lou

䁖〔瞜〕
*娄〔婁〕
偻〔僂〕
喽〔嘍〕
楼〔樓〕
溇〔漊〕
蒌〔蔞〕
髅〔髏〕
蝼〔螻〕
耧〔耬〕
搂〔摟〕
嵝〔嶁〕
篓〔簍〕
瘘〔瘻〕
镂〔鏤〕

lu

噜〔嚕〕
庐〔廬〕
炉〔爐〕
芦〔蘆〕
*卢〔盧〕
泸〔瀘〕
垆〔壚〕
栌〔櫨〕
颅〔顱〕
鸬〔鸕〕
胪〔臚〕
鲈〔鱸〕
舻〔艫〕
*卤〔鹵〕
〔滷〕
*虏〔虜〕
掳〔擄〕
鲁〔魯〕
橹〔櫓〕
镥〔鑥〕
辘〔轆〕
辂〔輅〕
赂〔賂〕
鹭〔鷺〕
陆〔陸〕
*录〔錄〕
箓〔籙〕
绿〔綠〕
轳〔轤〕
氇〔氌〕

lü

驴〔驢〕
闾〔閭〕
榈〔櫚〕
屡〔屢〕
偻〔僂〕
褛〔褸〕
缕〔縷〕
铝〔鋁〕
*虑〔慮〕
滤〔濾〕
绿〔綠〕

luan

娈〔孌〕
栾〔欒〕
滦〔灤〕
峦〔巒〕
脔〔臠〕
銮〔鑾〕
挛〔攣〕
鸾〔鸞〕
孪〔孿〕
乱〔亂〕

lun

抡〔掄〕
*仑〔侖〕
沦〔淪〕
轮〔輪〕
囵〔圇〕
纶〔綸〕
伦〔倫〕
论〔論〕

luo

骡〔騾〕
脶〔腡〕
*罗〔羅〕
〔囉〕
逻〔邏〕
萝〔蘿〕
锣〔鑼〕
箩〔籮〕
椤〔欏〕
猡〔玀〕
荦〔犖〕
泺〔濼〕
骆〔駱〕
络〔絡〕

M

m

呒〔嘸〕

ma

妈〔媽〕
*马〔馬〕⑳
蚂〔螞〕
玛〔瑪〕
码〔碼〕
犸〔獁〕
骂〔罵〕
吗〔嗎〕
唛〔嘜〕

mai

*买〔買〕
*麦〔麥〕
*卖〔賣〕㉑
迈〔邁〕
荬〔蕒〕

man

颟〔顢〕
馒〔饅〕
鳗〔鰻〕
蛮〔蠻〕
瞒〔瞞〕
满〔滿〕
螨〔蟎〕
谩〔謾〕
缦〔縵〕
镘〔鏝〕

mang

铓〔鋩〕

mao

锚〔錨〕
铆〔鉚〕
贸〔貿〕

me

么〔麼〕㉒

mei

霉〔黴〕
镅〔鎇〕
鹛〔鶥〕
镁〔鎂〕

men

*门〔門〕
扪〔捫〕
钔〔鍆〕
懑〔懣〕
闷〔悶〕
焖〔燜〕
们〔們〕

meng

蒙〔矇〕
〔濛〕
〔懞〕
锰〔錳〕
梦〔夢〕

mi

谜〔謎〕
祢〔禰〕
弥〔彌〕
〔瀰〕
猕〔獼〕
谧〔謐〕
觅〔覓〕

mian

绵〔綿〕
渑〔澠〕
缅〔緬〕
面〔麵〕

miao

鹋〔鶓〕
缈〔緲〕
缪〔繆〕
庙〔廟〕

mie

灭〔滅〕
蔑〔衊〕

min

缗〔緡〕
闵〔閔〕
悯〔憫〕
闽〔閩〕
*黾〔黽〕㉓
鳘〔鰵〕

ming

鸣〔鳴〕
铭〔銘〕

miu

谬〔謬〕
缪〔繆〕

mo

谟〔謨〕

馍〔饃〕
蓦〔驀〕
mou
谋〔謀〕
缪〔繆〕
mu
亩〔畝〕
钼〔鉬〕
N
na
镎〔鎿〕
钠〔鈉〕
纳〔納〕
nan
*难〔難〕
nang
馕〔饢〕
nao
挠〔撓〕
蛲〔蟯〕
铙〔鐃〕
恼〔惱〕
脑〔腦〕
闹〔鬧〕⑭
ne
讷〔訥〕
nei
馁〔餒〕
neng
泞〔濘〕
ni
鲵〔鯢〕
铌〔鈮〕
拟〔擬〕
腻〔膩〕
nian
鲇〔鮎〕
鲶〔鯰〕
辇〔輦〕
撵〔攆〕
niang

酿〔釀〕
niao
*鸟〔鳥〕㉔
茑〔蔦〕
袅〔裊〕
nie
*聂〔聶〕
颞〔顳〕
嗫〔囁〕
蹑〔躡〕
镊〔鑷〕
啮〔嚙〕
镍〔鎳〕
ning
*宁〔寧〕㉕
柠〔檸〕
咛〔嚀〕
狞〔獰〕
聍〔聹〕
拧〔擰〕
泞〔濘〕
niu
钮〔鈕〕
纽〔紐〕
nong
*农〔農〕
浓〔濃〕
侬〔儂〕
脓〔膿〕
哝〔噥〕
nu
驽〔駑〕
nü
钕〔釹〕
nüe
疟〔瘧〕
nuo
傩〔儺〕
诺〔諾〕
锘〔鍩〕
O

ou
*区〔區〕㉖
讴〔謳〕
瓯〔甌〕
鸥〔鷗〕
殴〔毆〕
欧〔歐〕
呕〔嘔〕
沤〔漚〕
怄〔慪〕
P
pan
蹒〔蹣〕
盘〔盤〕
pang
鳑〔鰟〕
庞〔龐〕
pei
赔〔賠〕
锫〔錇〕
辔〔轡〕
pen
喷〔噴〕
peng
鹏〔鵬〕
pi
纰〔紕〕
罴〔羆〕
鲏〔鮍〕
铍〔鈹〕
辟〔闢〕
䴙〔鸊〕
pian
骈〔駢〕
谝〔諞〕
骗〔騙〕
piao
飘〔飄〕
缥〔縹〕
骠〔驃〕
pin

嫔〔嬪〕
频〔頻〕
颦〔顰〕
贫〔貧〕
ping
评〔評〕
苹〔蘋〕
鲆〔鮃〕
凭〔憑〕
po
钋〔釙〕
颇〔頗〕
泼〔潑〕
䥽〔鏺〕
钷〔鉕〕
pu
铺〔鋪〕
扑〔撲〕
仆〔僕〕㉗
镤〔鏷〕
谱〔譜〕
镨〔鐠〕
朴〔樸〕
Q
qi
缉〔緝〕
桤〔榿〕
*齐〔齊〕
蛴〔蠐〕
脐〔臍〕
骑〔騎〕
骐〔騏〕
鳍〔鰭〕
颀〔頎〕
蕲〔蘄〕
启〔啓〕
绮〔綺〕
*岂〔豈〕
碛〔磧〕
*气〔氣〕
讫〔訖〕

荠〔薺〕
qian
骞〔騫〕
谦〔謙〕
悭〔慳〕
牵〔牽〕
*佥〔僉〕
签〔簽〕
〔籤〕
千〔韆〕
*迁〔遷〕
钎〔釬〕
铅〔鉛〕
鹐〔鵮〕
荨〔蕁〕
钳〔鉗〕
钱〔錢〕
钤〔鈐〕
浅〔淺〕
谴〔譴〕
缱〔繾〕
堑〔塹〕
椠〔槧〕
纤〔縴〕
qiang
玱〔瑲〕
枪〔槍〕
锵〔鏘〕
墙〔牆〕
蔷〔薔〕
樯〔檣〕
嫱〔嬙〕
镪〔鏹〕
羟〔羥〕
抢〔搶〕
炝〔熗〕
戗〔戧〕
跄〔蹌〕
呛〔嗆〕
qiao
硗〔磽〕

跷〔蹺〕
锹〔鍬〕
缲〔繰〕
翘〔翹〕
*乔〔喬〕
桥〔橋〕
硚〔礄〕
侨〔僑〕
鞒〔鞽〕
荞〔蕎〕
谯〔譙〕
*壳〔殼〕⑮
窍〔竅〕
诮〔誚〕
qie
锲〔鍥〕
惬〔愜〕
箧〔篋〕
窃〔竊〕
qin
*亲〔親〕
钦〔欽〕
嵚〔嶔〕
骎〔駸〕
寝〔寢〕
锓〔鋟〕
揿〔撳〕
qing
鲭〔鯖〕
轻〔輕〕
氢〔氫〕
倾〔傾〕
䝼〔賰〕
请〔請〕
顷〔頃〕
庼〔廎〕
庆〔慶〕㉘
qiong
*穷〔窮〕
䓖〔藭〕
琼〔瓊〕

茕〔煢〕
qiu
秋〔鞦〕
鹙〔鶖〕
鳅〔鰍〕
䲡〔鰌〕
巯〔巰〕
qu
曲〔麯〕
*区〔區〕㉖
驱〔驅〕
岖〔嶇〕
躯〔軀〕
诎〔詘〕
趋〔趨〕
鸲〔鴝〕
龋〔齲〕
觑〔覷〕
阒〔闃〕
quan
权〔權〕
颧〔顴〕
铨〔銓〕
诠〔詮〕
绻〔綣〕
劝〔勸〕
que
悫〔慤〕
鹊〔鵲〕
阙〔闕〕
确〔確〕
阕〔闋〕
R
rang
让〔讓〕
rao
桡〔橈〕
荛〔蕘〕
饶〔饒〕
娆〔嬈〕
扰〔擾〕

绕〔繞〕
re
热〔熱〕
ren
认〔認〕
饪〔飪〕
纴〔紝〕
轫〔軔〕
纫〔紉〕
韧〔韌〕
rong
荣〔榮〕
蝾〔蠑〕
嵘〔嶸〕
绒〔絨〕
ru
铷〔銣〕
颥〔顬〕
缛〔縟〕
ruan
软〔軟〕
rui
锐〔鋭〕
run
闰〔閏〕
润〔潤〕
S
sa
洒〔灑〕
飒〔颯〕
萨〔薩〕
sai
鳃〔鰓〕
赛〔賽〕
san
毵〔毿〕
馓〔饊〕
伞〔傘〕
sang
丧〔喪〕
颡〔顙〕

sao
骚〔騷〕
缫〔繅〕
扫〔掃〕
se
涩〔澀〕
*啬〔嗇〕
穑〔穡〕
铯〔銫〕
sha
鲨〔鯊〕
纱〔紗〕
*杀〔殺〕
铩〔鎩〕
shai
筛〔篩〕
晒〔曬〕
shan
钐〔釤〕
陕〔陝〕
闪〔閃〕
𫔍〔鐥〕
鳝〔鱔〕
缮〔繕〕
掸〔撣〕
骟〔騸〕
[illegible]
禅〔禪〕
讪〔訕〕
赡〔贍〕
shang
殇〔殤〕
觞〔觴〕
伤〔傷〕
赏〔賞〕㉙
shao
烧〔燒〕
绍〔紹〕
she
赊〔賒〕
舍〔捨〕

设〔設〕
滠〔灄〕
慑〔懾〕
摄〔攝〕
厍〔厙〕
shei
谁〔誰〕
shen
绅〔紳〕
*参〔參〕
糁〔糝〕
审〔審〕
谉〔讅〕
婶〔嬸〕
沈〔瀋〕
谂〔諗〕
肾〔腎〕
渗〔滲〕
瘆〔瘮〕
sheng
声〔聲〕
渑〔澠〕
绳〔繩〕
胜〔勝〕
*圣〔聖〕
shi
湿〔濕〕
诗〔詩〕
*师〔師〕
浉〔溮〕
狮〔獅〕
䴓〔鳾〕
实〔實〕
埘〔塒〕
鲥〔鰣〕
识〔識〕
*时〔時〕
蚀〔蝕〕
驶〔駛〕
铈〔鈰〕
视〔視〕

谥〔謚〕
试〔試〕
轼〔軾〕
势〔勢〕
莳〔蒔〕
贳〔貰〕
释〔釋〕
饰〔飾〕
适〔適〕㉚
shou
兽〔獸〕
*寿〔壽〕
绶〔綬〕
shu
枢〔樞〕
摅〔攄〕
输〔輸〕
纾〔紓〕
书〔書〕
赎〔贖〕
*属〔屬〕
数〔數〕
树〔樹〕
术〔術〕㉛
竖〔豎〕
shuai
帅〔帥〕
shuan
闩〔閂〕
shuang
*双〔雙〕
泷〔瀧〕
shui
谁〔誰〕
shun
顺〔順〕
shuo
说〔説〕
硕〔碩〕
烁〔爍〕
铄〔鑠〕

si
锶〔鍶〕
飔〔颸〕
酾〔釃〕
缌〔緦〕
丝〔絲〕
咝〔噝〕
鸶〔鷥〕
蛳〔螄〕
驷〔駟〕
饲〔飼〕
song
松〔鬆〕
怂〔慫〕
耸〔聳〕
㧐〔㩳〕
讼〔訟〕
颂〔頌〕
诵〔誦〕
sou
馊〔餿〕
锼〔鎪〕
飕〔颼〕
薮〔藪〕
擞〔擻〕
su
苏〔蘇〕
稣〔穌〕
谡〔謖〕
诉〔訴〕
*肃〔肅〕㉜
sui
虽〔雖〕
随〔隨〕
绥〔綏〕
*岁〔歲〕
谇〔誶〕
sun
*孙〔孫〕
荪〔蓀〕
狲〔猻〕

损〔損〕
suo
缩〔縮〕
琐〔瑣〕
唢〔嗩〕
锁〔鎖〕
苏〔囌〕
T
ta
铊〔鉈〕
鳎〔鰨〕
獭〔獺〕
㳠〔澾〕
挞〔撻〕
闼〔闥〕
tai
台〔臺〕
〔檯〕
〔颱〕
骀〔駘〕
鲐〔鮐〕
态〔態〕
钛〔鈦〕
tan
滩〔灘〕
瘫〔癱〕
摊〔攤〕
贪〔貪〕
谈〔談〕
坛〔壇〕
〔罎〕
谭〔譚〕
昙〔曇〕
弹〔彈〕
钽〔鉭〕
叹〔嘆〕
tang
镗〔鏜〕
汤〔湯〕
傥〔儻〕
镋〔钂〕

烫〔燙〕
tao
涛〔濤〕
韬〔韜〕
绦〔縧〕
焘〔燾〕
讨〔討〕
te
铽〔鋱〕
teng
誊〔謄〕
腾〔騰〕
䲢〔鰧〕
ti
锑〔銻〕
䴘〔鷉〕
鹈〔鵜〕
绨〔綈〕
缇〔緹〕
题〔題〕
体〔體〕
tian
阗〔闐〕
tiao
*条〔條〕㉝
鲦〔鰷〕
龆〔齠〕
调〔調〕
粜〔糶〕
tie
贴〔貼〕
铁〔鐵〕
ting
厅〔廳〕㉞
烃〔烴〕
听〔聽〕
颋〔頲〕
铤〔鋌〕
tong
铜〔銅〕
鲖〔鮦〕

统〔統〕
恸〔慟〕
tou
头〔頭〕
tu
图〔圖〕
涂〔塗〕
钍〔釷〕
tuan
抟〔摶〕
团〔團〕
〔糰〕
tui
颓〔頹〕
tun
饨〔飩〕
tuo
饦〔飥〕
驼〔駝〕
鸵〔鴕〕
驮〔馱〕
鼍〔鼉〕
椭〔橢〕
萚〔蘀〕
箨〔籜〕
W
wa
娲〔媧〕
洼〔窪〕
袜〔襪〕㉟
wai
㖞〔喎〕
wan
弯〔彎〕
湾〔灣〕
纨〔紈〕
顽〔頑〕
绾〔綰〕
*万〔萬〕
wang
网〔網〕

辋〔輞〕
wei
*为〔為〕
维〔維〕
潍〔濰〕
*韦〔韋〕
违〔違〕
围〔圍〕
涠〔潿〕
帏〔幃〕
闱〔闈〕
伪〔偽〕
鲔〔鮪〕
诿〔諉〕
炜〔煒〕
玮〔瑋〕
苇〔葦〕
韪〔韙〕
伟〔偉〕
纬〔緯〕
硙〔磑〕
谓〔謂〕
卫〔衛〕
wen
鳁〔鰛〕
纹〔紋〕
闻〔聞〕
阌〔閿〕
稳〔穩〕
问〔問〕
wo
涡〔渦〕
窝〔窩〕
莴〔萵〕
蜗〔蝸〕
挝〔撾〕
龌〔齷〕
wu
诬〔誣〕
*乌〔烏〕㊱
呜〔嗚〕

钨〔鎢〕
邬〔鄔〕
*无〔無〕㊲
芜〔蕪〕
妩〔嫵〕
怃〔憮〕
庑〔廡〕
鹀〔鵐〕
坞〔塢〕
务〔務〕
雾〔霧〕
骛〔騖〕
鹜〔鶩〕
误〔誤〕
X
xi
牺〔犧〕
饻〔餏〕
锡〔錫〕
袭〔襲〕
觋〔覡〕
习〔習〕
鳛〔鰼〕
玺〔璽〕
铣〔銑〕
系〔係〕
〔繫〕⑪
细〔細〕
阋〔鬩〕⑭
戏〔戲〕
饩〔餼〕
xia
虾〔蝦〕
辖〔轄〕
硖〔硤〕
峡〔峽〕
侠〔俠〕
狭〔狹〕
吓〔嚇〕㊳
xian
鲜〔鮮〕

纤〔纖〕㊴
跹〔躚〕
锨〔鍁〕
莶〔薟〕
贤〔賢〕
咸〔鹹〕
衔〔銜〕
挦〔撏〕
闲〔閑〕
鹇〔鷴〕
娴〔嫻〕
痫〔癇〕
藓〔蘚〕
蚬〔蜆〕
显〔顯〕
险〔險〕
猃〔獫〕
铣〔銑〕
*献〔獻〕
线〔線〕
现〔現〕
苋〔莧〕
岘〔峴〕
县〔縣〕㊵
宪〔憲〕
馅〔餡〕
xiang
骧〔驤〕
镶〔鑲〕
*乡〔鄉〕
芗〔薌〕
缃〔緗〕
详〔詳〕
鲞〔鯗〕
响〔響〕
饷〔餉〕
飨〔饗〕
向〔嚮〕
象〔像〕㊶
项〔項〕
xiao

骁〔驍〕
哓〔嘵〕
销〔銷〕
绡〔綃〕
嚣〔囂〕
枭〔梟〕
鸮〔鴞〕
萧〔蕭〕
潇〔瀟〕
蟏〔蠨〕
箫〔簫〕
晓〔曉〕
啸〔嘯〕
xie
颉〔頡〕
撷〔擷〕
缬〔纈〕
协〔協〕
挟〔挾〕
胁〔脅〕
谐〔諧〕
*写〔寫〕㊷
亵〔褻〕
泻〔瀉〕
绁〔紲〕
谢〔謝〕
xin
锌〔鋅〕
䜣〔訢〕
衅〔釁〕
xing
兴〔興〕
荥〔滎〕
钘〔鈃〕
铏〔鉶〕
陉〔陘〕
饧〔餳〕
xiong
讻〔訩〕
诇〔詗〕
xiu
馐〔饈〕
鸺〔鵂〕
绣〔繡〕
锈〔鏽〕
xu
须〔須〕
〔鬚〕
谞〔諝〕
许〔許〕
诩〔詡〕
顼〔頊〕
续〔續〕
绪〔緒〕
xuan
轩〔軒〕
谖〔諼〕
悬〔懸〕
选〔選〕
癣〔癬〕
旋〔鏇〕
铉〔鉉〕
绚〔絢〕
xue
学〔學〕
峃〔嶨〕
鳕〔鱈〕
谑〔謔〕
xun
勋〔勛〕
埙〔塤〕
驯〔馴〕
询〔詢〕
*寻〔尋〕
浔〔潯〕
鲟〔鱘〕
训〔訓〕
讯〔訊〕
逊〔遜〕
Y
ya
压〔壓〕㊸
鸦〔鴉〕
鸭〔鴨〕
铔〔錏〕
哑〔啞〕
氩〔氬〕
*亚〔亞〕
垭〔埡〕
挜〔掗〕
娅〔婭〕
讶〔訝〕
轧〔軋〕
yan
阏〔閼〕
阉〔閹〕
恹〔懨〕
颜〔顏〕
盐〔鹽〕
*严〔嚴〕
阎〔閻〕
厣〔厴〕
黡〔黶〕
魇〔魘〕
俨〔儼〕
䶮〔龑〕
谚〔諺〕
䜩〔讌〕
*厌〔厭〕
餍〔饜〕
赝〔贗〕
艳〔艷〕
滟〔灧〕
谳〔讞〕
砚〔硯〕
觃〔覎〕
酽〔釅〕
验〔驗〕
yang
鸯〔鴦〕
疡〔瘍〕
炀〔煬〕
杨〔楊〕
扬〔揚〕
旸〔暘〕
钖〔鍚〕
阳〔陽〕
痒〔癢〕
养〔養〕
样〔樣〕
yao
*尧〔堯〕㊹
峣〔嶢〕
谣〔謠〕
铫〔銚〕
轺〔軺〕
疟〔瘧〕
鹞〔鷂〕
钥〔鑰〕
药〔藥〕
ye
爷〔爺〕
靥〔靨〕
*页〔頁〕
烨〔燁〕
晔〔曄〕
*业〔業〕
邺〔鄴〕
叶〔葉〕㊺
谒〔謁〕
yi
铱〔銥〕
医〔醫〕
鹥〔鷖〕
祎〔禕〕
颐〔頤〕
遗〔遺〕
仪〔儀〕
诒〔詒〕
贻〔貽〕
饴〔飴〕
蚁〔蟻〕
钇〔釔〕
谊〔誼〕
瘗〔瘞〕
镒〔鎰〕
缢〔縊〕
勚〔勩〕
怿〔懌〕
译〔譯〕
驿〔驛〕
峄〔嶧〕
绎〔繹〕
*义〔義〕㊻
议〔議〕
轶〔軼〕
*艺〔藝〕
呓〔囈〕
亿〔億〕
忆〔憶〕
诣〔詣〕
镱〔鐿〕
yin
铟〔銦〕
*阴〔陰〕
荫〔蔭〕
龈〔齦〕
银〔銀〕
饮〔飲〕
*隐〔隱〕
瘾〔癮〕
䲟〔鮣〕
ying
应〔應〕
鹰〔鷹〕
莺〔鶯〕
罂〔罌〕
婴〔嬰〕
璎〔瓔〕
樱〔櫻〕
撄〔攖〕
嘤〔嚶〕
鹦〔鸚〕
缨〔纓〕
荧〔熒〕
莹〔瑩〕
茔〔塋〕
萤〔螢〕
萦〔縈〕
营〔營〕
赢〔贏〕
蝇〔蠅〕
瘿〔癭〕
颖〔穎〕
颍〔潁〕
yo
哟〔喲〕
yong
痈〔癰〕
拥〔擁〕
佣〔傭〕
镛〔鏞〕
鳙〔鱅〕
颙〔顒〕
踊〔踴〕
you
忧〔憂〕
优〔優〕
鱿〔魷〕
*犹〔猶〕
莸〔蕕〕
铀〔鈾〕
邮〔郵〕
铕〔銪〕
诱〔誘〕
yu
纡〔紆〕
舆〔輿〕
欤〔歟〕
余〔餘〕㊼
觎〔覦〕
谀〔諛〕
*鱼〔魚〕
渔〔漁〕
[illegible]〔[illegible]〕
*与〔與〕
语〔語〕
龉〔齬〕
伛〔傴〕
屿〔嶼〕
誉〔譽〕
钰〔鈺〕
吁〔籲〕㊽
御〔禦〕
驭〔馭〕
阈〔閾〕
妪〔嫗〕
郁〔鬱〕
谕〔諭〕
鹆〔鵒〕
饫〔飫〕
狱〔獄〕
预〔預〕
滪〔澦〕
蓣〔蕷〕
鹬〔鷸〕
yuan
渊〔淵〕
鸢〔鳶〕
鸳〔鴛〕
鼋〔黿〕
园〔園〕
辕〔轅〕
员〔員〕
圆〔圓〕
缘〔緣〕
橼〔櫞〕
远〔遠〕
愿〔願〕
yue
约〔約〕
哕〔噦〕
阅〔閱〕
钺〔鉞〕
跃〔躍〕
*乐〔樂〕
钥〔鑰〕
yun
*云〔雲〕
芸〔蕓〕
纭〔紜〕
涢〔溳〕
郧〔鄖〕
殒〔殞〕
陨〔隕〕
恽〔惲〕
晕〔暈〕
郓〔鄆〕
运〔運〕
酝〔醞〕
韫〔韞〕
缊〔緼〕
蕴〔蘊〕
Z
za
臜〔臢〕
杂〔雜〕
zai
载〔載〕
zan
趱〔趲〕
攒〔攢〕
錾〔鏨〕
暂〔暫〕
赞〔贊〕
瓒〔瓚〕
zang
赃〔贓〕
脏〔臟〕
〔髒〕
驵〔駔〕
zao
凿〔鑿〕
枣〔棗〕
灶〔竈〕
ze
责〔責〕
赜〔賾〕
啧〔嘖〕
帻〔幘〕
箦〔簀〕
则〔則〕
鲗〔鰂〕
泽〔澤〕
择〔擇〕
zei
贼〔賊〕
zen
谮〔譖〕
zeng
缯〔繒〕
赠〔贈〕
锃〔鋥〕
zha
铡〔鍘〕
闸〔閘〕
轧〔軋〕
鲝〔鮺〕
鲊〔鮓〕
诈〔詐〕
zhai
斋〔齋〕
债〔債〕
zhan
鹯〔鸇〕
鳣〔鱣〕
毡〔氈〕
觇〔覘〕
谵〔譫〕
斩〔斬〕
崭〔嶄〕
盏〔盞〕
辗〔輾〕
绽〔綻〕
颤〔顫〕
栈〔棧〕
战〔戰〕
zhang
张〔張〕

*长〔長〕④
涨〔漲〕
帐〔帳〕
账〔賬〕
胀〔脹〕
zhao
钊〔釗〕
赵〔趙〕
诏〔詔〕
zhe
谪〔謫〕
辙〔轍〕
蛰〔蟄〕
辄〔輒〕
詟〔讋〕
折〔摺〕㊾
锗〔鍺〕
这〔這〕
鹧〔鷓〕
zhen
针〔針〕
贞〔貞〕
浈〔湞〕
祯〔禎〕
桢〔楨〕
侦〔偵〕
缜〔縝〕
诊〔診〕
轸〔軫〕
鸩〔鴆〕
赈〔賑〕
镇〔鎮〕
纼〔紖〕
阵〔陣〕
zheng
钲〔鉦〕
征〔徵〕㊿
铮〔錚〕
症〔癥〕
*郑〔鄭〕
证〔證〕
帧〔幀〕
诤〔諍〕
𬮱〔闏〕
zhi
只〔隻〕
〔衹〕
织〔織〕
职〔職〕
踯〔躑〕
*执〔執〕
絷〔縶〕
纸〔紙〕
挚〔摯〕
贽〔贄〕
鸷〔鷙〕
掷〔擲〕
滞〔滯〕
栉〔櫛〕
轾〔輊〕
致〔緻〕
帜〔幟〕
制〔製〕
*质〔質〕
踬〔躓〕
锧〔鑕〕
骘〔騭〕
zhong
终〔終〕
钟〔鐘〕
〔鍾〕
种〔種〕
肿〔腫〕
众〔眾〕
zhou
诌〔謅〕
赒〔賙〕
鸼〔鵃〕
轴〔軸〕
纣〔紂〕
荮〔葤〕
骤〔驟〕
皱〔皺〕
绉〔縐〕
㤘〔㥮〕
㑇〔㑳〕
昼〔晝〕
zhu
诸〔諸〕
槠〔櫧〕
朱〔硃〕
诛〔誅〕
铢〔銖〕
烛〔燭〕
嘱〔囑〕
瞩〔矚〕
贮〔貯〕
驻〔駐〕
铸〔鑄〕
筑〔築〕
zhua
挝〔撾〕
zhuan
*专〔專〕
砖〔磚〕
䏝〔膞〕
颛〔顓〕
转〔轉〕
啭〔囀〕
赚〔賺〕
传〔傳〕
馔〔饌〕
zhuang
妆〔妝〕
状〔狀〕
zhui
骓〔騅〕
锥〔錐〕
赘〔贅〕
缒〔縋〕
缀〔綴〕
坠〔墜〕
zhun
谆〔諄〕
准〔準〕
zhuo
𬭚〔鐯〕
浊〔濁〕
诼〔諑〕
镯〔鐲〕
zi
谘〔諮〕
资〔資〕
镃〔鎡〕
龇〔齜〕
辎〔輜〕
锱〔錙〕
缁〔緇〕
鲻〔鯔〕
渍〔漬〕
zong
综〔綜〕
枞〔樅〕
总〔總〕
纵〔縱〕
zou
诹〔諏〕
鲰〔鯫〕
驺〔騶〕
邹〔鄒〕
zu
镞〔鏃〕
诅〔詛〕
组〔組〕
zuan
钻〔鑽〕
躜〔躦〕
缵〔纘〕
赚〔賺〕
zun
鳟〔鱒〕
zuo
凿〔鑿〕